Streams of Water Duet

Part Two

Echoes in the Tide

Dr. Michal Guter

ETERNUM

Publishing

Contents

Author's Note

Dear Reader,

Welcome back!

This book is the continuation of *Streams of Water: Written in the Waves* and picks up right where it left off.

If you haven't read the first part, I recommend starting there for the full experience. This is not a stand-alone part.

Trigger Warnings

May contain spoilers

This novel contains emotionally complex themes. For readers who wish to know more before beginning, a detailed content note is provided on the next page.

If you prefer to experience the story without potential spoilers, feel free to skip ahead.

This is a story of love, loss, healing, and emotional depth. It explores themes of identity, intimacy, abandonment, and the long journey home to oneself.

Your mental health matters. I've done my best to include all relevant content warnings, even for subtle themes. Please take care of yourself and prioritize your well-being, because I truly care.

Content warnings include, but are not limited to:

- Terminal illness

- Discussion of past illness and death of a parent due to terminal illness

- Medical trauma

- Hospitalization

- Refusal of treatment and end-of-life discussions

- Grief and prolonged mourning

- Explicit sexual content

Soundtrack

1. *Everything* – Lifehouse

2. *Numb* – Linkin Park

3. *Anchor* – Skillet

4. *Never Let Me Go* – Florence + The Machine

5. *Dying in LA* – Panic! At the Disco

6. *Bottom of the Deep Blue Sea* – MISSIO

7. *Speeding Cars* – Walking on Cars

8. *Milim* – Harel Skaat

9. *Fai Rumore* – Diodato

10. *Lookalike* – Conan Gray

11. *Let Me In* – Skinny Living

12. *Oceans* – Jacob Lee

13. *Soldier's Eyes* – Jack Savoretti

14. *Sing to Me* – Darren Hayes

15. *A Drop in the Ocean* – Ron Pope

16. *Take Me to Church* – Hozier

17. *You Are the Reason* – Calum Scott

18. *If They Only Knew* – Alfie Arcuri

19. *Hold Me* – Savage Garden

20. *Letting Go* – Dotan

For all who have beheld monsters crawling from the ground,
For those who once falsely believed monsters were merely outward
shadows,
To all who have learned that monsters breathe the same air as we
do,
For those still seeking the dawn's first light,
For those who were left behind in darkness,
For those who stood bravely when the hour came,
For those who never returned to shore,
For the souls whose lifesaver never arrived,
At least, not when it was truly needed.

Prologue

LOGAN'S SOUL HAD STAYED behind on that crumpled, sunburnt beach in Australia, tethered to the one man he ever truly loved. Logan had left, but it didn't. It clung to Adrian like seaweed in a tide pool, refusing to follow Logan's body across continents, refusing to let him leave Adrian entirely.

So, Logan had moved on. Or at least he told himself he had. He slipped into beds warmed by others, yet the chill within his soul remained unshaken. He brushed past lives that seemed flawless on paper, but beneath the surface, he's been drowning ever since. Drowning in silence, drowning in absence, drowning in a grief he couldn't name, even though Adrian's name had been written in bold on every scattered piece of his broken, suffocating soul.

Logan had tried to reach for the surface, gasping for air, clawing through, but nothing came. He told himself he was fine because he was alive, he was breathing, wasn't he? He had a career. He got married. He was the head of an entire industry. On paper, he was alive.

Yet, inside, he was drowning, suffocating, each breath splintered, hollow, wrong. It hadn't made sense. Nothing had. Not then. Not now.

There was that penumbral hovering over his life; he lingered half in the world, half in the ashen corridors of memory, where fragments glimmered like broken halos. In his mind they turned, slow and inexorable, a ring of heaven burning above him, while all around, the infernal flames rose to claim what little of him remained.

Logan's wife had begged for a child, and at night he had found himself seeking the fleeting warmth of Zack's arms, searching for something, anything, to quiet the ache that hollowed out his chest.

But he hadn't really been there.

He hadn't really been anywhere.

Not with her. Not with Zack.

His heart had still been lost on that Australian shore, wandering the drift, caught in the undertow, standing guard over a long-lost love that had never been meant to be abandoned.

And no matter how far he ran, or how many years unspooled behind him, he couldn't shake it.

Logan had asked himself, over and over: How could he have loved someone so completely, so deeply, in just a handful of months? How had Adrian, with his crooked smile and whisky-eyes, anchored him so profoundly that he hadn't been able to move on, even years and lifetimes later? Why Adrian? Why not Zack? Why not anyone else? What had made him different, special, irreplaceable? What had it been in Adrian's soul that had called to his like a lighthouse in a storm?

Or had it been his soul that had called to Adrian, summoned him from the bottom of the ocean to save him, to breathe life back into him when he'd forgotten how? Maybe it had been the bond forged in the presence of something greater than both of them—the waves, the salt, the rhythm of the sea. Maybe nature herself had given him a second chance, whispering under the crashing tide, promising him something eternal.

Or maybe it had been simpler than that. Maybe it had just been that Adrian was Adrian. And Logan had never been meant to leave. Because in every breath Logan had taken, in every dream he had woken from gasping, in every moment he had felt the emptiness press against his ribs, the truth had remained: Adrian hadn't just been someone Logan had loved. He had been the ocean itself. And no matter where Logan had gone, no matter how far, he had never been able to escape the pull of the tide, and the streams of water were coming to claim him back home.

Chapter 11

Ghosts of the Ocean

The sun, the sand, and the flowing streams of water remembered. The relentless current pulling Logan back could no longer be tamed, prompting him to gather what remained of his crumbled heart, his shattered bones, and his soulless existence as he sought to rediscover the breath in his lungs, the wind in his hair, and the whisky hue of his eyes.

November 16, 2020—Seattle, Washington—Two Years Later

LOGAN'S FINGERS TAPPED A restless rhythm on the staircase railing, his phone pressed tightly to his ear. He stared out the window, watching the world outside move at its usual pace, a cruel contrast to the turmoil raging inside him.

"Mr. Vaughn," the voice on the other end greeted, calm and professional. Logan wasn't surprised that the investigator recognized his number. He'd called too often these past few days for his number to be unknown to the man; he was probably saved in his contact list under an absurd name.

"Well?" Logan's voice was clipped, his patience razor-thin.

"Not yet," Mr. Boyed replied, his tone measured. "Look, Mr. Vaughn, we've only been on this case for three days. I assure you, our team is among the best, and—"

"No, you listen to me, Mr. Boyed," Logan interrupted, his voice hard, unsettled. "You have two more days to find him."

"Mr. Vaughn, we are exhausting every possible resource to locate the person you're looking for. There's no need to call twice a day or make threats."

"No threats," Logan snapped. "Just informing you. I pay you enough to expect results, yet you haven't found him. Two days, Mr. Boyed. If you fail, my money and I will take my business elsewhere." Without waiting for a response, Logan ended the call.

Shoving the phone into his pocket, Logan hurried back to his room. It had been three days since Sandy had moved out, and three days since his meeting with Mr. Boyed, the head of one of the most reputable private investigation firms in the area. Three days since he'd hired them to track down Adrian.

His chest tightened as he threw clothes into a suitcase, the empty house echoing with every movement. There wasn't much to pack. This house, a gilded cage bought by his father, had never felt like his. And now, with Sandy gone, it was easier to abandon it altogether. Logan had already met with a real estate agent and secured an apartment, a far cry from the opulence his family insisted on. He didn't care. He wanted small, simple, and his.

His father was away, sparing Logan the onslaught of questions that would inevitably come. His mother had already called, her voice dripping with concern. His sisters, too, had tried to pry, but Logan brushed them all off with vague reassurances. He couldn't explain now, not when his mind was consumed with one thing: finding Adrian.

By the next morning, he was back at his desk when the phone rang.

"Found him," Mr. Boyed said without a preamble. "I've just sent you photos. Please confirm if this is the man you're searching for."

Logan's fingers shook as he opened his laptop, quickly navigating to his inbox. He clicked on the email, downloading the attached photos, and as the first image appeared on his screen, his breath caught in his throat.

Adrian.

He stood upon the sunlit shore, his hair—still long, as Logan recalled, though now a deeper shade of brown than golden—waved gracefully in the gentle breeze. His broad, familiar frame appeared etched by the sun and caressed by the sea. The sight hit Logan like a fault line giving way beneath him, sudden, violent, impossible to brace for. His heart clenched and soared simultaneously, tears gathering in his eyes, igniting as his heart brimmed with the vision of Adrian. After so long, after everything, there he was.

For what felt like an eternity, or perhaps just a fleeting moment, Logan sat transfixed at the screen, his heart melting. The heavy weight he had borne for so long was finally lifted, allowing a breath of fresh air to fill his lungs.

There he was—the love of his life, his soulmate—still by the waves, still listening to their song, still gazing at the horizon.

"Yes," Logan managed, his voice cracking. "That's him."

"Excellent," Mr. Boyed said. "I'll send his address, phone number, and additional details shortly. Would you like us to investigate further?"

"No, that's fine," Logan replied, barely finding the words as he stared at the photo. "Just the address and number. Thank you, Mr. Boyed. I'll take care of the payment."

"Pleasure doing business with you, Mr. Vaughn," Mr. Boyed said before hanging up.

Logan leaned back in his chair, his hands trembling as his eyes stayed fixed on the photo of Adrian. His heart ached with longing, each beat echoing like thunder in his chest. But beneath the pain, something else stirred—hope. A spark reignited, spreading warmth through him.

He closed his laptop, the image of Adrian still burned into his cornea, as if the light itself had branded him upon his sight. Logan's tears came then, soundless as they spilled in a mix of grief, relief, and the overwhelming realization that he had found him. Finally. Logan sat suspended in time, running Adrian's photos in his mind again and again, in endless orbit, daring to hold him not as memory, but as living presence.

He drew out his phone and composed a brief message to his father; his fingers hovered, trembling above the keys, before he pressed 'send.'

> Taking a leave of absence. Don't know when I'll be back.

Logan shot upright, the chair scraping back, breath trapped somewhere between chest and throat. His pulse hammered against the side of his neck, loud, insistent, as if that organ itself wanted to claw its way out.

He staggered toward the door, stopped, turned back, paced. The office seemed to shrink around him, walls closing in, light swelling too sharp at the edges, too bright, as if the world had tilted. His fingers refused stillness—drumming the desk, twisting the hem of his shirt, clawing at the chain of his watch. He couldn't anchor himself.

Scenarios collided in his head, a thousand different versions of what would come next, each rising, crashing, burning out before the next began. What would Adrian say? What if he turned away? What if he never forgave him?

He pressed his palm flat against the cold glass of the floor-to-ceiling window. The city stretched below, indifferent. Cars moved like blood cells through veins. None of it could hold him.

His chest heaved. His body wanted to run before his mind caught up.

The truth fell heavy and undeniable, cutting through the storm inside him.

I found him. I'm going to him.

His pulse reverberated in his ears, a drumroll of anticipation. Yes. He was on his way to Adrian.

He tapped the pane with his knuckles, once, twice, again—too much energy with nowhere to go. His breath fogged the glass, then vanished, then returned, quick and shallow. He stood enveloped in a storm of thoughts and fears; yet above all, a more potent force surged within him: excitement. An overpowering need consumed him, the need to possess knowledge, to uncover the truth. He bolted back to his office chair and opened his laptop; it didn't matter that he could access it from his phone. Logic was a foreign concept to him, as his deepest desire grew from a faint hope whispered into an empty room and deaf ears, into a tangible reality he could hold as the most secret longing of his heart blossomed and expanded.

Opening the new email from Mr. Boyed, Logan carefully committed the nuances of the address to memory, his gaze lingering on the photographs and the mosaic of pixels that composed them. His fingers hovered over the screen, yearning to trace the contours of Adrian's skin, to feel the softness of his hair, the roughness of his stubble. Logan grabbed his belongings and left his office without a second thought.

"Ada Mae," Logan said as he strode past his assistant's desk. She looked up, startled, her bright red hair falling over her shoulders as she tilted her head in question.

"Look," Logan started, a faint smile tugging at his lips. "I'm leaving. I have no idea when I'll be back. If my father is upset with you, just leave. Cancel everything I have on my schedule for at least two weeks. I'll contact you when I can."

Ada Mae blinked, her expression shifting from confusion to concern. "You can't just cancel, Mr. Vaughn," she tried to reason with him, standing. "You have—"

"I know," Logan interrupted, shaking his head. "Trust me, I know. But I need you to do this. And one more thing, please book me the first flight to Israel. And *don't* tell my dad where I'm going."

Her eyes widened. "Israel? Logan, what's going on?"

"A lot of things, Ada Mae," he said with a deep exhale, his tone softening. "Please, just book the flight. I'll transfer the money to Mr. Boyed now. And take the rest of the week off, okay? You've earned it."

Before she could respond, Logan was already turning toward the elevator. "I'll call you," he called over his shoulder as the doors slid open, the words a promise left hanging in the air.

Ada Mae stood frozen for a moment, watching the elevator close. Then she sat back down, shaking her head as she muttered, "What the hell is going on with him?" But even as she sighed, she began typing, searching for flights to Tel-Aviv.

Logan tore through the building's underground garage like a man possessed, his chest heaving as he threw himself into the car and sped out onto the street. His hands gripped the wheel tightly, his mind spinning faster than the tires beneath him. On the way, he called the realtor, his voice rushed and breathless.

"I'm going away for a few weeks," he started, barely pausing to let her respond. "Please arrange for my stuff to be moved into the new apartment. I'll make sure you have access."

The realtor, professional as always, agreed immediately and told him she could meet him at his house in an hour with movers. Logan thanked her, ending the call before she could ask any more questions.

When he got home, Logan headed directly to his room and retrieved a black, empty suitcase. His movements were frantic, almost desperate, as he transferred clothes from suitcases and half-packed boxes, jamming them into the empty bag without much thought. Shirts, pants, shoes—it didn't matter what went in or whether it made sense. His mind was a whirlwind, teetering on the edge of panic and hope, and he couldn't focus on anything but the looming reality of seeing Adrian again.

Pausing for a moment, Logan sat heavily on the bed, his head dropping into his hands as he closed his eyes. His heart was pounding so hard it felt like it might burst, each beat a chaotic reminder of the fear and excitement coursing through him.

"Breathe, Logan," he muttered under his breath, forcing himself to take slow, shallow inhales. But even as he tried to steady himself, the thought of leaving things as they were, of not going, clawed at his chest like a physical pain. The idea was unbearable, nauseating. *No fucking way,* he thought bitterly, shoving the fear aside.

He stood abruptly, his hands shaking as he resumed packing. Even as anxiety gnawed at him, the thought of seeing Adrian again sent a flicker of warmth through him, a tentative sense of relief that soothed some of the pain still lodged deep in his chest. He didn't know what he would say, or how Adrian would react, but the idea of being near him again—of hearing his voice, seeing his face—was enough to keep him moving.

When the realtor arrived with the movers, Logan met them at the door. Together, they quickly loaded the few remaining items into the van. His belongings had already dwindled to almost nothing, the house more a reminder of what he'd left behind than a home. The realtor promised to email him once everything was set in the new apartment. She shook his hand with a polite smile before stepping away, already answering another call as she left.

Logan didn't linger.

The house—once a monument to everything his father wanted him to be—looked exactly the same. Perfect, polished, staged. The magazine-ready furniture his father and Sandy had chosen sat untouched, as if waiting for a version of Logan who had never existed.

Even after packing up all his things, he realized he had barely left a mark. He hadn't touched the surfaces, hadn't claimed the space. Nothing here had ever belonged to him.

The house no longer felt suffocating, just hollow. A relic of a life that had never truly been his.

Without a second thought, he locked the door behind him for the last time and called a cab.

The ride to the airport was a blur. His stomach churned with nerves, his thoughts flipping between dread and hope. His heart felt as fragile as glass, trembling with every possibility, every fear. But he couldn't stop now. He had to see Adrian. He had to try.

When Ada Mae texted him his flight details, Logan couldn't help but smile faintly. *What would I do without her?* He thought. She'd asked if he needed her to arrange a hotel, but Logan told her no. He could handle it himself. He asked her instead to keep an eye on emails from the realtor and to arrange for someone to drive his car to the new apartment once everything was finalized. Ada Mae, ever efficient, simply replied:

> Consider it done.

As the cab glided to a halt at the airport, a tumultuous wave of terror intertwined with exhilaration surged through Logan's veins. He grasped his suitcase tightly, exchanging a few bills with the driver before stepping into the enveloping anticipation of the terminal. Each footfall echoed like a heartbeat, propelling him deeper into the realm of the unknown. His heart quivered, caught in a fierce dance between trepidation and resolute determination. Yet, one truth shone brightly amidst the chaos; Logan was destined to find Adrian. He had no choice but to pursue this quest.

November 19, 2020—Tel-Aviv, Israel—Two Days Later

As LOGAN STEPPED ONTO the vibrant streets of Tel Aviv, the burden of the past two years crashed upon him, threatening to extinguish the flickering flame of hope that warmed his insides. He longed to gaze into Adrian's whisky-colored eyes, yearning for the moment when, if the heavens, the sea, and the currents conspired in his favor, he might glimpse Adrian's radiant smile. A pang of regret hit Logan for not buying a new camera; he wished to capture Adrian in a photograph that he could etch into his very memory. He craved to preserve the vivid image of those mesmerizing eyes, the joyful grin revealing perfect teeth, and his sun-kissed skin, ensuring that this beautiful memory would never fade away from him.

The twenty-hour flight, compounded by the endless hours spent waiting at the airport, had left him physically drained. His head throbbed, his limbs ached, and yet his exhaustion was eclipsed by the storm brewing inside him. Every breath felt heavier as he stepped into a world that was both foreign and achingly familiar, a world where Adrian existed.

It was midafternoon, and the sun bathed the city in a golden glow, but Logan barely noticed. His surroundings blurred as he hurried through the terminal, his focus sharp and singular. The bustling crowds, the chatter of travelers, the sunlight filtering through the glass windows—none of it mattered. His entire being was pulled forward by a single thread: Adrian. As if his heart had caught the faint susurrus of Adrian's soul and moved toward it, certain that redemption waited at the end, certain that its long echoing threnody had at last found an answering ear.

Outside, Logan climbed into the first cab he saw, gripping his phone tightly as he showed the driver the address Mr. Boyed had sent. The investigator, ever professional, had included the address in both English and Hebrew. The driver glanced at it and nodded, a flicker of curiosity crossing his face.

"Do you know where this is?" Logan asked, his voice tight.

"Yes," the driver replied, his eyes lingering on Logan for a moment.

Logan swallowed. "Can you take me to a hotel nearby? Please."

The driver nodded.

Logan couldn't quite put his finger on why he needed to stop at a hotel first. Maybe it was the nerves, an urgent need to compose himself before confronting the man who had dominated his thoughts for the past two years. Or perhaps it was the simple practicality of it: the idea of standing before the love of his life, luggage in tow, reeking of airplane air after over twenty grueling hours of travel, wasn't exactly how he wanted their reunion to begin.

As the cab rolled through the streets of Tel Aviv, Logan closed his eyes, trying to steady his breathing. His stomach churned with a mix of nausea and anticipation. His hands trembled in his lap, but within the chaos, there was a flicker of something else. Hope. The thought of seeing Adrian again sent a jolt of electricity through him, a spark that made him feel alive despite the chaos. He couldn't suppress the faint smile that tugged at his lips. *He's here. I'm going to see him.*

When the cab stopped, Logan handed the driver a hundred-dollar bill, not waiting for change. The driver's wide-eyed expression and blubbering suggested it was far too much, but Logan didn't care. He grabbed his suitcase and stepped out, finding himself in front of a modern and elegant hotel. Logan walked through the grand entrance, dragging his suitcase behind him as he approached the reception desk. "Hello, I need a room," he said, his voice flat with fatigue. "Just me. I don't know for how long."

The receptionist, a young woman with wide eyes and a shy smile, typed into her computer, sneaking glances at Logan every few moments.

"I'm sorry," she apologized eventually, her voice laced with a thick accent. "Only the suite is available."

Logan nodded, not hesitating as he reached for his wallet. "Then the suite it is," he stated, sliding his credit card across the desk.

The woman blushed faintly, clearly flustered. "Do... do you need help with your luggage?" she asked, her voice soft.

"No, thank you," Logan replied, taking his card back and pocketing it.

She offered him another shy smile while she continued typing on the computer. Then, she handed him the keycard, softly mentioning the room details and letting him know she's available for the night if needed, as he headed toward the elevator.

The suite was on the twentieth floor, high above the city. When Logan entered, he barely registered the luxurious surroundings. It was just a waypoint, a place to gather his frayed edges before the moment he both craved and feared.

He tossed his bag onto the bed, ignoring the neatly arranged amenities and the sweeping view from the floor-to-ceiling windows. All he wanted was a shower—to wash away the grime of the journey, the weight of the hours spent staring at his laptop, trying to distract himself from the emotions threatening to engulf him.

In the bathroom, the water poured down in a steady stream, hot and cleansing as it cascaded over his back. Logan leaned his hands against the wall, letting his head fall forward. "Breathe," he whispered to himself, the word almost drowned out by the sound of the water. He closed his eyes, willing himself to stay calm. The thought of seeing Adrian, of hearing his voice, was enough to make his heart race with both joy and terror.

What if he doesn't want to see me? What if I've already lost him for good?

But there was no going back now. The water carried away the dust and sweat, but it couldn't touch the ache in his chest or the hope that flickered brighter with every passing second.

Logan stepped out of the shower, tying a white towel low around his slim hips. The air in the suite was cool against his damp skin, brushing over him like a whisper he didn't ask for. As he moved toward the full-length mirror by the closet, his steps slowed. And then—he froze.

The reflection staring back at him was almost unrecognizable.

For the first time in two years, self-doubt struck him, not gently, not gradually, but with a force so raw it drove him back into his body. It was a cruel thing, self-doubt. Quiet and patient, it waited in the shadows until the right moment to break through. And now it did.

He couldn't remember the last time he'd felt happy. Not truly. There had been flickers, moments so faint they could be mistaken for joy. Fleeting glimpses where he wasn't aching for his breath to just stop. Sometimes, lost deep enough in a memory of Adrian, he might've passed for someone content. But it wasn't happiness. Not the real kind. Only the faint aftertaste of it, like perfume clinging to an empty room.

The past two years came back to him in fragments. Shards of days. Long, dragging hours heavy with silence. An ache that settled into his bones like winter. He remembered existing more than living, drifting, drowning, vanishing in slow motion.

There hadn't been enough of him present in those years to feel anything so trivial as vanity. He hadn't thought much about his appearance over that time. There hadn't been time or, truthfully, the will to care.

But now, standing there under the harsh hotel lamps, he was forced to look. What returned his gaze revealed no softness, no light; only the haunting silhouette of a man bleeding internally while the world continued to turn.

The man in the mirror bore the ballast of a soul too long unanchored, too long submerged, too long entombed in the eidolon of its long vanished half, dissolving like sea foam swallowed by the shore.

A face etched with the pain of surviving something that had already taken the best of him.

He didn't recognize himself. And yet, there he was. He was the living embodiment of the ruin of what love had made, and what loss had left behind.

Knowing he was about to see Adrian, he couldn't help but catalog the changes.

Back then, his life had revolved around the sea. Surfing every day had kept his body strong, his spirit free. He would run along the shore, race the waves, and bask in the golden light that seemed to follow Adrian wherever he went. But now... now he was simply lean, stripped of the vitality that had once been so integral to him. The sun had become a stranger. He had stayed away from beaches, from the water, from anything that reminded him of what he'd lost. His skin had thinned to a pallor, spectral, only accentuating the dark circles under his eyes, a testament to sleepless nights and restless days.

He wasn't the same Logan who had walked away.

His heart clenched painfully as his thoughts turned to Adrian. From the pictures Mr. Boyed had sent, Adrian hadn't changed much. He still looked strong, his body broad and tanned, his golden hair wild as the wind and waves seemed to embrace him. Logan hadn't let himself look at those pictures for too long; the sight of Adrian had been too much, too raw. And as for the others, the ones Mr. Boyed had sent but Logan hadn't yet opened... they remained untouched in his inbox, their presence a weight he wasn't ready to bear.

Logan dragged a trembling hand through his damp hair, breath breaking loose like something cornered. He knew this was not about appearances—Adrian had once loved him, not for flesh or form, but for the marrow of who he was. Yet the thought of standing before him now, emptied of the light Adrian had once kindled, left him hollow. Diminished. A ghost of a man, small beneath the weight of his own undoing.

He was no longer the Logan who had walked away.

That Logan had been burnished in gold, carved by sun and salt, hair stiff with seawater, arms forged from chasing horizons across continents. He had been beautiful without intent, magnetic without awareness. He had been a creature of radiance, and radiance had answered him in kind.

The man in the mirror was only his residue, a specter inhabiting the void husk of what remained. His reflection bore the sallow stains of neglect, the erosion of self-contempt, eyes dulled to ash, extinguished of their fire for two long years.

He looked like a man who had abandoned the labor of living.

And beneath all the fear, beneath the cracked layers of guilt and longing, a single truth pulsed like a wound:

What if Adrian looked at him now and saw a stranger? What if he no longer recognized the man he once loved? What if Logan—*this Logan*—was no longer enough?

It wasn't rejection he feared; he had long since braced himself for that. What hollowed him was the terror that he was no longer worthy of Adrian's memory, that even the echo of their love might find him inadequate.

He straightened, forcing himself to meet his own gaze in the mirror. *You're not the same Logan*, he thought. *But you're here. And you're trying. All I have left is to try.*

He was not the same Logan who had walked away, not just physically, but in every way that mattered. The Logan staring back at him from the mirror, hollow-eyed and threadbare, would have never left in the first place. Because *this* Logan *had been scorched* through loving and leaving Adrian, through the unbearable silence that followed.

The Logan standing here now was not the man he had once been. He was the one who had *survived* what happened, the one who had been shaped—no, *scarred*—by the absence of the love of his life. He was the Logan who had learned, too late, that love is not a thing you walk away from and expect to remain whole.

He was the Logan who lived in the shadow of what had been, who carried the weight of leaving like a stone in his chest. That magnificent, unbearable burden of his own making.

And he was the Logan who had lived through his own reckless choices, who had felt their sharp edges carve into him with every passing day.

Now, two years later, he had come back, not as the man who once left, but as the man who had been broken by it.

All I have left is to try. At the very least, after everything, try. Explain. See him again.

The reflection didn't argue. The man Adrian would see might not be the one who had left him, but Logan hoped, prayed, that Adrian could still see the man who had loved him with everything he had.

Logan had spent two years refusing to let the thought linger, banishing it every time it tried to claw its way into his mind. But now, as he stood in the quiet of the hotel room, staring at his reflection, it came crashing down on him, a tidal wave of fear and jealousy he couldn't outrun.

Adrian might have a boyfriend now.

The thought didn't just sting; it shattered, like a fragile glass breaking apart inside his chest. It carved through Logan's heart with relentless precision, splintering the profound silence that had taken root within him. Two long, agonizing years, two goddamn years of absence, of silence so deafening it reverberated through every fiber of his being. He'd walked away from Adrian like a coward—without a word, without a reason—merely the echo of retreat lingering in the air. And Adrian... Adrian had never been the type to falter in darkness. He was the guiding light that pierced through even the deepest shadows.

Logan's gaze sharpened with clarity as his mind betrayed him with a vision: Adrian in a sun-drenched café, his laughter ringing softly amidst the hum of conversation. Across from him, another man sat captive in his orbit, gaze fixed with unblinking devotion. A hand rested casually on Adrian's thigh, an intimate touch that hinted at unspoken stories, while lips brushed tenderly against his temple. It was a love story unfolding before Logan's eyes, one he had once believed was his fate, yet now Adrian leaned into it, unguarded, radiant, offering that perilous love he carried so effortlessly; the kind that made men believe in miracles, the kind that could turn a passing hour into eternal promises, vows sealed in flower arrangements and guest lists where another man took his place.

Because how could someone not fall in love with him? He was a walking eclipse, light and shadow at once, and men would line up to bask in him, to try and be enough. Maybe one of them had stayed. Perhaps one had pressed him to sheets still warm from their shared body heat, mapped the body Logan once worshipped, whispered into the dark the words Logan was too afraid to speak. Perhaps one had stayed when Logan had fled.

And worst of all?

Maybe Adrian let him.

Because when Adrian loved, he didn't ration it. He poured it, like wine, like blood, like rain. He gave everything. He didn't know how to withhold. Logan had known that. Had been on the receiving side of it. Had run from it. Had thrown it away.

And now someone else might be holding what he couldn't hold.

Someone else might have been able to heal the curved wounds he left behind. Another might have gathered the fragments he shattered and coaxed them back into wholeness.

Perhaps Logan should have implored the investigator to uncover that small yet profoundly significant detail.

Maybe Adrian had found someone better. Maybe someone had come along and treated him with the kindness and devotion Logan hadn't been able to give. Maybe he'd gone back to *Itay*, his ex. The name alone was a dagger to Logan's chest. Itay, with his easy familiarity, his shared history carved deep into Adrian's life. The thought of Adrian in Itay's arms, laughing the laugh that once belonged to Logan, leaning into him with that unguarded trust, whispering those fragile sounds Logan had worshipped, made bile rise in his throat.

Logan bore no right to ache, especially not after his actions. Two years ago, he had faced the world and taken another's hand in marriage, vows slipping from his lips while Adrian witnessed. If guilt ever found a home, it was not with Adrian; it forever dwelled within Logan, an agitated essence haunting his every moment. Yet the memory clung to him; it was as if the memory itself was smoke, choking him with every thought of the pact Adrian had made with his own heart. Two years ago, Adrian had taken the same journey, flown from his home to a foreign country, braved unfamiliar streets and languages, all for the sake of love.

Adrian had walked those streets with a fragile but determined heart, broken yet beating with the faint flicker of hope. Every step was a prayer, every breath a plea for this love to be enough. And when he finally reached his destination—when he stood before Logan with all of his love laid bare—Logan had turned him away. Cruel words had spilled from his lips, sharper than any blade, slicing through the fragile wings of Adrian's hope. Logan hadn't just refused him; he'd sent him away with nothing but the weight of rejection and the echo of shattered dreams.

Adrian had crossed oceans for Logan, only to be left standing in the wreckage of what should have been. And now, Logan dared to feel the sting of regret? The irony was a bitter taste in his mouth, as sharp and unforgiving as the memory of the love he'd lost.

Logan pressed a hand to his stomach, trying to quell the nausea that threatened to overwhelm him. His insides twisted, his heart pounding with a mix of fear, guilt, and something far uglier: jealousy. He hated himself for it, but the idea of Adrian with someone else was unbearable. It knotted his stomach, a sharp, persistent ache that wouldn't let him go.

What if Adrian had moved on? What if someone else now had the privilege of kissing those lips, running their fingers through that golden brown hair, hearing Adrian laugh in that soft, musical way that made the world feel lighter? What if someone else was holding Adrian at night, tracing the lines of his back, whispering words of love into the dark? What if Adrian was playing his guitar for another man, singing to him in the quiet of the night with shining eyes and his heart on his sleeve? What if Adrian was worshipping another's body? What if, at this very moment, another soul were to experience the tantalizing brush of Adrian's stubble against their skin, sending shivers cascading down like whispers of the wind? What if, in this vast universe, a fortunate being felt the gentle caress of Adrian's fingertips as they glided over their flesh, tenderly cradling their face in an embrace that spoke volumes beyond words?

What if Adrian didn't want to see him? What if he opened the door, took one look at Logan—worn down and waterlogged with regret—and just smiled? Not cruelly. Not with anger. But with a kind of quiet mercy that made it worse.

What if he'd say, *"You did the right thing, Logan. We would've never worked. I'm actually seeing someone now. And I love him."*

Logan could hear it in his mind, the calm, measured way Adrian might say it. Not out of spite. But because he *meant* it.

The words would drift gently, like an unstoppable rain. And Logan? He'd just stand there. Nodding, maybe. Pretending it didn't cave something in his chest.

Because that would be the worst part, not that Adrian had moved on, but that he had done so *gracefully*. That he had survived Logan's absence. Found love in someone else's arms. Built something stable from the wreckage Logan left behind.

And if that was true, if someone else now knew the sound of Adrian's morning voice, the shape of his laugh, the look he gave just before kissing you like he meant it—

Then what had Logan come back for?

Logan gritted his teeth, his hands trembling at his sides. He hadn't let himself think about this, hadn't let the idea creep too deeply into his mind because he knew—he *knew*—he wouldn't have survived the flight, wouldn't have made it this far if he had. But now, standing here, the thought had taken root, and it was tearing him apart.

And what was he even doing here? What was he hoping to achieve by finding Adrian after all this time? Did he think he could just show up, explain himself, and then leave? Did he want Adrian to forgive him and let him walk away again? Or was he hoping—desperately, selfishly—to get Adrian back?

And then what?

Logan stared at his reflection, his pale skin, his hollowed-out eyes, the man he barely recognized. What could he possibly offer Adrian now? He had broken him, walked away without giving him the love he deserved, and now he wanted to come back. For what? To ask for a second chance? To tear open wounds Adrian had probably spent years trying to heal?

The questions swirled in his mind, a tempest of guilt and longing, until his knees felt weak and he had to sit on the edge of the bed. His heart ached with every beat, pounding out a rhythm of regret and despair. The thought of Adrian happy with someone else was unbearable, but the thought of Adrian still hurting because of him was worse.

Tears pricked at the corners of Logan's eyes as he buried his face in his hands. He didn't know what he was doing, didn't know what he wanted, except that he needed to see Adrian again. To hear his voice, to look into those whiskey-colored eyes, to *know*, to *explain*.

Logan pulled open his suitcase, his hands shaking as he rifled through the clothes he'd hastily packed. His heart pounded against his ribcage, each beat a deafening reminder of the anxiety clawing at him. What was he supposed to wear? It was a stupid question, meaningless in the grand scheme of everything, but it consumed him in the moment.

He aimed to look good for Adrian, no, he needed to. It was essential for Adrian to see him and not think of the broken man who had walked away two years ago. His chest clenched at the memory of who he was then and who he had become. The Logan Adrian had known lived in board shorts and tank tops, always shirtless, with skin tanned and sun-kissed, barefoot more often than not. The Logan now standing here was a refined businessman, dressed in expensive suits and tailored clothing, a wardrobe carefully chosen to convey power and respectability.

But none of that felt right. None of it felt like *him*.

He tossed aside a blazer, then a pair of slacks, pulling out a gray button-down shirt and some black jeans. He ran his fingers over the fabric, his mind a chaotic mess. Maybe he should call Adrian first. *God, should I just call him?* he thought. *Talk to him before showing up at his doorstep? Test the waters before barging into his life again, uninvited?*

But no. Logan shook his head. He needed to do this right, face-to-face. Adrian deserved at least that.

Still, the indecision made his breath catch. His mind wandered to Ada Mae, and for a ridiculous moment, he considered calling her for advice. Should he go casual? Stick with something sharp and professional? Would a suit scream desperate? Would jeans feel too casual?

"Damn it," he muttered under his breath, running a hand through his hair. He felt ridiculous. Here he was—twenty-seven years old, a successful businessman, part of the most powerful shipping company in the world, and heir to an empire—and he was standing in front of a suitcase debating what to wear to impress a guy.

The weight of that realization made him laugh bitterly. "God, I'm pathetic."

He grabbed the gray shirt, slipping it on and buttoning it up with trembling fingers. If he chose it because Adrian always loved him wearing gray or light blue, as it made his eyes stand out, that was his own business.

The black jeans came next, followed by a spritz of cologne. He smoothed his hair back, trying to strike a balance between looking good and not looking like he'd spent an hour preparing to see Adrian. He stared at himself in the mirror, adjusting the collar of his shirt before stepping back.

His reflection stared back at him, pale and nervous. He looked good, he supposed. Polished, put-together. But he also felt like he might faint.

This is fine. It's fine, he told himself, shoving his feet into his shoes. Before he could second-guess himself again—or, God forbid, start changing his outfit in front of the mirror like a teenager—Logan grabbed his phone and left the room.

The cab ride felt like both an eternity and a blink. Logan handed the driver the address, barely looking at the screen as he asked if he knew where it was. The driver nodded, his English heavily accented as he reassured Logan he knew the place. The man chatted as he drove, filling the silence with small talk in broken English about the area, the weather, and the traffic. Logan barely processed the words, his mind too busy spiraling. Still, he was grateful for the distraction; it kept him from telling the driver to turn around and take him back to the hotel.

Logan's hands rubbed against his thighs, the rough texture of his jeans grounding him as he tried to steady his breath. The cab stopped suddenly, jerking him out of his thoughts, and his heart stuttered in his chest.

"House over there," the driver said, his voice kind as he pointed toward a small gray house nestled near the coastline in a line of houses. "Gray one, see, yes? Gray house, there, I'm talking about, yes? The last one in line. I with car, no get there, you... with legs, go, okay?"

Logan's gaze followed the man's hand, landing on the house. It wasn't much, modest and weathered, but its charm was undeniable. And it was so close to the ocean that Logan could feel the salt in the air, hear the faint rhythm of waves in the distance. Of course, Adrian would live here, never straying too far from the water.

"Yeah," Logan managed, his voice shaky as he stared at the house. "Thank you."

He handed the driver some cash, not caring how much, and waved off the man's protest that it was too much. Logan stepped out of the cab, the cool November breeze hitting him as he stood on the sidewalk. He watched the car pull away, leaving him alone with the weight of his decisions.

His feet felt glued to the pavement. He couldn't make himself move, his chest tightening as the first tendrils of a panic attack threatened to take hold. He knew he had to do this, had to face Adrian, no matter what he found inside that house. If Adrian had found another—if there was a man beside him, offering the devotion Logan had squandered—then Logan would bear it. He would stand in the ruin of his own jealousy, swallow the shards, and apologize for every betrayal. He would meet Adrian's gaze even if it split him open, and he would face the truth of what he had thrown away.

Hadn't Adrian endured the same? Standing at Logan's wedding, his eyes glistened with unshed tears until they finally fell, his voice breaking as he whispered love into a moment that crushed him.

So if Adrian had joy now, if another man carried the light that once belonged to Logan, then he would not fight it. He would slip away quietly, and perhaps he'd be blessed with a final embrace, a farewell pressed in silence, a last chance to feel Adrian in his arms, and he would take a breath that must last him the rest of his life. He would thank Adrian for this life, for the opportunity to be in his life, for the miracle of having been loved at all, and promise—no, pray—that when their souls met again in some distant universe, he would be braver, he would be worthy. And until that universe arrived, he would count the moments like rosary beads, each one burning in his hands.

Logan's legs finally obeyed, carrying him forward with unsteady steps. Each pace toward the gray house felt heavier, the air colder, the salt of the ocean cutting through his thin shirt and making him shiver. He tried to steady his breath, to calm the storm raging inside him, but it felt like a losing battle. The closer he got, the more the memories clawed at him;

Adrian's laugh, his touch, the way he'd looked at Logan as though he was the only person in the world.

I'm going to see Adrian again.

When Logan reached the front door, he stopped, his body trembling as the ocean breeze ruffled his hair. From here, he could see the beach stretching out behind the house, hear the waves rolling in, smell the brine of the sea. Adrian had built a life here, in the place where the water met the shore, where the ocean always whispered its secrets.

Logan's hand hovered over the door, his mind screaming at him to leave, to turn back, to run. But he couldn't. He wouldn't.

He knocked. Three quick, firm raps against the metal, the sound loud in the stillness of the afternoon.

Each knock seemed to echo back at him, hollow and accusing. The silence on the other side swelled until it pressed against his ribs, until every second dragged like a lifetime. His palms were damp, his breath caught between shallow gasps, and the world outside the door narrowed to nothing but the hinge, the handle, the hope.

When it finally creaked open, Logan's body jolted as if struck. For an instant, he saw him—Adrian, haloed by ocean wind, hair unruly, whiskey eyes widening in recognition. But the vision dissolved as the door swung wider.

Logan went still. His throat closed, his pulse stumbled. It wasn't Adrian.

The man at the door stared at him, eyes wide, his mouth hanging open in stunned silence. Logan recognized him immediately.

"Logan?" the man asked, his voice marked by his accent's rhythm. "Logan? Ma ata—" he began in Hebrew, but quickly switched to English as his mind caught up. "What are you doing here?"

"Dean," Logan acknowledged, bracing himself. He half-expected a punch, a shove, or, at the very least, a scathing insult. Dean was Adrian's best friend, his protector, and after everything Logan had done, it only made sense that Dean would hate him. Deserve it, even.

But instead of anger, Dean's face lit up with something Logan couldn't quite place. Relief? Joy? "You came!" Dean exclaimed, his voice filled with a mix of surprise and something close to elation. "How did you hear?"

"What...?" Logan stammered, completely thrown off by Dean's reaction. Before he could even process what was happening, Dean stepped forward and pulled him into a tight hug.

What the fuck?

Logan stood stiff in Dean's arms, his mind racing. Dean had never liked him. The last time they'd spoken, there had been barely veiled hostility between them. After what Logan had done to Adrian—walking out of his life without a word—Dean should be shoving him off the porch, not hugging him like some long-lost savior.

"Thank you so much for coming! Really!" Dean said, relief in his eyes.

And then another thought struck Logan, sharp and painful. Why was Dean even here, in Adrian's house? Were they together? Was that why Dean had hated him? Because Logan had been a threat to his relationship with Adrian? The possibility made Logan's stomach churn with a mix of jealousy and guilt.

When Dean finally let him go, Logan took a shaky step back, his confusion plain on his face. "Is... is Adrian here?" he asked, his voice rough and uneven, his heart lodged somewhere in his throat. Nothing about this made sense, and Adrian was the only one who could explain what the hell was happening.

"Yes, yes, of course," Dean said, stepping aside to let Logan in. "Come on in, he's at the beach."

Logan hesitated for a moment, but then stepped inside, his eyes scanning the space. The house was larger than it appeared from the outside, and though it looked weathered and worn on the exterior, the inside was warm and inviting. It felt lived-in, homey, like the kind of place where someone like Adrian could build a life.

"Where is he?" Logan asked again, his eyes darting to a hallway that seemed to lead to the bedrooms. But what caught his attention most was the large backyard visible through the sliding glass doors. Beyond it, the beach stretched out, the waves rolling gently against the shore.

The view was breathtaking, and Logan envisioned Adrian nestled within those walls, gazing at the horizon from the comfort of his home. Unlike Logan, Adrian could not escape the alluring call of the waves.

"The beach," Dean repeated, his tone patient but tinged with something Logan couldn't quite put his finger on.

"I'll wait for him there," Logan said, his voice soft as his gaze lingered on the shoreline. He assumed Adrian was surfing, his mind conjuring an image of Adrian cutting through the waves with that effortless grace Logan remembered so vividly.

"Sure, sure," Dean said, nodding as he moved toward the glass doors. "I'll take you to him."

Logan followed, still grappling with the strangeness of the encounter. Dean's happiness at seeing him felt out of place, incongruous with everything he knew. But he pushed the thoughts aside. Right now, all that mattered was Adrian.

The wind carried the scent of salt and freedom as Logan followed Dean, his steps hesitant, his mind racing. The sea roared in the distance, its eternal rhythm a backdrop to the storm raging within him. His heart pounded like the surf breaking on the shore, relentless and unforgiving.

Logan cleared his throat, his voice cracking as he asked the question that had been clawing at his mind. "Are you two together?"

Dean turned, a look of incredulity flashing across his face. "What? No. I'm straight," he said simply, shaking his head as they crossed a narrow road. "And Adrian's basically my brother."

Logan's chest tightened at that. "Is he... is he seeing someone?"

Dean glanced at him, his voice calm but firm. "Of course not."

The words settled like stones in Logan's stomach, heavy and confusing. Dean had said it as if the very idea was absurd, but Logan couldn't understand why. Adrian was *Adrian*—beautiful, warm, the kind of person who could captivate anyone. Why wouldn't he be with someone? The question swirled in his mind as they made their way to the beach, the sand shifting under their feet.

"There he is," Dean said, his voice softer now, almost reverent. Logan's breath caught as he followed Dean's gaze.

And then—there he was.

Adrian sat at the water's edge, back to him, still as stone. His gaze was locked on the horizon as though the ocean alone could answer him. The surf licked at the shore in hushed devotion, the wind tossing strands of golden hair into a restless halo, a flag raised in quiet defiance.

Logan stopped breathing. The world broke into silence, everything folding into this single sight: Adrian, alive, within reach. His chest constricted, ribs groaning around a heart that seemed intent on tearing

41

free. The air thickened, charged, as if the universe itself had been holding this moment in reserve, waiting to detonate it inside him. The long, decaying melody of his heart—once only threnody—suddenly surged into song, clear and commanding, as if the missing half of him had returned to the world.

Adrian. A few steps away. A lifetime away.

Dean's voice broke through the haze, warm and almost jubilant. "I'm so glad you came, Logan. I'll give you two some time." Without waiting for a reply, he turned and left, his footsteps disappearing beneath the soft hum of the ocean.

Logan barely registered it. His feet moved without thought, the sand soft beneath his expensive shoes, the grains clinging to him as if urging him forward. The wind grew stronger as he approached, carrying with it the cool bite of November. It bit at his skin, but Logan barely felt it. All he could see was Adrian.

He stopped just a couple of feet behind him, his throat tightening as he took in the sight. Adrian hadn't noticed him yet. He sat there, his hands resting loosely on his knees, his face turned toward the endless expanse of blue. The sun glinted off the water, painting golden streaks that matched the strands of his hair, as if the ocean herself had claimed him.

Logan's breath hitched, his chest constricting as tears burned his eyes. He took a shuddering breath, his voice catching as he finally spoke, his words as soft as the breeze, fragile as the moment.

"Ad."

The name escaped him, barely audible, but it carried everything he was, everything he had ever felt. It was a wave crashing against the shore, desperate and inevitable, eroding everything in its path. His name left

Logan's mouth like breath breaking the surface after too long underwater. It wasn't loud. It wasn't rehearsed. It came out raw, like something pulled from the deepest part of him—half prayer, half apology, all ache. A name he hadn't uttered in years, merely forming its contours with his lips, and on rare occasions summoning the courage to speak it aloud in hushed silence, now hung in the air between them, trembling and heavy with everything he could never say.

Adrian stilled.

The subtle lift of his shoulders, the pause in his breath—Logan saw it all. But he didn't turn around. He stayed facing the ocean, legs pulled close to his chest, arms wrapped loosely around them. He looked like he had been carved into the setting—sculpted out of stillness and sun, out of memory. That stillness was the loudest answer Logan had ever received.

Logan felt his heart shatter a little more, the silence slicing deeper than he had ever imagined. He had envisioned this moment a myriad of times, rehearsing every possible scenario in the theater of his mind: a furious slap, a bitter laugh, a tearful embrace. But not this—this unbearable quiet, this aching distance dressed in sunlight and salt air. He wanted to speak again, to explain, to fall to his knees if he had to. Yet now that he found himself here, gazing at the love of his life, his voice was silenced by an overwhelming tide of fear, guilt, and the heavy burden of unexpressed words, as everything he needed to say dissolved before reaching his mouth. Tears welled in his eyes, blurring the image of Adrian—his figure elegantly framed against the vast, azure embrace of the ocean.

Here you are, my love.

And yet, despite everything, they were here. Breathing the same sea-salted air. Standing on the same sand. Watching the same sky change colors above them. The same sky they used to chase from country to country, from wave to wave, as if they could outrun gravity itself.

Logan took a single step forward. The sand gave beneath his foot, soft and damp, and something in his chest crumpled under the weight of it. He was close enough now that if he reached out, his fingers could brush Adrian's shoulder, could thread through that familiar sun-kissed hair. But he didn't. Because touching Adrian now felt like waking a sleeping star. Like interrupting something sacred.

The ache to reach him burned in his palms. But instead, he stood still and let the ache speak. Let it seep into the silence between them. Let it say: *I came back. I never stopped loving you. I broke everything and carried the pieces here.*

Adrian's profile was etched in gold by the dying sun. Logan watched the wind stir the hem of his shirt, saw his fingers clench faintly in the fabric resting on his knees. He was right there, the man Logan had never truly left, not even for a breath. And for the first time in years, they were in the same orbit again. Not in memory. Not in dreams. Here. Now.

Adrian didn't move. Not a single muscle. But Logan could feel it, the way his name had struck him. The air between them was thick with something unspoken, a tension that neither of them could name but both could feel. Adrian's body was rigid, his shoulders drawn tight, and Logan's chest ached at the thought that his voice—the voice that once made Adrian smile—was now a source of pain.

Adrian closed his eyes tightly, as though willing himself to breathe. He knew that voice. He would always know that voice. It was etched into his very being, a melody he had tried so hard to forget but couldn't. It haunted him, followed him in the quiet hours, in the crashing waves, in the echoes of the life he used to have. It was raspy and soft, strong and light, all at once.

It was the sound of happiness.

It was *Logan*.

That single word—*Ad*—had unraveled something deep inside him, a thread he'd tried so desperately to keep knotted. Tears burned behind his closed lids, and Adrian saw him in his mind, as vividly as if he were standing there in front of him. The memory was sharp, aching: Logan's piercing eyes, his disarming smile, the way the sun seemed to love him, always dancing on his skin. Logan had lived in the depths of Adrian's mind for two years, and no amount of effort had ever been enough to let him go.

But now, reality was pressing in, and with it came the undeniable truth. That voice wasn't a dream. It wasn't a memory.

It was here.

Logan was here.

Logan is here.

Logan is here.

Logan is here.

Logan is here.

Logan is here.

A warmth spread through Adrian's chest, bittersweet and impossible to ignore, striking him to his very core. For a brief moment, he let himself feel it—the yearning, the pull, the piece of him that had always belonged to Logan. But with it came the pain, the hurt, the undeniable knowledge of what had been lost.

The waves continued their quiet rhythm, the wind whispering through the air, but neither of them moved. Logan stood behind him, his tears threatening to fall, while Adrian sat rooted in place, his heart pounding with every passing second.

Logan took a hesitant step forward, his chest tightening as he debated whether to sit beside Adrian. The idea of closing the distance between them felt both terrifying and necessary, but before he could move further, he saw Adrian shift.

Adrian pushed himself upright, each movement deliberate, fragile, as though rising cost him more than he could spare. Logan's gaze locked on him, unable to stray: the fists curling at his sides, bloodless knuckles pressed against sun-browned skin, the fabric of his shirt caught and twisted by the wind until it snapped and billowed like a sail fighting the storm. His hair whipped free, strands flaring gold in the dying light, wild and untamed.

The sight cleaved the breath from Logan's chest. Adrian's body was a battlefield of contradictions: rigid with restraint, yet trembling beneath the pressure of all he carried. The shock rippled through him in waves, invisible but violent, threatening to buckle his knees and drag him down into the sand. Still, he held his ground, eyes sealed shut, shoulders locked, bracing as though sheer will could keep him from collapsing.

He didn't want to turn. Logan felt it in the tautness of his frame, the desperate stillness of a man bargaining with himself: if he refused the moment, if he walked away blind, perhaps he could survive it. Perhaps he could keep the fragile pieces from shattering. But Logan knew the truth—that the instant Adrian turned, everything would break open, and neither of them would ever be the same.

Slowly, unbearably, Adrian turned, and in that instant, Logan's universe cracked down the middle.

Logan's world stopped as their eyes met. Adrian's face crumpled almost immediately, tears welling and spilling over before he could stop them. His whiskey-colored eyes glistened with pain, with anger, with a rawness that pierced him like ice splintering inside his chest. Adrian stood there, staring at him, his chest rising and falling unevenly as he struggled to breathe through the emotions surging in him.

Logan's pain plunged to depths he hadn't known existed as their eyes locked. It wasn't the tears that gutted him, tearing through flesh and setting fire to what lay exposed, but Adrian's gaze itself. Familiar, yet emptied, as if another soul looked out through the same whiskey shade, drained of its life. In the sunlight, his eyes glowed, fractured like citrine glass—still radiant, but shattered, altered forever, beautiful in a way that could never be whole again.

Logan had done this. He was the hand that had let the glass slip, the shatterer of what could never be mended. The knowledge seared through him, molten, merciless. Adrian's gaze was no longer the mischievous spark that once set Logan's veins alight; it was a ruin, a smoldering wreck, heavy with sorrow that clung to him like ash after a firestorm.

Adrian trembled, yet refused to retreat. Tears coursed in fragile, unstoppable lines, but his eyes did not falter. They were void of any light, burning only with the fractured brilliance of something crushed and reforged, jagged edges glinting, those citrine shards, beneath the sun. Fury flickered there, and grief, and a raw vacancy so profound it hollowed the air between them. Logan felt it carve through him, ruthless as crystal dragged across skin, each look a cut, each second an incision.

His breath came ragged, chest rising unevenly, every inhale like a body dragging chains across stone. The suffering of the beloved, Logan realized, is not thunder but silence; a silence so sharp it flays you open.

Adrian's lips quivered, his fists clamped tight as if he feared gravity might abandon him. For a single heartbeat, he allowed Logan to see the wreckage entire: the ruins still smoking, the raw fault-lines of a heart left to bleed for years. It struck with a violence that stole the ground from under him. His beautiful, broken Adrian stood there—scarred, trembling, yet unyielding, his body balanced on that unbearable edge between collapse and defiance. And Logan's heart splintered again, each fragment sharper than the last, cutting him from the inside out.

Adrian took him in, and it was like being thrown back in time. Those eyes, the ones that had once looked at him with so much love, now pursued him like ghosts. That face, which had filled his dreams and haunted his waking moments, was more vivid, more real, than anything he had dared to imagine. And those lips—soft, sweet, familiar—stung like a phantom touch, a memory that hadn't dulled despite the years.

Adrian could feel the wounds inside him opening again, tearing through him as if they'd never healed. Every scar he'd painstakingly worked to stitch together over the last two years burned anew, raw and bleeding. Logan's presence slashed through him like a rip current, dragging him back to the very moment his heart had broken.

The pain was unbearable, scorching him from the inside out. He thought he'd moved on. He thought he'd learned how to live with the ache. But seeing Logan standing there, his hands shoved into his pockets, his eyes filled with regret—it brought it all back. The anguish, the betrayal, the longing. It was as if time had collapsed, and the wounds had never been tended to at all.

In the blink of an eye, Adrian found himself alone once more in that secluded cabin in Australia. It was as if time itself had woven its threads around him, igniting a searing pain within his veins that danced like flames, pulling him back into the depths of memory.

Adrian's voice caught in his throat, his tears falling freely now, and all he could do was stare at Logan, the man who had once been his everything, and wonder how he was supposed to survive this.

The air between them was sharp and electric, the kind of tension that mirrors a storm at sea—beautiful, terrible, and ready to shatter. Adrian's eyes were burning embers, hot with anger and unshed tears as he faced Logan. But Logan could see it, beneath the surface. That flicker of something broken and betrayed, a light snuffed out but still glowing faintly beneath the waves.

When Adrian spoke, his voice was hard. "What are you doing here!?" he demanded, his words cutting through the air.

Logan flinched at the tone, but more than that, he yearned for the sound itself. Even in anger, Adrian's voice stirred something deep in him, a longing that clung to every word, as if it were a lifeline. "Ad, I—" Logan took a tentative step forward, the sand shifting under his weight.

"Who told you I'm here?!" Adrian's voice rose, almost a scream, but his tears betrayed him. They shone in his eyes, shimmering like the surface of the ocean before it breaks, turning his fury into something fragile, something heartbreakingly human.

Logan's chest tightened. He didn't want this version of Adrian, this anger, this pain. He wanted the husky laugh, the soft, joyful tone that once filled the spaces between them. But Logan knew he no longer had the right to want anything from Adrian.

"Dean," Logan started, his voice cracking as he reached for the words. "I came to your house, and I saw Dean—"

"Who told you to come here?!" Adrian roared, stepping back as if Logan's presence was a tide threatening to pull him under. He shook his head, his body trembling as he paced a few steps away. "Cut the shit out! Who was it? Tell me the truth, Logan!"

"No one!" Logan pleaded, his voice raw and breaking. "I swear to God, no one told me to come!"

Adrian's laugh was a sharp, bitter chime, out of place against his sunny personality and kind spirit. "Fucking liar," he sneered, shaking his head as he cursed under his breath. "Two years. Two fucking years of nothing, not even a goddamn word, and now you're here? Suddenly, you're here?"

Adrian pivoted, his shoulders a fortress of rigidity, bracing against the tide of his mounting anguish. Logan's reaction was swift and instinctive; his hand reaching out to grasp Adrian's wrist, a silent plea amidst the chaos. "Ad, wait—"

Adrian recoiled like he'd been burned, yanking his hand back with such force that Logan stumbled. "Don't you fucking touch me!" Adrian shouted, his voice a whip, his face twisted with so much pain it was unbearable to look at. "Take yourself and your pity and get the fuck away from me!"

"What pity?" Logan's voice was desperate, trembling. "What the hell are you talking about?" Tears traced silent trails down his face as he searched for words, those elusive whispers that might tether Adrian's heart, compel him to listen, and hold him here. "I left my wife—"

"Then you're a fucking idiot!" Adrian snapped, his voice cutting through Logan's words. "You left her for what? Six months? Go back to her. Run back home, Logan."

"Six months?" Logan repeated, his voice hollow with confusion. "What are you—?"

"Fine! Not six! Maybe eight. Maybe five. Does it fucking matter?" Adrian's voice broke, trembling with something deeper than anger. "What are you even doing here, Logan? What the hell do you want?"

Logan stepped forward, his hands trembling at his sides. "I came to explain myself," he whispered, the words tumbling out in broken pieces, hushed by the gushing wind. "I... I shouldn't have walked away. I shouldn't have said the things I said at the wedding. I was... I know I was horrible to you. I'm disgusted by the things I said to you. I'm sorry for all of it. I'm sorry I blocked you out. I'm sorry for leaving... I'm sorry for everything." His voice cracked as tears streamed down his face. "And I miss you. God, Adrian, I miss you."

The confession hung in the air, friable as blown glass, exposed and trembling.

But Adrian laughed.

And it was not the laugh Logan had once memorized, not the melody spun from sunlit mornings and salt-drenched days. No—this was something unrecognizable. Bitter, cavernous, hollow as a crypt, carrying the echo of a stranger's voice wearing Adrian's shape.

It was the sound of a man who had bartered away joy for silence, who had surrendered his brightest summers for winters of solitude. A soul scorched by memories hotter than fire, more merciless than any weapon forged by human hands.

It was a laugh wrested from a heart that never ceased to bleed; a heart that had once been laid, whole, in Logan's hands. And when Logan fled, he carried the shattered pieces with him, leaving Adrian only with the echoes, painfully bleeding. And Adrian, he had never truly learned to live in the wake of that absence. He had only ever learned to breathe within the desolation it left behind; to walk with the shadow it cast across every hour. He carried the wound in his chest until it became his heart, an unfaithful surrogate, raw and unclosing. He lived with that counterfeit pulse, with the gaping fissure, the endless seep of blood he gathered in trembling hands, smearing it over memory after memory, as though grief could be rewritten, as though love might be painted back into existence.

Adrian's lips curved, but it was no smile, only a rough contortion, a sour twist that cut Logan to the bone. "You really don't know, do you?" His voice was low, almost incredulous, though his gaze burned steady and unflinching.

Logan felt himself unraveling. "What don't I know?" he shouted, desperation raw in his throat.

Adrian's mouth tightened again, a grimace masquerading as mirth, warped in all the wrong ways, like thunder where sunlight once lived. His eyes glinted distant and cold, his face etched with something Logan couldn't name: anger, despair, perhaps resignation itself.

"You really don't know?" Adrian asked, his voice carrying a quiet disbelief that cut deeper than any shout. The smile lingered, brittle as glass, ready to shatter at the slightest touch.

Logan felt his chest constrict as if the air had been stolen from the world. "What don't I know?" he shouted, his voice hoarse with frustration and fear, as though screaming might somehow force the truth out of Adrian. "For God's sake, Adrian, what is it that I don't know?"

Adrian tilted his head, studying Logan with a searching gaze, as if trying to determine whether this was some cruel joke or an act of fate. "This isn't a scam? None of my friends told you anything? You didn't come because of them? No one had told you to come?"

"No!" Logan's voice broke, the single word echoing between them, raw and desperate.

Adrian nodded, head bowed, his eyes tracing the grains of sand as though each one carried a secret ledger of his existence. The sea breathed behind them, filling the silence, the tide's pulse erasing footprints even as they were made, mocking the fragility of bodies and their borrowed time. Silence thickened, and for a moment, Logan thought he might collapse beneath it. Then Adrian looked up.

And in that single upward flicker, the world reconfigured. His gaze was no longer merely human but the aperture of some deeper abyss, a clarity so merciless it stripped Logan bare, marrow to skin. His voice followed, low and steady, syllables knotted with resignation yet bright with a terrible finality, words that rewrote the horizon.

"Missed your chance, Lo," Adrian said. "I'm sick. Cancer. Six months."

The words hung in the air like a thunderclap, leaving nothing but devastation in their wake. Logan's breath caught, his knees threatening to buckle as his mind scrambled to comprehend what Adrian had just said. It wasn't possible. It couldn't be.

The world around him twisted, stretched thin like a film about to tear, the colors of the ocean too bright, the sky too wide, the air too thick. The sound of the waves became a roar in his ears, not soothing anymore but cruel—indifferent—as if the sea didn't care that the one person who had once saved Logan from drowning was now the one sinking. The one person in this world whom Logan loved so deeply was about...

He stood there, staring at Adrian, his jaw trembling as he struggled to voice a sound—a denial, a plea, anything at all—but silence engulfed him. His mouth parted, yet speech eluded him. His tongue felt weighed down, his throat constricted. His heart, a clenched fist within his chest, pounded fiercely against the ribs, yearning to be unleashed, to break free from this waking nightmare before it devours him whole.

Cancer.

Cancer.

Six months.

Cancer.

Cancer.

Six months.

The words rolled in his brain over and over, refusing to leave him, refusing to let go.

Cancer. Six months. Cancer. Six months. Cancer. Six months. Cancer. Six months. Cancer. Cancer. Cancer.

It pulsed, a drumbeat that cracked against his skull, a blast in the form of a handful of words.

His breath splintered, shallow and ragged, as if air itself had betrayed him. The world tilted sideways, colors draining, the ground beneath his feet nothing but shifting sand.

Cancer. The sound wrapped around his chest like barbed wire, cinching tighter, each syllable a thorn pressing deeper. His heart clawed against the cage of his ribs, desperate, suffocating, as if it, too, could not bear the weight of Adrian fading from the earth.

The man he had crossed oceans to find, the soul he had begged the stars to return, was dying. And the universe etched the word into his marrow until it burned: cancer.

Adrian's face didn't falter. No flicker of fear, no crack in the mask. His gaze was steady, his tone almost casual, as though he were speaking of a stranger's fate, not his own. The merciless and heavy words hung between them, but his expression carried the stillness of someone who had already surrendered to the surge. Then, with a grace that cut deeper than any violence, he turned. Each step back toward the house was measured, unhurried, as if time itself bent to his indifference.

Logan stood there, frozen, his feet anchored in the sand, and the roar of the ocean was the background sound to his entire world collapsing around him. The love of his life had just spoken the words that shattered everything, and yet he walked away as if he had said nothing at all. As if he had merely mentioned that it might rain later or that he was going to grab dinner, like it wasn't the equivalent of pulling the sun out of the sky and leaving the earth to stumble blind in the dark.

His chest burned, a fire with no oxygen, a scream that never left his throat. He wanted to protest, to undo, to demand that Adrian take it back, that it wasn't true, that it was a mistake, a lie, anything but real. But the words wouldn't come, wouldn't form, wouldn't save him.

Logan was still standing there, unable to move, as if his feet were cemented to the sand, while Adrian's figure disappeared into the distance, swallowed by the golden hues of the setting sun. The world around him seemed to blur, the roar of the ocean fading, leaving only the echo of Adrian's words reverberating in his mind.

Cancer. Dying. Six months.

The words transcended mere syllables; they dissolved, evaporated, then cascaded over him like rain, flooding the ocean within, conjuring waves that battered him and stole his breath. They were tearing Adrian from him, and his name hovered on Logan's lips, a silent prayer, a profound longing, a forsaken plea that echoed with vengeance when all others had fallen to desolation. He could feel the brumal chill seeping into his bones, freezing him from the inside as the realization began to settle in his chest, and the frost claimed all the space his lungs could no longer fill.

And then Dean's words clicked into place.

The realization slowly struck him, as his mind was overwhelmed, with three words ringing louder than all others. Adrian wasn't just walking away; he was slipping through Logan's fingers forever. Hot tears spilled down Logan's cheeks, burning his eyes, as a knot of emotion tightened in his throat. His bottom lip trembled like a child lost and yearning, and he let the tears fall. There was no stopping them. The pain clawed its way through him, overwhelming and raw, leaving him hollow.

Adrian was dying.

The thought made him stagger, bile rising in his throat as his stomach churned. He doubled over, pressing a hand to his chest as if that might somehow dull the ache that burned there. How had it come to this? How could the man who had pulled him from the ocean, who had saved his life in every way that mattered, who was the only source of comfort in Logan's miserable life, be fading like this?

But the despair didn't last. It couldn't. Adrian had left behind too many ghosts, too many fragments of things never spoken. The silence between them wasn't just empty; it was unfinished. And Logan could no longer live in the ruins of almost.

His breath hitched. His hands trembled. But he straightened, bone by bone, like someone remembering how to stand. Grief would have to wait.

Answers came first.

Movement. Action. *Something*.

He couldn't afford the luxury of falling apart, not when there was still a chance to put something back together.

The gray house was visible from where he stood, a stark reminder of where Adrian had gone, and Logan ran toward it, unsteady as the shifting sand beneath his trembling steps. His legs burned, his breaths sharp and labored, but he didn't stop. Couldn't stop. By the time he reached the terrace, his hands juddered, not with life, but with the shudder of something about to detonate. The sliding door opened beneath his touch, and then he was inside, his body moving before his mind could process the madness of it. The air was thick as stormwater, humming with rage, dripping with grief, heavy with longing, saturated with the unmistakable gnawing pang of regret, the pungent sillage of a love neglected until it soured into ruin.

Adrian stood in the middle of the room, his arms crossed, his jaw locked tight. He was thinner than Logan remembered, and it hit him like a gut punch, the way his skin seemed to stretch over sharper bones, the way his eyes—*God, his eyes*—smoldered with exhaustion beneath all that fury. When he saw the photos Mr. Boyed sent, he initially thought Adrian looked relatively the same. He was gravely mistaken; perhaps it was the excitement of seeing Adrian again, or the camera angle, or the distance between them, but Adrian was no longer the same. Logan was looking at someone who was ill, and that person was the love of his life.

Dean stood beside him, glancing between them with wary eyes, a silent witness to the storm brewing.

"Get out!" Adrian spat, his voice sharp as broken glass, and Logan felt them to his core, felt them slicing him, wounding him. Adrian turned on his heel, heading for the hallway.

"Ad—Adrian, please!" Logan cried, his voice breaking as he wiped at his tear-streaked face. "Please, just talk to me. Please! Just—just look at me."

Adrian froze for a moment but didn't turn around. "No," he said firmly, though his voice wavered, betraying the war inside him.

Dean, caught in the crossfire, hesitated before mumbling, "I'll let you talk," and moved toward the front door.

"No need," Adrian said sharply, his eyes flashing toward Dean. "Logan is not staying."

"Adrian, I'm not leaving." Logan's voice cracked as he took a step closer. "Please. Five minutes. That's all I'm asking. Five minutes to talk to you."

Dean's eyes softened as he glanced at Logan, then at Adrian, before slipping out the door without another word.

The silence stretched thinly between them. Adrian finally turned then, and Logan wished he hadn't. Because those eyes—those damn eyes—weren't just angry. They were hurt. They were tired. They were hiding something Logan didn't yet understand. And that made it worse.

"You have some nerve," Adrian spat, his voice shaking now, no longer as controlled as he wanted it to be. "Coming here... After everything. After the way you—" He laughed, bitter and cold, but he didn't finish that sentence. "You said you're sorry," he said coldly, his voice barely above a whisper. "I heard you. Now leave. I'm sure you know how."

Logan flinched, breath caught like a whisper in the night. Before words could dance upon his lips, before explanation could weave its tale, Adrian's voice, a tender hush, fell like silken rain. Yet within that softness, a sharpness gleamed, cutting through the still air, leaving Logan exposed, raw beneath the weight of unspoken truth. "Or would you rather wait until I fall asleep so you can slip out real quietly, just like last time?"

The accusation struck Logan like a blow, reverberating through his chest and before he could think, he strode forth with purpose, positioning himself in Adrian's path. "Adrian," he breathed, his voice trembling, quivering, a fragile note now that he stood so close to Adrian again. "I—I don't know what to say. I don't think 'sorry' is enough, but it's all I've got. Please, just—please hear me out."

Adrian's breath trembled. His jaw locked, his lips pressing into a thin, bloodless line, but the rage beneath his skin was restless—unstill, unquiet. A shudder rippled through him, a violent tremor barely contained, his fingers curling into fists at his sides as if gripping at the fraying edges of something breaking apart. His throat bobbed, his breath a stuttered thing, caught between fury and something too tender to name.

Then—he moved.

Suddenly, Adrian's hands seized Logan's shirt, and in the next breath, Logan's back collided with the cold, unyielding wall. The force of it rattled through his bones, stole the breath from his lungs, but none of it mattered—because there, mere inches away, was Adrian.

So close that Logan could feel the tremors dancing beneath Adrian's skin, the rhythmic rise and fall of his chest echoing like a restless sea on the brink of a storm, yearning to unleash its fury.

Close enough to kiss, to melt into that breathtaking proximity.

Close enough to disappear into the gravity that had never really let them go.

Close enough to behold the haunting ache mirrored in those whiskey-colored eyes, those deep, soulful wells that Logan chased endlessly through the corridors of his memories.

Close enough to reach out and undo the tie on Adrian's hair, like Logan had done countless times before. He could have touched his face, traced the lines grief had drawn, kissed the place where fury and pain lived beside love.

Even in anger, Logan wanted him.

No—he *needed* him.

And if Adrian offered anything, even rage, Logan would take it. Take it all. Take *him*.

Adrian's voice broke open, ragged and wrecked.

"You fucking left me!"

The words cracked like thunder, splintering through the air between them. They struck Logan forcefully, echoing through the silent house and spilling into the pain that separated them, where the ocean roared and crashed, unsettled just like the space between them.

Tears poured down Adrian's face, his anguish spilling out. "You left! You got up and walked away, like I was *nothing!*" His grip tightened on Logan's shirt, his body trembling with the force of his anger and heartbreak. "You tore me apart! You ripped me to pieces and didn't even look back!"

Logan didn't fight it, didn't try to pull away. He let Adrian's words crash into him, let them cut him open and expose every ounce of his guilt. Adrian's pain was a storm raging in front of him, his eyes screaming the truth of his torment louder than his voice ever could.

"I know," Logan choked, his own tears falling in rivers. "I know I did. And I hate myself for it, Ad. I hate myself every single day for what I did to you. I *am* sorry!"

Logan's tears fell freely, warm trails cutting down his face as if Adrian's words had unearthed him—dug down through layers of scar tissue and time, brushing dust from bones he thought were long buried. He didn't resist Adrian's grip when he was dragged forward, didn't fight back when he was shoved again.

He couldn't.

The anger, the sorrow, and the betrayal pouring from Adrian were raw, unfiltered, and well deserved. Logan could only stand there, silent and breaking, as Adrian unleashed everything he had kept buried.

"You never answered your phone!" Adrian's voice quivered. Tears streamed down Adrian's cheeks, revealing the depth of the wreckage Logan had left, the aching longing that still haunted him even now. "You fucking blocked me! Threw me away like I was nothing! You vanished after everything we shared—and then you got married!" His voice crescendoed, not just in volume, but in the unbearable weight behind each word—grief, betrayal, love twisted into something unrecognizable. It was thick with anguish, each syllable drenched in the heavy burden of years filled with heartbreak.

The words spilled from Adrian in a torrent, a mess of grief and rage born of sleepless nights, of replaying the same cruel moments over and over until they poisoned his very being. Adrian's body trembled, not with weakness, but with the sheer force of emotion that had gone unspoken for too long.

He had carried this hurt for years, letting it eat him alive, turning every memory into a weapon against himself. And now, faced with Logan, all of it erupted, raw and unrestrained. "You didn't even care what it did to me, did you? You ruined me!" Adrian shouted, his voice breaking as his fury gave way to despair. His words hung in the air, a chorus of betrayal that Logan knew he would never be able to erase.

"I'm so, so sorry!" Logan choked, his voice breaking, but the words sounded hollow even to him.

"I don't *care* that you're sorry!" Adrian spat, his voice trembling with rage and grief. He shoved Logan harder this time, his tears mixing with the venom in his voice. "How dare you come here like this! After *everything!*" The words tumbled from him, sharp and jagged, cutting Logan deeper than anything he could have imagined. "How could you leave—after *everything!*" Adrian's voice cracked as tears streamed down his face, his hands shaking as they held Logan. "How could you *leave me?!*"

Logan opened his mouth, but no words came. He could only cry, watching as Adrian unraveled before him. Adrian's tears fell faster now, his breaths coming in shuddering gasps as he repeated the question again and again, as though searching for an answer that didn't exist.

"After everything! After... after everything!" Adrian's voice broke, unable to fully articulate the depth of their connection, the love they had shared, the unspoken promises Logan had shattered. His chest heaved with the weight of unsaid words, unhealed wounds. His eyes, filled with anguish, locked onto Logan's for a fleeting moment before he turned his gaze away.

"I'm sorry," Logan whispered again, his voice trembling. "I'm sorry. I'm sorry…" It was all he could say, the only words his guilt-ridden mind could muster.

Adrian let him go, his hands falling to his sides as though they no longer had the strength to hold on. He turned his back on Logan and walked toward the sliding doors, the ocean stretching endlessly before him. He stood there, his silhouette framed by the fading light, his shoulders sagging as though the weight of Logan's presence was too much to bear.

"What cancer?" Logan asked, his voice barely audible as he straightened his shirt, his hands still trembling.

"It doesn't matter," Adrian uttered, his voice quiet and hollow, his gaze fixed on the horizon. He couldn't look at Logan, not now, not with every glance threatening to tear him apart. Every moment in his presence was a reminder of what they had been, and what they had lost.

"It matters to me," Logan said softly, his voice pleading. "Please, Ad… talk to me."

"Logan." Adrian's voice was softer now, somehow sounding more broken than his anger. "Please go. I'm begging you… go." Tears spilled from his eyes again, silent and remorseless. "I can't look at you."

Logan took a step closer, his heart shattering with every tear that fell from Adrian's eyes. He saw the pain written all over him, the love Adrian tried so hard to hide, but couldn't. It was all there, spilling out, raw and exposed.

Adrian clenched his jaw, his hands balling into fists at his sides as he tried to steady himself. He had thought about this moment so many times, imagined Logan coming back for him, begging for a second chance. But reality was crueler than any fantasy. Having Logan here, so close, only magnified the ache he had spent two years trying to bury.

"I can't," Logan said, his voice firm despite the tears streaming down his face. "I won't leave you again. Not like this. Not until we talk. I'll drive you crazy if I have to, but I'm not walking away this time."

"Why?" Adrian cried, spinning to face him, his tears glinting in the dim light. "Why now? Why? Two years, Logan. *Two years!*" His voice cracked with the weight of his pain. "And I didn't hear a word from you. Not one fucking word. And now—now you come? When I'm dying?"

Logan flinched as if the words had struck him physically, but Adrian wasn't done.

"You cut me out, Logan. You left me bleeding." His voice dropped to a whisper, trembling with anguish. "I had nothing. And now, when I'm finally at peace, when the pain is about to be stopped, *you show up?*"

Logan felt his knees weaken, his breath coming shallow. Adrian's eyes, usually so full of fire and life, were dark, distant, like a sea pulled too far by an unreachable moon. He searched for the words, something, anything, to stem the devastation he had caused. But there were no lifeboats here, no calm waters to be found.

"I know I hurt you," Logan whispered, his voice breaking against the silence between them. The words fell like pebbles into the ocean, swallowed instantly by the depths. "I know I don't deserve to be here. But I can't—I can't let you go through this alone, Adrian. I can't lose you." His voice cracked, tears spilling down his face. "I can't lose you, again."

Adrian's gaze, steady and hollow, pierced through him. His tears fell without sound, tracing the planes of his face, a testament to the storm he refused to unleash. Behind him, the waves mirrored his turmoil, their restless movement a reflection of his fractured soul.

"You already have," Adrian said, his voice soft but cutting, a whisper that echoed louder than any shout.

Logan staggered under the weight of those words, his heart splintering like driftwood in a tempest. "Ad..." he began, his voice trembling. "There wasn't a second—there hasn't been a second in the past two years when I haven't thought of you."

The words tasted like salt on his tongue, and he fought the urge to reach for Adrian, to close the unbearable distance between them. He longed to hold him, to anchor him, but his hands stayed by his sides, trembling with the weight of his guilt. He knew he had forfeited that right.

"Why?" Adrian's voice cracked, the anger surging to the surface like an undercurrent breaking free. "Why did you go, Logan? How could you leave me? How could you leave us behind, how could you leave that cabin without a second glance? How could you walk away like I didn't matter?" His voice broke again, and his hands clenched at his sides as though bracing against the flood of emotions threatening to drown him.

Logan's chest heaved, his own tears a stream flowing from his eyes. "I was a coward," he admitted, his words tumbling out like debris caught in the waves. "I was scared. Of my father. Of what the world would say. But not a day went by that I didn't regret it. Not a day went by that I didn't wish I had stayed. With you."

Adrian shook his head, a bitter laugh slipping past his lips, bleeding and sharp, like the cry of a seabird lost in the fury of a storm. His eyes glistened, not with hope, but with the sheen of heartbreak too familiar, too enduring. "And yet, you didn't," he said, his voice trembling, carrying the weight of injuries long left to fester. "So don't stand here now and tell me you care. Don't tell me you cared back then. Because if you did, Logan, you wouldn't have left. You wouldn't have shattered me into pieces too small to ever put back together."

His voice cracked as the truth spilled out, a flood of bitterness and sorrow that he could no longer keep contained. "You built a life with someone else, Logan. *Days. Days* after you ruined me. Days after I touched you, after I stood there with everything I had left to give, you went back to your life like I was nothing. Like I was disposable. Like I never even mattered."

Adrian took a shuddering breath, his shoulders rising as if he were summoning the last of his strength to keep standing. His gaze bore into Logan, his eyes filled with the kind of agony that only came from someone who had replayed every moment, every word, a thousand times over. "So even if, at some point, I might have believed you were scared—believed there was some part of you that cared about me—I've had a lot of time to think about it. To run it through my mind, over and over, until there was nothing left but the truth."

He stepped closer now, his voice lower, quieter, but heavy with an intensity that threatened to swallow them both. "And the truth is, Logan, you didn't just leave me. You erased me. You destroyed me and went back to everything like I never existed. And you don't get to stand here now, years later, and tell me you regret it. You don't get to claim you cared. Not after all of this."

The final words landed like a stone dropped into a still pond, their ripple spreading between them. Adrian took a step back, his movements slow and unpolished, his body aching with the weight of the distance he had no choice but to create. The space between them grew, an invisible chasm that felt vast and insurmountable—a divide that no apology, no tears, no desperate explanation could bridge.

His gaze held Logan's, a mix of fire and sorrow that burned with the fury of a man who had once given everything, only to be left with nothing. "You don't get to fix this now," Adrian said, his voice calm, but no less resolute. "You don't get to stand there and pretend you care after everything you've done. I've already had to learn how to live without you."

"Please, Adrian," Logan whispered, his voice raw, cracked, pleading like the mournful cry of a bird caught in the claws of a storm. His words trembled, each one clawing its way out of his chest, tangled and knotted with the desperation that bubbled inside him and now was spilling over. "Don't make me go. I can't walk away again. I won't." He swallowed hard, fighting against the suffocating lump in his throat, the burning tears that blurred the face of the man before him. Adrian's silence was a wall of pain, an unrelenting tide of sorrow that threatened to drown them both. Still, Logan forced himself to speak, his voice threadbare against the tempest. "You're right. What I did was unforgivable. I'm not here to erase it, or to ask you to forget it and move on. I'm just trying to explain, to make you see... why I failed you."

He stepped forward, tentative, his hands quaking like fragile leaves clinging to a dying tree. "I was scared, Adrian. Terrified. What we had... it was too big, too beautiful. It consumed me, and I didn't think I deserved it—or you. Instead of holding on, instead of staying and figuring out how to be the man you needed, I ran. I shut you out, blocked you, cut you off as if it would make the pain disappear. I thought if I made it impossible to go back, it would somehow get easier. But it didn't. It never did."

Logan's voice faltered, breaking under the weight of his confession, his tears now slipping freely down his cheeks. He pushed forward, desperate, vulnerable in a way he had never allowed himself to be. "And yes... I got married. I ran back to my old life, tried to convince myself that moving on was what I was supposed to do. But it wasn't marriage, Adrian—it wasn't love. It was a lie. A cruel, desperate lie I told myself because I couldn't face the truth of what I'd done to you. To us. And I dragged Sandy into it—God, I dragged her into my chaos, my brokenness. I hurt her too, all because I was pretending I wasn't destroyed. Pretending I didn't think about you every single day, regretting every single choice."

He paused, his gaze locking onto Adrian's with a depth of pain that could tear the heavens apart. "I've been miserable every day since we've been apart. Every. Single. Day. And I know—I *know*—I don't deserve your forgiveness. I don't even deserve to stand here in front of you. But I need you to understand: it wasn't because you didn't matter. It wasn't because I didn't care. I cared too much, Adrian. I cared so much it scared the hell out of me. You were the only thing in my life that was real, and I was too weak to hold on. Too selfish to be the man you deserved."

His voice grew softer now, like the last notes of a melody fading into silence. "I destroyed us. I destroyed you. And I've hated myself every single day for it. I know I can't undo what I've done. I know I've lost any right to ask for anything. But you weren't nothing, Adrian. You were everything. You still are."

Logan's words lingered between them, fragile as spun glass, heavy as an anchor sinking into the depths. The silence stretched, as if the air itself held its breath, waiting—hoping.

He didn't move. Couldn't. His heart pounded against his ribs, wild and desperate, clinging to the faint, impossible hope that his words might slip through the cracks, that somehow, in some quiet corner of Adrian's soul, they had reached him.

For a breath—just a single one—something flickered in Adrian's eyes. A ghost of the past, an ember of what once was. It danced there, weightless, aching, a half-remembered memory, a tenderly shaped whisper, fragile as seafoam and just as fleeting. In that instant, his soul loosened its grip on the hurt, the hollow in his chest closed, the bleeding stilled, and for the first time since his last night with Logan, he appeared to be someone who had finally gathered all his fragmented parts and composed them into a version of himself that knew how to find happiness.

But then it vanished. Extinguished without mercy. Like he was, in a single heartbeat, realizing he was too broken to ever be made whole again, like discovering cracks in the new version, seeing the façade and letting everything fall apart at once.

Logan felt it slip away, as though the universe itself had taken it back before he could reach for it.

He saw the exact moment Adrian's walls rose again, saw the war waging inside him—love and anger, longing and grief, hope and devastation. And then, the moment the war was lost. The part of Adrian that had shattered the night Logan left, the part that had never quite put itself back together—it won.

Logan felt it like a door slamming shut, like the final crash of a wave before the sea pulls back, leaving nothing but silence in its wake.

And God, it felt like losing him all over again.

"Logan," Adrian spoke at last, his voice low, weary, and final. "I don't have much time left. And I don't want to spend it fighting with you, reliving the worst moments of my life. Please... just leave the memories where they belong."

The words gnawed at him like rust, stripping the strength from his bones until he felt himself collapsing inward. He opened his mouth to protest, to plead one last time, but the look in Adrian's eyes silenced him. It was a look of quiet surrender, of someone who had carried too much for too long and was simply done.

Logan watched helplessly as Adrian turned away, his steps slow and careful, like a man walking into the sea, knowing he might not return. The sight of Adrian retreating toward the hallway, shoulders slumped, broke something deep inside him. Adrian didn't slam the door when he entered; he didn't need to. The finality of his steps was loud enough.

The ocean roared in Logan's ears, though he knew it was only memory, only blood rushing wild through his veins. Every nerve in him burned with the same command: *follow, fight, refuse the ending*. He would not lose Adrian to silence again. He would not leave another word unsaid, another wound festering in the dark. He would not surrender to absence, would not bow to the cruel whisper that Adrian was better off without him. No—he had come back to fight, and this time he would not let go.

He stumbled forward, desperation flinging him into motion. "Adrian, please!" His voice broke against the air as he reached the doorway. The door yielded easily beneath his hand, unlocked, and that small mercy struck him like a fragile victory, a crack of light in a collapsing world.

Adrian spun around, his face flushed with fury, his chest heaving as though the weight of his emotions was suffocating him. "Get the hell out of my room!" he shouted, the words bursting from him like a foundation finally giving way—loud, sudden, and devastating.

Logan froze, stunned by the intensity of Adrian's voice. "I just want to—"

Before he could finish, a strong hand clamped onto his shoulder, yanking him backward. Logan stumbled, nearly losing his balance, and found himself face-to-face with Dean, whose expression was a mixture of anger and pity.

Dean stepped between them like a barrier, his voice low but firm. "Enough."

Adrian didn't wait for further chaos. He slammed the door shut, the sound of the lock clicking like a final nail in the coffin. The silence that followed rang louder than the highest shriek, broken only by Logan's ragged breathing.

"What the hell are you doing?" Logan snapped at Dean, his frustration boiling over.

"What am I doing?" Dean shot back. "What the hell are *you* doing? You think you can just walk in here after two years, after the damage you caused, and demand anything from him?"

Logan's shoulders slumped as the weight of the confrontation settled over him. "I just want to talk to him—"

"You don't get to want anything!" Dean cut him off, his voice rising. "You don't get to make this about you. Not now. Not when he's..." Dean paused, his words catching in his throat before he steadied himself. "Not when he's sick."

Logan's stomach churned, his knees buckling slightly as he looked away. The word lingered in the air between them, reminiscent of the last note in a melody, resonating through the room with an undeniable finality that left the crowd breathless.

"Sick," Logan repeated quietly, his voice barely audible, that part hung there, and suddenly it was like he was learning about Adrian's illness all over again.

Dean nodded grimly, crossing his arms as he leaned back against the wall. "He's terminally ill. He's dying, Logan. Do you understand that? He's dying." Dean's voice broke slightly, but his gaze remained hard. "You don't get to come here, drag up the past, and upset him when every moment he has left counts."

Logan swallowed hard, his vision blurring with tears he didn't bother to wipe away. He felt like he was drowning, sinking into a sea of regret and helplessness. He moved toward the living room and sank into the couch, his hands trembling as he buried his face in them.

Dean followed, settling into a chair across from him. He leaned forward, his elbows resting on his knees, his expression unreadable. "God, Logan," he muttered, shaking his head. "I hate you so much. I don't even think *hate* is the right word for it."

Logan flinched at the venom in Dean's tone, but he didn't look up. "How much do you know?" he asked quietly, staring at the floor as though it held the answers he couldn't find.

Dean's laugh was humorless. "I know everything," he replied, his voice laden with bitterness. "I'm his best friend. Who do you think he called when you walked out of his life and left him in pieces? Who do you think picked him up from that cabin in Australia when he couldn't even stand on his own?"

Logan's chest tightened painfully. He'd spent two years suppressing those thoughts, locking them away in a part of himself he refused to visit.

"He was a wreck," Dean continued, his voice quieter now, but no less sharp. "I flew halfway around the world to find what was left of him. And let me tell you, Logan, you didn't just break his heart. You broke *him*."

Logan drew a sharp breath, the words not unfamiliar yet piercing all the same.

Dean sighed heavily, running a hand through his hair. "The thing is," he continued, the acerbity in his voice dulled, "I hate you, but that doesn't matter right now. What matters is him. And whether I like it or not, you're here now, and maybe—God help me—maybe you're what he needs."

Logan lifted his gaze, a fragile hope shimmering softly amidst the tear-streaked sadness that clouded his eyes.

"But," Dean said with resolve, leaning forward, "you don't make this about you. You don't push him. You don't demand anything. And when he needs space, you give it to him. Do you understand me? He's weak, he might try to conceal it and act like it's nothing, but those confrontations and high emotions are too much for him now."

Logan nodded slowly, his voice breaking as he said, "I understand."

Logan sat rigid on the couch, his hands clenched on his knees, as if grounding himself in a reality he wished he could escape. The faint scent of salt lingered in the air, a ghost of the ocean just beyond the walls, as ever-present as the ache in his chest.

"What about treatments?" Logan asked, his voice a low, gravelly whisper, raw from the endless tears that had carved trails down his face and shimmering with hope.

Dean leaned back in the chair; his expression indecipherable but heavy with something Logan couldn't quite place. "That's not my place to discuss," he said evenly. "If Adrian wants to tell you, he will."

He nodded, though the silence that followed settled over him like a suffocating mist.

After what felt like an eternity, Dean stretched, his movements slow. "I need to go to work."

"I'm not going anywhere," Logan announced quickly, his voice firm as he sank further into the couch, as if anchoring himself to the spot. The defiance in his tone felt hollow, born more from desperation than determination.

Dean paused, a wry smile tugging at the corner of his lips, though it didn't reach his eyes. "Good," he said softly. "Fight for him. He deserves that." He hesitated, then let out a dry chuckle. "You know, I knew from the moment I saw you that you were bad news." The words, though harsh, were spoken without malicious intent.

"Fuck you," Logan shot back, and while his voice was sharp, his expression betrayed the rawness beneath. "Adrian was happy with me."

Dean's smile faded, replaced by a thoughtful frown. "It's not about that," he started, his voice quieter now, almost pensive. He shifted his stance, folding his arms as if bracing himself against the current of his own thoughts. "Having your best friend dying really puts things into perspective. I don't have time for sugarcoating or beating around the tree, I think this is how the American expression goes? I don't know. I'll just say it like that: Adrian was the happiest I've ever seen him when he was with you."

Logan's chest tightened as the words affirmed his longing for Adrian, a bittersweet acknowledgment of guilt and desire.

Dean continued, his gaze distant, as though he were seeing Adrian in some long-lost moment. "I've known him my whole life. He's my brother in every way that matters. And when I saw that he had given you his mom's bracelet... I knew."

Logan felt himself go still.

Dean's eyes flickered back to him.

"I knew that in his mind, it wasn't just something to take lightly. It was a promise. A beginning. Adrian doesn't know how to do anything halfway, especially when it comes to love. If he gave you that bracelet, he was already thinking about engagement rings and proposals. He was planning a forever, because that is the kind of guy he is. And he looked at you... His eyes were shining every time he looked at you, it was so obvious."

The words didn't just land—they *lodged*. Logan felt them settle in his chest like shrapnel, burning him from the inside, a truth he had no armor for. He swallowed hard, throat raw. There was no air left in the room. No time left to rewind.

Dean, however, wasn't done. His voice softened, but it lost none of its weight, none of its sting. "But you weren't ready, were you? You couldn't give him that. And I get it, you were scared, it was too fast, too soon. You had your reasons. But Adrian?" Dean let out a breath, shaking his head. "He's the kind of person who throws himself into the deep end without hesitation, trusting the ocean will carry him. And you left him there, Logan."

A pause. Just long enough for the words to settle, to sink in, to twist the knife deeper.

"You left him to drown."

Logan closed his eyes, his head bowed as the tears spilled freely. His voice trembled when he spoke. "It wasn't like that," he said, the words sounding weak even to his own ears. "I loved him. I love him now. I never stopped loving him—not for a single minute."

Dean's silence hung heavy in the room. When he finally spoke, his tone was quiet but laced with undeniable truth. "Maybe you did," he said, his gaze meeting Logan's. "Maybe you still do. But love isn't just a feeling, Logan. It's a choice. And you didn't choose him when it mattered."

The room felt impossibly small, the weight of Dean's words pressing down on Logan until he thought he might break. He opened his mouth to respond, but no words came. The only sound was the distant crash of waves, as ceaseless and unforgiving as time itself.

Dean sighed, straightening as he glanced toward the door. "I hate you, Logan," he stated again, his voice devoid of venom but heavy with exhaustion. "I hate you for what you did to him. But that doesn't matter. What matters is that you're here now. And for whatever reason, Adrian hasn't sent you away. Because if he really wanted you gone, he'd tell me to get you the hell out of here, but he didn't, so I think he... on some level wants you here."

Logan looked up, hope flickering faintly in his tear-streaked eyes.

Dean's expression softened, but only for a moment. "So fight for him," he pleaded. "But remember this: he's dying. This isn't about you. If you're going to stay, you don't get to make this harder for him. When he needs space, you give it to him. When he needs you to back off, you do it. Understand?"

Logan nodded, his voice barely a whisper. "I understand."

And with a heavy sigh and a quick nod, Dean stood and turned away, his footsteps echoing faintly as he retreated into another room, before emerging once again moments later and leaving the house.

Logan remained still, his body tight as though preparing for an unseen tempest, and he felt a bitter taste of regret on his tongue.

He tried to focus on the space around him, to anchor himself in the present, but everything blurred into one undeniable truth: Adrian was dying. The thought churned in his mind like an undertow, pulling him deeper into his own despair.

The hallway felt impossibly long as Logan made his way to Adrian's door; each step echoed softly.

He paused, pressing his palm lightly against the wood, as though he could somehow reach Adrian through the thin barrier. Inside, he heard the faintest sounds—deep, uneven breaths and the occasional muffled sniffle. The realization that Adrian might still be crying twisted something deep in Logan's chest.

"Adrian," he called softly, his voice hoarse with emotion. "I'm still here."

There was a shuffling sound inside, faint but unmistakable. Adrian had heard him. Logan pressed his forehead against the door, words spilling out chaotically and without restraint. "I'm not going anywhere, you hear me? You can scream at me, curse me, hit me—whatever you need. But I'm not leaving. Because I'm so damn sorry. Because... *I love you.*"

It was a quiet tragedy that the first time Logan spoke those words to Adrian, it was through a closed door—a barrier that mirrored the distance he had spent years building between them. But that was all he had left now. And if speaking his heart through wood and silence was the only way to reach him, then he would do it, no matter how much it broke him.

Logan's voice cracked, but he kept going, the words tumbling out in a rush. "I'm sorry I ran away. I'm sorry I didn't wake you up that night to tell you I was scared. I'm sorry I blocked you. I'm sorry I married her in front of you, and that I acted like you didn't mean everything to me. God, Adrian, I've been sorry every single day since I walked away."

Logan wiped at his eyes, tears spilling from them in a wet trail that spoke of the pain. His body throbbed and trembled with longing, a restless ache seething beneath his skin as he was so close to Adrian, yet could not reach out and touch him. He longed for the comfort of Adrian's arms, the warmth of his skin, the quiet reassurance of his presence. It was a longing that had never left him, and now it seared like molten metal.

When it became painfully clear that Adrian wasn't going to respond, Logan's resolve crumbled. Slowly, he sank to the floor, his back pressed against the wall, the weight of his sorrow pulling him down. He let his head rest against the cool surface, just inches from Adrian's bedroom door, as if the nearness might somehow bridge the chasm between them.

The silence on the other side was smothering, a void that swallowed everything he had left to give.

He sat there, legs drawn up, as close to Adrian as he could get without crossing the line he knew he'd long since forfeited. The minutes stretched into hours, the stillness of the house broken only by the faint crushing of waves in the distance.

Now that he was so close to Adrian, the smallest distance between them felt unfathomably vast—too immense to confront, too painful to endure. With his soul recognizing its other half just beyond that door, separated by nothing more than a mere board of wood, he was left in a state of helpless longing.

At some point, sleep must have claimed him, because when Logan stirred awake, the house was cloaked in darkness. His neck throbbed from the awkward angle, and the hard floor beneath him should have seeped November's chill deep into his bones. But instead, he felt unexpected, comforting warmth. Blinking groggily, he cast a bleary gaze downward and discovered a blanket lovingly draped over him. The soft fabric exuded an unmistakable scent; Adrian's scent. The intoxicating smell, a blend that Logan's brain recognized too well—like a predator stalking his prey, it surged through Logan, awakening a torrent of memories that lingered inexorably in his mind. He recalled the peaceful moments spent lying in bed with Adrian nestled in his arms, enveloped by that familiar fragrance. It was a delicate blend of sweetness and cleanliness, intermingled with hints of his cologne and the shampoo he favored—all woven together with an essence that was purely Adrian, a scent imbued with warmth and comfort.

Beside him, a small portable heater hummed quietly, its glow casting faint shadows against the wall. Logan's breath caught in his throat. At some point, Adrian must have emerged from his room, seen him curled up against the wall, and chosen to help him. It was such a painfully Adrian thing to do, silent, tender, and full of a love that lingered, refusing to be extinguished, even after everything.

His eyes shifted toward the door beside him, still closed but no longer a fortress. No longer an impenetrable thing built to keep him out. Instead, it felt like a veil—thin, fragile, something he could almost slip through if he reached for it. He pressed a palm to the wood, fingers splayed out, feeling for something, some warmth, presence, a heartbeat on the other side.

"Ad," he murmured, his voice raw from sleep. The name barely rose above the hum of the heater, but it carried everything—years of longing, of regret, of love never given the chance to settle, to rest, to be enough.

Silence.

Logan swallowed against the weight of it, his pulse drumming in his ears. He thought of pushing the door open, stepping inside, spilling every word that had burned inside him for the past two years, but he stopped himself. He didn't have that right. Not anymore.

This is about Adrian. He reminded himself.

So instead, he pulled his phone from his pocket, the screen flaring to life with a harsh, bluish glow. His pupils shrank instantly, tightening against the sudden flood of light, and for a moment, his eyes stung, his vision swimming as they adjusted. He squinted, blinking rapidly, the brightness searing afterimages into the darkness. His thumb hovered over his contacts, scrolling with slow, thoughtful intent until it stopped on Adrian's name. Buried beneath years of neglect, beneath all the things he had tried to push away. But he had never really erased him.

A gasp slipped from him as his eyes caught the small, cruel reminder beside the name: Blocked. A severed connection, a wall of his own making. He had built it, steel-clad it, made damn sure Adrian could never reach him again.

And yet, Adrian had still left him a blanket. Still turned on the heat. Still saw him.

His chest ached as he tapped the screen, removing the block, as if the act itself could undo the damage, could bring back all the things he had let slip through his fingers. He sat there, staring at the name, at the thread of messages that hadn't disappeared—that hadn't let him forget.

That thread was the sole thing that made Logan cling to this cellphone, refusing to upgrade it no matter what.

Logan's breath hitched as he scrolled up, back through time, through every moment of Adrian reaching for him when he had refused to reach back:

November 13, 2018

You can't just leave. You can't do this to me.

This is us. You and me. Remember? It's me, Logan.

I'm begging you.

Please, answer the phone!

Please don't run. Please, not from me. Please pick up the phone!

I love you. Okay? There. I said it again. I LOVE YOU. So now what? You're gonna disappear on me?!

Logan, please. Come back. Please pick up the phone!

I'm not okay. I can't breathe.

I don't know what to do. I don't know how to lose you.

Please answer. Please just… let me hear your voice. One word. Are you okay?

The last message Adrian had sent him. A plea that had gone unanswered.

Logan squeezed his eyes shut, guilt clawing at his throat, at his ribs, at the spaces in between. He scrolled further, before everything shattered, before that night, before the running, before the silence.

And there it was.

A life reduced to pixels on a screen. The echoes of a love that had once been whole, woven into the quiet, mundane things, the kind of texts people send when they don't think there will ever be a last one.

Logan scrolled, his breath shallow, his pulse a dull, aching thrum in his ears. Fragments of them. Of the life they had built. Of the ordinary moments that had meant nothing at the time but now felt like everything.

His thumb hovered over the screen as the dates blurred together, time folding in on itself.

August 25, 2018

> I'm heading out.

September 4, 2018

> I'm grabbing dinner. They're out of your favorite. What do you want instead?

> Just get me what you get yourself. I've finished packing. We're all settled for tomorrow.

October 29, 2018

> Where's my hoodie? Did you steal it again?

> That's my hoodie now... I found the aloe vera gel brand you love and got some antiseptic cream and ibuprofen. I'm waiting in line to pay, and I'll be back in 15 minutes.

Ad, I just cut my arm on some coral... you're overreacting...

November 2, 2018

Where are you? I'm waiting for you at the market's entrance like we said.

Trying to barter with a local for fresh fruit. I think I accidentally agreed to help him move furniture.

What?!

Would you answer the fucking phone?

Sorry, he had a lot of furniture! I got like six kilos of mango, though.

Kilos?

American...

November 5, 2018

You are so beautiful when you sleep. I went for a run, didn't want to wake you.

Did you for real leave me in bed for a run?

You were sleeping...

> **Come back.**

> **I'm trying to run here.**

> ***attached photo***

> **Fuck. You are so hot. I'm on my way.**

Now, years later, the photo flickered back to life on the small screen, and Logan felt heat rise in his throat, his pulse hammering as if Adrian might appear in the doorway again. He scrolled past too quickly, as though speed could protect him, but the image clung like fire to the inside of his skull.

There he was, sprawled across tangled sheets, bare and unguarded, morning light dripping across his skin. His body was all heat and shadow, golden tones catching on the ridges of his stomach, the broad weight of his chest, the long cut of his flank, narrowing into the hips. His hair fell in loose disarray, his eyes half-lidded with that lazy, reckless invitation that made restraint impossible.

The camera caught everything: the thick line of his forearm, veins rising faintly beneath the skin, the casual sprawl of his shoulders that made the bed seem smaller beneath him. And lower—his hand curled loosely around himself, head exposed, flushed and wet with the promise of more. Not explicit enough to give everything away, but enough to taunt, enough to command Adrian back to him.

It was more than a photo. It was a challenge, a seduction, a trap. He had known exactly what he was doing.

And Adrian had fallen for it instantly.

Logan's thumb hovered over the screen, his body suddenly feeling too small for all the weight inside him. His fingers clenched around the phone, around the past, around the unbearable realization that he had spent two years pretending he didn't miss something that had been a part of him.

That Adrian had still seen him. Even when Logan had left him in the dark, Adrian had still reached out.

Though the weight of his choices and the separation from Adrian still burned in his chest, and the notion of being 'alright' felt foreign to him, he once again experienced that surge of hope swelling within. After everything that had transpired, it was the only thing he had left. It was this very hope that compelled him to board a plane, to come here, and to try to explain to the love of his life why he had left him stranded, why he had suffocated their love instead of letting it bask in the rising sun.

Adrian's gestures—the blanket, the heater—spoke volumes in their quiet simplicity. They weren't just acts of kindness; they were whispers of something that hadn't been completely extinguished. Maybe, just maybe, there was still a sliver of a chance to mend the devastation he had caused.

Perhaps Adrian hadn't entirely locked him out. Not yet.

With trembling hands and a heart burdened by years of unsaid words, Logan unlocked his phone. The faint glow of the screen illuminated his tear-streaked face as he began to type, every keystroke like a pebble dropped into an endless ocean, rippling outward with a mixture of hope and fear.

11:27 PM

> Ad, I'm sorry. For everything. For barging back into your life like this, for opening wounds that haven't healed. I know this is too much, too soon. I know seeing me again, after everything, is probably the last thing you need right now. And I don't blame you for shutting me out. I deserve that. But, Adrian, you have to know something. I love you. I've never stopped. Not for a single moment. You've been with

me in every thought, in every breath. Leaving you wasn't just a mistake, it was the worst decision of my life, one I've regretted every single day. I know I can't make up for the pain I caused. I can't take back the nights you spent alone, wondering why I left. But I can promise you this: I won't be leaving again. I will never leave you alone again. I realize now that standing outside your door like this is… invasive. Maybe even cruel. So I'll give you some space. I'll step back. But not too far, Ad. Not too far. I'm staying at the Light Beach Hotel here in Tel Aviv, room 717. If you ever feel ready, if you can find it in yourself to even speak to me, I'll be there. Every day, I'll come back here. I'll wait. I'll keep trying. Adrian, you are my everything. Always have been. Always will be. And I swear to you, I will spend every moment I have left proving that to you.

Logan's thumb hovered over the send button for a heartbeat that stretched into eternity. Then, with a deep breath, he pressed it. A muffled chime from the other side of the door confirmed the message's delivery, and Logan felt a faint wave of relief wash over him. Adrian would see it. He would read it. That, at least, was something.

Standing, Logan gazed at the door one last time, letting the silence settle around him like a cloak. "I'll give you space," he murmured. "But I'll be back." He promised.

And with that, he turned away, his gaze lingering for a moment on the softly humming heater. He bent down and unplugged it carefully. His footsteps were soft as he moved through the darkened house, each step echoing with unspoken regret.

At the threshold, he paused, his hand resting on the doorframe, hesitating as if the weight of the moment might pull him back. For a fleeting second, he almost turned around, almost whispered something to the silence. But instead, he drew a deep breath, steadying himself, and stepped outside. The door clicked shut behind him, the sound too gentle to match the enormity of what it signified, leaving Adrian with the quiet—and the unspoken promise—that lingered like a faint heartbeat in the stillness of the night.

Adrian spent the better part of the next day in his room, the four walls feeling both protective and suffocating, a fragile cocoon he wasn't ready to break. The sunlight streamed through the window in golden streaks, but he stayed buried under the blankets, moving only between the bed and the bathroom, each step heavy as though gravity had doubled overnight.

Dean had knocked a few times, his voice muffled through the door, but Adrian couldn't face him. Not yet. The words Dean offered were undoubtedly well-meaning, but they couldn't pierce the storm raging in Adrian's mind. Instead, he clung to the glowing screen of his phone, reading Logan's message over and over until the words blurred together, burned into his heart as much as his memory. Just above Logan's most recent message, Adrian saw the thread of his own words, still suspended in time, some undelivered, all of them unanswered. Dozens of messages he'd sent on that frantic morning, frozen behind the gray icon of rejection.

A graveyard of his own love, still marked undelivered like a wound that refused to close.

He despised the way his heart stuttered, remembering how it had once kept beating for a man who could vanish without a word. He despised the way his heart betrayed him, stirring to life the moment Logan reentered his world, an old injury reopening with a whisper of his name. He loathed the warmth that surged through his frail body when he found him there, asleep in the dimly lit hallway, curled into himself, so vulnerable, so unbearably familiar.

The sight of Logan—*Logan Vaughn*—sitting on the cold floor, waiting for him, his sandy hair tousled, his face softened in sleep, stole the breath from Adrian's lungs. Even in the quiet stillness, even in the hush of the night, Logan was a storm. A storm Adrian had spent years trying to forget, yet one he longed to be swept away by, just once more. It was cruel, the way memory laced itself into the present, the way the past refused to loosen its grip. Logan was thinner now, worn by time and the weight of regret, just as Adrian himself had withered, his body stripped of the strength it once held by a cruel illness. And yet, no matter the shadows beneath his eyes, no matter the way he carried his sorrow in the set of his jaw, Logan was still devastatingly, impossibly beautiful. And Adrian—dying, exhausted, terrified Adrian—was still hopelessly, helplessly weak for him.

At first, Adrian had convinced himself that Logan's presence was a hallucination, a cruel trick of his dying mind. The kind of cruel comfort a body offers in its final stages, blurring the edges of reality to make death feel a little less like an abyss, reshaping the contours of the truth to soften the ache of his dying body. Perhaps he had already traversed the fragile boundary between life and the unknown that lay beyond—Heaven, maybe? Or a realm resembling the haunting embrace of purgatory.

Yet if this was indeed Heaven, could it not be deemed a cruel irony?

Adrian stared at the message again, his fingers trembling slightly as he traced the words on the screen. He could hear Logan's voice in every letter, the rawness, the desperation, the weight of love tangled with regret. It was as though Logan had reached through the phone and placed his heart in Adrian's hands, fragile and bleeding.

Adrian exhaled shakily, his chest tightening with a pain that felt like both longing and grief. He was broken beyond repair—a shell of the person he used to be. He had accepted that. The cancer hadn't just ravaged his body; it had hollowed out parts of him he never thought could be touched. And yet, no agony, no sickness, no slow betrayal of his own body had ever carved through him as deeply, as mercilessly, as Logan had.

But then again, Logan wasn't every man.

Adrian knew, with a certainty as deep as the ocean herself, that Logan was his soulmate. The kind of love that felt written in the waves, etched into the fabric of who he was. And yet, that certainty was a double-edged sword, cutting into him with a question he couldn't silence: *Was he Logan's?*

He closed his eyes, his head resting against the pillow, as he tried to push the thought away. But it clung to him, like a half-remembered song that refused to fade. Logan's message offered promises, but Adrian wasn't sure if promises were enough. His heart whispered that Logan meant it, that this time would be different, but how could he trust it? How could he risk it?

The memory of Logan standing at his door, broken and pleading, flickered in Adrian's mind. The way his voice had trembled when he spoke, the way he'd said *I love you* as though it was the only truth he had left.

Adrian pressed his hand to his chest, feeling the faint, uneven rhythm of his heart beneath his fingertips. It wasn't just Logan's words that haunted him; it was the way they made him feel. Alive, even in the shadow of his own mortality. And that, more than anything, terrified him.

Because if he let Logan back in, he wasn't sure he could survive losing him again.

But did it matter anymore?

Adrian lay still, the faint rhythm of his breath filling the silence of the room. His gaze was fixed on the ceiling, where the morning light danced in soft, shifting patterns, like the reflection of water on a distant shore. The thought settled over him like a heavy mist: he didn't have the luxury of time anymore.

The cancer had already begun its slow, insistent erosion, pulling pieces of him away bit by bit, like waves licking away at the base of a once-solid cliff, wearing him down without mercy or pause. Piece by piece, it was claiming him. In a few short months, his body would betray him entirely, leaving him to the care of a hospice, where the world would grow smaller and smaller until it was nothing but a hospital bed and the quiet hum of machines pretending to be merciful. The world would be shrinking day by day, until time wasn't measured in months or seasons anymore, but in minutes... in breaths... in heartbeats. His life would dwindle to a countdown, to a metronome to the cruel music of oxygen drips, to the decaying rhythm of a withering, wuthering body.

And now, in the ticking of time itself, *Logan*—his name pulsed beneath everything, steady as a heartbeat, giving life. Logan's presence throbbed through the air, soporific, oneiric, a breath of dream against the vicissitudes of fate.

Adrian's heart had always perceived a symphony of undeclared words whenever Logan was near.

Would he allow it to dissolve into silence at the end?

Would he bear Logan's silent ache, unanswered, into his final breath—the doubt, the fading presence, the love that forever sought its shore?

Would that be the last testament of his soul, a story delicately frayed into stillness?

Would he cross the threshold with questions tearing at him, his heart raw and unspoken, that dark, woven hiraeth embedded deep within, haunting the empty corridors of years?

Would he venture into the cimmerian, where no light in the form of Logan's smile could follow, burdened by unspoken love that remains heavy, bleeding, yet unresolved, still undeniably his?

Adrian's chest rose and fell unevenly as he considered it. What did closure even mean now, when his days were numbered, when each moment felt borrowed from a life he was no longer certain was his to live? The stars above, the ones he had always imagined returning to when the end came, felt both infinite and indifferent. What was the meaning of all of this? Of Logan's return, of this love that refused to perish, even as his body prepared to?

The question wasn't about survival anymore; it was about choice. Did he want to leave this life with Logan's name still a wound he carried, or could he face him one last time, offer him something real—a chance for both of them to say the things they had left unsaid? Did Adrian want his final memory of Logan to be one of distance, or of closeness, even if it came at a cost?

Adrian turned his head toward the door, where just hours ago Logan's voice had seeped through, pleading. He could still hear the words as clearly as if they were etched into the walls: *I'm not going anywhere... Because I love you.*

His heart ached at the memory, but it also stirred, faint and uncertain, like the flicker of a candle in a room full of shadows. Did he have the strength to risk that flame, to let Logan in, knowing it might burn him one last time?

He sat up slowly, his body protesting the movement, each joint and muscle heavy with exhaustion. His phone sat on the nightstand, Logan's message still glowing softly on the screen. Adrian reached for it, his fingers trembling slightly as he reread the words for what felt like the hundredth time.

I'll be there. Every day, I'll come back here. I'll wait. I'll keep trying. Adrian, you are my everything.

Adrian closed his eyes, his thumb hovering over the screen. He didn't know if he could forgive Logan entirely, but forgiveness wasn't the point anymore. He wasn't searching for absolution or guarantees; he was searching for peace. For himself. For Logan. For the love that had bound them together, no matter how much time or distance had tried to unravel it.

The stars might take him soon, but before they did, Adrian thought, maybe he owed himself one final moment of truth. One last chance to decide what mattered in the end.

Did he deserve to feel the burn of Logan beside him again? That heat, that impossible gravity. It had scorched him in the end—left scars in places no eye could see. But God, the moments before the collapse... they had been galaxies. Every stolen glance, every laugh tangled in salt air, every night spent in the hush of a world that was only theirs. They were worth it. Every ember. Every ash.

He would burn for the rest of eternity, gladly, if it meant orbiting Logan's sun one final time.

Even now, with the illness hollowing him out from the inside, something ancient stirred beneath the decay. His soul. The atoms that built him. The blood and bones and sinew that had felt like nothing more than survival for so long—suddenly they remembered how to feel. How to long. How to live.

Adrian had never truly lived before Logan. And after Logan, there had been nothing. Just air that didn't fill his lungs. Days that didn't belong to him. Silence that didn't comfort, only echoed.

But now... now the memory of that love was waking the dead inside him.

All those years ago, Adrian hadn't known what compelled him to do it. He hadn't paused to think, hadn't questioned the primal force that surged through him as soon as he pulled Logan from the water. It was as though something ancient, something as timeless as the tides, had moved him to slip the bracelet from his own wrist and give it to Logan. It was instinctive, unspoken—an act that felt less like a choice and more like an inevitability.

Like the wind brushing against his skin, like the ocean's everlasting rhythm. It simply *was*.

The bracelet had been his most treasured possession, a link to his mother, who had been taken by the same disease that was growing in his body. It was the last thing of hers he had, a talisman that he'd clung to through the years, as if her essence was braided into the threads of its weave. Giving it to Logan had been a surrender, a prayer. A plea to his mother to watch over Logan, to guard his soul in the moments Adrian couldn't. And in some distant, childlike corner of his heart, Adrian had believed she would.

Even now, years later, he couldn't quite shake the belief that his mother was still out there, somewhere... somewhere just beyond the veil, stitched into the winds that followed him across oceans, hidden in the hush between crashing waves. Maybe she was woven into the salt in the air or the light that danced on the waves. Maybe she lingered in the pull of the tide, in the way the sea always seemed to answer when he felt lost. He knew it was a fantasy, the kind of thing you tell yourself to soften the ache of grief, to fill the void left by someone who had gone too soon. However, it was a belief that had taken root when he was a boy, and he had never fully relinquished it.

And now, as he sat on his bed, the weight of Logan's return pressing down on him like the heavy humidity before a storm, Adrian couldn't help but wonder if his mother had sent Logan back to him. After Adrian had passed the bracelet on, maybe she had whispered to him, guided him, nudged him toward Adrian when he needed him most. That maybe—just maybe—she had prodded him from whatever corner of the world he'd vanished to. That she had found him, reminded him, carried some piece of Adrian's voice to him through the settled emptiness between them.

But if that were true, wouldn't she be angry with him now? Adrian could almost hear her voice, sharp and warm, scolding him for the choices he had made since his diagnosis. For giving up before the fight had truly begun. For turning his back on life even as it clung to him, fragile but present.

It was all a conjuring, he knew that. A tapestry of longing plucked from the strings of grief, played by a heart too young to understand death, and too stubborn to ever let go. He had been just a child when she died. The memories he carried were soft-edged and uncertain, resembling old photographs left too long in the sun—half real, half imagined, blurred by time and the stories others told him, crumbling through his mind like friable earth slipping between his fingers, impossible to sift truth from dream. And her voice... it was long gone. Just broken syllables now, scattered echoes in his dreams, filled in by his own voice trying to remember how hers once felt, more than heard.

Adrian sighed, running his fingers through his hair as the thought twisted in his chest. It was a choice he'd made consciously, a quiet rebellion against the pain and the indignity of the disease. A choice he would carry to its inevitable end, as surely as the tide carries the driftwood to shore.

But now Logan was here.

The thought circled his mind, merciless, as if the universe itself was determined to hammer it into his consciousness. Logan was here. Logan, the man who had shattered him but who still held every piece of his broken heart. Logan, who had stood at his door, pleading and raw, spilling truths

Adrian had longed to hear and feared to believe. Logan, who had been a world away and was now just ten minutes down the road.

Adrian leaned back, his gaze fixed on the ceiling, his mind a whirlwind of emotions he couldn't untangle. It felt surreal, like a dream fabricated by the deepest recesses of his mind. Logan was suddenly in his life again, after years of silence and aching absence. And as much as it scared him, as much as it made his heart feel like it might burst from his chest, Adrian couldn't shake the thought that maybe—just maybe—this was heaven.

Not the kind he'd imagined as a boy, filled with clouds and angels and light. But this: the sound of Logan's voice murmuring through a locked door, the faint warmth of Logan's body blanketing him in the middle of the night, the knowledge that Logan had come back, that he had *chosen* to come back.

Adrian's breath hitched, his hands curling into fists. Hope burned in him, it was fragile, flickering, yet impossibly alive, refusing to go out, no matter how hard he tried to smother it.

Logan was here.

And for the first time in years, Adrian didn't know whether to feed that fragile flame or drown it in the rising tide of his doubts.

Eventually, Adrian left his bed and moved to the bathroom, his body heavy but his steps unflinching. He took a quick, scalding shower, letting the rush of water crash over him, jolting him from the fog that had clung to him ever since he had heard Logan's voice saying "Ad" in that wonderful American accent of his. He brushed his teeth, then toweled his long hair dry, tying it into a loose half bun that dripped faint droplets down his back. Dressing was methodical: jeans worn soft with age, a sweater layered over shirts to stave off the growing chill that seemed to settle deeper into his bones each day.

When he stepped out of the room, Dean was waiting in the hallway. He stood with his arms crossed, leaning casually against the wall, but his eyes gave him away. They were watchful, thoughtful, filled with a concern he never said aloud.

"Hey," Dean greeted softly, his voice careful, like he didn't want to startle Adrian from whatever fragile resolve he'd summoned.

"I'm going to him," Adrian replied simply in Hebrew.

Dean nodded, his jaw tightening as he studied Adrian for a moment. "I figured." His voice held a quiet resignation. He paused, his gaze searching Adrian's face as though looking for the answer to a question he couldn't ask. "I'm not his biggest fan, Adrian, and you know that. But I think..." He hesitated, then pushed forward. "I think you need this. I think you need to hear his side of the story. Because if you don't, it'll be something you carry with you forever. A question you can never answer. A regret you can't undo."

Adrian looked away, his hand brushing the wall as if he needed to feel something solid beneath his fingertips. Dean's words cut deeper than they should have, because he knew they were true. If he didn't face Logan now, the uncertainty would fester, leaving scars even deeper than the ones he already bore.

"Be careful," Dean added, his voice softening. "You've been through hell because of him before. I just... I don't want to see you hurt like that again."

Adrian nodded, unable to meet Dean's gaze. A silence settled between them, weighed down by two years of countless words, fights, and pleas. For a moment, Adrian could almost feel the ghost of two years ago—the cabin in Australia where Dean had found him hollowed out and drowning in heartbreak, and the frantic flight to the United States when Adrian had tried, futilely, to stop Logan's wedding. Every time, Dean had been there to pick up the pieces. Every time, Adrian had returned to Israel, with his heart bearing another crack and a strip of himself carried away by the wind.

Adrian wondered... did the future hold another heartbreak, another unraveling of the life he barely managed to stitch back together? Would some new fracture wait on the horizon, unseen, because he was too naïve to sense it coming? And if it did, would Dean be the one, once again, forced to gather his scattered pieces?

Dean didn't need to say what they both knew: that something inside Adrian had never fully mended after Logan left. It was as if a switch had been flipped, a light extinguished. It wasn't just a wound—it was an unraveling, a slow, merciless attrition of the man he used to be. It was in the way he no longer woke before dawn to chase the waves like he used to, his board gathering dust in the corner of his room only coming out on occasions, and every time Adrian spent chasing the waves in the depth of the ocean, he returned hunted. It was in the way that his drifting mind found working out too much to handle. It was in the way his laughter had faded, no longer the careless, sun-drenched sound it once was, but something hollow, something forced, as if it had forgotten how to be real. His smile was a fragile echo of what it once was, never quite drowning out the loneliness woven into his eyes, into his very foundation. Adrian used to move like the world belonged to him—wild and reckless, full of fire—but after Logan left, he moved carefully, deliberately, as though he had learned that one wrong step could break him, as if he knew his pieces were stacked together without any true tether, one fragile hold away from collapsing into the earth, breaking into a million shards that might never fit back together again. He spoke less, as if words were an unnecessary burden, as if silence was the only thing that didn't betray him. He stopped taking pictures, stepping out whenever someone held out a camera or a phone to take a meaningless selfie with friends, because after being the sole focus of Logan's lens, even that was meaningless. And the nights, Dean knew they were the worst, he knew Adrian didn't sleep much, he knew he was scrolling through photos and videos of him and Logan together, he knew that sometimes Adrian dreamed of Logan, of their time, and that would shatter him for the next day. Dean never spoke about it, never asked, even when he saw the remnants of it in Adrian's quietness, in the way he would turn his head too quickly at the sound of a familiar voice as if hoping—just for a moment—that it was Logan. He never mentioned the way Adrian had become a little less himself—a little less golden, a little less alive. Because some things didn't need to be said. Some things were written in the way a person exists, or in Adrian's case, the way he barely did.

But now, standing before him, Dean saw something shift. A flicker of that old light, faint but undeniable. Logan's return had stirred the ashes, breathed life into something long buried, something Adrian had convinced himself was lost. And though Dean resented Logan for what he had done, though the wounds ran deep, he knew—he *knew*—that Adrian would forgive him. That he had already begun to. The proof was there, shimmering in his eyes, in the way his soul seemed to drift toward the past, toward the man who had shattered him and yet, somehow, had also stitched him back together, mended him, and guided him back to safety.

"Just... don't let him crush you again," Dean murmured finally, though he knew the warning was futile. Adrian had never been able to guard his heart when it came to Logan. He gave too freely, loved too deeply. Even now, he was already gathering the crumbs Logan had offered and holding them as if they were treasures.

Adrian took a deep breath, squaring his shoulders. He didn't respond, but his silence spoke volumes. There was no logic to what he was about to do, no reasoning that could explain it. This wasn't about logic. It was about love—the kind that defied sense, the kind that hurt as much as it healed. And Adrian had made his choice.

Without another word, he stepped past Dean and headed for the door, the sound of the ocean outside echoing faintly in his ears. Logan was waiting, and Adrian was no longer sure if he was walking toward redemption or ruin. Logan was an unstoppable force that Adrian had always been too weak to resist, and now was no different.

Chapter 12
The Weight of the Surging Waters

In the heart of the ocean, a connection was born; we were destined to meet. How else can one explain this union, drawn together from the farthest corners of the earth? We shared the same breath, allowing the ocean's embrace to guide us as we emerged from the water's grace, revealing the light of day. Yet, a moment of folly, a human decision, severed our bond. But the ocean is stronger, the tide relentless, and the waves eternally return to the shore, so I returned. Not by choice but by the pull of something greater. The ocean called me home; its whispers threaded with your name.

I am the wave that, no matter how far it is cast, will always return to the shore.

To you.

November 20, 2020—Tel-Aviv, Israel—The Same Day

THE OCEAN SURGED WITHIN Logan as he fumbled with his thoughts, trying to anchor himself to the dull glow of his laptop screen while holding his phone to his ear. The faint voice on the other end of the call was nothing more than white noise, a distant hum beneath his own guilt and longing.

His mind floated aimlessly, like a castoff branch carried by indifferent surges, buoyed and battered by a current he couldn't control. Every thought was centered around Adrian. The echo of their last encounter, fresh and unresolved, merged with the sight of him now, two years older, two years farther away. And with every breath, his ache sharpened a reminder of what he had shattered with his own fear.

Logan's chest tightened as the reality of Adrian's illness gnawed at him. *Cancer.*

The word was slicing through his thoughts over and over again, each time gutting him and twisting him as if it were the first time he'd learned about it. It was a slow thief, stealing pieces of Adrian with every passing day. He felt paralyzed, drowning in a sea of his own helplessness. What could he do? How could he fight a war inside Adrian's body when he had already lost the battle within his own heart?

The room felt too small, the walls pressing in with the weight of his mistakes. He needed to do something, to break free from the inertia that held him.

A sharp knock at the door rattled Logan out of his fragile reverie.

"Ada Mae, I'll have to call you back," he said, his voice tight as he snapped the laptop shut with a decisive click.

"Alright," came her brisk reply, but Logan barely heard her. "I'm emailing you the calls to make and the meetings to reschedule. The ASAPs are going to your dad."

"Yeah, thanks," he muttered, already halfway to the door. "Good night."

The phone landed carelessly on the couch, a forgotten artifact in the rising swell of anticipation. His breath came shallow and quick as he crossed the room, each step weighed down by the gravity of what could be on the other side of the door. His hand trembled slightly as it hovered over the handle, the seconds stretching like the horizon at dusk, infinite and unknowable.

When he opened the door, it was as though the world tipped over and spilled into the room. Adrian stood there, a storm on the threshold, his face carved with the weariness of streams that had battered him too long. His eyes, the whisky-colored hue Logan adored, appeared darker under the hotel lighting, conveying pain that reverberated within the narrowed space. They were an immeasurable sea of yearning, heartache, and whispered secrets yet to be unveiled.

Logan's breath caught, a ragged sound torn from the depths of his chest. For a moment, neither of them spoke. Adrian's presence was like the scent of rain after a long drought—sharp, fresh, and overwhelming, filling the air with something electric, something alive.

They didn't speak at first. Their gazes met, a fragile bridge between them, carrying the weight of years in a silence that buzzed with all the words left unspoken. Logan couldn't tell if the intensity and hardness he saw in Adrian's eyes was edged with anger, layered with hurt, or if a softer, more hesitant warmth lingered just beneath the surface.

Logan stepped aside. A ghost of a smile flickered on his lips, unsteady, a flame in the wind. He couldn't help it—beneath all the uncertainty, a fragile thread of happiness coiled through his chest, tugging at the corners of his heart. Seeing Adrian here, standing in front of him, felt surreal. He held on to the hope that this wasn't just a fleeting echo of the past but the first step toward something real, something mended.

Adrian moved into the room, his presence a quiet thunder, filling the space with a gravity that seemed to pull the air taut. His eyes swept over the room—a polished expanse of muted tones, sharp lines, and gleaming surfaces. It was perfect in the way hotel rooms often were: clean, curated, and empty. When Adrian's gaze returned to Logan, there was a stillness in the air, thick and suffocating. Logan closed the door, his back resting against it as if bracing himself against the weight of what came next.

"You wanted to talk," Adrian said, his voice steady but distant. "Let's talk."

"Yeah, do you—" Logan began making his way to the middle of the room, but the words faltered when Adrian raised a hand, shaking his head.

"I waited," Adrian's voice cracked with the rawness of the memory. He stayed near the door, his posture tense, as though he might bolt at any moment. "When I woke up that morning and you weren't there, I thought... I thought maybe you'd gone to get coffee or something. You know? I didn't panic. The room looked the same. Your clothes were still scattered on the chairs, your board was leaning against the wall, just where you'd left it." He paused, exhaling a shaky breath. "So, I waited. I stayed in bed and waited for you to come back."

Logan lowered himself onto the back of the couch, his knees feeling weak under the weight of Adrian's words. He couldn't look away from him, couldn't do anything but listen.

"But you didn't show up," Adrian continued, his voice laced with hurt that seemed to ring in the room. "So, I called. Over and over. And there was no answer. But even then, I didn't think you'd left, maybe your phone was silenced, and you were on your way back, right? I couldn't believe it. Because..." Adrian's voice faltered, and he swallowed hard. "Because the memory book I gave you was still there, on the nightstand. And you wouldn't have left it behind. Not something that meant so much to both of us. Right?"

Logan closed his eyes briefly, the sting of tears burning behind his lids. He couldn't speak. When he opened his eyes, Adrian was still standing by the door, his arms crossed over his chest, as if holding himself together.

"Adrian," Logan started, his voice rough. "I—"

"No," Adrian cut him off, his tone sharp but trembling. "Let me finish."

The air between them was heavy, thick with the kind of tension that blooms from wounds left too long to fester. It was a quiet ache, raw and unhealed, the edges of their shared past still sharp and exposed. These weren't scars—scars were the marks of healing, of skin knit back together stronger than before. No, these were open wounds, tender and vulnerable, left to catch the sting of every passing breeze, to risk infection and rot. Always exposed, always on the verge of breaking open.

Logan hovered in a space that was neither standing nor sitting, his body half-perched on the back of the couch, as if suspended between the instinct to flee and the desperate need to stay. His hands were clasped tightly together, knuckles pale and straining, as though holding them so would keep the fragile pieces of him from scattering around the room. His breath came shallow, uneven, the kind of breathing that accompanies a drowning man seconds before surrendering to the deep. Adrian remained still, his knuckles turning white from gripping himself tightly.

"And I called again," Adrian continued, his voice trembling but firm, the emotion clawing its way to the surface. "Still no answer. So I got out of bed, and I started noticing things—things that were different. Your board shorts and wetsuit were still in the bathroom, Logan. Your toothbrush, too. But your bag? Your computer? Gone."

Adrian laughed bitterly, the sound sharp and hollow. "I kept calling. I kept texting. I became quite anxious when I saw our mugs still on the table, which clearly showed that you didn't go to get coffee. So I called again and again. And then you replied. Finally! You told me you were leaving. Just like that. Out of nowhere. And I thought—no, I *hoped*, I *prayed*—that it was some kind of joke. Because how could it not be? It didn't make sense. Nothing about it made sense."

Logan's breath caught as Adrian's vivid recounting drew him back to the past, plunging him into the chaos he had sparked. In his mind's eye, he visualized everything—the confusion, disbelief, and growing panic.

"When I got your text," Adrian went on, his voice breaking, "telling me you'd suddenly decided to go home, I panicked. I kept texting, kept calling, because I thought maybe... maybe something was wrong. Something must have happened to you. And then I tried again." Adrian's voice cracked, his shoulders slumping as tears slipped down his face. "And again. Until finally, I realized I couldn't get through to you because you had blocked me. You *blocked* me." Adrian closed his eyes, his breathing uneven as he tried to steady himself.

Logan felt the sting of tears at the corners of his own eyes, but he couldn't move, couldn't breathe.

"And you know what?" Adrian said, his voice rising slightly, a sharp edge to his tone. "I couldn't believe it. It took me *twenty-seven messages*—twenty-seven!—and at least fifteen phone calls before it even registered that you'd done it. Because I couldn't believe that you would block me, Logan. Not after everything. I thought, 'No, there's no way.' Not after what we shared, not after—"

Did Adrian seek the elusive words that could capture the essence of the tapestry they wove together over four fleeting months? Was he in search of phrases to immortalize the precious days they shared? That profound heart-to-heart on the cliff, those two treasured last days in the lavish hotel? The final night they shared, as Logan gave himself completely to Adrian? To the whispered moments in between—soft late nights and tender dawns, the playful dance among the waves, their bodies entangled in sheets, or the thrill of chasing their next adventure?

Adrian shook his head, his jaw tightening as his voice dropped again. "So I did the stupidest thing I could do. I got into a cab and went straight to the airport. And by the time I got there, you were gone. Gone, Logan. I begged security, I begged airport staff, I fucking had the entire place on its feet, trying to figure out where you'd gone, why you'd left. They showed me the footage. They showed me you were waiting, you were boarding, like it was just another day for you."

Logan's tears traced silent trails down his face, each drop carrying the heavy weight of Adrian's anguish. He had long imagined the pain he'd inflicted, but witnessing it, immersing himself in its depths, was an entirely different kind of torment. Every heartbreaking detail etched itself into his memory, a permanent scar of that moment.

"I was sure something had happened to you," Adrian said, his voice softer now, breaking around the edges, curling around his lovely accent. "Because I couldn't believe… I wouldn't believe… that you'd just *leave* me. Not after that night. Not after everything. So the only explanation I could come up with was that you were in trouble, that someone made you leave, because I thought I knew you, Logan."

Adrian stopped, his eyes fixed on the floor as his chest rose and fell with the effort of keeping himself together.

"Adrian—"

"Please don't," Adrian begged, his voice barely above a whisper. "I need to say this. If you talk, if I hear your voice, I won't be able to. And I need to."

Logan nodded, swallowing hard. His hands gripped the edge of the couch as though it were the only thing grounding him, but his whole body ached to move, to close the space between them. Adrian's tears fell in silent streaks, carving pathways down his face, and Logan felt as if each one was a blade cutting into his soul.

He wanted to stand, to reach out, to pull Adrian into his arms and beg for forgiveness with every ounce of his being. But he didn't. Not yet. He stayed where he was, waiting, because he knew that right now, Adrian needed to finish. And Logan owed him that. At the very least, he owed him to listen to the final notes of their love story.

"I waited in that room for three weeks," Adrian said, his voice raw, shaking, the words slicing through the space between them. "Three. Fucking. Weeks. I was sure you were going to come back. I… refused to believe you'd leave me alone, Logan. Every single day you didn't come back, it felt like a knife to my gut. It wasn't just emotional—my heart *hurt*. Physically hurt. And there was nothing I could do to stop it."

Adrian paused, his hands trembling at his sides as he stared at the floor. The silence was suffocating, broken only by the distant hum of traffic outside and the faint rhythm of their breathing. Logan swallowed hard, his throat dry, but he didn't dare interrupt.

"It hurt so much, Logan," Adrian continued, his voice dropping to a whisper, as though the memories were too heavy to bear. "I couldn't get through the days. I barely left the room. I was afraid—afraid I might miss you if you came back. But you didn't. Not for your board, not for your camera, not for me. *Not for me.*" The words choked out of him.

The way Adrian said it, his voice cracking on the last word, felt like a blow to Logan's belly. His hands clenched into fists at his sides, not out of anger but from the sheer helplessness of hearing just how deeply he had hurt the man standing before him. With the need to grab Adrian and tell him that he was loved, that he was missed, that Logan was here now, and God himself would not take him away.

"Each night," Adrian continued, his eyes unfocused, his words almost detached, "I broke down. And I called your number. Over and over again. Still blocked. Interestingly, you didn't block me on Facebook, but I couldn't do it—I couldn't let myself message you there. I didn't want to seem... desperate. Pathetic. Like I was begging for scraps of your attention."

Logan wanted to say something, to stop Adrian from continuing, but the look in Adrian's eyes held him back. It wasn't just pain—it was the need to be heard, to finally say everything that had been bottled up for years.

"I completely trashed that room. I was convinced you'd left a note or some explanation there. I searched everywhere like a damned fool, trying to find a reason—anything that would make sense," he said, letting out a dry laugh and mumbling "stupid" under his breath. "After two weeks in that room," Adrian whispered, his voice thick with emotion, "I was going insane. I couldn't take it anymore. You weren't answering me. You weren't coming back. So I called Dean. I told him everything, and he got on a flight and came to that room. The room *we* had shared." Adrian's voice cracked, and he paused to catch his breath.

Logan took a step forward, unable to stay seated any longer. "Adrian," he mumbled gently, seeing the way Adrian's body shook with the force of his memories. "Please, sit down. We don't have to do this all today."

"No." Adrian's reply was immediate and sharp. He straightened, his gaze locking onto Logan's with a fierce determination. "We *do*. You need to hear it, Logan. You need to hear all of it. Because you always get what you want. And now, now, when you don't, you'll understand why."

Logan felt his chest tighten at the words. Adrian's pain was no longer his alone; it was mist filling the space, curling into every corner, wrapping itself around Logan's lungs. It slithered into him, suffocating, until he could no longer tell where Adrian's anguish ended and his own began. Logan moved closer, but Adrian took a small step back, his arms crossed tightly as though holding himself together.

"Dean waited with me," Adrian said, his voice quieter now, almost like a confession. "I begged him not to leave that room, that was the last thing I had from you, and I thought you'd come back. I was so damn stupid." He muttered under his breath. "He agreed to another week. We sat in that room, day after day. And then he said, 'That's it. We're leaving.' But I couldn't keep traveling, Logan. I couldn't see the point. How could I keep going when... when you'd left? When everything felt like it'd fallen apart?"

Adrian's voice cracked again, and he looked away, his jaw tightening as he fought back tears. He didn't say how broken he'd been, how depressed, how he'd cried himself to sleep every night. He didn't have to. Logan could see it in the way Adrian's shoulders slumped, in the chasm of longing in his eyes. It mirrored Logan's own turmoil—a shared suffering that echoed between them. They both grappled with the same sorrow, wrestling against their own currents of despair, each of them teetering on the edge of surrender, separated by vast oceans of distance.

"Ad," Logan pleaded softly, his voice trembling. He took another step forward, closing the gap between them. "Please. I—I didn't know. I didn't realize... Please, sit down. Let me—let me help."

Adrian shook his head, his tears slipping freely now. "You don't get to help," he hissed. "Not after this."

Logan froze mid-step, his hands slipping uselessly to his sides, as if gravity had suddenly remembered them. The space between them stretched wide, not in measurable standards, but in memory, in the wreckage of everything. Adrian stood just a breath away, yet felt galaxies removed.

What spilled from Adrian's mouth wasn't anger; it was agony, stripped bare. His voice carried the texture of old scars being reopened, not with fury, but with truth too long caged. Logan hadn't known. Not fully. He hadn't realized that leaving had been like pulling the spine from a living body, that what he thought was escape had, for Adrian, been an unmaking.

Each syllable did not strike so much as twist, a blade long buried and turned slowly, unpityingly. These were not words but reckonings, carrying the ache of days left unanswered, nights collapsing in mute despair, the quiet brutality of a love left to rot in its own silence.

Logan stood there, gutted in his stillness, understanding too late that some things, once broken, don't shatter; they dissolve, slow and soft and irreversible.

"I thought I knew you," Adrian whispered, his gaze finally meeting Logan's again. "But you weren't the person I thought you were. And now, I don't know if I can trust the person standing in front of me."

Logan's tears spill over, his heart breaking all over again. He wanted to say something, to fall to his knees and beg for forgiveness, but he couldn't. Adrian wasn't ready to hear it. Not yet. So Logan stood there, silent and still, as Adrian's words were waves eroding a shore.

"And then," Adrian continued, his voice breaking as his tears streaked his cheeks, "when I came back here, to the country I ran from in the first place, there it was. A wedding invitation." He choked on the words. "It fucking killed me, Lo. Because while I was picking up the pieces of what you left behind, you were planning a fucking wedding."

Logan flinched as if struck, his hands curling into fists at his sides, though not from anger. It was the helplessness, the guilt, the unbearable reality of what Adrian was saying.

"I waited for you in that room," Adrian wept, his voice rising, each word drenched in anguish. "I waited while you were planning a life with someone else." Adrian stopped for a moment, looking around as if he was gathering strength for the next question. "So tell me," Adrian asked, eyes locking on Logan with a quiet fury that didn't need to shout, "how long... how long did it take?"

Logan's brows furrowed. "What...?" he started.

"How long before you went back to her?" Adrian demanded through clenched teeth.

Logan's face drained of color. "Adrian, please..."

"Logan," Adrian uttered. "How long?"

Logan shook his head. The answer was too painful, too shameful to be voiced in the presence of Adrian.

"No," Adrian cut in, sharp and cold. "How long before you went back to her?"

Logan looked down, as if hoping the answer might be hidden in the seams of the carpet.

"Logan." His name landed like a sentence.

Logan squeezed his eyes shut and pressed the heels of his palms to them, like trying to hold in something shameful that might leak out.

"The next day." It came out barely audible. But it didn't matter. Adrian heard it.

The sound he made wasn't quite a cry; it was more like a guttural noise torn from deep within, under his ribs, as if a fracture had occurred. A rupture through whatever fragment of hope remained in him, a tear through the very essence of his soul, a fresh fissure to his already broken, bleeding, vacant of a heart chest.

He stood there, swaying slightly, his hand coming up to his mouth like he was trying to stop something—vomit, maybe. Or words too cruel to survive.

Then, softly, as if doing the math aloud: "So you left me on the thirteenth... the flight's about seventeen hours. You would've landed the night of the thirteenth. And by morning—" he looked up, his voice caught like fabric on a nail, something inside him folding inward. "By morning you were..." The words were left to die on his tongue; betrayal required none. It was soundless, with no need for syllables or punctuation to reiterate the depth of deception, the cruel knife twisting in the absence of speech, without the courtesy of a final sentence, only guilt required.

And Logan—Logan felt it: the sharp, coiled fist of guilt tightening in his gut. Not just because of what he had done, but because of what he saw now: Adrian was unraveling, collapsing, crumbling in front of him.

His hands trembled, jaw locked tight, grief gnawing at his bones, pressing against the walls of his skin, yearning to shatter his soul, desperate to break through. The calculation was written all over his face: three weeks alone in that cabin, clinging to the last breath of something sacred. A silence full of belief. And meanwhile, Logan was already carving out a new life. Already erasing the one he'd promised without words to hold on to.

Logan saw it in Adrian's eyes: the impossible comparison between waiting and forgetting. He saw it and couldn't look away.

Adrian's voice, when it came, was low and ragged, more heartbreak than venom. "I thought... I honestly thought it had taken you two weeks to go back to her." He laughed. It was a hollow, bitter sound, more of a breath than a noise. "Turns out I gave what we had far too much credit."

Adrian drew in a long, deliberate breath, as if pulling oxygen into a collapsed lung. He needed to make space inside himself for this new truth. And he had a place for truths like this—dark, sharp-edged things that couldn't be held in daylight.

He found the box. He opened it. And gently, methodically, he folded this new betrayal and placed it inside, beside all the others. A private archive of pain. He would come back to it later, when he was alone, when the silence was loud enough to echo. He would take it out and hold it against his ribs like a blade.

But not now. Now, he had to stay upright.

He stood straighter, jaw tight, gaze fixed on some invisible horizon. He couldn't fall apart, not with Logan being five steps away, not while his hands still remembered the weight of that body, not while his skin still held the memory of a mouth that had whispered promises and then vanished.

He couldn't afford to think about the timeline. Couldn't afford to dwell on the math: Within twenty-four hours of leaving their shared bed, the one that still held the shape of them, their scent pressed into the crumpled sheets, heat trapped in the mattress, the ghost of their bodies tangled in cotton and sweat. A bed that hadn't cooled before Logan gave himself to someone else.

Within thirty-six hours of breathing and whimpering against Adrian's throat in the throes of passion, of tasting his skin.

Hours—mere hours—after their last kiss.

And still, Logan had gone back. To her. To the woman who would become his wife. With Adrian's name still clinging to his lips. With Adrian's breath still ghosting his skin. With Adrian's taste still on his tongue. With parts of Adrian's body still inside him.

That was the part that burned the deepest.

And Adrian knew: this was information he would use to destroy himself.

Not now. Not here. But later.

Later, when it was quiet.

Later, when Logan was gone again.

"And you know what?" he started again, feigning confidence, trying to finish his story. "Even after seeing the invitation and... it killed me. But... I wasn't even angry at first. I was hurt, I was...But I *understood*—I thought I understood. You panicked. You ran. You were trying to prove something to yourself, to the world, to your father. So I bought a ticket."

Adrian's voice cracked, and he took a deep, shuddering breath. "I didn't tell Dean. I knew he'd stop me if he found out. But I bought it anyway. Because I couldn't stand the thought of you suffering, Logan. I loved you too much to let you go through that alone. I thought I had to save you, rescue you, because that's what I do, right?"

Logan couldn't speak, couldn't even breathe, as Adrian's voice grew softer, his words heavier.

"I was sure," Adrian's voice trembled, caught between anger and the ghost of hope. "I was absolutely sure that once we saw each other—once I looked into your eyes and you looked into mine—you'd understand. You'd see what we had, what we still had. You'd realize it was a mistake, that leaving was a mistake." He drew in a sharp breath, the kind that seemed to scrape against his ribs. "I thought all I needed was a chance, just one chance to stand in front of you, to let you feel it. To let you see me. I thought it would be enough. But I was stupid, Logan. So damn stupid."

Adrian's eyes flickered around the room as if in thought, as if he was searching the wall for answers, for words, for strength to keep going. Like the bare walls of this random place would have anything to offer him.

"And I was selfish too," Adrian whispered, eyelashes heavy with tears that could not be contained. "Because I knew the pain of seeing you—seeing the man I love, the man I *adore*—marrying someone else... that was a pain I wouldn't wish on my worst enemy. To think..." His voice faltered, and he laughed bitterly, wiping at his tears with the back of his hand. "To think that it had only been a few days since I kissed you, since I held you, and there you were, planning a wedding."

Adrian's chest heaved with the effort of holding himself together, but it was futile. The tears came harder, and he muttered something in Hebrew, a broken prayer or curse, before switching back to English. "To think," he repeated, his voice hollow, "that so little time had passed. So little time between you leaving me and you building a life with someone else. I never knew you could be so cruel, Logan. I never knew you cared so little about us. About me."

Logan couldn't take it anymore. He closed the distance between them, each step slow, his heart pounding so hard it felt like it might break free from his chest. Adrian's pain was unbearable, and Logan couldn't stand to see him falling apart. He stopped just a whisper away, his tears spilling over, his emotions laid bare.

"Adrian," Logan pleaded, his voice raw and trembling. "I'm so sorry. I'm so fucking sorry, Ad. Please. I never let myself think about it, about how you handled it, about what you went through. I was a coward. I'm so sorry. Please..."

Adrian lifted his gaze to meet Logan's, his eyes red and brimming with tears. There was no forgiveness; only a lingering pain that merged with shattered dreams and tender memories. "Of course, you didn't think about it," Adrian said, his voice flat, his tone cutting like ice. "You don't care about anyone but yourself."

Logan shook his head frantically, the words slicing through him. "No," he whispered, his voice breaking. "That's not true. It's not true, Adrian. Please, sit down. Please... finish your story."

Adrian didn't move, didn't yield. He let the weight of his streaming tears speak for him in the silence, clinging to those memories—willing them not to slip away—because the sight of Logan, so close, was already eroding the last fragile defenses he had left.

The space between them yawned wide, an abyss that no hand could cross, though Adrian stood within arm's reach. Logan's fingers twitched with the urge to close the gap, to gather him in, to confess that he was not the man Adrian believed. He had cared. He still cared. He would always care. Yet the weight of restraint pinned him still, a silence heavier than touch.

Adrian straightened his spine, his hands trembling as he brushed away his tears, an instinctive movement that was useless.

"No," Adrian interrupted, his voice resolute, though it fractured like ice under pressure. He locked eyes with Logan, refusing to be the one to look away, to yield under the crushing weight of their dying love story. "The entire flight," he began, his words trembling on the precipice of emotion, "I felt sick. Like my heart was clawing its way out of my chest, desperate to escape. I was terrified, Logan. So fucking scared. But I told myself it was worth it. That you were worth it. That I had to fight for you." His voice faltered briefly, but he pressed on, each word carrying the rawness of an open wound. "Because you were *it* for me. You were everything. I was so damn in love with you that I couldn't let fear win. I had to go. I had to show you how much you meant to me."

Logan's breath stuttered in his throat, his chest clinching tight, the room had flooded, and he'd forgotten how to swim. His hands twitched at his sides, impractical, adrift, like they belonged to someone else. Adrian stood before him, not shouting, not accusing, but unleashing, his voice the kind of quiet that cleaves.

And Logan could do nothing. Just stand there, still and splintering, as Adrian's words swept through him—not like waves, but like undertow. Silent. Sudden. Merciless. They didn't crash. They *dragged*. Pulled him inward, downward, into the hollow places he'd spent two years pretending weren't there.

Adrian didn't need to raise his voice; truth was doing the shouting and tearing for him. And Logan felt it in his bones: not the rage of a man betrayed, but the sorrow of one left behind with too much love and nowhere to place it.

"And then..." Adrian continued, his voice softening, hollowed out like driftwood worn down by time and tide. "When I got there, I saw you. I saw your family. Your father, sisters, and you." He inhaled sharply, his chest heaving as though each breath cost him a piece of himself. "And I still didn't blame you. God help me, Logan, I felt sorry for you. You looked so fucking scared. Terrified. Like you were trapped in a life you didn't choose, a life that didn't belong to you. All I wanted in that moment was to help you."

A bitter laugh escaped Adrian's lips, sharp and raw, unraveling into something that sounded more like a sob. It was the sound of a heart breaking all over again. "I remembered what you told me. That you didn't have feelings for her—for Sandy. That you were just running. Running from yourself. Running to make your father proud. And I thought..." His voice cracked, and he paused, his shoulders trembling as he steadied himself. "I thought I made the right choice by coming there. That I could save you. That I could still be what you needed."

The words hung between them, weighted with a despair so sharp it toppled the fragile citadels they had once built from love. Logan felt Adrian's truth press into him and understood, with a hollow certainty, that no apology could ever mend what had already been broken.

"But then..." Adrian's voice cracked, and his hands clenched into fists. "Then you talked to me. And I didn't know who you were anymore. The man standing in front of me, in that suit, with that smile that didn't reach your eyes—I had no idea who that was. And that's when it hit me." He looked at Logan, and the tears did not thaw the ice in his gaze. "It was all a scam. The man I loved? The man I thought I knew? He wasn't real. The Logan I saw at that wedding... that was the real you."

"No!" Logan's voice was a roar, raw and desperate, as he surged forward. His hands grabbed Adrian's face, trembling with the intensity of his emotions. "No, Adrian, you're wrong. I swear to God, you're wrong. The real me was the man who was with you. That was *me*! The Logan you saw at that wedding was the fake. A puppet for my father. A shell. Please, Ad, you have to believe me. It was real. Every second of it was real. Me, you, us. It was the only thing in my life that *was* real. I was the happiest with you. I was *me*."

"I don't believe you." The honesty in his words struck Logan harder than any scream could have, the weight of Adrian's distrust tying knots in his gut.

Adrian reached up, his hands trembling, and pried Logan's hands away from his face. The warmth of Logan's touch, the familiar scent of him, the way his body felt so close—it was too much. Too much for Adrian to bear without shattering completely. His heart ached with longing, his body screaming for what his mind refused to allow. He wanted Logan so much it hurt, and that wanting was tearing him apart.

"And then I saw you getting married," Adrian uttered. "I stayed, Logan. I stayed because I had to. I needed to see it with my own eyes. To convince myself that what I thought we had was a lie. To prove to myself that I could never come back for you. That no matter how much my heart begged, I'd know—I'd *know*—that it was yearning for something that was never real."

Adrian's voice trembled, the words raw and serrated, like shards of shell driven into wet sand. "I stayed because my memories of us were too beautiful, too vivid, and I couldn't trust them anymore. I had to see the truth, to force myself to distinguish between what I thought we were and the reality of what you chose. I had to remind myself how foolish I'd been."

Logan's eyes burned, the world warping in a shimmer of salt, as Adrian's words crashed through every defense, leaving him flayed, every nerve exposed.

"You looked like shit," Adrian whispered, the words cracking like thunder. "You looked like you were in physical pain, like standing there in front of everyone was agony. Anyone could've seen it. A blind man could've felt it. But that didn't stop you. You still took a wife." His voice hitched, trembling as though the words themselves wounded him. "You still kissed her. And then... and then you vowed..."

Adrian broke, his voice shattering like glass against stone. "You vowed to love her. Until death."

The air seemed to shatter, the weight of his words cracking the fragile silence between them. Adrian's breath came unevenly, his chest heaving with the effort to hold himself together. But his body betrayed him, trembling as though the weight of everything he carried—the heartbreak, the betrayal, the loss—was finally too much.

Logan couldn't stay still anymore. The distance between them was unbearable, an ocean he refused to let separate them again. He stepped forward and reached for Adrian's hand, gripping it tightly but gently, as if grounding him. "Adrian," he said softly, his voice filled with desperation. "Please. Sit. You don't have to do this standing up. You don't have to carry it all right now. Just... sit with me. Please."

Adrian paused. His breath hitched—a fragile thread threatening to snap. Tears swelled in his eyes, shimmering like saltwater diamonds before trailing down, tracing the silent story of his grief across his cheeks, soaking into the collar of his shirt. Each drop a quiet surrender. His face trembled, not with fear, but the ache of love remembered and lost.

For a heartbeat, Logan feared he would turn away—retreat behind the walls time had built. But Adrian didn't. Instead, with the weariness of a man who knew he had lost a battle, he let Logan guide him to the couch. His body folded into the cushions, not sat, but *fell*, every limb heavy with unshed sorrow. He looked hollowed, as if the ocean he once conquered now lived inside him, crashing quietly against the bones and empty space of his chest.

Logan knelt before him, his knees pressing into the floor, his hands resting lightly on Adrian's knees. His eyes searched Adrian's face, pleading for a glimpse of forgiveness, of something that could undo the years of hurt he'd caused.

"I'm sorry," Logan whispered brokenly. "I'm so fucking sorry. For everything." His hands tightened slightly, trembling as he held on, afraid that if he let go, Adrian might drift away again.

Adrian didn't respond, his gaze distant as if he were still lost in the memory of that day. Logan's heart ached as he watched him, knowing that no matter what he said, no matter how many times he apologized, it would never undo the damage he had done.

Adrian sat with a rigid stillness that felt like a dam about to break. His gaze was fixed on his hand, where Logan's fingers had just been moments ago, on his knees, where Logan's hands touched faintly, burning him with sensations he had longed since felt. He stared at that spot as if it held answers to questions he couldn't ask, as if it were a wound he didn't know how to heal.

Logan's heart raced, the hazy flicker of hope sparking in his chest—a realization that his presence, his touch, still had some influence over Adrian, no matter how faint.

"Finish it," Logan breathed, his voice trembling with tears he didn't bother to hide. He knew he deserved this—deserved to hear every word Adrian needed to say. He also knew that Adrian needed to say it, to purge the decaying poison he'd been carrying. "Please, Adrian."

Adrian's voice was quiet, almost detached. "After the wedding, Dean... Like always. He was just... being my friend. Picking up the pieces you left behind." He paused, his jaw tightening as he gathered his thoughts. "I wrote that stupid song after that. Composed it for months. It was the only thing that helped me—helped me make sense of anything. And then one night, I sang it in some bar. Just a nothing place. But Tom and Dean filmed it. They said it was a good song. And... I later learned that Dean had put it online."

Adrian's words caught in his throat, his voice uncertain as he finally met Logan's eyes. "You heard it, didn't you?"

Logan nodded, his fingers curling gently against Adrian's knees, his touch a fragile lifeline. He needed that contact, however small—a reminder that this was real, that Adrian was here, solid and breathing.

"I knew it." Adrian's voice was low, heavy with something that felt too close to regret. His gaze dropped to where Logan's hand rested, the simple point of connection between them. "I never wanted you to hear that song. I didn't want you to know... to hear me at my lowest, at rock bottom. God, I felt so fucking pathetic when I found out it was on Facebook and you'd probably seen it. I tried to pretend it didn't matter, that it was nothing. But it wasn't 'nothing.' It was everything."

Logan opened his mouth, a response on the edge of his lips, but Adrian's words rushed forward, uncontainable now. They tumbled out with a sharpness, a raw edge, as if he had to spill them out before his courage dissolved.

"At the time the video went up, I was just trying to survive, my life was such a mess," Adrian said, his voice distant, as if he were talking to someone miles away. "I had enrolled in university, thought maybe I could start over. But it didn't fit. I didn't fit. I didn't even finish the first year. It was like trying to wear someone else's skin. So I quit. The day after the video went online, right after the diagnosis, I deleted my account."

Logan's breath hitched, the word striking him like a physical blow. Adrian barely noticed, his eyes distant as he continued, his tone hollow. "Dean and I were already roommates by then. We were renting the house you saw. Tom lived with us too for a while, but he moved out when he got a girlfriend. And then—Leukemia."

He said the word like it was nothing, a fact as casual as the weather. Logan wanted to scream at the indifference, to shake Adrian, to force him to stop minimizing what was happening. Adrian finally looked at Logan again, his eyes heavy with a sadness that seemed infinite.

"My mom died from this," Adrian murmured, almost to himself. "So when the first symptoms came... the fatigue, the weakness, when I couldn't work out, couldn't surf anymore... I suspected. Then my skin got pale, and I told myself it was just the lack of sun. But then the bruises appeared, out of nowhere. The bleeding. The bone pain." He shook his head, voice faltering. "I knew. I had seen it all before, on her. I knew even before the diagnosis. I didn't need a doctor to tell me."

Logan gulped, his fingers pressing into Adrian's skin as he whispered, "Treatments?"

Adrian shook his head, his gaze fixed on the floor.

"They didn't work?" Logan's voice cracked, each word stumbling over the thick lump in his throat.

Adrian let out a harsh breath, a sardonic laugh slipping through his lips like a shadow in the night, reverberating around the room. "No. I have turned them down," he murmured, the weight of his decision hanging in the air like a storm cloud ready to burst.

Logan's eyes widened, confusion and panic flashing across his face. "What do you mean you *turned them down*? You can't just—what are you doing, Adrian? Waiting to die?"

Adrian's face darkened, his body tensing as he stared at Logan with a fury that bordered on grief. "I don't *have* to do anything," he snapped, his voice rising. "Especially not because you say so. You don't get to come back into my life after all this time and tell me what I *have* to do."

"Ad!" Logan burst out, his voice desperate. "It's bigger than what happened between us! This is your *life*! You can't just... You can't just wait to die without even trying!"

Logan reached out, his hand trembling as he tried to take Adrian's, his knees still on the floor, the cold tile biting through his jeans. He was holding on to the last frayed threads of hope, praying there was still something left to salvage.

But Adrian recoiled, his body jerking back as if Logan's touch had seared his skin. He stood abruptly, the movement forceful enough to push Logan away. Adrian's chest heaved, his breath coming in ragged pulls as he backed away, the storm inside him breaking, winds fierce and unforgiving.

Logan scrambled to his feet, his own breath catching, the room suddenly too small, too tight. He could feel it—the end rushing toward them like a wave, the kind that crushed everything beneath it. And all he could do was brace himself, hoping somehow they could find air before the water closed over them both.

"I don't need your pity, Logan," Adrian snarled, his voice cracking. "And I don't need you to save me. Not now. Not ever."

Logan languished in the stillness of that quiet room, his hand suspended mid-air, reaching towards a man whose gaze refused to meet his. Adrian's shoulders were a bow strung too tight, trembling with the weight of silence, his body fraying at the seams, so weak, so impossibly weary that a single word from Logan might splinter him, might shatter the moment into shards sharp enough to draw blood.

"Adrian..." Logan's voice, hushed and raw, barely crossed the space between them.

Silence gathered, blooming, growing thick and dangerous, whispering secrets of looming peril.

Adrian drew a breath that seemed to cost him everything. When he spoke, the words cut clean, stripped of ornament. "So... I think we're done here, Logan. You can go back to your fancy life, and even get your beautiful wife back."

The words tore through him, each one a grain of salt pressed into an open wound, but still, Logan resolved would not be shaken. A shiver chased through his bones, then stilled, pinned down by something deeper than fear. His voice, when it rose, was ragged and sure all at once, tethered to the pulse hammering in his throat. "Ad, I'm not going anywhere. I don't care what you say or do. I'm staying."

Adrian's lips formed a hollow smile shaped by sorrow. It quivered at the edges, never quite reaching his tear-filled eyes.

"I don't want you to stay," he lied, his words tearing through the void between them, fragments masquerading as speech, born from the deepest shadows of Adrian's soul, where air was but a memory and sunlight forever out of reach. For an instant, he wanted to drag Logan there with him, to see if he would still reach out, even inside that darkness.

Logan froze, his lungs burned with ragged air, then shook his head, a raw frustration breaking through. "It's too bad. You need to get treatments! You can't just... wait here to die and do nothing. You *can't*! You need to take care of yourself." And somehow, though he could never have planned it, those words slipped past Adrian's armor, lighting something quiet and stubborn inside him, something that still remembered sunlight.

"You—" Adrian started, but Logan cut him off, his voice rising in desperation.

"Adrian! Please! Six months isn't long. We need to get you—"

"We?!" Adrian's laughter was sharp, almost cruel, the sound of a man who had been devoid of happiness for so long that he had forgotten the taste of it, only remembering how it burned him. "We?! How *dare* you say *we*!" Adrian was already gathering up the broken shield Logan had shattered with just a handful of words, piecing it back together with shaking hands, unwilling to let hope make a fool of him again.

"Adrian..." Logan tried to speak, but the words came out thin, as if he'd already lost the right to say them. He stepped forward, reaching, but there was nowhere to place his hands. "You... can't die."

Adrian's composure shattered, all the months of silence and sleeplessness, all the dreams that had soured into nightmares night after night, the hollow ache of Logan's heartbeat missing from his own, crashing through him in one unstoppable rush. "Fuck you, Logan!" he screamed, his voice breaking on the last syllable, as if it had been sharpened against every night he'd spent alone.

He turned abruptly, striding to the door and flinging it open with a force that echoed in the quiet room. The door then slammed shut behind him.

For a moment, Logan stood frozen, his breath coming in shallow, uneven gasps.

He knew he couldn't let him go.

Not like this.

Adrian stormed down the hotel corridor, inhaling sharply, knowing that the air might choke him. He wiped at his face with trembling hands, grief spilling from his eyes in a silent flood.

He moved with single-minded determination, not stopping even as his vision blurred.

The hallway stretched endlessly before him, the fluorescent lights above casting harsh shadows that flickered like ghosts of the past. He pressed the elevator button with more force than necessary, willing the doors to open and take him away from the swirling chaos in his mind. He wished he could stop thinking. He wished he could stop feeling.

What did I even think would happen, coming here? The thought spat through him like a cruel laugh. *That I could get closure? That I could scrape something real from him?*

Adrian had laid out his story, bared all of the raw parts of it, a confession he'd once dreamed of making, but it landed on the floor between them like a broken offering, leaving his chest emptier than before.

The numbers above the elevator ticked downward, agonizingly slow. And even though he told himself not to, he turned. His gaze drifted back down the hallway, back to Logan's door.

It was an instinctual glance—an echo from the depths of his soul, where a piece of him would forever be tethered to Logan, despite the struggles that raged within. This fragment of his being still clung to tender dreams, to the wistful yearning that perhaps Logan would pursue him, that he would leap through that threshold, seize his arm, and *whisper, "Stay. Don't go. I need you here with me."*

Adrian found himself entwined in a web of inner turmoil as his gaze went time and again to that closed door. He had sworn repeatedly, with a fierceness that echoed in his mind, to shut Logan out, to keep the heartache at bay. Loving Logan devoured him from the inside out, a ravenous burn that left nothing untouched, scouring every corner of him until only longing remained. In defiance of his own vows, his heart reached out in a desperate whisper, yearning for a connection, even as his rational thoughts roared persistently, urging him to turn away and retreat into the shadows, for Logan's light once more burned his soul.

The elevator dinged softly, the little screen above it showing that it was just two floors away. Adrian forced his eyes back to it, willing himself to move forward. But the part of him that still loved Logan, that *always* would, whispered for him to stay, to wait.

To give Logan the chance to prove him wrong.

But of course, Logan won't chase him.

Because he doesn't really care. Adrian reminded himself. *Logan came to clear his conscience and heard that I am sick, so he felt bad and stayed.*

Adrian wanted to kick himself for coming to Logan now, for unraveling every thread of his carefully entwined defenses. All the secrets he had guarded, the soft underbelly of his pain, lay exposed at Logan's feet. It felt like every note of their hurt-song, every tragic, fractured chord of the love story they had built and shattered, had been stripped bare. Again. A haunting melody emanated from a solitary violin, its screeching notes intertwining with the soft whispers of a broken heart as the streams of water dictated the bow and tore at the strings. Within each note, one could hear a deep yearning—a sorrowful lament for lost love, calling out to the ocean to reunite with the other half of a torn soul.

It was a cruel pattern—time and again, Adrian had bared himself to Logan, each time thinking he had nothing left to lose. He had spent two long years reprimanding himself, trying to harden the soft parts of himself that Logan had once held. But standing here now, the truth was undeniable: he was still weak when it came to Logan. Some things never change.

The realization burned through him, a slow ache that twisted beneath his ribs. He had opened himself up, let Logan see everything—the bruised parts of his heart, the raw edges of his grief—and once more, he found himself shattered. It was as if all the scars he thought had healed had split open, bleeding fresh and bright, and Adrian was left holding the pieces of himself, wondering why he had thought this time might be different.

And once more, like an interminable cycle of known scripts, where the end was incorrigible, Adrian was broken.

The elevator dinged softly, offering a lifeline, an escape from the hurricane of emotions spinning wildly between them.

Adrian moved to step inside, to leave behind the man who had once held his entire soul in calloused, surf-worn hands. But Logan's voice—hoarse, desperate—cut through the hum of the hallway, like that July storm breaking over Hawaii summer.

"Ad!"

The sound of it hit Adrian with the force of an unexpected wave, one that dragged him under and left him breathless. For a whisper, he hesitated, his feet rooted in place even as his mind screamed to flee, to stay, to run to Logan.

Logan ran toward him, his movements uncharacteristically frantic, the cool confidence Adrian had once adored replaced by a raw, unfiltered anguish.

"Please, don't go." Logan's voice trembled, and he blocked Adrian's path, his tall frame an immovable barrier. His gray eyes, stormy and rimmed with unshed tears, locked onto Adrian's. "Just... don't."

"Logan, move," Adrian said, his voice low but firm, as though speaking too loudly might crack the fragile shell of his resolve. He didn't dare touch him, couldn't risk the electric charge of Logan's skin against his own. Not again. He tried to sidestep, to slip past him like water through fingers, but Logan followed his every move, his determination as unyielding as the pull beneath a drowning man's feet.

And then, like a fallen warrior, Logan sank to his knees.

The sight was a visceral blow for Adrian, knotting his stomach in anguish. Logan Vaughn once again lowered before him, first within the confines of a walled room and now, heartbreakingly, in the hollow expanse of a hotel hallway. Tears cascaded down his pale, angular face, carving paths like sorrowful rivers through the memories that clung to Adrian's mind like ghostly engravings on ancient driftwood.

"Please, Adrian. Let me explain," Logan implored, his voice fracturing—a crack in a dam that had withstood the flood of his emotions for far too long. He grasped Adrian's hands, his touch both resolute and quaking. "I love you. Oh God, how I love you! Please, don't walk away!"

Adrian froze, caught in the tempest of those words. They weren't unfamiliar—they had been murmured through his bedroom door, woven into a hesitant text message—but now, hearing them spoken aloud, tumbling from Logan's quivering lips, it was as if all doubt had been stripped away. There was no escape, no deluding his racing mind or aching heart into believing he had misheard, that this was merely a cruel trick of fleeting hope.

Logan's voice carried a weight of raw emotion, his tears bleeding into the fragile fabric of time that hung so thin between them, a frayed thread threatening to snap. This moment was different. It was a devastating crescendo, an earth-shattering truth that resonated through every fiber of Adrian's being. He had never gazed upon a certainty as profound as the one reflected in Logan's eyes, as he bared his love.

"You don't get to say that," Adrian finally whispered shakily. He pulled at his hands, but Logan held tight, his fingers laced like the roots of a tree clinging to unstable earth.

"There hasn't been a second I haven't thought of you," Logan cried out, his voice rising, desperate; he was a man calling out to shore, the only shore he had ever known, after drifting too far. "I dreamed of you. I saw your face every time I closed my eyes. Adrian, you were the only thing keeping me afloat, even when I was drowning in everything else. I was lost without you. I *am* lost without you."

"Logan, stop." Adrian's voice cracked, his defenses crumbling under the weight of Logan's confession. He could see the truth in his eyes, the love that had never truly disappeared, the pain that mirrored his own.

"Nothing in my life is worth it without you," Logan insisted. "I made a mistake—a terrible, unforgivable mistake—but I can't lose you again. Not again. Please, Adrian. Let me fix this."

Tears blurred Adrian's vision, and he felt the sting of them as they carved paths down his face. His body wavered, caught between the magnetic pull of Logan's love and the crushing fear of what it would mean to let him back in. To give Logan his heart again was to stand on the edge of a cliff, knowing full well the fall could kill him.

The low cough of a bystander broke the moment, pulling both men from their raw, unfiltered emotions. An elderly couple, dressed to perfection, stood nearby, their presence a quiet reminder of the world outside this intimate storm.

"Perhaps you should hear him out, dear," the woman said gently, her British accent lending warmth to her words, her eyes filled with understanding.

Adrian swallowed hard, his throat raw with unshed words. The couple disappeared into their suite, leaving the hallway quiet but heavy with unspoken tension. Logan stayed where he was, kneeling before Adrian like a man praying for redemption. His tears shone in the dim light, a silent testament to the depth of his regret.

"Lo, get up," Adrian murmured, his voice trembling as his heart split in two—one part yearning to collapse into Logan's arms, the other terrified of being ruptured once more by the only person who held the power of making him whole again. He pulled at Logan's hands, but Logan held firm, his grip unmovable.

"Please, Adrian," Logan's voice was a tender whisper as he pleaded. "Don't make me let you go. Don't give up on us."

Adrian's tears cascaded like fragile raindrops, his heart aching with the gravity of the moment. In a fleeting heartbeat, he dared to dream—to envision himself melting into Logan's embrace, surrendering to the love he had fought so valiantly to entomb, allowing it to sweep him ashore like a tumultuous wave returning to land. Yet, the fear lingered—piercing and unbending, a ghostly specter echoing the ruins of their past.

"I can't..." Adrian breathed. "I'm not sure I can survive it again."

Logan's hands tightened, his eyes pleading, drowning in desperation. "Then let me show you. Let me prove it to you. Just don't walk away."

And there, amidst the silent hush of the corridor, with the ocean's gentle roar echoing faintly within their chests, Adrian felt utterly powerless, irrevocably shattered beneath Logan's imploring gaze, every fiber of his being yearning distraughtly for Logan.

Logan's voice cracked as he half-mumbled, half-sang the first fragile notes of a melody that, through the distance, had tethered them together. "I think of you when the sun climbs high, I reach for you when I breach the tide..." His voice was uneven, a whisper struggling against the weight of his tears, but the words were a lifeline cast into the storm that churned between them. It was Adrian's song—an elegy drawn from the depths of his heart, wrung out of the salt-stung strings of a soul shipwrecked by love's cruel tide. The words bled drop by drop onto the page, each oozing a testament to his sorrow, as he strummed a guitar that seared his fingertips, using the same strings that once resonated with the laughter of Logan, to weave a haunting ballad about their ossuary love.

"Lo, don't." Adrian's voice wavered, a thin veil over the sea of emotion threatening to spill over.

But Logan pressed on. "I search for you whenever I rise from the depths, I dream of you beneath the moon's soft embrace, I'll take a breath just to give you mine." He sang, his voice trembling but determined, each line a plea carved into the air between them.

Adrian's body betrayed him, reacting to the lyrics in ways he couldn't suppress. His shoulders shook, his chest heaved with the heaviness of memories carried on every note. Logan saw it—the way those words, born of Adrian's long-buried pain, still clung to him like seafoam on skin.

"When *I* left," Logan murmured, his voice low and raw, "*I left* the best of me with you. *It* was the *hardest* thing to rise and leave." His own words faltered, rewritten in the moment, his truth unraveling in the same breath as his regret.

Adrian closed his eyes, but the tears escaped anyway, carving silent rivers down his cheeks. His hands trembled as he gripped Logan's, forceful but fragile, and pulled him to his feet. For a heartbeat, they stood in silence, Logan waiting—breath held—until Adrian opened his eyes.

When he did, their gazes locked, and Logan saw every inch of the pain he had caused reflected back at him. Adrian's quiet sniffs punctuated the stillness, and Logan wanted nothing more than to pull him into his arms, to promise a tomorrow where this pain would no longer exist.

Instead, Logan brought Adrian's hand to his lips, his kiss as light as sea spray on a gentle breeze. "You are the real love, Adrian. Just you. Only you." His voice was soft, but his words carried the weight of an oath.

Logan led him back to the suite, their steps slow, hesitant, as if the ground beneath them might crack. The door closed softly behind them, and the tension in Logan's chest eased just slightly at the sound. Adrian stayed, and for Logan, that was everything.

They sat on the couch, bodies drawn together yet hesitant, like a current unable to choose whether to pull them closer or let them drift apart.

Logan held Adrian's hand, his fingers warm and steady despite the storm raging inside him. He didn't let go, afraid that if he did, Adrian might disappear like a phantom into the night.

"From the day I walked away from you..." Logan began, his voice breaking on the words, "I was drowning, Ad. Every day, every hour, I was sinking deeper. I thought I was doing the right thing, but it was a lie—I was a lie."

Logan's words poured out, a flood that had been dammed up for too long, surging between them with a force that neither of them could escape. His voice was unsteady, each word tumbling over the next, raw and unfiltered, as if the truth had finally broken free and couldn't be held back. He began with Sandy, letting out the tapestry of a life he had stitched together from lies and duty, not love. Each sentence was soaked in regret, each memory laced with the bitterness of a choice that had shattered both their hearts.

"I did everything I could to avoid her," Logan admitted. "I encouraged her to go on business trips, vacations, galas, conferences...anything to escape. I counted the hours she was gone as blessings. I spent most of the time at work..." He swallowed hard and avoided meeting Adrian's eyes. "I couldn't even touch her, Adrian. Not in the way she deserved, not in the way I wanted to touch you. My body shut down around her, like it knew I didn't belong in that life. I couldn't even be in the same room without feeling... trapped in someone else's skin. Fuck, I had to have porn in the background to get it up..." His hands clenched, and his shoulders curled inwards, trying to disappear.

Adrian sat motionless, his face a mask of exhaustion and sorrow, his head throbbing from too many tears. For a fleeting moment, Logan lifted his head and watched Adrian carefully, as though afraid of the strength of the confession.

"I turned to the bottle," Logan continued, his gaze dropping to their linked hands. "Every night, I'd drink until I couldn't feel anything. The pain, the regret...even my own body. I thought if I drank enough, I could drown the memory of you, but it didn't work. Nothing worked."

Adrian's lips parted as if to speak, but no words came. Logan pressed on, his voice faltering as he revealed the cracks in his fragile façade. "Sandy and I fought constantly. She wanted a child, but I couldn't do it, Adrian. I couldn't bring an innocent soul into that mess, into that kind of misery. I wasn't willing to be tied to her forever. Not when all I could think about was you."

The room felt oppressively small, with thick air and pain seeping into the space. Logan finally released Adrian's hand, standing to cross to the minibar. His movements were shaky, his frame a shadow of the man Adrian once knew. He rummaged through the bottles and cans, placing sodas and water on the table like offerings before cracking open a can. The sound of the carbonation hissing into the silence was almost jarring.

Logan drank deeply, the cool liquid soothing his raw throat. But there was no relief from the storm raging inside him. He sat back down and turned to Adrian, his voice quieter now, the weight of everything pulling him down.

"I thought about you constantly," Logan said, his voice trembling. "Every fight with Sandy, every night I couldn't sleep, every morning that I woke up, every time I took a breath...I thought about you. I missed you in ways I can't even put into words, Adrian. It was like losing a part of myself. No, it *was* losing a part of myself."

Adrian listened, silent but present, his tears falling steadily as Logan's words cut into him. He felt the truth of it in every syllable, every unguarded look in Logan's gray eyes. He wanted to speak, to say something—anything—but his voice was caught somewhere between his heart and his throat.

Logan had told him about the endless fights with Jane, how she had always felt something was off.

Logan continued, his gaze distant, his voice a hollow echo of the life he had lived without Adrian. "The first time I heard it—your voice..." His words caught, a tremor beneath the surface. "It broke me. I was a chaos. I cried so hard the bartender, Zack, told me to go home. But I couldn't. I just sat there, drinking and crying, saying your name like it was the only thing keeping me alive."

Adrian's fingers curled into the fabric of his pants, his knuckles white against his skin. His chest rose and fell with sharp, uneven breaths, but he made no sound. His lips pressed together, a thin, fragile line, as if holding back the flood that churned beneath the surface. He didn't trust his voice—not now, not with the image of Logan, broken and bleeding out his grief into the dark corners of a bar, lodged so deeply in his mind.

Logan's words hung in the air, and Adrian's vision blurred, not from tears but from the weight of everything he couldn't say. He could see it—the way Logan's hands might have trembled around the glass, the way his shoulders might have hunched, caving in around his own hurt.

"When I found out you deleted your Facebook account," Logan's voice was barely a whisper, a sound so fragile Adrian thought it might shatter if he breathed too loudly. "I broke down again. God, Adrian, I was stalking you. Every day. Just to feel close to you, to pretend you were still there, seeing you online... made me feel close to you, made me feel like... we exist in the same universe. It was stupid, but I... I needed it. And then, when I couldn't find you anymore, it was like losing you all over again."

Adrian's eyes stayed closed, his lashes brushing against his cheeks as if shutting out the world might soften the blow. But he could still see it all—Logan hunched over a phone, scrolling through digital remnants of their life, looking for proof that Adrian was still breathing somewhere, still under the same sky. His pulse thudded in his ears, the rhythm uneven, a drumbeat that had lost its tempo. His body felt too small to hold the hurt, like every breath was a stretch against the confines of his own skin.

A soft, shuddering exhale escaped him, and he bit down on his lip, hard enough to taste iron. His hand moved without thinking, pressing against his chest, fingers curling into the fabric of his shirt as if he could anchor himself to the present, to the room, to the truth. But beneath his touch, his heart thudded erratically, a reminder of the love that had never truly died, only buried itself deeper, waiting for a moment like this to rise again.

Adrian's breath hitched, and his tears came harder now. He had heard the same thing from Jane, on the day he survived the pain of seeing Logan marry someone else. But hearing Logan admit it, seeing the torment etched into his face, made it almost unbearable.

"I listened to your song on repeat," Logan confessed, his voice cracking under the weight of his emotions. "It was torture, but it was the only thing I had of you. Every lyric, every note...it felt like you were there, screaming at me, reminding me of what I'd lost. And every day, Adrian, I died a little more."

Adrian wiped his face with a trembling hand, his heart breaking anew with each word. Logan's pain mirrored his own, their shared suffering stretching like a vast ocean between them. For a moment, there was only silence, the quiet hum of the minibar filling the space where their voices had been.

Logan's voice faltered as he approached the hardest part of his confession, the part that felt like trying to navigate jagged reefs in a storm. He shifted in his seat, suddenly too aware of his own body, his own presence, like a trespasser in the space between them. His eyes flicked to Adrian's face, reaching—hoping—for an anchor in the very soul he'd once abandoned.

Adrian held his gaze, unmoving. Steady, almost calm. As if hearing Logan say he missed him, hearing the ache in his voice, had quieted some ancient, gnawing doubt—the fear that Logan had walked away from their love story untouched, unharmed, and unscarred. As if the words held the proof, the unmistaken declaration he hadn't been forgotten on that sun-kissed stretch of sand in Australia, akin to a chapter sealed shut and shelved to gather dust. That their time together hadn't been reduced to a hazy summer memory, something to be laughed about in passing—*What was his name? That surfer guy?*—a blur of harmless fun quickly filed away, never looked at again. That Adrian's name hadn't been carved in wet sand only to be swept away before it ever had the chance to set. He needed to hear it. Needed to know that the nights had been just as hollow for Logan. That he wasn't a memory discarded, but a heart carried. That he was missed. That he was *loved*—not just then, but still.

But in his eyes, the storm hadn't passed. It churned in silence—pain, restrained fury, and beneath it all, something quieter... more fragile. Not forgiveness, not yet. But the ghost of it, laying in the shape of Adrian's broken armor.

As if his heart, or whatever had been left in the gaping hole in his chest, had already given in—smashed and bleeding, held together by threads of stubborn hope and old devotion, delicate as cobwebs spun over a wound.

A heart that wanted to believe again. But didn't yet know how to survive the believing.

"I need to tell you about Zack," Logan began, his voice a low rumble that barely carried over the tension thickening the room. "It started after I found out you deleted your Facebook account. That night... I was... lost. I went to Zack's bar, and—" His throat tightened. "We slept together."

Adrian didn't move, not at first. His expression remained a careful mask, but Logan saw it—the smallest flinch, a ripple across still water. It was there in the way Adrian's eyelids fluttered, too quick, too controlled, like he was bracing for impact. His lips pressed into a thin line, the tendons in his neck tightening as if holding back the force of his reaction. Adrian's fingers twitched, a tiny, involuntary movement, as if he had reached out in his mind but reined himself back in reality. His gaze dropped to the floor, collecting himself between breaths.

"I didn't plan it, Adrian. I wasn't... I wasn't even present. It was like I was somewhere else entirely—half-dissociated, thinking about you." He paused, his hands gripping his knees as though grounding himself. "I know that sounds impossible, ridiculous even, but it's the truth. It happened that night, and it didn't stop there. It became... a thing."

Logan made himself hold Adrian's eyes. "Zack and I... we had this... sex-based relationship. I can't call it anything else. It wasn't love. It wasn't even a connection, really. It was just a way to not feel alone."

Adrian's chest rose sharply, his breath catching in that unsteady rhythm he knew too well, the one that came with grief, with shock, with the unbearable weight of things he wasn't ready to know. His fists tightened in his lap, the knuckles pale and straining, the kind of white that belonged to salt spray on a storm-wrecked sea. He didn't speak. Didn't move. But the silence around him swelled, thick and punishing. It was the silence of a man being pulled beneath the surface by something he couldn't fight—the silence of an undertow dragging him back through memories he had tried to drown with time and grit and the brittle armor of resilience.

In the years without Logan, Adrian had told himself stories. He had no choice. The nights were too long without them. Too hollow. Too filled with ghosts. So he stitched together versions of the truth to survive. Some nights, Logan had never loved him at all, and it had all been adrenaline, a fleeting high on sunburnt skin and saltwater kisses. In some of the stories, he wondered if he'd only hallucinated that surfer he had once loved; perhaps it was a fever dream so vivid it left scars behind. In other stories, they were written in the waves, a once-in-a-lifetime collision of souls that the world had torn apart. And sometimes, when the loneliness crept in so deep it ached in his bones, Adrian convinced himself it had all been in his head. That Logan hadn't meant any of it—that maybe he had imagined the look in his eyes, the tremble in his hands, the love that felt so impossible it had to be real.

But there was always one story that returned to him. The one he came back to more than any other. The story that made the most sense when the ache wouldn't fade.

That Logan had left because he was a man.

That the way Adrian loved, the way he *was*, made their love impossible. That even if Logan had felt it—even if he had truly, deeply loved him—it would never be enough. Not in the world Logan came from. Not with the family, the expectations, the weight of that old American dream pressing down on his chest.

And so Adrian had swallowed it. Swallowed the ache, swallowed the shame, swallowed every tender memory that still haunted his skin. He buried it under smiles and silence and the empty shell of a life that moved forward while his soul remained still. And every night, those stories played in his mind, soft and cruel, reshaping the truth into something he could live with. Or at least survive.

But now—

Now, Logan was telling him there had been someone else. Another man. And it didn't matter if Logan said it meant nothing, that it was just sex, just a way to silence the noise in his head. Because all Adrian could hear was the quiet shattering of every story he had clung to.

Logan *could* be with a man. Logan *had* been with a man. And not just any man, but someone who wasn't *him*.

That truth lodged somewhere deep in Adrian's chest, sharp and cold and breathless. It wasn't the sex that broke him. It was what it meant. That Logan had given someone else what Adrian had begged for in whispers and silences and trembling hands. That Logan had denied him not out of fear, but out of choice.

He had chosen someone else. Chosen convenience. Chosen what was easy. And Adrian—the man who had loved him through fire, through oceans, through the brutal quiet of being left—had been nothing more than the wave that carried Logan toward something else. Something less complicated. Something he didn't have to cross the world or break his life open for.

He had been left, not because he was impossible to love, but because he was *inconvenient* to love. And Logan, for all his tears and apologies, had not chosen him.

And that was the wound that would never close.

"I know it hurts to hear this," Logan whispered, his voice barely audible over the sound of their shared pain. "But I can't lie to you. Not again. Not ever again." His words hung in the air, climbing and pulling at Adrian's walls brick by brick.

Logan hesitated, watching as Adrian turned his head slightly, his eyes distant now, staring at the far wall as if searching for something to anchor himself. "It's over," Logan added, his voice breaking slightly. "It ended a week ago. I was barely there with him, Adrian. Physically, sure, but emotionally? Mentally? It was always you."

Adrian flinched again, this time more visibly, and Logan's stomach roiled. But he pressed on, determined to lay everything bare. "I never slept in the same bed as Sandy after that first night with Zack. I couldn't. The guilt... God, the guilt was unbearable. I hated myself for it, for everything. But I was too broken to stop, too far gone."

Silence fell between them like a heavy fog. Logan didn't dare reach for Adrian's hand, didn't dare breach the fragile barrier that separated them now. He saw Adrian's tears begin to pool again, saw the way his chest heaved with the effort of holding back whatever words or feelings churned within him. His tears, they lingered there, unshed, quivering like drops of water poised on the edge of a cliff. Logan saw the struggle within him, the battle to hold back the flood of words and feelings crashing against the walls he'd built to protect himself. Still, Adrian said nothing.

"I need you to hear this," Logan said, leaning forward, his voice was a castaway calling out to a ship on the horizon. "It was never about him. Never. Zack was just... a way to stay afloat. A way to keep breathing when it felt like I was drowning without you."

Adrian's eyes finally lifted to meet his, and the sharp intensity of his gaze hit Logan like a slap. There was something in those eyes—a tempest of emotions tangled and knotted so tightly they couldn't be unraveled. Pain, yes. But also envy, maybe. Anguish. Despair.

Logan took a deep breath, steadying himself against the pull of his own regret. "The bracelet... Adrian, I kept it. That lifesaver you gave me... I carried it with me through everything. Every fight, every disastrous day, every night I thought I couldn't make it. It was the only thing that kept me tethered to you, the one thing that made me feel like you were still here." His voice cracked, and he swallowed hard to force the words out. "It was my lifeline. You were my lifeline."

Adrian's expression shifted, the tiniest flicker of something—recognition, or maybe hope—passing across his face. It was so faint that Logan almost didn't see it, but he clung to it, desperate for the connection he thought he'd lost forever.

"One night..." Logan's voice faltered, and he ran a hand through his hair, his fingers trembling. "Zack... I don't know what happened. Maybe the band broke, or maybe it slipped off. I woke up, and it was gone. I searched everywhere. I tore the room apart. And then Zack..." Logan's voice grew hollow, a void where grief and anger swirled like a whirlpool. "He said he threw it away. Said it was just lying there on the floor, and he thought it didn't matter."

Adrian's face twisted, a new kind of pain taking root, deeper and rawer than before. His lips parted, but no words came out, and for a moment, Logan thought he might cry out, might scream or lash out. But instead, Adrian turned away, his gaze fixed on the dark expanse beyond the window, his shoulders trembling like the surface of a restless sea.

"Adrian," Logan whispered, his voice breaking. "I swear, I didn't let it go. I didn't. It was taken from me. And when it was gone, I felt like I was drowning all over again. Like I'd lost the last piece of you that I had left."

Something in Adrian's heart fractured anew, splintering into countless shards that cut deep as they fell. The memory of his mother flooded him, vivid and merciless: her frail hands trembling as she tied the bracelet around his too-small wrist, her voice a fragile whisper, filled with both love and finality, as he looked at her with big, confused eyes, too young to understand it. *"This is for you, my Adi,"* she had said. *"To keep you safe, even when I can't."* The bracelet had become his armor, a talisman of strength, guarding him through storms, wars and heartache, a tether to her love and protection.

And then Logan came into his life, and without hesitation, Adrian had passed that protection on to him. It hadn't felt like a loss—it had felt like a gift, a promise. Seeing Logan wear it every day had been a quiet joy, a comfort that Adrian hadn't fully realized until now, when its absence hung between them.

"I didn't realize..." Logan's voice trembled. "I didn't realize it until it was gone. And, Adrian, I lost my mind. I was devastated. It was like losing you all over again."

Words still evade Adrian. The storm in his chest swelled, too vast, too powerful to articulate. His wide, tear-filled eyes locked on Logan, as if searching for something he couldn't name. The weight of everything—the memories, the loss, the love—pressed between them, suffocating and yet alive, electric with possibility.

Logan reached for him then, his hand trembling, hesitating just inches away from Adrian's. His fingers hovered there, vulnerable and open, like a man reaching out to touch the surface of the sea, uncertain if it would welcome him or swallow him whole. He would let the streams take him, so he took Adrian's hand.

Adrian's gaze fell to Logan's wrist, and there it was—a faint discoloration, a ghostly imprint of the bracelet that had adorned it for years. The sight tugged at something deep within him, a bittersweet ache that radiated through his chest.

"I think..." Logan began again, his voice breaking as he met Adrian's eyes. "That was the thing that started the chain of events that led me here. I think... that on some level, I was always on my way back to you. I was a wreck. I *am* a wreck. And every day away from you, I was falling apart, piece by piece. Maybe I would've found my way back to you eventually... but losing the bracelet—it nudged me here, Adrian. Maybe just in time."

Adrian's breath caught, his heartbeat stumbling into a rhythm that was too familiar, too haunting. It was the rhythm of his mother's labored breaths in that sterile hospital room he had grown to despise, her life slipping away even as she smiled at him with infinite love. His chest ached now with the same unbearable weight, the same impossible pain. He fought the urge to clutch at it, as though he could physically hold the pieces of himself together.

But then, something else rose within him—a warmth, a flicker of belief, faint as a dying ember yet insistent. Perhaps Logan was right. Perhaps his mother, who had always seen him so clearly, had known. Perhaps she had watched over him from whatever shore she now resided on and had nudged fate itself, guiding Logan back to him. Not to mend the past, but to fill the time they had left with something whole, something beautiful.

Adrian would never confess it—not to a soul, not even to the whispering echoes of his own thoughts during the stillest moments—but his heart continued to pulse for Logan. Through the passage of time, Logan remained the tide that drew him in, the wave crashing violently against his heart, a longing so profound it robbed him of breath. He loathed the treachery of his own heart, clinging stubbornly to a love that had once been his ruin. Yet, interwoven within the fabric of his anguish, that very love was what fastened him to life.

Perhaps his mother had sensed it. Caught the essence of his most fervent, desperate yearning buried deep within the marrow of his being. Did she understand that on those haunting nights, when shadows loomed like the weight of the ocean, he breathed Logan's name into the silence, his voice quaking beneath the burden of unwept tears? Did she recognize that the countless hours spent on the cool, forgiving sand, gazing into the boundless sea, were his form of escape—a gentle surrender to the sweet memories of Logan? Memories that danced in his mind like the rhythmic lull of the waves, until the boundaries blurred and he could no longer decipher where he ended and where Logan began?

Did she know that, above all, Adrian's dying wish was to hold Logan once more? Not for an apology. Not for closure. Just—*Logan*. One final embrace, a lingering kiss, a fleeting moment to savor their lips meeting, and the intoxicating allure of being close to Logan, to experience the exhilarating rush, the sweet addiction he unwittingly ignited. No one bore witness to this truth. Not his closest friends. Not even the murmuring ocean that had silently observed his melancholic journey. Adrian had battled that wish with every fiber of his being, submerging it in the flow of pain that Logan had carved into his life. Yet even so, the slightest memory of Logan's enchanting, silvery eyes would crumble his defenses. Those eyes had been his undoing, sparkling beneath a warm golden sky on a breezy beach, brimming with vitality and promises that once felt as unbreakable as the earth beneath his feet.

Logan's voice broke through his reverie. "I know it doesn't change anything," his words trembling as if they might dissolve in the air. "I know I can't undo the damage I've done. But I need you to know, every second I was apart from you, I was breaking. And even when I was with someone else... it was always you. Always."

Adrian exhaled shakily, his breath catching in his throat as if the words had stolen the air from his lungs. His hands trembled, one gripping the edge of the couch as if it were the sole anchor to reality, while Logan held the other, his touch softening the pain that resided deep within Adrian's bones.

The silence that followed was almost unbearable, thick with the weight of two hearts still trying to find their rhythm after years of discord. For a moment, the only sound was their quiet and uneven breathing. Adrian didn't look at Logan, couldn't look at him.

But his heart, stubborn and traitorous, still beat for him. It always had. And despite everything—despite the fractures, the storms, and the years of unbearable silence—Adrian knew it always would. He understood now, with the clarity that came when time was running out, that the finite beats left in his chest were not his own. They belonged, irrevocably, to the beautiful, tall man sitting next to him—the man with sand-colored hair that glinted like sunlight on the shore, and storm-gray eyes that carried the weight of both the ocean's fury and its quiet depths.

Logan had taken Adrian's heart the very first moment their worlds collided, like two waves meeting, destined to crash together in an explosive, breathtaking moment of connection. Adrian had never truly reclaimed it, had never wanted to. And now, with his breaths numbered and his life waning like the surge retreating from the shore, he realized he wouldn't have it any other way. Every heartbeat, every inhale that remained, was his offering. His love—unwavering, unshakable, eternal—was all he had left to give.

Adrian hadn't said anything in what seemed like forever, but it didn't matter. His warm hand was wrapped around Logan's, giving small, reassuring squeezes, as though securing himself to the moment. It was the only response Logan needed to keep going, pouring his heart out with the urgency of someone finally set free.

Logan's voice trembled as he continued his story. He described the spiral that began the moment he realized the bracelet was gone—the way he'd torn Zack's apartment apart in desperation, yelling, breaking, crumbling into pieces. He'd gone home, broken and raw, and finally admitted the truth to Sandy. He told her he was gay. Finally, after years of hiding, the words were out.

"She left," Logan said quietly. "The divorce papers are on their way. She deserves more than the mess I was, and I knew it."

He went on, recounting how he'd returned to Zack, ashamed of his behavior, determined to apologize. He'd told Zack everything—about the bracelet, about Adrian, about the man he couldn't stop loving even after tearing himself apart trying.

"And Zack... he told me to find you," Logan said, his voice soft, filled with a kind of awe. "I was terrified. I'd been carrying this weight, convinced

I'd done so much damage that you'd never even want to see me again. But he told me you would. He told me I had to. So that's what I did, Adrian. I hired a private investigator, and I came here. I came to find you."

When Logan finished, Adrian was still in silence, staring blankly at the black screen of the television in front of them, though Logan could tell he wasn't really seeing it. Logan didn't dare push, didn't dare speak. He held Adrian's hand and waited, his heart pounding in his chest.

Finally, Adrian spoke. "Logan," he murmured, his fingers tightening around Logan's hand, holding on as if that touch alone could keep him grounded. His thumb brushed over Logan's skin, a slow, deliberate movement, as if savoring the connection, the proof that this moment was real.

"I think you've told me everything," Adrian continued, his voice a fragile thread weaving through the silence. "Even without me needing to ask." His throat worked around the words, and he swallowed hard, the motion sharp against his skin. It was as if every syllable cost him something, pulled from a place too tender to touch. "But..." His breath trembled, and the rest of his words slipped out. "The only thing I keep asking myself is... Why did you leave?" His voice cracked, the sound raw and unpolished, and the question hung between them, delicate and shivering. His eyes, glassy with unshed tears, destined to join the rest on his cheeks, searched Logan's face, looking for a truth that might heal the wound that had never closed. When a single tear broke free, it traced a slow path down his cheek, a silver thread against his skin. Adrian didn't move to wipe it away. He let it fall, a tiny echo of all the grief he had carried. "I spent so long asking myself," he continued, his words thin and frayed. "What did I do? What did I miss? I tore myself apart looking for the moment when I lost you, but I never found it. You left, and all I had were questions. I need to understand, Logan. I need to know why."

Logan dropped his gaze, his grip on Adrian's hand tightening, knuckles pale against his skin. He had known this moment would come—had rehearsed it, played out the words in his mind a thousand times. But now, with Adrian's eyes on him, with the raw weight of his question hanging between them, everything he had practiced crumbled into dust.

"I..." His voice fractured, a thin, brittle sound that barely escaped his lips. His throat tightened, and he forced himself to meet Adrian's gaze, even as the storm in those gray eyes threatened to drown him. "I was afraid," he whispered, the confession tumbling out like stones from a broken wall. "I panicked. I couldn't come out of the closet, I—I was too scared of what it would mean, of how my life would change. And... I told myself I was doing it for you."

A shiver rippled through him as he took a shaky breath, his thumb lightly grazing Adrian's skin and anchoring him in the warmth of the tangible reality of Adrian. "I convinced myself you deserved better than me. Better than someone too scared to plan forever with you. Someone who never spoke of the future because he couldn't imagine one that wasn't built on a lie. Better than someone who wasn't ready to give you everything, even when you deserved the world." His voice softened, a tremor beneath the words. "Because you are the world, Adrian."

Tears brimmed in Logan's eyes, his vision blurring as the truth finally broke free. His lips quivered, his breath hitching as he continued. "You told me you loved me, and all I could think about was how much I'd already hurt you. How much I'd keep hurting you if I stayed. So I left. I told myself it was the only way to protect you, to stop myself from breaking your heart any more than I already had."

He closed his eyes for a moment, a tear slipping free, trailing a cool path down his cheek. "I knew you were already deep inside my heart, and it terrified me. I couldn't see a future for us—not because I didn't want one, but because I wanted it too much. I wanted it so badly that it scared me to my core. And instead of being brave, instead of fighting for you, for us, I ran."

His voice dropped to a whisper, a fragile echo of everything he had never said. "I ran because loving you was the truest thing I'd ever known, and I didn't know how to hold on to it without..." Logan had to stop for a moment.

Adrian nodded, a flicker of tension cutting through his features, but he showed nothing else. Logan swallowed hard, knowing he wasn't finished.

"There's more," Logan admitted, his voice a thin thread stretched tight. He drew in a breath, the kind that seemed to scrape his lungs raw on the way down. The words he had kept buried for so long clawed their way up, each one sharp-edged and trembling. "To love you, Adrian—it means I'm vulnerable. It means I'm exposed in a way I wasn't ready to be. And if you love me, it's my job to hold your heart with care, to protect it." He paused, his grip on Adrian's hand tightening, as if the warmth there could secure him to this moment, keep him from unraveling. "I've always been reckless, Adrian. Always. When it came to the big things, I didn't think too hard, I just jumped. My dad picked up the pieces when I screwed up, so I never had to think about the consequences. I'll dive off any cliff, take any risk, I don't care. But you—*you*—you scared the shit out of me. This incredible, beautiful thing that happened to me, and I was terrified.

Because this wasn't a wipeout I could shake off and try again. I could ruin you. I could ruin us. And I didn't know how to handle that, so I ran." Logan's eyes searched Adrian's, the gray depths a storm Adrian couldn't navigate. Logan's voice dropped, a whisper barely above the pulse of his own heartbeat. "The thought of being responsible for your heart, for your love—it scared me to death. I couldn't stand the idea of holding something so delicate and precious when all I'd ever known was breaking things. You deserved someone better. Someone who wouldn't mess it all up."

Adrian let out a shaky breath, his tears falling freely now as he wiped at them with the back of his hand. His voice quaked as he finally asked the question that had been tearing at him since the day Logan walked away. "Is that really why you left?"

Logan nodded, his eyes brimmed with tears. "Yeah. I would never lie to you. Not again."

Adrian nodded slowly, as if bracing himself for what he was about to say. His hand stayed wrapped around Logan's, grip tight and unyielding, as if drawing strength from the renewed connection. His fingers twitched, a small, involuntary movement that betrayed the storm beneath his calm exterior. "I always had this thought in the back of my mind," he began, his voice quieter now, almost hesitant. He bit the inside of his cheek, his gaze fixed on the wall. "That maybe I pushed you. That I pressured you into...being in a relationship with me, to... having sex. That I coerced you in some way, and that's why you left."

The words hung in the air like a wave frozen mid-crash, their weight pressing down on the room. Adrian's confession bled with guilt, his self-doubt wrapped tightly around the admission.

"No!" Logan's response came sharp and immediate, the sound slicing through the stillness. His expression twisted, a mix of horror and disbelief, as he reached out instinctively. His other hand found Adrian's arm, his touch gentle but firm, a quiet insistence. "No, Adrian. You didn't. Of course you didn't. I wanted it. I wanted you."

Adrian turned to him slowly, his eyes haunted by the memories of countless sleepless nights spent digging into the past. He searched Logan's face, looking for the truth beneath the words, for a sign that the doubts he had nurtured like thorny vines were nothing but shadows. His mind had replayed those moments on an endless loop, every memory reframed and twisted by his fear. In the quiet solitude of his thoughts, everything had taken on a new and darker meaning, his own mind turning on him, whispering lies disguised as truths.

And now, Logan's words were light breaking through that darkness, a warmth that seeped into the cold corners of his soul. Adrian's shoulders slumped, the tension slipping away like sand through his fingers, and his hand tightened around Logan's, the grip not out of desperation but something softer, something that felt a little like hope.

"Come on, Adrian," Logan continued, his voice softening but losing none of its intensity. "We'd been having sex for months before that night. You know that. *I* know that. And that night was no different. I wanted you with every fiber of my being. I wanted you like I always had." He paused, his words trembling at the edges, a truth left unspoken. "I left because I was scared, not because of you. Never because of you."

Hearing Logan's words washed over Adrian in a wave of relief he hadn't known he needed. The tightness in his chest eased, replaced by a warmth that spread through him like sunlight breaking through a storm.

It was nice, a comfort he hadn't felt in years, but there was still one thing lingering, one question he needed to ask.

"Why did you act like that at the wedding?" Adrian asked the second question that haunted his nights. Because Logan was so mean that it wasn't fitting for the Logan he knew.

"Because I knew you wouldn't give up on me easily. I knew you knew me, and that you had figured out I was acting out of fear. My mind was really messed up, and I knew you would be able to call on me. I needed you gone, and it was the only way to get you to leave and to forget about me at the same time. I convinced myself it was somehow to your own good, to help you forget me." Logan muttered, hating his own words, hating everything he did. So, he took a breath and explained to Adrian the truth that was going on inside of him at that moment, all this time back. Honesty was the only thing Logan had left, and he took full advantage of it. "But I was bleeding inside. I begged you to stay while I said those vicious words. And when you left the hall, Adrian... when you walked out, and I was left behind, I creaked down and part of me died."

Adrian's grip tightened, not like a hand holding another, but like a man anchoring himself to the edge of the world. His fingers curled into Logan's with a desperate, bone-deep force—not just holding, but *remembering*. Years of silence, of aching nights and unsent messages, lived in that touch. His knuckles blanched, pale as moonlight on churning waves, while beneath his skin, his pulse galloped, frantic, erratic, a war drum echoing from somewhere too deep to name.

Logan felt it—not just the pressure of fingers, but the language of it. A plea that needed no voice. A heartbeat carved out of history, pulsing with every moment they had lost, every word that had spilled open between them. And something inside him gave way, a faultline splitting wide.

A sharp and unfiltered sob broke loose from his chest, tearing out of him. His body moved before thought could catch it, folding into Adrian, wrapping his arms around him with the fever of someone who had come back from the dead and still didn't believe it.

Adrian rose to meet him, just as fierce. His arms locked around Logan, hands digging into fabric, into skin, as if trying to prove he was real, as if he could press Logan's body back into the timeline where he'd never left. His fingers gripped like roots breaking through stone, pulling him closer, closer, like he could stitch them back together with touch alone. Neither of them spoke. There were no words. Only breath, only skin, only the fragile, sacred ferocity of being held by the one person who had broken you, and still, the only one who ever held all the pieces to make you whole.

They trembled together, their bodies heaving with the force of their shared sorrow and relief. The room filled with the sound of it, the broken, gasping cries, the wet hitch of breath, the soft, shivering echoes of their voices. It was the kind of crying that reached deep, pulling everything raw and vulnerable to the surface, leaving nothing hidden.

Logan's tears soaked into Adrian's shirt, the dampness spreading, a physical mark of his pain and his need. Adrian's cheek rested against Logan's hair, his breath a warm, uneven brush against his skin. His voice, when it came, was a rasp, a prayer spoken into the tenderness between them. "I can't believe I'm holding you again," he murmured, his fingers digging into Logan's skin as if to anchor himself in the moment. His heart pounded wildly, a drumbeat against Logan's chest, erratic and unsteady.

If this were a dream, Adrian never wanted to wake up. If this were the end, if death had come for him wrapped in the warmth of Logan's embrace, he would greet it with open arms, cradling his own mortality with the same fierce love he held for Logan. His world had narrowed to *this*, this heartbeat, this warmth, this undeniable truth.

Logan's breath trembled against Adrian's collarbone, a soft warmth that seemed to linger in the space between words. "I love you," he murmured, his voice a river beneath a whisper, flowing slow and deep. "So, so much."

His fingers wove into Adrian's hair, a tender pilgrimage through the dark strands. He moved gently, reverently, as if each curl were a prayer, each touch a promise. The hair tie held back the wild cascade, but Logan's fingers itched with old instinct, the kind that remembered the way those dark and golden waves would unfurl like ink through water. Still, he held himself back, hands trembling with the weight of restraint.

He breathed Adrian in, a quiet, aching inhale that tasted like a memory of sea salt and sunlight and something ineffable. It was a scent he had held like smoke in his lungs for years, always fading, never quite there. But now it was real, sharp and full, and it rushed through him.

The world outside blurred, a watercolor of muted sounds and softened edges. All that mattered was the heat of Adrian's skin, the steady beat of his pulse under the fragile arch of his neck.

"Ad... It's not a coincidence that I found you now, while you're... while you're sick. I know it's not. I've been sent to you, I know I have. I had to be here for you."

Adrian hesitated for a moment, his breath catching in his chest, before he pulled one hand away from Logan's, gently pushing him back just enough to meet his eyes. Their faces were close, their red, tear-streaked gazes locking together. Adrian's hands trembled as he cupped Logan's face, his touch both tender and resolute.

"I forgive you, Logan," Adrian whispered, his voice soft but steady, carrying the weight of everything he felt. "I really do. You can leave here with your heart at peace."

Logan froze, his eyes wide, shimmering with fresh tears. He started to shake his head, to protest, but Adrian's hands held him steady, forcing him to stay in this moment.

"I needed to forgive you," Adrian continued, his words heavy with emotion. "Not just for you, but for me. Because I love you, Logan Vaughn. I have loved you from the moment I met you, and I'll love you until the day I die. I can't let that pretend hate poison what little time I have left. I don't want to carry anger in my heart when all I want is to love you, even if it's selfish of me. I need this peace for myself."

Adrian paused, his chest rising and falling with unsteady breaths. His thumbs brushed against Logan's cheeks, wiping away his tears as his own continued to fall. "But before you say you won't go, please... listen to me." His voice broke, but he pushed forward, his hands trembling as they held Logan's face. "I don't want you here to watch me die, Logan. I don't want you to see what's coming. It's going to get ugly. And you're the one person I can't bear to say goodbye to. Not again."

Logan's face crumpled, a silent lament echoing in the silver-gray pools of his eyes, tearing at Adrian's soul. Adrian's chest clenched with unbearable ache, as if a blade had carved him from within. He loathed witnessing Logan in such torment, abhorring himself for the pain he had unwittingly inflicted on the man he loved.

"I can't," Adrian whispered, his voice shaking. "I can't do this with you again, only to lose it all over. I don't have the strength, Logan. Watching you look at me like this, with so much pain—it feels like I'm... and I can't... I can't take it."

Logan's hand came up to grip Adrian's wrist, holding onto him as though his life depended on it. "I don't care how ugly it gets," Logan said, his voice breaking, his tears falling unchecked, and Adrian's thumb could barely keep the pace of wiping them away. "I don't care about the pain, Adrian. I *won't* leave you. Not now, not ever again. Please... don't ask me to." A single tear slid down Logan's sharp, flawless nose, landing in the space between them.

Adrian shook his head violently, tears streaming endlessly down his face, his breathing shallow and erratic as Logan's words settled over him.

"Ad," Logan said softly, his voice barely above a whisper, though it carried a steady resolve that Adrian couldn't ignore. Logan turned his head, his nose brushing against Adrian's wrist where his face rested. It felt like an instinctive gesture, a motion driven by a deep yearning for the faintest warmth he could find. He managed a weak smile, though his own eyes glistened with tears. "If you don't get those treatments, I'm with you. No matter what."

Adrian flinched, his entire body recoiling at the sheer weight of Logan's words. His voice broke as he asked, "What do you mean?"

Logan leaned closer, his expression firm, his voice steady. "I'm not leaving you ever again. It means... if you die, so do I. I can't—I *won't* live without you, Adrian."

Adrian's breath caught, a sudden gasp caught in the dawn of the moment. In an instant, he recoiled, his hands flying back—one from

Logan's back, the other from his face—as if scorched. As if Logan's skin had turned to shimmering, almost transparent flame and his touch had branded something profound and unnamable upon him. He staggered upright, movement jagged and unsteady, rising like a man surfacing too fast from depths he dared not revisit. His legs trembled beneath him, barely holding his body, the air between them suddenly electric, unbearable. Adrian withdrew, not merely to create distance, but to escape the gravitational pull of Logan's touch—a force rooted in memories he longed to forget, yet still pulsed with life, too fierce to touch without shattering. "You wouldn't do it," he said, shaking his head in disbelief, his voice filled with a mix of fear and fury. "You wouldn't!"

"Try me," Logan replied, his tone calm, his silver-gray eyes burning with determination. That look—it was one Adrian knew too well. The one he had always called *Logan's look*, that reckless, stubborn resolve that bordered on madness. Logan wasn't bluffing; Adrian could see it, clear as day.

"Lo!" Adrian exclaimed, his voice cracking as he jumped to his feet, putting more distance between them. "Are you fucking crazy?" He clutched his chest, his heart pounding as if it might burst. "You can't do this! You *can't*! You're not serious."

But Logan was already on his feet, closing the distance between them. "Now you'll have to get those treatments for both of us," he said firmly, his words landing like a challenge. His hands reached out, though Adrian immediately retracted.

Adrian's voice rose to a scream, his anguish spilling over. "You have *no right* to do this to me!" he yelled, his voice trembling with raw pain. "You have no right to put me in this position!"

"I don't care," Logan shot back, his tone fierce, his expression hardened with purpose. "You need to get help. And I will do whatever it takes to make sure you do."

"You *wouldn't!*" Adrian said again, but this time his voice was softer, laced with denial, desperation leaking through every syllable. His legs threatened to give out beneath him as his mind spun, trying to grasp the gravity of Logan's resolve.

"Haven't you heard me?" Logan said, stepping closer once more, his hands trembling as he reached for Adrian again. "I cannot live without you! I meant it, Adrian. You're everything to me. You need to get better, for both of us."

Adrian snatched his hand back, his body shaking with the intensity of his emotions. "Don't you *dare* make me responsible for your life, Logan!" he shouted, his voice cracking as tears streaked his face. "Don't you *dare* put this on me. It's not fair. It's not—" His words choked off into a sob as he covered his face with his hands.

"It's already on you," Logan's voice thinned to a whisper, but his resolve remained unshaken. "It's been on you since the moment I fell in love with you, since the moment you pulled me from the waves and gave me your breath. And it's not a burden, it's a choice. My choice. I'm staying with you, no matter what, and if that means I have to fight you to save you, then so be it."

Adrian's hands trembled as he stood in the middle of the suite, his breath uneven, his chest heaving with the storm inside him. He had carried too much for too long, the weight of his past, the pain of his decisions, and now Logan's words, pressing down on him, taking the form of an anchor dragging him to the depths.

He could barely look at Logan, yet he couldn't look away. "Logan," Adrian began, his voice shaking, barely audible over the pounding in his chest. He felt his emotions rushing to the surface, threatening to spill over. "You can't do this to me. You *can't* take this decision from me."

Logan's brows furrowed, his silver-gray eyes filled with concern and something Adrian couldn't articulate. "Ad, I—"

"No!" Adrian cut him off, his voice rising, laced with a mixture of anger and heartbreak. His hands went to his hair, tugging at the strands as if trying to pull himself together. "You don't get to do this. You don't get to come here, out of nowhere, and put this on me! Do you have any idea what you're asking of me?"

Logan's lips parted, but Adrian didn't let him speak. His emotions surged forward, unstoppable. "You know me, Logan. You know what I've been through. You know about the soldier I lost. About how *that* has haunted me every single day. Saving you that day in the ocean—*that* was what finally let me heal. But this?" Adrian's voice broke into a yell, raw and unrestrained. "This would break me, Logan. I can't be responsible for your death. I *won't!*"

Logan recoiled as Adrian's words hit him, but he didn't back down. "Adrian, listen to me," Logan said, his voice steady but pleading. "I'm not asking you to be responsible for me. I'm telling you that I've made my choice. I will not live in a world where you don't exist."

Adrian's hands dropped from his hair, falling to his sides as he stared at Logan, disbelief written all over his face. His chest ached as though Logan's words were knives, slicing through his resolve. He took a shaky breath, rubbed the back of his neck, and turned toward the door, his steps hurried and uneven.

"You always do this, Logan," Adrian said, his voice quieter now but no less anguished. "You decide everything. You make your choice, and the rest of us just have to deal with it. Well, not this time. Not with this."

"Adrian—" Logan's voice was filled with desperation, but Adrian spun around, his eyes blazing.

"No!" he roared, every syllable vibrating with fury and pain. "You don't get to make this choice for me. You don't get to put *this* on me." His voice broke, and his breathing came in uneven, gasping sobs. "You don't understand what you're doing to me, Logan. You don't understand how much it hurts."

Logan took a step forward, his arms outstretched as though to comfort him. "Ad, please," he said, his voice trembling. "I love you. I just—"

"You love me?" Adrian interrupted. "Then respect me, Logan. Respect the fact that I can't handle this. That I won't." He turned back to the door, gripping the knob so tightly his knuckles turned white. "You do whatever you want. But you're not putting this on me."

And with that, Adrian yanked the door open and stormed out, the sound of the door slamming behind him reverberating through the suite. Logan stood frozen for a moment, staring at the door, his heart pounding as Adrian's words echoed in his mind. Slowly, as though weighed down by the gravity of everything that had just happened, he made his way to the bedroom and collapsed onto the bed, his body sinking into the mattress as exhaustion overtook him.

His promise from just a day ago surfaced in his mind, the one where he swore to Adrian he would respect his wishes and give him the time and space he needed. Now, after everything that had just happened, they both needed time apart—to breathe, to think, to *be*. Thus, even if his heart longed to race to Adrian, to seize him in fervor and pull him back to the sanctuary they've found tonight, he would grant him a moment of solace.

Logan stared up at the ceiling, his mind racing even as his body felt utterly drained. He couldn't even summon the energy to turn on the TV or distract himself with something mindless. All he could do was lie there, buried under the weight of his thoughts, trying to figure out what the hell he was going to do with his life now.

Because he had meant every word he'd said to Adrian. If Adrian chose to die, so would Logan. He wasn't bluffing, wasn't exaggerating. He *couldn't* live in a world where Adrian didn't exist, and he knew, deep down, that Adrian knew it too. Adrian, who carried the weight of the soldier he couldn't save. Adrian, who had saved Logan that day in the ocean, and in doing so, had found a way to begin healing his own scars. Adrian wasn't cruel—he didn't have a single evil bone in his body. And Logan knew Adrian would never take responsibility for Logan's life, just as he knew Adrian couldn't bear the idea of Logan giving up on his own life.

Chapter 13
I'll Guide You to Safe Shores, My Real Love

And if you truly perceive, if your eyes awaken,
To the vastness of the sky, its endless embrace,
You will come to understand that we were
A storm pausing to draw a breath, if only for a heartbeat.
Like shimmering waters cradled in the sea, like embers dancing in the wind,
You, who have just returned, you, who have never truly left my world.
You, who had been the deepest desire my heart ever knew, you who had
reshaped the fibers of my being.
Like footprints whispered away by the tides,
You graced this place, and your essence shall endure.
And should the day come when you choose to wander,
The ocean will hold our melody close to its heart.
And when the wind carries you beyond the horizon,
I shall remain here, counting lonely seconds until your return.

November 21, 2020—Tel-Aviv, Israel—The Next Day

WHEN LOGAN WOKE UP, it took a moment for reality to settle in. He didn't even remember falling asleep, yet the crushing weight of the previous night's events returned to him all at once. His body felt heavier than it had the night before, as though every ounce of him carried the weight of his unresolved emotions.

Logan hauled himself upright and moved into the sitting area, searching for his phone. His limbs felt sluggish, his mind clouded, but he sensed energy coursing through his veins. When he finally found the device, it was nearly dead, its battery hanging on by a thread. The moment he turned it on, a flood of missed calls, emails, and messages bombarded him, the notifications lighting up the screen like fireworks. Even as he held the phone in his hand, it buzzed incessantly with incoming calls.

Logan gritted his teeth, fighting the urge to hurl the thing across the room. Instead, he walked back to the bedroom, pulling his charger from the suitcase. With the phone plugged in, he grabbed his toiletries from the suitcase and headed to the bathroom. As the water ran, cold at first and then warm, he scrubbed the exhaustion from his face, brushed his teeth, and stepped into the shower. The hot water was soothing, but it did little to lighten the burden he carried.

Once he was clean, Logan dressed in a crisp blue button-down shirt and a pair of jeans. He grabbed his wallet and fully charged phone on his way out, determination hardening his resolve.

A plan had been forming in his mind since the early hours of the morning; an idea he couldn't quite shake. It was crazy, impulsive even, but it felt right. The only problem was figuring out how to pull it off in a foreign country where the language was an incomprehensible maze. Luckily, he had Google at his side.

Within an hour, Logan found himself standing in the doorway of a tattoo shop he'd found online. The reviews were raving about the art of this place, and the website had showcased some incredible designs—a blend of surrealism and bold, intricate detail. Logan wasn't one to be easily impressed, but even he had to admit that the portfolio was striking. A particular design, an ethereal phoenix rising through geometric patterns with the elements of raindrops and rainy clouds around, had been what drew him here in the first place. It was featured prominently on the website as a signature piece of the artist.

The shop was tucked into a quiet street corner, unassuming from the outside except for the bold, minimalist sign above the door that simply read: "Threads of Ink" and a pride flag hanging next to it. A small sticker near the door handle advertised that they sold exclusive merch, something Logan had already made a mental note to check out. He hesitated a moment before stepping inside, the bell's chime following him into an intimate small shop that felt more like an artist's studio than a tattoo parlor, with sketches and paintings lining every wall.

Logan felt himself drawn immediately to a wall displaying framed prints of the artist's work. The designs were captivating—bold, surreal, and brimming with intricate details that pulled at something deep within him. He took a step closer to the desk where a display of glossy merch caught his eye. T-shirts, high-end skateboards with jaw-dropping art, enamel pins, and prints—each piece unmistakably the work of the same artist whose portfolio had led him here.

"Shalom," said a voice from behind the counter. Logan turned toward a relatively short man with thick, unruly brown-red hair tucked into the hood of a sweatshirt featuring the shop's logo. The geometric designs on the hoodie flowed in a way that made Logan certain it was custom-made. The man's neckline was covered with a pattern of ink that climbed just to his jawline, and his bright hazel eyes fixed on Logan with a mixture of curiosity and warmth. "Eich ani yechul le'ezor lech?" he asked.

Logan blinked, utterly lost. "Uh... English?" he said, almost apologetically.

The man grinned, switching seamlessly. "Sure. Welcome to Threads of Ink, I'm Lucian, how can I help you? Do you have an appointment?"

"Not exactly," Logan admitted. "But I was hoping you could make an exception. It's kind of... an emergency."

Lucian hesitated, his tattooed fingers hovering over the keyboard. His hands were mesmerizing, covered in striking black ink that extended down to his knuckles. "An emergency, huh? Let me see if I can fit you in. What are we talking about here?"

Logan launched into an explanation, detailing the design he wanted, the specific location, and even pulling up some reference photos on his phone. Lucian nodded as he listened, his expression shifting between thoughtfulness and intrigue.

Just then, the back door swung open, and a woman stepped out, speaking in rapid Hebrew to Lucian. She handed him some cash, exchanged a quick laugh, and left the shop with a wave, clearly a customer on her way out. Lucian smiled and called after her before turning back to Logan.

"Good timing," he said. "Sasha just finished up. Let me see if he can squeeze you in."

"Sasha?" Logan echoed.

"Yeah, Sasha. He's the artist," Lucian explained as he glanced toward the back door.

Before Logan could fully process this, the door opened again, and someone stepped out.

Logan had to do a double-take. The man who emerged was tall, almost like him, with a long curtain of pale blond hair that fell over one side of his face, concealing it. As he moved closer, Logan caught a glimpse beneath the hair and felt his breath hitch. Half of the man's face was covered in burn scars—raised, uneven flesh that twisted across his features, warping the bridge of his nose and rendering one of his eyes a milky white. The other eye, however, was a piercing, electric blue that seemed to see straight through Logan.

Sasha was wearing a loose sweater, the sleeves pushed up to reveal tattoos crawling up his forearms, bold lines and intricate designs weaving into the burned flesh beneath. The scars extended past the ink, jagged and uneven, impossible to miss. Logan found himself staring for a beat too long before quickly averting his gaze. As Sasha moved, his steps carried a slight limp, a subtle hitch that was noticeable. And yet, there was nothing hesitant or uncertain about him. He carried himself with quiet confidence.

Reaching the counter, Sasha stepped beside the man Logan had been speaking to, Lucian, and with an almost absent gesture, leaned in and kissed him tenderly on the cheek. His arm slid around Lucian's back as though it belonged there, fitting into place effortlessly. "Hey," he said, his voice quieter now.

Lucian turned to him with a smile that was warm and familiar. They stood close, their body language easy and intimate, like two people who had shared a thousand such moments before. Logan's gaze flicked down, catching the glint of a wedding band on Sasha's hand where it rested lightly on the counter. The sight hit him harder than he expected, an ache tightening in his chest.

He thought of Adrian. Of the empty space where a ring should have been. The idea should fill him with so much hope, but in truth it left him hollow, a cruel reminder of what he'd lost. Logan blinked, forcing himself to refocus as Sasha turned his attention toward him. That piercing blue eye fixed on him again, unreadable, waiting.

Lucian gestured toward Logan. "This guy's got an emergency. Think you can take a look?"

Sasha's good eye flicked to Logan, cool and assessing. For a moment, there was only silence, and Logan's heart thudded as he struggled to decipher the man's expression as he wondered what had happened to him. Then Sasha nodded.

"Let's hear it," his voice smooth as silk, a Russian accent tingeing the words, laced with a kindness that stood in stark contrast to his rough exterior.

Logan began explaining his idea, showing Sasha the photo on his phone and weaving the story that tied it all together—the words, the image, the meaning behind it. Sasha listened intently, his focus sharp as he nodded along, occasionally asking clarifying questions. He pulled a notepad from behind the counter, his tattooed fingers deftly sketching as Logan spoke. With each word, the rough lines on the page became something more—Logan's scattered thoughts transforming into something vivid and alive.

Logan couldn't understand how Sasha managed it, how he could reach into his mind and pull out exactly what he'd imagined, but there it was. The sketch was perfect, raw yet precise. Sasha grabbed a liner pencil and, with the same sure movements, lightly traced the design onto Logan's arm to give him a sense of placement. "Like this?" Sasha asked, tilting his head slightly.

Logan nodded, unable to contain the flicker of awe in his voice. "Yeah. That's it. That's exactly it."

After Logan gave his approval, Sasha gestured for him to follow. They headed into the back room, where the sterile smell of disinfectant mingled with the faint hum of music from a hidden speaker and the air conditioner. Sasha motioned for Logan to sit in the chair, and as Logan settled in, Sasha set to work preparing his tools—disinfecting the area, slipping on gloves, and methodically organizing the inks.

As Sasha worked, Logan broke the silence. "So... the guy out there, Lucian... you... married?"

Sasha paused, glancing up from the ink bottles with a faintly amused expression. A slow, almost imperceptible smile tugged at the corner of his mouth. "Yes," he said simply. "He's my husband... and my entire life."

Logan nodded, feeling a faint pang in his chest. "Sorry about earlier," he said awkwardly. "I kind of stared at you. I didn't mean to, it's just, you know..."

Sasha didn't respond right away. Instead, he placed the tattoo gun aside, took Logan's arm in his hands, and gently disinfected the skin. "Don't worry about it," he said at last, his tone calm and measured. "It happens

a lot. There was a time when it bothered me, when I felt ashamed. But...
I've moved past that. Now, I don't let it define me. It's just a part of me,
nothing more."

Logan nodded again, his throat tight. He reached into his pocket and
pulled out his phone, hesitating for a moment before unlocking it and
scrolling to a song. "This is Adrian," he said, his voice quieter now. "My
Adrian. Well... if he ever forgives me. He gave me a bracelet once, and I lost
it. So..." Logan trailed off, unable to find the words to explain what he was
trying to do. "Yeah. You know." He already told Sasha about the bracelet,
but only in rough details of the image, not the deeper meaning behind it.

Sasha didn't say anything. He leaned closer as Logan pressed play,
and the soft strains of Adrian's voice filled the room. Sasha listened, his
expression unreadable as the melody unfolded. When the song ended, he
sat back, his piercing blue eye meeting Logan's. For a moment, Sasha said
nothing, but he gave a small, subtle nod—a gesture that seemed to say, *I
understand.*

The process hurt like hell. Every sharp sting of the needle drove deeper
into the skin, resonating with Logan's guilt and longing. But he welcomed
it, embracing the pain as a kind of penance. He deserved it, he told himself,
for everything he'd done and for everything he'd lost.

By the time Sasha finished, Logan was exhausted but strangely lighter,
the weight on his chest easing as he stared at the finished design. The tattoo
was perfect, more than he could've hoped for. It wasn't just art—it was
a reminder, a promise, and a piece of Adrian he would carry with him
forever.

Sasha cleaned the area carefully, wiping away the last traces of ink. He
reached for a roll of plastic wrap, unspooling it and carefully wrapping

it around Logan's arm. "This is just to keep it protected for the next few hours," he explained as he secured the edges. "Once you get home, take the wrap off and wash it gently with warm water and unscented soap. Don't scrub, just pat it dry. After that, use a thin layer of tattoo ointment. Repeat that process twice a day for about two weeks, and no swimming or direct sunlight for a while."

Logan nodded, trying to memorize the instructions through the haze of exhaustion. "Got it. Thanks," he said, flexing his arm slightly and feeling the slight sting of the fresh ink beneath the wrap.

Sasha gave him a small smile as he cleaned up his station, his movements precise. "Take care of it, and it'll heal beautifully. And if you have any questions, just call. Or come back in."

Logan stood, feeling a rush of gratitude and something else he couldn't quite name. "Thanks... for everything."

Sasha nodded, his gaze steady. "Good luck, Logan. And take care of yourself, too."

As Logan left the shop, he stopped at the counter to settle the payment, making sure to hand Lucian a generous tip for Sasha.

As Logan hopped into a cab, he made a mental note to rent a car. Relying on taxis was getting old; it was too slow and too inconvenient. But he didn't have the time to figure out a car right now. For now, there was only one thing on his mind: Adrian.

Logan was on his way, and this time, he wasn't leaving without being heard. No more running. No more avoidance. He was ready to fight for the man he loved, no matter how long it took or how hard it would be.

By the time Logan reached Adrian's door, the sky was bleeding gold into dusk, the sun melting like honey over the Tel Aviv skyline. He stood there for a breath—maybe three—his knuckles hovering just above the metal. In seconds, he'd be close to Adrian again, and he knew his heart would go off like a live wire the moment he saw him. When his knuckles finally found the door, the soft, tentative tap echoed with a delicate flutter, sounding so faint compared to the significance of that moment.

The door opened. And there he was.

Adrian.

A rupture in the world. A face Logan had memorized and forgotten all at once. The shock of seeing Adrian would never dull. It cracked something open in him every time, as if his chest wasn't made for this kind of reunion. As if memory and reality were fighting for the same space.

He stood there, caught in the gravity of him.

Adrian was light and shadow all at once—exhausted, beautiful, untouchable. Logan let himself bask in it, a man starved of sun finally stepping into morning. He drank in the sight with reverence, the way others might drink holy water, his soul stretching toward its missing half.

In that space, beneath the ruin and regret, beneath all the broken things between them, Logan could only thank the stars—whatever gods or ghosts or faith or streams had stitched this moment together—for letting him stand here. For letting him see him. For letting him try.

His heart whispered what his mouth couldn't: *You're still mine. Somehow, you're still mine.*

And there, in the pause between heartbeats, they just stood facing each other, silence pooling between them. Adrian's eyes were hollow constellations, impossible to read. He said nothing until he broke their spell and stepped aside, his bare feet softly sliding across the tile. Logan stepped inside, barely noticing the final click of the door closing behind him, his gaze fixed on Adrian.

Inside, the air carried the ghost of morning coffee despite the late hour and the distant breath of the Mediterranean drifting in through the open window. Beneath his shirt, the plastic film clung to his wrist, crinkling softly with every movement, the fresh ink beneath it still tender and concealed under the long sleeves of his button-down.

He followed Adrian into the kitchen, feeling both desperate and out of place, his pulse hammering with every step.

Then Logan's eyes caught movement from the corner of the living room. Someone stood up from the couch, and the sight of him was equivalent to a punch to the gut: *Itay.*

Adrian's ex.

Logan froze. An ache within his soul unfurled, weeping silently in anguish. He found himself caught in a haunting resonance of time, as though the walls had drawn inward, leaving only this stark reality: a figure from the past, suddenly, almost eternally, rooted in the heart of Adrian's present. The same Itay they had run into in the Philippines, the same man who had tried to win Adrian back. He was tall, with unruly blond curls and striking blue eyes, wearing a crisp black button-down and light jeans. Even now, looking disheveled and a little raw, with puffy eyes and a scowl etched across his face, Itay still managed to look like he belonged in a magazine spread.

But none of that mattered. Logan didn't care about the magazine-perfect details. What mattered—what thundered in his chest—was that this man was here. In Adrian's house. On Adrian's couch. In Adrian's orbit. Like he belonged. Like he'd never left.

Logan's mind raced. *Had Adrian said anything? Had he mentioned someone? Had he mentioned... him? Had Adrian dropped a hint of a second chance with him?* He couldn't think of a single word Adrian had said about having a boyfriend in the past two days. No whispers of a lover's return. No flicker of guilt. Nothing to brace against. Only this silence now, full of sharp corners. *So, what the hell was Itay doing here?*

Then Itay looked at him.

The stare was direct and unflinching—eyes bloodshot and shining with something darker than tears. Fury maybe. Or betrayal. Or the kind of pain that turns into fire if left unattended. His gaze sliced through Logan, an accusation without words: *You don't belong here.*

Logan clenched his fists at his sides, his entire body vibrating with the urge to yell. To tell Itay to get out. To stand beside Adrian like a guard dog and demand that this man—this audacious, smug reminder of the past—leave *his* Adrian alone. But Logan didn't move.

Because he had no right.

He'd made his choice. He'd stood in front of Adrian and married someone else. He'd walked away, and Adrian... Adrian had every right to find comfort in someone else's arms. Even if that someone was Itay.

Logan's chest ached, the sharp pain threatening to tear him in two. His jaw tightened as his gaze flicked to Adrian, who stood silently by the kitchen counter, his face unreadable. Logan wanted to scream. He wanted to demand an explanation. But he didn't. Instead, he swallowed the bitterness rising in his throat, his heart cracking a little more with every second that passed.

This wasn't how he'd imagined this moment. Not at all.

Itay completely ignored Logan as if he didn't even exist. He followed Adrian into the kitchen, speaking to him in rapid Hebrew.

Logan stood awkwardly in the middle of the house, sensing the tension thickening around him. Again, he felt left out, like an intruder in a space he had no right to occupy. He could hear Itay's voice, sharp and insistent, like he was trying to talk sense into Adrian.

Logan moved to the living room and sat on the couch, deciding to wait and see what Adrian would do. He clenched his fists, his thoughts a chaotic mess of frustration, jealousy, and regret. From the living room, he could see Adrian at the counter, his movements methodical as he made coffee. Every so often, Adrian glanced at Itay, his expression guarded, unreadable.

"You're not going to say anything?" Itay asked in Hebrew, his voice rising, tinged with anger. "You're just... back together with him?"

Itay's frustration filled the space of the small apartment. It was so poignant, so thick that Adrian felt it in his own body.

Over the years since Adrian and Itay had broken up, Itay had tried to move on. He'd dated here and there, half-hearted attempts to fill the void Adrian had left behind. But none of it ever worked. Deep down, Itay had never stopped chasing Adrian. The moment Logan walked out of Adrian's life—marrying Sandy and leaving Adrian broken and vulnerable—Itay had stepped in, trying to rekindle what they once had.

Itay had tried everything. Again and again, he reached for the ruins they'd once called love, he'd brushed the dust off old memories and tried to remind Adrian of the long years they'd shared, their history, the love they'd built. He'd begged him to see reason, to let himself be loved again. But Adrian had been impenetrable, a fortress of anguish and heartbreak. It didn't matter how many times Itay told him they could start over, that they could build something new—Adrian couldn't hear it.

His heart still belonged to Logan.

Even in the stillest hours, when the memories were too painful to bear, Adrian remained loyal to them. To *him*. His heart curled toward Logan's memory like a prayer, forgetting how to love anyone who wasn't that magnificent force. That beautiful man, with stormy eyes and a smile capable of liquefying rocks into flowing lava, had effortlessly dissolved Adrian's soul as well, merging it seamlessly with his own for the rest of eternity.

Adrian knew it would be a quiet cruelty to fall into Itay's open arms, knowing his heart drifted far from reach. Every breath, every fragment of his soul was already captivated by another, his existence tethered to a name that wasn't Itay's. How could he offer a love that burned half as brightly as the one he harbored for Logan? How could he present an absent heart that beat in sync with the rhythm of Logan's name? How could he feign that a flickering candle could embody the wildfire and fireworks he truly desired? To take what Itay offered so freely would be to weave tenderness into betrayal, and Adrian could not bear to wound a heart so unguarded.

When Adrian's diagnosis came, Itay had been devastated. Furious, even. He'd tried to reason with Adrian, to beg him to fight, to plead with him not to give up. "You can't do this," Itay would say, his voice trembling, his hands grasping Adrian's frail shoulders. "You can't leave like this." But

Adrian, pale and hollow-eyed, only smiled that faint, tired smile of his. A smile that spoke of surrender, not to fear, but to inevitability.

Night after night, Itay sat at his side, sometimes raging, sometimes weeping, sometimes begging in a silence so loud it seemed to crack the air between them. Yet every time, Adrian slipped further away—not in body just yet, but in spirit. His gaze grew distant, his words fewer, until it seemed he lived more in the echoes of memories than in the present.

One night, Itay had finally broken. "It's him, isn't it?" The words had cut through the stillness, sharper than the whettest blade. He didn't need to say the name. Logan's absence loomed as heavily as his return would. "It's him," Itay repeated, his tone a mix of accusation and defeat. Adrian hadn't answered, but his silence spoke more than words ever could. "You're willing to give up your life for him?" Itay's voice had cracked, his tears falling unchecked. "Adrian, it makes no sense! He's not worth this—he's not worth your life!" He would be shouting at that point, his hands shaking, his love turning to fury in the face of Adrian's refusal. But Adrian didn't flinch. He simply looked at him, his expression soft, almost pitying, and retreated once more into the quiet, impenetrable space inside himself.

How could a man with a vacant chest, a torn soul, and a shattered gaze feel anything, anything at all, when all of his tomorrows had been stolen, swallowed by a vast, black void that kept sucking the joy from his life?

What Itay failed to understand was that Adrian's life—the fire that once burned so brightly in him—was already gone. Logan had taken it with him that night two years ago when he walked away without a word. The candle had flickered, and when Logan left, it had gone out entirely.

And now Logan was back.

Itay's voice, raw with emotion, pierced the silence again, dragging Adrian from the depths of his memories. "Do you really think he's going to stay this time?" Itay demanded, each word trembling with heartbreak. "After everything? After what he did to you?"

Adrian didn't respond right away. He turned back to the coffee pot, his movements deliberate, the soft clink of porcelain against metal filling the space between them. He poured slowly, his hands steady, though his shoulders sagged under a weight only he could feel.

"Itay," he began, his tone the echo of a thousand conversations before, "we've been over this. You need to stop doing this to yourself."

Itay's jaw tightened, and his hands curled into fists at his sides. "*I* need to stop doing this to myself? What about you, Adrian?" His voice rose, trembling with hurt. "He broke you. He *ruined* you! He left you for her—*left you in pieces*—and now he just walks back in, and you're going to *let him*?"

Adrian's gaze shifted briefly toward the living room, where Logan sat on the edge of the couch, his body stiff and his head bowed low. Though Logan was within earshot, the words exchanged between Adrian and Itay—spoken in Hebrew—were a shield of privacy he couldn't penetrate.

Yet even without understanding, Logan wasn't blind to the storm brewing in the room. The tension radiating from Adrian and Itay filled the air like static before a lightning strike, and Logan's hunched shoulders betrayed that he felt every unspoken accusation, every lingering bruise, as if they were aimed directly at him.

Adrian turned from the counter, coffee forgotten as weariness settled in his eyes. "It's not that simple," he murmured. His voice was gentle, almost apologetic.

Itay's head shook in disbelief, his voice trembling, teetering on the edge of breaking. "It *is* simple, Adrian! He hurt you, and you're just—" His words faltered, the weight of his emotions spilling over in his tears. "You're letting him do it all over again. After everything..." His voice cracked, his love for Adrian bleeding through every word. "After *everything*..."

Adrian leaned back against the counter, his fingers briefly brushing his temple, as if the words were too much to hold. The silence stretched. Itay's eyes glistened with unshed tears, searching Adrian's face for any sign that he would change his mind, that he would choose differently this time.

"Itay," Adrian said softly, breaking the stillness, "please don't." His words were gentle but resolute, like the closing of a door that had been left open too long. His gaze lifted to meet Itay's, and the heartbreak in his familiar eyes was too much to bear. "Don't do this to yourself. Don't do this to me."

But Itay couldn't let it go. His voice rose again, desperate now. "I've asked you for another chance so many times. I would've done anything—*anything*—for you. And you always said no. But the second he comes back..." He couldn't finish, his voice faltering, caught in the tangle of his anguish.

Adrian stepped closer to Itay, his movements wary, as if every step carried the weight of a thousand unspoken apologies. His trembling hands rose to cup Itay's face, his thumbs brushing away tears that fell freely now. The intimacy of the gesture was comforting yet final, as though Adrian was holding not just Itay's face, but all the years, the love, the relationship, the laughter, and the heartbreak they had shared.

From across the room, the sound of a sharp gasp broke through the fragile moment. Adrian's chest tightened, his breath catching, but he didn't turn. He didn't need to look to know it was Logan. That sound—half shock, half ache—was unmistakable, and in his peripheral vision, Adrian could see the ripple of movement. Logan was no longer seated, his body taut and on edge, as though ready to intervene or perhaps flee, unsure which instinct to follow. He stood now, his presence an undeniable storm in the room, waiting, watching. Adrian could feel Logan's eyes burning into him, a silent plea for acknowledgment, for reassurance.

But Adrian didn't turn toward him. Instead, he focused entirely on Itay, his hands steady even as his heart wavered. He needed to do this—to close this chapter with the grace Itay deserved and free him from the burden of a love that had nowhere to go. "Itay," he whispered, his words tender but heavy with finality, "you have to stop. This is over. It's been over for a long time now." His voice cracked, but he pressed on, his heart breaking with each word. "I care about you, and I love you, but not in the way you deserve. You deserve a love that moves mountains, that gives you the world. You shouldn't have to beg someone to love you. You shouldn't have to fight for scraps."

Itay's tears spilled over, and his shoulders sagged under the weight of Adrian's words. Adrian pulled him into an embrace, holding him tightly, as though he could soothe the pain even as he inflicted it. "You deserve someone who will love you the way you love them," Adrian murmured against Itay's ear. "And that's not me. It's never been me. You miss what we had, I know, but that's all it is—a memory. You need to let me go. Please, Itay. Let me go."

The room fell silent except for the soft, muffled sound of Itay's crying. He clung to Adrian, his arms tightening around him, reluctant to release him into a future where he could no longer follow. But slowly, achingly, his grip loosened.

When he finally stepped back, his voice was hoarse and broken. "Will you seek treatment now?" Itay asked, his eyes brimming with hope and despair. "Now that he's here?"

Adrian hesitated, his face clouding with something unreadable. His gaze flickered toward Logan, who stood there watching them with fire and hurt in his eyes, ready to bolt. Then he turned back to Itay, and his expression softened. "I don't know. We just talked again last night. I'm still wrapping my head around it. I don't know what will happen."

Itay nodded, the motion slow, burdened with a quiet finality. His expression was heavy with the kind of defeat that doesn't come from losing a battle, but from knowing the war was never his to win. He stepped forward and wrapped Adrian in one last embrace—not possessive, not pleading, just full of everything he had never stopped feeling.

"I should've never let you go," he whispered, his voice low and breaking at the edges. "Not a single day has passed without me wishing I could take it back, and never break up with you on that damn day."

He pressed a soft and lingering kiss to Adrian's cheek and breathed him in like a man saying goodbye to a place he once called home. Then he pulled back, slower this time, his heart rising into his throat, swollen with the truth he could no longer deny: that he had lost. That maybe he had never even stood a chance.

And without so much as a glance toward Logan—the gravity he could never compete with—Itay turned, walked to the door, and slipped out. He closed it gently behind him, sealing a chapter with reverence, even if it wasn't his to end.

Logan had watched the entire exchange from the edge of the kitchen, the small space making it impossible to miss. He'd been silent as Adrian hugged Itay, holding him close, wiping his tears, the kind of warmth in Adrian's touch that Logan once knew so well. He'd seen Adrian smile at him—just a faint smile, but it was there. And Logan had stood frozen, unable to decipher the words they shared in Hebrew, his mind spinning with every possible scenario.

He wanted to cross the room, to wrap Adrian in his arms, bury his face in the place he once called home, and hold him like he'd never let go. He wanted to whisper into his ear: *I missed you yesterday when you left. I dreamed of you last night. I've dreamed of you every night. I wanted to wake up with you in the morning. Every fiber in my body longed for you. I love you. I cannot believe we are here again. I love you. I miss you. I love you. I will never leave again. I will never leave you alone once more, I will never leave you in the silence. I will love you till the day I die.*

But Logan didn't move. His hands stayed clenched at his sides as he wrestled with the demons inside him, trying to keep his emotions in check.

"Hey," he said finally, his voice low and hesitant.

Adrian didn't turn around. He picked up two coffee mugs from the counter and walked to the living room. Logan followed him, his heart skipping when Adrian handed him one of the mugs. A faint smile tugged at his lips. *He made one for me too,* Logan thought, the small gesture thawing something frozen deep inside him.

They sat in silence for a moment, the tension between them heavy but unspoken. Finally, Logan broke it.

"So, Itay?" Logan prompted, his voice strained, as he tried and miserably failed to sound casual. "Are you two... hooking up? Is he... with you?"

He almost choked on the words, the thought clawing at him. He would die right here if Adrian were seeing someone else. Even though both Adrian and Dean had told him Adrian wasn't with anyone, it didn't mean there wasn't *something* happening. Something casual, something like an arrangement. Maybe not a boyfriend, but friends with benefits. Logan's stomach churned at the thought, his chest aching.

Adrian sat down on the sofa, his gaze fixed on the ocean beyond the glass doors. For a drawn-out second, he didn't respond.

"We're not together," his tone was flat, stripped of any emotion. "He's a friend. He comes over from time to time. He... wants to be here for me."

Adrian paused, his words caught in the quiet struggle of his mind. Untold stories and unspoken fears circled like shadows around him, heavy with emotion. The haunting phrase "Because I'm waiting to die" hovered between them, a specter looming large, while the rhythmic whisper of the ocean's waves filled the silence, echoing the tumult within.

Adrian inhaled deeply, summoning the strength to continue. "We are friends," he repeated, as if saying it twice would make it true, or at least easier to believe. "I told him now that... he needs to let me go. He's still trying, though. He's been hoping, even though I've told him repeatedly." His voice faltered, a faint crack that betrayed the calm facade he had carefully constructed.

He shifted slightly, his gaze locking with Logan's. A surge of emotion washed over him as he surrendered to the depths of Logan's eyes, losing himself in their mesmerizing embrace—finally gazing into the eyes he had been longing to see for so long.

There was no anger in Adrian's gaze, no bitterness, only an exhausted kindness that cut deeper than any accusation ever could.

"But... I don't want to see him hurting. I care about him," Adrian added softly, the words carrying a weight they couldn't fully hold.

Logan exhaled, but the tension in his chest didn't ease. He set his coffee mug down on the table and sank closer into the seat beside Adrian. Logan couldn't help but compare his situation with Itay's; they had both broken up with Adrian, both had forsaken him. How could they have been so foolish as to let that man go?

Logan glanced at Adrian, his face lit by the fading sunlight, and the longing inside him surged. He wanted to reach out, to pull Adrian close, to say everything he hadn't said before. But for now, he remained silent, allowing the gentle sounds from the street—laughter, a child's shriek while playing, and groups gathering at the beach—to fill the space between them, as he awaited the moment when Adrian might finally let him in.

But for how long can a suffocating man deny himself the breath of life?

Logan knew small talk wouldn't get them anywhere. He took a deep breath, undoing the cuff of his shirt and carefully rolling up the sleeve, revealing the plastic wrapped around his wrist. He noticed the moment Adrian's eyes fell on it—how they widened slightly, how his gaze sharpened and glued itself to the tattoo beneath the translucent covering.

Adrian reached out before Logan could speak, his movement quick but his touch impossibly gentle. He cradled Logan's hand, his fingers trembling slightly as he turned Logan's wrist to examine the tattoo. Logan's body convulsed as electricity rushed through him, each nerve igniting in a burst of sensation. Adrian's touch was silky, reverent, but it carried an urgency that sent a warmth coursing through Logan's chest, striking his heart with a force he hadn't expected.

A set of whiskey-colored eyes, bright and piercing in the sunlight coming through the large windows, lifted to meet Logan's. They were wide, almost frantic, and filled with an intensity that sank all the way into Logan's soul. Logan's eyes grew tender as he looked at Adrian, love evident in their gentle glow. The quiet affection in his gaze spoke volumes, words unnecessary as he conveyed everything in that single, lingering look.

Adrian's fingers continued to move over Logan's wrist, tracing the edges of the plastic and the ink beneath it. It was as though Adrian wasn't entirely aware of what he was doing, his body responding on instinct, taking the touch he had long denied himself.

The tattoo, though small, held a powerful presence, wrapping around Logan's wrist just where Adrian's bracelet once rested. At its heart lay the symbol of the lifesaver, but it was the beautifully inscribed words encircling Logan's wrist, replacing the former leather thread, that captivated Adrian and steadied his trembling hands: *So when the end draws near, and life leaves you, I'll be here, waiting to save you.* The words wrapped around Logan's wrist, etched into his skin and framing the lifesaver symbol like an encore.

Adrian's heart clenched as the words sank in. He knew them too well—words he had whispered in his darkest moments, promises he had made to himself when he thought he would never see Logan again. His throat tightened as he struggled to breathe, the storm-gray eyes locking onto his with a longing that seemed to ripple through the air like a silent song. In that moment, words felt unnecessary, replaced by the unspoken storm of love and yearning pouring from him.

"Logan," Adrian whispered, his voice tender, trembling with emotion. He didn't need to say more. Logan's lips quirked into a small, soft smile, his eyes never leaving Adrian's.

Adrian shook his head, his gaze locked on the tattoo that now marked Logan's wrist. The words, looping around the lifesaver symbol, seemed to pulse with life, anchoring Adrian in the moment. He wanted to touch it, to trace the lines with his fingers, but the redness of Logan's skin stopped him. Instead, he held Logan's hand in his, his grip trembling as he spoke.

"Why are you doing this to me, Lo?" Adrian asked, his voice unsteady, shuddering with the weight of his emotions. His eyes didn't leave the tattoo, as if its existence alone might hold some impossible answer.

"Because I love you," Logan whispered, his voice steady despite the storm of desperation swirling in his chest. He squeezed Adrian's hand, leaning forward to place his other hand gently on Adrian's neck. The warmth of Adrian's skin against his palm grounded him, made his resolve even stronger. "I'm going to fix you," Logan said, his silver-gray eyes meeting Adrian's, full of a love that burned brighter than the fear threatening to consume him.

Adrian shook his head, his lips forming a thin line while tears filled his eyes. "Why not?" Logan asked, desperation in his voice as he fought to keep the panic at bay. He couldn't lose him—not again. He stroked Adrian's neck gently, his touch soft but insistent, as if willing Adrian to stay tethered to him. "Why didn't you start the treatments?"

Adrian's gaze flicked to Logan's, his expression distant but raw with emotion. "What for?" he said quietly. "My mom had it too. It killed her in two months. I've already had a year, it's more than she had. I can enjoy that year, at least."

"But, Ad..." Logan faltered, his words catching in his throat as his mind scrambled for something to say, something to convince him. "It's not fair."

Adrian exhaled, the sound shaky, filled with resignation. "You know, Logan," he said, his voice steady but laced with quiet pain, "those treatments themselves might kill me. They'll suck the life out of me without even the guarantee that I'll get better."

Logan gripped Adrian's hand tighter, his eyes pleading. "I know you will. I *feel* it, Adrian."

Adrian swallowed hard, tears stinging like fire behind his eyes. The sweetness of Logan's unwavering belief, his profound love, enveloped him in a bittersweet embrace. Here stood the man of his dreams, so long yearned for, yet an agonizing truth lurked in the shadows. The specter of loss loomed large, threatening to sever the fragile bond they had forged, a bond that might slip away all too soon. And then there was that voice in the back of his mind, whispering insidious doubts, telling him that maybe Logan was only here because he felt sorry for him. That voice reminded him of Logan leaving, of the cold, lonely nights when he had begged the universe for a miracle and only found silence in return.

Adrian's chest tightened as he spoke, his voice breaking as he opened up. "You know," he began softly, his eyes distant. "When my mom got sick, she spent all her time in the hospital. I didn't see her much, but one time, I overheard her begging my dad to take her to the sea." He hesitated, his voice catching as memories threatened to overwhelm him. "She just wanted to feel the water again, to be on the beach. But she couldn't, the doctors didn't let her go, and my dad was terrified to act against their advice. So... She had to stay there, in that sterile, stinking hospital bed, connected to all those machines." Adrian shuddered, his voice trembling as he relived the fear and sadness of those visits, from the standpoint of a boy with short legs looking up at those high walls and foreign surroundings machines. "And she died there, Logan. She died in that awful bed. That's not how I want to go."

Adrian wiped at his eyes, though the tears didn't stop. "I don't want to spend my last months locked in some hospital, suffering through treatments and surgeries. I don't even think I'd feel like myself anymore. I want to spend the time I have left doing what I love. Feeling alive."

Logan reached out instinctively, pulling Adrian into a tight embrace. He needed to hold him, to feel him, to let his love speak louder than his words could. "You won't die, Adrian," Logan whispered fiercely. "I'll get you the best doctors, the best treatments; whatever it takes."

Adrian shook his head against Logan's shoulder, his voice soft but resolute. "It won't matter," he said, pulling back enough to look into Logan's eyes. "Back in July, they gave me a sixty percent chance of survival—with treatments. Now?" He let out a bitter laugh, one that didn't reach his eyes. "Now, I'm sure it's even less."

Logan cradled Adrian's face gently, his thumb tenderly wiping away the tears that cascaded down his cheeks like fragile crystals, the stubble underneath his fingertips familiar to his finger pads. "I don't care what the numbers say, Ad, I'll rewrite them," Logan declared, his voice unwavering, a beacon of love and determination illuminating each word. "I'm not giving up on you. And I'm sure as hell not letting you give up on yourself."

Adrian's tears came faster, the weight of Logan's devotion cutting through his walls and carving through him like light through water, dissolving the last defenses he'd clung to for years. He felt seen, felt cherished, felt... like he used to feel when he was in the presence of Logan.

Adrian was at a loss for words.

Logan's love was a force he couldn't fight, a tide that threatened to sweep him off his feet, and part of him didn't want to fight it anymore. But fear still clung to him, whispering cruel truths about loss and the fragility of hope. But Logan Vaughn...

Logan was a hurricane wrapped in sunlight. He was every dream Adrian had dared to whisper into the universe. He was every sunrise he'd watched from the sea, every pulse of music in his veins. He was the breath between notes, the silence before the wave breaks.

He was everything. Simply, impossibly, everything.

In moments like this, Adrian longed to fold time. To reach back across years and find the boy he used to be, that awkward teenager with too-long limbs and too-loud fears, shoulders hunched under the weight of unspoken truths. The boy who stood in front of mirrors, wishing he were smaller or bigger or taller, or just *enough*. The one who was confused and afraid, who tried to kiss boys in secret, and learned that the kind of love he has to give must come with a bruise.

He wanted to kneel beside that boy, take his trembling hands, and point into the future.

"Do you see him?"

"That god of a man? Nearly two meters tall, shoulders like a harbor, hair the color of sunlit sand, and eyes like the sea before a storm? That heart—that wild, golden heart? One day, he'll be yours."

"And it will be the most terrifying, most beautiful thing you've ever known."

Logan held Adrian even closer, as if proximity alone could protect him from everything that threatened to pull them apart. His hands gently cradled Adrian's face, his thumbs brushing away the tears streaking his cheeks. "You won't die," Logan repeated, his voice steady but thick with emotion. "Do you hear me? You *won't*. We'll have all the time in the world, Adrian. Just us. It's going to be amazing."

Adrian nuzzled against Logan's neck for a few moments, drawing in the comforting scent of him, the warmth that made him feel safe despite the chaos churning inside him.

He was once again embraced within Logan's arms, and he just let himself bask in the feeling of it.

When he finally spoke, his voice was low, almost hesitant. "Did you really mean it, Lo? What you said yesterday?"

"Yes," Logan said firmly, his silver eyes meeting Adrian's, unwavering. "Every word."

Adrian sighed, his breath shaky as it fanned over Logan's skin. "I couldn't sleep last night," he admitted. "I just lay there, thinking about what you said. It freaked me out, Logan. The things I started thinking, the twisted ideas I couldn't stop from creeping into my mind." He paused, breathing deeply. "Why are you doing this? Do you really want me to spend my last months locked in a hospital, suffering through treatments? Do you want *that* to be how I go? Is that what you want to remember from me?"

"You won't die," Logan reiterated with heightened intensity. He gently grabbed Adrian's face, compelling him to meet his gaze. "You won't die, Adrian. Do you hear me? You're going to be fine. We'll have forever. We'll be together, and it'll be amazing. I promise you that."

"Don't make promises you cannot keep," Adrian pleaded.

"I will keep that promise," Logan replied fiercely, his voice quaking as tears streamed down his cheeks.

Adrian's eyes dropped, his voice trembling with pain. "Logan... you're giving me the worst thing a dying man can get." his voice faltered, stripped to the bone. "You're giving me a glimpse of what I could have had, what I could have been... and it's something I'll never get. You've made me hate this disease. I'd accepted it. I'd made peace with the fact that I was going to die. And now you're here, and it feels like the universe is just dangling what I can't have in front of me."

His chest heaved as he took in a ragged breath. "I don't want to die, Lo." He confessed silently, almost soundlessly, the terse whisper revealing the truth he had long kept shrouded in silence. He had believed he was at peace with fate, yet the weight of reality pressed upon him once more. "But I don't want to spend my last days suffering in a hospital either. I want to live—*really* live. And this cancer... It's going to take everything away, even you."

Logan's eyes burned with unshed tears as the old ones marked his cheeks, but his resolve didn't vacillate. "Adrian, trust me," he said softly, his hands still cradling Adrian's face. "You're going to be fine. We'll both be fine."

Adrian looked at him hopelessly, his voice barely above a whisper. "Wouldn't it be enough... if we spent those six months together? If I could just have that with you?"

"It'd be more than enough for me," Logan admitted, his voice cracking slightly. "But no. I won't let you go without a fight. If you die, Adrian... I die."

It was peculiar how Logan simultaneously mended his wounds and shattered his heart; a paradox Adrian had never conceived of until that very moment. He reached up, running his fingers through Logan's soft, silky hair, strands of molten sand slipping gently between his fingers, drawing him close. "Okay, Lo. You win. You knew I couldn't say no to you. I'll do it. I'll try the treatments. But only on one condition."

Logan's face lit up with a beaming smile that made Adrian's heart ache in the most bittersweet way. It was a smile so full of life and love that Adrian wanted to stay alive just to see it again and again.

Only now, in Logan's presence again, did Adrian truly grasp the depth of his own sorrow. He had felt it, yes—the weight of it pressing down over the years—but never understood how far he had fallen.

The chasms his soul had slipped into were darker than he'd known, vast and endless once its other half—once *Logan*—had been torn away.

How had he survived without that light? No wonder his body had turned against him. No wonder he had withered.

His heart, stripped of its axis, had collapsed inward.

Could a man grow ill from heartache? Could grief hollow out a body the way it hollows out a life?

Now he knew the answer.

It was *yes*.

He was not just sick; he had been starving. Starving for the warmth of Logan's voice, the gravity of his presence, the tether that had once kept Adrian from drifting too far into the dark.

"Lay it on me," Logan said eagerly.

Adrian's expression grew serious, his fingers still threading through Logan's hair. "If the treatments don't work—if they kill me—you have to promise me something. You have to keep living, Logan. I'm only doing this because you tied your life to mine. If it doesn't work, you need to let go. You need to move on. Promise me that."

Logan's smile faltered, his gaze searching Adrian's. The room seemed to grow quieter as the weight of Adrian's words sank in. Logan didn't answer immediately, and Adrian leaned back slightly, his eyes locking onto Logan's with an unyielding intensity.

"Lo," Adrian said again, his voice firmer now. "Promise me." He ran his thumb softly over Logan's temple, sensing the tension in his jaw, as his silver eyes filled with emotion.

Finally, after what felt like an eternity, Logan nodded, his voice barely above a whisper, "promise," he uttered, though the word seemed to tear something from him. "I promise."

And with that, Logan dissolved into him, drawing Adrian into his embrace and clutching him as fiercely as the moment demanded. The edges of reality blurred and faded, yet the richness of shadows deepened, embraced by the warmth of Adrian's body that seeped into him like a nourishing tide. His fingers traced the length of Adrian's flowing hair, while the faint, grounding scratch of stubbled skin whispered memories of solidity. This fragment of what had been lost brought serenity to his restless soul, erasing the chaos they endured and gently guiding the broken pieces back to wholeness. It was proof that forgiveness was not just a word but a pulse, a breath, a chance.

Adrian forgave him.

For so long, Logan had lived inside a prison built of his own making. Each brick was a whispered lie, laid carefully by the voice of his self-doubt. *He could never forgive you. You hurt him too deeply. You don't deserve this.* Those lies had become a constant murmur beneath his thoughts, a slow drip of poison. He had believed them, let them shape his world until all he could see were the walls he had built from the shadows of his mistakes.

But here, in the dim glow of the room, those shadows seemed to retreat, the bricks began to crack with a gentle patience, hairline creaks like veins winding around each form, releasing particles into the air, dust settling into quiet memory. Adrian's fingertips drifted through his hair, slow and tender, tracing silent lines of comfort and trust. Logan closed his eyes, each nerve attuned to the rhythm of Adrian's breathing, to the delicate, unspoken symphony of forgiveness echoing softly between them.

He had braced himself for a storm—anger, hurt, the finality of a closed door. And, at first, the storm had come. The moment Adrian saw him, Logan had felt the sharp sting of every emotion he deserved—rage, betrayal, the raw ache of a wound torn open again. But storms, even the fiercest ones, cannot rage forever. Adrian's anger cracked, revealing the raw, trembling hurt beneath. Logan watched as the fury softened, as the walls came down, leaving behind only the fragile truth of what lay beneath the wreckage. And then forgiveness moved in quietly, unexpected but undeniable, softening the sharp ache between them, disintegrating the wall Logan had built in his own mind.

Logan's lips grazed the curve of Adrian's shoulder, his breath catching in a jagged, broken sound that fractured the silence around them.

The voice of his doubt still lingered, a ghost at the edge of the room, whispering its old poison. *This isn't real. He'll change his mind. You'll lose him again.* But now, with Adrian's warmth against him, with the steady heartbeat beneath his palm, Logan gazed between the creaks, letting the truth rise above the lies.

Adrian had forgiven him. And they were here—tangled together not just in body but in the fragile, luminous promise of a new beginning.

Logan leaned back slightly, looking into Adrian's eyes, wanting so badly to close the space between them and kiss him. But he stopped himself. He couldn't, not yet. Not when he had only just begun to make things right.

"Lo," Adrian breathed, his voice was a melody that sent shivers down Logan's spine. "I'm sorry."

Logan grimaced, confusion coloring his face. "What?" he asked, his brow furrowing. "What could you possibly have to be sorry for?"

Adrian's eyes dropped, his hand falling from Logan's hair as he drew a shaky breath. "At your wedding... I told you I wished I'd walked away from you that day." His voice was quiet, filled with pain. "But it was a lie. My heart was broken when I said it, and my mind was at its breaking point, too."

Logan gently cupped Adrian's face, tilting it back up so their eyes met. Adrian's gaze was tortured, his emotions laid bare, and Logan could see that there was more he needed to say.

Adrian exhaled, his words trembling. "My broken heart, Logan, taught me the most. It taught me what wonders you could bring into my life. It taught me how to exist without you, even though every part of me didn't want to. And those broken pieces, they're what sent me to find you, to fight for you. Because my heart... it needs you. It's always needed you. No matter how much it hurt, I wouldn't change a thing. Not one moment. And I hated myself for saying I would. The only thing I'd do differently is hold you tighter that night. Make it last longer. Never sleep. Just talk to you until morning, because I should have known how much you were struggling."

A painful knot formed in his chest at Adrian's words. "Adrian," he whispered, his voice raw. "How could you have known? Don't blame yourself for something you couldn't possibly have understood. I wouldn't change a thing, either. I just wish I'd woken you up that morning and told you everything. You would've understood. You always did." He pulled Adrian into another hug, holding him close, as if trying to shield him from all the pain of the past.

Logan wanted to kiss him now—needed to—but he stopped himself again. Not yet. Adrian deserved stability, not impulsiveness, and Logan's priority was keeping him alive. He pulled back, letting himself take in Adrian's face, every detail burned into his memory.

"We have to start," Logan said with a smile that could melt iron, brushing a strand of Adrian's hair behind his ear and jumping to his feet. "Let's start by calling your doctors and setting an appointment? There's no time to waste. We might need to fly for treatment if there are better programs but—"

Adrian flinched, shoulders tensing, the color draining from his face. "Logan, slow down," he said, standing. "What do you mean, fly? This is Israel. The health care here is good—better than good—and it's free. I can't—"

"I'm not saying we have to," Logan broke in, voice taut as wire, "but we have to be ready. If there's a better program somewhere else, I want you to have it. I can't read the language here, Ad. I can't argue with doctors if I don't understand them, and if you fall through some crack because I couldn't fight for you, I'd never forgive myself."

Adrian's jaw clenched. "And if my doctors tell me the best chance is here?"

"Then we stay," he said. "No matter what. But if there's *anywhere* that can give you more, we'll go."

Adrian hesitated, folding his arms across his chest and taking a step back. "Lo... I don't have the money for this. You're talking about flying, hospitals, treatments... I... I *can't* afford it."

"Ad, I know," Logan said gently, stepping toward him. "It's okay."

Adrian dropped his gaze, his voice quieter as color tinted his cheeks. "I don't think you do. I don't own a car. I live with a roommate. I don't have a steady job." He trailed off, his embarrassment palpable.

He had been living simply, scraping by on savings and support, because he hadn't seen a future worth planning for. He had been preparing to say goodbye. He always thought: *just eleven more months, just eight more months, just six more months...* counting down the moment and trying to live in the little time he'd left.

"I know," Logan repeated, taking Adrian's hand and leading him back to the couch. "And it doesn't matter. It's all on me. Every single bit of it. It's not even a question."

Adrian frowned, conflicted as they sat down. "I don't like it. I agreed to the treatments, but I didn't think it would mean leaving here and—"

"Ad," Logan interrupted gently, intertwining their fingers. "This is the best way to save you. Please, don't worry about the money. I've got it. All I want is for you to fight. Let me take care of the rest."

Adrian stared at Logan for a moment, his heart aching at the determination and love in Logan's eyes. Finally, he nodded, though the hesitation in his eyes was clear. Logan saw it and reached out, gripping his hands tightly. "Ad, please," he said softly, yet his voice was steady. "It's just money. You hold my life in your hands now, *that* is what matters. Not a few pieces of paper. You're worth so much more than any of it."

Adrian's gaze dropped, his voice barely above a whisper. "It's... too much." He wasn't referring to the money, but to everything—Logan showing up, the whirlwind of changes, the chaos he'd brought into his carefully constructed resignation.

Logan bent slightly to meet Adrian's eyes, his voice firm but filled with warmth. "It's far from too much. I know it's scary, but we're in this together. We *are* together in this."

Adrian's lips curved into the faintest of smiles, a fragile thing, yet real. "I like the way that sounds," he murmured.

"So do I," Logan replied, his own smile radiant and genuine, lighting up his face. "So, why don't you start by calling your doctor and setting an appointment for as soon as possible?"

"Yeah, I'll do that."

"And then maybe we'll grab something to eat?" Logan blurted, voice tripping over itself, caught between hope and fear. He took Adrian's hand gently, grounding himself in the familiar warmth of that skin. "If... if you'd like, of course. Or, if you'd rather rest, I can head back, I mean—"

Adrian shook his head. "Do you want to maybe order in or get take-away?" Adrian asked in a calm, tentative voice.

Logan exhaled, relief flooding him, softening the tension in his shoulders. "Sure," he nodded. "So, do you want to go make that call, and I'll grab something to eat? I also need to get some ointment for the new tattoo."

"Or..." Adrian put one hand on Logan's cheek. "Or you could stay with me while I make the call. Then we can go together. Pick something up, stop by the pharmacy, come home...just...do it together?"

Logan felt tears welling up before he could stop them, the relief and the ache crashing into him all at once. "That," he whispered, pressing his lips to Adrian's knuckles, "sounds perfect."

Adrian got up from the couch and walked toward the bedroom to grab his phone. As he reached the nightstand, he spotted the device and stretched for it, but before he could reach it, Logan's voice called out softly from behind him.

"Adrian."

He paused and turned around, and the next moment Logan was hugging him so tightly it almost made him lose his breath.

"You're going to be okay," Logan declared, his voice brimming with certainty. He wrapped Adrian in a hug, his arms tightening around him as if anchoring him to the world. Logan buried his face in Adrian's shoulder, breathing him in, and Adrian felt his heart stutter in his chest.

Adrian nodded against Logan, his head resting against the warmth of Logan's torso, loving how tall Logan was, but doubt lingered. He wasn't sure if he could believe it. But his traitorous body didn't care—it reveled in the closeness, the feel of Logan's arms around him, and the way his own heartbeat seemed to be trying to leap out of his chest and settle next to Logan's.

And just like that, Logan Vaughn had blustered back into Adrian's life, as chaotic and unstoppable as a summer storm. He'd swept through, leaving nothing untouched, nothing unaffected. The wounds Adrian had spent so long nursing, the scars he thought he'd accepted, were eclipsed in Logan's presence. All that remained was the undeniable sense of wholeness, as the part of Adrian that had been missing was finally returned.

Logan had grown leaner, almost too thin, as though the weight of his own struggles had carved him down to the essentials. His face carried the wear of sleepless nights, and there was a fragility in his features that made something seize inside of Adrian.

But he was still *Logan.* The same beautiful, determined, kindhearted man who had swept Adrian off his feet two years ago. And now, against all odds, Logan had come crashing back into his life, just as unrelenting and irrepressible as ever.

Adrian placed a trembling hand over his chest, the uneven rhythm of his heart pounding against his palm, wild and erratic, as if it were alive with memory, as if it were trying to remind him of something vital. It pulsed beneath his fingertips with a desperate kind of loyalty, a quiet plea that whispered: Remember. Remember what it feels like to truly live. Remember what it feels like to be whole.

Logan had taken his heart once before, silently, painfully, and left him bleeding in his absence. And now, just like that, it seemed Logan had done it again—slipped past Adrian's carefully constructed defenses, stolen the fragile remains, and claimed them as though they had always belonged to him.

And they had.

Adrian closed his eyes briefly, his hand still pressed to his chest, as though he could hold the ache inside, contain the rush of feeling that Logan's presence had stirred. But it was futile. His heart, loyal to its thief, refused to obey, thrumming wildly with the thrill of living, the fullness of hope that he hadn't dared to let himself feel in so long.

Just like that, Logan had undone him.

Again.

Chapter 14
Linking the Loose Ends

There is nothing crueler than my own mind.

It plays the same scenes on repeat, again and again, until I can't breathe.

I sit here, alone, and I think of you with her.

I think of your mouth,

The same mouth that once whispered my name like a prayer,

now pressing against hers.

Do you kiss her the way you kissed me?

Do your hands know her like they knew me?

Do you say the same things you said to me?

Or did you save new words for her,

now that I've been erased?

I wonder if you laugh with her the way you laughed with me,

If you smile in that soft, silly way when she walks into a room.

I wonder if she knows the things I knew.

If she sees the parts of you I carried.

If she touched you while my fingerprints were still fading from your skin.

Because you still had my marks on you.

And you went to her anyway.

You married her.

After months. Months.

You chased her with the same heart that once beat for me.

With the same lips that tasted like goodbye when you left.

You gave her a life that I had built in my dreams.

A home that I had held for us.

And I—I am left with fragments.

Words you said.

Promises you never made to break.

Photographs that don't look like lies, yet.

Sentences that play like lullabies and land like knives.

Some clothes.

A toothbrush.

A mark on you from me in the shape of bracelet you kept on you.

Things. Just things. Not you.

Because you're gone. Not just gone—you're hers.

And whenever I think about it, I fall apart in places I didn't know could break.

At first, I cried.

I wept until my body shook and my voice vanished.

But now,

now, the tears are gone.

And what's left is worse.

A stone in my chest.

A bull of fire lodged in my throat.

A weight that has made a home inside me.

That pain,

it's part of me now.

As much a part of me as you were.

As you are.

As you'll always be.

The pain wears your face.

And every time I see it, more memories come.

More images I never wanted.

You, standing beside her in a house that was supposed to be ours.

You, holding her hand as if it had never held mine.

You, living a life I had once dared to believe in.

I wanted you. I hoped for you.

God, I yearned for you.

And you're there—

with her.

And I'm still here.

Losing my mind.

Losing my love.

Losing myself.

And about to end everything.

November 22, 2020—Tel-Aviv, Israel—Two Days Later

It had only been four days since Logan had found Adrian again—four days since his world had shifted entirely. Everything was different now. Logan was different. For the first time in years, he felt purpose coursing through him. The moment Adrian had said yes—yes to Logan staying, yes to being found, yes to letting him in again, yes to fighting the illness—Logan knew they had no time to waste. They needed to act, to do everything in their power to save Adrian from the grip of the disease that threatened to take him away forever.

Early that morning, Logan had video called Ada Mae. Her calm presence had been a cornerstone of his chaotic life for so long now, and he knew he could trust her. When she answered, her voice was as crisp and professional as always.

"Ada Mae," Logan began, his voice rough. "I need your help. It's personal, not work-related. If it's too much—"

"Logan," Ada Mae gently interrupted, using his first name to signal her willingness to move beyond work boundaries. "I'm here for you. Just let me know what you need."

Logan took a breath, steadying himself. He told her about Adrian—about their history, the love they had shared, and the years of silence between them. Her expression softened, a quiet understanding dawning in her eyes. "That makes sense," she said, as if a missing piece had clicked into place. Logan realized she had seen his struggles all along, his restlessness, his shadows, and now, at last, she knew why.

He moved on quickly, outlining the daunting logistics: cancer treatments, visas, doctors, insurance. He was covering every possible avenue in advance, refusing to let the ruthless march of time or the unyielding grip of bureaucracy defeat him.

Ada Mae didn't miss a beat. "Got it. Give me an hour to clear my schedule. We'll handle this."

Relief washed over him. "Thank you."

"You don't have to thank me. I've got you."

By the time they began sorting through the mountain of paperwork, Logan felt his determination solidify into something unbreakable. Ada Mae's efficiency was flawless: she assembled documents, coordinated with embassies for visas, and lined up preliminary consultations with top cancer specialists, navigating the scheduling chaos with practiced calm.

Logan took the research on himself, scanning studies late into the night, trying to decipher clinical jargon and chasing down every faint lead and asking Adrian's doctor so many questions that he was sure they thought him to be a madman. His jaw tightened each time a promising treatment turned out of reach, but his chest lifted with hope whenever he found even the faintest spark of possibility.

Through his family's connections—the Vaughn name that carried weight in rooms Logan had never cared to enter—he managed to contact several doctors and facilities, questioning doctor after doctor until he managed to get to one of the most renowned oncologists in the world. The call was brief, but Logan clung to every word, hope burning brightly for the first time in years.

"There's an experimental program," the doctor said, voice steady but weighted with caution. "It's a multi-center clinical trial, coordinated across several major sites in the United States, the UK, and Australia. The protocol was designed by one of my top protégés, Dr. Tierney, with myself and a team of international specialists involved as principal investigators. It's one of the largest prospective studies in its class, aiming to recruit enough patients to assess long-term survival outcomes properly. Early results are promising, especially for patients with a disease profile similar to Adrian's. But the eligibility criteria are strict, and time is critical. I'll email you a list of the screening tests Adrian will need, as soon as possible. Once we have those results, we can confirm if he qualifies."

The email arrived within minutes, and Logan sat staring at it, his pulse hammering as he read through the list of tests and procedures. It felt like a lifeline, a fragile, uncertain one, but a lifeline nonetheless.

Logan gently closed the lid of his computer, a twitchy energy coursing through him. Evening shadows stretched softly across the room as he settled beside Adrian in the cozy, sun-dappled corner of Adrian's little home. The golden hour light filtered through the window, casting a soft glow over the room, but it couldn't quite touch Adrian. Every time Logan looked at him, it was like seeing a faded photograph—a bit paler, a bit thinner, as if the world was slowly erasing him.

When Logan gently wrapped his fingers around Adrian's wrist, it felt so fragile, all bone and delicate skin, like he might slip through Logan's grasp if he wasn't careful. Adrian seemed to be withering away. His cheeks had hollowed, his lips often chapped. Logan knew how much Adrian slept—two hours here, another three there—but it was never restful. He would often wake with a soft gasp, a quiet moan, the pain in his bones too deep to escape even in dreams. Even now, as the room bathed them in warm light, Adrian looked exhausted. His eyelids drooped, and his breaths were measured, each one an effort.

"So, what did the doctor say?" Adrian asked with a timid voice.

"There's a program. A treatment. It's experimental, but it could... it could help."

Adrian turned to him, his expression unreadable, but Logan could see the exhaustion in his eyes, the deep weariness that went beyond the physical.

"We'd need to start with some tests, I have them in my inbox," Logan continued, his voice steady but thick with emotion. "If you're eligible... Adrian, I'll take care of everything. You don't have to do anything but show up. Please."

Logan had expected Adrian to smile, to show even the faintest glimmer of hope. He thought that telling Adrian about the experimental program and the possibility of treatment would lift some of the darkness that had settled over him. But when Adrian turned to him, his eyes heavy with sadness rather than joy, Logan's heart clenched in confusion.

"Why aren't you happy?" Logan asked, his voice breaking slightly as he leaned closer, taking Adrian's face gently in his hands. His thumbs brushed over the faint shadows under Adrian's eyes, as if he could somehow erase the weight of it all.

Adrian let out a soft sigh, leaning into Logan's touch for the briefest moment before pulling back just enough to meet his gaze. "You're too excited," he said quietly, his voice tinged with both affection and weariness. "Logan... I'm dying. It might not work. We need to... not expect much."

"You're not dying," Logan insisted, his voice firm but trembling at the edges. "You're going to be okay. We're going to fix this."

Adrian shook his head, a faint, tired smile playing on his lips. "You don't know that. No one knows that. I just... I don't want you to be disappointed if this doesn't turn out the way you hope. I need you to prepare for the worst, Logan. Please."

But Logan refused to relinquish the hope burning in his chest. "You don't get to give up," he asserted, his grip on Adrian's face tightening slightly as though he could hold him there. "You don't get to tell me not to hope. You are going to be okay, Adrian."

In the days that followed, Logan and Adrian took over the logistics and worked tirelessly to schedule appointments with the best doctors and hospitals in Israel to conduct the necessary tests for the trial. In the meantime, Ada Mae continued working on things in the US, ensuring that when the time came, everything would go smoothly.

Logan found himself in an unfamiliar position: juggling the staggering costs that came with trying to save Adrian's life. The doctor had explained that some aspects of the trial would be covered—the investigational treatment itself, certain lab tests, and follow-up visits. All of the other things would need to be paid separately.

The last two years have involved many expenses on his part. First of all, there was the recent search for Adrian, and then he purchased an apartment right away. On top of that, he was the one who assisted Sandy in opening her shops; most of her expenses were paid using his card, including the numerous trips he had bought her over the years.

Now, as Logan stared at the growing pile of expenses, he realized just how far he had let things spiral. The experimental treatment, even with

Adrian under his insurance, wouldn't be cheap. The Vaughn name opened doors, sure, but it didn't make him immune to financial strain. Logan scrambled to consolidate costs, cutting ties with Sandy wherever possible and redirecting his energy to Adrian's care.

He worked on getting Adrian covered under the Vaughn Global Lines' elite insurance plan, a benefit reserved for top executives and their families. Being the CEO's son and a founder's heir gave Logan leverage, and the Vaughn medical care was second to none, covering only the most advanced treatments and exclusive facilities.

That night, Logan called Adrian, and they spent hours on the phone. It was effortless, the kind of conversation that felt like slipping into a favorite song, familiar, warm, and grounding. Logan loved the sound of Adrian's voice, the way it softened in the quiet hours of the night, wrapping around him. As he lay in bed, the phone pressed to his ear, Logan felt like a teenager again, butterflies taking flight in his belly, a ridiculous smile stretched across his face. It was as though nothing else in the world mattered, just the cadence of Adrian's words and the warmth they brought to the dark corners of his heart.

He fell asleep that way, with Adrian's voice the last thing he heard, the sound of his laughter lingering in his dreams.

The next morning, Logan insisted on taking Adrian out for breakfast. They ventured through the winding alleys of Tel Aviv as Adrian led them to a café tucked away behind a tangle of bougainvillea, its petals like fuchsia kisses against the crumbling stone walls.

As they enjoyed plates of shakshuka and baskets of steaming bread, Adrian shared stories about his life in the city, his upbringing in Israel, and snippets of his military service, all while observing numerous men and women in uniform strolling through the streets.

Logan watched him, not just listening but absorbing every word.

But the truth hung in the air, a shadow in the sunlight. Adrian barely touched his food, and after the meal, as they walked through the city, he leaned heavily against Logan. His breath came in thin, ragged wisps, and sometimes his words tumbled into silence as he paused to gather air. When Adrian's strength ebbed, and his eyelids grew heavy, they did not push. They found a quiet bench under the canopy of a tree. Adrian rested his head on Logan's shoulder, and they sat in the soft hush of morning. The world moved around them, but they stayed still, a moment caught between breaths.

A while later, they flagged down a cab and made their way back to Adrian's home. As they stood outside his door, Logan lingered for a moment, reluctant to leave. "I've got some calls to make," he said, his voice tinged with regret. "But I'll see you later, okay?"

Adrian's response was a gentle nod, a faint smile ghosting across his lips, holding the promise of tomorrow. "Okay, Logan."

"Make sure to get some rest, alright, love?" Logan murmured, enveloping Adrian in a tender embrace, pulling him close. The warmth of their connection pulsed between them, and he felt Adrian nod against his chest, a soft hum escaping his lips, a melody of comfort and familiarity that lingered in the air.

The rest of the morning and early noon passed in a blur of logistics. Logan returned to his temporary workspace at his hotel room with Ada Mae, who had become so much more than just his assistant. Coordinating appointments across time zones was no easy task, and the hours were exhausting, but she never complained. Her two-year-old son, Henry, toddled around the room as they worked, occasionally tugging on Ada Mae's sleeve or looking at the webcam and Logan's face before smiling. It made the long hours feel a little lighter, a little more human.

In the afternoon, Logan and Adrian headed to the hospital for a series of appointments and tests. The day stretched on, each waiting room blending into the next, the sterile smell of antiseptic clinging to their clothes. By the time they returned home, the sky had already deepened into evening, a soft indigo wrapping around the world outside Adrian's small house.

The tests weren't meant to be brutal, but his body didn't have the strength to absorb them. Hours passed under fluorescent lights, needles, questions, waiting, and by the end of the day, exhaustion had lingered. He moved slowly, his body heavy with fatigue, and the medications they had given him for the pain left him groggy and disoriented. His steps faltered more than once on the short walk from the car to the front door, but Logan was always there, a steadying arm around his waist, a gentle hand guiding him forward.

Adrian's movements were sluggish as they stepped through the door, and he sank into the couch with a relieved sigh, his head tipping back against the cushions. Dean hovered nearby, watching his friend with a worried expression on his face. Logan crouched in front of him, brushing a strand of hair from Adrian's face. "You okay?" he asked softly.

Adrian blinked at him, his eyes heavy-lidded and hazy. "Mmm, yeah," he mumbled, a faint, loopy smile tugging at his lips. "Feel like I'm floating."

Logan chuckled, though a pang of sadness lay beneath it. "That's the meds," he said gently, his hand lingering on Adrian's knee. "You've been through a lot today."

Adrian nodded lazily, his smile fading as his gaze turned serious for a moment. "Thanks for… for staying," he murmured, his words slurring slightly. "I know it's… a lot."

"It's not a lot," Logan said firmly. "Never."

The doctor's words echoed in Logan's mind long after they'd left the sterile walls of the hospital. Pallor, fatigue, shortness of breath, infections, bone pain. The list seemed endless, a catalog of suffering, and the way the doctor delivered it—clinical, matter-of-fact—felt like a quiet verdict. Adrian didn't react much as the side effects were outlined, but Logan noticed the way his fingers tightened slightly on the armrest of his chair, a small, unconscious show of tension.

"It can be all of them, or just a few," the doctor had said. "It depends."

Logan hated the uncertainty. He hated that even this glimmer of hope came with the shadow of suffering. But he didn't let it show. He couldn't. Not in front of Adrian.

Two days ago, Adrian had told Dean about his decision to try, to fight, and Dean had practically glowed with relief and happiness. Logan suspected Dean's enthusiasm wasn't just about the treatment. He could tell that Dean had realized what Logan already knew: that Adrian's change of heart had everything to do with him. That Adrian was fighting because Logan had come back, because Logan was there.

"How was it?" Dean asked, his tone wary but hopeful as his eyes flicked to Adrian's pale face.

"Fine," Logan answered quickly. "Exhausting, actually."

Dean nodded, then turned his attention to Adrian. "You hungry?"

Adrian shook his head, his voice soft and distant. "No, thanks."

Logan's heart melted at the exchange. Both Dean and Adrian were speaking English, even though it wasn't their native language, even though it would have been easier to switch to Hebrew. It was a small, unspoken gesture of inclusion, one that didn't go unnoticed by Logan.

"I'll help you to bed," Logan suggested gently, reaching for Adrian's hand.

Adrian hesitated, then mumbled, "Shower first. Hate hospitals."

Logan nodded without hesitation. "Of course." He gave Dean a small smile before following Adrian to the bathroom, his hand steady on Adrian's back as they walked. Adrian moved slowly, his steps unsteady, his body swaying slightly under the lingering effects of the hospital's medications. Logan stayed close, ready to catch him if he faltered.

Once inside the bathroom, Logan closed the door behind them with a soft click and turned toward Adrian. Adrian leaned against the sink, his face hollowed by exhaustion, the corners of his mouth drawn in as if bracing for something harder than pain.

Logan turned the shower on, adjusting the water until it was warm enough, with steam beginning to rise like breath from the tiles. He turned back to Adrian, who stood motionless, fingers hesitating at the hem of his shirt. His eyes flicked around the room, avoiding Logan's gaze. He stared at the faucet, the grout between the tiles, the soft sway of the shower glass doors, anywhere but at himself in the mirror.

There had been a time when peeling off a shirt meant pride; muscles shaped by years in the ocean, skin kissed by the sun. Now it was something else entirely. A slow unveiling of what had been taken.

Logan stepped closer and placed a gentle hand at the nape of Adrian's neck, grounding him.

"I won't stay if you don't want me to," Logan said quietly. "But I want to make sure you're okay. That's all. Just that."

Adrian looked up, meeting Logan's eyes, and in them, he saw no pity, only a kind of reverent concern. He nodded once, the movement small but filled with trust.

With trembling hands, he pulled the shirt over his head.

Logan's breath hitched at the sight of the bruises beneath, the pale skin dotted with signs of the illness that was consuming him. At the hospital, Logan had caught glimpses of Adrian's body, the faint bruises, the signs of wear, but now, standing in the soft glow of the bathroom light, Logan could see the full extent of it. The marks on Adrian's skin were stark, red-purple bruises scattered like unwelcome reminders of how fragile his body had become. The muscles that once rippled with strength and vitality were all but gone, replaced by a thinness that made Logan's chest ache.

"I still surf," Adrian said quietly, his voice tinged with both pride and resignation. The words hung in the air, bittersweet, like a wave rising before it crashes. "Well... up until a few months ago, I did." He hesitated, the weight of his next words pulling his gaze down to the warm water rippling around them. "I barely can now."

Logan remained silent as Adrian continued, his voice steady but laced with vulnerability. "Even after just paddling, I have to stop to catch my breath." Adrian's fingers absently traced patterns on Logan's arm, but Logan could feel the tension in his grip. "With the cancer, every hit from the board, every fall... it turns into a bruise. And then there are the dots that come..."

Adrian trailed off, his free hand moving to his forearm, his thumb brushing over the faint, reddish-purple spots—*petechiae*, Logan remembered from his late-night research about leukemia. Those tiny dots, so small and insignificant to anyone else, were a glaring reminder of the war Adrian's body was waging against itself.

"I know," Logan interrupted gently, pulling Adrian into a hug. He pressed his lips to Adrian's neck, his arms wrapping around him with the kind of careful strength that spoke of both love and fear—fear of hurting him, of breaking something already so fragile. "I know. Come on, let's get you in the shower."

Logan helped Adrian with the rest of his clothes. Each button and fold of fabric was a moment of connection, a quiet ritual of care. When Adrian finally stepped into the shower, Logan perched on the closed toilet seat, his posture relaxed but his gaze attentive. He wanted to give Adrian space, but he also knew how easily exhaustion could turn into unsteadiness, how the smallest slip could lead to something worse.

The sound of water filled the small bathroom, a soothing rush that seemed to wash away the weight of the hospital. Through the fogged glass, Logan could make out Adrian's silhouette, thin and blurred, as if he were slipping away into the mist. It hurt to see how much the illness had changed him, but Logan's sadness was quickly overwhelmed by something stronger: admiration, love, an unyielding resolve to be there for Adrian no matter how hard the road ahead.

"Lo," Adrian called out, his voice faltering.

Logan's senses went on high alert. He stood immediately, one hand on the glass door, his mind already conjuring the worst—a fall, a head injury, blood spiraling down the drain.

"What happened?" he asked, his voice edged with worry as he cracked the door open. "Are you okay?"

Adrian turned off the water, his hair dripping, his skin pale beneath the droplets. "Hey. I'm sorry, I didn't mean to startle you."

"That's fine," Logan said, his breath settling as he took in Adrian's steady stance. Relief washed over him, cool and calming. "Did you need something?"

Adrian hesitated, a bashful look softening his features. "I do, actually."

Logan tilted his head, curiosity threading through the concern. "What is it?"

Adrian's voice dropped, almost shy. "Join me? Both of us had a long day, and... the hospital just makes me feel gross."

"You sure?" Logan asked, a hopeful note slipping into his words.

"I don't want to waste another second without you, Logan Vaughn." Adrian's tone was firm, his eyes clear despite the fog around them.

Logan didn't need to be told twice. He stripped off his clothes quickly. Stepping into the shower, he reached for Adrian, pulling him under the warm stream. Water cascaded over them, a gentle rhythm that mirrored Logan's hands as he washed Adrian with care. His touch was practical but infused with affection, his fingers tracing the outlines of bone and skin with a reverence that spoke of love more than lust.

Adrian leaned into him, his weight a soft press against Logan's chest. Logan washed himself quickly, his own needs secondary to Adrian's comfort. The heat of the water, the continuous hum of droplets against tile, it all created a cocoon where nothing else existed but them.

Once outside, Logan gently wrapped Adrian in a towel, drying him with the same care he had displayed all evening. He quickly dried himself as they headed back to Adrian's room, passing a startled Dean in the hallway.

Adrian turned on the heat in his room and threw Logan some clothes, which he accepted gratefully.

Once dressed, Logan leaned against the doorframe of Adrian's room, taking it in for the first time. It wasn't small, but it wasn't particularly spacious either; a cozy, personal space with little embellishment. The large window overlooking the ocean immediately caught Logan's attention; the view was breathtaking and calm, a mirror of the life Adrian had built here. Against one wall, two surfboards leaned together, one slightly propped over the other. They seemed like sentinels of a life Adrian still clung to, even in his illness.

At the center of the room stood a big bed under the window, the sheets slightly rumpled. Beside it, a guitar rested against the wall. Logan's eyes caught on it, studying it for a moment, and without meaning to, he found himself searching—searching for something that wasn't there.

Adrian's voice broke through his thoughts. "It's a different one," he said softly, his tone quiet, his gaze locked on Logan as though he'd been waiting for that moment.

Logan turned, eyes refocusing, and saw Adrian already fully clothed, leaning against the bed. He'd been watching Logan's unspoken question, and there was a flicker of sadness in his expression.

"Oh," Logan murmured, his stomach tightening with a small pang of disappointment. He remembered vividly the guitar Adrian had played in the video—the one he had given him, the one that carried the words he had scrawled on it in a moment of youthful devotion. He tried to act like it wasn't a big deal, even though it felt like something precious had slipped further from his reach. "On the video, you had it," he said, his voice light, but the weight behind his words unmistakable.

Adrian walked over to the bed and sat on the edge. Logan hesitated for a moment before following, taking a seat beside him. Adrian looked down at his hands, twisting his fingers together briefly before speaking.

"I burned it," Adrian confessed quietly, his voice steady but heavy with emotion. "Burned it all. I got the results that confirmed what I suspected, and I was so... angry. I took the guitar, the album I made you, and even the test results and burned them all. Everything I had that reminded me of you." He paused, his voice growing softer. "I left your other stuff, the things you didn't take with you. But the things that meant something to me? I couldn't keep them. I burned them along with the test results. It was the same day I decided I didn't want treatments." Adrian glanced around his room, his heart aching, intentionally omitting a specific item he had kept from Logan.

Logan sat in silence for a moment, letting Adrian's words settle over him. His chest ached with the weight of what Adrian had carried alone for so long, and once again, the only words he could manage felt woefully inadequate. "I'm sorry," he said quietly, for what felt like the hundredth time, his apology laden with all the regrets he couldn't begin to express.

Adrian didn't say anything in response. Instead, he reached for Logan's hand, his grip warm and reassuring, as though he were trying to tell him that some part of it, at least, was behind them.

Logan's eyes drifted to the surfboards leaning against the wall, and something caught his attention. He stood, crossing the room and moving the front board aside to get a better look at the one behind it. His breath caught when he saw it, the memories rushing back in an instant. "I see you didn't burn all of my stuff," Logan remarked, his voice tinged with satisfaction as he ran a hand over the surfboard he had left behind. "God, I missed this board."

Adrian's laughter broke the tension, light and easy. "Well," he started, a crooked grin tugging on his lips, "burning a surfboard felt like a violation. Especially an expensive one like that."

Logan glanced at him, a slight smile forming. Adrian's humor was gentle yet familiar, reminiscent of a long-forgotten song. "I haven't used it," Adrian went on, reclining on his hands, "but Dean was eager to sell it, said we could make a good profit. I believe he has a plan to steal it and then sell it off eventually." He playfully teased, his voice adopting a mock-serious tone.

Logan shook his head as he sat back down beside Adrian.

"Would you play something for me?" Logan asked after a moment, his voice quiet, almost tentative, as he motioned toward the guitar leaning against the wall.

Adrian glanced at it, then back at Logan, a flicker of hesitation crossing his face before he reached for it. He snatched the guitar and settled himself on the bed, shifting until he was comfortable, the instrument balanced on his lap. His fingers brushed the strings, testing the tuning, the soft hum filling the room like a whispered promise.

"What do you want to hear?" Adrian asked, his voice casual but tinged with something deeper.

Logan hesitated for only a moment before speaking his truth, his request as shameless as it was vulnerable. "My song," he said, his voice barely above a whisper. "I want to listen to my song. Live." A pause, then with a shy smile, he added, "It seems only fair; it is my song, after all. I should get to watch it live."

Adrian's mouth twitched with a resigned sort of amusement, and he gave a small nod. With no further words, his fingers danced over the strings, the melody washing over him, an echoing memory revived as it bloomed around the space. But this time, that memory was reimagined.

The song was born from the absence of Logan, crafted out of grief, out of longing, out of the unbearable silence where love used to live, and now it resonated in his presence, a tribute just for him. Although the melody and chords stayed constant, Adrian's feelings were no longer just remnants of the broken men who once played it. He performed that song for Logan, the love of his life, his heart reverberating with deeper emotions. Though he was still fragmented and far from whole, a new harmony began to heal within his soul as he played that tune for Logan.

Logan leaned back against the headboard, his eyes fixed on Adrian. The way Adrian played was mesmerizing—the natural grace of his movements, the way his eyes closed slightly as the music took over, the emotion in every note and word. And then Adrian began to sing. His voice, low and rich, filled the room, carrying the lyrics that Logan knew by heart.

By the fourth verse, Logan's throat had narrowed to a pinhole, breath scraping through, while his stomach writhed, tangled and tight. Tears slipped down his cheeks, unbidden, but he didn't try to hide them. He smiled through the tears, letting the music wash over him, letting Adrian's voice wrap around him like a second heartbeat.

He lifted his hand, his shaking fingers brushing against the still-healing tattoo on his wrist. The skin itched like hell, but he hadn't scratched it—not once. He had listened carefully to the tattoo artist's instructions, knowing how much this mark mattered. The words permanently marked on his skin belonged to Adrian, imprinted where the bracelet he cherished once lay. Now, they were a part of him in a way that no one could take away.

And as Logan watched Adrian now, his song spilling into the air like poetry, he felt the depth of that connection more than ever.

Adrian's fingers glided over the strings, coaxing out the melody as though it were an extension of his soul. His voice was low, raw, and hauntingly beautiful as he kept singing, the words filled with a deep ache that vibrated in the small, intimate room.

"I saw the parts you keep hidden from the light,

"I loved you in your darkest, most fragile fight.

"I always wonder if you ever think of me,"

Logan's breath hitched, and he couldn't stop himself from answering, his voice barely above a whisper but cutting through the charged air between them. "All the fucking time," he murmured, his eyes locked on Adrian. The words felt like they'd been carved from his very being, an echo of his truth. Adrian's lyrics, written with the blood of his broken heart, were a mirror to Logan's own.

"Does my memory soothe you like the sea?" Adrian sang, his voice quaking slightly, his fingers steady on the guitar.

"Yes," Logan whispered, his voice breaking. "It was reviving me, it was all I had."

Adrian smiled faintly, though his eyes were wet with unshed tears, as he sang the next line, his voice dipping into something even more vulnerable, something almost sacred. *"If you're broken now, I can't fix you."*

Logan straightened, leaning closer to Adrian. "Fix me by existing," he said, the words spilling out like a prayer.

Adrian's gaze lingered on Logan. *"Nothing of my soul survived the final dive,"* he sang, each word heavy with sorrow.

"Mine either," Logan replied, his voice low, their confessions intertwining in the air like a fragile thread, binding their shared pain together.

"But if you're damaged, maybe you need me as much as I need you?" Adrian's voice was tender, yet laced with quiet desperation.

Logan's hand reached out, brushing against Adrian's knee as he answered, his words came wrapped in ache and heartbeats. "Of course, I do. More than anything in the world, I needed you then, and I need you now."

Adrian's voice wavered as he sang the next line, his eyes flickering with something between hope and fear. *"I am fractured, but if you are whole, then I'll find my peace in your joy."*

Logan's reply came swiftly, his voice raw and aching. "I'm only fine when you're whole. I am only whole with you. There is no joy without you."

Adrian's fingers slowed on the guitar, his voice softening but losing none of its intensity. *"I believe my fate was to cross paths with you."*

"Our fate," Logan corrected.

"To be the one who saves you," Adrian sang, his voice trembling.

"Now it's my turn to save you, my love," Logan replied, his hand reaching out to touch Adrian's cheek, his fingers gentle against his skin.

Adrian's voice broke as he sang the final line, and Logan joined him, their voices blending together, rough-hewn and imperfect but deeply connected.

"So when the end draws near, and life leaves you, I'll be here, waiting to save you."

The final chord hung in the air, vibrating with the weight of their shared truths. Adrian's hand stilled on the strings, his gaze locking onto Logan's as silence enveloped the room. Without a word, Logan reached out, tenderly grasping the guitar from Adrian's hands and setting it gently on the floor, their eyes never leaving each other.

Before Adrian could say anything, Logan's hands were on him, cupping his face, pulling him closer until their lips met in a kiss that felt like it had been years in the making. Adrian responded instantly, his hand sliding to Logan's hip, the other cupping his cheek, grounding him as their lips moved together. The kiss was slow at first, soft and tentative, but the hunger beneath it quickly surged to the surface, their shared longing pouring into every movement.

Logan parted his lips just a whisper, his tongue softly grazing Adrian's in a quiet, loving caress, an invitation for more. Adrian didn't hesitate, his tongue sliding into Logan's mouth, meeting his in a dance that was both familiar and electric. Logan groaned softly, the sound pulsating against Adrian's lips, and his hands tightened on Adrian's face as though he never wanted to let go.

Adrian drew back briefly, his tongue retreating, only to slide back in again, coaxing Logan deeper into the kiss. Their lips moved together seamlessly, their breaths mingling, their shared need palpable. Logan's hands slipped to Adrian's shoulders, holding him firmly, grounding himself in the moment. He had forgotten how good a kisser Adrian was, how Adrian could make the world fade away with just a touch, just a kiss.

The kiss deepened, their bodies pressing closer as though they couldn't get enough of each other, couldn't close the space between them fast enough. It was more than a kiss; it was a reclamation, a promise, a surrender. It was everything they hadn't been able to say, everything they'd been holding back for years.

When they finally pulled apart, their foreheads rested together, their breaths mingling, their hearts pounding in unison. Logan's voice was soft, almost reverent, as he whispered, "You saved me then, Adrian. And you're saving me now."

Adrian's hand slid to Logan's neck, his thumb brushing gently against his jawline. "And you're saving me too," he whispered back. "Always."

Logan pulled away from the kiss reluctantly, knowing as much as he wanted to hold Adrian all night, he needed to let him rest. Tomorrow would be another long day filled with tests and the quiet agony of waiting. He gently brushed a delicate strand of hair from Adrian's face, his voice barely above a whisper as he breathed, "I love you."

Though he was aware of how often he had uttered those words—perhaps too often—he felt no remorse. Each time they escaped his lips, they carried the same aching sincerity, as if his heart had written them anew. He longed for Adrian to feel the essence of these words, to hear them resonate within him, to fully embrace their truth. He wanted to evanesce every glimpse of doubt from Adrian's mind, for, to Logan, the sunlight's true brilliance could only shine if Adrian genuinely understood the depth of his love.

With every proclamation, he reveled in the way Adrian's gaze would soften, how a playful smile would dance upon his lips, and how a faint blush would grace his cheeks, infusing life back into his spirit. Adrian craved those words, thrived on their warmth, and Logan would gladly scream them a hundred times a day if it kindled that radiant light in Adrian's eyes once more.

"I love you, too," Adrian whispered back, and it sent a wave of warmth through Logan's chest. It was as though his very soul had been set alight, the words igniting something deep and profound within him. He had waited so long to hear those words again, had longed for them in the emptiness of his nights. Now they were here, and they were everything.

Logan leaned down, pressing his lips to Adrian's one last time, a tender vow wrapped in a kiss. "It's late," he whispered, watching Adrian's heavy eyelids. "And you are exhausted... tomorrow we have another long day."

"Yeah. We must sleep."

Logan gently kissed his nose as he stood up. He picked up the guitar and put it back in its place by the wall. Adrian crawled under the blanket, feeling his muscles relax as he lay down on the bed.

"I'll see you in the morning," Logan promised, leaning down to kiss his forehead. "Goodnight, my love," he whispered before stepping away, flicking off the light, and opening the door.

"Lo?" Adrian called, a deep frown on his face.

"Yes?" Logan said, closing the door again instantly, and in the next moment, he was by his bed, leaning over him.

"Stay, please. I can't bear the thought of spending another night alone now that you're finally here." Adrian's voice trembled with urgency. "I understand you're trying to give me space—both now and earlier in the shower—but I don't want space. I need you, right here with me, close enough to feel your warmth. So please, no more distance between us." His plea was almost a cry, and Logan nodded, anguish flickering in his eyes.

How could he express his yearning for Logan to envelop him in suffocating love, to caress him with tender touches, to nurture him with devoted care, and to shower him with undivided attention? To admit that he craved Logan's presence incessantly? That he was aware of his own neediness, teetering on the edge of annoyance, yet still, he longed for Logan to be there, always?

Words floated away, leaving Logan marooned on the sandy shore of his own emotions. He moved swiftly, taking his place beside the love of his life, easing into bed, wrapping his body around Adrian's, drawing him in as tightly as he could.

As Adrian basked in the warmth of Logan's embrace, a dreamy gaze enveloped his eyes, accompanied by a whimsical, radiant smile that danced upon his lips—like an ethereal wanderer caught between the realms of slumber and something even more exquisite. Every fiber of his being radiated serenity, and the world unfolded in vibrant hues, more luminous and uplifting than ever before.

For the first time in 741 days, Adrian Leon and Logan Vaughn slept side by side.

For the first time in 741 days, they breathed the same air, their chests rising and falling in unison like waves in the quiet cover of night.

For the first time in 741 days, Logan's heartbeat found its echo in Adrian's pulse, a rhythm that matched the pull and push of the ocean they had once shared.

For the first time in 741 days, they lay entwined, warmth and safety woven into the space where their bodies met.

For the first time in 741 days, the emptiness that had stretched between them was filled, every mile they had been apart now folded into the hollow of their shared embrace.

For the first time in 741 days, the ocean inside them settled, their souls anchoring to one another, finding stillness where there had only been drift.

For the first time in 741 days, the bond forged in the heart of the sea rekindled—a flame cradled by the salt and the surge, a promise carried by the tide.

And with it, hope rose like the dawn, quiet but inexorable, spilling light into all the darkened corners of their hearts.

The next day, they run around the hospital corridors, moving from one test to another, each room filled with doctors' careful words and the hum of machines. Instructions and side effects crashed around them, a storm of information that left them clinging to each other. Adrian sat still under the fluorescent lights while Logan's hand stayed wrapped around his, a quiet promise.

They made it home earlier than the day before, slipping quietly into Adrian's house. The air inside was still, and Logan had also gotten used to this house, to this space that started to feel like home. Perhaps it was Adrian's presence next to him, or the faint traces that lingered around the space, echoing him.

Adrian explained, almost absently, that Dean was out—working late and then off to some date, said Dean hadn't specified with whom, but that he probably met someone new lately and was extra excited about it. His voice was tired, his words slower, but there was a quiet joy in having Logan beside him once again.

Without a word, Adrian laced their fingers together and drew Logan into the bathroom. They undressed each other in a hush, the fabric falling away like old fears. Logan traced the bruises along Adrian's skin as if reading a map only he could decipher, and Adrian shivered, steady-eyed and unafraid.

Steam rose when the water began, wrapping them in its gentle veil. They stepped beneath it, hands roaming in quiet conversation, each touch an unspoken promise.

When they emerged, towels wrapped loosely around their hips, the house was still silent. They moved through it like ghosts, barefoot and damp, leaving faint footprints behind as they made their way to Adrian's room. The door clicked shut behind them, and the world outside seemed to fall away. Adrian let the towel slip from his waist and climbed into bed, the sheets cool against his skin. Logan followed, his movements almost synchronized, and turned off the light before sliding under the covers. The darkness cradled them, intimate and tender.

Logan pulled Adrian to him, his arms wrapping around him. Adrian rested his hand on Logan's hip, fingers tracing the sharp lines there, a reminder of all Logan had lost. "You've lost so much weight, Lo," Adrian whispered, his voice carrying a mix of worry and love. His hand lingered as if he could somehow hold Logan's pain in his palm. "Even though you look better now... you still seem pale, drained."

Logan appeared as though the ocean itself had claimed a piece of him, never to return it. Like a man who had left his love behind in a distant Australian cabin, only to wander endlessly through the vast, empty expanse of his own regret. His eyes, once wild and luminous like the waves he once soared upon, now bore the dull, weary shimmer of one battered by unseen currents, too exhausted to resist. Adrian watched intently, sensing the hollow spaces, the toothed edges, the fractures beneath Logan's skin. And yet, amidst the weariness, Logan still radiated a kind of divine beauty—an unbreakable, eternal radiance that no tide of loss could diminish. He was a testament to the resilience of the soul, a reminder that even in darkness, there exists a radiant, indomitable light.

Logan hesitated, his words catching in his throat. "I... I haven't surfed since... since Australia," he admitted. "I tried once... when I decided to find you. But other than that, I haven't even touched the ocean. I drank instead. Every night. And then I'd go to work. Some days... I didn't even sleep."

Adrian lifted his head, his gaze piercing in the dim light. He cupped Logan's face, his thumb brushing over his cheek. "You gave up surfing?" he asked, disbelief threading his voice. "You, Logan? Surfing is your soul. I can't... I can't believe you let it go."

Logan's eyes were shadowed, the ocean behind them stormy. "You are my soul. It felt useless," he murmured. "Everything felt meaningless without you."

Adrian pressed his lips to Logan's neck, his kiss a soft balm against a wound. "And your weight?" Adrian asked, his voice quieter now, more tentative.

"Stopped eating," Logan said, the words almost inaudible. "I couldn't... I just couldn't. Ada Mae had to remind me to eat most days... sometimes I'd just ignore her."

Adrian blinked, a small, bittersweet smile flickering on his lips. "You, Logan, not eating? That doesn't even sound real," he said softly, but his heart ached as he kissed Logan's chin, a fragile gesture of comfort.

Logan's voice broke through the silence, serious but tinged with a faint smile. "What can I say? I guess... you're my appetite, Adrian."

The words lingered in the air, a tremor on still water, circles widening, drifting apart into silence. Adrian's voice cracked when he finally spoke. "I love you so much, Logan," he whispered.

Adrian's head sank back onto Logan's chest, his ear pressed to the steady rhythm of his heartbeat. "I'm going to take care of you, Lo," he murmured. "We'll take care of each other. Tomorrow, you're going to eat like a real Logan again."

Logan smiled, his arms tightening around Adrian like an anchor grounding them both. "Yes," he whispered. After a pause, his voice turned playful. "Though I hope you're on the menu, too." He leaned in, pressing a soft kiss to Adrian's lips, the touch more affection than desire. His hand slid over Adrian's waist, drawing him in, the space between them folding away.

But Adrian stiffened, his breath hitching. Logan felt it immediately, his body stilling, the warmth of his palm resting gently against Adrian's side. "Hey," he murmured, pulling back just enough to see him. "What's wrong?"

Adrian's eyes stayed closed, his lashes trembling against his cheeks. His voice, when it came, was thin and fragile, a thread unraveling in the dark. "I know you. I know... you want. I know you want to have sex. I just... I don't know. I don't know if I can give you that." His words fell out in fragments, each one a piece of his fear. "I love you," he added in a broken voice.

Logan's playful glint faded, replaced by a softness that reached deep, touching the places where only love could go. "Adrian, I wasn't—" He stopped, his words curling back into his throat. "I was just teasing you, like we used to. I just wanted to hold you, to kiss you. Nothing more."

Adrian's lips pressed into a thin line. "Yeah, but back then I could follow up with those teases." His voice was tight, laced with a sorrow that felt older than time. "I could give you what you needed. Now, I can't even..."

Logan's hand remained steady against his side, a warm, unyielding presence. "I don't need that," he said gently. "I just need you."

Adrian shook his head, his face turning into the pillow, hiding from the weight of his own insecurities. "But you could have anything," he whispered. "Anyone. You're young, beautiful, successful. You could have someone who's... whole. Not someone who's sick and..." His voice cracked, the last word dissolving into silence. "I don't want you to regret it, Logan. I don't want you to look back and see all the time you wasted on me."

Adrian broke into tears, the dam of his insecurities finally giving way. The weight of the past six days crashed over him—the shock of Logan's return, the sterile halls of hospitals, the sharp-edged words of doctors, the looming trial program, the thought of leaving Israel, of uprooting his fragile world to chase a chance away—it all pressed down on him, too much, too fast.

His breath came in uneven gasps as he fumbled for words, his mind a blur of fear and guilt. "I'm scared, Logan," he choked out. "I'm scared of leaving, of starting over, of hoping for something I might not get. I'm scared you'll regret this, regret me." Words were spilling from his lips, and then he uttered, "I'm afraid you'll... leave again."

Logan's arms tightened around him, but Adrian's body remained rigid, his own doubts keeping him distant. "I'm not... I'm not even a real boyfriend," he continued, his voice raw. "I can't give you what you need. I can't even... I don't feel like me anymore. I'm not the guy you fell in love with. I'm not strong or whole. I can't even give you something as basic as sex, like a normal boyfriend would. I want to, I do... I... Logan. I do. I... don't know—"

His words hung in the air, heavy and jagged. The truth of his fears exposed, naked and vulnerable. Adrian's chest heaved, his tears hot against Logan's skin as he pressed his face against his shoulder, hiding from the world, from himself.

"Adrian," Logan's voice cut through the air, firm and unwavering. "You look at me right fucking now."

Adrian's eyes fluttered open, and Logan's face was so close that he could feel his breath, warm and steady. His expression was fierce.

"I love you. Get that through your thick skull because I do not want you to doubt me, not even for a second. You think I came back here for sex? I've had sex, Adrian."

Adrian's face crumpled, his hand rising to cover his shame, but Logan caught it gently. He kissed Adrian's knuckles, his lips a soft promise against the rough skin. "Listen to me. It's important." He kissed Adrian's warm cheek then, before continuing. "I've had sex in the past two years." Logan's voice didn't falter, but his eyes shone with a different kind of truth—something painful, something real. "But I wasn't there. I told you, I didn't feel anything. It was empty, just a way to forget, to numb the ache of not being with you."

He squeezed Adrian's hand, grounding him, refusing to let him slip away into his fears. "If you think that what I care about right now is sex, then you're wrong. My love, you're so wrong." His voice softened, the sharp edges giving way to something tender. "I don't care about that. It's the last thing I'm worried about."

"I'm sicker than you are," Logan whispered, his voice thick with emotion. "I've been sick without you. You are what makes me better. You are what I want. I just want to be here with you, to love you, to hold you. That's all."

Logan's eyes bore into Adrian's, every word weighted with the truth. "If you think I would ever leave you again, and because of sex no less, then I am obviously doing a terrible job at showing you what you mean to me. You're everything, Adrian."

Adrian's lips parted, but no words came. His breath stuttered, and the dam broke. Tears spilled over, and Logan held him through it, his embrace strong and consuming. He didn't let go, not even when Adrian's sobs shook his frame, not even when the world seemed to tilt on its axis.

Logan was there, an anchor, a lifeline, a promise that the ocean between them had finally stilled.

Chapter 15
Hope at the Edge of Goodbye

And the thing that frightens me the most, the thing that coils tight around my heart, sharper than fear, heavier than grief, is that I don't care. I don't care if tomorrow never comes. I don't care if the sun rises and I am not here to see it. I don't care if tonight is my last breath, my last heartbeat, the final frame of whatever story I thought I was living.

It's a bad sign. I know that. I should be afraid. I should want to fight. I should claw my way toward something—toward life, toward hope, toward anything but this void. But I don't. I am hollow. I am an echo inside my own skin, a ghost haunting the empty rooms of my own life.

For so long, I've been moving through the motions, wearing someone else's skin, pretending to live. The diagnosis was like a key turning, a lock clicking open. It allowed me to finally peel back the façade, to shed that borrowed skin, to stop pretending. It was a permission slip to let go. To stop trying. To stop caring.

I told myself I needed time to think. To really decide. Maybe I didn't take enough time, maybe I didn't take any time at all. But what does it matter? Time feels like a trick now, a slow drip of seconds into a well with no bottom. Each breath is thin and wasted, each moment stretching out, elastic and empty.

The clock is ticking. I can hear it, a steady, taunting rhythm. And instead of wanting to stop it, to steal back the hours, all I want is to grab the dial and spin it faster, faster, until the hands blur and everything just... disappears. What is wrong with me? How did I become this—this numb, brittle thing, all splinters and silence, desperate not for more life but for less of it?

November 26, 2020—Tel-Aviv, Israel—The Next Day

LOGAN BLINKED AWAKE, REACHING for Adrian instinctively, but the other side of the bed was empty. He sat up, the sheets pooling around his waist, and his eyes caught the sight of his clothes, folded neatly on Adrian's pillow. They smelled of clean cotton and a hint of Adrian—fresh, familiar, and comforting. A small, involuntary smile tugged at Logan's lips as he realized Adrian must have washed and dried them while he slept.

They had spent most of the night tangled in the dark, Adrian's breath hitching against Logan's chest, his fingers clutching Logan's skin as if letting go meant falling apart. His tears rolled over Logan's bare skin, and Logan didn't move, didn't shift away from the dampness or the sharp edges of Adrian's sobs. He just held him, his hand moving slowly up and down Adrian's back, a quiet rhythm in the storm. Adrian had shuddered, his body curling tighter against Logan. His breath came in uneven bursts, like the remnants of a broken engine struggling to start. Logan kept his voice soft, a steady hum of half-formed stories and old jokes, words with no purpose but to fill the silence between Adrian's gasps.

Little by little, the tension ebbed. Adrian's grip loosened, his breathing slowing until it matched the quiet thrum of Logan's heartbeat. His eyelids fluttered, the fight slipping from him as exhaustion took hold. Logan stayed still, barely daring to breathe, watching the way Adrian's lips parted slightly in sleep, the remnants of salt on his cheeks.

And Logan observed him, weaving together the threads of transformation, seeking to unravel which of these shifts bore his fault.

Logan got dressed in a hurry, pulling on the freshly ironed fabric, then headed to the bathroom where he quickly washed his face and brushed his teeth.

When he stepped into the living room, the morning light had already spilled across the floor, golden and gentle. Adrian sat in its glow, a silhouette carved by the sun, his hair a tangle of soft highlights. He held a cup of tea, the steam curling up. Adrian lifted his head, and their eyes met. There was a hesitation there, a shyness that didn't belong on his face but had found a home there all the same. His cheeks held the faintest flush, a bloom of color in the otherwise pale landscape of his skin. He broke the gaze first, a small movement, the tea cup settling onto the coffee table with a soft sound.

Despite the light, despite the quiet, the marks of the night still lingered on him. Shadows clung to the edges of his eyes, his body still weighed down by the echoes of exhaustion. Logan saw it all; the remnants of their rough night etched into every line, every curve. He knew this would not be the last time, that the upcoming dawns would hold more weary mornings like this.

But he didn't say anything. Instead, he crossed the room with purpose, the space between them vanishing in a breath. He climbed onto the couch, straddling Adrian's lap, knees pressing into the worn cushions on either side of him. There was no hesitation as he leaned in, capturing Adrian's lips in a kiss that spoke where words would fail.

The kiss was a slow burn, a promise and a plea. Logan poured everything into it—the ache of their lost years, the raw edges of forgiveness, the quiet, stubborn certainty that this time he wasn't letting go.

Adrian's hands found his waist, hesitant, then firmer. When they finally broke apart, their foreheads pressed together, Logan's breath mixed with Adrian's, tangled in the small space between them. And for a moment, there was nothing else—no illness, no fear—just the soft rhythm of their hearts, finding their way back to the same beat.

Logan deepened the kiss, savoring the warmth of Adrian's mouth and the soft press of his tongue. When he finally pulled back, he leaned in to kiss the tip of Adrian's nose, a playful grin spreading across his face.

"Morning," Logan murmured, his voice still husky from sleep.

Adrian's lips curved into a smile, his arms tightening around Logan's waist. "Afternoon," he corrected gently, his voice sweet and teasing. He rested his forehead against Logan's for a moment, as if drawing strength from the closeness between them. Logan chuckled softly, his fingers finding their way into Adrian's hair, twisting and playing with the soft strands.

"I'm sorry about yesterday," Adrian murmured, his voice barely above a whisper. "I truly don't know what got into me—" Logan kissed him again, cutting him off, plunging into a deep kiss, tasting Adrian's tongue and moaning in pleasure.

"Adrian, we have a long journey ahead," he said, gently stroking Adrian's skin with his thumb. "It's frightening, and it's only been a week since I came back, so... please don't apologize for it, alright, love?"

He tilted Adrian's head back slightly, his thumb brushing along the curve of his jaw. "Okay," Adrian murmured again, transfixed by Logan.

"Go on a dinner with me tonight," Logan said, his tone low and intimate, but laced with hope.

Adrian arched an eyebrow, his smile growing wider. "A date, huh?"

"Not just a date," Logan replied, his gaze steady, full of meaning. "A celebration. Of us. Of being here. Of... everything."

Adrian's expression softened further, his eyes shimmering like sunlight on water, carrying a depth of emotion that words could never capture. "Alright," he whispered, his voice trembling just enough to betray the flood of feeling within. "Dinner it is."

The corners of Logan's lips curled upward, forming a smile so numinous it rivaled the divine. He leaned in to press a lingering kiss to Adrian's forehead before murmuring, "I'll pick you up tonight. I have to go, Ada Mae must be losing her mind." His voice held a note of apology, even as he reluctantly pulled himself away.

Adrian's fingers lingered on Logan's wrist for a moment, his eyes hesitant. "You sure you don't want to wait for the test results?" he asked, his voice wary, betraying the undercurrent of fear he worked so hard to suppress.

"They're going to be fine," Logan replied with a confidence that felt like a promise, though even he knew it wasn't one he could truly guarantee. He stepped back, walking toward Adrian's room to grab his cell phone.

"Dean hasn't come back?" Logan asked as he glanced around, noting the absence of any noise or movement.

Adrian shook his head, a small smile tugging at his lips. "Went straight to work from his date."

Logan chuckled, his laughter light and carefree in a way it hadn't been in years. "I think Dean scored!" he said with a wink.

"And on the first date!" Adrian added, his laughter mingling with Logan's, the sound filling the quiet house.

Logan's grin turned playful as he leaned against the doorframe, his eyes sparkling with mischief. "Let's see how you'll be doing on our first date," he teased, arching a brow and shooting Adrian a flirtatious wink. Despite their heartache the night before—and perhaps because of it—Logan didn't shy away from comments like that. Teasing each other and laughing were woven into the fabric of who they were, and he longed for their relationship to blossom anew, rivalling the depths of what they once shared. One way to nurture that was by trusting their bond to carry them through both playful jests and hurtful memories.

And it worked. Where yesterday a comment similar to that one made Adrian stiffen, today it painted his cheeks with a warm blush. He shook his head with mock exasperation, laughter bubbling between them, their embarrassment woven together into a tapestry of warmth and tenderness that enveloped them both.

When it was finally time to leave, Logan couldn't bring himself to rush. He kissed Adrian as if the world had stopped turning, as if time itself had folded in on them and nothing else existed but this moment. Five minutes passed, maybe more, but Logan didn't care. His lips moved against Adrian's like they were trying to memorize every inch of him, and when he finally pulled back, he laughed at himself, his forehead resting against Adrian's.

"I'm turning into one of those people," he said, his voice tinged with amusement. "You know, the disgusting ones who can't keep their hands off each other, even when they'll see their partner in a few hours?"

Adrian smiled softly, his eyes shining with affection. "Yeah," he agreed. "But you wear it well."

Logan laughed as he finally stepped away, his heart lighter than it had been in years. He was madly, hopelessly in love, and for the first time, he wasn't afraid to admit it, to himself or to Adrian.

As he left the house, the thought crossed his mind like a wave crashing against the shore: he wasn't just in love; he was starting to get used to the idea of *having* Adrian. Of waking up next to him. Of laughing with him over something as mundane as Dean's love life. Of holding him close and never letting go.

But there was one thing left to do—he had to make sure Adrian would stick around. And Logan knew, deep in his soul, that he would move heaven and earth to make that happen. Tonight's dinner wouldn't just be a date; it would be a step toward the future he could finally see on the horizon, one where Adrian would always be by his side.

The early evening sky was painted in hues of deep blue and gold as Logan parked his rented Maserati in front of Adrian's house. The engine purred to a stop, and Logan stepped out, brushing his hands over his jeans as he admired the sleek car for a moment. The decision to rent it had been impulsive, but he'd needed something to counter the frustration of cab rides, and besides, tonight was special. He wasn't going to let anything, not even a car, stand in the way of this moment with Adrian.

He made his way to the door, letting himself in as Adrian had instructed in his text. The house was quiet except for the faint sounds of movement coming from Adrian's room. Logan headed straight there, his heart skipping a beat as he reached the doorway and caught sight of him.

"Wow," Logan breathed, his eyes trailing over Adrian, who was buttoning up a sleek black shirt. His long hair was pulled back into a neat ponytail, and the navy jeans hugged his hips in a way that made Logan forget how to form words for a moment. Adrian looked like a vision, like something Logan might have dreamed up during one of his sleepless nights.

Adrian glanced up, a knowing smirk playing at his lips. "Not too bad yourself," he said, his eyes flicking over Logan before he winked and returned to his buttons.

Logan closed the distance between them, his hands sliding up to cradle Adrian's neck. "How are you feeling?" he asked softly, his gaze searching Adrian's for any trace of fatigue or discomfort.

Adrian smiled, leaning into Logan's touch. "Okay," he murmured before pulling Logan into a kiss. It was soft, slow, and grounding, and Logan's heart seized in the sweetest anticipation.

God, they were *playing house*. They were pulling off the whole boyfriend thing—kissing in doorways, teasing about dinner reservations—and Logan was completely in love with it. With Adrian. With every bit of this ridiculous domesticity.

"Let's go," Logan said after they broke apart, his voice filled with a barely contained excitement. "I made reservations, we still have some time but we can maybe look around before." Technically, Dean had suggested the restaurant when Logan called him in a mild panic, but Logan had made the call himself. "And I even scoped out a party we can hit afterward."

Adrian cocked an eyebrow, amused. "A party?"

Logan threw his hands up in mock defensiveness as they walked toward the living room. "Come on, I'm allowed to want to go to a party once in a while. Let me have this."

Before Adrian could reply, Dean's voice cut through the house like a fire alarm. "Adrian! Holy fuck, there's a Maserati outside our house!" Dean's footsteps thundered as he rushed into the room, his eyes wide with disbelief. "There's a *Maserati* parked outside! *Our house!*"

Logan smiled smugly as he dug into his pocket. Adrian's eyes sparkled with recognition just before Logan retrieved the keys and dangled them playfully.

"No fucking way, *princess*," Dean muttered, collapsing onto the couch as Logan dangled the keys in his hand.

"Yes way," Logan called back with a grin. "And you, you son of a bitch, you gave me a phone of a cleaning service twice when I called you for a recommendation about a restaurant!"

Dean's laughter echoed through the room, unabashed. "That was a good one," he said, clearly proud of his petty triumph.

Logan turned to Adrian, his grin softening into something more sincere. "It's rented," he admitted with a shrug. "I couldn't help myself." Then, with a flick of his wrist, he tossed the keys toward Adrian. "You're driving."

Adrian caught the keys, his expression a mix of surprise and amusement. Dean, on the other hand, groaned dramatically. "Damn it. I want a rich boyfriend."

Adrian snorted, his smirk taking on a mischievous edge. "I think you could definitely find yourself a sugar daddy," he teased, nudging Dean's foot with his own.

Logan, ever the troublemaker, chimed in without missing a beat. "I don't know... I don't think he's hot enough for that. And honestly, he's way too gruff—and let's face it, a bit too old—for the sugar baby role."

Dean's face twisted into a mix of offense and awkward indignation, and Logan nearly doubled over laughing at the expression. Adrian rolled his eyes, grabbing Logan's arm and tugging him toward the door.

"You're going to start a war," Adrian muttered, but he was smiling as they left, the keys jangling in his hand.

Logan looked over at him as they reached the car, his heart full as he watched Adrian slip into the driver's seat.

"Ugh, I forgot my jacket," Adrian grumbled, feeling unsure as he had been getting cold more easily lately. "I'll run back to grab it," he added, already half out of his seat.

"No," Logan said gently, resting his hand on Adrian's shoulder. "Tell me where it is, and I'll grab it. You can start the car."

"It's on the left side of my closet, on the hanging rack. It's the black one."

Logan leaned in and brushed a quick kiss across Adrian's lips, a gentle, almost shy press of warmth. "I'll be back in a sec," he murmured, slipping out of the car and heading back to the house.

Dean's door was closed, and through the wood, Logan could hear faint murmurs in Hebrew, a soft, awkward laugh following. He shook his head, a small, knowing smile tugging at his lips as he imagined Dean talking on the phone with the girl from last night. "Couldn't even wait a second..."

In Adrian's room, the air felt cool, and Logan could faintly hear the waves crashing on the shore. He opened the closet, instantly spotting the black jacket next to a heavy gray wool coat and a denim jacket. Adrian's wardrobe was a study in simplicity, comprising a handful of items. It made

Logan smile—Adrian had always been like that, valuing meaning over excess.

He reached for the jacket, and as he pulled it out, an unexpected motion jostled something free. A well-worn duffel bag tumbled from the dark recesses of the closet, its zipper gaping half-open, and its contents cascaded out in a sudden rush. Papers fluttered like startled birds, scattered across the floor, while cherished photographs slid and skittered in chaotic disarray. A thick book and a well-used notebook tumbled from the bag, landing half-open, revealing dog-eared pages, accompanied by a few mismatched items strewn across the floor.

"Shit," he breathed, the word barely breaking the stillness. He set the jacket on the bed and knelt down, his hands moving carefully as he began to collect the fallen items.

The papers were mostly in Hebrew, the text a river of dark ink that he couldn't navigate. He stacked them neatly, his fingers brushing over a folded envelope with his name on it, written in English in Adrian's handwriting. The ink was faded, the edges of the paper worn and soft, as if it had been opened and closed too many times, or perhaps never opened at all.

A quiet unease settled over him, a tightness coiling beneath his ribs. He didn't open the letter, couldn't bring himself to do it. Instead, he set it gently on top of the pile, his touch lingering as if the paper might speak if he waited long enough.

A notebook lay open, half in Hebrew, half in English, in Adrian's messy handwriting. His gaze caught a fragment of a sentence, a word hanging like a question in the space between languages before he snapped it shut, the sharp sound startling against the quiet. Adrian's privacy was a line he would not cross, not even now, not even with the ache of curiosity gnawing at him.

He continued gathering the scattered items, his hands brushing over a worn copy of Adrian's favorite book. The same one he had carried with him two years ago when they traveled together. The pages were bent, the spine cracked, a story that had been lived in, loved in. Logan swallowed hard, the weight of memory thick on his tongue. Logan remembered the way Adrian's lips would move as he read, the way he'd underline passages with a quiet, thoughtful smile.

He reached for the duffel bag, his intention to put everything back in order. But as he unzipped it fully, a piece of black fabric caught his eye. His breath stilled in his chest. He pulled out the hoodie—the one that had been his but had long since become Adrian's. The fabric was soft, worn down from years of being held onto too tightly. Logan's fingers curled into the material, the scent of Adrian wrapped around it, a ghost of warmth and comfort.

More items slipped from the bag, a pair of dog tags, the metal cool in his palm. One bore Adrian's name in Hebrew, a familiar shape of letters that Logan had learned to recognize.

His hand trembled as he picked up a framed photograph. Adrian as a small child, no older than four, his eyes a warm whiskey brown, his hair tousled by the sun. Beside him stood a woman with the same eyes, her smile wide and soft.

Another photograph lay beneath it, and this one pulled at Logan's breath. It was them, tangled together on the beach, their skin golden with sunlight, their mouths pressed together in a kiss that seemed to hold the whole world still, a love captured in the pixels, frozen in time along with the elements surrounding them. He remembered that day—the heat of the sand, the taste of salt, the feeling of Adrian's arms wrapped around him like an anchor.

Tears blurred his vision, the room slipping into soft focus. Each item he touched felt like a thread, pulling him deeper into the life Adrian had been building quietly, the plans he had been making for a future already foreclosed.

Logan wanted to collect everything and place it into the bag, but he found himself frozen, uncertain of what he had discovered, yet overwhelmed by a dreadful instinct. He sensed it could only be bad news, so he remained seated, clutching the hoodie with one hand while holding their photo along with a tidy stack of papers he had gathered beside him, with the bag still ajar.

"Hey, what's taking you so—"

Adrian's voice threaded through the quiet, soft but clear. Logan turned slowly, his vision blurred, the duffel bag still open at his feet. Adrian stood framed by the doorway, his expression shifting from curiosity to something raw and unguarded, a perfect echo of the ache in Logan's chest.

For a single heartbeat, the world held its breath. And then, everything came undone.

"I forgot it was there," Adrian's voice rushed forward, a hurried, fragile thread. He moved quickly, his hands darting to the spilled items, fingers curling around papers and photos, pushing them back into the bag with a kind of desperation that tightened the air between them.

Logan reached out, his arm finding Adrian's shoulder, the weight of his touch enough to still him. His own hand trembled, the edges of his world still blurred by the remnants of tears and the heavy press of realization. He didn't say anything, couldn't find the words, but his silence spoke for him, enough to make Adrian stop.

Adrian's hands stilled, a photograph half-crushed in his grip. He sank to the floor beside Logan, his body folding in on itself, as if he could make himself small enough to disappear into the space between them.

"It fell when I grabbed the jacket." Logan's voice was a hollow echo, his hand absently motioning to the bed where the black fabric lay crumpled. His gaze moved over the scattered pieces, the letter with his name, the old photographs, the hoodie draped over his knees. "I... what am I looking at, Adrian?"

Adrian's lips pressed into a thin line, his breath shuddering as he turned away, his gaze slipping to the window where the light filtered through dust and memory. "I don't want to say," he murmured, his voice barely more than a breath. His shoulders curled inward, a shield against Logan's searching eyes, against the truth that hung between them like a wound.

The silence settled around them, not empty but brimming—full of words unsaid, of years lost, of the weight of love worn down by time and pain. Logan's hand found Adrian's, their fingers tangling together, a quiet, desperate gesture. His thumb moved slowly, a soft, rhythmic stroke against Adrian's skin, a reminder that he was still here, still real.

Logan's heart shattered into a thousand fragile pieces, each shard lodging deep, the veins around it twisting tight, choking him from the inside out. He pulled Adrian into his arms, holding him with a strength that bordered on desperation. His grip was fierce, his fingers digging into Adrian's back as if letting go would mean losing him to the darkness already reaching for the edges of their world.

"Please tell me," Logan choked, his voice a raw whisper against Adrian's throat. The old black hoodie was still clutched in his hand, the fabric wrinkled between his fingers, a lifeline in the storm. "Please."

Adrian's hand found its way into Logan's hair, his touch light, soothing. His voice slipped out, soft and broken, the truth tangled in it. "I think you already know."

A sob tore free from Logan, a sound unbound and aching. He pressed his face into Adrian's neck, his breath warm and wet against the skin there, his tears smudging salt and grief into every kiss he pressed into the hollow of Adrian's collarbone.

Adrian drew in a breath, a shudder that ran through him, fortifying his bones against the weight of what he needed to say. He felt the shame gnawing at him, the bitterness of admitting just how close he had come to letting go, how foolish he felt for the remnants of hope he had tucked into that bag.

"My doctor... she told me how my final days might look," Adrian began, his voice trembling, each word like glass on his tongue. "She said I'd have to go somewhere, either a hospital or a hospice. She said I might not be myself. There could be delusions, fatigue, so much pain."

Logan's breath hitched, a soft, shivering gasp. His hands stilled, and he pressed his forehead against Adrian's, their shared breath fogging the thin space between them.

"So I started collecting things," Adrian continued, his voice barely above a whisper. "I knew I'd have to leave here, so I put together the things I wanted with me at the end. Things that I want to hold on to for as long as I can. Things... I didn't... things I knew I needed... things I couldn't bear to part with."

He hesitated, the truth pooling in his mouth, thick and hard to swallow. He couldn't voice it—that he had planned to put on Logan's hoodie, enveloping himself in the last lingering essence of him, refusing to part with it until the very end of his journey. That when he took his final breath, he wanted to be the closest to Logan, and it was okay to admit it toward the end, to be that vulnerable, as his time had already run out. He envisioned that when his phone grew too weighty to grasp, or when he wandered too far from the realm of clarity, he wished for that photo of them on the beach—the one where Logan sat nestled between his legs, their bodies harmoniously entwined, lips fused in an eternal kiss, and their joy shimmering like sunlight on the waves—to be the final image etched in his mind before the encroaching darkness swallowed him whole.

It rendered him pathetic, it stripped him of strength, it left him hopeless; yet, the truth was that in those final moments, when his breath slowed to a stop and the noise of the world receded, his heart yearned to be reunited with its other half. Thus, the hoodie and the photograph became his second-best choice, quiet stand-ins for what he could never ask for again.

In the final moments, the shame of loving Logan and enduring continual rejection by his lover felt as trivial as dust settling in a forgotten corner. He might be aware of its presence and recognize the need for cleaning, yet even if he chose to ignore it, what would be the consequence? One day, a ray of sunshine would illuminate that dust, revealing it in its entirety, but those minute particles of dust hardly held any significance at all.

He couldn't admit how he had run his thumb over the worn edge of the picture of his mother, memorizing her face, hoping to recognize her if there was another life after this. That the dog tags he carried weren't just his own but those of his fallen soldier, a reminder that maybe, just maybe, there was a reunion waiting for him.

Buried in the papers were his will, the last scraps of order he could give to the world. The notebooks held fragments of thoughts, scribbled in late-night clarity, and drafts of the song he had written and composed for Logan—music he had imagined would outlive him, a melody carrying his love even when he couldn't.

Logan pulled back just enough to look at him, his eyes red-rimmed and glistening, his lips parted as if he might say something but couldn't find the words. Instead, he cupped Adrian's face in his hands, his thumbs brushing away the tears that had slipped free.

"Adrian," Logan's voice was a whisper, wrapping and swirling around Adrian. His eyes held Adrian's, a steady, stormy gaze that saw through every wall, every shadow. It was as if he could read Adrian's mind, as if all the unspoken words between them had woven an understanding that needed no sound. Adrian had never been this close to anyone, never had someone who could slip into his thoughts so easily, who knew him so well that even the quiet of his soul spoke volumes.

Logan's hands framed his face, his palms warm against Adrian's cool skin. His thumb brushed gently over the curve of his cheekbone, a touch that felt both grounding and weightless. "There's a letter for me in the bag," he said, his voice tight, every syllable a thread pulled taut.

Adrian nodded, his movements small, vulnerable. "Just... just some thoughts. Things I needed to say. Stuff that I couldn't let go of." His voice cracked, and he swallowed hard, his breath catching in his throat. "I never thought you'd read it. I never thought you'd come back."

Logan's lips pressed into a thin line, the pressure of unspoken fears pushing against him. "I don't ever want to read that letter, okay? Never." His voice was fierce, the raw edge of a promise unraveling between them. He closed the distance, his mouth finding Adrian's, a kiss that tasted like salt and love and the desperate need to make sure he never had to say goodbye.

He tugged Adrian closer, pulling him into his lap so that Adrian was straddling him. Their bodies pressed together on the floor, the spilled contents of the duffel bag a quiet chaos around them. Logan's arms wrapped around him, holding him as if he could anchor Adrian's soul to this moment, to this life.

"We're gonna grow old together, you get it?" Logan's lips moved against Adrian's skin, his words seeping into every break and bruise. "We're gonna get old and gray, and we'll fight over stupid things like how you leave your shoes everywhere—"

Adrian's mouth twisted into a small, wobbly smile. "You're the messy one, if I remember—"

Logan kissed him again, a swift press of lips that cut off the words, a gentle rebuke wrapped in love. "We're gonna bicker over dumb things, and then you'll play for me in the evenings. And I'll melt all over again because even when you're a grandpa, you're still gonna be the hottest thing I've ever seen."

A rough laugh slipped from Adrian, his voice hoarse from crying, from speaking truths he had never planned to share. "Grandpa? We're just on our way to our first date, and you're talking kids and grandkids?"

Logan's hands slipped into his hair, fingers interlacing through the silky brown strands, his touch a soft hum against Adrian's scalp. "You don't want kids?"

"I do," Adrian whispered, his breath a warm brush against Logan's mouth. "You know I do."

"Then we'll have them," Logan determined. "We'll build a life together. A home. A forever." He kissed Adrian again, his lips moving softly, reverently. "And you'll only leave this world as an old man, surrounded by so much love you'll barely fit it all in your heart. You get it?"

Adrian's fingers threaded through Logan's hair, his grip tight, his face tucked against the curve of Logan's neck. His body shivered, not from cold but from the delicate weight of hope, something fragile and precious that had slipped into the spaces where only acceptance had been before.

"I get it," he whispered, his breath warm against Logan's skin. "I want it. But I'm so afraid of hoping. I've spent these past months just waiting, accepting... as if I didn't wish for anything more, it wouldn't hurt as much. Now... having hope—it's terrifying."

Logan's hand moved to Adrian's face, guiding Adrian to meet his gaze, his thumb tracing a slow, soothing line over his eyebrow and down the curve of his temple. His touch was a map of comfort, guiding Adrian back to the present, to the promise of a future. "But hope is all we've got," Logan murmured. "We need it, Adrian. It's the only weapon we have against all of this. I swear to you, I'll bring us that future. I'll fight for it, every day."

A shadow crossed Adrian's face, a flicker of fear threading through the warmth between them. "We still don't have the results. We don't know—"

"Say it," Logan cut in, his voice firm. His fingers slid to the back of Adrian's neck, his grip gentle but solid. "Say we're going to be together forever. Say you believe it. Say you have hope."

Adrian's breath shuddered, a moment of hesitation breaking open beneath the weight of Logan's stare. His lips parted, the words caught in the fragile space between what he feared and what he wanted.

"We'll be together forever," he said, the words a quiet vow, a candle lit against the dark. His voice was rough, but there was steel beneath it, a new thread of resolve winding through the softness. "I love you, Logan Vaughn. You're crazy, but I love you."

If there was anyone in the world who could stare down a room full of doctors, listen to every damning word, and still smirk with that defiant glint in his eye, as if to say, *watch me*, it was Logan Vaughn.

If fate were a script carved in stone, he was the one who would take a hammer to it. If time had a course, he was the storm that could bend it. If destiny had a plan, he was the flaw in its design.

Logan Vaughn had reached his limit with adhering to the rules; he realized that rules needed to be rewritten.

Logan's face broke into a smile, his forehead pressing against Adrian's, their noses brushing. "Good. Because I'm not going anywhere. Not now, not ever."

And in that quiet, tangled moment, they rewrote the story Adrian had been preparing to end, the pages of his life no longer filled with farewells but with beginnings.

For a long moment, they stayed on the floor, tangled in each other, their lips meeting in slow, unhurried kisses. The air around them seemed to hum, a quiet melody of breath and heartbeat, the echoes of their words still reverberating through the space between them. The weight of everything they had just unearthed settled around them, not crushing, but grounding, like roots digging deeper into the earth.

The axis of their relationship shifted beneath them, the ground both unsteady and solid.

After a while, Adrian pulled back, his cheeks flushed, his eyes rimmed with red but clear. He wiped his face, a soft, almost shy smile curling his lips as he looked at Logan. "We're going to be late for our date," he said, his voice warm and edged with a hint of teasing.

Logan's lips curved into a mischievous smile, his eyes bright. "I think they can hold our table. It's not every day a man gets to unpack his death duffel with the love of his life."

A laugh burst from Adrian, fresh and unexpected, the sound filling the room with light. He nudged Logan's chest, his touch both playful and gentle. "You're impossible."

"Yeah," Logan agreed, still grinning. "But you love me anyway."

Adrian stood, extending a hand toward Logan. Their fingers intertwined, and Logan let himself be pulled up, the connection between them a quiet promise.

"Help me put it all away," Adrian said, his voice steady, the strength beneath it woven with vulnerability. "And then we'll head out?"

They moved together through the quiet, their actions unhurried but deliberate. Logan handled the photographs with care, his fingers brushing over the worn edges as he placed them back into the duffel bag. Adrian lingered over each item, his touch a mix of reverence and relief.

When they had nearly finished, Adrian's hand tightened around the black hoodie. He looked at Logan, a question in his eyes, and then he slipped it over his head. The fabric slid over his skin, its softness settling around him like armor. It didn't matter that they were heading to an upscale restaurant with white tablecloths and candlelit corners. The hoodie wasn't about appearance; it was a statement. A reminder that he was still here, still fighting.

Logan didn't need to say anything. His expression softened, understanding threading through his features. He reached out, smoothing the hoodie over Adrian's chest, his fingers tracing the faded letters, lingering on the worn seams. His touch was gentle, a brush of warmth against the fabric, against the heartbeat beneath.

Dinner was easy, an upscale restaurant where Adrian's hoodie drew a few sideways glances. Neither of them cared. The soft hum of conversation and candlelight wrapped around their private table, offering them a small world of their own.

Logan noticed the way Adrian held himself, the subtle hesitance in his movements, the way his shoulders hunched as if bracing for something unseen. He avoided casual touches, his hands always finding something else to do—folding his napkin, tracing the edge of his glass.

Logan waited until the waiter took their orders, then reached across the table, hooking his hand with Adrian's. He watched as Adrian's eyes flicked down, landing on the tattoo inked into Logan's wrist—the lifesaver symbol that was as much a reminder as it was a promise. For a moment, Adrian seemed lost in thought, his gaze lingering before his lips pulled into a small, bashful grin. He squeezed Logan's hand, but Logan could see the flicker of anxiety behind his eyes.

Adrian still feared he might run again, that the love they'd rebuilt could crumble in a single moment. Logan's leaving had left scars, invisible but deep, and even as Adrian tried to bury that fear, it lingered, heavy and unshakable. Logan wanted to say something, anything to reassure him, but for now, he let their clasped hands speak for him. He wasn't going anywhere.

They shared a meal that stretched into laughter, teasing, and even dessert—Logan couldn't resist ordering something rich and indulgent, even though he'd eaten until he could barely move. By the time they reached the car, Logan felt both full and light, as if the weight he'd carried for so long had finally started to lift. He couldn't remember the last time he'd eaten so well, or enjoyed food so much. Adrian had been right—he needed this. He needed *him*.

As Logan slid into the driver's seat, he discreetly sent Dean a quick text, letting him know they were on their way. Shoving the phone back into his pocket, he looked over at Adrian, a grin spreading across his face without him even realizing it.

Adrian noticed immediately, his eyebrows arching in suspicion. "Why are you smiling like that?" he asked, narrowing his eyes playfully.

"Me?" Logan said, feigning innocence, though his grin only widened.

"Yeah, *you*. You look like a little boy who's up to no good," Adrian chuckled, shaking his head.

Logan couldn't hold back his laugh. He leaned across the console, cupping Adrian's face in his hand and kissing him deeply, as if the act itself could explain his mood better than words. Only the thought of where they were headed pulled him away, his lips lingering for a moment before he started the car. Adrian watched him, his expression softening, though the curiosity never left his eyes.

Ten minutes later, they pulled up outside the club, the neon lights painting the street in streaks of color. Adrian looked at Logan, surprise written all over his face. "What are we doing here?" he asked, but Logan was already out of the car, leaving Adrian no choice but to follow.

"Partying," Logan said simply, flashing his phone screen at Adrian. A text from Dean glowed briefly, instructing them to head to the bar.

Logan held Adrian's hand as they navigated the crowded club, weaving through the crush of bodies and the thrum of loud, bass-heavy music. When Logan spotted Dean with a group of people, he glanced at Adrian, watching for his reaction. He saw the exact moment Adrian recognized the faces in the crowd—his friends, the people he hadn't seen much of since everything had started. Confusion flickered across Adrian's face, and Logan leaned close, his lips brushing against Adrian's ear so he could speak over the noise.

"I heard you've been a little less social lately," Logan explained. "So I teamed up with Dean to fix it. He invited them all." His lips grazed Adrian's ear again, this time in a kiss, before pulling back.

Adrian's grin blossomed like the first light of dawn after a long, dark night. As he approached the group, Logan's eyes caught a flicker, a shimmering spark in Adrian's gaze as he warmly greeted his friends. It was a light so radiant, so full of life, that it seemed to draw Logan in, pulling at his heart with an irresistible tenderness. Gratitude surged through him just to witness Adrian alive in that precious moment. He had helped create this moment, and seeing Adrian happy, truly happy, made him feel whole in a way he hadn't in years.

Adrian danced, and Logan danced with him. On the crowded dance floor, Logan wrapped his arms around Adrian, holding him close, not caring who saw them. Nothing else mattered—not the fleeting glances, not the clamor surrounding them, not the heavy shadow of Adrian's illness that lingered brightly in the air yet remained hushed. All that mattered was this moment, and Logan was determined to hold onto it.

At some point, Logan noticed Dean at the bar, his face illuminated by the glow of his phone. He was grinning like an idiot, his fingers flying across the screen as he texted. Logan smirked, leaning closer to Adrian to point it out. "I think your roommate's got it bad," he murmured. Adrian laughed, nodding in agreement, though neither of them asked why Dean hadn't brought the mystery girl along.

Later in the night, Logan and Adrian found themselves tucked away at the bar, a quiet pocket in the otherwise lively club. Adrian sat perched on a stool, his posture slightly relaxed, though his movements betrayed the quiet fatigue setting in. Logan stood behind him, arms wrapped loosely around Adrian's waist, Adrian's head resting over his chest. It wasn't just a gesture of affection, it was grounding, anchoring both of them to the moment.

Adrian had taken a few breaks throughout the night, slipping away from the dance floor whenever his legs began to falter or the strain became too much. Logan hadn't minded in the slightest. If anything, those quiet pauses allowed him to savor moments like this, to hold Adrian close and feel the warmth of him against his skin.

Logan wasn't the only one watching over Adrian. Every one of Adrian's friends had their eyes on him, though they did it subtly, with the kind of quiet care born of love and concern. They paid close attention to how Adrian moved, when he paused, and when his laughter faltered, making sure to never let the shadow of his illness grow too heavy. No one said anything directly; there was an unspoken agreement to let Adrian enjoy the night without the weight of their worry, but their presence was a safety net, a silent act of solidarity.

Adrian closed his eyes, letting himself be lulled by the steady rhythm of Logan's heartbeat. It was a sound that anchored him, more comforting than the thrum of the music or the chatter of the crowd. With every beat, Adrian felt a sense of calm he hadn't known in years.

With a sigh that carried both release and longing, Adrian laced his fingers through Logan's and pressed a quiet kiss against his arm.

Logan drew him closer, answering with the gentle weight of his embrace, his lips brushing the crown of Adrian's head. In that touch lived the memory of battles fought, wrong turns endured, and the relentless pull that had carried him back here. All the pain, all the choices, all the restless searching, every fragment of it had carved the path to this man, to this moment.

"You wanna go home, Lo?" Adrian asked softly.

"Yeah," Logan murmured, his eyes closing. "But only if you want to."

"I do," Adrian replied, his voice warm and steady. "Come on."

Hand in hand, they wove through the crowd, stopping to say their goodbyes to Adrian's friends. Logan spotted Dean, who was beaming at his phone as he texted, "We'll be at the hotel tonight, so bring her to the apartment. Stop being a jerk and just texting her, take her out, and apologize to her for not bringing her tonight." He said over the music. Dean blushed, gazing at him in confusion, and nodded.

Logan could see the lightness in Adrian's step, the genuine joy that lingered despite the ever-present shadow of his illness. As they walked out into the night, Logan squeezed Adrian's hand, silently promising himself that he would keep making moments like this for both of them.

The drive to Adrian's house was silent. Once there, Adrian hurried through his home, collecting a small bag of necessities before rejoining Logan in the car and driving to the hotel. The city lights flickered outside the car, but neither of them seemed to notice; they were lost in the glow of the night they'd just shared.

At the hotel, Logan stopped at the reception desk to retrieve another key card. He handed it to Adrian without much ceremony, but the gesture spoke volumes. It was more than a card; it was trust, an invitation, and a quiet promise that Adrian belonged in his space. Adrian took it with a grateful expression, pocketing it before following Logan to the elevator.

Once inside the suite, the weight of the evening seemed to melt away. Logan moved toward the bathroom and began filling the hot tub, the sound of water bubbling to life filling the air. There wasn't much need for conversation; the kind of connection they shared didn't require words. As the tub filled with warm, inviting water, Logan stripped down and slipped in, the heat wrapping around him like a second skin. Adrian joined him, settling into the tub behind Logan.

Without hesitation, Logan leaned back, pressing his body against Adrian's, his head resting just beneath Adrian's chin. Adrian's arms encircled him, and Logan let his hands drift to cover Adrian's, their fingers lacing together under the water. The warmth of the hot tub mingled with the warmth of Adrian's embrace, and Logan felt a happiness so profound it almost startled him. How had he ever walked away from this? How had he ever thought he could live without Adrian?

Logan tilted his head slightly, brushing his lips against Adrian's chest, and the simple act made his heart swell. Adrian tightened his hold on him, his arms steady and grounding, as if he, too, was afraid to let go.

"Thank you for tonight, Lo," Adrian murmured, his voice soft but filled with emotion.

"You're welcome," Logan whispered, his eyes gently closing as he allowed himself to bask in that moment. "Your friends... they're amazing. They stayed with you through so much. You shouldn't let them go."

Logan reached for one of Adrian's hands, lifting it to his lips and pressing a gentle kiss to it. Adrian's breath caught for a moment, and then he nodded, resting his chin lightly on the top of Logan's head. He didn't say anything, but the way his arms were around Logan spoke louder than words ever could.

Logan felt Adrian's hard length pressing against his back, a quiet testament to the pull between them. He smiled to himself, his own body reacting in much the same way. It felt good, grounding, to know Adrian wanted him too, that the connection between them wasn't just something he imagined.

Sex lingered as an unspoken truth between them. The last time Logan had left things unsaid, it led to devastating heartbreak that shattered them. He was determined not to repeat that mistake, unwilling to let silence create another chasm of pain. Yet, sex had become complicated, especially given the intense emotions it stirred in Adrian. Their last conversation about it—just yesterday, though it felt like ages ago—highlighted how delicate this topic was for Adrian, revealing the intricacies involved.

He leaned back into Adrian's embrace, letting the warmth of the water and the strong arms around him ease his thoughts. Logan could have stayed like this forever, wrapped in Adrian's arms, safe and whole in a way he hadn't felt in years.

And yet, forever wasn't guaranteed.

Sex wasn't the priority, not now. Yes, he wanted Adrian—he *always* wanted him—but this wasn't just about desire. What they were rebuilding was fragile, and Logan knew trust came first. To complicate things with sex before they'd fully regained that foundation could jeopardize everything they were working toward. And then there was the haunting thought that Logan couldn't escape, the one that clutched at his chest like a rising tide: *What if we don't get forever?*

The reality of Adrian's illness loomed, its shadow darker than anything Logan could bear to acknowledge. He knew the truth of what was coming—pain, weakness, the inevitable march of time running out. Adrian didn't want to spend his last days in a hospital, but Logan also knew that the disease would soon make every moment more unbearable than the last. He tried to stay positive, never letting those fears spill out where Adrian could see them, but they crept in during quiet moments like this, flooding him with helplessness.

He thought of the last two years—the six months he'd spent numbing himself with Zack, trying to drown the ache of leaving Adrian behind. And now here they were, Adrian's time slipping through his fingers, and Logan was desperate to hold onto every second he had left. If only he'd come back sooner. If only he'd stayed. Maybe things could have been different.

A tear fell, warm against the cooler air above the water, followed by a whimper from his lips. Adrian's hand, gentle and familiar, brushed against his cheek. "Lo," Adrian said softly, his voice barely audible over the gentle bubbling of the hot tub. "Are you crying?"

Logan turned in Adrian's arms without answering, wrapping himself around the man he loved with a desperation he couldn't hide. He held him as tightly as he could, burying his face against Adrian's neck, his breath shaky and uneven. Adrian said nothing for a long moment, just held him, his hands skimming over Logan's back in soothing strokes.

Then Adrian kissed him. Softly, lightly, again and again. He pressed his lips to Logan's temple, his cheek, his jaw, each kiss a quiet reassurance that he was there, that Logan wasn't alone. Logan clung to him, his panic subsiding bit by bit under Adrian's steadying presence, until he could breathe again.

Silence thickened around them, dense as the tide, swollen with unspoken fears and the brittle shape of hope. Adrian didn't ask what Logan was thinking; he didn't need to. Instead, he leaned in, his lips brushing over Logan's cheek, a silent promise in his touch.

"I'm right here, Lo," Adrian whispered, his voice resolute despite the heaviness in the air. "We're here. Right now. We're hoping. We'll grow old and gray, remember?" He echoed the tender words Logan had whispered to him mere hours ago, carrying them like a delicate promise against the backdrop of uncertainty.

Logan nodded against him, his arms tightening around Adrian as if he could keep him from slipping away. For now, it was enough to hold him, to feel the strength of his heartbeat against his own, and to let the love between them speak louder than words.

Logan took a shaky breath, his hand coming up to cup Adrian's face, his thumb brushing over the strong line of his jaw. His eyes locked with Adrian's, intense and filled with a storm of emotions. He was ready to say it: to tell Adrian never to give up on him again, to beg him to fight, to rail against the quiet surrender that had seeped into Adrian's life long before the cancer could take him. Logan's anger wasn't directed at Adrian, not really; it was aimed at the illness that had already taken so much, at the way it had driven Adrian to retreat from the world. But just as he opened his mouth, he saw it.

A single drop of blood slid down from Adrian's nose, bright against his skin.

"Damn it," Logan gasped, a wave of panic crashing through him. He snatched a soft towel from the edge of the tub, his frantic movements causing the water's surface to ripple and dance violently. With urgency, he pressed the fabric against Adrian's nose, his heart pounding in his chest. "You're bleeding," he stammered, his voice barely a whisper, trembling as the chilling grip of fear constricted around him, threatening to suffocate his resolve.

Adrian blinked in astonishment, his demeanor inscrutable, a façade of tranquility that unnerved Logan. It was as if the chaos around them held no sway over him. "It's nothing," Adrian murmured, his voice a steady stream beneath the harsh reality of the crimson stains blossoming across the towel. For a fleeting moment, he peeled it away, before hastily pressing it back to his wounded nose. "I don't even feel it, Lo. It's just... nothing," he insisted, as if trying to convince not only his lover but perhaps himself of that chilling detachment.

Logan's eyes bore into Adrian's, his worry sharp and unrelenting. It was on the tip of his tongue to insist they go to the hospital, to demand that Adrian stop brushing this off like it didn't matter. The doctor had warned him about nose and gum bleeds, bruises, fatigue, bone pain, and all the various other symptoms that might creep in, but knowing didn't make it any easier to see.

When the bleeding finally slowed, Logan scooped water from the tub in his hands and gently cleaned Adrian's face. His touch was tender, as if he were trying to wash away more than just the blood—trying to erase the fear, the helplessness, the reminder of Adrian's fragility. He whispered reassurances to himself more than to Adrian, a quiet litany of *the doctor warned about this, it's normal, it's fine.*

Adrian's hands gently rose to cradle Logan's face, grounding him with a tender steadiness. He leaned in softly, his lips brushing against Logan's in a kiss that was both delicate and insistent, a quiet, irenic touch to chase away the phantoms of fear. With each kind press, Adrian sought to dissolve the trembling hurt within Logan. Gradually, the tension melted away as Logan surrendered, allowing himself to be enveloped by Adrian's warm embrace, finding solace in the comfort of his touch.

When the water cooled and their bodies began to chill, they stepped out of the tub. Logan dried Adrian off, his hands lingering on his shoulders, his back, as if afraid to let him go. Adrian mirrored the gesture, his eyes soft and watchful as he dried Logan's skin, neither of them speaking.

They crawled into bed together, their movements slow and almost ritualistic. Logan wrapped himself around Adrian, pulling him close, his head resting against Adrian's chest as he listened to the steady rhythm of his heartbeat. The sound soothed him, grounding him in the present moment. Adrian's arms tightened around him, his hand gently running through Logan's hair.

The next day, they sat in the quiet hum of the doctor's office, the faint sunlight streaming through the blinds doing little to ease the tension that clung to the air. Adrian sat still, his hands clasped in his lap, his face calm but pale. Logan, on the other hand, was a bundle of restless energy, his knee bouncing uncontrollably, his hand occasionally running through his hair.

The doctor, a woman with sharp eyes, looked at them both with a measured expression. She and her team had been in close contact with the team in Seattle that Logan had reached out to, and the two groups of doctors had worked tirelessly, running tests and poring over Adrian's case. Now, she sat before them, her voice steady but tinged with the kind of gravity that came from years of delivering life-altering news.

"We've reviewed everything extensively," the doctor began, glancing at the notes in front of her. "And after careful discussion with the team in Seattle, we've determined that Adrian is a candidate for the experimental treatment."

Logan exhaled audibly, relief washing over him as he reached for Adrian's hand, squeezing it tightly. Adrian's lips twitched into a faint smile, though his eyes remained fixed on the doctor, cautious, waiting for the other shoe to drop.

The doctor continued, "The experimental treatment will take place in Seattle, and we'll need to get you there as soon as possible. We have determined that you'll be conducting all of the treatment there. But I need to be upfront with both of you, Adrian, the cancer has progressed significantly. It's more advanced than we would have hoped for when considering this type of program."

Logan's grip on Adrian's hand tightened involuntarily, his heart sinking at the words. "Wh-what..." he started, his voice breaking slightly. "What do you mean by advanced?"

The doctor's gaze softened as she addressed Logan's question. "Adrian waited a long time before seeking treatment," she said gently. "I understand there were personal reasons, but that delay allowed the cancer to progress to a stage where it is more aggressive and harder to treat."

Adrian's head dipped slightly, a flicker of guilt crossing his face. Logan's stomach churned at the thought of those months when Adrian had been fighting this alone, retreating from the world instead of reaching for help. Logan fought back the urge to speak, sensing this wasn't the moment for reproach.

"However," the doctor continued, "despite the advanced stage, your overall health and age work in your favor. You're still a candidate for remission, and the experimental treatment gives us a real chance. But the first step is to start chemotherapy immediately. Our goal is to get the cancer into remission before moving forward with the next phase."

"What does the first phase look like?" Adrian asked, his gaze meeting the doctor's.

"You'll begin chemotherapy," the doctor explained. "It will be intensive and aggressive. You'll experience fatigue, nausea, and a suppressed immune system, among other side effects. The chemo will weaken your body, but it's necessary to target the cancer cells. Once remission is achieved, the

Seattle team will take over with the experimental program. That phase might involve targeted therapy, bone marrow transplant, and, if necessary, high-dose chemo."

Adrian nodded slowly, absorbing the information. "How soon do we start?"

"Immediately," she spoke. "I've talked with the team in Seattle, and the experimental program wants you at their facility as fast as possible. They've reviewed your case, and given the advanced stage of your leukemia, they believe it's critical to begin treatment immediately. They're prepared to admit you as soon as you arrive."

Logan's chest tightened. He'd known the situation was dire, but hearing the words spoken aloud, hearing how little time they had left to act, made it all feel unbearably real. He turned to Adrian, searching his face for any sign of hesitation or fear.

Adrian's expression remained calm, but Logan could see the weariness in his eyes—the kind of exhaustion that came from carrying a burden too heavy for too long. Slowly, Adrian looked at Logan, offering a small smile that didn't quite reach his eyes. "We'll do this," he said quietly, his voice steady despite the weight of his words.

Logan reached for Adrian's hand, his grip firm and full of determination. "We're doing this," he echoed, his voice raw but resolute. "Together."

The doctor slid a folder across the desk, filled with detailed instructions about the chemo schedule, dietary needs, and side effect management. "Adrian," the doctor said gently, "this is going to be a difficult journey. You'll need support—physically and emotionally. And Logan," she added, turning her attention to him, "you'll need to take care of yourself as well. Caregiving is as much a challenge as treatment."

Logan nodded, his gaze never leaving Adrian. "I'm not going anywhere," he said, his voice firm, leaving no room for doubt.

As they left the office, the weight of the diagnosis and the plan ahead pressed heavily on both of them. Logan didn't wait until they were in private to pull Adrian into a tight embrace. "I've got you," he murmured into Adrian's ear, his voice cracking slightly. "We've got this."

Adrian didn't say anything for a long moment, simply leaning into Logan's embrace. When he finally spoke, his voice was soft but certain. "As long as you're with me, Lo... I'll fight."

"Hope. Old and gray, remember?"

"I remember."

On the way back, Logan couldn't stop smiling, the kind of grin that stretched wide and refused to fade. He held Adrian's hand the entire way, as if letting go would break the fragile thread of hope they'd just been given. His voice was light, full of unbridled joy, as he called Ada Mae to share the news with her. She screamed with happiness on the other end of the line, her excitement infectious. It wasn't the end of the road; it wasn't even close, but it was the beginning, and that was enough to make Logan feel like the world had tilted back into place.

When they got to the house, Dean was waiting for them, and Logan barely got the words out before Dean lost his mind. His reaction was everything: arms thrown around Adrian in a tight hug, his voice loud and cracking with emotion. Logan was almost certain he caught the glimmer of tears in Dean's eyes, though Dean turned his head quickly enough to hide it.

"There's a chance, man, a real chance," Dean said, releasing Adrian just to hug him all over again. "You need to call your parents. And Tom. And Oz... and everyone," he added, rattling off their friends' names while Adrian laughed.

"I will, I will," Adrian promised, his voice lighter than it had been in weeks. He turned to Logan, his expression softening. "It's Friday tomorrow, so I'm going to my parents' for dinner. Tradition... kind of," he shrugged.

Logan's gray eyes met his, already knowing what Adrian was going to ask.

"I'll tell them then," Adrian added, his voice quieter. "Not over the phone. Would you come with me?"

"Absolutely," Logan replied without hesitation, leaning in to kiss him lightly. "I'll book us a flight for Saturday. Or maybe late Friday night? Sounds good?"

"Yeah," Adrian agreed, his hand tightening slightly around Logan's.

Dean, who had been scrolling through his phone, looked up. "You guys staying over?" he asked.

"Maybe. Why?" Adrian asked, turning to him but still holding onto Logan's hand.

"I was thinking," Dean started, his tone casual but his eyes serious. "If you're leaving after dinner with your parents, you won't have time to say goodbye to everyone. Maybe I'll invite some of the guys over tonight?"

"Yeah, tell them to come," Logan said, already pulling out his phone. Adrian smiled at both of them, the heaviness of the past days easing for just a moment, replaced by the warmth of the people who loved him.

Dean and Logan often bickered and teased, but beneath it all was a budding friendship. They had grown closer with each passing day, and Adrian could see that Dean was warming up to Logan.

Adrian nodded slowly, uncertainty flickering in his eyes as Dean continued talking on the phone in the other room. Logan saw it, the way his lips pressed together, as if he were trying to bury the weight of the word *goodbye*. Did Dean mean it as a farewell for a few years, until the treatments were over? Or as something heavier, something final, whispered into the cracks of a fragile hope? Adrian didn't ask, and Logan didn't dare.

While Dean called Adrian's closest friends to share the news and gather them for a farewell evening, Logan and Adrian withdrew to his room, beginning the delicate task of sorting through Adrian's possessions and packing them up. Logan moved with quiet efficiency, tucking clothes and belongings into a suitcase, while Adrian drifted to the back of his closet, his hands brushing against forgotten corners of his life. Then he froze.

"I completely forgot about it..." Adrian murmured, his voice catching on a faint tremor of pain as he pulled something from the shadows of the closet.

Logan glanced up from where he was zipping Adrian's guitar into its case. "What is it?" he asked, crossing the room to Adrian, his curiosity softened by concern.

Adrian turned, holding a small black box in his hands. His fingers trembled slightly as he passed it to Logan. "It's yours," he mumbled.

Logan's brow furrowed as he opened the box, and his breath hitched. "My GoPro..." he whispered, cradling the small camera like a relic from another life. The weight of it in his hands was both familiar and foreign, a piece of himself he hadn't realized he'd left behind.

"I forgot about it," Adrian admitted quietly, his voice barely above a whisper. "I found it in the cabin. After you left." The words hung in the air, suspended like raindrops before a storm. "I couldn't leave it there. It felt... wrong. Like abandoning a part of you." He hesitated, his throat moving as he swallowed a truth too heavy to carry. "But I never looked through the pictures. It felt too personal. Too much like trespassing on something... that is yours."

The spiraling tangles of guilt and longing swirl around Logan like a relentless storm, each knot tighter than the last, suffocating him, refusing to let him move forward. He managed a shaky laugh, trying to lighten the moment. "Thanks for not throwing it into the ocean," he tittered. "Or setting it on fire."

Logan had also set aside his love of photography, which once brought him joy. From the moment he first picked up a camera, he enjoyed capturing special moments. His passion for the ocean led him to take pictures of the scenery there, and he fondly recalls the pleasure of having his GoPro along during those adventures. Though he'd never pursued photography professionally or shared these videos widely—posting only the occasional photo—he simply enjoyed having those memories recorded.

Adrian smiled faintly, but his eyes stayed on Logan's hands as they clutched the camera. Logan grabbed his phone, opening the app that synced with the GoPro. "I don't even remember what's on it," he admitted, though his voice betrayed a mix of curiosity and dread.

Minutes later, the GoPro was plugged into the charger, and they were lying together on Adrian's bed, their bodies close, the phone screen glowing between them. As Logan scrolled through the photos and videos, the past unfurled before them like an old, forgotten film reel.

The videos blinked to life. Sun-drenched waves curled in slow motion, a cascade of crystalline blue. Logan's laughter echoed softly, the sound carried by the wind, and Adrian's voice followed—deep, warm, the kind of tone that had always felt like home. The screen captured their world as it had been—raw and beautiful, drenched in sunlight and the golden blur of happiness.

There they were, standing on a cliffside, the wind wild in their hair. Adrian's arm looped around Logan's waist, and Logan's face was a study in ease—eyes closed, head resting on Adrian's shoulder awkwardly because of the height difference, a moment of surrender caught forever in pixels.

Adrian's breath shivered beside him, and Logan turned, their faces close, the past dancing across their skin. Adrian's eyes reflected the screen's glow, but beneath it was something ancient and aching—a love that had survived, hidden beneath layers of scar tissue and silence.

Logan swallowed, his voice catching. "We were happy, weren't we?"

"I've never been happier than when I've been with you."

More images and videos were loaded into the app; they were snapshots of a time that felt impossibly distant and heartbreakingly vivid all at once. Waves crashing against golden shores. Their boards bobbing in the water, sunlit and alive. Faces lit with laughter, caught in moments of bliss so pure it seemed untouched by time.

Adrian's chest tightened as he watched, his heart twitching painfully with each image. He remembered every moment, every flicker of joy, but seeing it now—seeing them—it felt like a gut punch. They were so different then. Not just younger, though that was part of it. It was in their faces, their eyes, the way they carried themselves. They looked weightless, untethered, as if the world had belonged to them.

Logan felt it acutely, the realization descending upon him like a freight train—sharp, unyielding, and inescapable. He glimpsed his own reflection woven into those precious memories, particularly the way he had always gazed at Adrian. It was as if he had been smacked in the face by a truth he'd long been blind to, or perhaps too frightened to confront. He had loved Adrian in those moments; he had always loved him. It was inscribed on his very being. The way his eyes sparkled when Adrian smiled, how he laughed as if Adrian's voice were the sweetest melody to ever grace his ears, how the camera lingered on Adrian, capturing him as though he were the sun, the focal point of Logan's universe.

And Adrian. Oh, sweet God, Adrian. The warmth of his gaze trained on Logan through the screen, reflecting back with an intensity reminiscent of someone looking at the ocean—filled with awe, love, and reverence, as if embracing a vast, beautiful enigma that defied comprehension. Every facet of Adrian—his voice, his body language—sang in perfect harmony with Logan. They were entwined in synchrony, so much so that even the gentlest touch, the most innocent brush of fingers, ignited an undeniable charge, transforming the mundane into something profoundly electric.

Logan's throat tightened, his heart pounding painfully as the weight of what he'd done pressed down on him. He'd walked away from that. From *this*. From a love so profound it had been carved into the very fabric of their lives. He'd left Adrian behind, leaving him to wake up alone in that tiny cabin in Australia, with nothing but an empty room and a heart that was about to break.

And now... now the reality crashed down: time was slipping away. Logan's chest ached, heavy with the weight of urgency. It felt as though moments were cascading through their fingers like countless grains of sand, and every fleeting second they had left together transformed into a fierce struggle against the approaching inevitability.

Logan turned to Adrian, his eyes wet, his voice barely a whisper. "I was the stupidest man alive," he said, the words breaking as they left him. "I gave you up, and I don't even know how to forgive myself for that."

Adrian met his gaze, his expression soft but filled with an ache of its own. He reached out, his hand brushing against Logan's cheek. "You're here now, Lo," he said quietly, his voice steady despite the crack in it. "That's all I've ever wanted."

Logan pressed his forehead to Adrian's, his breath uneven, his body bracing itself against the tide of emotions threatening to overwhelm him. He held onto Adrian as if he might vanish into thin air, his arms locked around him, believing that alone could keep him safe. The weight of the past sat between them, and Logan made a silent vow: to fight for the time they had left. Even if it wasn't forever. Even if it was only now.

They continued scrolling through the footage, Logan's thumb swiping slowly as the images unfolded on the screen. There were videos of them paddling in the ocean, laughing as they splashed at each other, waves rolling beneath them. Back then, Logan's hair was long, wild, and sun-bleached, just as Adrian's was golden from spending countless hours in the sun. Now, Adrian's hair had darkened, returning closer to its natural shade, a subtle reminder of the time he had spent away from the water.

He watched Adrian's face as the memories flickered across the screen, afraid he might miss something. Adrian's gaze held a steady warmth, his expression gentle and inviting. Yet, beneath the surface, a subtle glimmer flickered, an elusive blend of nostalgia and bittersweet sadness that resonated deeply with Logan, stirring echoes of his own past.

Most of the videos were from those last few days in paradise, in the stunning resort Adrian had brought Logan for his birthday. The screen lit up with images of them, two men in love, carefree and utterly enchanted by each other. They looked like a couple on their honeymoon, the glow of happiness unmistakable. There was Logan lounging in the pool, his head tilted back as the water reflected sunlight across his face, when suddenly Adrian appeared in the frame, all radiant muscle and tanned skin. Adrian tackled Logan from behind, laughing as he kissed his neck, his lips lingering like he wanted to preserve the moment forever. There were clips of them on the beach, their arms tangled as they kissed passionately, the ocean stretching endlessly behind them.

And then, the camera shifted to Logan alone. He was surfing, cutting through the waves with grace and precision. Water droplets splashed the lens, distorting the image, but nothing could dull the brilliance of his smile. Logan's focus, his pure joy in the moment, was palpable even through the tiny screen.

"You're so good," Adrian murmured, his voice soft and almost reverent as he watched Logan carve through the water on the screen. "You have to go back."

Logan turned to him, his smile tinged with something bittersweet. "Only with you, babe," he joked, though the teasing tone couldn't mask the depth of his emotions. He swiped to the next video, but his voice turned quieter, more reflective. "God... that was such a good time," he whispered, glancing at Adrian. "I... it took me a long time to be able to open these photos. But when I finally did, it never failed to make me feel better—and worse."

Adrian nodded, understanding all too well. "Better because you could escape for a while," he whispered softly, his fingers gliding gently over Logan's, resonating with the unspoken feelings that he comprehended deeply, knowing he experienced it all within himself. "And worse because... because it reminded you how good it was. And then reality hit you again."

Logan exhaled shakily, the memories heavy in his chest. "Exactly," he admitted, his voice breaking slightly. "It's like I'd remember every perfect moment, and then I'd wake up, and it was gone. You were gone."

Adrian cupped Logan's cheek, his hand warm and grounding. "It's over," he whispered. "We're together now. That's all that matters."

Logan nodded, though his throat tightened with unspoken emotion. He hesitated, his words catching before he finally spoke. "I've been thinking about it these last few days. If things had been the other way around... if you'd been the one to leave me..." He paused, drawing in a shaky breath. "I tried to imagine it, but I couldn't. I tried, Adrian. I pictured myself waking up in that cabin alone, and suddenly it hurt to breathe. It was... it was terrifying."

Adrian kissed him then, pressing their lips together. It was like a gentle tale coaxing Logan out of the tumultuous spiral of his own thoughts, as if each press were a note in a delicate symphony, pulsing with unspoken emotions and vivid sensations. Logan let the phone fall to the bed, his arms tightening around Adrian as he deepened the kiss. There was no urgency, no rush—just love, pure and overwhelming, pouring from one to the other.

When they pulled apart, Logan rested his forehead against Adrian's once more, his breathing heavy but calmer. They'd been switching roles these past few days, trading hope and despair like a fragile thread passing between them. When Logan's positivity waned, Adrian stepped in, steady and reassuring, until Logan found his footing again. It was a dance, and one they'd mastered without even realizing it.

"Logan Vaughn," Adrian whispered, his voice low and full of affection, his fingers threading through Logan's hair. "If you'd decided we were meant to be together, there wouldn't have been a damn thing I could do to stop you. I could have walked a million kilometers away from you, and you would've tracked me down and demanded an explanation."

Logan smiled faintly, his lips curving against Adrian's cheek as he listened.

"And no matter what I said," Adrian continued, his voice warm with amusement, "you'd argue your way right back into my life. You're Logan. You'd charm your way into winning that argument."

Logan let out a soft laugh, the sound vibrating against Adrian's skin. "Damn right I would," he affirmed, his smile widening as he kissed Adrian's temple. He knew that Adrian was trying, as always, to lighten the heavy mood. Adrian had a way of easing the weight of the world, even when it was his own shoulders bearing it. Logan reached and picked up the phone again. Together, they scrolled through the captured moments of their past, letting the glow of the screen fill the space between them with memories that were bittersweet and beautiful.

Later, as Adrian's friends began trickling into the house, the atmosphere shifted. The living room buzzed with life, the sound of laughter, clinking glasses, and easy banter filling the air. Logan stayed close to Adrian, sitting beside him on the couch, their hands often finding each other's between bouts of conversation. Each time their fingers intertwined, Adrian would glance at Logan, his eyes brimming with something so pure it made Logan's heart skip a beat. That look—like Logan was the most perfect thing Adrian had ever seen—never failed to send a flush of warmth across his cheeks and a surge of love through his chest.

Snacks and drinks passed from hand to hand as jokes flew between English and Hebrew, the occasional laughter leaving Logan grinning even when he didn't understand the words. Dean and Adrian took turns translating whenever the group got tired of switching languages, though Dean's translations often came with exaggerated dramatics that left everyone rolling their eyes.

Adrian chuckled and shook his head, glancing at Dean. "So... translating for Logan now, huh? Things really have changed."

Dean smirked and gave Adrian a playful shove. "Just doing it so I can take the Maserati for a spin."

"That's it?" Logan teased, digging into his pocket before tossing the keys to Dean. "There you go, big boy. You can drive the grown-up's car. Just be back by midnight." The room erupted into laughter, with the other guys cheering and teasing Dean.

"Fuck you, princess," Dean shot back with a smirk, the keys spinning in his hand.

Logan's phone buzzed in his pocket. "It's Ada Mae," he said. "I have to take this, baby," he added as he kissed his temple and then stood.

Cat-calling and whistling erupted in the room, with the guys making exaggerated kissing noises and saying, 'I love you, baby!' to one another, mimicking them. Adrian grabbed a couch cushion and hurled it at Sergi, muttering a curse in Hebrew while the others laughed.

In Adrian's bedroom, Logan answered the call, listening as Ada Mae detailed the logistics. The flight was booked for late Friday night, and the hospital in Seattle was ready to admit Adrian the moment they landed. Logan thanked her for the hundredth time, gratitude heavy in his voice, and he was glad he had already emailed human resources about the bonus check and raise to her salary. As he slipped his phone back into his pocket and turned to head back to the living room, the door opened, and Dean stepped in, leaning casually against it.

"We need to have a little talk," Dean announced, his tone calm but laced with something sharp.

Logan nodded as he pushed his phone deeper into his pocket. "Okay."

Dean's eyes, piercing and unrelenting, locked onto Logan's. "The only reason I forgave you is because you're the only one who could get Adrian to fight for his life," Dean began. "I tried for months to convince him to start treatment, but he wouldn't listen. Then you showed up, and now he's finally agreed. I was right, you're the only one who could get through to him."

Logan opened his mouth to speak, but Dean raised a hand, cutting him off. "But don't think for a second that I've forgotten what you've done to him. He may have forgotten what you did, but I haven't."

Logan's breath hitched, and he dropped his gaze to the floor as Dean continued. "Four times, Logan. Four times you've wrecked his life." Dean's voice cracked slightly, but he pressed on. "The first was when I flew to Australia to see him after you left. That wasn't my friend in that room, it was a shadow of him. He was losing his mind. At the beginning, he'd told me it was nothing more than a crush, but I knew better. I saw it the day we met you. He was gone for you, completely gone, and you..." Dean shook his head. "You left him. Then, two months later, he disappeared for three days. When he came back, he told me he'd gone to your wedding." Dean's voice grew quieter, but the edge in it was unmistakable. "He was wrecked, Logan. Tom and I had to scrape him back together. And then..."

Logan swallowed hard, his voice barely audible. "And then?"

Dean exhaled sharply, as if the memory itself was painful to recall. "Then I heard the song," he said. "It was brilliant, painful, beautiful, heartbreaking. But it was proof he wasn't okay. I filmed it, I put it on YouTube and Facebook, trying to maybe get to you, trying to make you realize what you've lost, and maybe try to get him some fame, some good things in his life. And when he turned down treatment? I knew it was because of you. And now..." Dean's eyes darkened. "The fourth time was the day you came back. He didn't think you ever would, and when you did, it tore him apart all over again. I saw it, the anger, the sadness, the stress. He's sick, Logan. And he's good at hiding it, but I know him better than anyone. He's sick, and if you leave him again..."

Dean stepped closer, his voice lowering to a dangerous whisper. "If you leave him after everything you've put him through, if you turn his world upside down again and abandon him while he's going through this hell, I swear to God, Logan, I'll hunt you down. I'll put a bullet in your head, and I'll do the time without a second thought."

Logan's jaw tightened, his chest aching as he looked up at Dean. "I won't leave him again," he said firmly, his voice steady despite the weight of Dean's words. "Never. I swear to you, Dean."

Dean studied him for a long moment before nodding, the fire in his gaze dimming slightly. "You better not," he muttered, stepping back toward the door. His voice softened as he added, "You know, it's good you're back. I haven't seen him this happy in a long time."

Logan smiled faintly and crossed the room, pulling Dean into a brief hug. "Thank you, Dean," he said quietly. "For sticking by him when I didn't."

Dean didn't say anything, just gave Logan a firm pat on the back before stepping out. Logan lingered for a moment, the weight of the conversation settling in his chest. Then he turned, took a deep breath, and went back to the living room to find Adrian. He was home now, and nothing would take him away again.

The late afternoon sun spilled gold over Tel Aviv's skyline, a soft shimmer that kissed the glass windows of Logan's hotel suite. He exhaled, steadying himself as he zipped up his suitcase. With a quiet nod to the empty room, he checked out, tossing his luggage into the back of the rental Maserati.

The drive was a blur of shifting blues—the sea stretching endlessly beside him, whispering in its ancient tongue. It had always been the witness to their story. The ocean had first carried Adrian to him in a rush of white foam and saving hands. It had been their playground, their church, their silent observer. And it had swallowed Logan whole when he left.

Now, it watched as he pulled into Adrian's street, the sun dipping just below the rooftops.

Inside, Adrian sat on the edge of his bed, his form bathed in the amber glow of early evening. The man who once carved waves with effortless grace now looked slightly more fragile, his illness a quiet undertow pulling at his strength. But his smile—it was still the same. It was still the lighthouse Logan had spent two years pretending not to see.

"You're wearing a suit, Lo?" Adrian's voice was warm, amused, as Logan set his suitcase down beside his.

"Yeah, but it's not my best one," Logan admitted, rubbing the back of his neck. "I packed in a hurry when I left Seattle. Didn't have much time to think."

Adrian's gaze softened. "You're overdressed," he murmured, the corner of his lips tugging up into a knowing smile.

"But we're going to your parents' place, right? Thought I should make a good impression."

"You don't have to wear a suit for that." Adrian's hands found Logan's tie, his fingers curling around the expensive, slick fabric, pulling him closer. "But damn, you look so good in one." His voice was a hushed tide lapping at Logan's skin.

The heat between them ignited like the sun meeting the horizon. A gasp escaped Logan's lips as Adrian tugged, their lips colliding in a kiss that tasted like longing.

Adrian's hand slid up Logan's neck, fingertips tracing old paths, rediscovering, relearning. Logan swore he could die in that moment, from the way Adrian whimpered against his skin, the way his breath ghosted over the pulse at his throat.

"How good?" Logan rasped, his voice caught somewhere between desperation and devotion.

"Really, really good," Adrian murmured, his lips grazing Logan's jaw. "Like I want to tear this suit off you right now."

A shudder ran through Logan, the air between them thick with heat, with history, with the magnetic pull that had never really let him go.

"Fuck," Logan exhaled, his forehead resting against Adrian's. "We have to go."

Adrian chuckled, pressing one last kiss to his lips before pulling away. "Yeah, we do."

Logan inhaled deeply, willing his heartbeat to steady. He stepped back, tugging off the suit pants and replacing them with dark jeans, leaving the dress shirt on. He tossed the jacket onto his suitcase before turning back to Adrian. "Okay. Ready?"

Adrian gave him a once-over, a soft smile playing on his lips. "You really didn't have to dress up. Dinner's just homey, comfortable. You could've worn sweats."

"I'm not going to wear sweats when I first meet your parents!" he said indignantly. "I still want to make a good impression."

"You will," Adrian said, pocketing his phone and wallet as they stepped out of the room. "You charm every living soul on this earth; you'll be fine."

Logan hesitated, the sea of unspoken fears rising in his throat. "They don't hate me?"

Adrian paused at the doorway, turning to face him fully. "They did," Adrian said softly, his gaze steady. "I told them what happened. About how you left. And they saw how I broke." There was no accusation in his voice, no bitterness—just the raw truth, weathered by time but never washed away. "But they also know what you meant to me. What you still mean to me." He reached for Logan's hand, his fingers warm despite the chill of old wounds. A gentle squeeze, a tether pulling Logan back from the drifting void he had spent two years lost in. "And my mom?" Adrian's lips twitched into something between fondness and amusement. "She's so excited to see you. Prepare yourself, because both of them are going to be extra embarrassing, and she probably cooked for an army."

Logan smirked as they stepped out of the house and into the car. Adrian slipped into the driver's seat without a word, muttering something about knowing the streets better and having a long drive ahead of them. Logan didn't argue. In truth, he was glad Adrian seemed at ease—glad he wasn't burdened by the weight of Logan meeting his family.

The engine hummed beneath them as they rolled through the streets, the city lights flickering against the windshield like reflections on the water. Logan glanced sideways at Adrian, tracing the familiar lines of his face, the quiet intensity in his eyes as he focused on the road. He looked... different. Maybe it was the illness, or maybe it was just time, but there was something heavier about him now, something Logan hadn't seen before.

"Will your brother be there too?" Logan asked after a stretch of silence.

"Yeah." Adrian's answer was clipped, his hands tightening slightly on the wheel.

Logan hesitated before pressing further. "Are things... better between you two?"

Adrian didn't answer right away. The silence between them stretched, thick like the deep sea before a storm. Logan remembered the first time he had heard the name *Alon*. It had been an accident—just a passing mention in a conversation Adrian had with his parents one night when they were still traveling together. That was the time Logan learned that Adrian had a younger brother.

"Not really," Adrian finally admitted. His voice was steady, but Logan could hear the undertow beneath it. "He enlisted not long ago. Same unit I was in."

Logan frowned. "Is that... good?" He searched Adrian's face for some clue, but Adrian's expression remained unreadable.

"Don't really know," Adrian muttered, taking a turn onto a narrower street. "We're not talking much. He's been even more resentful since I came back two years ago."

When Logan stumbled upon the fact that Adrian had a younger brother, his curiosity was piqued, and he started to inquire further. Logan, who had spoken of his own sisters and shared little anecdotes about them, found it surprising that Adrian had never mentioned his little brother before. Adrian elaborated on their strained relationship, revealing that Alon had made hurtful and homophobic comments after Adrian came out of the closet. This antagonistic sentiment was not new; even prior to that event, Alon had nurtured an underlying resentment and animosity toward

Adrian, feelings that only intensified and festered over the years, casting a long shadow over their brotherly bond.

Logan didn't miss the way Adrian's grip tightened just slightly on the wheel, the way his jaw tensed at the words. He wondered what exactly had happened in those two years Adrian had spent without him—what wounds had been left open, what bridges had burned beyond repair.

Adrian's eyes flickered for a moment, his mind clearly elsewhere. Maybe back in those first few months after Logan had left.

"He said some things," Adrian murmured. "When I moved back home. When I was... trying to get back on my feet... it took us, me, Dean, and Tom a few months to find an apartment, so I lived with my parents for those months."

Logan didn't ask, but Adrian told him anyway. "*Your fag friend ditched you,*" Adrian repeated the words Alon had told him.

It had been a mutter, a careless cut from Alon that had sliced deeper than he would ever understand. In the early months, Alon drifted through the house like a ghost, the echoes of his cruel words hanging heavy in the air. Adrian, heartbroken and desperate, felt the chill of Alon's indifference seep into the very walls, a palpable hatred that threatened to suffocate him. With each moment spent in that stifling atmosphere, Adrian felt as though he might choke, teetering on the edge of despair.

And then, months later, when Adrian had told his family about the cancer, when he had told them he wasn't planning to fight it, his brother had looked *relieved*.

It had hurt.

Logan clenched his fists in his lap. He wanted to say something, but what could he say? He had no right to be angry on Adrian's behalf, not when he had been the first blade in his back.

The rest of the drive was quiet. Logan watched the city lights blur past, their glow fading into something dimmer, rougher, as they moved away from the heart of Tel Aviv. The streets grew narrower, the buildings more worn, the sense of abandonment sinking into the very air around them.

"We're here." Adrian declared. His stomach clenched as he looked up at the six-story building before them. It wasn't pristine, wasn't grand, but it stood firm. The beige paint was streaked with time; the balconies were lined with mismatched chairs, wind chimes, and the soft glow of potted plants reaching for the night air.

That was, in the simplest and most innocent way imaginable, home.

It wasn't the world Logan had imagined for Adrian, not the one his mind had built in the absence of truth. But it was real. And it was Adrian's.

Logan's gaze flickered down the quiet street, where similar buildings stood side by side, like weathered sentinels guarding a lifetime of memories. Some looked newer, some older, but all bore the same quiet endurance. This place wasn't luxurious, far from it, yet it embodied the essence of simplicity, a simple life well-lived and modestly flourishing.

This was the space that had shaped Adrian—the winding streets, the sun-cracked corridors, the quiet corners that had once cradled his boyhood dreams. Here, the man Logan loved had first been stitched together by time and tenderness and grief. If this place had birthed a soul as fierce and tender as Adrian's, then somewhere beneath its ordinary skin, it must hold a whisper of something divine.

Then, he glanced back at the car.

The sleek, black Maserati gleamed under the flickering streetlight, a glaring, unwelcome guest in this world. The sight of it made his skin crawl. It felt like an intrusion, an arrogance, a testament to just how little he had understood.

Adrian was already climbing the steps, and Logan followed, though something began to press in his chest with every stride, a quiet storm gathering under his ribs. He had never truly seen the world Adrian had come from, not like this, not the bones of it, not the walls that had once echoed with his footsteps, or the corners that might still remember his laughter.

Were these the hallways Adrian had raced through as a boy, beach-sand clinging to his ankles and sea-salt water drying on his skin after long days spent chasing waves? Were these the same stairs he climbed after the war, when the world had grown heavier, when his soul had become older and more fragile, when the silence between breaths had changed shape? Had he once walked here with sunburned shoulders and lucent dreams in his eyes, only to return years later, not with hopes but with memories too vivid to forget and an unheeded threnody crying Logan's name?

And now Logan was stepping into that same space, into that same past, as someone who belonged.

And it awakened something in him—something cold yet familiar. He had always existed on the periphery of places, never truly immersed in them. He had always been the outsider; adrift and unanchored, the one who never truly fit in, never truly belonged. The one persistently ready to flee. The one who avoided attaching to anything significant until he met a pair of whisky-colored irises and full, luscious lips framed by stubble, igniting a desire to connect with the man standing before him.

In that first meeting, without understanding why, Logan wanted to be known. Wanted to be held still in someone's memory, in someone's hands. And somehow, impossibly, Adrian had looked at him—really looked—and loved everything scattered and unfinished within him. It was the kind of love that didn't ask for permission, didn't seek to fix, only to hold, and the weight of that kind of love—pure, wild, undeserved—was almost unbearable.

"Did you grow up here?" The question left Logan's lips before he could stop it, a desperate need gnawing at his insides. He wanted to see it all, wanted to map Adrian's childhood, to touch the places that had shaped him, to stand where he had once stood.

More than anything, he wanted to take Adrian back to *his* own childhood home. Show him the bed where he had lain awake, night after night, drowning in heartbreak. Show him the walls that had absorbed his screams, his sobs, his mistakes, the ones he had made when Adrian wasn't there. Show him the spot where he had crashed and burned, after fleeing from the other half of his soul and the one person he had loved wholeheartedly.

"Hm... yeah."

Adrian's response came softly, clipped at the edges, but it wasn't the word that struck Logan, it was the way Adrian turned his gaze, just slightly. There was a flicker there, quick but unmistakable: shame. And that single flash of it tore through Logan like a rip current, silent and brutal, leaving him breathless. Adrian, who had never once been ashamed of who he was. Adrian, who had loved him without apology, who had stood in the fullness of his truth even when the world offered no shelter. But here, now, with

Logan beside him on these narrow stairs, something inside him had curled into itself, and that unspoken shift shattered Logan.

At the top of the second floor, Adrian stopped in front of a door. He lifted his hand to knock, but before his fingers could reach the steel door, Logan moved. He stepped forward, closing the space between them, and pulled Adrian into his arms. Their bodies aligned as if made to carry each other. And the way Adrian softened in his hold—the way the tension dissolved from his shoulders like ice melting under summer sun—told Logan he had done the right thing. He could feel it, the quiet surrender, the way Adrian let him carry what had become too heavy.

"I love you," Logan whispered, the words barely formed on his lips, as if afraid to disturb the stillness. "We're together." He pressed a kiss into Adrian's hair, then gently lifted his face, cupping it with both hands. "You are my entire life. Do you hear me? We're together."

Adrian looked at him, and his bottom lip trembled, his lashes flickering, as though he could hold back the storm building behind his eyes by sheer will. He blinked rapidly, fighting back tears, nodding but unable to speak. Inside, his thoughts rushed like floodwater. *This place—this life—it's not glamorous. It's not the kind of story that fits into Logan's world.* How could he explain the ache in his chest, the way these walls made him feel like the hollow version of himself that he was in the days after Logan had left? Every stair creaked with memory. Every corner whispered loss. He didn't know how to tell Logan that sometimes his mind dragged him back to those hollow nights, and that no matter how far he had come, part of him still lived there.

But I've survived worse, he thought. *I survived wars. I survived absence. I grew up in a country where sirens sang louder than lullabies, where you learned to fall asleep without comfort, where fear carved its place beside you like a second shadow. A place where you learned to flee in a heartbeat, where you buried your friends long before their grandparents, where every song was sung from the ashes, stitched with the pain of being Jewish, of being hunted, of carrying generations of sorrow in your bones. A place where joy was fierce because it knew how quickly it could be silenced—where every celebration could end in a blast.* He had faced things that should have broken him, and they hadn't. But Logan, this love, this moment, it unmoored him in ways nothing else ever had.

Adrian didn't have the words, not now, not yet. So instead, he leaned in and kissed Logan, soft and fleeting, as if to tell his body what his heart already knew: Logan was here. With him. Real. And for now, that was enough. That was everything. All the things Adrian had once whispered to the waves, all the wishes he had never dared to say aloud, were standing right in front of him, holding him close.

After a moment, his breath steadying, a soft, almost dreamy smile touching his lips, Adrian lifted his hand and knocked on the door. Logan stood beside him, his hand resting on the small of Adrian's back, a quiet anchor, a silent promise: *I'm here. I'm not going anywhere.* In the next second, the door creaked open, and a woman stood before them. She appeared to be in her late fifties, petite and soft around the edges, with light brown hair falling in gentle waves down to her chest. The color was touched by time, but still carried a quiet grace. Large glasses framed striking green eyes, eyes filled with too many emotions at once, joy and sorrow colliding, twisting, folding into something raw.

And once she looked at them both, she slowly smiled. A smile that melted the years from her face. A smile that didn't quite reach her eyes, a smile that had carried too much pain for too many years, but then she pulled Adrian into her arms, murmuring words in Hebrew that Logan couldn't understand, though their meaning was clear enough. Logan stood back, watching as Adrian held her tightly, her short frame almost engulfed by him.

When she finally let Adrian go, she turned to Logan.

"Logan, this is my mom, Tammi. Mom, this..." he glanced at Logan, his gaze soaring with admiration and awe, "is *my* Logan."

She looked at him with sharp, assessing eyes, the green behind her glasses brimming with something he couldn't quite place. Then, she smiled—that same bittersweet, world-worn smile she had given at the door.

"Is nice very to meet you, Logan," she said, her accent thick, her voice warm but measured.

"So do you, Mrs. Leon," Logan replied, extending his hand.

Tammi ignored it entirely, and instead, she wrapped him in a hug. She smelled like chamomile and something sweet, like bread baking in an oven. There was warmth in the way she held him.

"No, no," she said, releasing him, her voice firmer now, the Hebrew shaping her words. She patted her chest lightly. "Tammi. I Tammi." She stepped back and waved them inside with a quick motion before closing the door behind them. "I to remember you from calls. Videos."

Logan swallowed. "I do too," he murmured, feeling suddenly small, like a boy meeting his best friend's parents for the first time, instead of a man standing in front of the mother of the love of his life.

Tammi smiled up at him, lifting her gaze. "You... tall, so tall! So big!" she laughed, the sound light and unfiltered. Then she turned to Adrian and said something in rapid Hebrew that made Adrian's face flush almost instantly.

"Mom," Adrian groaned, rubbing the back of his neck.

"What?" Logan asked, glancing between them, a crooked smile forming despite himself. The language barrier had a way of reminding him that, even now, he was still learning Adrian's world—one word, one look at a time.

"Tell him," Tammi nudged Adrian gently. "I... sorry, English for me," she added, motioning with her hand to suggest it wasn't her strong suit.

"That's okay. Really," Logan said quickly. "Thank you for welcoming me." Then, turning to Adrian, he added with a grin, "Okay, what did she say?"

Adrian hesitated, cleared his throat. "She said... that you're very, very handsome. And..." he paused, looking like he regretted every second of translating, "hot. That you seem like a good man. Impressive. A man's man. That I chose well."

Logan felt his cheeks grow warm, the compliment catching him off guard. He looked at Tammi and gave a sheepish smile. "Thank you, Tammi. I just... I hope there aren't hard feelings. About before. About how I left. I know I don't deserve how kind you're being, but I'm really grateful to be here."

"No. Adrian is to decide. Adrian love you, I love you,"

From the hallway, another figure appeared, and Logan automatically knew that this was Adrian's father. There was no doubt about it. He was an older, heavier version of Adrian, with the same strong build and sharp jawline. However, while Adrian's eyes were liquid whiskey warm and endless, his father's were black, with deep lines framing them. Whereas

Adrian's physique had always been lean, bulky, and tight with muscles, his father carried a heavier gut and a set of wide shoulders.

Logan straightened instinctively. "Hello, sir," he said, extending his hand. "I'm Logan Vaughn, Adrian's boyfriend. It's a pleasure to meet you."

The words tumbled from his lips before he could even pause to reconsider them. *Boyfriend*. He hadn't sought Adrian's permission, hadn't lingered to verify if it was appropriate to embrace that title amidst all the chaos that had transpired between them. But it was undeniably true. After all the turmoil, Logan felt a resolute clarity. No more hesitations. No more running.

Adrian belonged to him, and he to Adrian. If there was a time and place to reveal the depths of his feelings, it was now with Adrian's parents.

He was Adrian's boyfriend, and the pride swelling within him was intoxicating as he embraced those words.

Adrian's father gazed at him, a fleeting emotion visible in his eyes—skepticism, maybe, or a subtle evaluation. Nevertheless, he grasped Logan's hand, his hold steady, and his face inscrutable.

"Hello, Logan." A pause. "Aaron."

Before Logan could respond, Tammi and Adrian exchanged a flurry of words in Hebrew. Then Tammi gestured toward the small living room and walked off without waiting for them to follow.

Adrian rubbed the back of his neck, a familiar gesture that told Logan more than words. "Their English isn't great," he explained, even though Logan had already understood that. "But they understand more than they speak. My mom said you should sit. Make yourself comfortable."

Logan nodded, but something sat heavy in his chest.

That language barrier.

There was still a gap between their worlds, not new, not hostile, but wide enough to feel. A chasm Logan had never tried to cross until now. Adrian moved between languages with ease, his English fluent, effortless, woven so naturally with Hebrew that it almost seemed like breathing. But Logan remained on one side of that divide, watching from a distance, unable to step fully into the language that had shaped the man he loved.

And sitting here now, in the quiet of this modest apartment, watching Adrian slip between sentences—translating, bridging two halves of his life—Logan felt the weight of that distance more than ever. He had promised himself he would show up fully, without fear, without retreat. That meant more than just presence; it meant learning the language, understanding not just the man, but the world that made him.

The apartment around them was small but carefully kept, every surface polished, every corner in order. The space felt lived in, respected. Family photos adorned the walls, tiny frozen moments of love and time. Some were of Adrian as a boy, his smile wide, his hair wild from the wind, standing next to a younger Tammi or a stern-faced Aaron. Others were placed carefully on the modest furniture around the room, snapshots of birthdays, Adrian about 14, standing near a young Alon with a big birthday cake featuring the number 5, beach trips with young Adrian sitting on Aaron's shoulders, capturing quiet, everyday happiness.

Logan's gaze drifted to the dining table, already set for five. It was a quiet gesture, but not a small one. Despite everything that had happened, despite the time and the silence and the way he had once walked away, someone had thought to include him. He was expected here.

Tammi returned carrying a tray with a kettle and glasses, her movements practiced. Logan opened his mouth to thank her, but Aaron was already rising from his seat.

"I go, ah... call Alon," he said, his voice thick with accent, then disappeared down the hall.

A few moments passed before they returned, Adrian's father first, and then a boy who looked no older than eighteen or nineteen. His black hair was buzzed close to the scalp, a haircut that belonged to someone in uniform. Lean, angular, still growing into his frame, he moved with the tentative posture of someone trying to seem older than he was.

But it was his eyes that caught Logan; they were dark, hard, guarded. He didn't look at Adrian so much as through him, his stare edged with something bitter, a quiet, simmering resentment that bubbled there. The resemblance was clear—the same bone structure, the same sharp line of the jaw—but where Adrian carried warmth, even in his silence, Alon was all frost. There was no welcome in his expression, only a tension that settled over the room like a held breath, his lips pressed into a thin, contemptuous line.

And he ignored Adrian entirely.

Every movement, every shift of his body, from the way he stepped into the room to the way he carried himself or moved an arm, was calculated to pretend his older brother did not exist, to ignore his brother's presence entirely, as if Adrian had vanished into the furniture.

But Logan wouldn't be ignored.

He stood, extending his hand, steady and open. "You must be Alon," he said calmly. "I'm Logan Vaughn. Adrian's boyfriend. It's nice to meet you."

Alon's eyes narrowed slightly, something flickering there—maybe curiosity, maybe defiance—before he reached out and took Logan's hand.

"I am." Then, without hesitation: "Are you the one who ditched him?" Alon's English was better than his parents', crisp and direct.

Logan felt a twist in his stomach, although he wasn't as taken aback by the question itself. What genuinely rattled him was the venomous tone laced within the question. What unsettled him was the weight packed into those words, the unmistakable edge beneath the surface. There was no curiosity in the question; it was no question at all, only a pointed kind of cruelty, as if he'd been waiting for the chance to throw it like a stone. That unsettled Logan.

He caught the way Adrian's posture changed, how his shoulders dipped inward, almost imperceptibly, like he'd just taken a hit. And that was what truly got to Logan: not the accusation, but the way it landed.

Alon knew exactly where to aim.

In just seven words, a striking impact was unleashed. Seven clean, deliberate words, and Adrian crumpled within himself. Logan felt his jaw tense, rapt with attention on Alon, and for a fleeting moment, a fierce urge to lash out surged within him. He recognized it with unnerving clarity—the precise instant Adrian diminished, the way his silence enveloped the room, brimming with all the words left unspoken.

Before Logan could answer, Adrian's voice cut through. "Ignore him."

So, Logan attempted to do so. However, the damage had already been inflicted, and the ensuing silence was charged with tense energy.

Aaron and Tammi turned toward Alon in unison, their voices rising in clipped Hebrew. Logan couldn't follow the language, but the stern and fast rhythm was unmistakable; the kind of scolding that didn't need translation. Alon didn't answer. He crossed his arms and sank into the chair beside Tammi, his jaw tight, his glare fixed somewhere far from the room.

After a while, Adrian cleared his throat. "I actually wanted to tell you something," he began, his voice trying to be steady.

Tammi turned to him fully, Aaron's brow furrowed, Alon's eyes flicking up in reluctant attention.

And then Adrian glanced at Logan. "I'll explain to them in Hebrew, okay?"

Logan felt a tightness in his chest, a visceral tug that resonated deeply. It was just a small moment, perhaps, yet its impact on Logan was more profound than he had anticipated. Adrian, with endless understanding, chose not to sever their connection. He could have effortlessly slipped into another language, left Logan in the shadows of conversation, but instead, he lingered. With a gaze fixed on Logan, Adrian extended an unvoiced invitation. In that simple act, there was a richness that conveyed: *You belong here. You're no longer on the periphery; you are part of this moment now.*

Logan nodded. "Of course."

Adrian drew in a breath, then turned toward his family, his voice slipping into Hebrew. Logan couldn't follow the words, but he could follow the meaning. Adrian was telling them that he had made a choice—that he wasn't giving up. The tests had already started, and tonight, he and Logan would be flying to the United States. In two days, the treatment would begin.

Tammi reacted before the words had even finished leaving Adrian's mouth. Her hands flew to her face, and then she was on her feet, arms wrapping around her stepson with a force that came from the deepest part of her. Her sobs broke free as she held him, crying into his chest, her small frame shaking as though the relief was too much to bear.

"Ben sheli, ben sheli, yeled sheli," she cried. *My son, my son, my boy.*

She didn't need to say more. Logan could feel the truth of her love in the way she held Adrian, not gently but tightly, fiercely, like someone who had feared they were losing him and had just been handed a second chance. Her voice trembled with everything she had been holding in: the fear, the helplessness, the fragile thread of hope she hadn't dared name. She rocked slightly, whispering things Logan couldn't understand but didn't need to.

He remembered what Adrian had told him once—how Tammi hadn't inherited the title of mother, but claimed it, fought for it. How she took him to the beach when he was a boy, how she made herself present even when he resisted her. She didn't replace his mother, but she became one anyway, because Adrian had needed someone, and she had chosen to be that for him. And now, in the middle of this small living room, she was holding him the way only a mother could, crying not just from fear, but from the sudden, overwhelming hope that maybe—just maybe—he was going to stay.

Aaron stepped forward next. He didn't say a word at first. He simply wrapped Adrian in a strong embrace, and Logan saw how his shoulders trembled, how his breath caught, how he held his son like a man who had run out of ways to be brave and was finally allowing himself to break. Like a man standing on the precipice of despair, poised to lose his son to the same cruel disease that snatched away his beloved wife, yet is suddenly granted a second chance, a flicker of hope amidst the shadows.

He whispered something, low and rough, and Adrian leaned into him, nodding slowly, holding on.

Logan's eyes shifted to Alon, who hadn't moved. He sat with his arms crossed, his jaw tight, his gaze hard. But something was shifting under the surface. Logan noticed the way his fingers curled slightly, the subtle bob of his throat as he swallowed. His eyes didn't settle on Adrian, they landed on the space between Adrian and their parents, as if he wasn't sure whether he wanted to step into it or not. For a moment, Logan thought he might say something, but then Alon rolled his eyes and looked away. The posture was practiced, the indifference intentional, but the crack had already shown. And Logan had seen it.

Before Logan could brace himself, Tammi grabbed him, crushing him in an embrace so fierce, so desperate, it nearly stole the breath from his lungs.

"Thank you so much, thank you!" she sobbed against his shoulder. "You save my boy."

Logan's throat tightened as he wrapped his arms around her. The weight of her gratitude pressed against him, heavy, overwhelming. He didn't know what to say—*I didn't save him, I just came back*—but the words wouldn't come. So instead, he held her.

His return had saved Adrian all the same. Logan was the only force fierce enough to break through the ramparts Adrian had built around his heart; the only light bright enough to pierce the starless night where Adrian's spirit had caged itself during the barren years of Logan's absence. Logan was the sea crashing against a fortress, insistent and unstoppable, until even stone had to yield.

His presence flooded Adrian's darkness, sweeping away the silt of hopelessness, revealing something painfully human beneath. It made Logan's heart convulse with a sharp, almost unbearable ache, made his lungs twist with a suffocating anguish: if he had arrived a moment later, the consequences would have been catastrophic.

Before Logan could fully collect himself, Aaron stepped forward and pulled him into a hug. It caught him off guard. Aaron didn't seem like the kind of man who reached for closeness so easily, but in that moment, he wasn't guarded or distant, he was simply a father. A man who had nearly lost his son and had been given the smallest flicker of hope in return.

"Thank you," Aaron said, the words rough around the edges, thick with emotion. "I..." He paused, his brow furrowing as he searched for the right English, translating each word carefully. "I never no... could to thank you. Thank you. You... to save my son. I forever thank you."

There was nothing polished about it, but Logan had never heard anything more sincere.

"When you leave?" Tammi asked, wiping at her tear-streaked face as Logan took his seat next to Adrian again.

"Our flight's at four," Logan answered gently. "So we'll have to leave in a few hours."

As the words left his mouth, Adrian reached for his hand. Logan didn't hesitate—he took it instantly, lacing their fingers together. The touch grounded him. It reminded him that even in the middle of all this uncertainty, this was real. This was theirs.

He felt Adrian's thumb move slightly across his skin, just once, and that simple motion settled something inside him.

But not everyone in the room felt the same peace.

Logan caught the way Alon's expression shifted the moment he noticed their joined hands. His eyes darkened, his mouth tightened, and something in his face twisted—not just anger, but something tangled deeper: pain, maybe, or grief, or the confusion of a boy watching a brother he couldn't reach. Tammi turned to Alon and said something in Hebrew, her voice gentle but firm.

Whatever it was, it was the final crack in the dam.

Alon stood so suddenly that his chair scraped loudly against the floor. His body was rigid, his fists clenched at his sides.

"LO!" NO.

He shouted in Hebrew, the word tearing through the space as he continued, his voice tumbling over itself in a torrent of syllables, each one cracking open the brittle silence of the room.

And then he was gone—pushing past the front door, slamming it open, and vanishing into the night.

Adrian's face fell, his head dropping as if a weight had settled on his shoulders.

"What happened?" Logan asked, his heart pounding. "What did he say?"

Adrian let out a slow, uneven breath before answering.

"She told him to get up and hug me," he said quietly. "'Hug your brother,' she said." A pause. Then his voice dropped even lower. "And he screamed back, no, and that he's not my brother. That he's my half-brother."

Logan clenched his jaw.

"Then he said she's not even my mom," Adrian carried on, his voice raw. "Told her to cut the act."

Logan's heart ached. Not just for Adrian, but also for Tammi.

She had been *his* mother. The only one who had stepped into that role, who had fought to love him, to make him hers. And now, in front of everyone, Alon had torn that down, had thrown it back at her as if it was nothing.

Logan gave Adrian's hand a gentle squeeze, a small gesture, but one that tried to convey comfort, as if steadiness could be transferred through skin. Across the table, Aaron and Tammi shared a quiet, brief glance, the kind that said more than words ever could.

"I'll go to him," Aaron suggested, already starting to rise.

But Adrian raised a hand, stopping him before he could stand. "No." His voice was quiet but firm. "I'll go. This is long overdue."

Aaron hesitated, but after a moment, he gave a small nod.

Logan met Adrian's gaze, searching for something, for reassurance, hesitation, anything.

Adrian gave him a small, tired smile. "Be right back."

Adrian jogged down the stairs; the stairwell felt longer than it used to, but even that small effort left him winded. His breath hitched, his ribs straining against the weight of his own body. He hated how the disease crept in during moments like this; the smallest reminders that he wasn't who he used to be, that time and illness were stripping him down piece by piece. It was the ordinary moments that spoke the loudest.

But he pushed forward.

Alon was sitting at the foot of the stairs, back turned, a cigarette burning low between his fingers. His gaze was locked onto the Maserati, as if it held all the answers to the rage simmering inside him. The smoke rose in thin spirals, catching the yellow porch light and twisting toward the dark.

Adrian lingered at the final step, torn between speaking up or retreating, feeling that it would be easier to declare defeat, endure the dinner, and move on.

But no, Alon was his brother. Adrian understood that beneath the harsh words and cruelty, there was something more profound.

Then, sharper than he intended, the words came out, in Hebrew, rough and raw. "What's your problem?"

Alon didn't move, didn't flinch. The harsh tone rolled away from him. He took a long pull from the cigarette and exhaled through his nose, the sound edged with something between a laugh and a scoff.

"So now you smoke?" Adrian said, quieter now, stepping onto the pavement and standing directly in front of his young brother. "Since when?"

Alon's shoulders shifted slightly, but his eyes stayed fixed ahead. "Up until a few days ago, you didn't even have a car," he muttered. "Now you show up in a Maserati?"

"It's a rental." Adrian crossed his arms. "Logan got it because he wanted the experience for a few days. That's all."

"Oh, so your rich boyfriend just happened to get you a Maserati? Just your rich boyfriend doing rich boyfriend shit," Alon let out another humorless chuckle. "Man, you really don't even hear yourself, do you?"

"What the fuck are you talking about?" Adrian stepped closer, frustration sharpening his voice. "I was taking the bus two days ago."

Alon's mouth twisted into a smile, but it didn't reach his eyes. "Oh, yeah, right." Alon took another drag, exhaled through his nose as he stood.

"Always the perfect excuse. It's never you, huh? It's always something else—a coincidence, bad timing, someone else's decision. Nothing's ever really your fault, is it?"

Alon looked at him then, really looked, and for a second, just long enough to be real, the anger cracked. There was something else behind it. Something quieter. But it passed quickly, and the wall went up again.

"You don't even know how easy it's been for you," he muttered, barely audible. "You've always had everything."

Then, without breaking eye contact, Alon flicked the cigarette to the ground and crushed it beneath his boot. His movements were intentional, almost theatrical, as if daring Adrian to react.

The muscle in Adrian's jaw twitched. Patience slipped through him like seawater through rope, slow at first, then all at once. "What the hell is going on with you?"

Alon didn't answer. He pulled another cigarette from the pack, lit it with a snap of his lighter, the brief flare casting shadows across his face.

Adrian stepped forward, voice rising. "Are you out of your mind? You just got into an elite unit, and you're out here chain-smoking like nothing matters? Do you have any idea what kind of training is ahead of you? Cut that shit!"

Something in Alon's expression shifted—a flash of something darker, deeper—and then it snapped.

"I'M NOT ONE OF YOUR SOLDIERS!" he exploded, the words ripping into the quiet night like a shot. He dropped the second cigarette to the ground and stepped on it. "So stop talking to me like I am! Stop giving me orders like you've always fucking done!"

Before Adrian could respond, Alon shoved him—hard. Adrian stumbled back a step, caught off guard, but his feet held. Instinct moved faster than thought, and a second later, he shoved back, his palms slamming against Alon's torso.

"I'm so fucking done with this," Adrian snapped. "I've put up with your crap for years, because you were a kid and I thought you'd grow out of it, but guess what? You didn't. So go ahead, yell at me, punch me, whatever the hell you need to do. Just say it already. Stop skulking around with this silent, bitter bullshit. Get it out of your system!" Adrian's voice tore through the stairwell, bouncing off the cracked walls.

Alon stood rigid, breath loud in the space between them, his hands balled into fists, his chest rising and falling like he was holding something in; something too heavy to carry anymore. His eyes were wild, but not just with rage. Beneath the blaze of fury, something else sparked in his eyes, a confusion steeped in pain, raw and mute, still searching for a name it had never been given. It was as if it had been quietly dormant within him all those years, concealed in silence, never having been able to take the form of language.

And then it all broke open.

"I've got two fucking days at home, Adrian!" Alon roared, his voice ricocheting down the stairwell. "Two fucking days before I go back! And even in that time, all I hear is you!"

Adrian froze mid-step, hand gripping the rusting railing.

Alon's laugh was jagged, almost a choke. "High school wasn't enough? You think it was easy? Everyone knew I was your brother. The gay brother's kid. They mocked me, they beat the shit out of me because you decided you weren't gonna hide. And I got the fire for it. I carried it." His fist slammed into the peeling plaster beside him, leaving a faint smear of dust on his knuckles.

"But I thought, okay, high school's over. I'll have the army. I'll be my own man. Finally. Not in your fucking shadow." His voice cracked into a half-sob, half-snarl. "But no. Even there. Even in the one place that was supposed to be mine, you're still everywhere."

Adrian tried to cut in, "What—" but Alon overrode him, louder, fiercer.

"I make Shayetet 13, the fucking elite naval commandos, and guess what?" Alon's laugh was sharp, bitter. "No one cares! You know what they say? 'Oh, you mean like Adrian?' I call Dad during my one fucking hour of phone time, after a week that nearly kills me, and what does he say? He doesn't ask about me. No, he doesn't care about it. He says, 'Oh yeah, Adrian did that too. He was great at it.'"

Alon's breath hitched, his voice growing wilder, more frenzied.

"They came to my rank ceremony, Adrian. And guess what I heard the entire time? 'Adrian finished his training with honors.' 'Adrian was number one.' 'Adrian aced every test.' 'Remember when Adrian was here? He was the best.' Always you!"

Adrian swallowed, something thick and hot lodging in his throat. "You didn't tell me you got your first ranks," he said quietly.

Alon scoffed, eyes burning. "Yeah. Because I didn't want you there."

The words hit like a slap, but Adrian didn't move.

"Everything in your life is so perfect," Alon spat, voice dripping with resentment. "You're always the golden fucking boy. The one they worship. The one who gets everything. The one who gets everything handed to him just by walking into a room. And don't you dare stand there and tell me that's not true." He turned half away, then whipped back, the last confession ripping out of him. "Everyone chooses you," he said, the edge of his fury trembling into something else. "Every person I've ever wanted... chose you."

His voice cracked on the last word, the confession slipping out before he could stop it. He dropped his gaze, turning away sharply, like he could shove the feeling back down if he just didn't look at Adrian. A breath hitched in his throat—not quite a sob, but close—and then he blinked hard, jaw clenched, as if anger might save him from the softness that had just broken through.

Adrian felt his pulse pounding in his skull.

And then, something inside him snapped.

"Are you out of your mind?!" he burst. "I'm dying, Alon! Do you get that?!"

Silence slammed down between them, dense and suffocating in the familiar street where they'd grown up. Adrian caught glimpses of neighbors behind half-drawn curtains, faces drawn to the spectacle of their Friday night shouting while the rest of the block shared Sabbath dinners in warm, hushed rooms.

Alon's jaw tightened. His lips parted, but no words came.

And then—so quietly it was almost a whisper—he said, "Even with your fucking illness, I would still take your life over mine."

Adrian's stomach twisted.

"Shut your mouth." His voice was barely above a growl. "Don't say that bullshit."

"Bullshit?" Alon let out a broken laugh, shaking his head. "You have any idea what it's like to live in your fucking shadow? Have you ever—*just once*—asked what it's like being me? To never be enough? To never matter as much as you? To live in your shadow and watch everyone fall over themselves to love you, to see you, and never once looking back to notice me?"

Adrian didn't answer. He couldn't.

Because for the first time, he saw it—not just the anger, but the exhaustion, the helplessness, the weight Alon had been carrying for years.

"Adrian made it to commando. Adrian's a lieutenant. Adrian was number one." Alon's voice turned mocking, venomous. "Adrian's an amazing musician. Adrian is coming home. Adrian is going back. Adrian is traveling the world. Adrian has a special man in his life, so beautiful, so perfect. Adrian is surfing, Adrian is jogging, Adrian is training, Adrian is so good at sports! Adrian's heart was broken! Adrian is dying—poor, poor Adrian, dying of the same thing that took his mother—"

"Alon, STOP—"

"And even then, when you were a mess, when you couldn't eat or speak or sleep without breaking, Dean was there every day for you! Every fucking day and night, he was at that house after you. Held you when you cried. Slept beside you so you wouldn't wake up alone." He let out a sob that was masked as a laugh. "Can't you see a pattern here? I'm invisible."

"Alon..." Adrian's voice faltered, unsure. "What—"

"You know what I think?"

Adrian's stomach coiled with unease. "What?"

Alon's voice dropped, quieter, more dangerous. "That even when you're dying, your life is still fucking perfect. Even when everything should be falling apart, you still have everything."

Adrian felt his breath stutter, his skin prickling, his heart aching in ways he couldn't name.

"You think it was easy?" Adrian's voice cracked, shaking with something raw. "Do you have any idea—"

"Yeah, yeah," Alon interrupted with a bitter smirk. "I remember. I remember when things weren't perfect for you. But, of course, even when something bad happens, everything just falls back into place."

Adrian's fists curled at his sides. His lungs burned. But beneath the anger, something shifted.

Because for the first time, he realized—

Alon wasn't just angry at him.

He was *hurting*.

"Alon..." Adrian's voice wavered, brittle as autumn leaves before they crumble.

"You got out," Alon whispered, his face twisted. "You left this place behind. You got to start over. You moved in with Dean—" his voice caught hard on the name, as if saying it cut him open. "So not only did you have it all back then, now you've got a fucking American boyfriend too. And you still act like you don't understand. Like you didn't take something from me..."

Adrian stared at him, speechless. His little brother—his Alon—stood before him, a storm unraveling, years of anger, hurt, loneliness spilling out all at once. His hands trembled at his sides. Adrian knew that look, the tears threatening to fall. But they weren't tears of sorrow. They were furious, resentful, the kind that sting because they've been held back too long.

And yet... what he said—about Adrian, about Logan, about Dean—wasn't making sense. He spoke like he had been keeping score, like Adrian had stolen something from him without ever realizing it.

Oh, shit.

"And you flying away, off you go—"

"To have treatments!" Adrian snapped, voice sharper than he intended. His body ached from just speaking. "I'm not going on a fucking vacation!"

"Every fucking person alive is fighting for you to live. And you—" Alon's voice dropped to something venomous, something broken. "You just want to be left alone and die."

"Alon..." Adrian whispered. His hands clenched into fists. "Why didn't you ever say something?"

"To whom?" Alon's laugh was hollow, bitter. "To Mom? To Dad? Dad doesn't even see me. When he looks at me, all he sees is you. Every time he talks to me, it starts with you and somehow ends with you. Even when I'm doing well, it's never just mine—it's always compared to you. Always, Adrian, Adrian, Adrian." He took a step back, shaking his head. "You are the star of that house. And me? I am just the echo, the spare, the one who came after you."

Adrian felt his heart crack; the pain was not just physical anymore. It ran deeper than that, into places he didn't even know existed. His little brother—his baby brother—had been drowning all this time, and Adrian never noticed.

"Why didn't you come to me?" His voice was hoarse now, barely above a whisper. "Why, instead of being such an asshole, instead of mocking me, why didn't you just come to me? I never knew, Alon. I had no fucking clue." He exhaled shakily. "I wasn't home much, but—"

"Yeah, because 'kind-hearted Adrian' was always working to help Mom and Dad—"

"Go to hell," Adrian spat, voice cracking. "You think I wanted that? You think I chose to work instead of being a normal teenager? Dad was about to lose the house, Alon! And then what? You were, what, thirteen? You wanted to live on the fucking streets?" His breath shuddered, his ribs a cage of fire. "Believe me, I would rather have gone to school. I would rather have had a childhood." He swallowed hard. "You don't know shit about what I had to do to make sure you never had to worry about any of it."

Alon's anger flickered, like a candle caught in the wind. His shoulders slumped, the fight starting to drain from him.

"I'm sorry," Adrian said, softer now, voice laced with regret. "I had no idea you felt that way. I should've. But I didn't. And I'm sorry."

Alon didn't answer right away. But he looked at him—really looked—and though his gaze still held pain, it wasn't the same kind. It wasn't sharp and fresh anymore. It was older, quieter. Bruised, not bleeding.

Adrian knew what he had to do. He had always been the big brother, whether he wanted to be or not. And maybe he hadn't always been good at it. Maybe he'd been too consumed by his own pain and struggle to notice his younger brother gradually disappearing. While standing in the same room, his brother was being erased, ignored, and dismissed, fading into silence that no one bothered to break. But he saw him now. He saw everything—the bitterness, the loneliness, the hollow ache of being the one always left behind. The one always in the shadow. Alon wasn't really angry. He was hurt. Deeply, deeply wounded in a place no one had ever thought to reach. And Adrian had never noticed. Never realized how much Alon had been waiting—craving—just to be seen.

So Adrian took two steps forward, closed the space between them, and pulled his little brother in. A short hug, but real, nonetheless. Solid. He felt the tension in Alon's body, the way he hesitated for a fraction of a second before melting into it, like he wasn't used to being held this way anymore. Like he had forgotten what it was like.

Adrian let go but kept his hands on Alon's shoulders, grounding both of them in this moment. "I don't want to leave like this," he admitted, voice heavy with exhaustion, with regret. "Alon, you're my brother. I love you. I care about you."

"Half-brother," Alon remarked silently, not meeting his eyes, clinging to the one piece of distance he had left, as if it could protect him.

"No," Adrian said quietly. "Not that half-brother shit. You're my little brother. That's it." Adrian took a breath. "I am sorry. I've failed you, I should have talked to you sooner, to try and understand. I should have seen it, and I am so damn sorry, Alon."

Alon didn't say anything, but something flickered in his expression—something raw, something close to breaking.

Adrian hesitated. He had spent so many years looking forward, trying to survive, that he had forgotten to look back. To remember. But now it hit him—hard, sharp, like a blade twisting in his ribs.

He remembered when they were kids, when Alon was just four or five, clinging to Adrian's every move. Back then, it had felt natural, his baby brother following him around, asking endless questions, tugging on his sleeve, wanting Adrian to play with him. He had loved it. Loved having Alon there, a tiny shadow always at his side. They played catch, ran wild at the park, and spent entire days at the beach. Because Dean had been a consistent part of Adrian's life since he was six, he accompanied them on most of those adventures. Back then, the three of them had been inseparable.

But then, slowly, things began to change. Alon started pulling away.

At first, it was little things: choosing to stay home instead of joining them, keeping to himself, and rolling his eyes at Adrian's jokes. Then it became something more, something colder. The distance between them stretched year after year, widening until Adrian barely recognized the boy who had once followed him around.

And now, standing here, Adrian saw what he had been too blind—or too distracted—to see.

Had he missed the way Alon used to look at Dean? The way his face lit up when Dean entered the room? The way he blushed when Dean gave him attention, or how small he became when he didn't? Had Adrian overlooked the way Alon's admiration had twisted into something deeper? Something quieter. The way that unspoken affection festered, year after year, when Dean always came for Adrian... and never for him?

It hadn't just been their parents who overlooked Alon.

Dean had, too.

And so had Adrian.

And maybe—just maybe—Alon had been resenting him all along.

Adrian swallowed hard. "I never meant for this to happen," he said softly, meaning so much more. "I should've seen it, Alon. I should've been there for you."

Alon's throat worked like he wanted to say something, but he just nodded.

The night wrapped around them like a vast, endless ocean, deep and dark and unknowable. The air was thick with salt and cigarette smoke, the remnants of old battles fought in silence, words swallowed like seawater, choking but never spoken.

Adrian held his brother's gaze, searching for something, anything, that told him they weren't still adrift in the wreckage of all the years between them.

"Are we good now?" His voice was quiet, holding too much weight behind it.

Alon's lips twitched, a flicker of something fragile, before he gave a small nod. "Yeah."

A single word. So simple, so insufficient, and yet it held multitudes. But Adrian hesitated, lingering in the silence that stretched between them. Just in case. Just in case Alon needed to say something more. Just in case this was the last time they would ever stand together like this.

Because Adrian knew.

Even if no one else was brave enough to say it out loud, he knew. The ocean was calling him back, but not to the waves—to the abyss. There was no coming back from this. He could feel it in the marrow of his bones, in the quiet certainty that settled in his chest like an anchor dragging him deeper, deeper. This might be the last time he got to look his baby brother in the eye, the last time he got to hear his voice, to touch his shoulder, to feel, even for a fleeting moment, the bond that time and grief had nearly severed.

A man can only be given so much in a lifetime before fate comes to collect its debts. And Adrian? He had already stretched his luck thin, had already taken more than he had ever deserved.

His life had never been kind, not in the way stories promised, not in the way children dream. He had lost his mother too young, had grown up in the shadow of grief, had learned too quickly that love did not make a home safe, that money did not stretch far enough, that no one was coming to save him, that not everyone came back home.

And yet, there had been light, too.

Tammi, who had chosen to love him, though she never had to. His little brother, who followed him around and was a constant source of cuteness in his life. Brothers who had flown across oceans to stand by his side, who had lifted him from the depths when he had nothing left but the ghosts of war clinging to his skin. He had found purpose in the army, had thrived in the fire of it, had felt, for the briefest time, like he was whole. Even when it took everything from him—even when it broke him, shattered him, spat him out into the world as something lesser—he had never regretted it.

And then there was love.

Real love.

The kind that poets wept over, the kind that bent the laws of time and logic, the kind that no man, no matter how broken, ever truly believed he would find. Four months of chasing waves and stolen kisses and laughter that echoed across continents. Four months of waking up to gray eyes that felt like home, of knowing—deep in his soul, in the very marrow of him—that he had found the other half of himself.

And maybe that had been his limit.

Maybe the universe had given him all the love he was allowed before it came back to take the rest.

Because now, the streams of water that had once given him everything were pulling him under, and this time, there was no one who could save him.

Adrian forced a smile, even as his chest ached, even as his ribs felt like they might crack beneath the weight of all the things he would never get to say.

"Come on," he urged, his voice calm despite his heart's turmoil. "Mom likely cooked enough to feed an army."

And then, with one last touch, a firm hand on Alon's shoulder, one last silent promise, he turned toward the stairs and together they climbed back up. As Alon pushed open the apartment door, Logan's gaze found Adrian's the moment he stepped inside, like he felt him coming. Those silver eyes, sharp yet full of quiet warmth, searched his face, asking a silent question.

Adrian nodded, just a small dip of his chin, a reassurance without words. Everything was okay.

Logan's shoulders loosened slightly, and he gifted Adrian one of those half-smiles—beautiful in its simplicity, effortless. Then, without missing a beat, he took another bite of the cookie in his hand, his eyes flickering with amusement.

Adrian smirked as he slid back into his seat beside him, raising a brow at the half-empty plate of cookies and the cup of tea nestled in Logan's hands.

"Your mom forced me to eat cookies," Logan explained, holding up the half-eaten treat as proof, his voice laced with a boyish kind of mischief. "And she made me tea." He took a dramatic sip, then turned to Tammi with a charming smile. "By the way, the cookies are amazing, Tammi. Thank you."

Adrian snatched a cookie from the plate and handed it to Alon, grinning. "He's not lying. She does that. She weaponizes food."

Tammi let out an affectionate laugh, waving a hand dismissively. "I to make sure, you... a guest. You need to welcome." Then, she asked, "You hungry?"

Adrian scoffed before Logan could even answer. "It's Logan. He was born hungry."

Logan elbowed him discreetly, his laughter spilling into the room like sunlight dancing on the waves.

Tammi shook her head, pleased, and motioned for them all to take their places at the small dining table. The chairs scraped softly against the floor as they settled in, the table suddenly feeling full. Bowls filled with steaming dishes were placed in the center, the rich scents of home-cooked food curling through the air.

Dinner unfolded with an easy rhythm. Tammi, ever the doting host, kept slipping food onto Logan's plate, watching him with the same quiet care she gave Adrian. Conversation circled around his life and work, and Logan answered with a surprising openness, sketching the steady shape of his career and degrees while quietly omitting the fractures beneath. They surely knew about his marriage, about his sudden vanishing and storm-like return into Adrian's world, but no one asked, and for that, he was grateful.

For the first time in a long while, Adrian let himself sink into it—the warmth of family, the sound of Logan's voice folding into the rhythm of the room. He caught the way Logan laughed at something Tammi said, how easily he reached for another bite, how natural he looked here, as if he had always belonged. And Adrian thought, maybe some things really do find their way back to shore.

At some point, Tammi and Aaron asked about how they had met, and Logan hesitated.

He had expected them to already know, had assumed Adrian had told them the story in full. But as it turned out, Adrian had only ever given them the simplest version: *Hawaii. We met in Hawaii.*

As if the ocean itself hadn't rewritten both of their lives that day.

So Logan told them everything—every last detail he could remember.

He recounted how the water had devoured him entirely, plunging his senses into darkness. He spoke of Adrian's fearless dive into the abyss, of his grasping hands that had yanked him back from the brink of death, restoring him to the world with a trembling hope.

"And you gave me CPR," Logan said, glancing at Adrian with a small, grateful smile. "How long was it again?"

Adrian shifted, a flicker of something deep in his eyes before he shrugged, a soft breath escaping him. "I don't know. It felt like forever."

His father had never looked prouder. And his mother looked at them like they had walked straight out of a fairytale.

The warmth of the moment lingered, stretching over the table like the last golden rays of sunset. Plates were cleared, cups refilled, and just when it seemed like the night might carry on in its quiet, steady rhythm, Adrian spoke.

"So, Dad," he said, his voice measured, his tone deceptively light, "how come you never told me about Alon's first ranks ceremony?"

He spoke in English, though his father would understand. A deliberate choice.

Aaron barely looked up. "It wasn't a big deal," he dismissed, slipping back into his native tongue. "You had better things to do."

Adrian went still. His fingers curled slightly against the table, a quiet tightening. "No," he insisted, his voice unwavering. "I wanted to be there."

"Adrian, not now," his father said, his gaze flicking briefly to Logan, as if the presence of a guest should be enough to bury the conversation.

But Adrian had never been the type to swallow the tide when it came crashing in.

"Yes, now," he protested. "I might not be here for another time."

The words hit the dinner table with startling force, like a bomb bursting in midair.

His mother let out a small, broken sound, covering her face with her hands.

Aaron exhaled sharply, exasperation lining his features. "Adrian, you're *dying*, and you wanted to drive three hours and stand in the sun for some first ranks ceremony? It's not even a staff sergeant, or a captain, or a second lieutenant, or a lieutenant like you were. It's just *first ranks*."

Across the table, Alon shoved back his chair, the legs screeching against the tile like a wounded thing, slicing through the tension around the table. He didn't say a word—just stood and strode away, disappearing into his room, his absence heavier than his presence had ever been.

Adrian's patience snapped, the last fraying threads coming apart all at once.

"Dad, it needs to stop! I also started from first ranks, you know that, right? It's not like you just enter and are instantly given your lieutenant rank with a 'congrats!'" he shouted, switching to his father's language now, making sure there was no room for misunderstanding. "You have to stop treating him like that! Do you even know how hard it is to get to where he got? Do you have any idea what it means to him?"

His father straightened, his expression unreadable, but Adrian didn't stop.

326

"No, Dad. Come on. Go talk to him. Go talk to your son. You've got two, you know." His voice trembled slightly, but he pushed through, shaking his head.

Beside him, Logan's hand found his under the table, warm, grounding. Adrian exhaled sharply and covered it with his own fingers, tightening around Logan's as he forced his voice lower and steadier.

"Go talk to him," Adrian said again, quieter now, the fire in his voice dimming into something softer. "He feels bad. He's been standing in my shadow for years, and you—you never noticed. But I see it now, and I should have seen it before. He is his own person. So ask him about himself."

For the first time, something in his father's face shifted. A crack in the stone.

Aaron pushed his chair back, moving more slowly this time. He looked shocked. *Distressed.*

Like he had never seen it before.

As soon as the tension ebbed, Adrian leaned toward Logan, murmuring an apology for switching languages so abruptly, for leaving him stranded in a sea of unfamiliar words. Logan just waved him off with a quiet smile, as if to say *it didn't matter. None of it mattered, as long as you're here.*

Still, there was something fragile in Adrian's expression, something that only deepened as he rose from his chair and walked toward his mother. Without hesitation, he wrapped his arms around her, holding her close as if to anchor her, as if to anchor himself.

"I'm sorry," he murmured, his voice barely above a whisper.

She cupped his face, said something soft, something only for him, and he kissed her cheek in return before moving to help clear the table.

Logan tried to stand and assist, but before he could so much as reach for a plate, Tammi pushed a thick slice of cake into his hands and pointed toward the couch with the authority of a woman who would not be questioned.

"Sit," she ordered, her accent thick with warmth. "You guest."

Logan, knowing better than to argue, grinned as he took his seat.

A few minutes later, Tammi and Adrian returned to the living room, but something in their quiet conversation made Adrian's expression twist in immediate horror. His head shook—once, twice, over and over. "No. Mom, please—no."

But it was too late.

Tammi smiled sweetly as she walked to the wooden sideboard, her movements deliberate, her intentions clear. Logan immediately knew what was happening the moment she pulled out the four thick photo albums and placed them on the coffee table with quiet reverence.

He beamed.

"Oh, this is going to be amazing," his voice was a mix of gleefulness, teasing, and affectionate mockery, as he barely held back his laughter while Tammi sat beside him, opening the first album in her lap.

Adrian groaned, sinking onto the couch beside him, his face already in his hands. "Mom, please."

But there was no escape.

Tammi flipped to the very first page, pointing at a picture of a tiny, round-cheeked baby wrapped in soft blankets. "This is Adrian when he a.... baby," she said, her accent adding a melody to the words.

Logan grinned. "He is adorable."

Adrian muttered something under his breath that sounded a lot like 'kill me now'.

Tammi turned the page, revealing a photo of a beautiful young woman holding baby Adrian in her arms. She smiled, softer now. "And this," she said gently, "this the mother of Adrian."

Logan's smile wavered as his gaze fell upon the woman who had nurtured Adrian into existence. Her gentle kindness radiated from her face, a tenderness in her eyes that spoke volumes as she cradled her son, making him the center of her universe. Amongst the memories captured in the faded photograph, Logan's attention was drawn to a bracelet adorning her wrist. Though the image was a blur, the quality was low and faded with time, there was no doubt that it was the very same bracelet that Adrian had bestowed upon him with love.

Tammi said something in her native tongue, glancing at Adrian as she spoke, and Adrian quickly translated, his voice softer now, quieter.

"She's saying that I probably haven't talked much about her," he explained, his fingers grazing the edge of the page. "But her name was Aliana." He paused, swallowing thickly. "Dad told her I used to keep them awake all night long."

Logan's heart ached at the memory. Because he *had* heard about her. He had heard the story of the bracelet, the one Adrian had carried across continents, the one he had pressed into Logan's palm as though giving him something more than just a piece of jewelry. A piece of his past. A piece of himself.

And now, that bracelet lived on Logan's wrist forever, inked into his skin, never to be lost again.

He met Adrian's gaze, a quiet understanding passing between them, a remembrance of that night on the cliffs in Australia when Adrian had laid his soul bare.

Without thinking, Logan reached for Adrian's hand and brought it to his lips, pressing a soft kiss to his knuckles. Adrian gave him a small, watery smile before turning back to the album, flipping the pages forward.

The pictures painted a story—one of childhood, of summers spent at the beach, of scraped knees and ice cream-stained smiles. There was Adrian, no older than three, playing in the sand, his tiny hands grasping at seashells. Another of him, sticky-fingered and wide-eyed, gripping a half-melted ice cream cone.

Logan chuckled, shaking his head. "You were too cute."

The laughter dimmed when they reached a picture taken in a hospital room.

Aliana lay in the bed, her skin pale, her head wrapped in a soft kerchief. And there, sitting at the edge of the bed, was Adrian—just a little boy, no older than five, his small hands wrapped around hers, his face solemn as if he understood, even then, that the world was about to take something from him that he could never get back.

Logan swallowed hard, but no words came.

The pages turned, and time passed with them. Adrian grew older in the photos, his face sharper, his stance stronger. Most of the pictures were at the beach—his first surfboard, his first real wave. There was something breathtaking about seeing him like this, young and fearless, salt in his hair and sunlight in his smile.

"I..." Tammi started, then stopped, miming a camera with her hands, pressing an invisible shutter. "Those," she said, pointing to the album, her eyes shining with pride.

Logan, still mesmerized by the images before him, turned to Adrian and whispered, "You're beautiful."

A betraying warmth bloomed in Adrian's skin.

They were halfway through the third album when the sound of footsteps brought them back to the present.

Aaron and Alon had returned.

Logan didn't miss the redness in Aaron's eyes, the way they looked swollen, puffy—like maybe, just maybe, something had finally cracked open inside him.

Alon, oblivious to the weight in the room, plopped onto the couch beside Adrian and peered at the album. "What are you doing?" he asked.

"Mom is showing Logan embarrassing pictures of me," Adrian muttered, resigned to his fate.

Logan laughed, flipping another page.

"Have you seen him naked as a baby? Or the one where he thought he looked cool with a skateboard?" Alon smirked.

Adrian groaned. "You both suck."

But Logan just grinned, his fingers still laced with Adrian's.

"Yeah... it was a tough phase with the skateboard and those... rapper clothes, huh, Ad?" Logan teased, his silver eyes glinting with amusement as he glanced over at Adrian with a smirk.

Adrian groaned again, rubbing a hand down his face. "Shut up, or I'll post your embarrassing pictures on Facebook, Alon."

Alon just grinned, unbothered, while Logan chuckled and turned the page.

The laughter faded slightly as the next set of photos came into view.

Adrian, standing ahead of his unit, clad in crisp white navy dress uniform—sharp, immaculate, a stark contrast to the Adrian Logan had met chasing waves and sunrises. His hat sat perfectly in place, his black shoes gleamed, his posture was rigid, disciplined, and *god*, he looked *so* different. His body had been even more muscular then, his hair cropped neatly, his expression unreadable.

He was so damn hot in uniform.

Not now, Logan scolded himself. *You're in his parents' living room, for god's sake. This is not the time to picture Adrian in that uniform and then taking it off. Slowly.*

He shifted uncomfortably, clearing his throat, and flipped to the next photo before his thoughts betrayed him further.

Then, suddenly, he stopped, his eyes widening with recognition. His lips curled into a smile.

"Wait... is that Dean?" Logan laughed, pointing at a young man in the photo standing beside Adrian, looking every bit as disciplined and severe as Adrian had.

"Yeah," Adrian affirmed, his tone infused with glee.

"Oh my god, I would never have recognized him," Logan said, shaking his head.

"Why not?" Alon asked, leaning in slightly to look at the picture.

"I don't know, just look at him," Logan gestured at the image. "He actually looks... uptight here, like a serious person. Nothing like the Dean I know now."

Adrian snorted at the assessment, while Alon, still staring at the photo, mumbled absentmindedly, "I think he looks just fine."

Adrian glanced at him, catching the slight blush on his brother's face before he turned away, feigning indifference.

Ah. So his suspicions were right.

Alon had a crush.

It made sense now, the extra bitterness in his voice when talking about Adrian's friend, the subtle defensiveness. If he was gay or bi, if he had spent years struggling with it the way Adrian had once struggled, then of course some of that anger was about more than just standing in his brother's shadow.

Adrian didn't say anything. He didn't let his face betray the realization. He just let it pass—let Alon have his moment—and turned his attention back to his mother, who, miraculously, with her broken English, still managed to share story after story, each more embarrassing than the last, about his childhood to Logan.

"He not know that... ah... she want him—" Tammi laughed, slapping her knee. "He take her to movie and ice cream. He think, *'we friends!'* She paused for dramatic effect, eyes gleaming. "She kiss him... and he to run!"

She burst into full laughter, clearly delighted with her delivery. Adrian groaned and buried his face in his hands. "Mom, please."

Logan was already laughing, leaning back on the couch, completely enthralled. "You were quite the heartbreaker, weren't you, Ad?" he teased, nudging Adrian's leg.

Of *all* the embarrassing stories she could've chosen, she had to tell *that* one. Adrian had been fifteen. The girl from the next building had chased him down for weeks, asking him to take her to a movie—some random action thing—and then for ice cream. He'd finally caved, assuming it was friendly. But at the end of the night, she leaned in to kiss him, and Adrian, overwhelmed and blushing to his ears, mumbled a goodbye and practically bolted.

"He was!" Tammi said, proud as ever. "After he... gay, come out the closet," she nodded seriously at Logan, as if clarifying something important, "I have boys—*many many boys!*—come to house. Try talk to him. Boys all over. Boys from school, army, neighbors. Cute boys. All of them."

"Many, many boys? Boys all over? You don't say," Logan asked, eyebrows raised, smirking at Adrian, his voice low and full of mischief. His eyes had gone dark—warm, amused, a little possessive.

"But my boy, he is gentleman," Tammi said, tapping her chest. "He... picky. Very very. Want..." she gestured with her hands, searching for the word. "Connection. Not just kiss-kiss. You know?" She winked. "Feeling. Real love, yes? He... ah...ah... sensitive. My boy, sensitive, very."

"*Mom*, please," Adrian groaned again, his ears now a deep shade of red. "She is exaggerating." He said to Logan.

But Tammi was already launching into the next story. "Once, he in beach, yes?" she started again. "No shirt, tan, my boy beautiful—"

"Mom," Adrian cut her off.

"No, no, I want to hear it," Logan said, flashing Tammi a charming grin, and she melted on the spot, grinning right back.

Logan, of course, was eating it all up, wearing a satisfied smile like a man who had just discovered treasure.

By the time the night began to wind down, dessert plates were empty and Adrian's parents had managed to parade out every embarrassing story they could remember. Tammi, in particular, seemed delighted to recount every boy who had ever shown interest in Adrian—from classmates to army buddies to a barista who once left his number on a napkin.

To Adrian's quiet relief, Alon had joined in the jokes, had laughed with them, and—most importantly—his father had made an effort to include him, asking him questions, acknowledging him in a way Adrian *knew* hadn't happened often enough before.

And with that, Adrian's heart eased.

Maybe—just maybe—things would be *better* for Alon now.

As the evening came to a close, Logan exchanged numbers with Tammi, Aaron, and Alon, promising to keep them updated about Adrian's treatments.

And then, the moment Adrian had been dreading: the *goodbyes.*

Tammi wrapped him in her arms first, hugging him so tightly it almost hurt, holding onto him as if she could keep him from slipping away.

They all said it wasn't a goodbye.

But it *felt* like it could be.

Adrian buried his face in her shoulder, inhaling the scent of home, of warmth, of *her.*

"Love you, Mom," he whispered, so softly only she could hear. "Thanks for being my mom... even when you didn't have to."

Tammi let out a soft, broken sound, clutching him tighter. "Don't be silly," she scolded through her tears. "You are *my* son."

She held him for several minutes, unwilling to let go. And when she finally did, her hands lingered on his face, smoothing his hair back like she was committing every detail to memory.

Then came his father.

Aaron didn't say much—he never had been the type for long, emotional speeches—but when he pulled Adrian into a tight embrace, Adrian felt the tremor in his grip, the way his breath hitched against his shoulder.

His father was crying.

And so Adrian held on, pressing his hand against his father's back, holding onto this moment.

"Love you, Dad."

Just in case.

Alon was next.

His little brother didn't say much either, but his hug was firm, his voice steady when he said, "Good luck."

And that was enough.

Finally, after saying their goodbyes to Logan, Adrian and Logan stepped out of the apartment, making their way back to the car in silence. The air was cooler now, crisp against Adrian's skin.

Logan unlocked the car but didn't get in right away. Instead, he turned to Adrian, his silver eyes searching his face.

"You okay?" he asked softly.

Adrian let out a slow breath, staring up at the sky for a moment before looking back at Logan.

"I don't know," he admitted.

Logan nodded, as if he understood.

And then, wordlessly, he reached out, taking Adrian's hand and lacing their fingers together.

Adrian squeezed his hand in return, and for now, that was enough.

"So... many, many boys, huh?" Logan simpered. "School friends, neighbor's kids, army buddies, baristas, surfers...? I'm sure I've missed a few," he flashed a teasing smirk at Adrian.

"Shut up," Adrian muttered, his voice low and mortified as a deep flush climbed up his neck, blooming across his cheeks. He buried his face into the curve of Logan's neck, trying to hide from the world—or at least from his mother's wildly exaggerated matchmaking memoir.

"She thinks every guy who looks at me wants me," he grunted against Logan's skin. "And I told you how it usually goes. My height..." He exhaled slowly. "Let's just say I'm fun to flirt with, but not the one they take seriously. No one wants to *date* the short one."

Logan's arms tightened around him in reply. "You are perfect," he said, kissing the top of Adrian's head.

The drive back to Adrian's house was quiet, filled only with the hum of the tires against the asphalt. Logan held Adrian's hand the entire way, his fingers a steady anchor, a silent promise.

Adrian's throat burned with the emotion choking him, the kind of ache that had no release, no words strong enough to carry its weight. So neither of them spoke. They just breathed together in the hush of the night.

At some point during the drive, Logan made a call to the rental agency, arranging for them to pick up the car. By the time they pulled into the driveway, a man was already waiting. The keys exchanged hands, and just like that, another chapter closed.

Inside Adrian's bedroom, Logan moved with tender urgency. He drew Adrian into his embrace, pressing him close against his chest as if to shield him from the world's harshest trials. In that silent shelter, he held him not just with arms, but with strength, offering solace and resilience to both, entwined in a moment of shared vulnerability. "I love you," Logan murmured, his breath warm against Adrian's temple. "And everything will be okay."

Adrian didn't believe it. Not really.

A deep, haunting fear lingered within him, echoing the reality that he may have just spent the night wrapped in the warmth and familiarity of his family for the last time.

But hearing Logan *say it* made breathing just a little easier.

Then, there was a gentle knock on the door.

Logan kissed Adrian once, gently, before pulling away and heading toward the door.

Dean stood on the other side, his face calm but his eyes saying everything his voice hadn't yet.

"I'll take you guys to the airport," he offered, his voice rough, thick.

Logan nodded. "Thanks."

They gathered their bags, rolling their luggage into the trunk, and then Dean started the car. The engine purred to life, and they were off. One step closer to leaving, one step further from home.

Adrian sat in the back with Logan, their hands intertwined between them. And as the city blurred past, Adrian spoke. He told them about what had happened at dinner, about Alon, about his father.

But not about what he suspected. Not about Alon's crush on Dean, or the way it had hit him with sudden clarity. No. That was something Alon had to figure out on his own.

Dean listened, eyes fixed on the road, the tension in his shoulders betraying how deeply he heard every word. His hands were tight on the wheel. He nodded occasionally, but said nothing. Logan, beside Adrian, stayed quiet too, tracing gentle circles on the back of Adrian's hand, grounding him, reminding him that he didn't have to carry everything alone.

By the time they reached the airport, something had shifted. Not just between them, within them.

Dean parked in silence, his grip on the wheel a little too firm, his jaw locked the way it always was when he was holding something in. He didn't say goodbye. He just got out, grabbed a bag, and started walking.

He insisted on taking them all the way inside. Through security. To the gate. Until the very last possible moment, as if, by staying close enough, by refusing to let go, he could slow time down. Maybe even stop it.

Adrian let him.

Not because he needed help. But because Dean did.

And, if he was being honest, he needed it too.

But then, there was no time left.

They had to cross the gate alone.

And just as Adrian turned to step away, Dean grabbed him. His fingers curled tightly around Adrian's arm, his grip firm, desperate.

"We got through—" Dean started, but his voice faltered.

He didn't have to finish.

Adrian knew what he was thinking.

He was thinking about all of it. The years. The training. The diving into depths no one else had dared to reach. The wars that had reshaped them into something neither of them fully recognized. The missions that had turned them into ghosts of themselves. The nights spent standing watch over each other's backs, both knowing that death had brushed too close too many times.

The blood.

So much blood.

The fallen friends they have mourned and grieved together.

It was the strength and sacredness of their friendship—founded on sacrifice and deeper than anything Adrian had ever experienced. They had been bound by things that no one else could understand, by the silent oaths spoken in gunfire and sea spray and the metallic taste of adrenaline on their tongues. By the dark nights when Adrian cried so loud that Dean came into the room and held him.

And Adrian knew, without question, without hesitation—Dean would die for him.

He almost *had*.

And Adrian would have done the same.

"A lot," Adrian finally said, his voice quiet but steady, a small, painful smile tugging at the corner of his lips.

Dean swallowed hard, his Adam's apple bobbing, his eyes burning with unshed tears. "You didn't survive all this shit just to die from cancer..."

Adrian had no answer.

Because he *couldn't* say everything would be okay.

Because they both knew the truth.

Dean clenched his jaw, blinking rapidly before nodding once. "I'll come visit you in a few months. Tom and I."

Adrian nodded. "Keep an eye on Alon, okay? He's in our unit now. Make sure he's handling it. It should be my job, but... I don't know if I'll be able to. And he might need some help."

Dean didn't hesitate. "Of course."

And then Adrian pulled him into a hug.

Dean clung to him fiercely, as if striving to etch this fleeting moment into eternity, yearning to rewind time itself. He held his best friend—his brother, his everything—so tightly, as though anchoring him against an impending departure. The heart-wrenching reality hit: he was about to board a plane, facing the uncertainty of whether he would return.

Then, all too rapidly, it slipped away. Dean discreetly brushed away his tears, trying to catch his breath.

Logan grabbed his suitcase. Adrian grabbed his.

They turned to go.

And then—

"Hey, Princess."

Adrian and Logan both turned.

Dean stood there, his shoulders squared, his chest rising and falling in deep, measured breaths. But his eyes—his eyes were red, and when the tears finally slipped free, he didn't wipe them away.

"Remember what I told you," Dean said, his voice cracking, raw. "I wasn't kidding."

Logan met his gaze, something unreadable flashing between them.

Logan looked at him. Something flickered behind his eyes, something quiet, protective, knowing. "I know," Logan said. He smiled, just barely, just enough to mean something. "See you in a few months, Dean."

And then, with one last look, one last breath, they turned and walked away.

Dean lingered at the airport, the weight of emotions anchoring him in place, as he observed the bustling crowd around him. The bright lights and distant announcements faded into a blur, mirroring his scattered thoughts. Finally, gathering his resolve, he turned away, navigating through the labyrinth of memories in his mind, eventually making his way back to the car. With a heavy heart, he steered toward the solitude of an empty apartment, each kilometer echoing the silence he felt within.

Chapter 16

I Only Ever Looked for You

I didn't know if we would ever find our way back to this. To each other, to this version of us that still knows how to hold, how to stay, how to trust. So much time passed. Too much silence. Too much damage. But that night, when you looked at me, not like someone who had left, but like someone who had never stopped waiting, I understood. We had both been surviving in the absence of something sacred.

And now, in the quiet between your breath and mine, I know this: you are still my home. You always were. And this time, I am not afraid to be touched by you. This time, I let you see everything. Because this time, we both know: we never stopped belonging to each other.

The streams of water came again—this time to bring us back.

November 29, 2020—Seattle, Washington—The Next Day

SEATTLE'S NIGHT AIR SEEPED into his very being, a sting of icy chill—a stark contrast to the warm, gentle embrace of Mediterranean winters that Adrian had known all his life. Logan barely flinched. He had weathered colder things—loneliness, regret, the hollow ache of missing Adrian. But Adrian, wrapped in the delicate warmth of the Israeli sun for most of his life, shivered.

Without a word, Logan ripped open his suitcase, pulling out the thickest coat he could find, and wrapped it around Adrian's shoulders, his fingers lingering there, pressing into the bones that jutted out sharper than they used to. He murmured against Adrian's skin, his voice low, solid, "Now that you're no longer in the Middle East, we'll get you proper winter gear." Then, with the tenderness of a man who had lost too much to ever take anything for granted again, he kissed the tip of Adrian's nose, as if to warm him from the inside out.

They moved through the night like two drifters on a vast and empty sea, tossing their luggage and Adrian's beloved guitar case into a cab's trunk. Logan leaned forward, giving the driver the address of the home he had barely seen before choosing on impulse.

It felt unreal. The last time Logan had traced these streets, he had been drowning, every familiar building a rip current pulling him under, every familiar smell, every whisper of wind, a reminder of what he had lost. He had walked through this city with his hands in his pockets and his heart in his throat, stifling in the absence of Adrian. He had told himself Adrian would never want him again. That he had shattered something beyond repair.

And yet now, impossibly, Adrian was here.

His body had changed, his frame slenderer, his muscles softened by time and sickness, but his eyes, those molten-whiskey eyes, still held that same quiet kindness, that same depth, as endless as the horizon. And his smile—God, his smile—was still the same. It cracked something inside Logan, something he had kept locked away, something he had feared he'd never feel again.

Love.

Love so deep it eclipsed reason, so vast it could pull the tide. Love that had survived two years of distance, of silence, of regret. Love that sat right beside him now, in a cab in the middle of a city that had once felt like a graveyard, but tonight... felt like home.

The cab weaved through the streets near Seattle-Tacoma International Airport, where the roads stretched wide and empty under the dim glow of streetlights. The rain-slick pavement shimmered like black glass, reflecting the neon hum of convenience stores and the occasional lonely restaurant, their windows fogged with warmth against the biting night air.

"We need to stop at my parents' place," Logan croaked, gripping Adrian's hand more tightly as if braced for impact.

Adrian peeked at him, his fingers lacing through Logan's, offering silent reassurance as the cab hummed forward. "Is there a particular reason?" he asked, his thumb pressing gently against Logan's wrist.

"A few, actually." Logan exhaled, his breath uneven. "I left at a haste. Walked out of work. Walked out of everything. My mom's beside herself. She and my father don't understand the divorce from Sandy, don't understand why I just disappeared." He paused, swallowing, his fingers tightening around Adrian's. "And... I want them to meet you. I want to explain to them what happened. I want them to know why I left."

He came to a stop, the words and their meaning too vast to be conveyed all at once.

Adrian's warmth was comforting in a way that gutted him. "I get that," Adrian murmured gently. "Do you want me there?" Always, the kindness in Adrian roared louder than any storm.

Logan turned to Adrian, his gaze fierce. "Always. I want you with me always. Everywhere, every time. Clear?"

Adrian's cheeks flushed, his lips parting slightly in silent surrender. He nodded.

Logan studied him for a moment, then exhaled, his fingers tightening around Adrian's. There was something raw in his eyes, something tender and desperate all at once. "I don't have enough money for the treatments." Those words were stones dropping into a deep, dark abyss. "I need to borrow it from my dad. And before you get angry, I didn't tell you because I knew you wouldn't agree. But I need you to get better. And money won't be the reason you don't."

Adrian stiffened, his jaw tightening as he tried to pull his hand away.

"Logan, I don't want your dad to pay—"

"It's not about you." Logan's grip held firm, his voice steady but urgent. "It's me taking the money. And I will pay him back."

Adrian's eyes flashed. "Logan, I am not some charity case—"

He tried again to free his hand, but Logan only held on tighter.

"Ad?" Logan's voice softened, cutting through Adrian's frustration.

Adrian turned, exasperated. "What?"

Logan swallowed, his thumb tracing slow, absent-minded circles on Adrian's wrist. "Let me take care of you." His voice was quiet, pleading. Then, as if sealing a promise, he brought Adrian's hand to his lips and kissed it.

Adrian's breath hitched, his anger faltering.

"Logan, I don't want to be the needy person who comes begging for money." His voice cracked slightly, the words scraping at his throat. "I don't even want those treatments."

"Yes, you do." Logan's response was immediate and firm. "You're keeping me alive, remember?" His tone softened into a teasing whisper as he nestled his head against Adrian's chest, inhaling deeply and savoring the delicate texture of the fabric brushing against his cheeks. Against his face, he felt the firm strength of Adrian's chest, a comforting presence he memorized with each breath. He could hear Adrian's strong heartbeat, each one an echo of life for which he was grateful. He allowed himself to be enveloped by this sensation, letting it wash over him like a soothing balm, numbing the chaotic noises of the world outside.

Adrian's resistance crumbled in an instant, his arms moving instinctively around Logan, fingers threading into his hair.

"You're not begging for anything, Ad. You're just coming with me." Logan whispered against his shirt. "Or would you prefer I go alone?"

"No, of course not." The answer came without hesitation.

"Then let me deal with my father." Logan sighed, closing his eyes as he relished Adrian's warmth.

There was a beat of silence before Adrian huffed, shaking his head. "Lo, if you don't have money, why the hell did you book the most expensive suite and rent a Maserati?"

Logan smirked against Adrian's chest. "It's not that I don't have money. I don't have enough money. Plus, I told you, the suite was the only one available. And I've always dreamed about driving a Maserati."

Adrian groaned but couldn't hide the ghost of a smile tugging at his lips.

The cab came to a gentle halt, the rhythmic patter of rain dancing against the windows creating a soothing backdrop between them.

"Don't you dare," he warned Adrian, who was reaching into his pocket. With a firm gesture, Logan commanded Adrian to exit while swiping his card and thanked the driver.

Adrian retrieved their bags from the trunk, carefully placing them onto the slick sidewalk. As Logan joined him, he inhaled deeply, the crisp, cold air filling his lungs, and watched in fascination as his warm breath mingled with the Seattle night, a fleeting wisp against the dark, star-studded sky.

The apartment building rose like a glass-and-steel monolith against the night sky, towering above them, its windows glinting with the fractured light of the city. Even at this late hour, Seattle was still breathing—cars slicing through the rain-slicked streets, headlights casting silver streaks on the pavement, pedestrians bundled against the cold, their hurried steps whispering against the sidewalk. Beyond the buildings, patches of darkness hinted at parks, trees swaying in the wind, silhouetted against the electric hum of the skyline.

Adrian took it all in, the urban sea so different from the sun-drenched shores of home. He turned to Logan as the cab pulled away. "You live here?"

Logan nodded, bending to grab his suitcase. "Yeah. Close to work and the airport." He smirked slightly.

Adrian hesitated, his fingers ghosting over Logan's wrist before he caught his hand properly, stopping him just before he reached the large glass doors.

"Have you..." Adrian's voice was careful, his fingers squeezing slightly, "lived here with her?"

Logan closed his eyes for a moment, setting the suitcase down again, his heart shrinking from the hurt in Adrian's voice as he asked it. Without a word, he stepped closer and wrapped Adrian into his arms, breathing him in. "No." He leaned in and kissed him, slow and certain. "I moved here after we split up. Actually... I haven't even been here since I bought the place."

Adrian pulled back just enough to search Logan's face. "How so?"

Logan's hands moved absently, tracing Adrian's back over the thick coat that wrapped him. "Everything happened so fast," he murmured. "Basically, the house Sandy and I lived in? My father bought it for us. And when I told her I was gay... she left. Walked out and never looked back. And I—" He stopped, taking a breath. "I couldn't stay there. The house felt haunted. Not by her; by me. By all the things I tried to be, all the ways I tried to force myself to live a life that was never mine."

Adrian's hold on him grew firmer.

"So, I started looking for you." Logan swallowed, his voice quieter now, but no less intense. "And then I found this place. Signed the contract. But before I could even move in, I got the call." His fingers curled against the back of Adrian's neck, holding him close. "That they found you. And I did the only thing I knew how to do. I ran to the airport and got a ticket to the fucking Middle East."

Adrian let out a short, breathy laugh, shaking his head. "You're insane."

349

"Completely." Logan grinned. "You love it."

Adrian just hummed in response, but his fingers brushed lightly over Logan's wrist, lingering.

They hurried inside, the glass doors sighing shut behind them, locking out the cold and wrapping them in the building's quiet, artificial warmth. The lobby stretched before them, polished and modern. The concierge barely looked up.

"Where to?" he asked, his tone as routine as the ticking of a clock.

Logan straightened, shaking off the weight of the past few hours. "Penthouse."

A flicker of curiosity crossed the concierge's face as he turned to his computer, fingers gliding over the keys. A quiet moment passed, the hum of the city barely pressing against the glass, before he nodded.

In the elevator, Logan swapped the fob, and the doors sealed them off from the rest of the building. The ride up was silent, broken only by the soft hum of the elevator and the occasional shift of their suitcases.

When the doors finally slid open, Logan stepped forward first, fishing the key from his pocket and unlocking the door.

He had expected emptiness, a few boxes standing in the middle of the room in disarray, furniture scattered, some still unpacked, others covered. But when the door swung open, the space was pristine. Polished floors gleamed under soft, recessed lighting. The scent of fresh wood and clean linen lingered in the air.

"Huh," Logan muttered, stepping inside.

Adrian arched a brow. "Expecting chaos?"

"Honestly? Yeah." Logan let out a quiet laugh.

He turned back, reaching for Adrian's hand, pulling him across the threshold. "It's your home too, you know that, right?" His voice was softer now, a promise rather than a question.

Adrian tilted his head, studying Logan's silver eyes, searching. "Is that so?"

Logan held his gaze. "Yeah." There was no hesitation, no doubt. Just certainty.

Adrian exhaled, shaking his head slightly, but his fingers curled into Logan's.

"Let's look around," Logan offered, squeezing his hand. "I barely had time to see it when I signed for it."

Adrian followed him through the space, both of them moving slowly. The apartment was modern, sleek, but not cold. Dark wooden floors stretched beneath their feet, soft against the quiet hush of their steps.

There were two master bedrooms, one larger than the other, each with its own bathroom and a large walk-in closet attached.

Logan's belongings, still packed in boxes, were neatly stacked in the smaller room. He let out a quiet chuckle. "I guess the movers figured I'd rather have one room without my mess."

"That's really considerate of them," Adrian remarked.

"Let's freshen up before we go?" Logan suggested, running a hand through his travel-worn hair. His voice was casual, but there was something beneath it, something careful, something measured. He glanced at his phone. "I already texted my mom. She's really excited. I told her I was coming... and that I wasn't coming alone."

Adrian nodded. "I'm a bit nervous about meeting them," he admitted, letting out a small chuckle.

"Do you trust me?" Logan asked, holding his gaze.

"Of course."

"Then don't worry about it," he whispered softly, taking Adrian's hand and gently pressing his lips to the back of it. "It will be okay."

Every cell in Adrian's body seemed to melt as Logan's lips brushed softly against his skin. His silvery eyes bore into him with a wildfire of longing and admiration, creating a gaze so forceful it should be outlawed by the heavens.

All he managed was a nod.

"So, how about freshening up before we head out?" Logan asked again, planting another quick kiss on Adrian's cheek before walking toward the bathroom door.

Adrian shook his head in an attempt to clear his mind. He let out a sigh, stretched his arms, and tried to shake off the stiffness from the long flight. "Yeah, almost a whole day on a plane. That's brutal." He followed Logan to the shower, massaging the back of his neck. "Forgot it was that long."

But then the words settled, and so did the silence.

Because the last time Adrian had been on a flight here... had been for Logan's wedding. And the flight back? That was something Adrian had spent the last two years trying to erase from his memory. A slow suffocation at 12,000 meters, his heart breaking in quiet, invisible ways, with no one to see and no way to escape.

His throat tightened. "Sorry," he murmured, eyes flicking away. "I didn't mean it like that."

Logan didn't hesitate. He reached for Adrian's hand, lacing their fingers together like an anchor. "I know," he said softly. And with that, they stepped inside the bathroom, and Logan shut the door behind them.

Logan rummaged through the bathroom cabinets, finding a neatly arranged collection of toiletries: new bottles of soap and shampoos, fresh toothbrushes and toothpaste, everything untouched. He figured the cleaning services he hired upon signing had ensured the apartment was stocked with essentials. He made a mental note to thank them, but right now, all that mattered was Adrian.

And then the shower.

What should have been a quick rinse stretched into something else, something slower, something deeper. Their lips found each other between the steam, between the rivulets of water tracing over skin and scars, between the unspoken apologies and the weight of everything they had lost. It was desperate, not just from longing but from time itself, from all the months and miles that had separated them. Hands mapped out what was once familiar, as if trying to remember—no, trying to make sure they never forgot again.

By the time they finally pulled away, breathless and warm, they had lost track of how long they had been in there.

"We have to go," Logan murmured, even though the last thing he wanted was to leave this room, this moment. He wanted to crawl into bed with Adrian, press close, let sleep take them somewhere softer. But instead, they finished their shower and stepped out.

"My dad's leaving in a few hours. Flight to Denmark. Business stuff. He could be late since he is taking his private plane, but he wouldn't."

Adrian, still towel-drying his hair, gave him a small, tired smile. "Then let's go."

He finished pulling on his clothes, and together, they stepped back out into the world.

The drive wasn't long, but it felt like an eternity. Logan's grip on the wheel was too tight, his pulse hammering at his throat. The confrontation with his father loomed like an approaching storm, dark and inevitable. But this was exactly why he had to do it, why it had to be now.

Adrian needed to be hospitalized in the morning. Logan wasn't going to let this moment slip past. It was time to stand his ground.

He reached across the center console, taking Adrian's hand in his, feeling the warmth of it, the solidity of him. "I'll show you the city someday," Logan said, stealing a quick glance before returning his eyes to the road. "I promised you that a long time ago... and I plan to keep that promise."

Adrian's fingers tightened around his, his smile a mix of love and sorrow, as if he were holding something fragile between his teeth. "I know," was all he said, and that was enough.

The iron gates of the Vaughn estate had rolled open, revealing a world so far removed from Adrian's that it might as well have been another planet.

The private road leading up to the mansion was lined with sculpted trees. On either side of the driveway, marble fountains sprayed arcs of water over sculptures that he could barely make out in the night light.

Adrian glanced out the window and spotted a cluster of smaller homes scattered across the estate. These homes were at least three times the size of his small Tel Aviv apartment, boasting sleek stone, sweeping terraces, and the kind of upscale living that probably included servants and private pools.

The main house stood at the top of the hill, all glass and pale stone, its walls catching the night like mirrors. Light from inside spread in a steady, artificial glow that made the place seem detached from everything around it. It was vast, too much to take in at once. Adrian found himself tracing the memory of the long drive from the gates, the manicured trees, the perfect lawns. Whoever lived like this probably had other estates just like it, scattered across the world, identical in their perfection.

The drive curved into a wide circular court where a black Rolls-Royce waited under the portico. Logan slowed the car and gave a small nod to the driver, who straightened from where he'd been leaning against the car, dressed in a sharp black suit.

Adrian barely registered the soft purr of the engine shutting off. His body had gone rigid, hands gripping his jeans like he was bracing for impact. A stray thought crossed his mind, maybe he should've gone shopping first, bought something that looked like it belonged here. Or at least cleaned his shoes before stepping onto that driveway, before walking into a place like this.

Logan stepped out, rounding the car in an easy motion before opening Adrian's door himself. "Come on," he said softly.

Adrian forced himself to move.

He had been in a lot of places that made him feel like he didn't belong: war zones, military bases, foreign cities where he barely spoke the language. But nothing had ever made him feel as small as this place did.

The driveway alone was bigger than the street he lived on.

And God, the sheer perfection of it all. The silence, the faultlessness. In the estate's impeccably arranged domain, not a single blade of grass dared to be out of line, nor was there any imperfection to sully the pristine atmosphere. He had encountered wealth in various forms, had witnessed opulence, yet this experience transcended all. This was generational wealth, old money woven so deeply into a bloodline that it no longer felt like wealth; it felt like divinity.

His gut twisted.

This world—*Logan's world*—wasn't just wealth. It was an entirely different existence.

The kind where people didn't ask for things, they simply expected them to appear. If Adrian measured his life in hundreds of shekels, equivalent to about a third of a dollar, those individuals spoke in hundreds of thousands and millions of dollars.

It was a place where money wasn't just a luxury, it was a force, a weapon, a birthright. It built empires, erased problems before they could even be spoken aloud. It made sure people like Logan never had to fight for anything in their lives, because the world had already surrendered to them before they were even born.

And standing here, beneath the towering columns of the Vaughn estate, Adrian had never felt smaller.

A wave of shame crashed over him, so sharp it nearly stole his breath. Shame for ever thinking he and Logan could be equals. Shame for that tiny, secondhand-furnished apartment in Tel Aviv, the one he had so proudly called home. The one where Logan had stayed with him, where they had spent the recent nights curled up on his sinking old couch, laughing, kissing, whispering dreams into the dark.

It felt ridiculous now.

He felt ridiculous.

Had Adrian really been fantasizing? Had he truly believed that Logan—the heir to this, a world of private jets and marble mansions, of polished sculptures and luxury cars—could ever belong with someone like him?

The poor boy from southern Israel?

And worse... had he actually taken Logan to his family home? To that tiny apartment with its creaky floors and peeling paint? Had he truly let himself believe that was enough?

What had he been thinking?

Now, more than ever, Adrian understood why Logan had left.

It had nothing to do with fear. It had been inevitable. Adrian longed to transcend time, yearning to revisit those early weeks in Hawaii. He envisioned himself advising his younger self to bury those ambitious dreams deep within, for there was simply no chance of fulfillment. With a wry smile, he imagined encountering his younger self, chuckling at the naivety of that young man. 'Do you truly believe you could get that guy? Not in a million years, my friend.'

Logan had nothing to gain from being with him. He could offer him nothing. No money, no status, no effortless security. Just a life of struggle, of working-class exhaustion, of a future that could never match the one he was destined for.

And suddenly, Adrian wanted to run.

He wanted to turn around and tell Logan to take him back to the airport. He could catch the next flight home, disappear before they even knocked on that godforsaken door.

Because they were crazy.

Both of them.

This was never going to work.

But before Adrian could step back, Logan moved.

A firm grip closed around his wrist, pulling him forward, forcing him to stop. And before Adrian could say anything, before he could voice the panic clawing at his throat, Logan grabbed his face in both hands—big, warm, steady hands—his thumbs brushing over Adrian's cheekbones as he bent down, pressing their foreheads together.

"Stop."

Just one word. Steady. Commanding.

Adrian swallowed hard, trying to look away, but Logan wouldn't let him.

"Look at me."

Adrian did.

And all he could think as he gazed into those storm-colored eyes—eyes filled with a fire so raw, so certain, so unshakable—was that Logan could do so much better than him.

Logan, with his expensive suits and that effortless charm. With his brilliant, wicked mind, his degrees from universities that Adrian could only dream of attending. With a last name that carried weight in exclusive circles where Adrian had never set foot. With a wonderful sense of humor and a caring heart. With his magnetic smile and kind eyes that sparkled like the most beautiful star in existence. With his fiery personality that was laced with persistence, courage, and bravery.

Logan, who had every possible door open to him.

And yet, here he was. Holding Adrian's face like he was something precious. As if he were the only thing that mattered.

And then Logan spoke, his voice thick with conviction, with love, with devotion.

"I chose you, Adrian. Don't you dare think for a second that you don't belong with me."

How had he known, from a single gaze, exactly what was going on in Adrian's mind? How did he recognize it so quickly and accurately? Was Adrian that obvious, or was Logan just that perceptive?

Adrian squeezed his eyes shut, his breath shaky, his heart breaking open.

But Logan wasn't done.

"I don't care about this place. I don't care about the money, or the house, or what my father thinks. I care about you." His voice dropped lower, softer. "And now that I finally have you, I will never, *never*, Adrian, let you go."

Adrian's chest ached.

Logan had no idea just how much Adrian wanted to believe him.

And yet, as Logan's grip tightened around him, as the fire in his eyes blazed like the molten heart of the sun sinking into the horizon, Adrian knew—

Maybe, just maybe, he *could*.

Because standing before him, beneath the weight of years lost and the ache of time slipping between their fingers like sand, was *his* Logan.

Not the man in tailored suits and polished shoes, not the heir to empires built on steel and saltwater trade, not the son of wealth and expectation.

No.

This was the same Logan who had once slept beside him in cabins with roofs that leaked like broken seashells, who had curled against him on too-small motel beds where the sheets smelled of strangers and dreams half-lived.

The same Logan who had eaten food from questionable diners, who had worn the same sun-bleached shirt for days on end, shrugging with that lazy smirk, saying, *"I wore it for like ten minutes, then it's off, it's basically clean."*

The Logan who had walked endless trails with him, their feet bruised and their spirits wild, who had jumped into roaring waters with him, letting the ocean pull them under, letting the waves roll over their heads like the sky's embrace, because they knew, together, they would always rise.

This—this—was the Logan who had claimed Adrian's heart, flowing with the inevitability of the tide caressing the shore.

The house, the wealth, the legacy, it was just background noise, a distant hum, a mirage shimmering on the horizon.

What mattered was here, now.

The man in front of him.

The man he had always loved.

So when Logan raised his hand to knock, his fingers trembling ever so slightly, Adrian stayed beside him.

The heavy mahogany door swung open, and there they stood.

Logan's mother, Samantha, was dressed in casual yet elegant loungewear, the kind of effortless luxury that looked simple but made a statement. Her diamond earrings and necklace caught the soft light, and her hair was styled. She had clearly been expecting them, and the late hour did not seem to bother her.

His father, Robert, stood beside her, dressed in dark jeans and a crisp white shirt, appearing more casual than what Logan was accustomed to seeing him wear. It was obvious he was preparing to leave; his tailored suit was probably waiting somewhere, perfectly pressed, alongside a private jet ready to fly him across the world.

Logan wondered if the man ever slept, if there was even a second of his life he didn't devote to work. Or if, even now, standing here at the doorway of his own home, he was thinking about profit margins and shipping routes.

The moment his father's gaze locked onto him, Logan felt the shift.

"Logan." Robert's voice carried the weight of both distress and fury, his sharp blue eyes narrowing. "Nice to see you. Now, where the hell have you been?!"

Samantha let out a quiet sigh and placed a hand on her husband's arm. "Robert, not now." Her voice was even, controlled, as though she had spent years smoothing over the cracks in this family. She turned back to Logan with a warm, if slightly cautious, smile.

"Come on in, Logan," she said, stepping aside to let them through. "And who is this lovely guest you've brought with you? You look so familiar..."

Her gaze landed on Adrian, studying him with mild curiosity.

Adrian stiffened. Logan felt it immediately, the tension coiling in his frame.

"I'm Adrian," he said cautiously, his voice measured. After a brief pause, he added, "I think we crossed paths at Logan's... hum... ahh... wedding."

At the word *wedding*, Logan caught the subtle recoil in his tone. The syllables dragged against Adrian's throat, his vocal cords tightening and stretching around them, an instrument straining to reach a note beyond its range.

Logan's arm gently encircled Adrian's hips, drawing them closer as they moved through the house's silent corridors. The touch was a whisper of comfort, easing the tension that lingered in Adrian's grip. He responded with a quiet, grateful smile, a small gesture of thanks. They entered the grand room, where Samantha's warm invitation beckoned them to sit. She offered Adrian a soft, reassuring grin and pointed to the plush couch, "Make yourself at home, dear."

"Oh, do you want to start, Logan?" Robert's voice was razor-sharp, slicing clean through the room. "Shall we begin with your sudden departure? Or the fact that you're filing for a divorce out of nowhere? Or maybe we should talk about the customers and business partners calling me because you've been canceling your meetings?" His words came rapidly, with questions firing off one after the other like gunfire.

"Or maybe," he continued, stepping closer, "we should talk about why Ada Mae has been calling me to take over your responsibilities because, apparently, you were in Israel? What the hell were you doing flying half a world away without a word?"

The room held a charge, the air trembling in the pause before a storm broke.

And then, Robert turned his gaze to Adrian.

His expression didn't change; there was no warmth, no hostility. Just indifference, like Adrian was a minor detail in the grand equation of his frustration.

"Hello, Adrian," he said, almost as an afterthought. "How lovely to have you here."

His voice was utterly flat, a passing remark, a polite acknowledgment before turning his full attention back to Logan, his eyes steely, demanding answers.

The room held its breath.

And Logan stood there, heart pounding, jaw clenched, realizing that this was it; the moment he had to face everything he had spent years running from. Shoulders squared yet trembling beneath his coat of composure, like a man stepping barefoot into a fire he'd built with his own hands. The air tasted like memory, and his father's silence was a mountain between them.

"I need money, Dad," Logan said, cutting straight to the point. His voice was steady, but beneath it, there was an urgency, a quiet desperation he couldn't mask. "A lot of it. And I need it now."

Robert didn't react right away. Instead, he simply studied his son with an unreadable expression. "Of course you do." His tone was dry but not cruel. "How much?" he asked as he sat down.

Logan followed his father's lead and took the chair opposite, palms pressed to his knees, aware of Adrian taking the seat beside him.

"Five hundred grand, for starters."

Time seemed to stop. Even the light filtering through the curtains looked frozen, suspended mid-breath.

Adrian's head turned sharply toward Logan, his expression a stunned echo of everyone else in the room. Samantha's lips parted, her hand drifting instinctively to her chest. And Robert—stoic, immovable Robert—lifted a single brow like a man peering over the edge of something he didn't want to see the bottom of.

"I'll probably need more down the line," Logan added.

Robert leaned back in his chair, a slow exhale escaping him like he was trying to release something that wouldn't be let go. His fingers dragged thoughtfully along the line of his jaw. "You don't just drop a number like that on me, Logan, and expect me to sign a check. What's going on? Are you in trouble? Gambling? Debt? What the hell did you do?"

There was a flicker of genuine concern beneath his usual strict businessman exterior.

"It's not like that," Logan was hurried to say. "It's a long story."

Robert scoffed. "Then you better start talking."

"Adrian has leukemia," he said, forcing the words out before his nerves could stop him. "He needs treatment."

There was a long pause where no one seemed to know what to do with the truth now sitting between them like a third presence.

Robert finally gave a slow nod, subtle, almost imperceptible, but it was there. "I'm sorry to hear that," he said, and though the tone was neutral, something in Adrian's eyes shifted; he blinked, clearly not expecting even that small acknowledgment.

"But what does that have to do with my money?" Robert finally asked.

Logan clenched his jaw, his hands curled into fists on his knees. His voice, when it came, was thick with the effort to remain composed. "I don't have enough for the treatment."

Robert's lips pressed into a thin line. His father didn't react with fire. Instead, there was a chill to him, calm in a way that made the room feel colder, the silence between each word deliberate and controlled. "Interesting," Robert said, the word falling from his mouth like a dropped coin. "And why exactly don't you have the money, Logan? You should have the money. I gave you and your wife a house. I know your salary. I know your shares in the company. So where is it?"

Logan bit the inside of his cheek until the copper taste of restraint filled his mouth. He knew this was coming. The interrogation wrapped in numbers, the audit of his life delivered with boardroom precision.

"I paid some of the first investments for Sandy's clothing line. I bought her vacations. She used my credit card for... basically everything. I also bought an apartment, by the way, so you can sell the house you gave us. And..." Logan took a deep breath. "I spent some money... finding Adrian."

Samantha's brows knit together in concern.

"Finding Adrian?" Robert repeated, his sharp eyes narrowing.

Logan vacillated long enough to feel himself poised at the edge of a cliff. He drew in a breath and remembered the ravine they had once crossed together, a jungle vine clenched in his fists, Adrian's presence around him. He felt that same vertigo now, and once more he leapt.

"I'm gay."

The room seemed to fall away from itself. Air grew thick, unmoving, the walls holding a silence so complete it almost hummed.

Samantha's hand flew to her mouth, her eyes wide, not cruel, not disgusted, just stunned by the way truth can arrive without knocking.

Robert, by contrast, barely moved. A small, nearly imperceptible twitch in his jaw, the only betrayal of shock. But Logan saw it. He saw everything.

"And Adrian is my boyfriend," he continued, steady now, steadier than he had been in years. "I think that explains the divorce."

His father didn't blink. Didn't breathe, it seemed. He just looked at his son as though trying to decipher a language he'd never cared to learn.

Then, with a calmness that scraped, Robert asked, "How the hell are you gay?"

"Robert!" Samantha snapped.

But he kept his eyes locked on Logan, like the truth might dissolve if he stared it down long enough.

"No, I'm serious." Robert looked at Logan, his brow furrowing. "For twenty-eight years, you were straight. You were happily married. And now, suddenly, you're gay? Out of nowhere?" He turned his gaze, sharp and cutting, to Adrian. "Is he... blackmailing you, Logan?"

"Oh my God, Dad, no!" Logan pressed his fingers to the bridge of his nose, trying to breathe through the sting behind his eyes.

Adrian flinched, not visibly, but inwardly; Logan could feel it like a shift in the air beside him. A wound not yet spoken.

Robert shook his head, his expression unreadable. "I don't get it. What changed?"

Logan exhaled, something bitter clawing at his throat. "Nothing changed." His voice was raw, cracked open like a wound. "I just... got the courage to pursue what I wanted."

But that wasn't enough. It was never enough.

His father sat there, assessing him, just as he assessed board meetings and mergers, calculating profits and risks. Logan clenched his fists against the rising frustration.

"When you saw Adrian at my wedding, he wasn't just a guest." Logan's voice wavered but didn't break. "He was trying to stop me. Because he knew. He knew I was lying to myself."

Logan swallowed hard. "My marriage was a nightmare. For both of us. I didn't love her. I couldn't. We spent six months sleeping in separate rooms, pretending to be something we weren't. Do you know what that does to a person?" He let out a breathless, humorless laugh, shaking his head. "I was drowning, Dad. And when I finally came up for air, the only direction I knew was back to him."

He turned and met Adrian's eyes across the charged air of the room, and without hesitation, he reached for his hand, openly and unapologetically, a man who had at last stopped concealing the only thing that had ever made him feel real.

"I love him," he declared, the words cracking in his throat yet spilling into the silence with the weight of a stone breaking the surface of still water, undeniable in their descent, reverberating through the room, impossible to take back, impossible to ignore, not a plea or a defense but truth, confession, surrender.

Robert didn't speak, didn't blink, didn't shift a single muscle, but Logan could feel the machinery grinding behind that stillness.

It wasn't enough. It had never been enough.

So Logan did something he never imagined he could.

He pressed Adrian's hand to his lips, a fleeting kiss brushed upon his skin before he rose gracefully to his feet. With fingers that barely obeyed him, he pulled his phone from his pocket and moved across the room. He paused—just for a breath, just for a heartbeat—but in his mind, it felt like a lifetime of silence. Then he unlocked the phone and opened the folder.

The hidden one.

The digital shrine to the sole thing that had ever given his life significance. The only companion in the past two years that had helped him regain a moment of fleeting happiness, allowing him to feel human once more.

A digital embrace from the love of his life, pixels filled with memories that would eternally be engraved in his heart.

He placed it into his father's waiting hand.

"Look at it."

Robert frowned, but he took the phone. He scrolled while Samantha leaned in, glancing at the photos with him as they moved through them together.

Logan didn't need to see the screen to envision the moments unfolding beneath his father's fingers. The images shimmered in his mind, effulgent and indelible, etched deep as a palimpsest of memory. He had lingered in that material reverie so long he could summon the photos in perfect order, each one a fugitive fragment of a life already lost.

He recalled the shimmering sunlight reflecting off the water, where the two of them floated on surfboards, hair soaked and laughter spilling forth, eyes narrowed against the bright sun, smiles beaming.

He could almost feel the peacefulness of night in foreign cities, the golden glow of streetlamps illuminating their path as Adrian guided him through winding alleyways, their fingers intertwined like a silent prayer upon which they both depended.

There was a blurred photograph, one that Logan snatched in a fleeting moment, where the world around smeared into motion and light. Yet Adrian's gaze, his expression, was the single point of sharpness—clear, arresting, luminous. The sunlight struck him at just the right angle, and in that suspended instant, he seemed to truly see Logan, to gaze inside him as he smiled that jaw-dropping, heart-beat-increasing smile of his.

In a symphony of love, there existed a collection of roughly fifty photographs capturing their tender embraces and soft kisses, each moment forever preserved in time. An eternal kiss, framed against a skyline that stretches into forever, envelops their passion in a timeless embrace.

Love. Unsullied, uncharted, raw love.

His chest tightened; his ribs felt like they might split under the pressure of his heartbeat.

"The only reason I ever came back here," he whispered, "was because of him."

Robert didn't respond. He just kept scrolling, his face unreadable.

Logan took a breath, a trembling, unsteady inhale that barely reached his lungs.

"The first time I ever stepped into the ocean in Hawaii..." His voice was softer now, not fragile, but reverent. "I drowned."

Samantha gasped, a sharp, visceral sound.

Robert's entire body stiffened. His grip on the phone tightened.

Logan pressed forward, making them listen, making them see.

"I fell from my board. Hit my head. I lost consciousness. And do you know who saved me?"

Silence.

"Adrian."

The name echoed. It didn't just hang in the air; it *rooted* there.

"He happened to be on that beach. He didn't know me. He saw a stranger go under and ran into the storm without thinking. Without any hesitation, straight into the water, and he pulled me out." His throat constricted again, his words strained but sturdy. "He gave me CPR. Over and over. Minutes passed. He didn't stop. He wouldn't stop. He nearly drowned saving me." Logan swallowed hard, his vision blurring at the edges. "He fought for me in the water, and then he fought for me on the beach."

A flicker of something in Robert's gaze—fear? Pain? The terrifying realization that his son could have been lost, just like that?

Logan dropped his head, eyes closing as he tried to gather himself, piecing together the fragments of his resolve and searching for the courage to keep standing there, his breath shallow, his hands clenched tight at his sides. And then—suddenly—warmth: a presence at his back, the gentle press of a hand against the small of it. He turned, and there was Adrian, and before his thoughts could catch up, before fear or shame could crawl their way back into his spine, before he could second-guess the wild cry of his own heart aching for release, he pulled him close, arms wrapping around him as though clutching the very edge of the world, gripping him with the desperate strength of someone who could not afford to let go—and Adrian held him just as fiercely.

Logan exhaled, pulling back, turning to face his parents again. His eyes burned, but he didn't let the tears fall.

"This is how I knew him. This is how we found each other. And when I got scared, when I didn't think I could do it, I ran. I ran from him. From myself. And I have never, not for a single second since, felt whole again."

The words floated gently in the silence, akin to breath hanging in the crisp winter air—fragile, perceptible, on the verge of falling.

And then, quiet.

Not the kind that comes from absence, but the kind that fills a room to its edges. A silence so complete it echoed in the chest, pressed behind the eyes.

Samantha stood so abruptly that the chair shrieked across the polished floor, and before Logan could even register the sound, she was across the space, wrapping him in her arms, gathering him into the kind of embrace that doesn't ask for permission.

"Oh, honey..." she murmured, and her voice cracked like porcelain under too much pressure.

He sensed the tremor in her arms, the almost uncontainable relief, and the trembling grief of a mother who hadn't realized she was nearly mourning her son.

She pulled back just enough to hold his face in both hands, her thumbs brushing his cheeks as tears traced paths down her own. She pulled his head down, and kissed his forehead, then his temple, whispering something too soft for the room to catch—just for him, for his heart alone.

"I love you, Logan. No matter what."

The words landed like a stone in deep water—sinking straight through him, anchoring him in place, cracking something wide open inside his chest.

He tried to swallow, but his throat burned too much to let it through. His body trembled under the unfamiliar weight of being held *as he was*, no edits, no conditions.

Her arms tightened around him again.

"My son almost drowned, and I didn't even know?" Her voice cracked, thick with grief she hadn't even known she should carry, that she almost carried. "I don't even want to think about what I would have done if I lost you."

Logan squeezed his eyes shut, pressing his forehead into her shoulder for just a second longer, letting himself be held, be loved.

"Thanks, Mom. I love you, too."

When she finally let him go, her hands lingered on his face, one last touch, one last reassurance, one last silent benediction, before she turned, and her gaze fell on Adrian.

Adrian stiffened, just slightly, but Samantha only smiled, a soft, warm thing, filled with something far deeper than politeness. "Welcome to the family."

And before Adrian could speak, before he could question it or flinch from it, she stepped forward and wrapped her arms around him.

He froze for a heartbeat, the reflex of someone unaccustomed to unconditional affection, but then, slowly, he leaned in. His arms rose. And he returned it.

"Thank you," she whispered, voice trembling. "Thank you so much for saving my boy."

Adrian felt something twist inside his chest, tight, splintering, the cracking of ice across a still lake. Samantha leaned back just far enough to look into his face, and her eyes—shining, soft, aching with everything she hadn't said yet—met his.

"Thank you," she repeated, firmer this time, as if the word itself were failing her, as if it could never possibly contain all that she meant. "You saved the most precious thing I have." She pulled him in again, this time not gently but fiercely. "My children are everything to me." She spoke. "And I couldn't lose Logan."

Adrian's breath hitched, caught somewhere between disbelief and the quiet ache of being seen. His hands tightened around her without thinking.

"I just... I did what anyone would do," he said, swallowing hard.

She pulled back slightly and looked at him with a smile that was more knowing than tender, the kind of smile that mothers give when they see right through you and decide to love you anyway.

"Not everyone would have," she murmured. "Not everyone has that kind of heart, sweetheart."

He felt his face flush, the heat creeping up his neck, and he looked down, unable to meet her eyes.

She squeezed his hands once more before turning, moving back toward Robert.

"Dad—" Logan started, but Robert raised a hand, slicing the air clean between them.

"I've heard enough," Robert said, glancing at his son.

His voice was flat, unreadable, too calm. Still holding Logan's phone, his fingers curled tightly around it like the images inside weighed more than he was willing to carry.

He exhaled long and slow, eyes locked on the screen, yet he seemed to be gazing at something beyond, something more distant and colder.

He shook his head. "I really thought I raised a son." His voice was low and collected. "A man. But no, you have to keep up with this... nonsense." He waved the phone as if referring to said nonsense.

Logan's stomach twisted.

"You were doing well." Robert's voice edged with something dangerously close to disappointment. "You were the son I raised you to be. Even after you disappeared for four months, you came back and you stepped into your role. It's in your blood, Logan. I saw it in you. When you were doing business, you had the fire, the instinct. You took the right risks, and you were brilliant. You were ruthless when it counted. And then, suddenly, you went off for a few days, and I figured, fine, you needed a break after the separation from Sandy. But this?" He gestured sharply at

Adrian. "This is too much. You come back, and now I find out it's for this?" He turned his gaze back toward Adrian, voice cooling even further.

He took a breath, scanning the room, his mind clearly working, calculating, measuring.

"And now you expect me to just hand over half a million dollars to some guy I don't even know? Just because you say he matters?" He tilted his head, eyes narrowing, scanning Adrian like he was parsing a résumé. "Who are you?" Robert asked, voice like a scalpel. "What do you do for a living that you can't take care of yourself? Where are you from? Where have you been for the last two years?"

"Dad—" Logan started, anger simmering in his voice.

"Robert!" Samantha snapped, shooting him a glare.

But he didn't look at her. He kept his eyes trained on Adrian, face unreadable but full of judgment. "I think I have the right to ask these questions, considering you're asking me to give this man half a million dollars." His voice hardened. "You tell me, out of nowhere, that you're gay. That you have a boyfriend. That he has cancer. And now you need my money to save him?"

"Enough!" Samantha's voice cracked through the room like a thunderclap, sharp and final as a gunshot.

The tension cracked like a dam bursting.

Robert blinked, startled, as his wife rose to her feet with a grace that didn't ask permission. Her voice, always soft, always measured, now burned with something unyielding.

"He is the one who jumped into the ocean and rescued your son!" she defended, every word like fire across stone. "Logan could have died, Robert. He *was* dying. And this young man—this brave, *selfless* man—risked his life to pull him back from the edge. And after everything, after all that, they *fell in love.*"

She jabbed a finger toward him, not in accusation, but in defense.

"Do not dare diminish what that means. Do not belittle the magnitude of our son's life, or his happiness."

Silence rang loud and heavy.

Robert's jaw tensed, his hands curling into fists. He opened his mouth, but before he could speak, Samantha shook her head. "You're in denial."

Robert froze, his eyes widening in surprise as he looked at his wife.

Samantha turned toward Logan now, her expression softening with something painful, something motherly, something raw. "Do you know how many times Jane came over to voice her concerns about Logan?" She looked between her husband and son, searching for recognition in their faces. "Jane told me she feared he was depressed. That she thought he was *hurting*, truly hurting. That he was self-destructing. She spoke to Ada Mae, who confirmed Logan was drinking and barely eating." She paused, breath catching in her throat. "And no one knew why." Her voice cracked on the last word, but she pushed through it.

And then, without hesitation, she turned to the grand wall of family photos. Every inch of the house was adorned with them; framed memories capturing milestones, holidays, birthdays, and celebrations. The grand moments of her three children were proudly displayed throughout the space. Adrian's gaze fell on a few photos of Logan's graduation, where he wore a colorful cape and a traditional graduation hat, proudly clutching his diploma. In another photo, Logan appeared youthful, no older than 16, his face lighting up with a radiant smile as he held a large camera, looking directly at the shot's taker. In the left corner, another large photo of

Logan standing on a bridge, with a stunning landscape in the background, suggested a beautiful place that resembled Spain. Despite a fleeting look of concern on his face, he exuded a captivating beauty that was forever captured in that moment.

She reached for one in particular.

Logan's wedding day.

A picture of Logan and Sandy.

Robert watched as she held it up, turning it slightly to let them get a good look. She held it like a weapon, but instead of a threat, she was carrying proof; a proof that had just as much lethality as a firearm.

Logan's stomach tightened as an unsettling emptiness washed over him.

He appeared hollow, a fragile shell of himself, a ghost wandering through the world. His suit was a sharp toast to elegance, his tie a perfect knot, his hair a carefully crafted crown. Yet beneath this polished veneer, an emptiness seeped through, a silent scream behind the pixels, the echo of neglect. His eyes were vacant pools, reflections of a love lost, the rare gem of his soul now gone. His smile, a fragile masquerade, veiled some pain, and his stance was stiff with the weight of unseen burdens, whispering stories of longing and regret.

It was as if he were merely acting in a play, trapped in a character he could not embody fully.

Standing next to a woman he had already lost, even before the first note of their duet had sounded, not yet begun, yet irrevocably ended.

And then Samantha picked up Logan's phone from the table, where the screen still glowed with images of him and Adrian. She held the two pictures side by side.

Logan and Sandy—lifeless, scripted, barely touching.

And then Logan and Adrian—entwined on an Australian beach, basking in sunlight and carefree joy, gazing at one another with a brilliance that rivaled the sunniest of days.

The difference was staggering.

She turned to Robert, daring him.

"Look at that," she demanded. "And tell me that this is nonsense. Tell me that you haven't seen your son fading away with each moment. Tell me they were happily married."

Robert's gaze dropped to the pictures.

He didn't speak.

But he didn't look away either.

Something in his stoic expression wavered.

Samantha softened. "Don't be like your father, Rob. Don't pass down another generation of silence and control." She put the framed photo and the phone on the table and placed a gentle hand on his shoulder. "There are things far more important than the business."

Robert inhaled sharply, closing his eyes for just a moment. When he opened them, the anger had softened, replaced by something else, something that would irrevocably change the course of this conversation. He was a father realizing, far too late, that he had missed the whispers of his son's silent struggles, that the boy had been drowning long before that day in Hawaii.

"I love him," Logan repeated. He wondered if his father even heard him—truly heard him—or if the words simply crashed against his ears, simply striking that fortified exterior and sliding off, unnoticed, like water against stone, dissolving before they could leave a mark.

"Adrian refused treatment. He is dying. And if he dies..." Logan exhaled, his breath trembling like the wind before a hurricane. "If he dies, I die too."

His father's expression barely wavered. A fortress, weathered and immovable. Logan had spent his whole life throwing himself against those walls, trying to carve his name into the steel of a man who never let anything in.

"You don't understand," Logan pressed on, the words burning his throat. "I have already been through hell, Dad. I have drowned in it. And you didn't notice. Or maybe you did, and you didn't care. Either way, I can't—*I won't*—go through that hell again." His voice faltered, but his stance remained unshaken. "Adrian wouldn't fight for himself, so I told him I'd do it for him. I told him that if he let this thing kill him, I'd follow. That's how much he means to me. That's how much I've already lost."

"Logan, please." Samantha's voice was a threadbare whisper, barely holding together. Her fingers clung to the arm of the chair as if it were the only thing anchoring her. Her glassy eye searched his face for a place to land.

He turned to her, and for a moment, something inside him softened. She had always been the one watching from the shore, never stepping in, but always hoping he'd make it back to land. He wanted to tell her that he had—*just barely*—but he wasn't sure if he believed it himself.

"It's true, Mom," he murmured. "I mean it."

His father exhaled slowly and measuredly. "You've always been like this," he said, and there was something in his tone—exhaustion, perhaps, or disbelief, or the reluctant awe of someone facing down a mirror they had spent decades avoiding. "All or nothing." He looked briefly at his wife before his gaze returned to Logan, sharp as a broken shell beneath the sand.

"It's a pattern with you. When you close a deal, it's on your terms or not at all. When you left, you vanished without a word. When you came back, you chased everything you abandoned, full speed ahead. You threw yourself into that marriage, clawed your way up in the company, and now this." He gestured toward Adrian, toward the photos still glowing on the phone. "Big or nothing. This is the next all-or-nothing." His voice was cold but resigned. "You're gay, and in the span of a day, you have a boyfriend, that you're in love with, he's dying, and you're willing to die for him?" He shook his head slowly. "Just like that?

The air pulsed between them, dense with unspoken words. Logan could feel the rage begin to swell in his chest again.

"You taught me how," he spat through gritted teeth, his voice thick with emotion. Was the anger flickering within him, born from his father's dismissive words? Or was it the way his father spoke of his love for Adrian as though his absence had not inked his heart atramentous, nor planted abulia in the soil of his soul. Perhaps, it was something more profound, his father reaching into the depths of Logan's innermost instinct, stirring a storm beneath his skin.

"No, I didn't," Robert said simply. "That, son, is something you learned all by yourself."

Logan's breath hitched, a flicker of disbelief curling in his chest like seafoam swirling around a half-buried shell.

But Robert continued. "But you are my son. And regardless of what you think of me, I care about you." He paused for a moment, considering his words. "I thought you were stressed from learning the business. I thought maybe you and Sandy were trying for a child, and the pressure was wearing you thin. It never crossed my mind that you were living in hiding, that you left behind someone you loved. But I did see you struggling. I just didn't understand why."

The words weighed heavily on Logan's ribs, not in a crushing manner he anticipated, but like the soft whisper of an incoming wave.

"No man's life is easy, Logan," Robert said, softer now, no longer the executive but just a man trying to get through to his son. "And I would never trade your suffering for my business." He stepped forward, slowly closing a space between them that had stretched for years. "You are my son. My heir. My legacy. And no matter what I have failed to say in the past, I do not want you to suffer anymore. I do not want you to be unhappy, not even in the smallest way. I want you to thrive. I want you to have it all. That includes happiness... alongside the company."

Logan's heart clenched. His father had never spoken this way before. These were not the words of a man who bartered with power, who measured love in terms of success. They were something else entirely—something more raw, more real.

Robert stepped closer, the distance between them suddenly feeling smaller than it ever had. "I will give you all the money you need, an initial half-million, and whatever future expenses arise. I will ensure that Adrian is admitted to the best care facilities and treated by the world's top doctors. I will fly him out for treatment or bring the doctors to him, whichever he needs." His eyes, usually so guarded, softened just a fraction. "But I need you to step up, Logan. I need you to pull yourself together. Not because I am punishing you, not because I am holding your love hostage, but because I am retiring soon. And I want my children to lead the company I built."

Logan swallowed hard, his pulse roaring in his ears.

"Jane is the head of the entire legal department. If she wanted to run the company, I would give it to her, but she belongs in the law, and you... you belong in business, in management. You always have. You have a mind for it, an instinct." Robert studied him for a long moment. "I am not asking you to abandon Adrian. Of course, take the time you need to care for him. But when you come back, I need you to be present. I need you to stop walking into meetings reeking of whiskey, to stop missing deadlines and blowing meetings, and disappearing on clients. It looks bad, unprofessional, and your behavior tarnishes our reputation."

Logan felt something crack inside him, something heavy and worn down by years of resentment.

Logan saw the deal for what it was: not merely a transaction, not just another power move, but something deeper.

For the first time, it looked like his father *cared*.

This wasn't just about money; it wasn't just about the company. This was his father's way of making sure Logan *had it all*—not just stability, not just success, but a life worth living. It wasn't a handout, not entirely. It was his father giving him the means to fight for Adrian while also pushing him toward independence.

A test, perhaps. A challenge, as always. But beneath it, there was something else.

It was strange, unsettling even, to realize that the man he had spent his entire life resenting might have been reaching for him in the only way he knew how. That all the years Logan had spent believing his father was only a businessman—calculating, distant, always weighing the value of things before committing—he had never considered that maybe, just maybe, *this* was how he showed love.

Not with sentiment. Not with softness.

But by giving Logan the means to stand on his own.

And in the end, that was what made Logan's stomach twist, what sent a slow, creeping understanding through his bones.

Because for all the ways he had hated his father for being a businessman *first* and a father *second*—

Now, standing in front of him, staring at the deal laid out like a lifeline—

It looked like *he* was his father's son, after all.

The city hummed outside, distant and muted, as Logan and Adrian stepped into the quiet sanctuary of Logan's apartment.

Everything was ready to go. His father simply texted his personal banker: "Wire my son $500,000 today." Even though it was the middle of the night, she replied within minutes: "Understood, funds will be cleared in the next hour." No one left Robert Vaughn waiting.

But the only thing that mattered in this moment wasn't money, or hospitals, or treatment plans, or the silent countdown of time slipping through their fingers like fine grains of sand.

It was Samantha, standing at the threshold of their home, pulling Adrian into a gentle embrace, whispering, "You are always welcome here. You are family now. And I can't wait to get to know you better."

Or Robert shaking Adrian's hand with a nod, wishing him good luck, and refusing to hear the slightest thank you from Adrian, no matter how much he tried to express his gratitude.

They accepted him wholeheartedly, welcoming him into their family as part of Logan's life, and gave Adrian, in a span of mere hours, more than he would ever get in his lifetime.

And it was Logan's hand, steady around Adrian's wrist, as they left, as they returned to a space that had been empty for far too long.

The door had barely clicked shut when Adrian turned to him, his breath brushing Logan's mouth like a secret. His fingers rose, hesitant but reverent, tracing Logan's jaw as though trying to memorize the geography of something holy.

"It's happening, isn't it?" Adrian whispered softly against Logan's lips, his voice barely audible but filled with anticipation.

"What?" Logan replied, his brow furrowing in confusion, as he cupped the back of Adrian's neck. He should have understood what Adrian was referring to, yet Adrian was so close to him—body pressed against body, their lips almost touching—that not a single logical thought could remain in Logan's mind. Rationality had long abandoned him.

"The fight... it's... really about to start," Adrian continued, his breath warm against Logan's skin as their foreheads pressed together. "I know it sounds foolish, but it's real now. It felt so far away before, like it belonged to someone else. But now... it's here. I feel it breathing down my neck." He inhaled sharply, his chest rising and falling quickly as anxiety coursed through him.

Logan didn't speak at first. He let his hands speak for him, running through Adrian's hair, down the curve of his back, settling against the rhythm of his pulse. "It is," he said finally, voice like the beginning of a vow. "And we're going to win, remember? You and me. Old and gray. That's the promise, my love."

Adrian kissed him, soft at first, a brush of gratitude, of ache, and then deeper, fuller, as if trying to press the memory of Logan into every cell of his body. A shiver of urgency passed between them. Logan's breath caught in his throat as Adrian whimpered into the kiss, all need and devotion.

"I want you," Adrian muttered, the words trembling. "Now. Before everything begins. I want to feel alive in your arms. I want to remember *this* moment with you when it gets hard. When I'm scared. I want *this* to be the last thing I feel before everything changes."

Logan said nothing, only nodded, only wrapped his arms around Adrian's waist and pulled him in, pressing their bodies together. His hands roamed, mapping every inch of Adrian's body like a man relearning something sacred, like a ship returning to the harbor after too many years lost at sea. It wasn't just hunger; it was possession, and it was reverence. It was a homecoming. It was the ache of knowing this body once lived in his dreams and was now, impossibly, here again, solid, warm, breathing, beating.

Adrian tangled his fingers in Logan's hair, his grip firm, his touch gentle, as if anchoring himself in this moment, as if afraid to move too fast, afraid that the fragile bubble around them would burst and reality would come rushing in too soon. His breaths were shallow, caught between hope and fear, between this moment and all that waited beyond it.

Logan drew back just far enough to meet his eyes—those molten-whisky eyes that had once pulled him from drowning, and now, years later, were saving him all over again. A thousand words passed in a single breathless glance. And then Logan took Adrian's hand, kissing his fingers with a sacred touch, and led him to the bedroom.

Because this had to be *right*.

After all the time he had spent apart from him, after all the nights haunted by his absence, after all those desperate, hopeless reaches for another body, wishing it was this man, this love—after the many mornings waking in a familiar bed with another person beside him, Adrian's name still lingering on his tongue. After all the occasions of feeling another's touch yet yearning for that man, the ache of longing intertwined with memory.

Logan needed this to be *right*. Not just because he had lost Adrian once. Not just because time was no longer a luxury they could take for granted. But because Adrian was *everything*.

And tonight, Logan would remind him of that.

As Logan backed Adrian against the bedroom wall, a realization washed over him: it was deeper, far deeper than skin against skin, more profound than the desperate mingling of lips and hands. It was something carved into the marrow of his bones, stitched into the very fabric of his soul, written into the breaths he took.

It was love, not spoken, but remembered.

It was the soul remembering the body it once called home.

And tonight, Logan would remind Adrian—with every breath, every whisper, every shiver of skin—that he was everything. That he had always been everything.

Because in every kiss, in every touch, he wasn't just claiming Adrian's body, he was trying to hold onto something *forever*. A forever that might already be slipping between his fingers.

The thought closed over him, a stygian curve of water where no light survived. He shook it away and let the brightest light of all guide him back. He unzipped Adrian's coat, which was actually Logan's, and let it slip from his shoulders, pooling at their feet. Next, Adrian's shirt fell to the bedroom floor, leaving him bare-chested in the dim light.

Two years ago, love had been something effortless, an endless summer, a wave he rode without fear, carried high by the warmth of Adrian's laughter, the softness of his touch. Back then, his hands had known only happiness. They had learned Adrian like scripture, traced the shape of devotion across his skin like poetry, caressed him with the kind of tenderness that belonged only to those who believed love would never end.

But now—now Logan touched Adrian like a man who had *lost* him once.

A man who had *drowned* once.

A man intimately familiar with the chilling depths of despair, who had plummeted into the ocean's abyss, lungs aflame, vision clouded, limbs feeling as though they had become weightless, lingering in a silence for a rescue that never arrived. He touched him like someone who had endured the unbearable, bone-deep ache of emptiness, of nights spent reaching for an elusive specter, of calling out in dreams only to hear the echo of silence, awakening to a world that had lost its vibrancy. Someone who had begged the sky for one more chance.

Someone who was branded by dolor.

And yet, as his lips pressed tenderly against Adrian's, and his fingers trembled with cautious reverence over the familiar warmth of his skin, Logan felt himself sinking once more, deeper, more fervently, giving in to the boundless ocean that embraced him, filling the emptiness within, permitting the water to soothe his aching soul, allowing them to fill the vacant husk he had become.

Adrian moved against him, with him, responding to every touch, every unspoken plea expressed by Logan's fingers, their bodies, and breaths in a perfectly synchronized rhythm. He smiled into the kiss, the quiet curve of his lips sending a tremor through Logan's chest, and Logan wanted to memorize the feeling, wanted to bottle this moment and drink from it forever.

He wanted to carve that smile into memory.

Adrian's hands found the buttons of Logan's shirt, undoing them with a frenzied urgency, as if trying to erase the years of distance between them, as if trying to claim back the time they had lost. When the last button gave way, he pushed the fabric from Logan's shoulders, letting it pool at their feet before his palms found Logan's hips, sliding lower, gripping him with a possessiveness that sent a shiver racing down Logan's spine.

"Some moments, I still can't believe it's real," Adrian murmured against his skin, fingers ghosting over the ridges of Logan's chest before pressing a reverent kiss there, right over the place where his heart beat the strongest. "You're here. We're together."

Logan exhaled shakily, the weight of those words settling deep inside him, anchoring him in a way nothing else ever had.

"Me too."

He took a slow step backward, pulling Adrian with him, their bodies still fused together, unwilling to part even for a second.

"But it is real. " His voice was soft, edged with wonder, thick with something unbreakable. He brushed his knuckles along Adrian's cheek, his touch lingering, memorizing. "At this moment, I'm the happiest I've been in so long." His lips curved into a small, aching smile. "Actually... since the moment I saw you again, I have been the happiest. No matter how hard it was. No matter everything. Because it was always you, Adrian. It's only ever been you."

Adrian lowered Logan onto the bed with a tenderness that felt almost sacred, as if laying him down was an act of worship, as if he were something precious to be handled with care. He made sure Logan's head rested against the pillows before crawling over him, his body a familiar weight, a warmth that melted into Logan's own.

Then his lips pressed delicate, lingering kisses along Logan's neck, trailing down to his shoulders, his breath hot against bare skin. Logan let his eyes flutter shut, surrendering to the sensation, feeling the warmth coil in his spine, his pulse quickening beneath the gentle onslaught of Adrian's mouth.

"I love your smell," Adrian murmured, inhaling deeply against Logan's throat before sealing his lips over his once more.

Logan chuckled softly, a sound both light and full of longing, before tilting his head back, letting Adrian take whatever he wanted, however he wanted. He *needed* this, this press of Adrian's body against his, the familiar slide of lips and hands, the way Adrian touched him like a man savoring something he never thought he'd have again.

His fingers slid into Adrian's hair, the strands silk-soft against his touch. He found the tie and, with aching slowness, drew it loose, letting the dark cascade fall. Adrian's gaze locked on his as he hovered above, their world veiled by that sudden spill of hair. A laugh broke from Logan, strange, near frantic, as his hands threaded through the locks he had once undone with care, knowing now it might be the last time, that those beautiful strands carried only numbered hours. The laugh broke, fading into a sob as he drew Adrian into a kiss, melting against him, his voice trembling between their mouths: "I missed this so much. I can't believe I get to do it again. I love you."

For a moment, time stilled as they lay entwined, kissing, Adrian's touch soft with solace and love. There was no urgency, no weight of tomorrow, only the quiet need to remain in each other's arms.

After a while, Adrian started to kiss his way downward, taking his time, refusing to rush as he traced every inch of Logan's skin with his lips, his tongue, his breath. It was slow, unrushed devotion, a silent conversation between mouths and fingertips, and the occasional giggle as Adrian's strands tickled his skin.

When he reached the waistband of Logan's jeans, he didn't hesitate. With practiced ease, he unbuttoned them, dragging the zipper down with an almost agonizing slowness. Logan's breath hitched, his body arching slightly, anticipation thrumming in his veins.

Adrian hooked his fingers into the fabric, gripping the denim and pulling both jeans and underwear down in one smooth motion, peeling them away and doing a quick work on his shoes and socks, until Logan lay bare beneath him, stretched out like a vision, a dream made flesh.

"You're so fucking beautiful," Adrian whispered, his voice thick with hunger, admiration laced in every syllable. "It's driving me insane."

His hand slid down, wrapping around Logan's length as if his hand grazed the ethereal. Logan gasped, his head tipping back, a raw sound escaping his lips that made Adrian throb with need.

"I need to taste you," Adrian crooned. The things he craved were not merely a desire but a deep calling, something that surged through his veins like molten fire, reverberating in his chest, igniting a yearning for Logan that no torrent could extinguish. He pressed soft, wet kisses along the length of Logan's cock, each one slow and aching, his breath warm, his lips tender.

Then he took him into his mouth, starting with just the head, tongue circling, teasing, before swallowing him deeper, inch by inch, until Logan was buried fully, his tip brushing the back of Adrian's throat.

"Fuck," Logan moaned, his voice hoarse, his hands flying to Adrian's hair, fingers threading tight. His hips moved without thinking, a helpless thrust into that velvet heat, into the warmth of Adrian's mouth, so hot, so perfect it nearly undid him.

There was an overpowering beauty in witnessing Logan fall in surrender to the softness of the mattress, a quiet void of voices and reason, as Adrian became the one to bring him pleasure.

"Ad—" Logan choked on the name, his voice breaking. He thrust twice more, unable to help himself, wanting to get lost in that sensation more and more, savoring it—savoring *him*—before he pulled Adrian back, panting, quivering.

"I don't want to come yet," he managed to get out as his chest was rising and falling just the way it did when he surfaced from deep underwater.

Adrian nodded, his lips wet, his eyes dark with desire and love and something deeper, something *hungry*. He wiped his mouth slowly with the back of his hand, gaze never leaving Logan's cock, then flicked his eyes up with a look that made Logan's knees weak.

"I could live off the taste of you," Adrian whispered, and Logan swore his heart stopped. "I missed it so much."

When Adrian climbed back over him, Logan caught the wicked glint in his eyes, and before Adrian could settle, Logan smirked and rolled them over in one fluid movement, pinning Adrian beneath him.

He kissed him again, it was hungrier now, deeper and more consuming, his hands pressing into Adrian's sides, feeling the heat of him through his clothes. He rocked against him, his own bare skin dragging over the rough fabric of Adrian's jeans, feeling where he was already hard beneath the constraint, already aching for more.

Logan's kisses drifted lower, sliding over Adrian's chest, his ribs, his stomach. He lingered over the bruises that marred his lover's skin, kissing them softly, whispering against them, "You're perfect."

Because for Logan, he was.

Bruises and all. Scars and all. The past and all.

Adrian was everything.

He had always been.

Logan quickly removed Adrian's jeans and boxers in a fluid movement, pausing briefly to take off his shoes and socks before biting Adrian's toe playfully, earning a giggle from him. He let the fabric fall away and tossed it aside, exposing the warm, golden skin beneath. He took his time kissing his way back up, his lips tracing a path over Adrian's thighs, his stomach, the sharp lines of his ribs, savoring every inch, taking every touch so he would never starve for it again.

"Be right back, don't move," Logan murmured against Adrian's lips, stealing another kiss, before pulling away.

Adrian let out a breathy chuckle, his accent curling around his words. "Like there's anywhere else I'd rather be."

Logan smirked and slipped off the bed, hurrying toward the walk-in closet where their suitcases sat, untouched since they had arrived. His hands moved quickly, unzipping his bag, pulling out the little plastic bag they had bought at the pharmacy in the airport, a quiet promise made in the space between then and now.

He retrieved the small bottle of lube and the box of condoms, the weight of them in his hands a reminder of all the nights he had dreamed of this, of Adrian beneath him again, skin against skin, nothing between them but heat and love and the desperate need to make up for lost time.

When Logan returned, he didn't hesitate—he crawled back onto the bed, back over Adrian's body, pressing him into the mattress with his weight, their mouths crashing together in a kiss that tasted of urgency, of devotion, of years spent waiting.

Their hips found each other instinctively, a rhythm neither had forgotten. Logan rolled against him, grinding down, and the friction sent a sharp, aching pleasure shooting through him. The sound Adrian made, those breathless moans, only spurred him on, made his movements more frantic, more desperate, as their cocks slid together, trapped between their bodies, slick with heat and sweat and Adrian's saliva that still coated Logan's cock.

"Fuck," Logan gasped against Adrian's lips, moving harder, his entire body trembling from restraint, from wanting more, from needing everything.

Adrian's hands found Logan's hips, gripping them tight, his fingers pressing bruises into his skin as he stilled him, stopping the movement with a quiet groan.

"If you don't stop, I'm going to come," Adrian panted, his voice wrecked, his lips curved into a breathless smile. "It's been a long time for me."

"How long?" Logan asked, too fast, too sharp. The words escaped before he had a chance to reel them back, before he could soften the demand buried in them.

He hadn't given much thought to Adrian being with another man, hadn't let himself dwell on it, on the inevitable, on the reality of time moving forward even when his own heart had been frozen in place. But now, with Adrian beneath him, with their breaths mingling and their bodies pressed together, it felt like something they *had* to talk about.

The questions burned in his throat like salt rubbed into an open wound, forcing his heart to wail with that threnodic song Adrian had soothed not so long ago.

Who?

How many?

Where?

When?

Were they good?

Did they touch you the way I did?

Did they make love to you, or was it just fucking?

Did you think of me while someone else had their hands on you, the way I thought of you?

Did you softly sigh and whimper as you did with me?

Can you remember the precise position in which it was made?

Could you trace for me that very path they had caressed you, so I might glide my hand along the exact contours and endeavor to erase those lingering memories?

Will you recount, in precise detail, what it felt like, for I believe I need this to unravel myself?

How did their eyes linger on you when they touched your skin?

Adrian looked away, tilting his head slightly, and the shift in his body was enough to change the air between them, thickening it. Logan felt it in his chest, in the sudden tightness of his ribs, in the way his fingers twitched against Adrian's skin.

"I'm sorry, forget it," Logan blurted, reaching out, his fingers brushing against Adrian's jaw, tilting his face back toward him. The pulsing pain in his voice betrayed him. "It's none of my business."

Adrian exhaled softly, a breath that barely reached the space between them. "No, it is." His voice was quiet but steady. Still, he didn't meet Logan's eyes. Not yet. "Something like...." Adrian took a deep breath, "Two years," he concluded, his chest moving sharply under Logan's hands, as though the words themselves were contingent and, in being spoken, conjured a reality in which they became real.

Logan flinched. His whole body tensed, a sharp pull of muscle and breath, because two years ago—

That was them.

Which meant that whoever Adrian had been with had come right after Logan left.

A rebound, maybe?

A flash of nausea gripped him. Had it been between Australia and the wedding?

Had Adrian—*my Adrian*—been with someone else in their room, in their bed, where Logan had once held him, as if he were the only thing that mattered? That horrible bed. That ugly, scratchy comforter. That stupid, cheap little cabin that had meant everything because it had been theirs.

And now, the thought of someone else there, in *his* place, made him feel like a fool.

But screw it.

That bed was no place for Adrian to fuck anyone else.

Muscles bunched along Logan's jaw, feeling the sharp edge of jealousy slice through him, even though he knew—*God*, he *knew*—he had no right. He had been the one to run. He had been the one to leave Adrian bleeding in a hotel room while he boarded a plane back to a life he didn't want.

He had gotten married.

And yet, the idea of Adrian bringing someone else into his bed so soon after, the idea of someone else taking what had once been Logan's to hold, made his stomach twist with something ugly and possessive. The idea of Adrian going to a random bar and picking someone up, bringing that man to their room and...

But then—

Adrian's eyes fluttered open, their hue a storm-dark amber, limned with unshed sorrow. They glistened—no, they *ached*—with something more than grief: a fevered yearning, in which gentleness and devastation were intertwined.

And beneath that dark, forsaken swirl, innocence lay.

"Since that night?" Logan's voice barely made it past his lips, thick with disbelief, with something dangerously close to hope. His throat tightened, his heart pounding erratically in his chest. "You mean... no one since me?"

Adrian swallowed, his gaze never wavering, his hands curling against Logan's skin like an anchor.

"No one," he whispered.

And Logan felt something inside him *break*—something deep, something he hadn't even known he was holding onto. "But... why?"

Adrian nodded, just slightly, as if confirming it was a good question; it was a movement so small it might have been missed if Logan weren't watching him with the kind of wide-eyed shock that stole the breath from his lungs.

"I thought about it myself..." Adrian began. "There were the weeks I waited for you there... in Australia," his voice was low, quiet, raw. "Then your wedding happened, and the months that followed... I wasn't really into dating. I couldn't even bear the thought of someone else touching me. It made me sick just thinking about it. Like my body didn't know how to belong to anyone else. Like my skin had memorized only your touch, and anything else—anyone else—felt wrong, felt *vile*."

His voice trembled on that last word, as if even saying it left a bitter taste in his mouth. Logan swallowed, unable to speak, unable to move, unable to do anything but listen as Adrian continued.

"During university, I tried." He exhaled a soft, almost hollow laugh. "Dean pushed me into it. He signed me up for so many dating apps and practically forced me to go on dates. He even dragged me to a gay bar once."

That should have been funny. The image of Dean in a gay bar—Dean of all people—was something Logan would have loved to tease him about. But right now, it was nothing more than background noise to the only thing that mattered.

"And?" Logan asked, his voice almost a whisper as he gently caressed Adrian's face with his palm.

"And... nothing." Adrian's gaze met his. "I wasn't ready."

Logan felt his heart squeeze in his chest.

"I was too broken to start something new. And you know me... I don't really do the whole one-night stands, it's not for me... I need an emotional connection to be with someone, I need to feel something for them, or sex is just... hollow for me. But I couldn't form it; I couldn't... even look at a guy after you. And the few guys I did go on dates with, well... they just weren't it."

Logan blinked, his throat constricted, his hand tightening over Adrian's face while he clenched the sheet with his other fist, trying to hold himself together as he felt himself being unmade from the inside out.

Adrian's voice softened, his words laced with something achingly bittersweet, something that tasted like longing and old wounds still healing.

"They were nice, even great guys, actually. But..." He inhaled, and the breath he let out was fragile, like seafoam dissolving into sand. "None of them had gray eyes that turned storm-dark when they were angry, or softened like silver under the sun. None of them had sand-colored hair that the ocean kissed gold. None of them were reckless enough to jump off cliffs like it was nothing, or dangle over a ravine just to prove a point, just because they could."

Logan let out a small, wet laugh, shaking his head as he remembered exactly what Adrian was talking about.

"None of them were moody enough to throw a scene at me for talking to another guy at a party, nor were they possessive enough to make any other guy that looked at me run away with one glare," Adrian continued, smirking faintly. "Or were about to leave me altogether when I spent an hour with my friends instead of being with you."

Logan groaned, covering his face for a moment, and Adrian's laugh was soft, but full of something real.

"None of them made me laugh loud and honest, to the point where it hurt to laugh. None of them had that ridiculous smirk of yours, or the wild look in their eyes when they came up with some insane, reckless, yet somehow brilliant idea. None of them said my name the way you did, with that thick, hot American accent, that low, strong, sexy voice that made me shiver every damn time."

Logan swallowed thickly, his hands trembling as he listened, as Adrian's words stripped him down, leaving him bare and vulnerable.

"None of them made me feel like myself, not the way you did."

Adrian's gaze burned into him then, something unshaken, something final. He reached out, cupping Logan's face in his hands, his thumbs brushing softly over his cheeks, grounding him in the moment.

"None of them were you, Logan."

The words hit like a wave breaking over him, like the current pulling him under, like every breath he had ever lost since the moment he walked away from Adrian.

"And I only ever looked for you," Adrian confessed. "So, to be honest, none of them ever had a chance. Every word they spoke, every touch they offered, every love they tried to give, every moment they tried to make special, it was always measured against you. Against us. And it paled in comparison. It was unfair of me to make them fail before they even began, so eventually, I just... stopped."

Logan's breath caught, his throat tightening as if constricted by a tangle of unspoken words, lingering regrets, and countless I love yous he had been trembling to voice when it mattered most.

Adrian exhaled, and the weight of it settled deep in Logan's chest.

"I don't take words lightly," he whispered. "When I told you I loved you that night, I meant it. And I had loved you for a long time before I ever said it out loud." Adrian ran his fingers through Logan's hair. "So when my wounds finally started to heal, when I finally thought that maybe—just maybe—I could move on... and I convinced myself to give guys a true chance, to be them and not search you in every guy I meet," Adrian's voice broke just slightly, and he took a breath before finishing, "I got diagnosed. And suddenly, nothing mattered. Everything felt meaningless."

Logan's world tilted.

"That's why I burned your things. I didn't do it because they were *yours*. I did it because they were *ours*."

And Logan, unable to withstand the torrent within any longer, seized Adrian, drew him into his embrace, and clasped him with the utmost ferocity, inhaling his presence, hungering for proximity.

Logan pressed his lips to Adrian's like a man drowning, clutching at the only thing that could bring him back to the surface. His hands trembled as he held him, his body wracked with sobs, salt from his tears marking Adrian's skin.

"I'm so sorry," he whispered into Adrian's lips, his voice breaking around the edges.

But Adrian pulled him closer, arms wrapping around him like the warm embrace of the sea after a lifetime spent fighting against the current.

"No," he murmured. "We've already passed it." He gazed at Logan then, the molten whisky of his eyes full of something vast and endless. "I'm just grateful you came back to me. And don't you dare apologize for it ever again, okay?"

Logan nodded, unable to speak, his throat thick with grief, with love, with the weight of everything he had lost and found again in Adrian's arms. Adrian's thumb brushed the tears from his cheeks, the touch reverent, soft, caressing his face with a tenderness unmatched in its intensity.

"I love you, Ad. So, so much."

And then Adrian kissed him, and Logan melted into it, let himself fall, let himself be carried away like a wave surrendering to the pull of the moon. His tears kept falling, but he let them, trusted Adrian to catch them, to wash them away, to make them disappear like footprints in the sand at high tide.

And he did.

Adrian's hands were rough but tender, his fingers threading through Logan's hair as he kissed him deeper, as if sealing up every wound Logan had ever carved between them.

Then Logan felt Adrian's cock stirring against his, causing him to gasp against his lover's lips as his own body readily reacted to Adrian's desire. Logan pushed their hard lengths against each other as he started to press a trail of kisses down Adrian's neck, tasting his skin and feeling the shiver that ran through him.

His lips mapped the ridges of Adrian's body, worshipping him in a way he never had the words for. He traced the curve of Adrian's collarbone, his breath warm against fragile skin, his tongue drawing invisible poetry over a body he had once known so well. His hands joined, too. Roaming with a tenderness that bordered on the rhythmical, exploring with a gentleness that captured the essence of the moment, weaving a narrative through every touch and caress, his fingertips ghosting over ribs that stood more prominently now, along the lines of Adrian's stomach, the jut of his hipbones. Logan pressed his lips there, letting them linger, breathing him in. There was something numinous in the way Adrian trembled beneath him, the way his breath hitched when Logan kissed lower, the way his body arched.

Adrian's fingers tangled in Logan's hair, anchoring him, tethering him to this moment. There was no rush. No frantic, desperate hunger like there had been in the past. This was something else. This was measured, careful, a love letter written with mouths and hands and the weight of the truths uncovering. It was a whisper in the dark, a prayer pressed into skin.

Logan kissed the inside of his wrist, where his pulse fluttered weakly, and whispered against his skin, "I've got you."

Adrian exhaled a shaky breath. "I know."

Logan's hands gripped Adrian's thighs, his fingers pressing into the soft flesh just enough to leave the faintest imprint, as if he needed to mark him, to claim him. Adrian's chest rose and fell in uneven breaths, his fingers twisting into the sheets like they were the only thing keeping him tethered to this world. His lips were parted, his eyes dark with pleasure, and Logan thought he had never seen anything more devastatingly beautiful. He wanted to ruin him. He wanted to worship him. He wanted to take his time, to savor him, but there was also a hunger simmering in his veins, a need that started to burn through him like wildfire.

"Fuck," Adrian choked out, his voice raw, wrecked, as Logan's tongue licked over his cock, from base to root, leaving a wet trail behind. Then, Logan took him into his mouth, both of them groaning with longing, with satisfaction as Logan started to work Adrian's dick, taking it as far back into his throat as possible.

Logan's mouth moved over Adrian's cock with reverence, the taste of him intoxicating, a familiar elixir that went straight to his head, giving him a heady feeling. Every slide of his lips and flick of his tongue carried intention, forming a language unique to them, filled with longing and regret, love and redemption. The weight of Adrian's beautiful cock on his tongue sent a shiver through Logan as desire coiled tightly within him, and he sucked more intensely, his tongue gliding over Adrian as he took him deeper into his throat.

But it wasn't enough. It could never be enough.

With a growl that reverberated through both of them, Logan released Adrian's cock, the wet sound of his mouth leaving him echoing in the room. Adrian's eyes, dark and wide, blinked down at him in dazed confusion, but Logan was already moving. He slid off the bed, falling to his knees on the hardwood floor, the roughness grounding him even as his mind spun.

He grasped Adrian's legs and pulled him forward, the friction of sheets whispering under him until Adrian's hips were perched at the edge of the bed, legs thrown over Logan's broad shoulders. Adrian's surprised gasp filled the room, a sharp intake of breath that sent a bolt of desire straight to Logan's cock.

Logan looked up, meeting Adrian's gaze, a devilish smirk curling his lips before he lowered his mouth to that tender stretch of skin behind Adrian's balls. He placed soft kisses there, then opened his mouth to lick, to suck, the sensation tearing another moan from Adrian's throat, a mellifluous sound, the very echo of Logan's dreams, had haunted his thoughts, tormented his nights, and breathed fire into every failed attempt to bury the desire he carried.

Logan's grip on Adrian's thighs tightened, his thumbs stroking gentle circles as he lavished attention on that sensitive spot, his tongue moving in slow, purposeful strokes. The way Adrian's body responded, the way he twisted on the bed, fingers clutching desperately, made Logan's heart clench and his cock throb painfully.

But it still wasn't enough.

Logan pressed Adrian's legs back, exposing him fully, baring him in a way that was both vulnerable and powerful. The sight of Adrian like this—spread open, glistening, his entrance twitching in anticipation—was enough to make Logan's vision blur, his restraint nearly snapping under the weight of his desire.

He licked his lips, savoring the eagerness, the heat between them. Logan leaned forward, pressing a tender kiss to Adrian's inner thigh before letting his tongue drag over that sensitive ring of muscle, tasting him, feeling him, driving him to the edge.

Adrian's hands plunged down, one entangled in Logan's hair, the other gripping the sheets as his head tilted back, a string of jagged gasps and curses escaping his lips. Logan's name became a prayer, a plea, and a curse—merged into one—igniting the fire within him, the unfulfilled hunger that had smoldered for two long years.

Logan closed his eyes, losing himself in the taste, the scent, the sounds of Adrian coming apart above him. Every twitch of Adrian's hips, every shuddering breath, was a victory, a reminder that despite everything—despite the time, the distance, the sickness—they were still here.

Together.

Logan could never undo the pain he had caused, could never take back the nights Adrian had spent alone, but here, on his knees with Adrian's taste on his tongue, he could at least show him that he was loved. That he was cherished. That he was worth every breath, every beat of Logan's heart.

And as Adrian's spine lifted in a sharp curve and his body tensed, Logan's tongue deepened, his hands holding Adrian open, grounding him, worshipping him, wholly, completely, eternally.

"Fuck," Logan growled against Adrian's opening. "I forgot how good you taste." He said in passing before diving back in. His own cock throbbed in time with Adrian's gasps and moans, with the way his thighs trembled, muscles taut and quivering. Each sound, each shudder, was a symphony he had longed to hear, a song that resonated deep within his bones. Logan licked, sucked, pressed his tongue inside, slow and careful, tasting Adrian's vulnerability, his trust, his love.

Adrian's raw cries filled the room, his voice breaking as Logan worked him open, eating his hole like a starved man. Logan could feel the way Adrian's body trembled, could hear the way his breath hitched, the way his words flowed into a frantic Hebrew, with half-coherent, unfiltered curses and half-prayers spilling from his lips.

And Logan loved it.

Loved that he could unravel Adrian like this, that he could push him past language, past thought, until all he could do was feel. He growled against Adrian's hole, flickering his tongue, sucking the flash. He felt his eyes roll back as he lost himself in the sensation of eating him out.

Logan didn't stop.

Not when Adrian begged, not when his body shook, not when his hands pulled at Logan's hair, trying to ground himself. No—Logan wanted to ruin him completely. He licked into him, deeper, firmer, his tongue flicking and pressing in frantic, messy movements, his saliva slicking Adrian's entrance, his own cock aching from the unadulterated beauty of it. It was the perfect waking call: surrendered to the cries that spilled from Adrian, intoxicated by his taste, smothered in the echo of his sounds, a sound torn brutally from the fabric of his dream, wrenched straight from the fragile sleep where he had wandered, even as his waking life lay shrouded in darkness.

Adrian panted, his thighs flexing, his fingers twisting in the sheets before they found Logan's hair again, tugging hard. "Logan," he choked out, his voice wrecked, desperate.

Logan hummed against him, the vibration making Adrian cry out again. "Yeah, baby," he murmured, lips brushing over the sensitive skin before diving back in, tongue fucking him open, slow at first, then more relentless, more demanding. Adrian's legs spread wider, inviting Logan deeper, his body completely open to him, vulnerable.

"Need to come," Adrian pleaded, his voice breathless, shaking, his body arching off the bed. "Please, please, I need to come."

Logan smirked against his skin but didn't stop. Instead, he pulled back just enough to spit, watching as it dripped down Adrian's hole, glistening, before diving back in, his tongue teasing for a second before disappearing inside again. Adrian snarled, a ragged sound of pleasure and frustration, his head thrown back, exposing the long column of his throat.

Logan palmed Adrian's cock, wrapping his fingers around it, stroking in slow, torturous movements, using the slick of his precum as lube. Adrian shuddered violently, his muscles clenching as Logan played with him, dragging him closer and closer to the edge.

"Yes, yes," Adrian chanted, his voice cracking, but still not loud enough.

Logan wanted him wrecked. Wanted him screaming. Wanted to pull every ounce of control from him until all that was left was the raw, primal need between them.

So Logan brought his free hand to his mouth, sucking one of his fingers, drenching it with spit, before pressing it against Adrian's entrance. He went slow at first, gentle, teasing, letting Adrian feel every single moment, letting him adjust to the stretch.

Adrian groaned, his breath stuttering, his legs shaking. "Fuck, Logan," he gasped, his back arching as Logan worked the finger deeper, pushing past resistance until he was all the way in.

Then Logan found it.

That spot. That soft, sensitive gland inside Adrian that made his body jolt, his breath catch, his hands clench desperately in Logan's hair. The second Logan pressed against it, Adrian *screamed*.

Logan grinned, wicked and satisfied.

There it is.

So he did it again. And again. Pressing, rubbing, teasing, pushing Adrian closer to the edge with every single motion.

Adrian was lost now, his moans wild, frantic, his body writhing beneath Logan, hands yanking at his hair, his hips bucking helplessly into Logan's hand, chasing his own pleasure. His cock pulsed, throbbing in Logan's grip, precum spilling onto his stomach, glistening under the dim light.

Logan's mouth left his hole, but his finger stayed, fucking into him as he moved up, his lips brushing over Adrian's cock before he took him to his mouth in one gulp, sucking hard and desperate to taste him, to drink him down.

Adrian screamed his name.

His whole body tensed, every muscle locking tight, back arching, before he *broke*—his orgasm crashing over him, shaking him apart, leaving him gasping and helpless beneath Logan's mouth. Logan felt Adrian's cock pulse, felt the warm spill of him against his tongue, and he moaned, drinking it down, sucking him through the aftershocks until Adrian was nothing but a trembling, spent mess.

Slowly, Logan pulled away, pressing kisses to Adrian's stomach, his hipbones, his inner thighs.

Adrian was still panting, still shaking, his eyes glazed, his body lax and boneless.

Logan smiled against his skin, pressing one last kiss over his fluttering pulse before whispering, "I missed you."

Adrian exhaled a shaky breath, his fingers running gently through Logan's hair. He tilted his head back against the mattress, eyes fluttering closed as he murmured, voice hoarse, "I missed you too." When Logan kissed him, Adrian devoured him, sucked the taste of himself from Logan's tongue, deep and desperate, like he was pulling pieces of himself from Logan's mouth, wanting to merge, to lose the spaces where they ended and began.

Two years. Two fucking years. And now, Logan was here, touching him, loving him, ruining him all over again.

"That was…" Adrian tried to speak, but his voice was lost, wrecked from moaning, from screaming Logan's name like a man lost at sea, calling for the only shore he's ever known. He sucked in a breath, his chest still heaving.

"I know," Logan smirked proudly. He kissed Adrian again, and it wasn't a kiss meant to tease, it was a claiming, a confession, a vow unspoken.

But it wasn't enough.

"I want you inside me," Adrian whispered.

And fuck, the way his voice shook, the way his cheeks flushed like he was vulnerable, like this was something delicate, sent a shiver straight down Logan's spine. Adrian lifted his gaze, burning, dark with desire, with need.

"I want to feel you, Lo." Adrian's voice was nearly a whisper of a plea, his fingertips tracing along Logan's naked and damp back, nails softly pressing to assert his presence, to remind Logan that this moment was real, that everything between them was undeniably happening.

Logan nearly shattered.

But he swallowed down the ache, forced himself to move, and gently guided Adrian back onto the soft pillows. He reached for the condom on the bed, fingers shaking slightly as he ripped it open, rolling it over his aching length with the kind of urgency that felt unbearable, because he needed this more than his own breath.

When they got that box together, Logan had murmured awkwardly that they would have to use it in the meantime, because even though he always used protection with Zack and Sandy, it was unsafe, especially with Adrian's condition. And the shame he had felt then equaled the shame he felt as he finished putting the condom on his length. It was the kind of shame that curled in his stomach like smoke, curling up his spine, whispering ugly things in his ear—Zack's hands, Zack's mouth, the nights spent trying to drown out Adrian's ghost.

"Lo," Adrian whispered, breaking him back from his thoughts. "I love you. I don't care about it. We all have a past." He said it gently, just as he had in the store. Adrian had made peace with Logan's past, and though a shadow of pain flickered in his eyes at the thought of Logan with someone else, it lingered only briefly, as if swept away by the wind of acceptance. "Be here, with me, right now in that moment. Okay? I want you so much. I've been dreaming about having you again, ahuv sheli."

Logan whimpered, his heart leaping in a moment of fragile despair. Something within him shattered at the echo of words he had once held close, memories of Adrian's voice etched in his mind yet forever elusive in repetition. He had longed for those words, only to forget the depth of his love they carried, a bittersweet reminder of what once was.

"Say it again," Logan begged.

"I've been dreaming about you, every night, every day, every millisecond that lingers between heartbeats. Ahuv sheli." Adrian captured him in a tender kiss, pulling him close as if to shield him from the world. "Put the past where it belongs, okay? Let it rest, let it drift away. We are together, our love is all that matters." He kissed Logan's lips again, his hunger for Logan forever insatiable. "Stop punishing yourself for what's behind us; it doesn't concern me." Adrian paused, his voice softening. "I know I have moments of jealousy, of doubt... but you are my anchor, you are mine, and I've released the past. Okay? Don't carry that burden. We have a long journey ahead, and I need you to be strong. If you carry it, ahuv sheli, it would only make the road even harder."

Logan nodded against him. "What does it mean? You never told me."

Adrian let out a little laugh. "I was afraid to tell you that back then."

"Spill it," Logan ordered, giving him a harsh pack on the lips and grabbing his face a bit harder.

"You are bossy," Adrian mumbled. "I like it." He wiggled his brows.

Logan snorted and bit his nipple lightly before kissing it better.

"It means, 'my loved one' or 'my beloved,'" Adrian whispered. In that fleeting moment, Logan captured his lips with fervor, savoring every taste, his tongue intertwining with Adrian's, absorbing his soft whimpers like a fine wine. From the very beginning, almost from the first heartbeat, Adrian had loved him.

Logan had loved him too; he simply lacked the words to articulate that yearning back then.

Adrian widened his legs, pulling Logan back to him, guiding him close until their bodies aligned, until the heat of him was pressed against Logan's stomach, their breaths mingling in the space between them.

They kissed like they were memorizing each other, like their mouths were the only things tethering them to the earth. Adrian held him, his fingers gripping Logan's ass, pulling him in, needing more, while his other hand cupped Logan's jaw, like he wanted to feel every word they couldn't say.

Logan groaned into Adrian's mouth when his cock throbbed, painful with need, and he broke the kiss with a sharp breath. He sat back, just enough to reach for the lube Adrian had already ripped open and handed to him, their fingers brushing.

Their eyes met, and Logan felt his entire body pulse with something overwhelming.

He slicked himself up, coating his cock with generous, shaking hands, then rubbed the excess onto his fingers, shifting back over Adrian, kissing him again, swallowing the gasp as he lifted Adrian's legs and hooked them around his waist.

And then finally, he pressed two well-lubed fingers inside, sliding them into Adrian's primed entrance without any resistance.

Adrian's head dropped back against the pillows, his mouth falling open, a ragged moan tearing from his throat. Logan watched him, utterly transfixed, captivated by the fluid motion of Adrian's body. He marveled at how Adrian shuddered and arched instinctively, gripping him desperately for stability. Every detail was etched into his memory: the soft parting of his lips, the trembling of his breath, and the flutter of his lashes against his rosy cheeks, creating an intensely vivid tableau in his mind.

Logan buried his face in the curve of Adrian's neck, panting, pressing kisses against his pulse, his collarbone, his jaw, as he took his time, letting Adrian adjust, his fingers buried deep inside him, feeling the way Adrian's body clenched around him, soft and tight and wanting.

Adrian's hand found Logan's bicep; he clung to him hard, his touch electric against sweat-damp skin. "I'm ready," his voice was heavy, breathless, thick with need. He kissed Logan, his lips moving slowly and deeply, their tongues entwined as Adrian savored his own taste in Logan's mouth. "I want you inside me."

Something inside Logan shattered. Something inside him that had been frozen for so long cracked open and caught fire. The years between them collapsed in an instant, the weight of longing folding in on itself until only this remained, only now, only this body beneath him, this man he had loved through silence and distance and regret.

His fingers slid free, slick and trembling with something deeper than want. With shaking hands, he reached for himself, guided his cock into Adrian's slick and loose opening.

He pressed in, slow at first, the head breaching that tight ring of muscle, and—

Fuck, fuck, fuuuck—

Adrian was burning, his body pulling Logan in, sucking him deeper. Logan let out a ragged moan as he folded forward, his forehead resting in the crook of Adrian's neck, drinking in the scent of his skin, the warmth of him, the impossible truth of him. This was real. Adrian was real. He was here.

Adrian bore down on him, his legs locking tighter around Logan's waist, his fingers pressing into his back, his body taking Logan in. Logan sank deeper, inch by inch, until there was no space left between them, no breath, no thought untouched. Logan forgot his breath somewhere in the space between the moments of Adrian's body taking him inside. He was buried to the hilt, his entire body trembling at the sheer overwhelming rightness of it.

A broken sound escaped him, half sob, half groan. "So good," he purred, voice raw and shaking, fighting the tide of instinct that told him to move, to take, to lose himself completely. He forced himself still, trembling with restraint, giving Adrian time to adjust.

Adrian whimpered, soft and wrecked, and that sound—*that sound*—undid him. Logan pressed his mouth to Adrian's shoulder, teeth grazing the skin, a low moan vibrating against him. Slowly, so slowly, he began to move, dragging out until the friction stole his breath, then pushing back in with aching precision, every inch meant to be felt, meant to be remembered.

His restraint began to slip, the years of hunger rising in him like a storm. His thrusts deepened, quickened, driven by longing too vast for words, too heavy for thought.

Adrian greeted him with an intense fervor, his embrace welcoming and full of unspoken longing. His hands wove into Logan's hair, fingers threading through the strands with gentle insistence, then he moved, his nails lightly etched into Logan's biceps and back, a subtle reminder of the tension and desire that simmered beneath the surface. With each pull, he drew Logan closer, until the space between them dissolved completely, leaving only their entwined presence and the electric hush of anticipation. Their mouths crashed together, breathless and starving, their tongues a tangle of desperation and devotion. Their bodies spoke in the only language they had left, in the only way they knew how to say, *I missed you, I love you, I will never leave you again.*

Their breath was heavy and ragged, fusing together in the air between them. Adrian held Logan close, his forehead pressed to his, his hands firm and trembling, as if the only way to keep this moment alive was to anchor them both in it. His fingers curled around Logan's neck, the heat of his skin beneath them, the wild pulse thrumming there, a rhythm that matched his own frantic heart.

"You feel amazing inside of me," Adrian moaned against Logan's lips. "Yes, harder." He pleaded as Logan slammed home again and again.

Logan's gaze never wavered, those silver eyes burning into him, not just watching but seeing him, all of him, as if the years had not passed, as if the distance had never existed. He moved within Adrian in long, deliberate thrusts, each one dragging a sound from Adrian's throat, each one unraveling them both a little more.

Adrian reached for more, always more. He caught Logan's wrist, pulled him in, guided that arm around his neck, drawing their bodies impossibly tighter until they could not tell whose breath was whose.

Logan gasped, lost to the sudden closeness, the overwhelming press of skin on skin, and he collapsed into it, into him.

Now there was nothing left between them, no air, no hesitation, only the feverish heat of their bodies, the slick glide of skin, the pounding of two hearts that beat true only when the other was near, hearts destined to live in one another's symphony and keep it from ever turning to lament.

Adrian's cock throbbed between them, caught between their bodies, trapped in the heat and friction, every desperate thrust sending sparks through his veins, every grind of Logan's stomach against him drawing him closer to the edge.

Adrian let out a choked whimper, his head thrown back, his body writhing beneath Logan, taking everything, giving everything.

Logan groaned, pressing messy, open-mouthed kisses to Adrian's lips, stealing his gasps, his moans, his breath.

"Come for me, Lo," Adrian whispered, the words soft and rough all at once, a plea carried on the edge of a broken breath. "I want to feel you. I want to watch you. I want you to finish inside of me."

And fuck. That broke something in Logan.

His rhythm faltered, hips stuttering, breath catching, as heat coiled sharp and bright along his spine. The pleasure rose in him, unstoppable now, drowning thought, erasing everything but this, this moment, this man beneath him.

And then he exploded.

A moan broke from his throat. His body convulsed, the waves of release rolling through him, his fingers digging helplessly into Adrian's skin as if anchoring himself there, as if the strength of his grip might somehow make this last forever.

He pulsed deep inside him, again, again, his body undone, his heart spilling open with every trembling thrust. "I love you," he gasped, the words raw and unguarded, torn from somewhere deeper than breath or bone, a truth too vast to be silenced.

Adrian moaned softly, drinking in the wreckage of him, the way Logan shook, the way his body shook against his own. He held him through it, felt every last wave of Logan emptying into him, each stuttering pulse a promise, a tether, a plea not to be left again.

When Logan finally collapsed, spent and boneless, his body sinking into Adrian's, Adrian caught him there, held him close, and kissed him, slow and deep. Their mouths met in a kiss that was not hunger now but reverence.

Logan floated, adrift in the afterglow, his mind thick with the remnants of pleasure, of love, of Adrian. And when the haze began to clear, when his senses returned, it was to Adrian's mouth still moving softly against his, grounding him, keeping him tethered to the world they had reclaimed together.

Beneath him, Adrian trembled, breath ragged, body taut with need, hands gripping Logan's back. His hips rolled upward, chasing friction, lost now in his own rising storm. Logan felt it, the desperate rhythm of it, and reached between them, wrapped his fist around Adrian's cock, slick and hot and straining.

Logan took his time, every movement deliberate, every breath measured. He savored this, savored *him*, the weight of Adrian's cock in his palm, the way it filled his hand, the familiar smoothness of the skin, the way it twitched with each slow, steady drag of his fingers.

He leaned in, his mouth brushing Adrian's ear, voice low and dark and thick with everything he felt, everything he had kept locked inside for too long.

"I can still taste you on my tongue," he whispered, the words spilling like smoke. "Do you think of our future?"

"Al...ways," Adrian gasped, lost in sensation, voice barely a breath.

"Me too," Logan rasped, the words rough against his ear, his hips rolling in a slow, deliberate rhythm. "Let me tell you about it." Logan chuckled, smiling.

"I'm going to fuck you in every way you've ever needed, until you cannot walk, until your body aches for me in the dark. I want you to feel me every time you close your eyes, to wake up still swollen and wet from me."

Adrian moaned, the sound torn from him desperately, something that might have been Logan's name.

"That's it, baby, moan for me," Logan breathed, voice thick with want. "We'll have a house, a bed, our own world. And I'll keep you open for me, take you apart until you're shaking, until you're begging, until the only thing you can say is my name."

He slowed his hand, tightened his grip, savoring every tremor in Adrian's body.

"I want to wake you in the middle of the night with my cock inside you, slow and deep, feel you slick and aching for it. I want your come on my tongue, on my cock, on my fingers, on my face. Again and again, until you forget every second we were apart."

He kissed Adrian's ear, breath shuddering.

"I want to fuck you through the sunrise, through every morning, until you belong to me in every way. And I want you to break me too. I want to be yours, wreck me, take me, own me. Because I've only ever been yours."

Adrian whimpered, his body taut with tension, his thighs quivering around Logan's hips, the sound of Logan's voice driving him closer to the edge with every filthy, reverent word. His fingers dug into Logan's sweat-slick skin, desperate now, his whole body trembling.

A raw, shattered cry tore from his throat, wild and unbound, as his body locked tight, as the pleasure consumed him. He spilled over Logan's hand, across their stomachs, between them, the heat of it painting their skin as his release pulsed through him in waves that seemed to steal the breath from his lungs.

Logan never stopped, his hand moving, stroking him through it, holding him in place, watching him with something more than hunger. Something closer to awe.

Because God, he was beautiful like this.

Utterly undone. Completely his.

Logan waited until the tension drained from Adrian's muscles, until his limbs went loose and spent, until his chest rose and fell in soft, uneven pants.

Only then did Logan slowly pull free, dragging his hips back, his body aching from where they had been joined.

Adrian opened his eyes, heavy-lidded, exhausted, blissed-out, and when he saw Logan looking at him, he smiled.

He smiled back.

Without a word, Logan slipped off the bed, padding to the bathroom, disposing of the condom, and grabbing a warm washcloth.

When he came back, Adrian was exactly as he left him—spread out on the sheets, a mess of sweat and release, his dark brown hair that used to be kissed by the sun, tangled against the pillow, his lips parted, his eyes watching Logan, waiting.

Logan tenderly wiped Adrian down with the warm washcloth, tracing the lines of his body with devotion. Adrian barely stirred, his body boneless, but Logan took his time anyway, memorizing every inch of him, knowing that moments like this weren't infinite.

He cleaned himself next, then tossed the towel onto the floor, searching blindly for his phone. When he found it, the screen glowed in the dark, reminding him of the world waiting outside this room, outside this bed.

Three hours.

That was all they had before the hospital. Before IV drips and sterile rooms and quiet beeping machines. Before the fight.

Logan swallowed hard and set the alarm for two hours. Just a little more time.

He climbed back into bed, the sheets still warm from their bodies, and pulled Adrian into him, against him, into the space where he belonged. He wrapped an arm tightly around Adrian's waist, buried his face in the mess of his long strands that soon, too soon, would be lost, breathed him in, let his warmth settle into his bones.

Adrian stirred just enough to murmur, "How long do we have to sleep?" His voice was soft, sleep-heavy, a little hoarse from moaning Logan's name.

Logan pressed a kiss to the top of his head. "Two hours."

Adrian nodded against Logan's chest. Within moments, his breathing evened out, his limbs heavy and trusting, as if even in sleep he knew Logan would hold him together.

And Logan did. Held him close. Held him tight. Held him like he was afraid the night would steal him away.

He intertwined their fingers and felt the warmth of Adrian's palm resting against his own, a quiet weight settling in his chest, yet sleep did not come.

Instead, he devoted himself to memory, counting the measured cadence of Adrian's breaths, memorizing the rise and fall of his chest, the faint flicker of lashes against his skin as dreams moved through him. His hand traced slow, tender circles across Adrian's back, each touch an act of remembrance, knowing he might never be granted this again, knowing that tomorrow carried no certainty.

So he remained awake, holding on, because this mattered, because it was everything, because if time proved merciless and fate sought once more to take Adrian from him, he needed this moment carved into his very being: the weight of Adrian in his arms, the way their bodies met and fit as though shaped for one another, the way love, revealed itself in the stillness between breaths. And so Logan kept his vigil, and he loved Adrian in the only way he knew, by refusing to let go for as long as the night would allow.

Chapter 17
Beneath the Surface, Still Breathing

Time is running out.
The sands slip through my fingers,
Each grain a moment I should have had with you.
You are the last wish I whispered to the world,
The last prayer I wept into the night.
And for a moment, I had you.
I always believed in the next world.
I always hoped there would be something beyond this,
Somewhere I could love you forever,
Somewhere where bodies do not break,
Where the ocean does not take,
Where time does not steal what is sacred.
Your touch is the remedy of death.
This is the power you carry,
To chase away the shadows,
To drag me back from the edge,
To anchor me to life when I am drifting toward the dark.
But the end is near now.
I feel it creeping into my bones,
Settling in the spaces where warmth once lived.
The weight of it presses against my lungs,

The hush of it lingers in my breath.
Life is slipping through me, slow and silent.
And when the last moment comes,
When the light in me flickers,
I will reach for our picture.
I will hold it like a lifeline,
Like a prayer pressed between shaking hands.
My last breath—
My death—
My dirt—
My burial—
My farewell to this world—
They will all be written in the blood and tears
Of our burning love.
My life was your joy.
My heart was your touch.
My happiness was the light in your eyes.
And your love, even for the short time I held it,
Was the greatest privilege of my life.
Everything of me, everything in me,
It belongs to you.
I am eternally yours,
In this life and the next.
And now, the ocean is calling me home.
Its voice hums at the edges of my mind,
A siren's song whispering of peace, of surrender.
The waves rise like open arms,

The tide beckons me into its depths.

It tempts me with visions of you—

Of us, of love, of being whole again.

And in the breaking waves,

I still hear your laughter.

I still see your eyes in the glow of the rising moon.

So I reach.

Further and further into the abyss,

Chasing the love that was lost to the tide.

Chasing you.

Chasing us.

Chasing forever.

December 24, 2020—Seattle, Washington—A Month Later

LOGAN PULLED INTO THE hospital parking lot, his heart pounding, his fingers tightening around the steering wheel as he took a steadying breath. It was Christmas Eve, and even the bitter Seattle cold couldn't dull the warmth curling in his chest at the thought of seeing Adrian again.

Had it really been just a handful of days since he last saw him?

He reached into the passenger seat and grabbed the paper bag that was sitting there before leaving the car and venturing outside into the freezing cold.

Logan's breath hitched as he stepped through the sterile, whitewashed corridors of the hospital, the scent of antiseptic thick in the air. Christmas Eve lights twinkled faintly through the glass-paneled windows, but inside, time moved differently. Slower. Heavier. Every step he took toward Adrian's room felt longer than it should have felt.

In his hands, he clutched a small paper bag containing a collection of things Adrian loved. A book, though Adrian was often too tired to read now, and when he did read, he preferred audiobooks so he could listen with his eyes closed. Socks, warm and soft, for feet that were always cold. Chamomile tea. And cookies from the small bakery they had discovered early in treatment, when the doctors had cleared Adrian for a brief walk. Bundled in layers against a Seattle December his Middle Eastern body was still learning to endure, Adrian walked hand in hand with Logan to the lake. They sat on a nearby bench, the bakery bag resting between them, and although his appetite was thin, Adrian closed his eyes in quiet delight after every bite.

Logan clung to these small, human things; they were the ones who gave a homey feeling to those corridors and walls. They were the ones, in his mind, anchoring Adrian here, preventing him from drifting away from this world just a little longer.

When Logan reached the door, he didn't knock.

This was home. This was all that was left of it.

Inside, the machines hummed their quiet, merciless symphony. The beeping of the heart monitor, the slow drip of the IV. And there he was—Adrian. Smaller now. Hollowed out. His once golden skin was almost translucent under the fluorescent lights, his breathing steady but fragile, as if his lungs were made of glass. The sight of him, the undeniable truth of his frailty, punched the air from Logan's lungs.

But then Adrian opened his eyes, those deep, honey-whiskey eyes that had once stared at him across salt-sprayed waves, full of fire, full of life. And he smiled. A small thing, barely there. But real.

He set the bag down without a word and went straight to the sink to scrub his hands; it was hospital protocol.

When he turned back, Adrian was watching him with quiet amusement, his lips twitching in the faintest ghost of a smirk.

"You're still washing your hands like a surgeon," Adrian murmured, voice hoarse but teasing, as his dry lips fought to smile.

Logan huffed a laugh, but it cracked at the edges. "Can't be too careful."

He moved to Adrian's bedside and leaned down, pressing a soft, lingering kiss to his forehead. Then, lower, to the corner of his mouth. It was barely more than a brush of lips, but it was everything. A thousand unspoken apologies. A million silent I love yous.

Then he sank into the chair beside him, fingers tangling instinctively with Adrian's, anchoring himself in the illusion of warmth that still remained.

Warm.

God, he needed that warmth.

Adrian sighed, his lashes fluttering as exhaustion pulled at him. "You don't have to be here every second, you know."

Logan tightened his grip around Adrian's hand, his throat thick, his voice barely more than a whisper. "Yes, I do."

Adrian studied him for a long moment before his lips curved, just slightly, into something delicate and knowing. The kind of smile that had once driven Logan mad with longing, the kind that had felt like the sun breaking through heavy clouds. Now it was quieter, softer, like the last ember of a fire refusing to go out.

"Merry Christmas, ahuv sheli."

Logan swallowed past the ache in his chest, his fingers tracing absent patterns along Adrian's knuckles, feeling the faint tremor beneath his touch. "Merry Christmas, love."

Adrian's fingers curled around his, weak but steady. A reminder that he was still here. That there was still time.

"Missed you," Adrian murmured.

Logan exhaled, his breath shaking. "Me too."

Adrian's gaze grew distant for a moment, his mind drifting somewhere far away, somewhere untouched by sterile hospital rooms and the war waging inside his own body. "You know, I never really celebrated Christmas."

"Really?"

Adrian hummed, shifting slightly against the pillows, wincing as the IV tugged at the tender skin of his arm. "Yeah... I always wanted to, though. It seems fun. With the tree and the gifts and those ridiculous matching pajamas."

Logan huffed out a quiet laugh, rough around the edges but real. "Well, then, I believe you are definitely due for a Christmas." He lifted Adrian's frail hand to his lips, pressing a kiss to his bruised knuckles, the touch lingering. "A hybrid Christmas-Hanukkah extravaganza."

Adrian's smile was tired but genuine.

Logan swept his eyes over Adrian, still not quite accustomed to how intensely his pulse raced at the sight of him. His gaze dawdled on the gray knit cap on his head, knowing it wasn't just for warmth.

He remembered the morning Adrian was admitted, the way they had stood in the bathroom at their apartment—because for Logan, it was their apartment now—staring at the long, dark ponytail in the mirror. Adrian had washed his hair carefully, combed it back one last time, before turning to Logan and saying, "Do it."

Logan hesitated, scissors trembling in his grip. But Adrian met his gaze in the mirror, eyes steady, and nodded.

So, Logan did.

Tied the tail. Cut it. Shaved the rest.

Adrian sat there, staring at his reflection, his fingers ghosting over the buzzed skin of his scalp. He tried to make light of it, saying, "Reminds me of the army. Guess I won't have to use all those ridiculous hair products anymore."

But Logan heard it. The way his voice had caught. The way his throat had worked around the words.

They donated the hair. And on the drive to the hospital, Adrian ran his fingers over his shaved head, adjusting to the strange lightness. Logan stole glances at him the whole way home, thinking, *different, but still Adrian. Always Adrian.*

Now, a month later, there was nothing left to run his fingers through.

The chemo had been merciless.

From the start, the doctors had been brutally honest. Adrian's cancer was advanced and aggressive. There was no easing in, no slow burn. They had gone full force, hitting him with everything they had.

No mercy.

No time to waste.

It had taken everything from him. His strength. His appetite. His sleep. Some days, it even felt like it was taking his spirit.

But not tonight.

Tonight, Adrian smiled at Logan with that same quiet, unshakable love, the love that had carried them across oceans, through lost years and broken hearts. The love that still burned, even now, even in the face of something neither of them could control.

Logan studied him, his heart aching at the sight. Of how much Adrian had lost, how his body had withered under the weight of the battle. His collarbones jutted out sharply, his fingers thin and delicate, wrapped around Logan's hand like they might disappear if he let go.

But he was still here.

Still fighting.

And that was all that mattered.

Adrian's voice, soft and hoarse, pulled him back. "How was your flight?"

Logan tore his gaze away from the sharp edges of Adrian's face, from the ghost of the man he once knew, and met his eyes.

"Fine." He shrugged, forcing a smirk. "Hate flying."

Adrian hummed, a tired sound, his eyelids flickering. "Your dad still being... your dad?"

Logan huffed a quiet laugh, shaking his head. "Oh yeah. Classic Robert. Confused why I'd rather be here than flying around the world closing deals."

Adrian squeezed his hand, the pressure barely there but enough. "Because you're here with me."

Logan's throat tightened. "Yeah," he murmured. "Because I'm here with you."

He tried to smile, tried to keep the weight of everything from showing on his face, but Adrian saw it. He always did.

"I think he's trying, though," Logan admitted after a beat. "I can see it. He struggles, but he's trying. And I'm... I'm trying too. Work is a lot. I push through, but my head's not there."

Adrian watched him, silent. Logan could feel the weight of his gaze, heavy despite the frailty of his body.

He didn't say *It's okay*. He didn't say *I understand*. Because he *did* understand. And they both knew it wasn't okay.

Logan glanced at the machines beside the bed. The IV bags were filled with chemicals designed to save Adrian's life, dripping slowly into his veins. The monitors were beeping in rhythm with his heartbeat, each sound a reminder of how fragile that heartbeat really was.

"How are you feeling?" Logan asked softly, his voice barely above a whisper. "I haven't had a chance to speak with Dr. Tierney yet."

Adrian sighed and moved against the pillows. "Like I got hit by a truck. Then backed over for good measure."

Logan tried to laugh, tried to keep the moment light, but the sound barely made it past his throat. Because none of this was fair.

His grip on Adrian's hand tightened, his thumb tracing slow, absentminded circles over the fragile bones beneath his skin. Holding onto him. Holding him here.

"I'm kidding, I'm good," Adrian murmured, his voice softer now. "Though I think Dr. Tierney left for the rest of the evening. It's Christmas Eve, after all."

Logan nodded, but he wasn't thinking about Dr. Tierney. He was thinking about how much weight Adrian had lost. About the way his body seemed too small for the bed now. About how his pulse felt fragile beneath his fingertips, like it could slip away at any moment.

"And," Adrian added, forcing a small, teasing smirk, "I can go home the day after tomorrow. After that, another round starts."

Logan swallowed hard. He forced himself to smile, to match Adrian's attempt at humor. "Lucky you."

Adrian chuckled, but it was a breathy, weak sound, and it broke something inside Logan.

He didn't say what he wanted to say. That he would give anything to trade places with him. That if he could take all of Adrian's pain, carry it himself, he would. That it should be him in this bed instead.

Instead, he just lifted Adrian's hand again, pressing another kiss to his knuckles, lingering there, breathing him in.

We are not losing this fight.

Adrian exhaled slowly, his gaze drifting over Logan's face, studying him like he was memorizing him, like he was afraid he might forget the way he looked if he blinked for too long.

"Aren't you going to spend the holiday with your family?" he asked.

Logan barely hesitated. "You're my family."

The words left his mouth without thought, without calculation. Simple. Unshakable.

Adrian didn't say anything for a moment. But Logan didn't need him to.

Because he squeezed Logan's fingers just a little tighter, just enough to say, *I know. I love you, too.*

Logan cleared his throat, forcing his voice lighter, teasing. "But no, I spoke to Jane and Ann, and they're coming tomorrow. Ann is really excited. She wants to talk to your doctors, see your test results."

Adrian grinned, his dark eyes crinkling at the edges. "Of course she does."

As a med student, she was in her element.

"She actually texted me," Adrian admitted. "Said she's considering oncology for the long run."

Logan blinked, then let out a small breath of laughter, his expression softening, something warm and tender slipping into his features.

"She texted you?" he asked, his voice almost disbelieving.

Adrian nodded, shifting against the pillows, the weight of exhaustion dragging at him. "Yeah. And Jane sends me videos of her baby girl." His lips curled, shaking his head slightly, like he still wasn't sure how he had become so effortlessly woven into Logan's life like this.

Logan sat still, his chest tightening with something deep, something indescribable. It was an ache, but not the kind that hurt.

It was something bigger. Something fuller.

Adrian had slipped into his life so seamlessly. Like he had always belonged there.

As if he was always meant to be part of his family.

Logan remembered the moment Jane had found out about Adrian's cancer.

It wasn't a dramatic confession or a grand revelation. Their mother had just called her and mentioned that Logan had a friend who was sick, a friend he wouldn't abandon, and slipped that Jane should probably check on that friend.

And Jane, being Jane, had run to the hospital without a second thought.

Logan had been sitting outside Adrian's hospital room when she found him, his hands shaking, his heart lodged somewhere between his ribs and his throat. She had taken one look at him, at the weight he carried, and sat beside him without a word.

So he told her.

Told her everything as briefly as he could manage, like if he said too much, he might collapse under the weight of it.

That he was gay. That the man inside that hospital room wasn't just his friend—he was his love, his soul, his home, his entire damn universe. That he had been too scared to say it out loud. That for years, he had been terrified, ashamed, and lost. So damn lost. That Adrian had been the only thing that had ever made him feel whole. That he had run from it. Run from *him*. And that now, he was here, fighting for him, praying for him, loving him the way he should have from the very beginning.

Jane cried.

And then she hugged him so tightly it stole the air from his lungs.

And when Logan, with his voice cracking and his whole body trembling, apologized for shutting her out, for the way she had always, *always* known something was wrong, but he had never let her in—

She only held him tighter. "You were scared," she had whispered fiercely. "You don't have to be scared anymore."

And when he admitted—choking on the words—how terrified he was now, how he didn't know if he could survive losing Adrian, if he could survive losing *everything*—

She cupped his face, looked him straight in the eyes, and said with all the certainty in the world, "It's going to be okay."

And somehow, at that moment, Logan believed her.

The incredible part wasn't that Jane had accepted it.

It was that she had already known.

Because when Logan finally spoke the truth, when he had finally dared to *say* Adrian's name the way he had always felt it—like something holy, something fragile, something infinite—Jane had only smiled.

"It's him, isn't it?" she said.

Logan blinked, confused. "What?"

Jane's eyes shimmered with something between joy and heartbreak. "The guy from the wedding," she clarified, grinning through her tears. "The one who flew over twenty hours just to see you."

Logan stared at her, stunned. Because *how?*

How did she know?

How did she connect the dots—the way Logan changed after that wedding, the way he had spent years afterward spiraling, drowning, unraveling?

Jane had always seen him.

"He looked at you…" she started, then hesitated, her lips parting like the words were caught somewhere deep in her chest. She glanced away, as if she was trying to piece together something that had always been there, waiting to be spoken.

Then, her gaze snapped back to Logan. "Like he was seeing the light," she eventually said. "Like you were the only thing in the room that mattered," she continued, her voice barely above a whisper. "Like the world had stopped turning just so he could look at you a second longer."

Logan forgot how to breathe.

Because *yes*. Adrian had always looked at Logan like that.

And now, Adrian wasn't just Logan's anymore. He had become part of the family.

Ann hadn't met him in person yet, too busy with med school and routines to fly home.

She came to know him through late night phone calls and fleeting glimpses via video chat, and through that learned the story. But more importantly, she knew what he truly meant to Logan. Logan never needed to voice it aloud. It was in the way his breath caught when he spoke of him, in the lingering silence that stretched too long when words failed.

Tomorrow, she would finally see Adrian for herself.

Logan let go of Adrian's hand and reached for the bag he'd brought with him, emptying the contents into the bedside table.

This was their life now.

A balancing act between hope and fear, between exhaustion and resolve. A life held together by whispers in the dark, by desperate prayers to a God neither of them fully believed in, by the silent promises exchanged in the press of fingers against skin.

It was terrifying. It was painful. It was fragile.

But it was *theirs*.

And Logan, who had once been so afraid of love, of himself, of *them*, was holding onto it with everything he had.

Adrian had always been there. Woven into the fabric of his life in ways Logan hadn't even realized until he was gone. Like the rhythm of the ocean, like the pull of the tide, like something inevitable, something constant.

Something he had once taken for granted.

But not again.

Never again.

Adrian stirred, a faint shift beneath the thin hospital sheets. Even that small movement cost him something now.

"Lo," he whispered. "You can go. It's okay." His gaze flickered, weary but determined. "You look exhausted. Go home. Take a shower. Get some real sleep."

"No." The answer came without hesitation, sharp and low. "I've already stopped by the apartment to take a shower." Logan would never risk exposing Adrian's frail body to airport germs, so he took a quick shower and put on clean clothes before coming in.

He grasped his hand once more, as if the mere idea of leaving Adrian drove him into a frenzy. "I want to be with you." The words came rough, caught on something deeper than exhaustion, thicker than fear.

For a moment, Adrian's lips twitched, almost a smile, though there was no strength behind it.

"Are you tired?" Logan asked, his thumb brushing lightly over the fragile line of Adrian's knuckles.

Adrian hesitated. Just for a beat. "No," he whispered.

They both knew it was a lie. Logan could see it in the way his body sank deeper into the mattress, could hear it in the rasp of his voice, feel it in the way his pulse fluttered faintly beneath his skin.

But Logan didn't press.

He nodded, letting the lie stand, offering the small mercy of pretending to believe it.

"I thought you would go to sleep for a while before coming," Adrian added.

"I'll sleep later."

Adrian exhaled, the sound soft but deep, an unspoken ache wrapped inside it. He didn't argue. Instead, with slow movements, he shifted beneath the thin sheets, his hand slipping from Logan's grasp, and scooted over an inch.

"Come here," he whispered. The word hung in the air between them, tender and fragile, part invitation, part plea.

Logan moved without thought.

He shrugged off his jacket, let it fall to the chair, kicked off his shoes with the absent grace of a man who had done this too many nights now, whose body moved on instinct even when his mind spun with everything it could not fix.

Then he climbed into the narrow bed, careful—always careful.

Careful of the IV in Adrian's arm, thin and pale beneath skin that bruised too easily now. Careful of the central line threaded into his chest, a lifeline and a threat all at once. Careful of the dark blooms of bruises along his ribs, the new sharpness of bone beneath skin that had once been golden and strong. Careful of how easily the body he loved seemed to be slipping away beneath his hands.

He slid an arm around Adrian, drew him in with infinite gentleness, fitting their bodies together in the small space. He pressed his face into the hollow where Adrian's neck met his shoulder, breathed in the scent that was still his, beneath the antiseptic and the faint odor of saline.

And in that moment, there was no hospital. No beeping machines. No time ticking away at the edges of their fragile peace.

This was home.

Adrian sighed softly with content, melting into Logan's embrace, into the warmth, into the familiarity of *them*. His body, fragile as it was, still fit perfectly against Logan's, like it always had. Like it always would.

"You need to sleep, Lo."

Logan answered not with words but with a kiss, pressed to Adrian's cheek, slow and lingering, lips resting there as though he could drink him in, absorb him, carry him beneath his skin. As if the sheer force of loving him might be enough to keep him here, in this bed, in this life, for just a little longer. "I'll just close my eyes for a while," Logan mumbled.

Adrian breathed out quietly, a sound that held understanding and love and grief all woven together.

And as Logan began to drift, the weight of wakefulness loosening its grip, pulling him gently toward dreams, the last thing he heard was Adrian's voice singing to him, a low hum, rough and thin.

Their song, unfurled in a low, smoke-rough murmur meant for his ears alone, a private lullaby, a spell uttered softly enough to carry him into that long-known ethereal garden of dreams, where the almost-s loosened their hold and sank back into the soil. What had once survived only as a sanctuary of the imagined, conjured from hunger and ache, at last took form and weight. Adrian was no longer a figure dreamed into being, but flesh and warmth and gravity, held, undeniably, within his arms.

Logan didn't know how long he had slept, only that when he blinked himself back into consciousness, the room was softly glowing with lamplight, the low murmur of voices filling the air. The sterile scent of the hospital was still present, but now it was mingled with the aroma of home-cooked food. A soft draft brushed across his face, and as his eyes adjusted, he noticed the window slightly cracked open, letting in the December air. It was freezing outside, but someone had opened it for Adrian. The smell of food must have been too much.

His family was there.

He could hear Ann's hushed, rapid-fire words, the excitement buzzing in her voice as she spoke to Adrian.

"Ann, be quiet! Your brother is sleeping, you know how exhausted he is," Samantha scolded, but there was affection in her voice.

Logan stirred, rubbing the sleep from his eyes, and felt the solid warmth of Adrian still beside him. His heart tightened, his breath settling just knowing that Adrian was still there.

The soft rustling of bags and containers being placed on the small hospital table made Logan glance toward the cluster of people now filling the space.

Jane was unpacking something from a bag—food, from the smell of it. Samantha was watching Ann with amusement, while Ann, practically vibrating with curiosity, was already leaning toward Adrian, talking animatedly, her eyes bright with something between fascination and genuine care.

And then there was his father.

Standing by the door, still in his business suit, the tie loosened just slightly.

Their eyes met across the room.

His father was here.

That alone meant more than Logan could fully comprehend.

For years, his father had ignored him whenever he stepped out of line, whenever he wasn't who he was supposed to be.

But now, he was standing in Adrian's hospital room, holding a large bag filled with gifts while Cole carefully placed a small plastic Christmas tree in the corner.

And that meant everything.

"What are you doing here?" Logan asked, his voice hoarse with sleep, his fingers absentmindedly squeezing Adrian's where they still lay between them.

He turned to Adrian, who was already looking at him with that small, knowing smile, the one that made sweat beads form on Logan's skin and butterflies flutter in his stomach.

"It's Christmas Eve," Jane said matter-of-factly, like it was the most obvious thing in the world. She arched a brow at him, her tone caught somewhere between exasperation and affection. "You didn't think we'd just sit at Mom and Dad's like everything was fine while you were here, did you?" She had that big sister voice, the one that was lined with "you're stupid vibes" without ever saying the words.

Logan blinked at them—at all of them—his throat tightening as the weight of it settled behind his ribs. No. He hadn't thought they would come. But here they were, every one of them, carrying Christmas with them into the pale light of this hospital room.

And so they stayed.

Through the night, through the slow passing of hours beneath the soft hum of machines, they sat together, sharing food, passing plates, laughter rising in gentle waves against the sterile air.

Samantha sat comfortably beside Adrian on the small couch in the softly lit room. Her voice was bright and inviting, imbued with warmth and a relaxed ease, as if they had known each other for years. She asked him questions effortlessly, her tone friendly and curious, eager to learn more about him. Logan could see how it steadied Adrian, how it drew something soft across his features that had not been there in weeks.

And Logan, with Jane's little girl tucked in his arms, let himself lean into that moment. He played with her through the evening, making faces, whispering nonsense sounds that sent her into fits of delighted giggles, her tiny hands reaching for his nose, for his chin.

Adrian watched them with a gaze that shimmered, the corners of his mouth tilting up in a smile that spoke of longing and love all at once.

"Wanna meet Uncle Adrian?" Logan cooed, voice soft as he shifted Olivia closer, mindful of the lines trailing from Adrian's body, of the fragility beneath the smile.

Olivia gurgled, babbled something that might have been agreement, her hands reaching again. Logan held her carefully, close enough for Adrian to see her, to let her tiny fingers curl against his own trembling ones.

And Adrian melted, a soft sound leaving him, a tenderness pooling in his gaze as he traced every inch of her with his eyes, as though memorizing her for some future that felt both too near and too far.

Later, over dessert, Jane leaned back in her chair with a knowing smirk. "You know," she said, her voice full of teasing affection, "you used to swear you'd never be the kind of guy who got all gooey-eyed over a baby. I think I'm watching you eat those words, little brother."

Logan rolled his eyes, but there was no heat in it, only a quiet glow beneath the weariness.

Even their father, slow to thaw as he always had been, began to soften by degrees. A word here. A faint smile there. And in the hush that followed one shared glance between them all—a breath caught between one heartbeat and the next—the world, for just a moment, felt almost okay.

March 18, 2021—Seattle, Washington—Three Months Later

LOGAN STOOD ALONE NEAR the arrivals gate, hands buried deep in his coat pockets, the seams worn thin where he'd been rubbing his thumb raw these past weeks. Logan spotted them before they saw him—Tammi and Aaron, their faces worn by time and worry. In just four months, grief had carved its way into their posture, their expressions, the very way they walked.

Logan stepped forward without hesitation, heart pounding. The Hebrew he'd been practicing wasn't perfect yet, but it was enough. He wanted them to know they were safe, that they were wanted here. He had insisted on picking them up himself, despite their protests.

His mother had been the one to insist they stay in the guest house, not a hotel. "They're family," she said simply, and that was that. No argument had stood a chance against her quiet conviction. Logan was grateful for it—for her, for all of them. His family had folded Adrian into their lives without pause, and when Logan had begun to break under the weight of it all, they held him together.

The drive home passed mostly in silence. Logan watched them in the rearview mirror, saw their quiet awe at the sprawling trees and wide streets, the way their fingers fidgeted in their laps, the silent worry in their eyes. He filled the silence with what he could—updates on Adrian's treatment, reassurances laced with honesty.

At the house, Logan carried their luggage despite Aaron's half-hearted protest. He didn't say much, but Logan saw something flicker in his eyes—relief, maybe, or something gentler. The guest house was modest, warm, tucked into the quiet edges of the property.

They stayed just long enough to drop their bags, take a quick shower, change into fresh clothes, and exchange a few gentle words with his mother, who welcomed them with open arms and her calm, steady demeanor unique to her.

And then it was time.

The walk through the hospital was quiet, and every step seemed to weigh a little more than the last. Logan could feel the tension in the way Tammi clutched her purse, in the slight tremble in Aaron's jaw. He guided them gently, like you might guide someone blindfolded through a dream they never wanted to enter.

The nurses greeted Logan with soft and knowing smiles as they passed through the corridors. They had seen him every day, had watched him fold himself into the chair beside Adrian's bed, memorizing every shift in his breath, every tremor of pain, every exhausted whisper. They had seen him fall asleep with his forehead pressed against Adrian's frail shoulder, as if willing his strength into the body that once held so much life.

When they reached the door, Logan paused—just long enough to steady himself—then opened it and stepped aside to let them in first.

What waited inside was not the boy they had raised.

Adrian was thin now, achingly so, his skin pale and nearly translucent. The vibrant flush that once lived in his cheeks had faded, and the soft gray knit cap on his head covered his completely bald head now. Long gone were the beautiful strands of hair Logan adored. But his eyes still watched the world like it mattered. They dimmed, for a moment, when he saw the pain on his parents' faces.

Logan crossed the room without a word. He leaned down and pressed a kiss to Adrian's temple, soft and reverent.

Adrian's lips barely moved, but they curled into the faintest smile. That was enough.

No matter how worn down his body was, seeing Logan changed everything. He was still looking at him the same way, like nothing had changed. With love. With certainty. With that quiet devotion that said: I'm here. I'm yours. I'm not going anywhere.

And Adrian, somehow, was the luckiest person alive, held in the gentle, heady embrace of Logan Vaughn's love, a feeling that made his heart soar.

Logan took Adrian's hand, fragile and cool in his own, and they held each other's gaze, no words needed.

Then his parents stepped forward, slow, hesitant, overcome. Tammi's hand reached for his face; Aaron brushed his fingers along Adrian's shoulder. They spoke softly, voices breaking.

Logan caught enough of the Hebrew to understand. "How are you, my son? How much does it hurt? How can we help you? What are the doctors saying?"

But beneath the fear and sorrow, Logan saw something else flickering in their eyes, relief.

Adrian kept glancing toward Logan between words, his gaze pulled again and again to the one person who kept him grounded. And every time, Logan smiled back with the same quiet promise.

I'm here. I'm not leaving.

Logan settled into the seat next to Adrian's bed, while his parents sat on the other side, watching their son with thinly veiled concern. The conversation moved cautiously, treading the fragile line between pretending at normalcy and the truth that hovered just beneath every word. Even in the lightest moments, fear lingered in the pauses, in the glance Aaron cast toward the IV line, in the way Tammi's fingers curled tightly in her lap.

At some point, Adrian shifted, pushing himself up with quiet determination and moving to the small half-couch, half-chair by the window. Logan followed, settling beside him, slipping his fingers through Adrian's with quiet familiarity.

Their hands rested together on Adrian's lap, Logan's thumb tracing slow, comforting circles against his skin. A silent rhythm reverberates—a heartbeat that exists outside his own chest.

It is a wondrous thing that Logan had two heartbeats, each pulsing with life in its unique cadence.

Adrian translated quietly, his voice soft and fraying. He told them what he could: the doctors were adjusting his treatment plan, tracking every shift, fighting for remission. He had just finished his fourth round of chemo.

No one mentioned the pain. No one spoke of the nights when Adrian could barely lift his head, or of the mornings when his hands shook too much to hold a spoon. But Logan saw it—in the way Adrian leaned against him more heavily now, in the quiet tremor beneath his words, in the stillness of his hand when Logan held it.

Then Aaron reached across the space between them, folding Adrian's hand in both of his. And Logan watched the soft unraveling of the man's face, the thin control giving way beneath the years.

He had seen this before.

Aaron had once held another hand in another hospital bed, beneath a different sun, beneath the same shadows. He had already lost the love of his life to this disease. And now, across the fragile span of years, he faced it again.

Adrian tried to steady the moment, his voice soft. *"Abba,"* dad, he whispered. *"Ani beseder."* I'm fine. *"Ani sameach she'atem po."* I'm glad you're here. *"Ani mekabal et hatipol hachi tov."* I'm getting the best care possible.

But Aaron's breath caught, and his fingers tightened. His voice broke as memory bled into fear.

"Your mother said that too," he said in Hebrew. "She told me she was fine. And that cancer..." His voice broke. "It killed her."

Adrian stilled beneath the weight of it.

Because this was the deeper wound. Not only the fight for his own life, but the knowledge that his father had already walked this grief once.

Aaron didn't say the rest, but it lived in his eyes. The terror that he would be asked to bury his son.

Adrian tightened his grip. "Dad," he said gently, "it's different."

And Logan, watching them, watching how tightly they clung to each other—father and son, both trying not to fall—wished, with everything in him, that it was true.

July 17, 2021—Seattle, Washington—Four Months Later

Beneath the sorrow, past the pain,
Across restless nights and settled loneliness,
Like an angel's whisper, like a devil's taunt,
You dance within my dreams,
Just as they flutter, about to slip away.
You are here, flesh and bone,
My deepest wish, at last, comes true.

ADRIAN LAY IN THE hospital bed, unmoving, eyes locked on the ceiling. He memorized it in the same way a prisoner memorizes the cracks in the wall, simply because there was nothing else to do. Every line, every shift of shadow in the sterile white tiles had become part of his world, more familiar than the reflection in his own mirror.

Time no longer moved forward. It circled, caved in, dragged itself over, and over, an irrepressible wheel. He was still here.

Still in this bed.

Still in this body that refused to work.

His body had become a traitor. A place he didn't recognize anymore. Weak, foreign, constantly betraying him in small, humiliating ways. The pain was not sharp, not always. It was worse than that. It was constant. Dull and dragging, woven into the fabric of his being. Some days, he couldn't even tell where it started or ended; it just was. It had become part of him.

His phone sat beside him, untouched.

No messages. No missed calls. No, *I'm sorry, I'm swamped, baby. I'll call tonight.*

They had made a rule. One rule in the middle of all this chaos, this war. One promise they had clung to in that first time they had been apart, and Adrian was too weak to sit up or answer the phone, when Logan had paced the floor with the weight of silence pressing against his ribs.

Never go to bed without speaking.

One call. Every night. No matter where Logan was. No matter how long or how short the words might be. One line of connection. One thread of love stretched across whatever distance the world tried to put between them.

But last night, for the first time, Logan broke that promise.

Logan had been gone for nearly a week now, off on a business trip he couldn't reschedule. Adrian hadn't protested. He'd nodded, said *I understand*, even smiled. But it wasn't the truth. Not really.

It wasn't that he didn't understand. Logically, he knew Logan had to work. Logically, he also understood that Logan was scheduling all his meetings to the minimum amount of time so he could return sooner. He knew that a week, in the grand scheme of things, wasn't all that long. He knew Logan loved him, had shown it in a thousand ways since this nightmare began. But logic had little weight when your world was reduced to four white walls and the steady hiss of machines. When days no longer unfolded but blurred together like water over glass, until the edges of time disappeared.

When the life outside this room began to feel like a dream you had once touched but no longer belonged to.

In that space, a week became a lifetime. A single day grew heavy as stone. And a few missed calls could hollow out a chasm that no words could cross.

And after so many nights spent side by side, Logan's absence felt vast. Adrian hated how much he noticed it, how much he needed him. Hated the quiet shame curling in his chest as he stared up at the ceiling, wondering if he was being too much. Too dependent. Too broken.

Was it selfish to want to hear his voice? To want to feel his hand on his cheek, his breath against his skin? Was he being clingy? Needy? Was he asking too much of someone who already carried so much? Someone who, if he was honest, could have an easier life with someone whole?

He shut his eyes, allowing those intrusive thoughts to settle in his mind, persistent and hard to ignore, while the silence continued to gnaw at him.

There was nowhere to retreat.

And what hurt more than the pain, more than the chemo, more than the nausea and fevers and cold sweats, was the ache of being forgotten.

Because he wasn't just sick. He wasn't just dying.

He was starting to feel invisible.

He turned his head toward the window, the light slanting in across his face. Even the sun looked bored with him.

He thought of home, but not his apartment in Tel Aviv, not the life he used to live.

He thought of Logan's apartment.

Of their home. A place he was eager to return to every single time.

He thought of warm blankets and soft lighting. Of lying on the couch with Logan's arm around him, head against his chest, listening to the heartbeat that had become more comforting than any medication. He thought of pretending to eat the soup Logan got after a failed attempt to cook a home-made one that somehow turned solid, just so he wouldn't worry. Of late-night walks where Logan held him up without ever making him feel small. Of the beach trip. They never made it out of the car that day. Adrian had tried—God, he had tried. But the moment the cold air hit his lungs, the nausea surged, pulling him under before he could even unbuckle his seatbelt. He'd curled into himself on the passenger side, shaking, humiliated, too tired to even cry.

And still—before the sickness claimed him—he had seen the ocean. Just for a second. That endless stretch of blue. He had closed his eyes, breathed in the salt, and let himself pretend. Pretend that he was still someone. Still the man Logan had fallen in love with. Not a body unraveling molecule by molecule, not this fragile ghost of a life. That he was a man who deserved Logan Vaughn's love.

He hadn't cried in weeks. Not because he wasn't hurting, but because the weight inside him had become too heavy to move. Too heavy for tears. So instead, his fingers curled into the stiff sheets, white-knuckled, clinging to something that wouldn't give.

A long time ago, before Logan was back in his life, Adrian accepted his death. Or at least he thought.

But...

He didn't want to die. But worse than that, he didn't want to fade.

He was fading.

The walls of this room had grown smaller by the day. The window might as well have been a painting for how static and unreachable it had become. Time folded in on itself, and the outside world became a myth. Life happened elsewhere now, in places with noise and wind and laughter.

But here, inside this sterile, fluorescent cage, Adrian felt like nothing. Like less than nothing.

The Adrian he used to be—the one who surfed before sunrise, who chased light, who could laugh without effort or catch his breath without thinking—that version of himself was gone. Drowned somewhere in the weeks of chemo and fever and IV drips. And whatever remained... didn't feel like a person. Just a patient. Just an echo.

And the silence didn't help.

It gave space for the voices that lived in the corners of his mind. The ones that whispered Logan deserved better. That no matter how tightly Logan held his hand or how often he said *I love you*, it was only a matter of time. Time before he realized the truth:

That this—this hospital bed, this frail shell, this life built on survival—wasn't what he signed up for.

Adrian tried not to believe it. He told himself love was stronger than this. But some days, when the pain curled up in his spine and wouldn't let go, when Logan hadn't called in days and the silence stretched too long, he couldn't stop it from creeping in.

This was not the man Logan had fallen in love with.

The man Logan fell for had salt in his hair and a reckless grin that dared the world to contain him. He was sun-drenched, loud, shamelessly alive. He climbed cliffs barefoot, chased waves like they owed him something, jumped into rivers without checking the depth. In airports, strangers' laughter followed him like a song. Under inky stars, he slept wild and kissed as if the end of the universe was only the beginning.

Back then, Adrian had been made of motion, of sweat and sea spray and adrenaline. He was strong. He was magnetic. Men noticed him, wanted him. They watched him surf, asked for his number, and leaned in too close at beach bars. He hadn't needed anyone, but with Logan, he *wanted*, and that made all the difference. Logan had fallen in love with him in that golden hour of his life, when the world was wide and the body was obedient.

But now...

Now he was small. Tethered. Fading.

His body had thinned to something almost foreign, fragile, translucent, shaped more by sickness than by will. He lived in a bed that wasn't his, surrounded by plastic tubes and machine murmurs. His skin carried the scent of hospital, sterile, sour, permanent. His muscles, once taut with purpose, had softened into surrender. There were days he no longer knew the face in the glass, and worse, days when the not-knowing didn't matter. He was drowning in a single, merciless refrain, a kind of auditory torment dressed up as care. The hospital composed its own song: the hiss of oxygen, the drip of chemicals, the unyielding metronome of machines. Footsteps passed, voices rose and fell, the staff moving in and out like a surrogate family he had never chosen. It was a music that hollowed him, a chorus that made silence the only mercy he craved.

He hadn't heard from Logan yesterday. Just a day, just a call, but it hit like an absence carved out of bone.

He didn't blame him. Not really.

Because this version, this aching, trembling shadow, was not who Logan had fallen for. Logan had fallen for the wild in him, the fight, the fire. And now all of that was ash.

Adrian couldn't help but wonder: what did Logan see when he looked at him now? Was it love? Or mercy? Was it memory that kept him coming back or guilt? Pity?

The silence pressed harder against his ribs.

Because once, they had conquered countries. Now, he couldn't even leave the room. Once, they ran barefoot through unknown cities, swam in cool lakes, made love on the beach and under the stars. Now, he could barely stand without help.

And he hated it. Hated that his own body was betraying the love they had built. Hated that somewhere deep inside, a cruel voice whispered that maybe Logan deserved more than this husk he had become.

Because Logan had loved a man who could carry him out of a riptide.

Not the one barely holding onto himself.

Adrian knew, in theory, that Logan loved him.

He said it often. Gently. Fiercely. Without hesitation. He brought him flowers even when Adrian couldn't smell them, told bad jokes just to see Adrian's laugh, played old songs on his phone, curled beside him in the too-small hospital bed just to hold him through the nausea. Logan loved loudly, persistently, stubbornly.

And still, Adrian couldn't feel it.

Not really.

Because love, to him now, felt like a relic belonging to another lifetime. A dialect he once spoke fluently but could no longer comprehend. It echoed around him, cleaved, split from its meaning yet clinging to him all the same, beautiful but incomprehensible, like music underwater.

He knew Logan meant every word. But he didn't know *why*.

Why would someone love this?

This body that betrayed him. This face that had hollowed. This version of himself that couldn't even stand up straight without clutching the rail of the bed like an old man. He was vanishing piece by piece, and Logan kept insisting there was still something here worth holding on to. But Adrian couldn't see it. Couldn't feel it. He felt like driftwood, a vestige of something once alive, now just a shape washed ashore.

Logan said *I love you*, and Adrian tried to believe him.

But how could he? He didn't love himself. Didn't even like himself. Most days he barely recognized the person in the mirror, and on the days he did, he felt only shame.

Because somewhere in the quiet rot of his mind, a voice whispered: *He didn't fall in love with this. You're a burden now. You're not beautiful anymore. He'll stay, but only because he's too kind to leave.*

Adrian tried to shut it out. He tried to summon the way Logan used to look at him, like he was made of sunlight and seawater, like he was something wild and holy. But memory was a fragile, elusive thing, especially when grief made the past feel like a lie.

Depression was louder.

The whispers turned into screams that drowned out all memory.

It spoke in absolutes. It rewrote truths. It turned love into obligation, tenderness into pity. And all the warmth that Logan offered—the soft hands, the whispered I love yous, the way he stayed even when he didn't have to—was entirely consumed by the static in Adrian's mind, by venom that infected his brain and gradually seeped into his heart.

Every kind word drowned beneath the weight of that brutal inner voice.

You're not him anymore. You're broken. You're a burden. He's lying. He has to be.

No matter how tightly Logan held him, Adrian could still feel himself slipping away. The force of his self-hatred was tidal, dragging him under, again and again. It was relentless. Merciless. Coldblooded. Stronger than love, some days. Stronger than memory. Stronger than him.

And that was the cruelest part of all: That something so dark, so small and invisible, could undo everything beautiful he'd ever believed about himself.

And so he lay there, wrapped in sterile sheets, drowning in love he couldn't feel, with a heart that still wanted to believe, but a mind too broken to let it in.

The fear. The shame.

What if Logan woke up one morning and saw things clearly? Saw how young he still was. How much life he had ahead. How much easier it would be to love someone whose body wasn't a battleground.

What if the phone did ring one day—not with warmth, not with love, but with the soft, careful unraveling of everything? A voice low and tired. A pause too long. And then the words: I can't do this anymore. I want someone I can build a future with... not someone fading in a hospital bed.

And Adrian would understand. Of course, he would. That was the worst part. He wouldn't scream or beg or accuse. He would nod. He would whisper, *I get it,* and mean it.

But afterward—quietly, invisibly—it would destroy him.

Because if Logan left, really left, Adrian wouldn't just be sick.

He'd be *lost.*

He'd be *gone.*

He'd still be breathing, but there would be nothing left inside to hold onto.

Tears came before he could stop them. He turned his face into the pillow, pressing down hard, hoping the weight might stop the flood. His fingers curled into the sheets, grasping and clinging to the fabric.

He hated this.

Hated the way grief softly curled up in his chest, as if it belonged there, like a dark, silent companion.

Hated that he cried so easily now, hated that even his emotions had become soft, exposed, raw.

This fear, this hollow, gnawing ache that lived at the edge of everything, it wasn't about death anymore. It was about being left behind before he was even gone. About watching someone he loved carry the unbearable weight of him, and knowing—deep down—that one day, that weight might be too much.

Because cancer didn't just take the body. It took the self. It wore Adrian down in layers, first his strength, then his voice, then his light, and finally it came for his sense of worth.

And Adrian could feel it now. The unraveling. The part of him that used to believe he was enough. That he was worthy of being chosen.

Even on the good days, even when Logan was there, whispering *I love yous* into his skin like a prayer, something inside him pulled away. Because love—real as it was—didn't always survive sickness.

And no matter how tightly Logan held him, Adrian couldn't stop wondering when it would happen. *When the hand would loosen.*

When the goodbye would come.

Because some part of him believed it already had.

Then the door opened.

Adrian didn't move. Didn't sit up. Didn't even turn his head.

He just listened, to the soft click of the latch, the shuffle of familiar footsteps, the rustle of Logan's jacket as it hit the chair, the water rushing, the sterilized soap dispenser being pressed, the sound of a paper towel tearing, and finally, the slow exhale as Logan stepped fully into the room, like he'd been holding his breath until now.

"Missed you," Logan murmured as he leaned down, pressing a kiss to Adrian's forehead. His arms wrapped around him without hesitation, like instinct, like home. Like nothing had changed.

Adrian let him. Let the weight of Logan's body settle near his. Let the scent of him—warm skin, lingering cologne, body wash—fill his lungs. And then something else. Something foreign. A trace he couldn't name, and didn't want to.

"You just landed?" he asked, voice flat, his body unmoving.

Logan eased onto the edge of the bed beside him, fingers seeking Adrian's hand, holding it gently. As if he hadn't noticed how stiff Adrian had gone. As if he hadn't felt that his fingers didn't return the touch.

"Yeah... horrible flight," Logan groaned, rubbing his temple. "My head's killing me."

Logan wasn't wearing his suit; he was dressed casually in jeans and a sweater. He was frantic about keeping Adrian away from germs, so either he changed into clean clothes in the car or stopped at home. Adrian thought it was the latter.

Adrian stared at the ceiling, breath steady, until he couldn't hold it in any longer. "You didn't call last night." It was soft. Almost laidback. But the words cut like glass in his own throat.

Just a whisper of accusation. Just enough to betray the ugly thing curling in his chest, the bitterness he hated, the desperation he refused to name.

Logan sighed, shifting in his seat.

"Yeah, by the time I got back to the hotel, it was late. Didn't want to wake you up or something."

He said it as if it were nothing.

Like it hadn't mattered. Like Adrian hadn't spent half the night staring at his phone, counting the minutes, waiting for a screen to light up with his name.

Adrian nodded, looking away.

Didn't say *it would have mattered to me*. Didn't say *I waited for you*. Didn't say *every fucking second without you feel like another part of my body dying, and you didn't even think to send a text?*

He said nothing.

But Logan noticed.

"I'm sorry I didn't text either," he said, his voice careful now, like he was trying to read Adrian, trying to navigate around something fragile. "I was tired. And... a bit drunk. I just fell asleep."

Adrian blinked.

"Drunk?" His own voice betrayed him, too quiet, too raw, too exposed.

Logan nodded. "Yeah. Closed the deal. The team wanted to go get some drinks. Couldn't say no." How many times had he whispered those words to Sandy, fabricating stories in the dim glow of deception? Too many to count. Now, he spoke them to Adrian, and for the first time, they were true. The irony of it was not lost on him.

And that was it. The last piece of rope in Adrian's chest snapped.

Because of course.

Of course, Logan had been out drinking with his team, with people who weren't trapped inside the walls of a hospital, who weren't rotting away from the inside out, who weren't *dying*.

Of course, he had forgotten.

And why wouldn't he?

Adrian wasn't something you remembered anymore.

He wasn't something you longed for.

Not like before. Not like when he was still beautiful, still alive, still whole.

And on some level, Adrian was happy for him. Logan needed to have some moments like this. But...

He could picture it so fucking clearly—Logan, in a dimly lit bar, surrounded by easy laughter, by bodies that were strong and alive and desirable. Maybe someone had looked at him a second too long. Maybe Logan had looked back. Maybe there had been a hand on his arm, a touch against his back, a voice that didn't tremble with exhaustion, a mouth that didn't taste like sickness and hospital air.

Maybe, for a moment, Logan had forgotten what was waiting for him here.

Forgotten who was waiting.

And maybe—just maybe—Logan had felt something close to relief.

Adrian let out a quiet laugh.

Small. Bitter. A sharp, self-inflicted wound.

"Okay."

Just that. A single word spoken quietly and flatly, but it carried everything Adrian didn't have the strength to say. *I don't belong to your world anymore. You don't need to lie to me. Just go.*

In a gentle yet firm movement, he pulled his hand from Logan's, needing space he didn't know how to ask for. He couldn't bear to be touched like this. Not like he still mattered. Not when every cell in his body was screaming that he didn't. That it was ridiculous—*pathetic*, really—to be lying here, in this bed, in this failing body, waiting for a man far too good, far too alive, to remember him.

And he hated himself for it.

He hated how quickly the thoughts turned on him, how easily they spiraled into something cruel. Hated the jealousy that curled inside his veins, poisonous and quiet, burning slow. It wasn't fair, and he knew that, but knowing didn't stop the ache. It didn't stop the sharp sting of resentment that flared in his chest at the simple fact that Logan still got to exist out there, in a world that wasn't defined by IV lines and blood tests. That Logan got to *live*, while he was here, rotting from the inside out.

He hated what this had turned him into.

"What's wrong?" Logan asked, sitting up, his voice careful, the edges lined with concern. His brows knit together as he studied Adrian, trying to read the storm he could already feel.

Adrian didn't answer. He just stared at the blanket bunched in his lap, focused on the creases, the folds, the places where the fabric had thinned.

"Nothing," he eventually said, and it sounded like a lie even to his own ears.

Logan's voice softened. "It's because I didn't call, isn't it?"

Adrian turned his face away. He couldn't look at him. Couldn't meet those kind eyes, still full of warmth, blind to the hollowed-out ruin he had become. Because Logan, perfect Logan, was still here. Still trying. Still choosing him, over and over. And Adrian... Adrian was turning into a bane, a venomous vexation, cloaked in a deadly aroma with jagged edges—an unbearable burden no soul should have to bear.

He heard Logan's sigh; it was long, slow, patient, as if he were searching for the right words in a minefield.

"Ad," he whispered, reaching out again, fingers brushing toward his hand. But Adrian didn't move. He couldn't. Because if Logan touched him now, Adrian knew he'd come undone. Everything he'd been holding inside—the bitterness, the shame, the guilt, the grief—it would all spill out in a flood he wouldn't be able to stop. He would say too much. He would confess that he hated the way Logan still looked at him like he was beautiful, like he was still whole, when all Adrian could see in the mirror was a stranger. A gaunt, fading version of the man he used to be, skin pale, bones sharp beneath it, eyes hollowed out by pain. He would admit how much he despised the need, the desperation, the craving for Logan's voice, his touch, his warmth, how, without it, the silence seemed to scrape his insides raw, like it was hollowing him out from within, like his body was giving up piece by piece.

He would admit that he was afraid. Not just of dying, that fear had settled into him long ago, quiet and constant, but of being left behind *before* death ever came. He was afraid that Logan would wake up one day and realize he was already grieving. That he would look at Adrian and see not the man he loved, but the fading outline of someone he used to know. That he would grow tired of pretending. Tired of carrying this weight. Tired of watching someone disappear in slow motion. And if that day came, if Logan reached the edge of what he could bear, Adrian wouldn't blame him. He would only blame himself. For holding on too tightly. For being the one who begged him to stay. For making him stay.

Logan had been warned. Dr. Tierney had said it early on, calmly, gently, as though clinical language could soften the truth. This will happen. The mood swings. The withdrawal. The hopelessness. The guilt. The anger. The treatments take their toll not just on the body, but on the mind as well. *Be patient. Be prepared.* Logan had nodded, said he understood. But nothing—*nothing*—could have prepared him for the way Adrian looked at him now. Not with love. Not even with pain. But with something colder. Like Logan was the villain in the story. Like he was the reason Adrian was here.

Adrian sat stiffly, arms crossed over his too-thin chest, the lines of his body drawn tight with tension. He looked like he could snap with the slightest touch. Logan thought the storm might pass. That if he just waited long enough, the silence would settle. That maybe Adrian would let it go. But then—

"Why did you even do it?" Adrian suddenly said. "Why did you bring me here? Why did you force me into those treatments? I didn't want this. I don't want to be here."

Logan's breath caught. His whole body tensed, instinctively straightening like a soldier under fire.

"Ad, you don't mean that."

"I do." Adrian's voice cracked as it rose, hoarse and trembling but full of something that had been building for weeks. "I'm so fucking tired, Logan. Tired of this hospital. Tired of the fucking machines. Tired of being—"

He stopped. The rest of the sentence clung to the silence between them, unspoken but deafening.

Logan felt it. Knew what he didn't say. *Tired of being without you.*

But he was here. He *had* been here. Every day, every hour he could spare. He had held Adrian through fevered nights, whispered to him through vomiting fits, carried his weight when his legs couldn't. He had slept in stiff hospital chairs, answered every nurse's question, and memorized every medication schedule. He had stayed, and stayed, and stayed.

And still, this.

Still, this chasm between them—wide and aching, emerging unexpectedly, tearing through the beautiful connection they had been nurturing like a crater.

Adrian didn't see that. Couldn't. Because there was a voice inside him louder than Logan's presence, louder than reason, louder than love. A voice that said: *You're not worth staying for. You're not enough. You're not lovable like this.*

And that voice, that cruel, inner gravity, was dragging everything down.

"I'm tired of being this," Adrian said, and his voice trembled under the weight of everything it carried. "Of being so goddamn lame. Of being stuck in this fucking bed, in this body that doesn't even feel like mine anymore. Of the pain. God, Logan, I'm in constant pain. Everything hurts. Everything."

Logan's stomach twisted, his fists tightening in his lap, helplessness clawing its way up his throat like a scream he couldn't release.

"I can't do anything," Adrian continued, and now his voice cracked—raw, exposed, bleeding. "I get exhausted just walking to the damn bathroom. I can't run. I can't surf. I can't even eat without throwing up. I feel like I'm not even here, like I'm some fucking ghost of myself. And I can't even be your equal like this." His chest was heaving now, every word tearing itself out of him like it had been buried too long. "I hate that I can't work. That I depend on you for everything. That I'm not... enough."

The silence that ensued was an inertia, a stifling inert air that refused to budge. Adrian's breath shuddered as he exhaled, his shoulders sagging, the words draining the last flicker of strength from his being.

"I refused treatment because I knew how it would be," he said, voice quieter now, shaking his head. "And I was right."

Logan looked down, his throat tight, his eyes stinging.

"You're sick, Adrian," he uttered, gently, trying to steady the crack in his voice. "Sick. Don't you get it? This is temporary. Just until you get better."

Adrian let out a sharp, humorless laugh. "But what if I don't get better?" The bitterness in his voice nearly tore Logan open. "What if this is all for nothing?"

Logan's head snapped up, panic rising in his chest.

"What if I end up exactly where I would've been anyway," Adrian pushed on, eyes glassy, burning, "just dragged through months of this—this humiliation, this fucking hell—for nothing?"

"It won't be for nothing," Logan insisted, desperate now, but Adrian wasn't listening. He was spiraling, unraveling, the small drops swelling into a flood as the dam gave way—every fear, every resentment, every unspoken thought crashing through the breach, tearing him apart from the inside out.

"Why did you do this to me, Logan?" The words carry the same impact as a punch, strong enough to shatter something between them. "Because you felt guilty? Because you felt sorry for the sick guy? Because you needed to fix something in your own fucking head—"

"Ad—" Logan tried, but the name barely passed his lips.

"I told you I forgave you!" Adrian's voice broke completely now, tears spilling down his cheeks, his chest rising and falling too fast. "So why did you have to do this to me?! Why couldn't you just let me go? Why couldn't you have just left me alone?!"

Logan froze. Everything in him stilled. He wanted to argue, to scream, to beg Adrian to see him—see what he'd done, what he was still doing, all of it for love. He wanted to say that the thought of losing him had been worse than anything else, that dragging him into this fight had never been about guilt, only desperation. That he would rather burn through hell than live in a world without Adrian.

But before the words could rise, Adrian cut him down again.

"You should have just gone back to the States and left me at home."

Logan flinched like he'd been slapped.

"Adrian—"

"No!" Adrian choked, his whole body trembling with the force of it, hands clutching the sheets like they were the only things keeping him tethered. "I can't. I can't do this, Logan. Please, just leave."

And then the room went still, not the peaceful kind of stillness that settles gently, but the kind that presses against your chest like a hand that won't let you breathe, the kind of stillness that occurs the moment before something irreversible happens, something that can't be taken back or forgiven or undone. Logan stood motionless, not out of fear of being hurt again, not even out of shock, but because something in him had broken loose and gone silent, something he didn't have the words for, didn't even have the instinct to name. He didn't blink. He didn't speak. He simply stared at Adrian, as if seeing him for the first time, his fingers clenching unconsciously around the back of the chair he had spent what felt like hundreds, maybe thousands of hours in, counting breaths, counting IV drips, counting days that never passed fast enough and yet somehow still managed to disappear.

He looked at Adrian—*really looked*—and what he saw was heartbreaking: it was the shadow of the love of his life, a fragile, flickering outline drawn in exhaustion and pain and something far more dangerous than either—resignation. There were deep violet hollows under his eyes, his fingers trembled not from cold or fear, but from something more insidious, some slow unraveling of will, of self. And the rage, that wild, sharp burst of anger, wasn't rage at all, not really. It was the echo of grief misnamed. It was sorrow in a borrowed costume. It was heartbreak without direction, hopelessness that had run out of places to hide, pain that had filled his body until it could no longer be contained by skin or words or silence.

And for the first time in weeks—or months, if Logan were honest, if he dared to look back far enough to trace when things began to splinter—he had nothing to say. No comfort to offer. No cleverness to hide behind. No denial left intact. The man he loved was dying, not just in the clinical, quantifiable way that doctors spoke of in hushed voices outside closed doors, but in the slow, devastating way that eats from the inside out: the kind of dying that starts in the spirit before the body gives out. And Logan, who had once believed he could love Adrian hard enough to keep him here, now stood rooted to the floor, a witness to something he could neither fix nor stop nor flee.

"It's not easy for me either, Ad," Logan said finally, his voice shaking, breath unsteady. "I don't like this either. The flights. The meetings. That damn phone that never stops ringing, I only go when I have to."

Adrian scoffed, shaking his head, hostility curling at the edges of his mouth. "Great," he muttered, sharp and small.

"I know you feel like shit, but it's not like I'm enjoying it."

Adrian chuckled, if that distorted semblance of humor could still be classified as laughter. Tears blurred his vision as they welled and refused to cease, streaming down his face since the fight erupted, and then, quietly, devastatingly, he said, "Then go." The quietness with which the words were said was more deafening than a scream could ever be.

The words were sharp—not because they were loud, but because they were quiet. Measured. Surgical. "Leave, Logan." It echoed in the stillness, a dagger disguised as language, slipping beneath the skin without force, only precision, because Logan saw it in his eyes. Saw the truth behind the anger, behind the jagged words—something soft, something terrified. A silent plea, too strangled to say aloud: *Don't go. Don't leave me. Not really.* But Adrian didn't say it. And Logan couldn't make him. So he turned away.

He didn't even know why—whether it was to leave, or just to breathe. To escape the look in Adrian's eyes, the one that made him feel like both the safest place in the world and the most dangerous. To get a break from the flowing tears in his eyes, because seeing Adrian crying was worse than being burned alive. Adrian had told him to leave—*thrice now*—and Logan knew why. Knew this wasn't really about the phone call, or the bar, or the distance. But it still cut deep. Deeper than he thought it would.

He pressed his hand to his forehead, dragging in a breath that rattled in his chest. He didn't want to leave. He just didn't want to *fight*. Not like this. Perhaps if he stepped outside, just for ten minutes, they could both catch their breath. Maybe Adrian would soften. Maybe Logan would stop feeling like he was drowning in a room with no water. Maybe Adrian would stop looking at him like he was both the thing he loved most in the world... and the thing he hated most for it.

The whiplash between being everything and not enough was brutal.

Some days, Logan was always with him. He would curl up in the impossibly small hospital bed, kiss the sweat from Adrian's forehead, trace soft lines on his arm to lull him to sleep, whisper *I'm here, I'm here, I'm here* until the monitors slowed their rapid beeping. On those days, he felt connected to Adrian's breath and blood, and it was his only source of comfort. But on others, he had to leave.

And those days felt like a kind of dying.

Because Logan knew what the distance did to Adrian. Knew that his entire world had shrunk down to the four walls of this room. That his sky was now fluorescent lighting. That the only sounds he heard were footsteps, beeping, and machines. That his hours stretched endlessly between nurse visits and nausea. That he was lonely—*so lonely*—even if he never said it.

And Adrian wasn't crafted for solitude. Adrian had always belonged to the vibrant tapestry of existence. He was forged for the warmth of sunlight, the rich embrace of conversation, the soothing touch of saltwater, and the beautiful chaos of strangers transformed into family. He carried joy as if it were intricately woven into the very fabric of his being. Trapped within a body that betrayed his very essence, he found himself ensnared in a language that felt foreign and in a place devoid of warmth and belonging. All that he once was—every thread of his identity—had been cruelly stripped away, leaving only echoes of the person he had been.

And when Logan left, Adrian was truly, achingly alone.

Logan loathed himself for it, that insidious guilt adhering to him like perspiration on a sweltering day. He despised the stark contrast of his breath, the rhythm of life pulsating through him, while Adrian lay withering away, facing the eternal silence. It wounded him that despite every ounce he poured into giving, it remained a mere drop in the ocean of need, never enough, always aching for more.

But what else could he do?

He was exhausted. The flights. The boardrooms. The calls. The constant pressure to perform, to provide, to hold it all together. Adrian was trapped in a hospital bed, and Logan was trapped in a life pulling him farther from everything that mattered. And through it all, Adrian's body was being carved apart by medicine. Examined. Prodded. Broken down and built back up again. Every week. Every day.

Logan had watched it happen.

Watched the chemo burn through him. Watched the man he met in the ocean dissolve—inch by inch—into someone thinner, quieter, smaller. Someone he still loved. *Desperately*. But someone who was barely holding on.

And the worst part? The thing that woke Logan up at night with his hands shaking and his lungs gasping?

It was working.

The chemo was working. The treatments were working. It was keeping Adrian alive.

And it was killing him.

Not all at once. But in pieces. Slow, quiet pieces. Taking little things first—the appetite, the strength, the joy—and then bigger things. Adrian's voice. His laughter. His fight. His hope. And Logan was terrified that by the time this was over...

There would be nothing left.

Logan clenched his eyes shut, a shuddering breath lodged painfully in his chest. Uncertainty washed over him—he felt adrift. Not about Adrian, never about him, but about how to navigate this situation.

Remaining here felt like a wound reopened, while the thought of leaving the room cut even deeper. The very idea of being away from his other half suffocated him.

And then he felt arms wrapped around his waist. A trembling weight pressed into his back, soft and desperate, curling around him like gravity, like surrender. Adrian's chest shuddered against him, his breath broken, his voice no stronger than shattered glass.

"I'm sorry," he whispered. "I'm sorry. Don't go. I'm so sorry."

Logan froze completely as Adrian clung to him, face buried in his back. Adrian's arms tightened, holding on desperately, fearing that if he loosened, Logan might walk through that door and never come back, like this time would be the moment when Logan would just disappear from his life.

"I didn't mean it," Adrian continued, his voice trembling as he struggled to breathe through tears, cries, and hiccups. "I didn't mean any of it. I'm sorry."

Logan could feel the tears soaking through his shirt, could feel the way Adrian's hands trembled as they clung to him, the desperation pouring out of him in uneven breaths. "I don't know why I said it. Please don't go, Lo. I love you so fucking much. I'm so grateful for you. I'm sorry."

Something cracked open in Logan's chest. He sucked in a breath, sharp and ragged, his throat burning as emotion pressed up hard behind his ribs. His hand found Adrian's, fingers sliding over his skin, gentle at first, then gripping tight.

A small, broken sound slipped from his throat. He didn't even know what it was—a cry, a gasp—as he turned in Adrian's arms and pulled him in with everything he had, crashing into him with such force it knocked the breath out of both of them. He embraced Adrian's fragile frame, clutching him so tightly it felt like Logan's heart was holding him, not just his arms.

Adrian clung back just as hard. His fingers dug into Logan's back, desperate, trembling. Like he didn't believe this was real. Like he still expected to be left.

"I missed you," Logan choked out, his lips pressed against Adrian's temple. His voice was hoarse, cracked open, his breath shivering between the words. "I missed you so fucking much."

Adrian made a sound—not quite a sob, not quite anything—just raw feeling caught in his throat. And then he just held him. Held onto him like Logan was the only thing in the world not slipping through his fingers.

"Me too," he breathed, barely audible. "The thought of you... it's the only thing that makes being here bearable."

His hands, still frail but warm, skimmed the back of Logan's neck, fingertips tracing the shape of him like it was a map—familiar, grounding, something real in a world that felt increasingly fading at the edges.

"But it's been so long, Lo," he whispered. "And it looks like it's gonna be even longer."

Logan didn't flinch. He only tightened his arms around Adrian's waist, steady, unwavering, like he was trying to hold the pieces together with nothing but touch and breath.

And then, in a voice so small it nearly disappeared—

"I keep waiting for you to go."

Logan's hand brushed softly against the back of Adrian's neck, a gentle and rhythmic caress before his fingers glided upward, curling around the soft edge of the knit cap. Adrian had three of these beloved caps. Logan got them for him as gifts from a special place where he had paid a handsome sum for their quality. Adrian cherished them deeply, especially the gray one, which was his favorite. "It reminds me of the color of your eyes," Adrian had said, as if it were obvious. Little did he know, those words made Logan's heart skip a beat and the sky change color as he breathed them into existence.

"Why would I go?" Logan whispered, his breath warm against Adrian's skin.

Adrian let out a bitter, hollow laugh. "Look at me," he said, and Logan could feel the ache in every syllable. "I'm a joke compared to who I used to be. Stuck in this hospital, in this body that barely works. Why would you stay? That's the real question. You have more reasons to go than to stay."

Logan exhaled, a sound full of frustration and disbelief. "You are so damn stupid sometimes."

Adrian flinched, not from the words, but from how gently they were said. And then Logan's hand was on his cheek, reverent, slow, like he was touching something sacred. Not a body ravaged by sickness. Not a fading man. But *Adrian*.

"You're my reason to stay," Logan said, and his voice wasn't soft now—it was *raw*, threaded with something fierce and unshakeable. "You don't get it, do you? I love you. Even when I'm gone, even when I'm buried in meetings or flying across the country, I'm counting the seconds until I can come back to you. Because I *have* you to come back to. You are my home, Adrian. You were my home ever since we met, and you always will be."

Adrian shuddered, unable to hold back the tears. Logan's thumb slid across his cheek, warm and steady, and the look in his eyes—that look of undiluted love—shattered whatever defenses Adrian had left.

It was too much. Too much to be seen like this. Too much to be *loved* like this.

But it was real. And he held onto it.

"It's like you don't understand how much I need you," Logan said, his voice fraying at the edges, his thumb catching a tear before it could fall. "How much I want you. If this—if this is what we have to go through to be together, then so be it."

Adrian could only nod. He didn't trust his voice. Didn't trust the flood behind it. But Logan wasn't done. He reached out, fingers curling under Adrian's chin, lifting his face with a tenderness that made something in Adrian's chest shatter. Their eyes met—molten whisky and aching silver—and Logan's voice broke as he whispered, "Tell me you didn't mean it. The part about not wanting the treatments. Tell me you want them. Tell me they're going to give us a future together."

His voice cracked on the last word, and Adrian saw it, saw the shimmer in Logan's eyes, the tears clinging there, refusing to fall. "A future with a house," Logan whispered, barely breathing now. "With kids. With surfing and sitting on the beach at night. With going to sleep together, waking up next to each other. Old and gray. Tell me."

And Adrian let out a sound that barely escaped his throat—small, cracked, helpless—and nodded, another tear slipping down his cheek. "I want it," he muttered, and his voice was nothing more than breath. "I want all of it."

Logan exhaled and pressed his forehead to Adrian's, their skin burning with shared heat, shared fear, shared everything. His hands trembled slightly as he cupped Adrian's face, thumbs brushing against damp cheeks.

"Ad..." Logan breathed.

Adrian lifted one hand, weak but certain, and laid it flat against Logan's chest, right over the heart that had carried him through the worst of this. The beat was strong, steady, real. "Of course you're my equal," Logan murmured, as if it were the simplest truth in the world. "I love you so damn much, Adrian."

Adrian swallowed, his throat thick, his eyes closing against the pressure behind them. "I love you too," he said, his voice tender, small. And then, softer still—"You are the best thing in my life."

Something in Logan's face changed. A flicker of light, of breath, of release. Adrian watched it happen—watched the weight lift from his shoulders, watched the shadows leave his eyes. And for that moment, for that breath, Adrian understood exactly why he had said yes to the treatments. Not for himself. For *him*. For Logan, who deserved all of it—life, love, a future. Even if Adrian didn't know how much of it he could give, he would give every second he had left.

So he pulled him closer. Pressed their foreheads together, then their lips. The kiss was slow. Gentle. Nothing frantic or desperate—just them. Soft and sure. The kind of kiss you fall into, not because you're trying to fix anything, but because it's the only way to be close.

"How are you feeling?" Logan whispered, his lips brushing over Adrian's.

"Fine," Adrian lied, and let his head fall against Logan's shoulder, the weight of exhaustion tugging at his body again.

"Liar," Logan murmured, pressing a kiss to his cheek. The words were playful, but soft, woven through with care, with knowing. He didn't pull away.

Instead, Logan helped him shift toward the small half-couch tucked beside the bed. Adrian's limbs were heavy, muscles aching from the weight of standing too long in one emotional place. But he didn't want to let go of Logan. Not even for a second. So when Logan sat beside him, Adrian curled into him instinctively, resting his head on Logan's chest, letting the steady rise and fall anchor him. Letting the warmth sink deep into his bones.

Then Logan reached out and plucked Adrian's gray knit cap from his head. Before Adrian could protest, Logan tugged it over his own head, pulling it down until it hugged his curls snugly.

"How do I look?" Logan asked, lips twitching, trying for cocky but landing somewhere between adorable and utterly transparent.

Adrian just stared. "Sinfully hot," he whispered, voice soft, gaze open in a way it hadn't been in days. "It complements your eyes."

Logan chuckled. His nose brushed Adrian's cheek, followed by a kiss so sweet it made Adrian's heart squeeze. "I've heard it before," he muttered, trying to sound smug, but Adrian could hear the love beneath the teasing, the relief threading every word.

And for the first time in days, Adrian felt safe.

He leaned into Logan, his body finally relaxing, his breathing evening out. Logan began to talk about his work, about deals he'd closed, people he'd met, boardroom politics, and stubborn executives and late-night hotel check-ins, and Adrian just listened. Not to the words so much as the voice. That familiar, steady cadence. That quiet strength. He let it wash over him like warm water.

His eyes were half-lidded now, his fingers curled lightly around Logan's hand, not gripping—just resting. Anchoring. "You're so damn smart," Adrian murmured, a small smile playing on his lips. "It's kind of unfair, really."

Logan smirked, gently squeezing his hand. "Oh, I know."

Adrian laughed and lovingly smacked Logan's chest. And for a moment, it felt like before. Before hospitals. Before fear. Before the world had shrunk to a bed and an IV drip. For just one moment, it was him and Logan. A couch. A kiss. A quiet night.

And then Logan's phone rang.

The sound shattered the moment, sharp and sudden, slicing through the soft cocoon of their closeness like a crack in glass.

"Sorry," Logan muttered, already reaching for his pocket. "Forgot to turn it off when I got here."

Adrian didn't think anything of it at first. Another call, another meeting, another echo of the outside world trying to reach in and pull Logan away. But then Logan glanced at the screen and something in him stiffened. His whole body held tension. And Adrian saw the flicker of something across Logan's face. Not fear. Not guilt. Not quite. But something close enough to both. His fingers hovered, uncertain, twitching with hesitation, like he didn't know whether to decline the call or throw the phone out the window.

And then, without a word, Logan turned the screen toward Adrian.

Zack.

It landed with a sting, bitter on Adrian's tongue even before he said it. "Zack?"

"Yeah." Logan swallowed hard, his voice almost too soft.

Adrian's gaze lingered on the screen a moment longer. Too long. His features schooled themselves into calm, but inside, something pulled taut. The truth was there, suspended between them like a wire strung too tight.

"It's the—"

"Yeah," Logan cut in quickly, his voice sharp. "Don't."

Adrian nodded. He didn't need to say it. They both knew. They had talked about Zack once, long ago. Back in that hotel room in Israel, back when Logan was still trying to explain the ache of losing him and what he'd done to survive it.

"I'll just let it go to voicemail," Logan muttered, moving to silence the call.

But Adrian stopped him.

"No, answer him."

Logan's eyes snapped to his. "No."

"Yeah, answer him," Adrian pressed, giving Logan's hand a small, measured squeeze. His voice was light, easy, but there was something darker curled beneath it. Something unsaid.

You want to ignore him? Because I'm here? Because you don't want me to hear?

"It's fine. Really."

For a long moment, Logan hesitated.

Then, reluctantly, he slid his finger over the screen and answered the call, pressing the phone to his ear.

"Hello, handsome," Zack's voice purred smoothly through the receiver.

Adrian felt everything inside him coil tight. And then—he watched Logan blush. Deep, five different shades of *fuck, this is awkward* red.

And Adrian didn't like it. Not one bit.

His fingers twitched in Logan's, and Logan must have noticed, because he visibly winced.

"Hey, Zack," Logan said, quietly, hesitantly.

"Haven't seen you in ages," Zack drawled, his voice warm, full of something that made Adrian's stomach churn. In the background, there was the sound of clinking glasses, the low hum of bar chatter.

Adrian could picture it so clearly—Zack, behind a counter, flirting with customers, with Logan, the way Logan had gone there once, twice, more, the way Logan had touched—

He stopped himself.

"Found your guy?" Zack asked casually.

Logan tensed beside him. "Yeah," he said quickly. "I'm back in the States, actually. He's right here next to me."

"So..." Zack's voice curled through the speaker again. "Am I going to see my favorite customer soon? The tips have been awful since you left," Zack chuckled, but even Adrian could hear the truth behind it.

Adrian's chest burned.

Logan had been a regular at that bar.

A favorite customer. What the fuck does that even mean? Adrian did not need to guess; he remembered his and Logan's conversation all those months ago, clear as day.

"I don't think—" Logan started, but Zack cut him off.

"Oh, come on, don't be like that. You could bring your guy. I'd love to meet Adrian, after everything you said about him."

Logan's mouth snapped shut.

Adrian's stomach twisted.

Even though Logan hadn't put Zack on speaker, he was close enough to hear every word.

He forced a small, tight-lipped smile and kissed Logan's knuckles, like he wasn't seething. Like he wasn't burning alive.

Logan looked at him, reading him, knowing, before clearing his throat. "It's... a bit complicated."

"Oh shit," Zack said, his voice shifting, dropping lower. "You found him, and he didn't want to try again? But wait—you just said he's there..."

"No, not that. We're together."

A pause.

"We're in a hospital."

There was silence on the line.

Logan swallowed, then, carefully, briefly, explained.

The leukemia. The hospital. The reality of everything.

Zack was quiet for a long time. And when he finally spoke, it wasn't flirtation. It wasn't teasing. Just—"I'm sorry, man. Really. I didn't know."

Adrian exhaled slowly, his fingers loosening slightly from their grip on Logan's hand.

"Thanks," Logan said, voice heavy, his thumb tracing over Adrian's knuckles in slow, steady circles. "I huh... guess you need to get back to your shift."

"Yeah, yeah..." Zack said softly. "See you around."

The line went dead.

Logan turned off his phone.

And then he leaned into Adrian, pressing their foreheads together, his breath uneven.

"I love you," Logan whispered.

"I know."

And Adrian wasn't angry.

Not really.

But something in his chest ached.

"You did great," Adrian murmured, pressing a soft kiss to Logan's head, his lips brushing against the fabric of the knit cap. He loved seeing it on him, loved the way it sat slightly askew, loved the quiet way Logan had claimed something of his as if to say, *We belong to each other. No matter what.*

Logan let out a dry laugh, his eyes closing briefly as he wrapped one arm around Adrian, pulling him in. "Yeah, right. I think you might be the only boyfriend on earth who encourages me to talk to a guy I used to hook up with."

Adrian smirked, shifting closer, letting Logan's warmth seep into his bones. "Well... technically, he sent you back to me. I think I owe him for that. And honestly? I'd rather be okay with it than have you hiding things from me."

Logan's expression turned serious, his grip on Adrian tightening slightly. "I would never hide anything from you," he said quickly, fiercely, like the thought alone unsettled him.

Adrian nodded, his gaze soft. "I know. But still. I don't ever want you to feel like there are things you can't tell me because you're afraid I'll get angry. I know you love me, Lo. That phone call wasn't easy to hear, but..." He exhaled slowly, his fingers brushing over Logan's knuckles. "I'm okay."

Logan studied him, searching his face like he was looking for any sign of a lie.

Then, his expression softened. "Thank you," he whispered, lifting his head just enough to look Adrian in the eye.

Adrian smiled at him, the dry, pale skin of his face stretching slightly, his lips—almost white now—curling at the edges.

And Logan *hated* that.

Hated how even a smile—something so simple, so *Adrian*—looked *exhausting* now.

Hated how time had stolen from them, how even now, even in this moment of warmth and quiet intimacy, the sickness was still there.

"You're going home tonight," Adrian suddenly declared, interrupting Logan's thoughts. "You need to sleep in a real bed and rest for a bit."

Logan blinked, then scoffed. "Huh... no. I'm staying."

Adrian sighed, but before he could argue, Logan was already reaching for Adrian's phone, his fingers moving swiftly across the screen.

"And I'm ordering food," Logan continued as if the matter was settled. "I'm starving. And you need something that didn't come in a plastic bottle."

Adrian raised an eyebrow. "You know that stuff is actually good for me, right? It's designed to keep me alive."

Logan snorted. "Great. You'll drink it," he said, his tone matter-of-fact. "And you'll have a slice of pizza. Because let's be real, Ad, surviving on hospital nutrition alone isn't living, it's just not dying."

Adrian let out a small, tired laugh, shaking his head.

Logan woke slowly, his body heavy with exhaustion, the scent of antiseptic and Adrian clinging to his skin. He blinked, adjusting to the morning light, stretching slightly, only to realize he was alone.

The space beside him was empty, the sheets barely disturbed, still faintly warm from where Adrian had been.

Logan sat up quickly, his heart lurching, but then he saw Adrian sitting in one of the chairs, gazing at him with a quiet and amused expression.

"Morning," Adrian said, his lips curling into a small smile. "You were really tired."

Logan groaned, rubbing a hand over his face, then pulled the blanket up higher and closed his eyes again. "Morning."

"You didn't even wake up when the nurses came in. Or when Dr. Tierney stopped by."

Logan peeked at him, eyes still heavy with sleep. "Did he say anything important?"

Adrian shrugged, standing and padding over to the bed. "Not much. Though he did suggest examining you, since you looked like shit."

Logan scoffed. "I bet."

Adrian chuckled softly before leaning down, pressing a lingering kiss to Logan's head, his lips warm against his skin.

"How long have you been up?" Logan asked, pushing himself upright.

Adrian hesitated. "Two hours."

"You woke up from the pain, didn't you?"

There was no need to ask. He already knew.

Adrian nodded silently.

Logan exhaled sharply, guilt settling deep in his stomach. "I should've slept on the couch or something, given you more space."

"No, no, Lo. Come on." Adrian reached for his hand, squeezing it tightly. "I love when you sleep with me. You have no idea how much strength it gives me just to have you here."

Without another word, Logan jumped to his feet and pulled Adrian into his arms. He pressed his lips close to his ear, whispering, "You owe me a good morning kiss."

Adrian smirked, tilting his head, his nose brushing against Logan's in a teasing nudge. "Oh really?" he murmured, his voice smug and light, something almost playful lingering in his tone.

Logan didn't answer. He just kissed him.

Deep and slow, holding Adrian's face with one hand, cupping the back of his neck with the other.

It wasn't rushed.

It wasn't desperate.

It was them.

When they pulled apart, Logan rested his forehead against Adrian's for a moment before sighing. "I'm going to get us something to drink and try to find Dr. Tierney. You rest for a while, okay? You look exhausted."

Adrian gave a small nod, though Logan could still see the exhaustion dragging at his features, the way his body seemed too heavy even as he stood there, even as he smiled.

But he didn't argue.

He just kissed Adrian's fingers before letting him go.

And then Logan was gone.

Adrian eased back into bed, sinking into the mattress and trying to relax despite the persistent, dull pain deep within his bones. His head pulsated with a throbbing ache. His stomach churned uncomfortably in that familiar, subtle way that never quite led to vomiting but remained constant. Every movement felt heavier, with his limbs weak and uncooperative.

None of it was new. He closed his eyes, feeling exhausted and vaguely unwell in that all-encompassing manner—an unnameable sensation, while the sterile smell of antiseptic and clean linen filled the room. He allowed himself to drift into sleep.

Then, the door creaked open.

A smile flickered across his lips. *That must be Logan,* he thought to himself. *Maybe he forgot his jacket, or he wanted to speak to me about something Dr. Tierney mentioned.*

But the air shifted.

The presence in the doorway was different. He felt it before he saw it.

Adrian lifted his gaze, and the smile vanished.

A stranger stood before him, tall and commanding, dark eyes holding something unreadable—something Adrian couldn't name but felt immediately in his chest. His hair, jet black, was slicked back, save for a few rebellious strands that fell over his forehead, blending with the dark stubble lining his jaw. His face was a perfect study of sharp angles and smooth arrogance, but there was something softer in his expression, something that made the air feel heavier.

The man tilted his head, a smirk curling his lips, but his eyes seemed insightful as they gazed upon Adrian. "Adrian?" The voice was smooth, even, yet laced with something restrained—curiosity, maybe. Or something else.

Adrian's stomach twisted.

"Yeah." His voice came out quieter than he intended.

The man stepped forward, his presence stretching into the space between them.

"I'm Zack."

The name landed like a quiet explosion in Adrian's chest.

The 'Zack.'

The ghost that had lingered between him and Logan, the man who had filled the void Adrian left behind, the one who had touched Logan when he could not, held him when Adrian had become nothing but a painful memory.

Something dark curled in his gut.

Adrian sat up slowly, ignoring the ache in his limbs, straightening as Zack's eyes raked over him, not cruelly, not possessively, but assessing.

And fuck.

Zack was hot. Unfairly so.

He exuded a kind of effortless sensuality, like someone who knew exactly what to say, how to move, how to make the world tilt in his favor. He was built strong, broad-shouldered, like he could carry the weight of the world on his back and still walk with that quiet, unshaken confidence.

This was the man Logan had turned to.

And now, he was standing in front of Adrian, watching him, measuring him.

The air between them felt electric—charged with something undefined.

Adrian swallowed, forcing himself to push past the sudden, unwelcome awareness in his chest. He shouldn't be thinking about how the dim hospital light cast soft shadows on Zack's face, or how the loose strands of his hair made him look like he'd just stepped out of a storm.

No.

This was Logan's ghost.

Adrian clenched his jaw, pushing past the exhaustion, the wariness, the sickness that looped around his ribs like a snake.

He was dying.

He could feel it, creeping in slowly, curling its fingers around his breath, his energy, his strength. The chemotherapy had stolen so much already—his hair, his appetite, the weight he had once carried effortlessly. The poison ran through his veins like fire, burning away the sickness, but also burning away him.

He had spent months drifting between pain and hope, between defiance and despair. Some days, he felt strong enough to fight. Other days, the thought of surrender felt like a quiet mercy.

But Logan... Logan made it impossible to let go.

And now, Zack was here.

Adrian took a slow breath, leveling his gaze.

"I... hah." Zack exhaled sharply. He shifted his weight, his dark eyes flickering with something Adrian couldn't quite place. "Logan told me about you... about the cancer. You already know that. I just—" He hesitated, rubbing his shoulder. "I wanted to check how you're feeling."

Adrian studied him, the way he took a small step backward, as if unsure whether to stay or go.

"Fine, I guess." He shrugged, forcing the words out, though they felt hollow. His gaze lingered on Zack for a second too long before he pulled it away. It was too hard—too painful—seeing him and knowing that Logan had chosen this man when he left.

Zack let out a quiet breath, a smirk curling the corner of his mouth, but it didn't reach his eyes. "I figure Logan must've mentioned me, based on how you haven't even asked who the hell I am." He bit the inside of his cheek, watching Adrian with careful precision.

"He did." Adrian nodded, his voice calm, but there was a storm beneath the surface.

Silence stretched between them, thin and fragile.

"So..." Zack cleared his throat. "How are you, really? Are you going to be okay?"

Adrian swallowed. He had expected the question. What he hadn't expected was the concern in Zack's voice. It softened the edges of something sharp inside him.

"I'm not sure," Adrian confessed. The truth tasted strange on his tongue, unfamiliar. He wanted to ask Zack if he was here to check how long Logan would be tied to him, but something in Zack's face made him stop. There was no jealousy, no hidden motive, just quiet, steady worry.

Zack's expression faltered. His face dropped.

"How's he dealing with it?" Zack asked, his voice softer now, almost fragile.

"Better than me." Adrian tried to smile, but it barely made it past his lips. "Logan will be back soon."

The silence between them thickened, pressing into the room like a held breath.

Adrian let out a slow exhale. "You're worried about him, aren't you?"

Zack nodded, his jaw tensing. "When he told me last night, I started feeling—" He stopped, looking away for a moment before turning back, his eyes darker than before. "I was terrified. That's why I'm here. I needed to see how you're doing."

Adrian frowned slightly, but Zack continued before he could respond.

"I saw him without you, Adrian. And it wasn't just hard—it was unbearable." Zack's voice was raw now, stripped of the cool detachment he had carried before. He leaned against the wall, exhaling like he was trying to steady himself.

"He drank." Zack shook his head, staring at the floor for a second before looking up again. "A lot. More than I could keep track of. I don't know if he ever told you, but... he was just... gone. Checked out. He wasn't living. He wasn't even surviving."

Adrian's breath hitched.

He had known Logan suffered. He had known Logan was broken. But hearing it from Zack, from someone who had witnessed Logan when Adrian couldn't... it made the reality of it insufferable.

"He'll be fine," Adrian murmured, though the words barely held weight. They sounded weak even to his own ears. More for himself than for Zack. "Logan... he knows it's a possibility."

Zack remained silent for a moment, simply staring with an unreadable expression.

But Adrian knew what he was thinking.

Zack didn't believe him.

Because Logan wouldn't be fine.

And in truth, neither would Adrian if the roles were reversed.

The atmosphere between them had taken a more delicate and tentative shape. The bitterness, silent rivalry, and envy seemed to dissolve, leaving a space filled with muted vulnerability. They were just two men standing in the wreckage of Logan's heart, both holding pieces of him, neither knowing what to do with them.

Finally, Adrian spoke. "Thank you, Zack."

Zack's dark brows furrowed slightly. "For what?"

Adrian let out a breath, a small, tired smile breaking through the weight of everything. "For sending him to me."

Zack blinked, as if the words caught him off guard.

"If it weren't for you, Logan wouldn't have come." Adrian's voice was quieter now, tinged with something almost like reverence. "I needed him. I have needed him for so long. And I think, on some level, I was always waiting—praying—for him to come back." He met Zack's gaze, holding it with a sincerity that made his own chest ache. "You granted me my biggest wish."

For a long time, Zack didn't move, didn't speak.

"No problem," Zack finally murmured, but his smirk, usually laced with arrogance, was different this time, softer, touched with sadness.

Then, the door creaked open.

Logan stepped in, the scent of coffee and the crinkling sound of crisp paper bags trailing behind him. In one hand, he carried a large brown bag, in the other, a cardboard tray with two steaming cups. He stopped dead in his tracks.

His eyes flickered from Adrian to Zack, and the air in the room shifted.

Logan swallowed. His heart pounded.

"Zack?" Logan's voice wavered slightly. "Hey. What are you doing here?" He felt his face grow hot, an involuntary blush creeping up his neck as he glanced between Adrian and Zack, his stomach twisting.

Zack stuffed his hands into his jeans pocket, his fingers moving restlessly, fumbling with something unseen. Then, as if shaking himself out of it, he let out a breath and spoke.

"Came to check on the guy you drank oceans of whiskey over," Zack said, smirking, though it didn't quite reach his eyes.

It was meant to be a joke.

And yet, Logan felt it.

Adrian let out a small chuckle, and Logan, almost instinctively, smiled back at him—a silent, *Are you okay?* in his gaze.

Adrian gave him a soft nod, his lips tilting up just a little, and Logan hadn't even realized how tense he had been until it suddenly eased from his body.

He exhaled.

Zack cleared his throat, drawing Logan's attention back. His hand was still fidgeting in his pocket, fingers twitching like they were clutching something important.

And then—

Zack pulled his hand out.

In his palm sat a small, familiar object.

A bracelet.

Logan froze.

His breath caught. His heart stopped.

"Oh my god." His voice came out as a whisper, barely there, like a prayer. His feet moved before he could think, taking him toward Zack, toward the object in his hand—toward the last piece of Adrian's soul he had ever been entrusted with.

"Is that—?" Logan gasped, his voice tight.

"Yeah." Zack nodded, clearing his throat as he handed it to Logan.

With trembling fingers, Logan took it, the familiar woven threads brushing against his skin, delicate yet unbreakable. He felt as if he was holding time itself. Like holding Adrian's past, his love, his sacrifice.

Adrian inhaled sharply, his eyes locked on the bracelet—the one he had once given away with his whole heart.

A tear slipped down Adrian's cheek, silent and unannounced, as Logan reached out and placed it in his hands.

Adrian clutched it instantly, his fingers curling around the worn threads, his chest rising and falling unevenly. His mother's bracelet. The last tangible piece of her, the last thing she had given him before the sickness had taken her.

Imma. Mom.

The room felt too small.

Too full of emotions none of them knew how to hold.

"Did you find it?" Logan asked breathlessly. "How? When?"

Zack shifted, exhaling slowly.

"I didn't find it." He glanced between them before settling his dark gaze on Logan. He took a breath. "I took it."

Logan's head snapped up. "What?" He blinked, stunned, confused, unraveling. "What do you mean?" His voice was softer now, almost afraid.

Zack's voice faltered, his dark eyes drifting somewhere beyond the present, as if he were rewinding through the nights, the moments, the quiet suffering that had led them all here.

"You were..." he started, then stopped, inhaling sharply.

Zack was remembering it. The empty bottles at the bar, the shadow underneath his eyes, remnants of countless sleepless nights. Logan would sit in the dim, flickering glow of his apartment, staring into the abyss, lost in the phantoms of his own creation. Logan was physically beside him, yet a thousand miles away in spirit. There was always a sadness lingering at the edge of his gaze, a perpetual shadow that seemed to cling to him. It was as if he was everlastingly teetering on the brink of a collapse, his smile a rare and almost wistful sight. His demeanor was forced, a mask of feigned normalcy, struggling to conceal the turmoil that brewed just beneath the surface. It was a painful dance of existence, where connection felt elusive and the weight of his unspoken thoughts loomed heavy in the air.

"You were spiraling," Zack finally remarked, his voice softer now. "You were... absent." Those words barely captured the depth of the sorrow residing within Logan, which Zack had observed, but that was all he offered.

Logan felt something heavy press against his chest, something suffocating, something familiar.

"I couldn't watch you like that anymore," Zack continued, his voice raw. "You weren't just drinking—you were disappearing. You were disconnected, guarded, drowning in your own misery, and no matter what I said, no matter what I did, I couldn't reach you."

He exhaled, glancing at Adrian, and for the first time, something flickered in his expression—something like jealousy, but softer. More resigned.

Because Zack had always cared for Logan.

Perhaps it had begun as something casual, an ease between them, yet somewhere along the way it deepened, almost imperceptibly, until it was no longer casual at all but something heavier, more luminous, dangerous in its tenderness. And Adrian, watching, had recognized it at once, because he knew the signs too well; he had, after all, surrendered his own heart to Logan in a single instant, a surrender so complete it had frightened him, and it was that very knowledge—that soft and devastating recognition—that made him see it mirrored in another without effort, as if pain could recognize its twin in love.

"I knew there was no breaking through to you. No saving you. You were too far gone, too lost in your own pain." His voice dipped, quieter. "But I knew you had a weird attachment to that bracelet."

Logan stiffened.

"And I knew about Adrian." Zack smiled faintly, but it was laced with something bittersweet. "You called for him that night. Over and over. You begged me to find him. You don't even remember it, but you did. You were wasted, barely able to stand, and yet... you called his name."

Logan's stomach twisted in a mix of anxiety and confusion, the events of that fateful night shrouded in a fog of forgotten memories. It was the night when he first listened to Adrian's song, each note weaving through his mind like a bittersweet spell. But the night spiraled out of control as he drank deeply, drowning the haunting refrains until they blurred and vanished from his thoughts, along with any trace of Adrian himself.

Zack told him, on the same day when he sent him to search for Adrian, about the event of that night, which Logan could only imagine.

"So I thought... maybe if you no longer had it, maybe if I took away the one thing tying you to the past, it would force you to move. To do something—anything—other than just sitting there and letting yourself decay." Zack let out a slow breath, shaking his head slightly, as if still uncertain whether it had been the right thing to do. "And I was right."

Logan stared at Zack, his fingers tightening around the bracelet, his heart pounding.

"You took it?" His voice was quiet, but laced with something else—something he couldn't even define.

A part of him wanted to be angry.

Wanted to yell.

Because Zack had seen him in those dark, miserable moments—without the bracelet, without anything to hold onto. Zack had seen the hopelessness, the madness that had crept into Logan's bones, the empty, aching rage that consumed him.

And he had done nothing.

Or had he?

Logan's chest heaved, his thoughts tangled in knots.

Because Zack hadn't done nothing.

Zack had forced his hand. Zack had unknowingly set everything into motion.

Because without the bracelet, Logan had felt an unbearable emptiness. And in that void, he had finally realized what he had to do.

That loss had pushed him.

That absence had led him home.

His throat felt tight.

He looked down at the bracelet in his hands, then up at Zack, and something shifted inside of him.

"Thank you."

Zack blinked, as if he hadn't expected that response.

"And thank you for giving it back," Logan added, a small smile breaking through the storm in his chest.

Then, before he could think too much about it, he stepped forward, pulling Zack into a brief but firm hug.

Zack stiffened for a second—surprised, maybe—but then relaxed, patting Logan's back awkwardly before they pulled apart.

Logan met his gaze. "You are a good friend." His voice was steady now, certain. "And I'm lucky to have you."

Zack swallowed, looking away for a second, then smirked, but it was softer this time—more genuine.

"Yeah, yeah. Don't get all sentimental on me."

But his eyes told Logan he had needed to hear that.

The door swung open again, and Dr. Tierney walked in with his usual calm, professional demeanor.

"Adrian," he greeted warmly, his voice smooth as he approached the bed. "How are we feeling? Has anything changed since the morning? Any nausea? Irregular pain?"

He approached the bed with quiet confidence, scanning the tablet in his hand while Adrian lifted his head slightly, answering in a voice that tried to be stronger than it felt. Logan sat beside him, one hand resting on the blanket near Adrian's hip, thumb tracing slow, mindless circles into the fabric—a silent form of grounding, or maybe prayer.

Dr. Tierney listened, nodding, tapping something into his tablet. His brow furrowed with concentration, but not concern. Not yet.

Logan noticed the shift before it happened.

From the corner of the room, Zack straightened. It was subtle—shoulders back, chin lifted, a quiet tension building like a ripple across still water. His fingers ran through his dark hair with casual flair, and then he tugged the hem of his sweater, adjusting it just enough to let it fall better across his frame.

Logan sighed internally. *Here we go.*

As Dr. Tierney leaned forward slightly to check Adrian's vitals, Zack took a step closer. Not intrusive, but deliberate—like gravity had shifted slightly and pulled him into the orbit of the doctor. His gaze had sharpened, eyes scanning Dr. Tierney from head to toe with a look that was somewhere between admiration and slow undressing.

Dr. Tierney, for his part, remained focused. At least, he tried to.

Zack cleared his throat, it was a little too loud, a little too performative. "Doc,"

Dr. Tierney turned, polite, measured. "Yes?"

Zack's mouth curved into a smile, one that radiated wicked charm.

"Could you maybe check me out too?"

Logan froze mid-breath. *Oh no. Not here. Not now.*

Dr. Tierney blinked in surprise, a fleeting flicker of amusement—or perhaps disbelief—dancing across his features. A subtle blush crept onto his cheeks, a clear indication of the double entendre that Zack had intended with his words, fully aware of the effect they would have. After a brief pause, Dr. Tierney took a moment to gather himself, restoring his composed demeanor once more.

"If you're not feeling well," he said carefully, "you can head to the nurses' station. They'll—"

"No," Zack replied, drawing the word out like melted caramel. He tilted his head, letting his voice drop an octave. "I'm actually feeling... very, very weak."

Adrian coughed—whether from the remnants of laughter or illness, it was hard to tell.

Zack stepped forward again, closer now. Too close.

"It started," he continued, voice thick with mock seduction, "right when you walked into the room."

Logan dropped his face into his hands with a groan. "Oh my god."

Adrian let out a soft, wheezing laugh and quickly pulled the blanket over his face, shoulders shaking with silent amusement.

Dr. Tierney stood completely still, the tension in his posture betraying how hard he was working to maintain composure. His grip tightened on the tablet. His jaw clenched once, then relaxed. Very slowly, he turned back to Adrian, as if Zack had simply ceased to exist.

"I'll come back once your... visitor is finished," he said with surgical neutrality.

Adrian, still catching his breath from laughter, simply nodded, wiping the moisture from the corner of his eye. It had been so long since he had laughed like that, really laughed.

The door clicked softly shut behind Dr. Tierney, and the moment it did, Logan turned slowly to Zack, giving him a look so dry it could've been dust.

"Really?" he said, voice flat, unimpressed, the rim of his coffee cup hovering inches from his mouth.

Zack, utterly unfazed, simply placed a dramatic hand over his chest, feigning a swoon like some lovesick character in a play.

"What?" he said, blinking innocently. "I think I'm coming down with something. A fever. Maybe even a... burning sensation. Somewhere serious."

Adrian wheezed.

He burst out laughing all over again—loud, uncontrollable, and full-bodied. The kind of laugh that made his chest ache, that left his lungs searching for breath. He curled slightly to the side, gripping the blanket like it was the only thing keeping him anchored. For a few glorious moments, the weight of his illness lifted. He was just a man in bed, laughing with two idiots.

The sound of it cracked something open in Logan. He fought it, tried to keep his face neutral, but then his lips betrayed him—curling into a smile, then a grin, and finally, he gave in and started laughing too.

Zack, ever victorious, leaned back against the wall with the smug satisfaction of a man who'd just won a silent war.

"But seriously, though," he mumbled under his breath, "that doctor is hot."

Logan let out a long, exhausted groan, scrubbing his hands over his face like he could erase the moment.

"Please," he muttered through his palms, "don't mess with the doctor. I'm paying him *way* too much money, and I really need him to focus on Adrian. Not on... whatever seduction campaign you're currently strategizing."

Zack didn't even pretend to hear him.

His gaze was still locked on the door Dr. Tierney had disappeared through, eyes narrowed like a hawk tracking prey.

"You think he swings my way?" he asked, tilting his head, genuinely pondering the odds.

Logan just stared at Zack. "He's literally here to help Adrian not die."

Zack pushed off the counter like a man with purpose, smoothing the front of his sweater and running a hand through his hair one more time. His smirk had returned—sharpened, lethal, impossible.

"Well, my dear friends," he declared, voice all velvet and mischief, "before the hot doctor slips away forever, I'm going to finish what I started."

Logan's eyes went wide. "Zack, no—"

But Zack was already halfway to the door, striding out like he was walking into a battlefield he planned to seduce.

Adrian was shaking his head before the door even closed behind him.

"He has *no* limits," he said, grinning.

Logan sighed heavily, surrendering to the inevitable chaos of Zack's wake. He handed Adrian the tea he had gotten him and then slumped into the chair beside the bed, rubbing the bridge of his nose. "None at all."

Chapter 18
The Way the Light Doesn't Leave

Sometimes I dream. I dream of the past, of the present we built with our hands, and of the future we almost had. And sometimes I dream of losing it all. There are nights when the dreams slip into nightmares, when they become too vivid, too sharp, and I wake up gasping, caught between memory and fear. I feel like something has already been taken from me. Like I'm already mourning a life that hasn't yet ended. On those nights, when I can't breathe past the grief, I dive into memory. I reach for it like a lifeline. I pick a moment—any moment—and fall into it, hoping it will hold me together. I often find myself slipping back to our first kiss. I think about how we fought it for so long, how we resisted what had already been written in the way we looked at each other. And when it finally happened, when we let it happen, it was like something inside both of us shattered and reformed all at once. I remember how terrified I was. I truly believed you would pull away, that you'd regret it, that you'd stand up and leave, and with you, my light would leave too. My warmth. My sense of safety. My center. You were already my soul by then, and I don't think I fully understood it until that night. I once overheard my mother say that anything hidden for too long will begin to die. She said flowers need sunlight, and if you bring them home and forget to place them in the light, they'll wither. Love is the same. I couldn't keep it inside anymore. I couldn't let my love for you curl up in the dark and die

quietly. So I told you. I didn't know if you were ready to hear it, but I couldn't
live another day without speaking the truth out loud.

I had been gone, completely gone, for so long, carrying it all inside me. Every
time I wanted to kiss you and didn't. Every time I wanted to reach out and
touch you but forced my hands to stay still. And I kept telling myself you
didn't know. That you had no idea what you meant to me.

But that night, when you got jealous of Itay, I remember how stunned I was,
not by your jealousy itself, but by the fact that you truly believed there could be
someone else. I sat there watching you, trying to hold back my disbelief, and
all I could think was: Is he serious? Does he not know? It was laughable, not
in a cruel way, but in the kind of way that breaks your heart a little. Because
the man I was already in love with thought I might want someone else.

You actually believed I could glance at another soul. That I could let another
man touch me. That I had room in my heart for anyone else when the best
man I had ever known was already giving me the time of day. And not just
any man—you.

You, who I would have burned the world for.

You, who I woke up thinking about and fell asleep praying for.

You, who didn't yet realize that I was already yours, hopelessly, entirely,
without escape.

It was laughable. It was absurd.

Because if you had even an ounce of perspective, you'd know—I was gone for
you. Ruined for anyone else. There was no one else. There never could be.

So I gathered everything I had—my pride, my fear, my trembling
heart—and I gave you the truth. I tried to say it carefully, gently, like I wasn't
setting fire to the air between us. I tried to shape the words into something

that wouldn't frighten you away. And then—before I could even finish—you crossed the room. You kissed me.

And just like that, everything changed.

No one had ever kissed me like that before. It wasn't just a kiss; it was a claim. I finally knew how a kiss, how a real kiss, should feel. You owned me in that moment, and I let you. More than that, I wanted you to. I had never felt so relieved in my life, because finally—finally—you knew.

January 12, 2022—Seattle, Washington—Six Months Later

ONE YEAR AND TWO months. That was how long Adrian had been fighting. That was how long Logan had been watching him slip through his fingers.

The hospital doors parted with a mechanical hiss as Logan stormed through them, a gust of winter air chasing him inside. Snow clung to the shoulders of his coat, forgotten and melting fast, soaking into the wool. His breath came in ragged bursts, fogging the air in front of him. His heart no longer beat in the ordinary rhythm of life; it battered against the cage of his ribs, wild, frantic, like a bird bewildered by its own wings. Within that tumult it seemed to answer some hidden summons, some revelation not yet unveiled, some script still being inscribed upon the corridors through which he wandered. The cadence of those desperate pulsations bore intimations of knowledge his mind could not yet name, as though the blood itself were deciphering a secret alphabet while the intellect, obstinate or unready, remained in darkness, whether by its refusal of the truth or by its helpless bewilderment before it.

He hadn't heard much, just a low and calm voice with something trembling underneath, saying: "Come" and "Now." Logan knew there were other things Dr. Tierney had mentioned; there were sentences in that phone call, but all his mind could process were those two words. And that was all it took.

He'd been in the middle of a meeting, some polished corporate cathedral filled with leather chairs and glass water pitchers, surrounded by men who measured power in quarterly profits and silent nods. His father had sat beside him, all jaw and certainty, speaking in that clipped tone he reserved for boardrooms and battlegrounds. But the moment Logan saw Dr. Tierney's name flash on his screen, the rest of the world fell away. The voices blurred. The light dulled. Everything narrowed down to that single point of gravity.

He didn't excuse himself. Didn't explain. He simply stood up, turned his back on all of it, and walked out.

Now, under the harsh fluorescent glow of the hospital corridor, Logan gripped the nurses' station like a man holding onto the edge of a cliff. His fingers were numb, knuckles white, his body vibrating with a storm of urgency he couldn't contain.

"Dr. Tierney," he rasped. His voice cracked under the strain, too loud, too desperate. "Where is he?"

"Here."

Logan spun around, breath catching in his throat as Dr. Tierney approached, his footsteps quiet against the linoleum.

"Where's Adrian?" Logan's voice faltered, a single thread unraveling. "Is he okay?"

His composure fractured in a heartbeat. The bubbling of panic gave way to insidious fear. Not fleeting, not shallow, but real fear, glacial and enduring, the kind that seeps into the bones and draws nourishment from the core itself, hollowing from within until only brittle scaffolds remain. Such bones, emptied of their secret strength, were fated to crumble beneath the crushing burden that Logan, trembling, strove to bear.

Dr. Tierney's expression remained professional, but Logan could see past it. There were shadows under his eyes, stiffness in the way he held his shoulders. A man carrying more than his own exhaustion.

"His condition took a turn early this morning. His white count is dropping," Dr. Tierney said.

Logan forgot how to breathe and how to exist. He knew what it meant. A drop in white blood cells meant Adrian's immune system was collapsing, his body's last line of defense thinning to almost nothing.

"He spiked a fever... We were able to stabilize him, but he's very weak." Dr. Tierney continued, his words resembled a scalpel more than syllables.

Logan's breath hitched. The air in the hallway felt thinner now. He tried to pull it in, to hold it in his chest, but it slipped through him—like trying to breathe underwater. Grief was already expanding inside him, slow and thick.

Tierney studied him, silent for a moment, the way someone looks before breaking a truth open. Not cold. Just careful.

"The chemo isn't working the way we'd hoped. It's held things off longer than we expected, but it hasn't been strong enough. We've managed to slow the disease... but there's no remission. No regression."

The silence that followed spoke with a gravity no clinical term could ever summon. The fear he had known before Dr. Tierney's explanation was but a single drop of blood in a crystal sea, insignificant beside the deluge that now consumed him. This fear was no longer formless; it had grown sinew and substance, had carved itself into his essence, riving him with merciless precision. He was left desolate, stripped of even the faintest promise of healing, a vessel not of recovery but of ruin.

Behind him, he could feel the presence of his father. Silent. Watching. A shadow of concern cloaked in expensive wool. Somewhere nearby, a monitor beeped in uneven rhythm. Footsteps squeaked past. A nurse cleared her throat. All of it drifted around Logan like a world half-sinking underwater.

"What are you saying?" His voice was barely there. A rasp. A question already afraid of its answer.

Dr. Tierney's gaze didn't waver. It softened, just slightly, but not enough to shield the truth.

"I'm saying... we're out of time for waiting. His marrow is failing. If we want to keep fighting, we need to move forward with a stem cell transplant. Now."

A pulse of silence passed between them.

Logan could barely swallow. His throat burned. The words hovered, but he couldn't speak them. Because underneath it all, he already knew.

They were past the edge. This was the last chance.

"My sample?" he whispered, though part of him already knew. He was grasping for a miracle, for some loophole the universe might have missed.

Dr. Tierney hesitated, then shook his head. "We tested it. It's not compatible."

The words hit like a fist to the gut. Logan's breath hitched, his ribs straining against the silence that followed.

"So—"

"As I told you before," Dr. Tierney interrupted gently, "a compatible match depends heavily on ethnicity. The best-case scenario would be a full biological sibling. Does Adrian have any?"

Logan's mind reeled. "A half-brother," he said finally. "Same father. Different mothers."

Dr. Tierney's lips pressed into a line, and his expression betrayed the composer he always wore. "Not ideal," he murmured. "The chances are slim, but he still needs to be tested. If he's a match, and if he agrees, Adrian will need the transplant soon. But before we even get there... we'll have to increase his chemo. Aggressively."

The words hung in the air like a death sentence.

More poison. More nights curled into himself, too weak to speak, too sick to eat. More days where Adrian's body trembled under the strain, where his skin turned paper-thin and clammy, where his voice broke just trying to say Logan's name. Logan had watched him suffer through the last rounds, seen how hard Adrian fought to hold on, and now they needed to make it worse? He could not even fathom that a *worse* existed, that the torment had a deeper level.

He wanted to scream. Instead, he nodded, his focus narrowing to a single purpose: *find the brother. Find the match. Save him.*

His hand trembled as he reached into his coat pocket, fingers fumbling for his phone. His thoughts were scattered, his body buzzing with useless adrenaline.

"Is he awake?" he asked, wincing at how frail his voice sounded, like it barely belonged to him.

"No." Dr. Tierney's tone softened. "Rough night. He needs rest. You can see him soon, but let him sleep a little longer."

Rough night.

Those words pierced deeper than any clinical term. Logan could already picture it: Adrian curled into himself in that too-white bed, the machines around him murmuring, steady and cold. He saw him there in his mind's eye: his skin pale, lips dry, that slight tremble in his fingers when the pain crept in. And sometimes, in those moments, he would reach out blindly, his hand finding Logan's wrist and holding it tight.

Logan had left just after midnight. Adrian had insisted—again—that Logan would go home, shower, and get a real night's sleep. "You've been here all week," he'd whispered. "Go. Please." His voice had been barely audible, a breath wrapped around a smile. And Logan had gone. Against every instinct, against the tight ache in his chest, he had left.

He shouldn't have.

There had been meetings scheduled at the office, ones his father insisted he attend. Clients. Stakeholders. People who didn't know, or didn't care, that Logan's heart was breaking on the fifth floor of the hospital. Adrian had told him it was okay, again and again. "You don't need to sit at my bedside all day," he'd said, trying to smile like it didn't cost him everything to do it.

But he was wrong.

Logan *had* needed to stay. He should have stayed. Because this wasn't just illness anymore. This was the edge.

He was terrified that Adrian was getting too tired to keep fighting.

Dr. Tierney gave him a gentle nod and turned away to check on another patient, his coat trailing behind him, his voice low as he greeted someone down the hall.

The second he disappeared from sight, Logan's composure collapsed.

He bowed his head and stared at the floor, squeezing his eyes shut, willing back the burn building behind them. His hands curled into fists at his sides, nails biting into his palms. The pressure helped, a small, physical ache to keep the other one at bay.

He would not cry here. Not yet. Not in the sterile hush of a hospital hallway where time had slowed to a crawl, where every breath felt borrowed. Not when Adrian still needed him to be strong.

But *God*, his chest hurt. Not in the way of broken bones or bruised ribs, but in the deep, hollow place where grief had begun to nest, quietly, insistently.

His soul ached.

Beside him, his father stood in silence, solid and still. Logan could feel the weight of his gaze, not judgmental, not even inquisitive. Just there. Watching. A man who had seen too much and said too little. There was something like understanding in Robert Vaughn's eyes, something that might have been compassion. But Logan didn't want compassion. He didn't want sympathy or comfort or even hope.

He wanted Adrian to live. That was all.

He sucked in a sharp breath, trying to anchor himself in his body again. His hand went to his coat pocket, curling around the smooth edge of his phone. Cold metal. Something real. Something he could do.

He had to make the call.

Alon. Adrian's half-brother. A long shot, and Logan knew it. But still—*a shot*. If he wasn't a match, there was a possibility, a sliver of hope, that Adrian's father might be. The odds were thinner than thread, but thinner than thread was still something.

And then there was the international donor registry. Maybe, somewhere across an ocean, someone carried the same genetic imprint. A stranger with matching marrow, a stranger who could unknowingly save a man they'd never met.

But *maybe* wasn't good enough. Not anymore. Not when the clock was ticking so loud it drowned out everything else.

Then—

"Logan."

The sound of his name, spoken low and steady, cut through the storm in his chest.

"Son, look at me."

Logan swallowed hard, dragging his gaze upward, trying to hold himself together. His father was looking at him the way he always did when things fell apart—with calm, with command, with a steel spine that had weathered too many storms.

"Make the call," Robert said simply. There was no space for panic in his voice, no room for doubt. "Come on."

Logan hesitated, thumb hovering over the screen of his phone. The silence stretched between them.

His father stepped closer. "I'll talk to the authorities," he said. "I'll contact the organizations in Israel. If we need legal channels, embassies, whatever it takes. We'll go through the proper people. We'll move fast."

There was no emotion in his tone, but that was what made it feel real. This was what his father *did*. He didn't fall apart. He didn't lose control. He made things happen.

Logan nodded once, but his fingers trembled where they rested against the cool glass of his phone. Everything felt distant, surreal. His feet were still in the hallway, but the rest of him? Gone. Drifting in a haze of helplessness. In that other place—where Adrian's hands were cold, where his eyes fluttered shut and didn't open, where Logan couldn't reach him fast enough.

Adrian's getting worse.

Not better.

That thought sent chills through his veins, freezing his blood as it ran through his body like ice.

His world was cracking, piece by piece, and he couldn't hold it together with just his bare hands.

"Logan."

His name again, sharper this time, cutting clean through the fog.

It jolted him. Pulled him back into his body.

His spine straightened, his hand steadied, even as the rest of him threatened to fall apart. There was something about his father's voice—solid, commanding, undeniable. It was the tone he used in boardrooms and behind closed doors, the one that had turned empires around and silenced rooms full of men with just a few clipped words.

But this wasn't business. This wasn't a deal to close or a market to sway. This was Adrian.

Logan couldn't afford to collapse beneath the weight of it, no matter how badly he wanted to. Not now.

There had always been something in Robert Vaughn that demanded control. It was in the way he stood, the way he spoke, the way he moved through the world like gravity bent to him. People listened when he talked. People followed when he led. And growing up, Logan had hated that. He had felt like a product on an assembly line, molded and measured against an image he never asked to be.

His father wasn't warm. He wasn't gentle. He didn't offer praise or patience. He offered expectations. Pressure. Dismissal, when Logan didn't meet the mark.

So Logan stopped trying.

He pulled away in college, stopped calling, stopped returning home. They became little more than two names in the same family tree, linked by blood, separated by everything else.

In the past year, something had shifted.

At first, it was subtle. His father covering all of Adrian's medical expenses without a second thought. Then, giving Logan time off work, only requiring him for crucial meetings and deals.

Then, it became more.

His father visiting the hospital, sitting beside Adrian's bed. Small talk, at first. Then genuine interest. Kindness, in his own quiet, awkward way. Inviting them both over when Adrian was home for brief moments between treatments.

Not just tolerating Adrian's presence, but accepting it.

Acknowledging that Adrian was Logan's heart.

That Adrian was his whole damn life.

And now he stood beside Logan, not as the cold, unreachable patriarch he had once feared, but as a man who had finally seen his son for who he was.

And who Adrian was to him.

Not a phase. Not a mistake. Not a deviation from the path.

But his heart.

His everything.

Robert Vaughn didn't say any of that aloud. He didn't need to. It was in the way he stood with him now, in the silence he held, in the steadiness he offered without ceremony. It was in his unflinching presence. It was in the way he carried this nightmare with Logan like it belonged to him, too. It was in the way he left that board meeting and ran after his son, for the first time, putting him first.

And Logan wanted—so badly—to lean into it. To let someone else be strong for him for just a moment.

Because if Adrian died—

If he was gone—

Then Logan would cease to exist.

He would fade into nothingness.

His father seemed to understand that.

And for the first time in his entire life, Robert Vaughn spoke to Logan not as an executive. Not as a son he wished had made different choices.

But as a father.

Robert Vaughn was one of the strongest individuals to ever walk this Earth. For a brief moment, Logan yearned to be the child who trusted his father to take care of things. Because if Robert Vaughn promised him he could retrieve that sample from the registry in Adrian's country, then it could happen; Robert Vaughn had the power to make it so, and Logan desperately needed that power, as he felt completely empty inside. He longed to be that little boy again, wishing his father would shoulder that burden for just a moment. He wanted him to take on the weight he had been carrying.

"Take out your phone," his father said, firm but gentle. "Call his brother. Now."

Logan's breath hitched.

"Stay calm," his father continued. "Take a breath. Panic achieves nothing. If you want to help Adrian, be strong. Take care of what needs to be done." And then, softer—softer than Logan had ever heard from him. "Then let yourself break. But not now."

Logan's throat tightened around something sharp. His fingers curled around the cool weight of his phone like it might ground him, like it could carry the unbearable.

He nodded once—more to himself than to his father—and swallowed hard against the ache rising in his chest. His thumb trembled as he unlocked the screen. The faint click of each motion sounded louder than it should have, like the whole world had gone silent around him.

His father was right.

He couldn't fall apart. Not yet. Not while Adrian was still here, still breathing, still fighting beneath pale sheets and blinking monitors.

So he searched for the name and hurriedly clicked on the call button.

The line rang once. Then twice.

"Logan?"

Alon's voice came through thick with sleep, scratchy and unfocused. Disoriented.

Logan closed his eyes for a moment, trying to find his voice in the tangle of grief and fear choking his throat. His hand tightened around the phone, his knuckles aching. It felt like his entire chest was splitting open, like if he said the wrong thing, it would all come crashing out—every tear, every scream, every second of the last year.

"Hey, Alon." His voice was low, taut with restraint. "Sorry about the hour. I know it's late over there."

He forced himself to breathe. In. Out. Steady.

There was a pause, the sound of movement on the other end. The faint rustle of sheets. The creak of a mattress. Then the subtle click of a door closing.

"It's fine," Alon murmured. "Give me a second."

After a few moments Alon's voice returned, softer now. More awake. "Yeah, I hear you. I'm at the base, so I just didn't want to wake the others."

Logan nodded reflexively, though he knew Alon couldn't see it. His throat burned. His pulse was a thunder in his ears. His father stood silently nearby, a quiet sentinel. The world felt suspended.

"Yeah," Logan said. "Of course."

For a moment, Logan couldn't speak. The words sat like stones on his tongue, too heavy, too sharp. Because saying them aloud would make them real, and once they were real, there was no going back.

"Logan?" Alon's voice was clearer now, alert and tinged with concern. "Is everything okay? How's Adrian?"

His chest clenched. His fingers curled tightly into his palm, nails biting skin. It was like trying to breathe through concrete.

"Not so good," the words barely escaped. "He needs a bone marrow transplant," Logan said finally, his voice cracking on the edges. "As soon as possible."

The silence that followed wasn't empty. It was thick. It pressed in, the way silence does in hospital rooms, in places where lives dangle by threads.

Alon didn't flinch. His voice held steady. "You want me to give it?" No resistance. No fear. Just a quiet sinking into the gravity of it. A man walking into the ocean because someone he loves is drowning.

Logan inhaled sharply and tried to steady himself. "Yeah. We'd test you first," he said, voice catching. "It's easy... a cheek swab or blood, just to see if you're a match. If you are, then... then they'll give you shots, for a few days. To make the stem cells leave your bones, go into your blood. And after that, they hook you up to a machine... it takes the blood from one arm, pulls out the cells... and gives the rest back through the other." A breath. A quiet exhale. It came out messy. Half-formed. Too clinical and too human at once.

"Fuck," Alon muttered under his breath, barely audible. Then, after a beat, "Can I talk to him?"

Logan's eyes fluttered shut. He leaned his forehead into his hand, the weight of everything pressing inward.

"No," he said softly. "He's sleeping. He's... he's really weak."

He paused, swallowing hard. It felt like the truth was slicing its way out of him.

"In the past two months, his condition has declined rapidly. The bleeding's worse. He gets sick constantly. He can't eat. He's in pain all the time."

Each sentence felt like glass. Shards in his throat.

On the other end, Alon's confusion surfaced.

"But when we talk to him... he sounds okay," he said, uncertain, like he was trying to reconcile two versions of his brother, the one on the phone, and the one Logan was describing.

"He's lying," Logan whispered. And this time, his voice broke completely. "He's lying because he doesn't want to scare you. Because he thinks that if you know the truth, it'll make it real. But it *is* real, Alon. It's worse than you know. And I—" He choked on the words, pressing shaking fingers to his forehead. "I can't lose him."

There was a pause.

"Would you do the test?" It came out quietly. Raw. A plea wrapped in hope and desperation.

And after a moment of silence that felt like it might break the world in two—

"Of course," Alon said.

Logan exhaled sharply, staggered by the sheer force of relief. His knees nearly gave beneath him.

"It's a bit complicated," Alon added, tone careful. "I'm on base. I'll have to talk to my commanders, get approval... see the medic here."

Logan nodded, even though Alon couldn't see him, already anticipating every barrier, every potential delay.

"You won't have to fly out here," he rushed to say. "Not unless you want to. They can do the test where you are—just a quick swab or blood draw—and they'll send the results here. If you're a match..." He trailed off for a moment, the weight of hope catching in his throat. "We'll figure it out," he finished quietly.

The call ended.

His hands trembled as he shoved the phone into his pocket, his breath shallow, disjointed, as if his lungs no longer knew how to hold air. He didn't think. He didn't listen. He just moved; turned down the hall, and walked toward Adrian's room.

He didn't care what Dr. Tierney had said.

Adrian needed him. And Logan needed Adrian like lungs need oxygen, like waves need the shore.

When he pushed open the door, the quiet hit him like a wall.

The stillness inside was louder than noise. The soft beeping of monitors, the rhythmic hum of machines, those were the only signs of life. Adrian lay motionless beneath sterile white sheets, the IV lines coiled like delicate threads around his arms. His skin was pale, nearly translucent. The strong body Logan had once known—tanned, vibrant, powerful in the surf—was reduced now to something breakable. His face was hollowed, shadowed, but still impossibly beautiful.

Still Adrian.

Still the man who had pulled Logan from the ocean and into love. Still the man who had given him something sacred to believe in. Still the man who carried the soul of Logan's life in the beat of his heart.

Logan leaned against the wall, eyes fixed on him. Watching. Counting each rise and fall of Adrian's chest like a prayer, as if his gaze alone could keep him tethered to this world.

Each breath was a victory.

Each breath was a battle won.

Tears slipped down Logan's face, silent and relentless. He didn't try to stop them. He just stood there, feeling the quiet ache of inevitability creeping in like a shadow on the floor.

He wasn't ready.

He would never be ready.

"Son."

The voice came from behind; it was gentle, but threaded with the kind of command that never had to raise its volume to be obeyed. Logan turned, startled out of his spiral, and saw his father standing in the doorway.

But something had shifted. There was a softness in the set of his shoulders, in the line of his brow. The unshakable man who had run boardrooms like battlefields now stood in a hospital hallway, smaller somehow. More human.

"I'll go back to the meeting later," Logan said quickly, his voice rough with tears, trying to wipe his face with the back of his hand, as if erasing the evidence of his unraveling could make it less real. "We'll reschedule everything and I—"

"Come, Logan." His father interrupted quietly. "I want to talk to you."

Logan hesitated, eyes flicking back toward Adrian's bed.

He didn't want to leave. Not even for a moment. Not when it felt like death was circling, waiting for an opening.

But his father's gaze was steady—rooted. And in it, Logan saw something he had never seen before.

So he followed.

They walked in silence, down the pale hallway, shoes echoing softly on tile. They stopped only when Logan did, still stiff, fists clenched, shoulders braced for another kind of battle.

"I know you've taken over some of the bills," Robert began. His voice was quieter now, measured. "I just spoke to the nurse. She said you've been covering expenses behind my back."

Logan exhaled sharply, looking away.

Of course, he had. Of course, he would.

Because this was Adrian.

And Logan would spend everything—every cent, every breath, every piece of himself—if it meant Adrian could live.

"The hospital will return the money to your account," Robert said. Then, after a pause that felt heavy with finality: "Our deal is off, Logan."

Logan blinked. "What?"

"I want you off the business. Completely. At least for now. When you're ready to come back, it'll be on your terms. But right now... You need to be here. Full-time. Even the few days a month you're working, it's too much."

Logan staggered back a step, like the words had landed a blow.

"Why?" he asked, and his voice was raw, scraped down to the nerves. His anger cracked through it, unsteady, desperate.

His father let out a slow breath. "Because I realized, too late, that it wasn't the right way."

And something inside Logan broke.

The right way.

Coming from his father, those three words carried more weight than any apology ever could.

Robert Vaughn, the man who had always believed in control over compassion, discipline over tenderness, was standing here, admitting he had been wrong.

The air felt different. Like something in the world had shifted.

Logan turned his gaze back to the hospital door, his heart thundering. Adrian was behind it. Pale, shrinking, slipping.

He swallowed the knot in his throat.

"Thank you," he whispered.

There was no reply. Just the sensation of strong and certain arms wrapping around him, and, for the first time in years, not stiff or brief or obligatory.

But real.

And Logan, who had held the world on his shoulders for so long, let himself lean into it. Just for a moment.

"I love him," he choked into his father's shoulder, the words so soft they might've been missed, but so full of truth they vibrated in his bones.

His father pulled him a little tighter.

"I know."

They stayed like that, locked in something that wasn't forgiveness exactly, but maybe something just as rare: understanding. They breathed in the same air. And in that breath, something between them began to heal.

Then, Robert spoke low and steady, the way only a father could speak. "Do you remember, son," he started, "when you came back and told me you were going to marry Sandy?"

Logan froze, his jaw clenching tight. The memory was dim, disfigured by shame.

"I asked you if you loved her," Robert said.

Logan closed his eyes.

"You didn't give me a real answer. You mumbled something, but it wasn't yes." His father's voice was calm, even. "I told myself maybe you liked her. Maybe you wanted a life with her because it felt safe. Predictable."

It had been all of that. And none of it.

A way out. A shell. A lie.

"I had no idea," Robert whispered. His voice cracked slightly. "I didn't know what you left behind. What you were escaping from. What you were running *toward*. Who you loved."

And Logan stood there, barely breathing, staring at the door that held the man he had once left, and swore he never would again.

Because Adrian was on the other side.

And Logan would do anything to keep him there.

The room hadn't changed in days. Same hum of machines, same thin light bleeding through the blinds. Adrian was asleep—or something close to it—his face turned toward the window, pale beneath layers of fever and fatigue. Logan sat slouched in the same vinyl chair he'd spent too much time to count, his body stiff from hours without motion, his hand still loosely wrapped around Adrian's wrist.

That was when Dr. Tierney came in.

There was no dramatic pause, no buildup, just the soft shuffle of shoes and the clipped, clinical voice that somehow still hit like thunder.

"He's compatible," he said, glancing at Logan first, then down at the tablet in his hands. "Alon's a match."

For a single beat, Logan's world stilled; the room contracted into a hush. The chair creaked as he rose, absurdly loud in the sudden silence.

He didn't cry—not fully—but the sting was instant, burning behind his eyes before he could even speak.

Adrian stirred, blinking awake slowly as if surfacing from deep water. Logan turned toward him, eyes glassy, a smile tugging at the corner of his mouth.

"Alon's a match," he said, voice catching.

Adrian didn't answer right away—he just stared at Logan, then toward the ceiling, then back. A smile broke across his face, tired but real. It lived in his whole body.

He asked for his phone.

When Alon answered, Adrian's voice was barely more than a breath. "You're a match," he said, raw with disbelief. *"Toda, achi."* Thank you, my brother.

As Adrian and Alon talked on the phone, Hebrew came naturally. It was a language that Logan could now navigate and understand without needing translation.

He didn't speak Hebrew well—not yet—but he understood enough. Enough to follow and listen. Enough to be part of this moment and all the in-between moments of Adrian's life, the side of his that always eluded Logan because of the language barrier that had become smaller and smaller.

They had spent so many hours in these hospital rooms, long, half-lit afternoons where the beeping monitors played background music to grammar drills and pronunciation corrections. Logan would stumble over vowels, raise his eyebrows for clarification, scribble notes in the margins of whatever notebook he could find.

"Let me get this straight," Logan had muttered one evening, brow furrowed as he squinted at his notes. "The *table* is masculine... but the *door* is feminine?"

Adrian snorted. "Correct."

"But it's a door."

"Still feminine."

"But both are just—objects! How would I even know which object is which?"

Adrian shrugged dramatically. "Ahh... I guess you'll just have to memorize them?"

"So all of the objects are either feminine or masculine, and this is entirely random. Great," Logan muttered. He studied the page again, frowning like it had personally insulted him. Then, hesitantly: "So... *ha delet hagadola niftach?*" *The large door was opened.*

Adrian winced like he'd been slapped with a wet grammar book. "Almost. But no. It's actually *ha delet hagdola niftacha.* The verb needs to be feminine too."

"I quit," Logan announced, dropping his pen with a theatrical sigh.

Adrian laughed, eyes lighting up as he looked at him. "I love you struggling with Hebrew."

Logan groaned. "I'm so glad my misery brings you joy."

"Do you know how hard it is to translate everything in my head constantly?" Adrian shot back, still grinning. "Now you get it!"

But even in the teasing, there was warmth.

Adrian always softened when Logan got it right—when he landed a word, even clumsily. When the verb agreed with the noun, or the feminine adjective, fell into place by accident. There was something quietly sacred in those moments. Logan cared enough to try. "I am so proud of you," Adrian said. "So proud to have you in my life."

Sometimes Logan would practice under his breath while Adrian dozed, his voice barely a whisper, the syllables strange and sharp in his mouth. Other times, he'd murmur short phrases when nurses walked past, trying them out like test flights. Little things. A verb here, a greeting there.

And then one day, as the afternoon light spilled across the floor in long, golden strips, Logan looked at Adrian and said, soft but certain:

"Ani ohev otcha." I love you. The words caught in the air between them, real and unshakable. And he even pronounced *otcha* right. The *you.* The

singular masculine form. One of six (or more!) ways to say it, depending on gender, number, person, context—a linguistic maze he'd been quietly navigating for weeks. But this time, he got it right.

Now, as Adrian spoke to Alon, Logan nodded along, catching the flow of their exchange. When Adrian paused, Logan leaned in and added a few slow, careful words of his own.

Adrian watched him in awe. Logan's wickedly smart brain had managed to catch the language in just a handful of months, he was able to understand Hebrew very well and was even starting to speak.

When the call ended, Adrian let the phone rest on his chest, fingers curled lightly around it. "He's coming here," he said. "Didn't want to do it from Israel."

Logan nodded. Of course, he was.

They hadn't seen each other in over a year. And depending on how this went... it could be the last.

Logan didn't wait for Alon to bring up logistics. He told him he'd buy the ticket before the question even landed.

When Alon mentioned he wanted to check if the army could help with the cost, Logan cut in. "There's no time for bureaucracy," he said, firm but calm. "As soon as Dr. Tierney gives us a date, you get the leave and you're on a plane. I'll handle the rest."

Adrian shifted slightly, wincing as the IV pulled at his skin. "The recovery's going to knock him out," he said quietly, more to himself than to Logan. "He'll be behind when he gets back. His team..."

Logan reached for his hand again, fingers wrapping around his gently. "Then he'll be behind," he said. "That's what brothers do."

February 3, 2022—Seattle, Washington—13 Days Later

MORNING ARRIVED WITHOUT FANFARE. No sunrise worth noticing, just a thin layer of winter light pressing against the windows like a second layer of glass. The world beyond the hospital walls remained suspended in gray—colorless, hushed. Inside, time lost its edges. Minutes slipped into one another. Nothing began. Nothing ended.

Adrian lay in the center of the room, small beneath the folds of white cotton blankets, a slender central line tracing upward from the hollow of his chest, a fragile lifeline. The machine beside him pulsed in quiet rhythm. A bag of deep red fluid hung above, the color of rust under fluorescent light, the stem cells collected from Alon days ago. Alon had undergone the peripheral blood stem cell donation process, which involved five days of injections to coax the marrow's most vital cells out of his bones and into his bloodstream, followed by hours hooked up to a machine that drew blood from one arm, separated the stem cells, and returned the rest through the other. It was exhausting, draining, but it was the best option.

They moved slowly now, drop by drop, into the core of Adrian.

There was no sound but the hush of filtered air and the low, metronomic beep of the monitor. No great ceremony. No sudden transformation.

This was the moment.

Not a climax. Not a miracle. But the gentle, invisible beginning of a war.

Logan sat beside him, wearing a mask and disposable gloves for added safety, since nothing could be brought into that room because Adrian's immune system had been erased. Any infection could be deadly before the new marrow had a chance to take hold.

Logan barely moved as he lingered there, his hands clasped between his knees to stop their trembling. His gaze never left the drip. He counted each drop as if it might be the one to change everything.

His throat burned from the silence. There were things he wanted to say—to Adrian, to God, to no one. But the words stayed buried in the back of his mouth. He hadn't slept, not really, in three days. Not since the doctors had said this was it. The window. The narrow corridor between life and death, and they were walking it barefoot, blindfolded, breathless.

He looked at Adrian's face—pale, still, half-lit by the soft green glow of the vitals monitor. His lips were parted, dry. His eyelids didn't flutter. The body Logan loved was barely recognizable now, thinner in places he once kissed, ribs casting long shadows across translucent skin.

The cells made their way through him. Somewhere inside, they would either take root or fail. There was no middle ground. Logan could not stop imagining them—microscopic, glowing, searching for purchase in Adrian's marrow, in the place where blood begins.

Alon had arrived six days earlier, stepping off the plane with the quiet gravity of someone bearing more than his youth should carry, his presence marked not just by duty, but by love, by blood, and by something deeper still. He wasn't alone. At his side was Dean, Adrian's closest friend, his shadow through sickness, the one who had picked up the pieces when everything else had come undone.

Initially, Logan had argued regarding logistics with fervor. He adamantly insisted on covering every aspect—from the plane ticket to the hospital arrangements, and even the accommodations. It was evident to him that Alon, just nineteen and valiantly serving in the Israeli military, could hardly shoulder any financial burden associated with it all. But Dean had brushed it all aside, he stepped in without asking, without pause, like it was a foregone conclusion. As though carrying burdens that weren't his had become second nature.

Logan shouldn't have been surprised. The past year had redrawn their relationship; it was a slow process, marked by the erosion of grief and the repeated struggles of care. A bond formed not through affection, but through devotion. The calls, the texts, the late-night messages that tracked blood counts and fevers and weight loss—those weren't logistics. They were lifelines. They were the threads that bound two men who loved the same person more than they knew how to say.

Logan vividly remembered the fateful moment he first encountered Dean in the Philippines, a time before the world crumbled around them. Dean's gaze was piercing, imbued with a stillness that felt akin to judgment—a judgment not laced with cruelty, but with a clinical detachment. It was as cold as reef stone yet instinctively protective. Dean had perceived something deeper, something hidden from both of them; he foresaw the impending shutter before it descended. He recognized the heartache unfolding; he noticed that his best friend fell head over heels for someone who was not fully ready to reciprocate this, and by that, he feared the chaos that would soon envelop them both. As the earthquake struck, when Logan vanished without a trace like fog dissipating in the light of dawn, it was Dean who remained steadfast, the observer of the devastation, who endeavored to piece together the remnants of Logan's shattered world, who took the broken shards and tried to rebuild them knowing the fallout was too hard to bear.

There was a time when Dean couldn't stand to look at him.

But Logan had returned. And more than that, he had stayed. And through that stubborn, aching commitment, something in Dean had shifted. Not with warmth, not with sentiment, but with something even rarer: respect. Like spring thawing the edge of winter, that change had taken time. It was never spoken aloud. But it lived in the quiet between them now. Not forgiveness, not exactly—something harder. The kind of trust born only from shared suffering, from watching someone you both love teeter at the edge of life.

And that was why Dean being here meant everything.

In a quiet room down the hall, Alon lay in his recovery bed, his skin a shade of pale that hinted at his recent ordeal. Grogginess enveloped him, a lingering aftermath of the apheresis that had tethered him to the machine for what felt like an eternity.

And beside him, oddly enough, was Dean.

Dean, who had unofficially, quietly, and unshakably made himself Alon's guardian. He was the one coordinating updates for Adrian's parents in Hebrew, as both their children were going through one of the most important operations. He was the one speaking to the transplant nurses, the coordinators, and the specialists. He took care of the smallest details with the same reverence he gave to the largest—a blanket adjusted without being asked, water cooled with lemon wedges, a book or a TV show to pass the time. He hadn't slept more than an hour at a time since they arrived. He barely left Alon's side for more than a few minutes, not even for a snack or coffee.

Dean had never left Adrian's side in the past.

And now, he wouldn't leave Alon's.

For eight days before the transplant, Adrian had undergone high-dose conditioning chemotherapy, not the slow, sustained kind meant to manage symptoms, but an aggressive, full-body wipeout designed to destroy his bone marrow completely. The chemo had wrecked him, nothing like the earlier rounds; this was a scorched-earth protocol, a brutal purge to make space for new marrow. He could not keep food down; even water made him gag. Fever arrived in searing waves, burning through the sheets, soaking his back and thighs until he lay trembling in a pool of his own sweat. His teeth chattered, his jaw clenched with chills that gnawed at the bones; nurses kept time with ice packs and warm blankets, a futile rhythm. He vomited, blood ran from his gums and nose, he could not even swallow his own saliva; sleep abandoned him. Hollowed and shaking, a vessel emptied by the treatment, he lay waiting for the storm to abate.

Forty-eight hours ago, the chemo had ended.

Now, the infusion had begun.

Logan's gloved fingers were threaded gently through Adrian's. His other hand trembled against his knee.

And softly, barely louder than the hum of the IV, Logan began to sing.

The melody was threadbare on his tongue, fragile in the sterile air. He sang the song Adrian had written for him—the one he'd composed on a guitar that was ashes now, beneath the skies of his homeland back when he was in pieces. A song stitched from saltwater and soul, from surf breaks and silence, from glances held too long and words neither of them had dared say.

It carried the story of them—all of it. The ache. The wonder. The quiet roar of love that had never stopped burning, even when it had been buried under fear.

He didn't know if Adrian could hear him.

He just knew he had to sing.

"I believe my fate was to cross paths with you,

To be the one who saves you,

So when the end draws near, and life leaves you,

I'll be here, waiting to save you."

Three to four weeks, that's how long Adrian would need to stay. A month of waiting. A month of holding his breath, of watching numbers rise and fall, of praying that what had been given would take root and grow. That the cells would graft. That his body wouldn't turn traitor. That his immune system wouldn't see salvation and mistake it for a threat.

And if he made it through all of that—if the transplant held—he could go home.

Finally, home.

Logan sat slumped in a vinyl chair just outside the isolation wing, his head tilted back against the cold wall, eyes half-shut. His body didn't feel tired so much as emptied. There was no fight left in his muscles, no thought left to chase. Just silence. Just breath. His limbs had gone heavy with the kind of exhaustion that came not from lack of sleep, but from carrying too much for too long.

His family had come earlier. Brought sandwiches he didn't eat, coffee that had gone cold, and hugs that tried too hard not to feel like goodbyes.

One by one, they'd drifted out, quiet squeezes on the shoulder, soft reassurances, doors whispering shut behind them.

Now, the hospital was still.

He let his eyes fall closed.

The moment sleep began to drag him under—

"Princess, go home."

Logan's eyes snapped open. Dean had dropped into the chair beside him with a heaviness that the hospital corridors witnessed too often.

Logan rubbed his face, already bracing. "Later," he muttered. "How's Alon?"

Dean stretched, arms behind his head, legs kicked out long in front of him. "Recovering," he said with a yawn. "Still cranky about missing training. Mostly just pissed that he's falling behind."

He flipped his phone lazily between his fingers, a mischievous glint catching in his eye as he glanced toward Alon's room.

Logan narrowed his gaze. "What did you do?"

Dean's smirk grew like it had been waiting all night. "Well," he drawled, dragging the word out, "Adrian and I were in the same unit as Alon's in now. I might've... pulled a few strings."

Logan blinked. "What kind of strings?"

Dean shrugged, far too pleased with himself. "Alon's going to be here a while. They need to monitor him anyway, make sure the transplant worked, see if anything shifts. You know that already. You and Dr. Tierney have had those talks. More routes, more options, more waiting."

Logan nodded, slowly.

Dean leaned in, eyes bright. "So I made a few calls. Said a few things. When Alon's cleared to return, he'll slot back in with his team like he never left. No penalty. No falling behind. It's already sorted."

"You can do that?" Logan asked, incredulous.

Dean just grinned and leaned back again. "I did."

Logan exhaled, scrubbing a hand over his face. "That's... good."

"I know." Dean stretched like a cat, arms overhead, spine popping, and let the quiet settle.

For a moment, neither of them said anything. The silence wasn't awkward. It was just there, like breath or time or gravity.

Then Dean turned again, quieter now. "Come on, Logan."

Logan looked over, jaw already tightening.

"Call a cab," Dean said. "Go home. Sleep for a few hours."

"I'm fine," Logan insisted.

"You're not," Dean replied, voice soft but steady. "You look like shit. I'll stay here tonight. I know you don't want to leave him. But you need to rest."

Logan didn't move.

Dean gave him a look, not cold, not hard, just human. "He's going to need you tomorrow."

Logan inhaled sharply, he tipped his head back until the ceiling tiles blurred, feeling the air thin against his ribs as though Dean had compressed the entire future into that single sentence. He knew Dean was right. Of course he was. Tomorrow... Adrian would need him tomorrow.

But still—How did he walk away?

How did he leave Adrian alone, even for a few hours, when the line between life and loss felt so impossibly thin? When tomorrow could be...

He couldn't finish that thought; he could not even think that thought.

For a long moment, Logan didn't move. His fingers twitched faintly in his lap before he reached into the pocket of his jacket. The motion was slow, almost reverent—as if the thing he was about to pull out was too fragile to handle casually.

Then, with a breath that felt like it had taken weeks to gather, he drew out a small black jewelry box and held it out.

Dean blinked, momentarily taken aback. He gazed at the box for a heartbeat longer than necessary before gently accepting it from Logan's hand. His fingers moved with an odd clumsiness as he lifted the lid—

And then he froze in awe.

Inside, nestled against luxurious black velvet, lay a ring.

A band of white gold, glowing softly under the subdued hospital lights. A delicate array of perfectly cut diamonds dazzled along the center, embraced by two sleek silver edges. It exuded elegance yet possessed a reassuring solidity. Quietly radiant, it was a ring crafted to endure the passage of time.

Dean turned it in his hand, and that's when he saw it, the engraving on the inside of the band.

My lifesaver.

The words were delicate, etched in a script so fine it almost shimmered when the light caught it just right. A secret, meant only for one person.

Dean exhaled, a breath that lingered between them like steam in winter. Logan's voice followed, threadbare.

"I really can't lose him." The words came from Logan's throat like a prayer—cracked, hoarse, barely there. When Dean looked up, Logan had buried his face in his hands, his shoulders trembling with the effort of holding everything in.

Not crying.

Not yet.

Just holding on.

Dean slipped the ring gently back into its box, closing it with a soft snap. He looked at Logan again, something gentler behind his eyes now.

"How long have you been carrying this around?" he asked, his voice quieter, steadier.

Logan dragged his hands down his face, resting them in his lap.

"Two months," he murmured. "I've been looking for the perfect one for so long..." His voice cracked, just enough to betray the weight he'd been carrying alone. Then, softer, almost ashamed, "But I don't know if I should ask. Not now."

Dean's eyebrows lifted. "Wait—what?" He let out a quiet, disbelieving laugh, shaking his head, incredulous, almost affectionate. "Are you seriously worried Adrian might say no?"

Logan didn't answer. He just stared at the floor like the thought was a knot he couldn't quite undo. Dean reached over, pressing the box back into his hand.

"Logan. Trust me. It's a big fat yes."

Logan let out a breath of a laugh, but it was hollow, his shoulders still braced like he couldn't exhale all the way.

"I know it's a yes," he said quietly. "But what if it upsets him? What if it's too much? What if he's scared, or overwhelmed, or..."

Dean cut him off firmly. "No what-ifs."

Logan looked up.

"Ask him," Dean encouraged. "He'd be so damn happy. Trust me... Adrian is a bit cheesy and overly romantic when it comes to that stuff; he'll be the happiest man alive when you ask." Then, softer, with a knowing glance, "But not here. Not in this place. Wait until you're home. It'll be more meaningful."

Logan let out a slow breath before nodding. "Then in three weeks, I'll be engaged."

And for the first time in so long, he smiled. A real, unguarded smile. The idea of it, the certainty of it, settled deep in his chest like light returning to a place that had been dark for far too long.

Dean, of course, couldn't resist. "Yeah. Isn't it, like, your second engagement?"

Logan shot him a glare and promptly elbowed him in the ribs.

Dean let out an exaggerated groan, rubbing his side dramatically. "Hey!" he protested.

"You're a mean person," Logan muttered, shaking his head. Then, softer, more genuine, "I can't believe you're the first person I told."

Dean just smirked. "I'm sorry, but you basically set me up for that one. And let's be honest, I'm growing on you."

Dean grinned, stretching lazily as he pulled out his phone. The glow of the screen reflected off his face, casting a soft light over the teasing smirk tugging at his lips.

"Get out of here, Princess. I'll see you in the morning." He stretched out in the chair, all long limbs and lazy ease, tapping on his phone screen. The soft blue glow lit his features, casting gentle shadows across his face. There was a smirk tugging at his lips, yes, but something else had crept in.

A softness. A stillness. The kind that came from what—or who—waited on the other side of the screen.

Logan rose from the bench, stretching the stiffness from his spine, his limbs unfolding with the slow, aching reluctance of someone who'd been sitting far too long. He turned toward the elevator, ready to call it a night, or at least pretend he could, but something made him pause mid-step.

Dean hadn't moved.

Still rooted to the same spot, still staring at his phone, but the expression on his face had shifted. This wasn't the easy grin he wore when laughing at something stupid, or the cocky smirk he threw around like spare change. No, this was quieter, softer. A smile that didn't reach for attention, that didn't perform. It hovered on his lips like something half-remembered and wholly cherished.

He looked at the screen as if it held more than pixels, like it carried meaning. As if what glowed there wasn't just light, but something delicate, something alive. Something *real*.

The phone buzzed gently in his hand, the sound barely more than a sigh, and Logan watched as Dean's eyes softened further, the faintest shift in his expression betraying everything. He bit down on a smile that wasn't meant to be seen, and a breath caught in his throat like it had to make space for whatever had just reached him through the glass.

There it was, that stupidly tender look, all soft edges and quiet reverence. Like someone reading a letter they'd memorized but still couldn't get through without feeling it all over again.

His thumbs moved slowly, deliberately, as though each word he typed was a string of glass beads he didn't want to crack. His whole body had gone still, except for that barely-there smile, the kind people wear when they think they're alone with something beautiful.

And Logan just stood there, watching the whole thing unfold with a slow lift of his brow.

"Who's that?" Logan asked, voice casual, but laced with quiet curiosity.

Dean blinked, momentarily pulled out of whatever space he'd disappeared into. "Huh?"

Logan gestured to the phone. "The one that's making you grin like a fourteen-year-old girl scribbling hearts next to the name of her crush in her diary."

Dean's mouth twitched. Not quite a grin. Not quite a smirk. His gaze flickered—briefly, instinctively—toward Alon's room, then dropped again to the screen.

"Oh, fuck you," he said lightly, like it meant nothing. "We're just dating. Four months now."

The words floated away, intended to vanish before taking root. Yet, Logan perceived their underlying meaning: the subtle curl at the edge of Dean's mouth, the calmness of his hands, and the slight dip in his voice that hinted at something more serious. All of this was evident in the silence that surrounded their exchange. He noted how Dean's shoulders relaxed, his body appeared eager, the brightness in his eyes, and the smirk that formed—along with the change in his gaze.

Logan tilted his head, a slow, knowing smirk creeping across his face.

"Dude... if you're counting the months, that's not just dating, she's your girlfriend."

Dean hesitated. Just long enough for Logan to know he'd struck something deeper. His thumb stilled on the phone screen. His posture changed—not tense, just uncertain.

And then, slowly, carefully, Dean dropped his gaze.

He was quiet for a beat. Then another. Like he was sorting through the thousand ways not to say the thing he'd already decided to say.

When he finally looked up, his voice was quieter than before. Less sharp. Less armored.

"You let me in on a secret," he murmured. "So I'll tell you one too."

He didn't look at Logan. He didn't have to.

A breath passed. The kind of pause where something important waits.

"It's a he," Dean said finally. "Not a she."

And just like that, the world didn't change—*but something did*.

There was no cinematic stillness, no collapsing ceilings or dramatic hush of fluorescent lights. The hallway buzzed with the same tired hum, nurses still moved past with quiet efficiency, machines still blinked behind closed doors. But inside Logan's chest, something shifted—quiet and seismic. A thread pulled loose. A beat caught between his ribs.

Dean. Of all people—*Dean*—had just come out to *him*.

Logan didn't move. Didn't reach for a joke or let some reaction stumble out. He just looked—really looked—at the man in front of him. At the edges of him. At the way the usual armor had fallen away without fanfare. No smirk. No deflection. Just a softness, a fragility that hadn't asked permission to be seen.

Dean's gaze stayed low, flickering near Logan but not quite touching him. A smile ghosted at the corners of his mouth—not playful, not performative. Tentative. Like a door half-opened.

Then Logan blinked, and the words spilled out with a lopsided grin, unable to hold back the rush that followed. "Dude! Welcome to the other side." It wasn't mockery, it was joy, too stunned and too sincere to be filtered. His grin broke wide across his face. "Have you told Adrian?"

Dean shook his head, "No…" The word was barely audible

Logan's eyebrows shot up. "Your literal best friend in the entire world is as gay as possible—"

"What does that even mean?" Dean cut in, half-exasperated.

"You get the meaning," Logan said, waving a hand. "Point is, your best friend is gay and you're *dating a guy* and you haven't told him? For four months?! He's going to lose his mind." He laughed—sharp, delighted, somewhere between disbelief and admiration. "Who is he?"

Dean chuckled, rubbing the back of his neck in that way people do when they're caught off-guard but don't mind being seen. His eyes dropped for a second, not shy exactly, but something adjacent. Like the feeling you get before saying a name that matters. His smile changed, softer, almost hushed. It wasn't fear, but something far more delicate: reverence. Like the name he carried was too new to expose, a fragile thing he was keeping warm in his chest until it was strong enough to stand in the open.

Before Logan could press further, a soft ding broke the moment.

Dean's phone illuminated in his hands, transforming his entire demeanor, his eyes gravitated toward the screen as if drawn by an instinctive force, bypassing thought entirely. A spontaneous grin spread across his face, bright and unguarded, appearing before he even recognized that he was smiling. A delicate flush brushed his cheeks, genuine and revealing, exposing his emotions far more than any words could. His fingers danced across the screen with urgency and excitement, almost trembling as he crafted a reply—oblivious to the rest of the room, his focus entirely ensnared in a world that felt singular, intimate, and intensely personal.

"Does he know about Adrian?" he asked gently.

Dean blinked slowly, his gaze flicking upward before landing somewhere distant. "Yeah," he said. "He knows."

"Wasn't he upset you're gonna be away for at least a month?"

Dean gave a small, guarded shrug. His hands were in his pockets, but his shoulders spoke louder than anything his mouth could've formed. There was something unsettled about him. A low static, humming just beneath the surface.

Logan stepped in a little closer, not imposing, but deliberate—his voice dropping to a near whisper, something meant to stay just between the two of them.

"You could've asked him to come," he said, almost gently. "Make it romantic. I would've helped you plan it... it's not too late, you know. You could call him. Tell him to come. We'll figure something out."

Dean didn't respond right away. Something in him paused, not in hesitation, but in exposure, a truth that had accidentally been touched.

His jaw clenched, then relaxed again. His leg began to bounce, a nervous tell that betrayed the armor he tried to present. He bit at his lower lip, flicking his gaze between the two hospital room doors down the corridor.

Adrian's.

And then—

Alon's.

Logan didn't say anything. He didn't have to.

He just watched.

He watched the way Dean's gaze lingered too long on the second door. The way his shoulders stiffened, like he was holding something too heavy for casual denial. The way his breath subtly changed caught somewhere between confession and restraint.

It came to Logan not in a flash, but gradually. A realization that didn't strike but rather *rose*, inevitable and soft.

He thought back.

To the way Dean had shadowed Alon from the moment they arrived. The way he'd insisted on carrying his bags, the way he hovered, never obvious, always close. The way he sat by his bed without needing to be asked, the gentle way he'd reached out to adjust a pillow or offer water, as if Alon might break if he moved too fast.

The way his voice softened when he said his name.

The way his eyes never seemed to *leave* him.

There had been something there, something tethered and tentative, unspoken and raw. Something sacred. And now, it clicked. All of it.

Dean hadn't just come here for Adrian.

He tilted his head, a slow smile forming as he watched Dean carefully, the way a person looks when they've finally put together a puzzle that's been in front of them all along. "It's Alon, isn't it?"

Dean went still.

Frozen, breath caught, eyes wide in a look that was half shock, half surrender. A deer blinking against the glare of headlights he knew were coming. For a suspended moment, he didn't move, as if motion itself might give the truth too much shape.

Then finally, with a sigh that held more than fatigue, he ran a hand over his face and let out a dry, reluctant breath. "Don't tell Adrian yet, okay?"

Logan's smile blossomed, a deeper warmth rising from within, quiet but steady. Something in him—soft, gentle, and quietly expanding—began to unfurl, delicate as a flower finding its way back to light. In the midst of all the chaos, somehow, against all odds, he and Dean had grown into each other's closest confidants. Through grief and healing, through the stillness of long-distance silences and the unexpected intimacy of late-night conversations, over half-meant insults and fully-meant laughter, through their relentless teasing and the sharp-edged comfort of banter that only ever masked care, trust had taken root. Not loudly, but deeply.

"Of course," he said simply. Sincerely. "But... how did it even start?"

Dean flushed instantly. It was subtle, but unmistakable—color blooming at his cheeks, climbing his neck. Blushing. Actually blushing.

That's gold.

"You remember when you were in Israel?" he began, shifting in his seat, his voice a little faster now. "That night we went to the club? I kept texting someone the whole time—yeah, that was Alon. I was just checking in, making sure he was okay. He was just starting his military service, and I knew it must be hard on him, and with Adrian... I should have reached out sooner. And then we met up the next day. Talked for hours." His voice softened. A memory threading itself into the air. "I've known him since we were kids, you know? But now... now he's just..." Dean drifted for a moment, his eyes unfocused, a distant smile tugging at his lips. "Amazing," he whispered. "I couldn't stop thinking about him after that."

It wasn't performative. It wasn't for show. It was honest. Raw. Real.

And Logan felt it—the weight of what it meant. This wasn't a fling. This wasn't a crush. This was something that had taken root.

Dean ran a hand through his hair, that shy, lopsided smile still there. "It's new... but Alon's basically been living with me."

Logan blinked. "Wait, *what*?"

Dean chuckled. "You know how it was, me, Adrian, and Tom got that place together. Then Tom moved in with his girlfriend. And Adrian..." A beat. "Well. He left."

There was no bitterness in the words, just history.

"After that, I asked Alon if he wanted to move in. Maybe he needed a break from his parents. Maybe I just... needed someone around."

A soft, almost breathless laugh.

"I'd see him every month or two when he was on leave. And somehow... it just happened. It became more."

Dean's voice had gone quiet again. Not uncertain—just full.

And the look on his face told Logan everything. There were no questions left.

"Damn, man," Logan grinned, joy sparking through his chest. "That's... that's really something."

Then his grin turned mischievous. He couldn't help himself.

"Please," he said, hands raised in mock prayer. "I am begging you—let me be in the room when you tell Adrian. I *have* to see his face when he finds out his best friend is banging his baby brother."

Dean's face went slack. Emotionless. For half a beat.

Then—

"You son of a—!"

Logan was already on his feet, laughing, turning on his heel and sprinting down the hall as Dean launched after him, feet pounding, curses flying in sharp, echoing bursts through the quiet corridors of the hospital.

The past three weeks had been a blur of recovery and stolen moments.

Alon was healing. His body was still sore, his strength slow to return, but each day brought a little more color to his skin, a little more steadiness to his step. He no longer stayed overnight in the hospital. Instead, he crashed into the spare room at Logan and Adrian's apartment while Dean took the couch.

Or at least, that's what Dean told them.

Logan had no doubt they were sharing a bed. He wasn't an idiot.

And every time Dean casually mentioned sleeping on the couch, Logan made sure to raise his eyebrows, smirk knowingly, and make the most exaggerated, ridiculous faces—especially when Adrian was around.

It had become something of a ritual—Logan teasing Dean, Dean refusing to flinch, and Adrian caught somewhere between confusion and amusement.

But the first time it happened—the very first jab—it was over coffee.

Adrian had only just come out of isolation. It was early, the world still gray through the windows, and the three of them had gathered in Adrian's hospital room.

That's when Logan struck.

"How's the couch treating you, Dean?" he asked innocently, sipping his coffee with exaggerated calm, eyes gleaming with mischief.

Dean, too proud to take the bait, barely glanced up. "Fine."

"Oh, yeah? Not too stiff? Not too cold? No back pain from those terrible cushions?"

Dean's jaw tightened, fingers twitching around his mug like he wanted to throw it across the room.

"It's. Fine." He hissed.

"Huh." Logan tilted his head, all mock innocence. "Weird. I could've sworn I heard the guest room door open in the middle of the night. And close. And then open again. And closed. Any idea why, Dean?"

The glare he received could've melted steel.

"And this morning when I was getting water... I didn't see you on the couch... where did you sleep?"

"I was probably in the bathroom," Dean said dryly, as his look suggested that he was thinking of a burial place for his body.

Logan winked at him when Adrian was not looking. "That must be it..."

Adrian, blissfully unaware of the full implications, raised an eyebrow. "Why are you annoying him?"

"Because it's fun," Logan grinned, and Dean muttered something under his breath that definitely included a curse, which only made Logan laugh harder.

Riling Dean up had become one of his favorite pastimes.

"Have you noticed that Dean's being weird?" Adrian's voice was hoarse one afternoon, thin from fatigue but still sharp, still full of that old, suspicious edge as he picked disinterestedly at his lunch.

Logan froze for half a beat.

Adrian sat slumped against the pillows, pale in a way that gnawed at Logan's stomach. His skin looked translucent under the fluorescent lights, and the dark circles beneath his eyes were etched too deeply to ignore. Still, there was a spark behind them—that glint of observation that never left him.

"Like... he barely leaves Alon's side," Adrian continued, pushing his spoon in lazy circles around the tray.

Logan shifted in his chair, gaze dropping. "Maybe it's just... the situation, you know?" he said too quickly, too casually.

Adrian didn't press—not yet—because in the next moment, his body tensed, his face paling further as his stomach rebelled against even the thought of food.

Logan knew the signs.

Adrian swallowed hard, trembling fingers setting the spoon down like it was made of lead. His whole frame tightened, bracing.

"Ad..." Logan leaned forward, his voice low, coaxing. "You have to keep eating."

Adrian shook his head weakly. "Can't."

The word barely made it past his lips.

Logan sighed, heart aching, and reached out, cupping Adrian's face gently in his hands. His thumb brushed across the sharp line of Adrian's cheekbone, where there should've been softness.

"Just a little more," he whispered. "For me?"

Adrian closed his eyes. A long, quiet breath. Then, slowly, he nodded.

He picked up the spoon again. Small bites. Painfully slow. Each swallow looked like it took everything he had, but he did it—not for the hospital, not for survival. For Logan.

Because somewhere, deep in the tired shell of his body, the fight was still there.

By the time he finished, he was shaking.

His hands trembled in his lap. His legs were weak. But Logan knew that if they didn't keep moving—if they didn't push—the strength wouldn't return on its own.

"Come on," Logan murmured, rising to his feet. "Let's walk."

Adrian hesitated. His teeth sank into his bottom lip. He knew it would hurt. Everything hurt.

But after a long breath, he nodded.

Logan reached out again, arms steady, unwavering, wrapping around Adrian's waist as he pulled him upright with care. The moment Adrian placed weight on his legs, pain shot through him, a sharp, searing ache that pulsed through his joints like fire.

His jaw locked. His breath hitched.

"I'm here," Logan whispered.

Adrian's fingers clutched at Logan's arm, knuckles white, muscles trembling with each step. His legs felt like they belonged to someone else—useless and burning. But Logan's grip didn't waver. He held him like a lifeline, guiding him forward through the ache.

"Just a few more steps," Logan said softly. "Then you can take a shower."

Adrian let out a breathless, broken laugh. "You make it sound like I'm running a marathon."

Logan smiled, pressing a kiss to his temple. "To me, you are."

And Adrian, despite the fire in his limbs, despite the bone-deep fatigue, took another step.

And another.

Because Logan was there.

Because love, in its quietest form, was movement.

Chapter 19

A Memory That Exists in My Broken Heart

I will never love another.
I have already seen the world without you.
I have already drowned in the days that stretched too long,
Swallowed nights that tasted of regret. I drank oceans to forget you,
But every tide still carried your name.
I will never love another.
Not after I have felt the shape of your soul,
Not after I have traced the map of your body,
Not after I have known what it is to be whole.
For I have lived without you,
And it was not life—it was the shadow of a breath,
The echo of a heart that once beat.
If the streams of water take you away,
If I wake to a world where your voice is only a memory,
If the sunrise spills gold over an empty bed,
If the ocean roars and you do not hear it—
Then let it swallow me whole.
Let the waves pull me under,
Let the current take me where you are.

I don't want to be old and gray without you.

I don't want to be a ghost wandering through years

That were never meant to be lived alone.

I don't want to breathe air

That does not belong to the same sky you stand beneath.

I don't want to walk this world

Where you are nothing more than an absence.

I will never love another.

The time we had was a borrowed dream,

A fragile thing made of salt and sky,

Of whispered laughter between waves,

Of hands pressed together in the dark,

Of love too deep to speak aloud.

I ran from you once.

I was afraid of the fire we built,

Afraid of the weight of loving you.

But I burned in your absence.

I turned to ash in the silence.

I was a man unmade.

And now, if the tide pulls you away from me—

If you go where I cannot follow,

If your breath stills before mine,

If the light in your eyes fades into nothing,

If your smile is nothing but a memory,

Then I will never set foot in the water again.

I will never cross the tide,

Never chase the horizon,

Never let the wind carry me forward.
Because my heart is no longer mine to give,
And the ocean is no longer my home.
Without you, I belong nowhere.
Without you, I am nothing.
Without you, my breathing is worthless.
Without you, my heart forgets its rhythm and stills.
I will never love another.

THE DAYS BLED INTO each other, slow and bruised, the air inside the hospital room thick with sterilized silence and the rustle of too-clean sheets. Adrian was unraveling—not all at once, but in the quiet, cruel way life sometimes leaves. His body shrank into itself; his skin thinned until it seemed the light might pass straight through him. There were mornings when Logan could barely recognize the man lying in that bed—not because he looked different, but because he looked like he was fading.

His movements grew sluggish, like he was wading through water too deep for his limbs. Even the act of lifting a glass became a negotiation. His breath caught more often. His eyes dulled under the fluorescent hum of hospital lighting. Logan watched, helpless, as exhaustion draped itself over Adrian's frame like a second skin.

The fight was a storm that never quite broke, hovering over them like a restless tide, swelling, retreating, but never fully gone. It came in waves—first, a quiet resistance, a sharpness in Adrian's voice that hadn't been there before. "Stop treating me like I'm fragile," he'd snap, though his body told a different story. "I don't need you hovering, Logan." But his hands trembled when he reached for his phone. His voice cracked when he whispered Logan's name in the middle of the night. His anger wasn't real rage, it was a shield, a wall of thin glass, cracking under the weight of things he couldn't control.

Logan didn't argue. He stayed. He fetched ice chips and rewound movies they didn't finish. He adjusted the blankets Adrian kicked off in his sleep, read him parts of books they both pretended to care about. He didn't ask permission to stay; he knew that Adrian wanted him there, even in anger. But he stayed anyway. Because he had once walked away, and the guilt of that still burned in his chest like something half-swallowed and stuck.

Sleep evaded Adrian, broken by sweats and shivers that came in fits. Fevers left him soaked, breath hitching against the pillow. Logan would press cool cloths to his face, whisper nonsense, and count heartbeats. Nights stretched long and unkind. Sometimes Adrian talked in his sleep, fragments, confessions, apologies. Logan never told him what he heard.

And then there was Zack.

Zack, who moved like a shadow in the hospital hallways. Zack, who Logan swore was nothing, just a relic of a past life, a mistake made in the dark. But to Adrian, it was another thing taken from him. He saw the way Dr. Tierney and Zack exchanged quiet, easy smiles. He saw Logan say hello and it made something sour churn inside him. It wasn't about Zack. Not really. It was about the betrayal of his own body, the war he couldn't win, the mirror he now avoided. It was about how Logan looked at him sometimes—carefully, like he might break apart with the wrong kind of touch.

He'd never been jealous before. Never needed to be. But illness didn't just strip away strength. It stripped away certainty, too, peeled a man down until all that remained was fear dressed up as fury draped over weak bones.

So he pushed.

He snapped. He withdrew. He said things he didn't mean in voices that weren't his. He turned away when Logan reached for him, not because he didn't want the comfort, but because needing it made him feel like he was already losing.

And still, Logan stayed.

Through the fights. Through the moments Adrian refused to speak. Through the apologies that came not with words, but with tearful eyes and fingers reaching for his hand in the dark. Through the way Adrian's back sometimes stayed turned long into the night, and Logan would trace the curve of his spine with his eyes, praying for morning.

Logan stayed.

Because he knew now—knew in his bones, in his blood, in the marrow of him—that leaving Adrian was never the answer. That love like this didn't just come and go like the changing tides. That love like this was as wild, merciless, and infinite as the ocean that had first brought them together.

So no matter how hard Adrian pushed, Logan would not drift away.

The hospital room was dimly lit, the soft hum of machines filling the silence between them. The scent of antiseptic clung to the air; at that point, it had become so familiar to them both that it never even registered. Outside the door, life moved on—nurses pacing, visitors murmuring—but here, in this quiet space, time felt frozen, suspended in a moment too fragile to touch.

When Adrian spoke, his voice was barely a whisper, rough from exhaustion, from the sickness eating away at him. His body was now a battlefield of scars and bruises, of veins burned from chemo, of hands that trembled even when he tried to steady them. But his eyes—they were the same. The same whisky clear depths that had once pulled Logan under, the same gravity that had always drawn him back.

"If you want…" Adrian's voice barely rose above a breath, the sound of it delicate and unraveling, like a single thread pulled from an old sweater. It trembled with something not quite defeat, but something dangerously close, not because he wanted to let go, but because he loved Logan so much that letting go might be the last thing he could still give.

His eyes lingered on the hallway where Zack had just passed—a blur of movement, a polite, half-smiled hello, the kind of presence that knew its weight and tried not to take up space before he slipped back, no doubt in search of Dr. Tierney. Adrian swallowed hard, as if pushing something sharp down his throat.

This was love. The kind that hollowed you out. The kind that stood in the doorway of your own heart and said, *take what you need, even if it leaves me empty, even if it kills me.* It wasn't grand or noble. It was silent and cruel. It tasted like rust and blood. It felt like dying with your eyes open and your heart beating. And still, he offered it.

He closed his eyes. Just for a moment. Just long enough to steady himself. And then he forced the words out, raw and brittle and breaking.

"If you want to be with him… I'll understand."

The room shrank in an instant. The air, which moments ago had felt bearable, turned thick and suffocating. Logan could feel his lungs tighten around the shape of those words as they choked him. They didn't belong in Adrian's mouth. They didn't belong anywhere.

He didn't need to ask what Adrian meant.

He saw it in the way Adrian's fingers curled into the hospital sheets, trembling, as if they were the only thing keeping him from falling apart.

In the way his breath caught and refused to leave his body. In the quiet collapse of his shoulders, like he was already grieving a goodbye that hadn't yet happened.

Like he had rehearsed this moment too many times in his head and hated himself more with every draft.

Oh yes.

This wasn't a spontaneous act. This was rehearsed. Over and over, in the quiet hours when Logan had fallen asleep in the chair beside him. In the silences between test results. In the dark. Adrian had imagined this moment, practiced it like a wound he'd need to bleed clean.

"I really would understand," Adrian said again, softer now, his voice fraying at the edges. "I know we haven't—"

He stopped.

The silence that followed wasn't empty. It was swollen. Dense with everything he couldn't force through his mouth. Shame coiled tight around his ribs, a slow suffocation he didn't have words for. He wasn't crying—not yet—but Logan saw it in his eyes: the shimmer of tears not yet shed, the way grief perched behind his lashes like something waiting for permission to fall. Adrian wouldn't let himself break. Not all the way. Not here. Not now.

Adrian was doing something that burned more than chemo. Something that made his soul feel like it was blistering inside his body. This was the part that hurt more than the nausea, the weakness, the vomiting, the hair loss. This was the part that stripped him of dignity, of manhood, of feeling like he was someone who could still be wanted.

"I know I can't," Adrian whispered, and now his voice was small—smaller than Logan had ever heard it. "I know I haven't touched you. I know it's been so long. And I don't feel like—" He paused, swallowed hard, looked away. "I don't feel like a man anymore, Logan. I don't feel like I have anything left to give. Not like *that*."

His hand twitched on the blanket. Not reaching. Just bracing.

"So if you want to be with him or with another man," he said again, "just for the night. Just for sex. Just to feel like someone wants you. Just to feel something. Just... you know, for sex."

He tried to make it sound casual—*just sex*, he'd said, like it was nothing, like it didn't matter, but the words carried the weight of something holy being handed away. And he said it like it was a gift. Like his heart wasn't shattering into dust as he let the words leave his mouth.

"You don't need my permission," he added, barely audible now. "But you have it. I would understand."

Logan didn't move. He couldn't. The sound of Adrian giving him away—like a man laying down a weapon, like a soldier surrendering not to an enemy but to love—it hit him with the force of a fist to the chest.

Logan didn't speak.

Not right away. Not for a long time.

And the longer the silence stretched, the more unbearable it became.

Adrian sat frozen in it, trapped inside the stillness like it was a cage. He couldn't breathe. Couldn't swallow. The IV beside him beeped rhythmically, indifferent to the way his heart was stalling in his chest.

He couldn't look at Logan—not directly. But in the cruel, flickering theater of his mind, he saw it all unfold.

He *saw* the moment Logan was considering it. Saw the calculation behind his silence. Saw him weighing desire against duty, loneliness against loyalty.

He imagined the quiet decision—Logan rising slowly, maybe brushing Adrian's arm with a gentle thank you, something kind enough to ease the edge of it. Then the door would whisper shut, and his footsteps would fade down the hallway. Maybe toward Zack. Maybe not.

Adrian imagined him waiting now—easy smile, that casual lean. No need for words. No need to ask. Some people just know when the door's about to open.

And Adrian... Adrian would lie here in this bed, IV line snaking into his arm, mouth dry, chest hollow, listening to the space where Logan used to be.

He wouldn't cry.

He would clench his jaw. He would stare at the ceiling and count the seconds. He would pretend it didn't burn more than the chemo. Pretend he wasn't measuring every minute by the sound of Logan not coming back.

If it wasn't Zack, it would be someone else.

A stranger, faceless and charming. Met through a screen, or the blurred edge of a bar. Someone younger, someone whole. Someone who didn't flinch when touched.

He would understand.

He *meant* that.

But meaning it didn't make it hurt less.

He would understand, and it would still tear through him like a slow blade. He would never truly recover.

But he would understand.

He would.

Because Logan was still whole. Still *alive* in ways Adrian no longer was. His blood still surged with want, with fire. His hands still itched for touch. His body hadn't been rewritten by poison.

And Adrian, as much as it tore him open to admit it, couldn't give him that. Not anymore. Not now.

He was too thin. Too tired. His skin no longer felt like his. He barely recognized himself in the mirror. Whatever version of manhood he had once carried so easily, so instinctively, had long since burned away in hospital lighting and the cold sterility of survival.

He was still Logan's boyfriend, technically. But not really. Not in the ways that mattered. And maybe that's what hurt the most—the slow erosion of being *his*. Of being *enough*.

So when Logan still said nothing, when the silence thickened into something sharp, Adrian's mind filled the gap with every terrible possibility. Every imagined betrayal. Every truth he had tried not to name.

And suddenly, it became unbearable.

His voice came out cracked and fragile, more exhale than speech. "You go now?" It barely made it into the room. A whisper shaped like a surrender. His eyes stayed forward, fixed on nothing, because he didn't think he could survive looking at Logan if the answer was yes.

He'd read once—years ago, in a life that felt like it belonged to someone else—that people could die of a broken heart.

He didn't believe it at first.

But then Logan had married *her*.

And Adrian couldn't breathe for weeks.

The pain in his chest wasn't metaphorical. It was pressure, constant and dull, like something sitting on his lungs, waiting. He had nearly gone to the hospital once, had imagined walking into an ER and saying, *someone left me, and I think it's killing me.*

Instead, he'd searched it online at three a.m., curled around a silence that wouldn't let him sleep. "Can heartbreak cause real pain?" "Heart hurting after breakup?" "Dying of grief?" And somewhere, buried between poorly written articles and medical journals he didn't fully understand, he found it.

Broken Heart Syndrome. A real thing. Triggered by intense emotion. A surge of stress so brutal it stuns the heart into failing.

He remembered staring at the words, numb and trembling, whispering to no one, *so I'm not crazy.*

And now—Here. In this room, with Logan silent beside him and love threatening to slip through his fingers, he didn't need the internet to tell him what it was.

If Logan left now, if he walked out that door to the arms of another—Adrian's heart would not survive it.

Not poetically.

Not figuratively.

Literally.

It would flicker once—and then fall quiet, simply... cease.

"Stop." Logan's voice was low, but it cracked with something too fierce to contain.

Adrian's gaze pierced through the silence, and Logan felt the weight of it, the remnants of war etched into his irises, a haunting guilt swirling in the depths. An aching desire flickered there, a longing to feel enough yet lost in uncertainty. Love glimmered alongside a deep-seated fear, clinging to him like a shadow. The anguish of unfulfilled cravings mingled with doubt, resonating in the silent spaces between them.

Logan clenched his jaw and tightened his fists, fixing his gaze on the ground while a fire ignited in his chest. His mouth remained drawn tight, without any hint of a smile. He lacked the gratitude or joy Adrian had anticipated; instead, only a simmering rage lurked just beneath the surface.

"Stop that," Logan said again, more urgently. He reached out without hesitation, threading his fingers into Adrian's—cold and fragile and trembling. "Right now. Stop."

He held his hand like it was the only lifeline that mattered. Like it was the only truth in the room.

"Don't you dare give me away," Logan ordered, his voice thick, his throat burning. "Don't you ever let go of me like that again. You're still mine. You're still *you*. I'm yours. You don't have to earn me back."

Adrian's eyes filled, finally, but still the tears didn't fall. He blinked furiously, his jaw clenched, his shoulders rigid.

"You silly, stubborn, impossible man," Logan murmured, brushing the lightest kiss against Adrian's temple, against the fever-warmed skin that had once tasted like the sun, like salt, but now tasted simply like home. "I love you. I am in love with you. Cancer or not. Healthy or sick. Here or anywhere. Do you understand that?"

He turned his head away, swallowing against the hard knot in his throat. It wasn't only from the raw, ulcerated lining that stretched from his mouth down through his gut, though every attempt to swallow felt like fire. The lump now also took the pain of fear and shame. But Logan wouldn't let him go, not this time, not ever again.

"I don't want anyone else. Ever. Not Zack, not anyone. If it's not you, it's nothing. If it's not sex with you, I don't want it. If it's not waking up next to you, falling asleep next to you, spending every breath, every second, every stupid, beautiful moment with you, then I don't want it. Do you get that?"

Adrian's breath hitched, his fingers curling around Logan's with what little strength he had left.

"I love you," Logan whispered again, voice breaking now, his forehead pressing against Adrian's, their breaths tangling between them. "I dreamed about being with you when I was with Zack. Hell, I think I've only ever wanted you. Maybe I'm not even gay, maybe I'm just—" Logan let out a half-laugh, half-sob. "Maybe I'm just Adrian-sexual, because you are it for me. You have always been it for me."

Adrian let out a trembling breath, his other hand lifting—slow, weak—to rest against Logan's cheek, thumb brushing against the stubble there, as if he were memorizing the feel of him, as if this moment, this love, were something he could take with him, even into the dark.

"Say it again," Adrian whispered.

Logan kissed his knuckles. "I love you."

"Again."

"I love you."

Adrian closed his eyes, exhaling softly.

"Again," he begged.

"I love you, Adrian. And I will *never* love another."

More days came and went, folding into each other like soft, worn pages of the same book. Time began to lose its shape. Mornings bled into afternoons, afternoons into evenings, until the light outside became just another thing to ignore. Dr. Tierney insisted on keeping Adrian longer—"for observation," he said. The hospital has long since become a second home, not just for Adrian and Logan, but for the people who drifted in and out—friends, family, nurses who stayed an extra five minutes to chat, visitors who brought soup, books, stupid jokes.

Ada Mae, who started as an assistant and has become more of a friend, made it a point to visit at least once a week. Jane and her husband came twice a week, engaging in quiet conversations and expressing care through small acts—fluffing pillows, straightening blankets, and distracting Adrian with stories unrelated to illness.

His parents came too, their worry never quite masked by polite smiles. Adrian's parents, thousands of miles away, called often, their voices breaking slightly over the line as if distance made everything worse. But they had come twice since their last visit, unwilling to let their son fight this alone.

And Tom, one of Adrian's oldest friends, who had flown in for a two-week stay with his now fiancée.

Adrian sat propped up against the pillows, a gray knit cap snug over his head, his skin pale but his eyes bright. He sipped slowly from a cup of green tea, his fingers trembling only slightly as he lifted it. They were watching something mindless on TV, one of those shows neither of them truly cared about but kept on for the noise, for the illusion of normalcy.

And then, there was a soft knock.

Logan turned his head, already used to people coming and going, and called out, "Come in."

The click of heels against the linoleum floor was the first thing he noticed, measured, steady, familiar. Then, the sight of her. Sandy. Dressed to perfection, long golden waves cascading over her shoulders, her deep brown eyes scanning the room before locking onto his. Uncertainty flickered across her face, a moment of hesitation filled with so much unresolved tension between them.

And then, her gaze drifted past him, to Adrian.

And she winced.

It wasn't pity. It wasn't even shock. It was recognition, the moment when you see someone not just as a person, but as the truth you spent years avoiding. The truth that had unraveled her marriage, stolen her peace, shaped her pain.

Behind her, a man entered. Tall, broad-shouldered, neatly dressed in a crisp suit. His posture was relaxed but protective, one arm instinctively resting against Sandy's lower back. He was older than Logan, mid-thirties, composed, someone who didn't enter a room unnoticed.

Logan smiled at her. Because, despite everything—despite the pain he had put her through, despite the lies and the years wasted, Sandy had been a close friend once.

"Hey, Sandy," he said, warmth in his voice.

She met his gaze, something unnamable flickering there. "Hey, Logan." Her voice was steady, but then her eyes found Adrian again, and her composure faltered.

"Hello, Adrian," she said quietly. Her fingers twisted in her lap. "I remember you... from the wedding. We never met officially but I...

remember seeing you." She glanced at Logan again, a thousand unspoken words passing between them. A thousand moments of what ifs and could-have-beens and it was never meant to be.

She inhaled sharply, straightened her back. "A few months ago, I ran into Samantha, and she told me... most of what happened."

She swallowed, casting a glance at the man beside her before exhaling slowly. "I don't really know why I came. I just—when I heard everything, I felt like I needed to. So, here I am."

Adrian, despite the obvious effort it took, offered her a small, genuine smile. "Thank you for coming. It means a lot."

Sandy paused before sitting in one of the chairs close to Adrian's bed, but not too near. The man who joined her took the seat right next to her, gently taking her hand as he settled in. His movements were soft, and he gazed at her intently, as if she were the only person in the room.

"Hello, I'm Chris," he introduced himself, his voice smooth. He extended a hand toward Logan and then to Adrian. "I hope we're not imposing."

Logan shook his hand, returning the smile. "Not at all. It's always nice to have visitors."

The conversation was light, inconsequential. They spoke of Sandy's stores, of Chris's work. The kind of talk that felt safe. And then, as naturally as a wave smoothing the rough edges of a stone, Sandy lifted her hand to brush some hair off her face, revealing the glint of a diamond ring.

For a heartbeat, Logan felt the weight of a different kind of tide, one that pulled at something deep inside him—guilt, relief, gratitude all tangled together like seaweed in a current.

"You seem..." she hesitated, her gaze sweeping over him. "Happier? I guess. I know this isn't ideal, but... you're lighter somehow." Her voice carried the weight of understanding, of something that had taken years to form.

She turned to Adrian then, her eyes gentle and full of kindness. "I really hope you'll be okay," she said, her voice holding the quiet ache of someone who knew loss too well.

Then, after a breath, she looked back at Logan, something raw surfacing in her gaze. "It's been a while since we divorced, and for a long time, I blamed you. I hated you, Logan." Her voice didn't waver, didn't break, but it carried the echo of those years, the ones they both spent drifting in separate, storm-tossed waters. "But now... I understand. We both rushed into something we didn't understand. And for what it's worth, I forgive you."

She hesitated, then glanced at Chris, her fingers unconsciously brushing against the fabric of her dress. "We're expecting now," she admitted, her words like a pebble dropped into deep water, rippling outward. "So I guess everything... happened for a reason."

Logan felt something warm bloom in his chest—not regret, not sorrow, but something closer to the sun breaking through storm clouds. He stood, crossing the space between them, and she rose to meet him. When he pulled her into a hug, he was grinning like a man who had just touched the horizon.

"Congratulations," he said, his voice unshaken, unburdened. "Really, Sandy. I am so happy for you."

His grip tightened for just a second, enough to say all the things words never could—*I'm sorry. You deserved better. I'm glad you're okay.*

When they pulled apart, she smiled.

"Well, Adrian," Dr. Tierney remarked, glancing between the two of them, carrying measured optimism that came with years of bad news. "It's been eight long weeks since the transplant, and I won't lie—it hasn't been easy. But your counts are holding, your body isn't rejecting the graft, and your latest biopsy results look promising." He smiled then, small but genuine. "I think you're ready to go home. For a few weeks, at least."

The words felt like sunlight breaking through a storm—*Adrian could go home*. After eight long weeks of sterile walls and the unrelenting hum of machines, after the agony of waiting for his body to decide whether it would accept or reject this gift of marrow, after blood draws and transfusions and nights spent drowning in exhaustion—he could finally *go home*.

Adrian blinked as if he hadn't heard correctly, his lips parting, but no sound came out. Then, slowly, a breathless laugh escaped him—shaky, disbelieving. His fingers twitched where they lay against the hospital blanket, and Logan could see the war in his eyes—the joy, the fear, the exhaustion.

Logan clung to those words like a lifeline, like a surfer spotting the shore after too long at sea. The battle wasn't over, not by a long shot. They would have to return every few days for blood tests, for checkups, for more waiting, more hoping. But at least, for now, Adrian could sleep beside him, breathe the same air that didn't reek of antiseptic and bleach, exist somewhere that wasn't a hospital bed. That was enough. That was everything.

But freedom had never been so fragile.

By the time they reached the apartment, Adrian was struggling to breathe, his breaths coming in short, sharp pants. Logan could see the effort in every step, in the slight tremor in Adrian's hands, in the way he leaned against the wall, in the way his eyes shut down to compose himself. The sight of it was unbearable, like watching the ocean pull back only to crash down in a furious wave.

Logan didn't hesitate. He wrapped an arm around Adrian, guiding him through the door with a tenderness that broke his own heart.

The journey from the garage to the elevator had been hard. The walk from the elevator to their apartment had been brutal. By the time Adrian sank onto the couch, he looked like he'd just fought through a storm.

Logan crouched in front of him, his hands already reaching, steadying. "Are you okay?" His voice was gentle, but the fear beneath it was sharp, undeniable.

Adrian closed his eyes tightly, his face pinched with pain. *Maybe if I don't see it, it won't be real.* But the pain didn't listen. It never did. Even now, after everything, it still found new ways to surprise him, to steal the breath from his lungs and the strength from his body.

He nodded, even though it was a lie, and they both knew it.

Logan didn't argue. He didn't push. He just moved, maneuvering Adrian gently, guiding his head onto Logan's lap. The weight of him there, so real, so alive, made something in Logan's chest tighten.

Then, without a word, he reached for the blanket draped over the back of the couch, the same one Adrian loved to wrap around himself for those rare moments when he was home. *It smells like home*, Adrian had said once. Logan spread it over Adrian, tucking it around his shoulders, pressing a hand to the center of his chest as if to remind him—*I'm here. I'm not going anywhere.*

Adrian exhaled, long and slow, his body finally beginning to relax.

"You're home," Logan murmured, his voice thick with unexpressed emotion, raw and untamed.

On the seventh day of Adrian being home, Logan felt like he was floating.

Not in some dramatic, euphoric way, more like the quiet kind of buoyancy that comes from breathing evenly again. From moving through the day without dread clinging to your heels. Things weren't normal, not really. There were still near-daily hospital check-ins, medications lined up like soldiers on the kitchen counter, the central line needing its quiet ritual of care, and a constant vigilance that buzzed just under the surface.

But they had a rhythm now. A softness. A kind of almost-life. And, at the end of the day, Adrian slept next to him. After so long sleeping alone in that bed, Logan was thrilled to have him there.

Every morning, just after sunrise, they took a short walk around the block, ten minutes, on good days. Five, if Adrian was dizzy. He always wore a mask, avoided people like shadows, and sanitized his hands often. And when they came home, he went straight to the shower, where Logan hovered outside even though Adrian told him about one hundredth time, "I remember how to use soap, you know?"

"Can't a man watch his boyfriend take a shower anymore?" Logan would say dramatically, watching Adrian through the glass door, not missing how he rolled his eyes.

Logan decided to just join him on most showers. "Can't be too careful, you know, germs," and he kissed Adrian under the spray of water.

Adrian said the walks made him feel *normal*. Said that after so long in a hospital bed, the simple act of stepping outside felt surreal, like recovery was something he could taste in the air. Like maybe things would be okay.

So they walked. Hand in hand.

And they talked, not about the transplant or medication, or prognosis, but about nothing: Logan's next grocery trip or whether they should just order online, the new series they planned to watch, or the movie they wanted to see. For ten minutes each day, it felt like they were just two people in love, reclaiming a little normalcy from the world.

At home, Logan cooked while Adrian sat nearby, still queasy but smiling at the smell of butter in a pan. They ate what they could. They took naps in the early afternoon. Sometimes they drove aimlessly—sightseeing, Logan called it—but really, it was just to give Adrian something other than white walls to look at.

They even made plans to visit Logan's family in a couple of weeks. If Adrian felt up to it.

At night, they cooked together—or tried to. Logan would toss a slice of carrot at Adrian's chest just to get a laugh, and Adrian would retaliate by leaping at him like a cat, only for Logan to catch him mid-air and lift him onto the counter, where they'd stay tangled together until the pasta boiled over.

The past few days at home had worked quiet miracles. They followed Dr. Tierney's recommendations: speaking honestly, even when the words trembled; taking medication on time; they tried to keep to their routines—regular meals, sleep that came in fuller stretches, mornings that didn't begin in dread. They talked about counseling, too, as another door they might open together.

And through it all, they stayed close. Closer than before, somehow, woven into each other not by urgency, but by choice.

At that moment, they sat on the balcony watching the sunset, Adrian's favorite part of the day. Just a few minutes each evening, they sat side by side with Logan's arm around Adrian's back, as Adrian lay his head on his shoulder, both wrapped together in a blanket, watching the sun slide behind the buildings with a look that always hovered between wonder and exhaustion.

Today was a hard day.

The nausea was worse. The lightheadedness came in waves. They barely made it five minutes outside before Adrian had to stop and lean against Logan's arm, breathing carefully through his mask. Dr. Tierney said healing wasn't linear. That this was normal. Expected. But Adrian had a hard time believing that when even getting out of bed felt like climbing a mountain in his own skin.

He spent most of the day buried under blankets, silent, worn thin. Logan didn't push. He stayed close, brought water, took his vitals, read quietly, and kept Dr. Tierney updated.

But by evening, Adrian seemed a little steadier—clearer-eyed, less pale. He made it to the balcony again and took Logan with him to watch the sunset, like he cherished their small routines just as Logan did.

And that felt like enough.

As the air turned brisk and nipped at their skin, they retreated inside, crushing into the soft embrace of the couch. The muted glow of the screen flickered to life as Logan dialed down the volume, setting the mood just right. Adrian nestled against him, arms wrapped tightly, seeking warmth and affection, their connection radiating like a gentle flame against the encroaching cold.

Outside, the city murmured—the soft, distant hush of traffic, of life continuing. Inside, the only sounds were the screen's low murmur and the quiet rhythm of Logan's fingers tracing lazy circles along Adrian's arm.

Adrian's breathing slowed. Less strained now. Less guarded.

He drifted. Dipped in and out of sleep like a leaf caught in water. Every time he blinked awake, he tried to pretend he hadn't missed anything—eyes flicking to the screen, lips parting like he might ask a question, and then thinking better of it.

Logan had been watching him throughout, his gaze imbued with a profound intensity, laden with desperation. It was a fear that had nestled deep within his soul, flourishing in the quiet cavities between his ribs, like an ache that refused to diminish.

Then, gently, he reached for the remote and turned the TV off.

Adrian opened his eyes and saw it there—the terror, the helplessness. He hated it. Hated that Logan had to carry this, that he was the one causing it. So, with what little strength he had, he reached up, his fingers tracing over Logan's face, brushing along his jaw, his neck. His skin was soft, smooth, warm under Adrian's trembling fingertips.

"Lo..." Adrian breathed, barely audible.

Logan was already there, fingers weaving through his like muscle memory, lifting Adrian's hand to his lips. He kissed the fragile skin gently, reverently.

"Yeah, baby," he murmured. "I'm here."

Adrian swallowed, his throat working slowly. "You remember your promise, right?" His voice was thready, worn down at the edges, but his grip tightened, shaky but insistent, needing something solid to hold onto.

Logan didn't ask which one. He didn't need to.

The pain in his chest swelled, thick and suffocating, as he nodded. Adrian promised to get treatment, and Logan would keep living, not give up. That was what Adrian had made him swear. To not drown when the inevitable tide came to take him away.

Adrian exhaled shakily and pulled Logan's hand closer, turning it over so he could run his fingers along the tattoo inked into his wrist—the one Adrian had traced a thousand times, the one that had the life-saver bracelet with the line from their song in delicate, curling script, forever etched into Logan's skin. On top of it rested the original lifesaver bracelet after Zack had returned it.

"God, I love how crazy you are," Adrian chuckled, pressing a kiss against the ink.

Logan laughed, but the sound cracked down the middle. It was too full, too layered: part amusement, part grief, part plea. It sounded like someone trying to hold everything in at once and failing.

Adrian looked at him, whisky-colored eyes shining with something unreadable, something fragile and infinite all at once. He hesitated, then spoke, his voice no more than a whisper. "I need to ask you for another promise."

Logan swallowed hard. "Anything." His free hand drifted to Adrian's knit cap, his fingers ghosting over the soft fabric, as if memorizing the shape of him.

Adrian took a slow breath, pulling his head away from Logan's chest to sit upright, facing Logan. Logan instinctively wrapped his arm around him, and in that embrace, Logan's love radiated a healing power that surpassed anything chemotherapy could offer. "If this... if this isn't working, I know you already talked to Dr. Tierney about other options." His voice wavered, but he kept going. "But please, if it's not working—no more."

Logan stiffened. The air in his lungs vanished. "No."

"Lo—"

"No." Logan shook his head, his grip tightening around Adrian's fingers like he could anchor him here, like he could fight back the tide by sheer will alone. "You promised. You promised you'd keep getting the treatments."

"And I did." Adrian's voice was soft, but the weight of it crushed Logan's chest. "I did, and they gave me more time with you. More moments. More memories. But, Lo..." His voice quivered, and he briefly shut his eyes, gathering his composure, before locking his gaze directly into Logan's shimmering silver irises, his tone pleading. "Please. No more. I can't do it again. Everything hurts. *Everything*. I can't—I can't go through another chemo."

Tears burned down Logan's cheeks, hot and unrelenting. His entire body ached with the weight of it, the reality of it. He wanted to fight. To argue. To *beg* Adrian to hold on, to promise him more time, more days, more nights, more of *them*.

But Adrian was already looking at him with those deep, aching eyes, with something like peace written in the quiet corners of his face.

"Please," Adrian whispered, bringing Logan's hand to his lips again, pressing a kiss against his knuckles, lingering. "Don't ask me to go through it again."

Logan released a heart-wrenching sob, grasping Adrian's hand as if it were the sole anchor preventing him from completely fracturing. And somehow, it was.

He found himself caught in a wordless battle, unable to whisper a yes, yet too paralyzed to utter a no.

As their foreheads met, Logan's breath quivered, tears cascading between them like raindrops merging with the vast ocean. His fingers clutched Adrian's with a fervent desperation, unwilling to loosen their grip, a silent plea for connection amid the storm within.

"Ad, I can't do that," Logan whispered, his voice fractured, as if speaking the words alone might split him apart.

Adrian closed his eyes, pain flickering across his face—not just the pain in his body, but the pain of knowing what this was doing to Logan, the pain of watching the man he loved fight against a stream that could never be turned back.

"I'm not giving up on you."

Adrian exhaled, shaking his head weakly. "I don't want to die in a hospital bed." His voice was quiet but firm, pleading. "That was the one thing I wanted to avoid. I wanted to leave this world on my own terms, not hooked up to machines, not with strangers whispering about how much time I have left."

His fingers wove through Logan's, their hands locked like a final vow as their eyes held each other's gaze. "Please... it's not giving up, it's accepting. You need to accept it, ahuv sheli. It'll be easier that way."

But Logan shook his head fiercely, tears slipping past his clenched jaw. "No. Not easier. Never easier." His voice broke completely. "You can't ask me to be okay with this. You can't ask me to let you go."

Adrian swallowed, blinking up at him, his gaze soft and filled with something ancient—something infinite. "I never wanted to say goodbye to you." His voice was so small, so unbearably full of love that it made Logan's chest ache. "I love you too much."

"Not goodbye," Logan choked out. He was trembling now, his entire body unraveling beneath the weight of it all. "You are going to be okay, Adrian. You are going to be okay. Those past days, you... You've been feeling better. You will be okay." He repeated it like a prayer, like an incantation that might rewrite fate.

Adrian closed his eyes, exhaustion pulling at him, but his fingers brushed against Logan's face, grounding them both. "Lo... I have overcome death too many times." His voice was quiet, but unwavering, as if he were telling Logan a truth as old as the sea itself. "I survived four wars. I survived rescuing you from the ocean. I even survived the last time death came for me, when you left."

Logan's breath hitched, a sob breaking through his throat, but Adrian kept going. "When you walked away that night, something inside me died. My soul died from how much I loved you." He paused, letting Logan hear the weight of those words, letting them sink into his bones. "But when you came back? I lived again." His lips trembled. "Every moment with you is worth a lifetime of agony, even if it was always going to end like this. And now, my soul will live even if my body won't."

Logan pressed his forehead firmly against Adrian's, allowing their breaths to entwine, his tears cascading onto Adrian's delicate skin. One arm embraced him tightly, while the fingers of the other glided over Adrian's cheeks, tracing down his neck, yearning to etch every contour into his memory.

"No." Logan's voice cracked, breaking like waves against jagged rock. "I'm sorry, Ad... no."

His sobs fell against Adrian's forehead, raw and uncontained, his body shaking with the force of his grief. "No. I'm not ready for you to become a memory that only exists in my broken heart. I'm not. And I'm sorry. Maybe it's selfish, but I don't care."

His hands clutched at Adrian as if holding him tighter could keep him here, as if love alone could defy time, defy fate.

"I don't care," Logan whispered again, his voice drenched in agony.

And Adrian, despite the pain, despite the exhaustion, just held him. Held him like the ocean cradles the shore, like the sun holds the horizon before it disappears. He held him as if he could carry Logan's grief for just a little while. "I understand," Adrian breathed, his voice carrying all the quiet acceptance that Logan wasn't ready to give.

Logan closed his eyes for a second, gathering himself, wiping away the tears that refused to stop falling. Then, as if making a silent decision, he shifted, reaching for his back pocket. Adrian watched him with quiet curiosity, his brows furrowing as Logan pulled out a small black box.

"Ad," Logan said softly, and Adrian's eyes fluttered open, locking onto the delicate object cradled in Logan's hands.

A wave of confusion washed over Adrian's face, swiftly followed by disbelief, and then a flickering emotion that eluded description, a feeling that made Logan's heart miss a frantic beat. He held Adrian's gaze steady as he carefully opened the box, unveiling the glinting ring nestled within.

Adrian inhaled sharply, his eyes darting between the box and Logan's insightful gaze, as if he were assessing the very fabric of reality. Logan beamed at him with a radiant and beautifully reckless smile, laced with a hope so profound that it almost hurt to behold.

With a mix of wonder and vulnerability, Adrian's gaze fell on the small, shimmering band resting inside the cocoon of velvet, only to rise once again to the man who held it with hands that trembled in anticipation.

"Adrian," Logan whispered, voice thick, tears pooling in his silvery eyes, "will you marry me?"

Adrian stared at him, stunned, overwhelmed, his lips parting as a shaky laugh slipped out. "What are you doing?" he asked, even though the answer was obvious, even though his heart already knew.

"What does it look like, you silly man?" Logan chuckled, though his voice wavered.

Adrian let out a breathless laugh, shaking his head in disbelief. "You are crazy."

Logan grinned, the kind of grin that lit up his whole face, that made the entire world disappear. "And you just love it."

Adrian swallowed hard, his fingers brushing over Logan's as he stared at the ring. "You can't... You can't want to marry a dying man." His voice was quieter now, hesitant, filled with sorrow he couldn't hide.

But Logan's grip on the ring tightened, his jaw setting. "I have the ring to prove I do." His voice was fierce, unwavering. "Is that a no?"

"What? No! Of course not!" Adrian blurted out, his heart pounding so hard he thought it might break through his fragile ribs. "I mean—yes. It's always a yes." His hands trembled as they hovered over the ring, as if he couldn't quite believe it was real.

Logan stood then, tugging Adrian up with him, slow and careful, making sure not to strain his body. A playful smirk danced upon his lips as he leaned closer and whispered, "I want to do this right, now that I'm positive I won't be humiliated." He winked at Adrian, and oh that wink, a subtle gesture, tugged at the very strings of Adrian's heart, igniting a warmth in his cheeks and making his smile blossom impossibly wide, filled with uncontainable joy.

And before Adrian could process what was happening, Logan dropped down on one knee.

Adrian let out a choked laugh, covering his mouth with his hand, his entire body trembling—not from weakness, not from sickness, but from the sheer depth of emotion drowning him.

Logan took a deep breath, his own voice struggling past the weight of his heart. "Adrian," he began, and his eyes were stormy oceans, endless and filled with love. "Will you marry me?"

Adrian let out a broken sob, nodding furiously. "Yes. Of course. Yes."

Logan's face split into the most radiant smile Adrian had ever seen, a smile that could chase away every storm, every shadow. With unsteady hands, Logan pulled the ring from the box, slipping it onto Adrian's trembling finger.

Adrian didn't even let him stay on his knees for another second—he pulled Logan up, and then Logan practically jumped to his feet, arms wrapping around Adrian as tightly as he dared, as if holding him close could somehow fuse their souls together forever.

Adrian buried his face into Logan's shoulder, inhaling him, clutching him, grounding himself in the only thing that had ever truly mattered.

After a long moment, Logan whispered against his temple, "Now, we're going to take a bath together."

Adrian let out a breathless laugh, his lips brushing against Logan's neck as he murmured, "Okay."

Logan squeezed him tighter.

Adrian sighed against him, feeling the warmth, the love, the life that pulsed between them.

"Logan Vaughn..." he whispered, his voice full of wonder, full of love. "I really don't know what I've done right in my life to deserve you."

Logan pulled back just enough to meet his gaze, his hands framing Adrian's face with infinite tenderness.

"You were you..." Logan murmured, his voice full of quiet reverence. "Jumping into twelve feet waves to save the idiot who went surfing in the middle of a storm, with his mind messed up and no sleep."

Adrian let out a weak chuckle, squeezing Logan's fingers. "You know, Lo... I checked it."

"Checked what?" Logan asked as they stepped into the bathroom.

"The weather. Before going out that day, I checked the forecast." Adrian's voice was quiet, thoughtful, laced with something almost... mystical. "There were supposed to be ideal surfing conditions, like two- or three-foot waves, nothing major. Barely something you'd even notice. But the storm we had? It came out of nowhere. It had no forecast, no warnings.

And that kind of storm? It wasn't normal for that time of year. It wasn't supposed to happen. At all."

Logan turned to look at him, watching the way Adrian's tired eyes flickered with something... something he had never spoken of before.

"I didn't think much about it back then," Adrian continued, watching Logan turn on the water, steam rising slowly from the filling tub. "But after you left... and then when I got my diagnosis... I wanted to look at it again. I wanted to find something—some meaning, some reason for everything that happened." He swallowed. "And I realized... it shouldn't have stormed that day. It was like... something made it happen. So we could meet. So you could be there."

He let out a small, self-deprecating laugh. "It's stupid, I know. But I held on to that."

Logan shifted his gaze, his face an unreadable mask, yet beneath it, his heart thudded with trembling uncertainty, a secret storm he couldn't quite name. "That's not stupid at all," he declared, his voice carrying the steady, commanding weight of a boardroom, echoing strength and conviction that seeped into Adrian's soul, transforming that moment into an almost oneiric state because Logan Vaughn was out of this world. And when he spoke in that low, deliberate register, something in it held the weight of oceans, the hush of cathedrals. And Adrian, like the rest of the world, stood no chance. He was already undone.

Slowly, Logan's hands reached for the hem of Adrian's shirt, peeling it away, careful with every movement. Adrian let him, watching as Logan's fingers ghosted over his bruised skin, the sharp rise of his ribs, the ghost-blue bruises blooming like dusk, the pinprick scars left by weeks tethered to machines.

But he was here. He was alive.

Logan swallowed hard, the sound thick in his throat, his pulse thudding like a drum under skin. He leaned in and pressed a lingering kiss to Adrian's shoulder; his lips were warm and reverent, landing a kiss that echoed a quiet vow. Then, slowly, he reached for the drawstring of Adrian's sweatpants, fingers moving with careful patience. The fabric slid down inch by inch, pooling at Adrian's feet with a hush.

Adrian exhaled shakily. His breath trembled on the way out. He let Logan undress him. Let himself be softened by that care, by hands that touched him not like he was broken, but like he was sacred.

His voice, when it came, was barely a whisper. "Can you dim the lights?" he asked, his breath brushing the shell of Logan's ear, quiet as a confession.

He wasn't hiding. Not really. Logan had already seen the map of his pain, the bruises that bloomed along his ribs, the pale scars that traced his arms like fading ink. He had witnessed the wreckage. But tonight was different. Tonight, Adrian wore Logan's ring. And with it came a fragile need, not to disappear, but to feel strong again. To cloak the edges of his vulnerability in shadows. The dim light would soften him. Give him back a sliver of pride, of presence, of manhood.

Logan didn't hesitate. He simply nodded, a quiet understanding passing between them, and crossed the room with graceful intent. The switch clicked, and the overhead light dissolved. Soft amber replaced it, low and warm, curling around the walls like dusk spilling into a room. A single lamp remained, casting faint lines across the tile. Just enough light to find each other. Not enough to expose.

They finished undressing in silence, and when they were bare, Adrian stepped into the tub first. The water welcomed him gently, lapping at his skin with the warmth of a long-awaited embrace. A sigh slipped from his lips as he sank in, eyes fluttering closed, steam rising in soft ribbons around him. The heat wrapped around his sore body, easing the tension from his muscles.

Then Logan joined him, moving slowly, the water shifting to make room. He settled in behind Adrian, arms folding around him beneath the surface, the way rivers curve around stone. Adrian shifted, pressing himself against Logan's chest, letting his body melt into him. Logan's arms came around him instantly, holding him close, one hand resting over Adrian's heart, the steady rhythm of it grounding them both.

After a long moment, Adrian raised his hand, staring at the ring on his finger, the tiny silver band that now carried so much weight.

"I think you're right," Logan said thoughtfully, gazing at the light glinting off the ring's smooth surface. "The storm appeared out of nowhere. I remember suddenly feeling the shift in the water; it was so bizarre. I hadn't thought much about it, but now that I do... I... I think you're right."

Logan leaned in, pressing his lips against Adrian's ear, gently nipping at the lobe. "I love seeing my ring on you," he added, voice thick with emotion.

Adrian smiled softly, tilting his head as Logan trailed kisses down his neck.

"You're so beautiful." Adrian exhaled, his free hand coming up to rest over Logan's, his fingers tracing the veins beneath his skin. "I think the storm wasn't just so I could save you," Adrian murmured. "Maybe it was so you could save me, too."

Logan pressed a kiss to the side of his head, his grip tightening.

"Then I hope we have a thousand more storms, Ad. Because I'm never letting you go."

The warm water lapped gently around them, their bodies sinking into the quiet intimacy of the moment. Logan's fingers traced absentminded circles against Adrian's damp skin, his arms wrapped securely around him as if anchoring him in place.

Adrian tilted his head back slightly, pressing a slow, lingering kiss to Logan's lips. It was soft, unhurried, one of those kisses that wasn't about passion but about feeling, about remembering.

"Sometimes... I wish we could go back to your cabin in Hawaii," Adrian murmured, his voice low and steeped in nostalgia. The words drifted through the steam like a memory reborn, delicate and aching. "Of all the places we traveled, that's the one I loved the most. Probably because... it's where we met."

Logan hummed in agreement, a soft sound vibrating against Adrian's skin as he rested his chin on his shoulder. "I feel that, too." His voice was soft, lost in memory. "There's something about Hawaii that just... stayed with me. I mean, Australia was incredible, sure, and the Philippines—God, the waves there were unreal. But nothing compares to that night at that tiny, lame bar where we first met."

Adrian chuckled, a breath of sound that danced between them. His fingers traced slow, absent-minded lines across Logan's forearm, skin to skin. "You think that was a date?"

Logan smirked, tilting his head in thought. "Hmm... tricky question." He pretended to consider it, even though the answer was already written across his heart. "But I'd have to say yes. I mean, we got to know each other, right?"

"Definitely," Adrian agreed, lips curling, his voice warm as sun-drenched sand.

He shifted in the tub, turning until he faced Logan fully, one leg slipping to each side of him. The water lapped around them in lazy waves, steam rising in gentle coils. The scent of soap mingled with a calming oil—lavender or sandalwood—something that made Adrian's body feel lighter, more his again. Logan's arms wrapped around him, drawing him closer, and Adrian melted into the embrace like breath into air.

"I was excited as hell that night, don't know about you." Logan's smile was playful, but his eyes were filled with something deeper.

Adrian stole another quick kiss, his lips ghosting over Logan's before pulling away. "You know I was."

Logan grinned. "And there was even an invitation for a second date."

Adrian chuckled, shaking his head. "Yup. You totally invited me for a second date after that night."

"What? I was terrified I wouldn't see you again!" Logan defended himself, feigning indignation.

Adrian smirked, turning slightly to face him. "Don't worry, ahuv sheli. If you hadn't invited me, I would have invited you." His voice softened, a gentle smile gracing his lips as he reached up to brush his fingers along Logan's jaw.

Logan let out a laugh, his nose nudging against Adrian's. "Of course, you would have." His voice dropped to a teasing whisper. "You had a crush on me from the start."

Adrian rolled his eyes, though his smile only widened. "Yeah, and you were jealous most of the time."

Logan scoffed, his laughter a soft rumble against Adrian's chest as he tightened his arms around him, pulling him closer. "What can I say? I was going through a lot."

Adrian melted into him, letting himself be held, letting the weight of time blur around them. The past and the present weren't separate anymore—they were intertwined, stitched together by love, by loss, by them.

"I know," Adrian murmured, resting his head on Logan's broad shoulder, feeling the steady rise and fall of his breathing.

For a while, there was nothing but the hush of the water and the quiet hum of their heartbeats syncing. Then, Logan whispered, "Ad?"

Adrian hummed in response, his body completely relaxed against Logan's.

"What did you say to me?" Logan asked after a pause. "That day, when you pulled me out of the water. You murmured something in Hebrew. I know now."

Adrian's eyes fluttered open, locking onto Logan's face. He saw the firm set of his jaw, the intensity in his gaze, the way his damp skin glowed in the dim light. And God—Logan was beautiful. He always was, but there was something even more devastating about him like this—wet, warm, holding him as if the world outside didn't exist.

A small smile touched Adrian's lips as he reached up, cupping Logan's cheek with a trembling hand.

"I asked if you were okay," he whispered, repeating the words he had spoken so long ago, words that had been lost to the wind and waves that day.

Logan let out a soft laugh, turning his face into Adrian's palm. "I didn't believe you then, and I don't believe you now."

Adrian chuckled, pressing a lingering kiss to Logan's lips before pulling back slightly. But in his mind, he wasn't here, in a bathtub, wrapped in Logan's arms. No—he was back on that beach, staring at a man who had just cheated death, a man who had already changed his world without even knowing it.

"Ani me'olam lo ra'iti mishehu kol kach yafe," Adrian uttered, repeating the words. "I said that I'd never seen someone so beautiful."

Logan grinned, and God, Adrian loved that grin. The cocky one, the one filled with mischief and a hint of arrogance. He loved all the versions of Logan—the confident one, the know-it-all, the smug and spicy one who could argue with a wall just for fun.

Adrian tilted his head, a playful smirk curving his lips as he peered up at Logan. "How'd you know?"

Logan's grin widened, a mischievous glint flashing in his eyes. "You were all red—"

Adrian scoffed. "I just swam and dived to get your sorry ass—"

"And you looked all confused—"

"Again, rescuing—"

"And you couldn't stop staring at me like I was some kind of a statue—"

Adrian groaned, rolling his eyes. "I didn't know you!"

"And you're a really lousy liar."

Adrian huffed dramatically, covering his face with his hand, though the smile betraying him was clear. "That doesn't explain it..."

Logan smirked, shifting slightly so he could look at Adrian better. "Oh, it explains everything," he said, dragging out the last word.

"How?" Adrian challenged, raising a brow.

Logan grinned like a man who had just caught the biggest wave of his life. "Let's break it down, shall we?" He held up a finger, playfully professorial. "First of all, when I woke up, you could not stop looking at me, like you were staring at me, like I was a painting in a museum."

Adrian gasped in mock offense. "I did not!" He totally did.

Logan pointed at him, his smirk widening. "See? That right there? Lousy liar."

Adrian groaned, shoving Logan lightly, though his lips twitched in amusement. "I had just saved your life, excuse me if I needed a moment to process the ridiculousness of it all!"

"Ridiculousness?!" Logan's eyes widened in fake scandal. "How dare you!"

Adrian snorted, shaking his head. "Me? You—"

Logan ignored him, fully committed now. "Second," he continued, holding up another finger, "you lingered."

"I lingered?" Adrian repeated, deadpan.

"Yeah, you lingered." Logan nodded like he was presenting a case to a jury. "Your hands were on my chest for an extra few seconds after you realized I was alive."

Adrian scoffed. "You could not possibly know that!"

Logan smirked. "Sure, but you looked like you were contemplating something."

Adrian opened his mouth, then closed it, glaring. His ears were turning pink now, and Logan lived for it.

"Uh-huh," Logan said, leaning in, smirking. "And what exactly were you contemplating, then?"

Adrian huffed dramatically. "Whether or not I should throw you back into the ocean."

Logan laughed, his eyes crinkling at the edges. "Yeah, yeah. Sure you were. But third—" he grinned, tapping Adrian's nose, making Adrian scrunch his face—"you kept looking at my mouth."

Adrian groaned loudly, his face heating up, because he remembered. He had looked at Logan's lips too long, remembering the feeling of them as he had given Logan his breath on the edge of the water, the way Logan's lips had been soft even in the middle of a raging storm.

"I was making sure you weren't foaming at the mouth from lack of oxygen!" he tried to cover, but his voice was an octave too high to be convincing.

"I was already breathing and sitting down on the beach!" Logan countered, grinning like he had won. "You," he wagged a finger, "are really, really bad at lying, Ad."

Adrian gave up, flopping back dramatically against Logan's chest. "God, I should've just let the sea keep you."

"Fourth," Logan continued smugly, "you ran to find me my board. That was really chivalrous of you, by the way."

"You were not breathing! You had just drowned! I was being considerate!"

"Fifth, you gave me that bracelet, and while I still didn't fully grasp its significance to you, come on, no one gives a gift to a virtual stranger without some intention behind it," Logan remarked, his voice light, imbued with a laughter he was keeping at bay. Adrian contemplated a clever retort, but his mind drew a blank. He felt his cheeks flushing, warmth creeping all the way to his ears as he was caught off guard. With a swift motion, Logan captured his lips in a fleeting kiss, a moment that both pierced through him and whisked him away to his next thought. "Sixth would be the way you were all over me for like the entire evening," Logan went on, waving a hand. "But that is beyond the point."

Adrian gasped, hitting Logan's chest. "You're impossible!"

Logan just chuckled, clearly reveling in Adrian's fake outrage. It felt like them again, bantering, laughing, falling into the easy rhythm they had always had.

"I should have left you and your board there!" Adrian muttered, but his voice was all fondness, all warmth. "So smug."

Logan snickered. "You say that, but admit it—" he wiggled his brows, "—you were already into me."

Adrian groaned into Logan's shoulder. "You are unbearable."

"And yet, you love me," Logan sing-songed, happiness basically pouring out of him as he pressed a wet, teasing kiss to Adrian's temple.

Adrian sighed heavily, so dramatically, as if this were the greatest burden of his life, though his arms were already winding around Logan's neck, pulling him impossibly closer.

"Yeah, yeah," he muttered softly. A breath lingered between the words as he gazed at Logan, with shine in his eyes, the spark of life, of happiness, of something like bliss. He took in the bright, magnificent smile Logan wore and felt his very soul and every one of his cells melt. It was impossible not to smile back. To be loved by him felt unreal, almost beyond what he deserved. "I do. More than anything. And I was gone for you from the first moment I saw you." He admitted it like Logan hadn't already known that.

Logan's teasing grin faded, his gaze softening into something devastating, something endless. "Yeah?" he murmured.

Adrian nodded, running his fingers absently over Logan's arm. "Yeah."

Logan exhaled, his lips brushing against Adrian's hair. "Good," he whispered. "Because I've been yours since the moment I woke up and saw you looking at me like I was the most beautiful thing in the world."

Adrian closed his eyes, resting his forehead against Logan's chest, his heart full, heavy, overflowing.

Logan smirked, his voice dropping to a near whisper, low and teasing. "Truth?"

Adrian swallowed, nodding.

"On the beach, I suspected it. Nothing more." Logan traced his fingers along Adrian's shoulder absentmindedly, his touch gentle, a slow caress, his touch drifting over skin like an angel passing through a private heaven. "After our first date, I kinda knew there was something there. And the fact that you gave me the bracelet just after I woke up? And later, when I realized what it meant to you..."

He hesitated for a moment, pressing a soft kiss to Adrian's temple before continuing, his voice gentler now.

"From the first moment, I felt it, Ad. That's why I held on to you so tight. And I figured, based on how you were looking at me that day—and how terrible you are at lying—that you said something else."

Adrian blinked at him, his breath catching, his heart swelling with something too big to name. He had always known Logan was smart—too smart for his own good, too perceptive when it came to him. But knowing Logan had thought about it, held onto that moment, analyzed it in his overthinking way?

His voice was barely above a whisper. "You really spent time thinking about it, huh?"

It was meant to be a light, teasing comment, but his voice cracked slightly under the weight of emotions, betraying him.

Logan exhaled softly, his fingers tilting Adrian's chin so their eyes met in the dim light. His gaze was warm, knowing, steady.

"Of course, I did." His thumb brushed over Adrian's jaw. "I was trying to figure out what the hell was happening to me. Why couldn't I stop thinking about you? Why, after one night—hell, after one conversation—I felt like I'd already known you forever."

Adrian swallowed hard, his throat tight.

Logan's smirk softened, dissolving into something devotional, almost disbelieving, as his thumb brushed over Adrian's ring. The silver glinted in the soft glow of the lamp, a fragile star between them.

"My future husband," he murmured, almost to himself, like the words were too sacred to say out loud, too large to fit in a single breath.

Their mouths met suddenly, fervent and urgent—no prelude, no hesitation. An unquenchable desire that first ignited on that Hawaii shore and had been shimmering through the heartbreak and the destruction and the pain until it blustered again.

The kiss was a collision of memory and need, lips parted, breath shared. Adrian's hands explored with intent, not just hunger but ache. He traced the solid line of his shoulder, the curve of his bicep, the strength still humming in him. His fingertips glided down the slope of Logan's chest, then his stomach, memorizing the heat of him.

He moved on Logan's lap, hips rolling with slow precision, grinding gently where their bodies met, feeling the heat of Logan's arousal rising against him. He wasn't imagining it—Logan's cock thickening under the water, responding to his touch, to his presence. And the feeling of

Logan's thick cock touching his own made his eyes roll back, made him feel powerful.

The friction drew a sound from Logan, something deep, half-gasp, half-groan. "What... what are you doing?"

Adrian smiled, barely. His voice came quietly, threaded with breath. "I want to touch you."

Their lips met again, slower now, reverent. Adrian reached between them, fingers curling around Logan's shaft, solid, growing harder by the second. That sound again, Logan's moan, unfiltered, helpless, made Adrian's own breath catch.

Inside him, something flickered. Arousal. Desire. But as it rose, it stuttered, like a flame in the wind. He felt his body trying, wanting, but not responding the way it used to. His cock twitched, swelled halfway... then faltered. The fullness never came.

He froze. His movement on top of Logan's and his hand as it jacked Logan off just stopped, and for half a second, the room felt colder. The steam couldn't hide it. His heart pounded more rapidly, not from longing, but from a wave of shame.

This again.

The doctors had warned him. He remembered their words: low testosterone, hormone disruption, erectile dysfunction, delayed response. Clinical terms, cold syllables. He'd nodded through those appointments like a soldier taking orders, but none of it had prepared him for the hollow pause in his own body. For the way desire could rise without being met by function. Those words that sounded clean on paper but tasted like failure when they lived in your body. He was supposed to understand this, accept it, not define himself by it.

But still, he wanted. Wanted to be a man. Not just a survivor. Not just a patient. A man who could take his partner apart with his hands, his mouth, his body. A man who could still *give*.

He looked at Logan, flushed, panting, eyes hazy with pleasure. Adrian's heart clenched with *love* so consuming it eclipsed the rest.

He didn't need release. He didn't need performance. He needed *this*—to give, to touch, to make Logan feel everything he couldn't always feel himself.

"Ad," Logan gasped, breath hitching as pleasure rolled through him, but even in the haze, he saw it. The shift.

The way Adrian stilled.

Not in hesitation, but in something quieter, heavier.

Logan knew that look. The flicker of sadness. The glint of shame behind Adrian's eyes. He'd seen it before, felt it in the way Adrian's body went tense, in the way his own arousal pressed against the soft, limp weight of Adrian's cock, twitching but unresponsive.

And it was okay. *It was okay.*

Logan's hand found Adrian's cheek, thumb stroking gently across damp skin. "Look at me," he whispered, not as a command, but as an invitation.

Adrian's eyes met his, wide, searching.

"That doesn't matter," Logan breathed. "Not to me. Not ever." He leaned down, pressing their foreheads together, breathing into the silence. "I feel you," Logan whispered. "Every time you touch me. Every time you kiss me. That's desire. That's love. And it doesn't need to be hard to be real."

He let the moment sit, let Adrian feel it, not just the words, but the weight behind them.

"There's nothing broken in you," he said softly. "You're still the man I want. The man I *choose*."

"I need this," Adrian murmured, voice low, rough with honesty. "Let me... let me make you feel good."

"Adrian, we don't—"

"Shhh." A kiss silenced him. "I need this," he said, voice low, raw with truth. "I need to make you feel good. I need to *give* you this. I want to touch you, okay?"

Logan nodded, his breath catching as Adrian's hand slid back to his cock, wrapping around him with deliberate tenderness. Adrian kissed him again, moaning softly into his mouth, not from his own pleasure, but from Logan's. As if Logan's ecstasy lived in his bones now.

Logan's hands gripped Adrian's ass, squeezing firm handfuls of flesh, grinding their bodies together with mounting need. Water splashed between them, steam rising around their skin like a veil. Adrian gasped, smiling against Logan's mouth, drunk on the sensation.

"Yes..." Adrian moaned. "Touch me. Please."

And Logan did.

He touched him the way lovers do, no fear, no apology. Not like a caretaker. Like a man who remembered every inch of Adrian's body and wanted to worship it all over again.

His hands slid up Adrian's back, down to his hips, his palms mapping the body he had missed for too long. He grazed Adrian's nipples, teasing until they hardened beneath his touch, then moved lower, down the swell of his ass, kneading the flesh, slow and thorough. His fingers teased gently at Adrian's entrance, not pressing in, just grazing, searching for a response.

Adrian moaned, loud and open, his head falling back. His own cock remained limp, twitching faintly between them, but that didn't matter. Not to Logan.

Because desire wasn't in the hardness of flesh, it was in the way Adrian's body arched into his touch, in the gasp he made when Logan teased him, in the way his hand moved over Logan's cock with growing intensity.

Logan saw it in his eyes. *The need was there.*

Not for orgasm. Not for dominance. But for closeness. For contact. For the right to feel like a man again, not in defiance of what he'd lost, but in honor of what he still carried.

After a moment, Adrian broke the kiss, breathless, lips swollen, eyes burning with hunger, not just lust, but need. Raw and unfiltered.

"Sit," he whispered, voice tight with urgency. His hand stilled on Logan's cock, and he looked up, pupils wide, cheeks flushed. "On the edge of the tub. Sit. I want to taste you."

Logan blinked at him, a brief flash of hesitation passing through his eyes. But then he saw the fire behind Adrian's request; this wasn't about sex, not only. This was about power, about *giving*, about Adrian wanting to *be a man* again, just for a moment, and Logan knew better than to deny him that.

Water cascaded off Logan's body as he stood and shifted, his skin slick and steaming. He perched on the edge of the tub, thighs parting instinctively, his cock hard and glistening in the dim light.

Adrian paused, just for a breath, to take in the sight of him. His soon-to-be husband. Strong, flushed, gorgeous. Waiting—for *him*.

And then, he didn't waste any more time, he knelt between Logan's legs, hands steady on his thighs, and leaned in. His mouth opened with devotion, and he took Logan in—slowly at first, the head, the shaft, inch by inch, until his lips stretched around him and the weight of Logan's cock filled his mouth.

Logan's moan cracked open the silence. One hand reached out blindly, gripping the edge of the tub, knuckles white. The sound of his pleasure echoed off the tiles, soft, helpless, real.

Adrian's head bobbed, his lips sliding over hot skin, tongue circling, throat working.

"Yes... baby," Logan moaned. "Fuck, that feels incredible."

The steam curled around them. Water lapped against the sides of the tub. And all the while, Adrian gave himself to the rhythm—focused, driven, not performing but *offering*, as if this act were a sacrament.

At that moment, he wasn't a patient. Wasn't fragile. Wasn't broken.

He was just a man, loving another man, in the most primal way he knew how.

Logan's breath grew ragged, hips twitching under Adrian's control. "I'm... I'm about to come," he gasped, voice hoarse.

Adrian didn't pull back. He didn't slow down. He swallowed around him, humming softly against Logan's skin, holding him there as Logan came, hot, sudden, and shuddering into his mouth.

Logan cried out, the sound breaking into a gasp, his whole body shaking as pleasure overtook him. His hand clutched Adrian's shoulder, grounding himself in that touch.

When it passed, when his breath returned, Logan sank back into the water, pulling Adrian with him, arms wrapping tightly around his lover's damp body.

"Damn," Logan panted, still breathless, pressing his lips to Adrian's temple. "That was... incredible."

Adrian buried his face in Logan's neck, his voice gravel-soft. "I needed that."

And he had. Not for orgasm. Not for validation. But for *wholeness*. For the quiet, sacred knowledge that even in the wake of everything, he could still love and be loved through his body.

They stayed in the tub until the heat faded, until the warm water turned cold around them. And even then, neither of them wanted to move, wanted to break the fragile spell that held them there, in that moment, where time didn't exist, where they had everything.

Eventually, they climbed out, shivering a little while drying off with fluffy white towels.

When they finally collapsed into bed, skin damp and hearts still racing, Logan pulled Adrian into his arms without a word. He wrapped himself around him tightly, like a man afraid the world might reach in and steal him away. His arms weren't just holding, they were anchoring.

They lay there, tangled under the soft breath of linen sheets, and spoke in hushed voices about the wedding. Logan's fingers toyed with the ring on Adrian's hand, spinning it slowly like a ritual.

They let fantasy envelop them, their whispers weaving through conversations about cake, suits, and the venue, bickering and compromising over trivial matters, as they laughed together. They debated how to blend Judaism and Christianity into their ceremony, as they envisioned and built their dream wedding.

"Old and gray," Logan murmured, voice thick with sleep and something heavier. "Right, baby? Old and gray."

Adrian smiled against his chest, his reply muffled but sure. "Old and gray, *ahuv sheli.*"

They kept talking, their words growing slower, softer. The kind of conversation that feels like dreaming out loud. Logan chuckled at something Adrian said, but Adrian's laughter had already begun to fade—blurring into whispers, into sighs, until eventually, silence settled in.

Sleep pulled Adrian under gently, his body relaxing into the curve of Logan's own, his breath evening out into a rhythm that Logan clung to.

Logan didn't sleep. Not yet.

He stayed awake, eyes open in the dark, watching Adrian with reverence. Memorizing the lines of his face, the soft rise and fall of his chest, the way his lips parted just slightly in sleep.

With infinite care, Logan lifted Adrian's hand and brought it to his lips, pressing a kiss to the silver ring on his finger—the ring that now meant *everything*.

"I love you," he whispered into the hush of the room, his voice barely more than breath. "I love you so much."

And as the night held its silence, Logan held Adrian tighter. As if he could keep time from moving. As if love alone could hold the world together.

But for some reason, the same threnody melody that had repeatedly filled Logan's chest during their separation began to echo once more after a long silence. Was it the haunting backdrop of impending melancholy? Could it be the ominous foreboding of eldritch sorrow to come? Did the universe possess secrets that Logan refused to acknowledge?

Epilogue

Logan,

And when all is said and done, when the flames of our love have smoldered into ashes, and only the ghost of our story lingers in the quiet corners of this world, I need you to remember this: I loved you. I loved you with a depth and a fury that could crack the bones of the earth, with a tenderness that softened even the sharpest edges of my soul.

I loved you so fiercely that without you, I unraveled. My existence became a hollow shell, an echo that had lost its source. My breath stumbled, lost in the labyrinth of my chest, and my heart—oh, my heart—it became a tide out of sync with the moon, crashing and pulling with no rhythm, a ripple swallowed by the deep. My blood turned to river stones, heavy and unmoving, and the colors of the world drained into shades of gray.

You were the sun that drew the tides of my being. Without you, I was a sea at low ebb, an expanse of barren sand and forgotten shells. But even as the world darkened around me, you were the ember, the glimmer of light in my dying sky. Your presence was the last warmth I felt, a soft glow that held back the cold.

In those final moments, when the world was fading and my body was slipping through the seams of time, you were there. You were the breath in my lungs, the beat in my chest, the melody that played softly at the edge of the silence.

You became my salvation, my lifeline, the thread that held me together as I frayed.

And when my time came, it was not death that claimed me. It was love—your love. It was the peace of your hands, the safety of your arms, the echo of your voice whispering me into the dark. You revived me, my love. You brought me back to life, even as I let go of it. You were the final note in my song, the soft hum that carried me into the quiet.

So when the ashes settle and the world moves on, promise me this: that you will carry the flame. That you will burn bright with the love we shared, that you will breathe and live and laugh for us both. And when you close your eyes, I hope you feel me there, in the space between heartbeats, in the soft rush of the tide, in the quiet moments where love still lingers.

Because my love for you is not bound by this life. It is the wind in your sails, the salt on your skin, the whisper of the ocean calling you home. It is eternal, infinite, and it will live as long as you do.

And when you finally join me, when our souls meet again on some distant shore, I will be there—waiting, still loving you, still burning for you, forever and always.

Yours forever,

In this lifetime and all the countless lives that await beyond,

Adrian.

July 10, 2026—North Shore, Oahu, Hawaii—Four Years Later

THE MORNING LIGHT SPILLED into the cabin like warm honey, stretching long golden arms across the floorboards, climbing the walls, breathing life into every grain of wood. It filtered through the shutters in narrow beams, illuminating the dust that hung in the air, turning it to something sacred. Outside, the ocean whispered low against the shore—steady, rhythmic, familiar—a lullaby only memory truly understood. There was salt in the air, and the faint scent of distant rain, the kind that never quite reached the earth but lingered in the clouds like a promise.

Logan lay still beneath the soft weight of the covers, his body cradled in warmth, in silence, in something that felt so much like a dream he was almost afraid to open his eyes. But he did, gradually, his eyes fluttering open to the wooden ceiling that loomed above, fixating on the same intricate knot in the beam—a knot he had gazed upon in a lifetime that felt like another world entirely. For a moment, he didn't move. He simply existed. In the quiet, in the weight of something unspoken, in the ghost of everything that had ever been lost and found in this place.

The ocean called to him from beyond the walls, not loudly, but intimately, like an old friend with a secret. The sound of it—the hush, the pull, the deep exhale—wove itself into his breath. Time moved differently here. Slower. Softer. More sacred. The kind of time that forgets to count itself.

He turned his head.

Nestled beside him in the crisp, linen-white sheets lay a tranquil figure, still lost in slumber. Golden tresses, like liquid gold, even in the gentle dimness of the room, cascaded across the pillow in soft, ethereal waves. A cheek rested delicately against the cool cotton, while long lashes fluttered in peaceful repose. Each breath, a quiet, deep rhythm, rose and fell, embodying the serenity of the untouched morning light.

Something pressed against Logan's ribs—a flutter, an ache, a sharp bloom of tenderness. He didn't reach out. Not yet. He only watched, his fingers curling slightly against the sheets as if anchoring himself to the moment. There was too much fragility here. Too much beauty to risk breaking.

Hadn't he already said goodbye to this once? Hadn't he stood in the ruins of it, chest cracked wide open, heart hollowed out by silence?

Yet this—this was not merely memory. It was not the whimsy of grief twisting reality. The sunlight enveloped him in its warmth, too inviting to be ignored. The breath that mingled with his was undeniably real, a tangible presence. The world around him pulsed with a vibrancy that could be nothing less than the essence of truth itself.

A small smile graced his lips as he watched the sleeping figure beside him. A profound sense of serenity enveloped him, accompanied by a whisper of happiness.

He rose from the bed, careful not to wake the figure still dreaming beside him. His feet met the cool wooden floor, grounding him. Each step was gentle, reverent, as if the cabin might sigh beneath him.

In the bathroom mirror, the man staring back at him was both someone he knew and someone who had lived a thousand lives since the last time he stood here, in this very cabin, on those same floorboards, gazing into the same mirror with the same name etched into his soul. The lines around his eyes were deeper, the sun had carved stories into his skin. His hair was shorter, and his gaze held weight—but not the weight of sorrow. Not anymore. It was something else now. Something steadier.

He splashed his face with cold water, letting it chase away the last shadows of sleep, and when he looked up again, his reflection didn't waver. He was here. Present. Whole.

He had looked into this mirror before; he remembered the cracks in the bottom left corner that were still there after all those years.

Returning to the bedroom, he paused at the threshold.

The figure in the bed hadn't moved much. His cheek was still tucked into the pillow, lips parted in sleep, the soft rise of his chest a quiet rhythm that had become Logan's favorite sound.

For a moment, Logan simply stood there. Watching. Remembering. Feeling. Letting the ache in his chest consume him and live inside of him. How many times had he watched another sun-kissed-haired man like this?

The cabin was exactly the same. The ocean still whispered the same song. Even the date, he realized, was almost exact.

The weight of memory pressed in again, filling the cabin like a tide rolling in.

Eight years ago, he had met him.

Eight years ago, in this very place, his life had changed.

Eight years ago, in this very place, Logan's heart had learned how to love.

Eight years ago, in the pull of a wave and the reach of another man's hand, Logan had been pulled back to shore, not just from the water, but from everything he'd been drowning in long before that day.

His gaze drifted across the cabin, landing on the kitchen counter. And suddenly, he saw it, the past unfurling like mist from the sea, vivid and tangible. So real, he half expected to see his younger self standing there, nervous and sun-flushed, getting ready for what would be known later as his first date with Adrian. Past Logan didn't know he was about to fall for a man whose smile felt like sunlight breaking over water.

Amid the morning mist and glimmering light, he could see them there, him and Adrian, leaning against the counter, young and sun-kissed, leaning toward each other with the magnetic pull that had been present from the very first moment. The air between them had been thick with it, that soft, crackling tension of two people standing on the edge of something neither of them dared name.

Adrian had looked at him with those whiskey-colored eyes, warm and endless, full of something dangerous and fragile and infinite all at once. His full lips, framed by stubborn dark stubble, had curved into a half-laugh at something stupid Logan had said, head tilted just enough to show he was listening. Really listening.

He saw Adrian's sun-kissed hair spilling down his back, his arms tanned and strong beneath his rolled-up sleeves, his whiskey-colored eyes burning with something Logan hadn't understood at the time—but oh, he did now.

He saw it all, felt it all.

Their laughter, overlapping, easy. The way Adrian had absentmindedly traced patterns against the countertop while they talked about traveling the world together. Their entire future stretched out before them, unformed and limitless, still untouched by loss, by fear.

Still untouched by the cruel hands of time.

And then—Logan glanced toward the bed.

For a breathless second, he could almost see young Adrian again, sprawled on his stomach, half-buried in the sheets, hair mussed and mouth curved in that sleepy smirk. Murmuring something about Logan's snoring. Teasing, soft, full of love.

Like nothing had ever gone wrong.

Like nothing bad had ever happened.

Logan swallowed hard.

The golden-haired figure stirred.

"Jay," Logan whispered the name of his heartbeat, as he sat on the edge of the bed and gently brushed the tousled strands from his face.

Big green eyes blinked open—sleepy and unfocused at first, then slowly warming, brightening. They looked up at him like he was home.

"Good morning, my love," Logan murmured, pressing a soft kiss to his forehead.

Jay stretched with a small groan, then his arms wound around Logan's waist as he pressed his cheek against his chest, clinging like a sleepy barnacle. That familiar, wordless affection undid him every time. Logan closed his eyes and just breathed him in.

"Are we going to surf?" Jay asked, his voice still raspy with sleep.

Logan let out a quiet laugh, his fingers combing gently through the soft gold of his hair. "Of course. But breakfast first," he said.

Jay groaned dramatically, rubbing his eyes with the back of his hand.

"Why don't you brush your teeth, and I'll make you something?" Logan offered.

Jay nodded with a sleepy hum and peeled himself away, slow and heavy-limbed, vanishing into the little bathroom with the sound of bare feet padding across the wooden floor.

Logan sat there for a moment longer, the room quiet again.

Exhaling, he dragged a hand over his face, fingertips brushing the corners of eyes that had weathered so many storms. His heart still ached, an ache that had settled into him long ago, a quiet companion he no longer tried to silence. It would never truly leave him, and that was a truth he had come to accept.

But sitting here now, in this cabin by the sea, with the gentle rhythm of another breath beside him and sunlight stretching across the floor like a blessing, he knew he was no longer alone.

Four years ago, he had believed grief would consume him whole. That it would pull him under like the riptide he once feared more than death. But love—God, love—had found a way to rise.

It had clawed its way back to him, even when he had stopped searching.

It had pulled him out of the dark.

It had brought him here.

Back to where everything had begun. Back to where Adrian had saved him, not just from the sea, but from himself.

He gazed out the window, where the waves crashed in a rhythmic dance, their wild melodies echoing softly against the glass. They moved with the same untamed, relentless spirit as on that first day. He watched the surf swell and fold, watched the light break across the water's back. The streams of water that had nearly taken him had also given him everything.

He stepped into the tiny kitchen. The air was thick with salt and morning, and something in it made his chest ache in that sweet, familiar way. He reached for the bowls, hands moving on instinct, quiet and sure. Cereal spilled against porcelain, followed by milk. He placed two spoons beside the bowls, the clink of silver gentle.

Footsteps padded softly across the floor.

Jay emerged from the hallway, sleep still clinging to his lashes, his golden hair a chaotic crown. Without a word, he climbed into the chair and began eating like he was making up for lost time.

Logan watched him, a quiet smile spreading across his lips, slow and full of wonder.

Jay. Jay was Logan's heartbeat in another body.

There was an abundance within him, a hidden beauty behind those soulful green eyes that had witnessed so much. They reminded Logan of a hazy sunrise, often masked by clouds yet always glowing, like sunbeams awaiting to warm a distant shore. His laughter came like thunder sometimes, his joy sudden and bright, his tears fast and whole. He was chaos and sunlight.

Logan reached for his spoon, but paused as his eyes caught the ink circling his wrist.

The tattoo, carved not in ink but in the marrow of meaning, was no mere adornment: it was elegy and augury, a psalm of scars, a litany of love and ruin. The script coiled round his flesh like a sacred ouroboros, a covenant etched in dolorous grace, binding what was to what shall be. Each letter burned with the afterglow of vanished things: a vow whispered through the wreckage, a hymn born of ash and breath. In that aching tread, where sorrow wore its ceremonial skin, lay a truth so resplendent it refused oblivion, a flame kindled here, in this very place, that outlived ephemera and named the only verity Logan's heart had ever dared to hold.

"So when the end draws near and life leaves you, I'll be here, waiting to save you."

Adrian's voice echoed in his mind, as clear as the night he first heard it and crushed and burned inside. The words had stayed with him, carved into his skin the way they'd been carved into his soul.

His gaze drifted away from the ink and the life saver bracelet that adorned his wrist to the silver glint of his wedding band, caught in the morning light. It rested quietly against his pulse, the very ring Adrian had slipped onto his hand the day they promised forever, against all odds, despite the darkness.

And then, without warning, the ache returned: a quiet deluge, blooming behind his sternum, rising like floodwater to the gates of his throat, not screaming, but insisting, insisting. It was the ache of a love too vast to hold, too woven into his bones to ever leave, blooming again in the quiet of a morning that felt too gentle to carry so much sorrow.

But he did not weep.

He did not let the grief spill over.

He had learned how to carry that ache with dignity, how to let it live beside him like a shadow that no longer haunted but simply remained; present, undeniable, part of the architecture of who he was now. And so, instead of giving into the tears pressing behind his eyes, he let his mind wander, let it drift like a surfboard on calm water, backward through time, toward the memory of their wedding, the moment they had stolen from the chaos, carved out like a sanctuary in a world that never promised them peace.

It had been a day unlike any other. The ocean had been their cathedral, the sky their witness, and the light had spilled over them in golden threads, as if the universe itself had bent to acknowledge what they had survived. There was just a small crowd of close family and friends, no spectacle, only the salt on their lips, the sand beneath their feet, and the raw, trembling honesty of two men who had lost everything and somehow still found their way back to each other. A modest altar stood nestled in the dunes, a soft fusion of tradition and defiance—a chuppah-by-the-sea, its pale fabric fluttering like sails in the breeze, adorned with handwoven flowers that swayed as though they, too, were bearing witness. Beneath it, a rabbi and a priest stood shoulder to shoulder, smiling quietly, sharing some small joke between them. Logan could barely register it. He saw only Adrian.

"I'll go first," Adrian whispered, brushing at his cheek with the back of his hand, his voice hoarse with held-back tears. "Otherwise, I'll break down halfway through."

He took Logan's hands, held them as if anchoring himself to the earth.

"Not many people get to say this," he began, his voice trembling like a struck string, "but I've lived all of my dreams." He paused, exhaled, the sea wind tugging at his shirt.

"You are all of them, Logan. Every single one. I will love you with every breath I have, for as long as I have. And I will spend that time—however much we're given—doing whatever I can to keep that smile on your face. You're my peace. My storm. My home. And wherever the streams of water decide to take us, in this life or the next, I will walk beside you, as your husband."

And Logan, already full to the brim with everything he couldn't say, could only nod as tears slipped down his cheeks, not from sorrow but from the unbearable weight of joy. To be loved like that. To love like that. It had been more than he ever believed he was allowed to have. "All my breaths, all my heartbeats—they're yours. Without you, breathing is just noise. Without you, my heart forgets its rhythm and stills. I will spend the rest of my life making your wishes come true," his voice trembled as he spoke, low and rough.

Adrian watched him through tears, lips parting around a breath, and mouthed the words softly. "You already have."

"I left us once," he said, shame a shadow in his tone. "I left you. And somehow, I was given another chance. To make it right. To show you what you are to me. Because, Adrian—you are everything."

"So when the end draws near and life leaves you, I'll be here, waiting to save you." The words left both their mouths in perfect unison, like a shared breath.

His eyes opened again, the present pressing gently against his skin, and he looked around the cabin.

That cabin.

And now, even in the hush of morning light, even in the stillness, the memories returned, not like ghosts, not like pain, but like waves that came to get him back. He saw Adrian in every corner, not just in this room but in the world they had built together, scattered across the globe like footprints in wet sand. He saw him in every shoreline, every mountain path, every passport stamp, every laughing photograph that still hung in his heart.

He remembered nights spent lying beside him, long before the words were ever spoken, before either of them dared to admit the magnitude of what they were falling into. He remembered floating beside him in the sea, their bodies moving like they belonged there, like they were made not just to ride the waves but to become part of them. He remembered the ridiculous dares in foreign cities, the sleepless nights tangled in unfamiliar sheets, the way they chased sunrises across continents, not because they were running, but because they believed—fiercely, stupidly, beautifully—that time could not touch them if they kept moving.

It had been a life of motion, of wildness, of wonder. They had fought, too, but even the arguments had been full of love, full of desperation, full of the fear that maybe they wouldn't get to keep this thing they had found, this rare, glittering miracle between them.

And then came the stillness. The years after Adrian had gotten sick had slowed the world to a crawl. Hospitals. Waiting rooms. The unbearable silence of test results. The soft, mechanical beeping of machines that tried to hold a life steady. But through it all, Logan had stayed. He had fought. He had begged the universe and then defied it. When Adrian could not find the strength to hope, Logan had lent him his. When Adrian gave up, Logan clung tighter. And somehow, impossibly, through a storm that should have ended everything, they had made it.

At least for a while.

And now... now, Logan sat in this cabin by the sea, and it felt like the past and present had collapsed into each other. It felt like he was back at the beginning, standing again at the edge of something he could not name. But it was different, too. Because now, there was Jay, breathing softly in the room where Logan had once learned to love. Jay, with sunlight in his hair like Adrian's, and that sly, crooked grin that Logan adored.

And even as Logan moved through the morning rituals, there was a weight in his chest that would never fully lift. Not grief. Not anymore. Something gentler. Something quieter. A kind of holy ache, a reverence for what had been, and what had miraculously, against all logic, endured.

Because Adrian had taught him how to love. Not just love as a feeling, but love as an action. As a rebellion. As a promise. He had taught him that the moon didn't need the sun to matter. That it could shine in its own soft light, and that sometimes, that light was enough to guide you home.

Across the table, Jay finished his meal, dropping his spoon with a clink before jumping from the chair, his body already filled with energy. He sprinted toward the bathroom, where his wetsuit hung from the day before.

Logan laughed under his breath, the sound rising up from somewhere tender and quiet, watching the echo of so many yesterdays dance across the floor.

Logan pulled on his board shorts, feeling the light fabric against his skin, a sharp contrast to the stiff, tailored suits he had worn for too long. He didn't mind it now; he didn't resent it anymore. He'd learned to respect the work, to own it. It gave him the means to provide, to protect, to build a life worth keeping. And in time, it gave him something else: a way back to his father. As they worked together, their bond grew stronger, and they both attempted to make up for lost time. The man had been hard, distant, but when Logan needed him most, he showed up. And now, years later, Logan carried that legacy with a pride he hadn't expected to feel.

He slipped a T-shirt over his head, stretching his shoulders with a contented sigh as the ocean breeze flirted with the soft fabric. Here, the air was lighter, and for a moment, the burdens of the world seemed to drift away.

"Jay," he called softly, reaching for his board, the waxed surface familiar beneath his palm, "you need sunscreen before we hit the water."

Jay reappeared like a burst of sunshine, swallowed by his wetsuit, clutching his little surfboard, which still looked too big for him, like it was a sword forged just for his tiny hands.

"No, Daddy," he said, chin raised in bold defiance, "I don't want to, it's sticky." His voice was tiny but full of conviction, the kind of adorable defiance that made it nearly impossible to argue.

Logan opened his mouth to protest, ready to make his case, but then that single word, so casual and yet so loaded, struck him with full force: *Daddy*.

It wasn't the first time Jay had said it, but somehow, it hit differently every time. Like sunlight breaking through a cloud-covered sky, sudden and disarming, the kind of sweetness that made his chest ache before the heart even catches up. He felt it settle into the space behind his ribs, warm and endless.

There was a time, not long ago, when he believed he had given his whole heart away to one man, that there was no more to offer, no room left to love anything else with that kind of ferocity. But then Jay came, and Logan realized that love was not finite, not a measured portion to be emptied once and for all, but an ever-expanding universe, making space where there was none, writing new constellations with every heartbeat.

He had loved Adrian—still loved him—with a depth that reordered the waves and defied the streams, with a force that taught him the language of gravity and devotion, of what it meant to be known completely. But this? This love for Jay was not lesser. It was not more. It was different. It was primal. Wordless. The kind of love that burrowed into his bones and reclaimed a home there. A love that was silent and screaming all at once, existing peacefully and all-consuming.

With a soft sigh, Logan shook his head, a smile pulling at the corner of his lips. "I got you a new one, that one is not sticky," he said, relenting like he always did, "we'll put it on at the beach. But you have to wear shoes."

Jay groaned in theatrical defeat but didn't argue. Instead, he dropped his board with a thud, flopped onto the wooden floor with all the drama of a performer taking his final bow, and began wiggling his feet into a pair of blue flip-flops. When he stood again, triumphant, he grabbed his board with both arms and marched toward the door, posture exaggerated, expression full of mischief, tapping his little foot with comical impatience.

Logan chuckled as he grabbed a small bag, tossing in the sunscreen, two bottles of water and Jay's beach toys before he tucked his wallet inside one of the bag pockets, leaving his phone behind. He didn't need it here. Didn't want it here.

"Daddy, come on! The waves are killin'!" Jay called, bouncing on his heels as Logan locked the door behind them. Jay grinned up at him, and Logan smirked, recognizing the phrase—his phrase—coming from his son's mouth. He probably picked it out from himself.

"Killin' waves, huh?" he said, ruffling Jay's hair, his voice thick with wonder. "What do *you* know about that?"

They walked hand in hand toward the beach, Jay's small fingers curled around Logan's in that unconscious, instinctive way that only children do, like it was the most natural thing in the world, like they had always belonged to each other, like his hand was the only place safety could live. Their steps sank into the sand with a rhythm that echoed somewhere deep in Logan's chest, a quiet drumbeat of something steady and sacred. The shoreline opened before them like a page being turned, golden and vast and endless. The waves rolled in smoothly and glassily, surfers dotted the lineup, the sun casting a silver fire over the water, scattering light across it until it shimmered like a living jewel.

And it was here.

Here, on this very stretch of sand, where the tide still kissed the shore with the same familiar hush. Here, where the salt in the air clung to the skin like memory. Here, where the wind spoke at the same rhythm it had always known. Here, where everything had changed.

This was the sacred place where Adrian had rescued him from the relentless grip of the sea, pulling him ashore through the turbulent waters. His breath had been stolen not solely by the water that day but also by the man who had reached into the chaos without knowing his name, diving unwaveringly after him, a stranger then, driven by a silent, desperate urge to save. Adrian hadn't understood at first, and perhaps it took a long while for him to truly realize, but in that fleeting moment, he had dove after something deeply intertwined with his soul.

Maybe Adrian's soul recognized his other half and lingered on the sun-kissed beach, longing and solemn. Perhaps it heard the distant cry of his counterpart and sprinted into the crashing waves, chasing the echo of what once was. And maybe... Logan's soul, too, sensed the stir of its missing piece, wandering with a fractured mind, pulled by an irresistible pull, carried far away from the familiar shores, straight into the embrace of the arms he'd waited a lifetime to feel again.

Maybe, on some profound level, the lost piece of himself was always Adrian's, the elusive reason behind Logan's hollow disconnect, his inability to forge bonds or feel deeply. Logan was adrift, uncertain of who he truly was, because his soulmate had existed on the other side of a distant world, unanchored and unbound, wandering through conflict and chaos.

Unbeknownst to both, they were each searching for the missing part—the fragment that completes their whole—destined to find each other across the void, bound by forces beyond understanding.

This was the place where Logan had first met his future, without knowing it, where hands on his chest had jump-started not just his lungs and his heart, but his soul too.

Where the missing pieces finally fell into place.

Something in Logan's chest tightened, ancient and immediate, but when he looked down and saw Jay, his hair catching the wind, his eyes wide with wonder, his joy pouring out of him like sunlight, there was no pain. There was only love. The kind of love that doesn't just heal wounds, but makes them sacred.

That managed to elicit beauty from the pain.

That had brought Jay, the brightest light, to his life.

"This is the best vacation *ever!*" Jay shouted, his voice breaking through the morning.

And Logan smiled—*God*, he smiled—because that joy was real, and because, for the first time in years, the ocean did not feel like a thief. It didn't feel like a reminder of what had been taken, of what had been almost lost. No, not today. Today, it felt like an offering. A return. A gift.

"Yeah, buddy," Logan murmured, his voice thick with something unspoken as he gave Jay's hand a gentle squeeze. "It really is."

They stepped closer to the edge of the world, feet sinking deeper into the sand, the water reaching toward them with every passing wave, like it remembered them too, like it had been waiting. The wind wrapped around them, warm and salt-heavy, carrying the scent of a hundred yesterdays, and Logan knew—*this* was home. Not a place, not a building, not even a beach—but a moment, a breath, a presence. This was what love became when it refused to die.

And then—

His heart fell silent, his soul sang.

His body lit up like it had been struck by lightning, every nerve waking in unison, his breath catching. Because there, rising from the water with the kind of grace that felt otherworldly, was a lone surfer stepping out of the sea like something the tide had returned to him. The sunlight caught him first, pouring over his shoulders in molten gold, illuminating every angle of his body—broad, tanned, and glistening—carved into the shape of someone who had never stopped moving, never stopped *fighting*. His board was tucked beneath one strong arm, water dripping in slow rivulets down his chest and stomach, down the long muscles of his legs to the edge of his black boardshorts, soaked and clinging to him like second skin.

And then—*his eyes.*

Whiskey-colored. Wide and warm. Familiar in a way that made the world tilt sideways.

They found Logan as they always had, without hesitation, without doubt, as if all this time had been nothing more than a pause between heartbeats. And there was no question in them. No fear. Only love. The kind that had survived cancer and silence and two oceans' worth of separation. The kind that knew the cost of being alive. The kind that *chose* again, even when it had every reason not to. The kind that burned with love for Logan like the hottest flames. The kind that bled Logan's names and molded his shape to his chest, and said his name like a prayer.

Logan's lips parted, breath caught halfway between disbelief and wonder, and his heart clenched—not from pain, but from the unbearable weight of joy. *That's my husband,* he reminded himself, blinking against the light that suddenly felt too holy to hold. *That's him.*

As Adrian approached, his steps quickening into a gentle jog to meet Logan halfway—almost as if their time together hadn't carved their familiar rhythm—Logan caught a faint glimmer of awareness. The surrounding beachgoers had turned, their gazes drawn by the quiet energy of the moment, watching silently. How could they not? Adrian's presence demanded it. The curve of his shoulders, the calm in his gait, the way he smiled like sunlight belonged to him. He was unforgettable. He always had been.

But Logan didn't care.

And neither, thank God, did Adrian.

"*Abba!*" Jay's voice shattered the stillness, high and bursting with light, his small body already in motion, legs pumping, arms outstretched. "Daddy, let's go to Abba!" His tiny surfboard dropped into the sand behind him, forgotten in his urgency, and Logan barely had time to react before Jay took off like a storm of joy, racing down the beach with a speed that only love could give.

Jay used the Hebrew word for "dad" for Adrian, a small thing that carried the world for Adrian. Logan remembered the first time Jay had said it, how Adrian had broken down, tears spilling freely, as he processed it.

Adrian's expression softened instantly, and without missing a beat, he ducked down, collecting Jay in his arms, murmuring that he missed him and how fast of a runner he was. He lifted him effortlessly, one arm wrapped securely around him, while the other still gripped his board.

Jay's little arms and legs wrapped around Adrian, clinging to him like a koala, his small hands gripping his shoulders.

"You went surfing without me," Jay huffed, his voice filled with playful accusation.

"Didn't want to wake you and Daddy," Adrian said, pressing a lingering kiss to Jay's forehead before his gaze shifted, landing on Logan.

The kind of gaze that always said more than words ever could.

"We have the whole day to surf together."

Logan closed the space between them, reaching up to cup Adrian's jaw as he leaned in for a kiss, his lips brushing against Adrian's; they were salty, warm, familiar.

"How dare you leave the bad so early on vacation?" Logan murmured, smirking against his lips.

Adrian chuckled, nuzzling their noses together. "Wanted to go and feel the water." He stole another kiss. "You two were sleeping so well, I couldn't wake you."

Logan exhaled, resting his forehead against Adrian's for a beat longer than necessary, his hands slipping over his husband's arms, feeling the shape of him.

Adrian was here.

Alive. With him.

Something he didn't dare take for granted.

"Daddy! Look at that wave!" Jay's excited scream shattered the moment, his head snapping toward the ocean where a set was rolling in, powerful and perfect.

Adrian and Logan turned, following his gaze, their expression shifting into one of playful scrutiny. "Hmm... those are too high for you, buddy," Adrian said.

Jay pouted. "I can do it."

"You will do it. One day." Logan promised, grinned, and Adrian set Jay down before ruffling his messy blond hair. "But for now, I have a very cool trick to show you."

Jay's entire face lit up. "What trick?" he asked.

"I'll show you in the water."

"Come on, Lo, let's go," Adrian called, removing the leash from his ankle. He stood barefoot in the sand, his sun-kissed hair damp from surfing earlier.

But Logan didn't move yet. Instead, he reached into the bag, pulling out the bottle of sunscreen and a water bottle, handing the latter to Adrian before turning toward the small, excited boy in front of him.

"Jay-Jay. Sunscreen first," Logan said, kneeling in the sand, watching as a deep frown formed on his son's tiny face.

Jay sighed dramatically but shuffled over, standing in front of Logan like a reluctant warrior facing his fate.

Logan grinned, smearing the cool white cream onto Jay's small arms, then down his legs, before Jay started squirming at the feeling. Logan took full advantage of the moment, fingers slipping to tickle his ribs, making the little boy shriek with laughter, wiggling in place.

"Daddy, stop!" Jay giggled, trying to break free.

"No can do, buddy, this is important," Logan said between chuckles, smoothing the last of the sunscreen over Jay's nose.

Jay pouted, but the moment Logan pulled his hands away, he grabbed his little board, kicked off his flip-flops, and bolted toward the water, screaming in excitement.

"Jay—wait!" Logan called, but the kid was already charging toward the waves, his tiny feet kicking up sand as he ran. Adrian dropped the bottle and took off after him, laughing as he chased after their son, the ocean calling to all of them like an old friend. Logan tore his shirt off and sprinted after them, meeting them both in the water as they grabbed a laughing Jay and helped him jump into the water.

Five-year-old Jay had entered their lives like a whisper at first, a distant echo of a child neither of them had met, spoken about in the past tense by strangers who had never known what he was capable of becoming. He had lost his biological parents in a devastating car accident when he was barely two years old, too young to remember their faces, too young to understand that the fragile world built around him had already shattered before he ever had the chance to walk steadily inside it. By the time he was three, the world had told him again and again that he was too much, that there was no place for him to be safely held. Five foster homes in less than one and a half years. Moved like furniture. Returned like a product that didn't meet expectations.

Logan still remembered the night that started it all. The night he and Adrian sat in the dim hush of their home, no TV, no distractions, only the soft breath of the evening moving around them. They had already survived so much; walked through fire, through grief, through the edge of death and back again, stitched themselves together in the quiet aftermath of war. And somehow, all of that hadn't broken them. It had deepened them. It had made their love something weightier, something urgent. In that quiet moment, as Logan gazed into Adrian's tired yet resolute eyes, he felt not fear of the uncertain future but a powerful clarity, an urge to shape, seize, and turn it into reality.

Nothing was promised. Not time. Not love. Not the luxury of waiting for the right moment. They had learned that the hard way. So instead of waiting, they decided to build. To begin.

"I want a family with you," Adrian had said softly that night, his voice trembling from the burden of how long he had held these feelings. He gently intertwined his fingers with Logan's, then brought them closer and kissed them reverently. "That conversation we had in Tel-Aviv... before everything began, before I started treatment, it never left me. I used to lie in the hospital and dream about that future. About a home. With... with a child. A life we could call ours. The whole dream... You know? Like... a place with a family, with you."

And Logan had known—without hesitation, without calculation, without fear—that he wanted the same.

So, they had made it happen.

They completed the paperwork, ensured all boxes were checked, and attended every course. They participated in interviews where strangers assessed them, underwent a background check and home study, and registered as foster parents. They also applied to adoption agencies and expressed openness to foster-to-adopt.

They wanted to be a family.

And then, on a warm July afternoon in 2024, the call came, like a prayer answered, like a soul that needed a home.

A voice, professional but tired, stretched thin with the burden of too many children and not enough hands to hold them all, spoke plainly: "There's a child." The caseworker had said. "A three-year-old boy, his name is Jayden."

By the time the call came, Jayden had already been placed in five different foster homes, and returned from every one of them. Passed along like a problem no one could solve. Moved from house to house like an afterthought, like something temporary, like a question mark no one wanted to answer.

"He has severe behavioral dysregulation," the caseworker had said over the phone, her tone clipped but not unkind. "He's highly emotional. He lashes out. Severe tantrums. He throws things, and sometimes hits. Families keep bringing him back. They say they can't handle him." She didn't sugarcoat it. She didn't try to soften the edges.

One quiet and certain glance passed between them. No words, only a shared breath that said *yes*. Their home was a threshold flung open to any child who needed a way in. They had rushed out that afternoon, hearts taut with hope and fear, to meet the child psychologist who knew Jayden's case better than anyone. Logan still remembers her gaze as she evaluated them, as if she were trying to determine whether they would be just another failure.

"He lost his biological parents before he was two years old. The accident was bad; it was a miracle that he survived it. But even before that, the environment wasn't stable. We don't have all the details, but we suspect his parents weren't equipped to raise a child. So, before the loss, there was chaos. Then he was pulled out of it abruptly, and he hasn't had a single consistent caregiver since. His system doesn't know what safety feels like. That kind of instability, it rewires everything. He's not trying to be difficult." The child psychologist explained. "His brain is just doing what it learned: fight, flight, freeze. When something upsets him, even something small, it feels like an emergency. That's how his body responds. He's a kid who's never had a reason to believe the world is safe."

Logan had sat in silence, the words landing hard in his chest. Next to him, Adrian's face had gone still, his eyes dark and unblinking. Logan took Adrian's hand in his and held it tightly as they learned more about Jayden.

Back then, he was just a child's name and a case file that read more like a map of wounds than a biography. A three-year-old boy who had already been rejected five times. Who had been taught—repeatedly—that he was too much. That his pain made him unlovable. That the harder he tried to be seen, the faster people turned away.

They'd heard the worst of it. The screaming fits, the violent outbursts, the way he shut down when anyone tried to touch him. But it wasn't the behavior that haunted them, it was what sat underneath it. That he had never known calm. Never known what it felt like to be chosen and *kept*.

That night, they came home hollowed out, utterly drained, stretched thin beneath the weight of hope. They sat side by side, barefoot and quiet, Adrian tucked against Logan, listening to the silence of the house they'd worked so hard to make feel like a home, and imagined a child who had never had one.

They cried for him.

Because they knew.

They knew what it felt like to be lost. To not know where you belonged, or if there was any place at all where you might land and stay.

So when they said yes, it wasn't out of impulse. And it wasn't charity. It was a choice. A conscious one. They weren't naïve. They weren't trying to save anyone. They just knew what it was to hurt, and what it meant to be met there.

They didn't go into it thinking it would be easy. And it wasn't.

And then they met Jay in a hospital.

He'd been assaulted by another child—older, bigger—in his most recent foster home, and no one had intervened in time. Jay had taken the full weight of it, every blow, every sharp word, every failure of the adults meant to protect him. And when it was over, they didn't hold the other boy accountable. Instead, they turned their judgment on Jay—called him difficult, said he was uncooperative, that he provoked the other children and refused to be kind. As if a child that small could be anything other than frightened. As if cruelty from the world had somehow taught him how to be cruel.

When Logan and Adrian walked in with the caseworker, they didn't know what to expect, only that nothing could prepare them for what they saw: a small figure curled tightly beneath a thin hospital blanket, fists clenched and tucked close to his chest, jaw set like stone, the way a fighter stays coiled even in sleep, ready to defend, ready to flee. His skin was marked with fading bruises, his body shrunken into itself, and his eyes, God, his eyes, far too old for someone barely three years old, eyes that held the weight of every disappointment he'd learned to expect.

The moment his eyes settled and registered the presence of strangers standing beside the caseworker he had come to know far too well, he snapped loose. It was as if his body recognized the pattern before his mind could catch up: new faces, more promises, more leaving. And he erupted.

Screaming. Kicking. Clawing the air like the only language he had left was resistance. He tried to bite the nurse who came in to check his IV. He screamed at Logan to leave, shouted at Adrian to go away, knocked over the toy someone had left on the bedside table without ever looking to see what it was.

He wasn't difficult. He wasn't violent. He was terrified.

Terrified in the way only children can be when the world has already broken its promises. He had learned early that nothing good lasted. That when someone came close, it meant they were about to disappear. That being wanted always came with conditions. That home had a short shelf life.

But Logan and Adrian—they didn't flinch.

They didn't recoil when he shouted or scrambled away from their voices. They didn't glance nervously at the caseworker when he threw the stuffed turtle they brought across the room and shouted a garbled curse they didn't even know he'd heard before.

Because they weren't afraid of him.

They weren't afraid of the sharp edges, of the anger, of the way he seemed to push at them just to see how far he could go before they vanished like everyone else. They had both worn armor like that. They had both lived inside bodies that didn't feel safe. They knew what it meant to be shaped by pain.

So they stayed.

They stayed when he refused to speak. When he ignored the snacks they brought. When he shoved the blanket to the floor and stared at them like he was daring them to keep coming closer. They stayed when the nurses asked if they needed a break. When the caseworker asked—more than once—if they were still sure.

That was it, in the beginning. Just that.

They stayed.

Not with grand gestures or endless reassurances, but with stillness. With presence. With the quiet, steady rhythm of people who understood that trust could not be coaxed, only earned—and only slowly. Days bled into weeks, and in that hush, in that space where no one asked too much and nothing was expected in return, something shifted.

Not in any way that would have been noticeable without close attention. But it was there, real, fragile, and impossibly brave.

His shoulders, once locked like armor, began to soften, to settle. The tight fists that had curled against his ribs loosened their grip. His eyes, wary and restless, flicked briefly toward Adrian, then Logan, then dropped again to the wrinkled blanket tangled at the foot of his bed.

They offered him another toy—gentle, uncomplicated, a soft blue dolphin with stitched eyes and worn velvet skin. He took it wordlessly, held it for half a heartbeat, then flung it hard across the room. It hit the wall with a dull thud, bounced once, and came to rest near the window. Adrian said nothing, only picked the dolphin and placed it gently on a chair beside the stuffed turtle Jayden had rejected days before.

And then—almost imperceptibly—he looked up.

His voice, when it finally broke free, was raw, sandpaper-thin, as if it hadn't spoken gently in far too long. "Are you leaving, too?"

The words didn't rise like a question. They landed like a wound. Quiet, direct, devastating.

Logan felt Adrian draw in a breath beside him, the kind that meant something was breaking inside. Logan reached forward slowly, lowering himself into the plastic chair next to the hospital bed, steady as he could manage.

"No," he said, voice even, clear.

"Never, Jayden," Adrian added, crouching beside him, his eyes fixed on the boy who had just handed them his deepest wound.

"My name's Jay," he said, barely above a whisper.

It was the most he had said to them in the three weeks since they'd first walked through that door. And somehow, it felt like more than just a correction; it felt like a reclamation.

Logan's face softened. "That's a beautiful name."

Jay looked at him—eyes wide, searching, blinking once, twice—but said nothing.

"I'm Logan," Logan offered, gently pointing to himself, keeping his movements slow, careful. "And this," he gestured toward Adrian, "is Adrian."

Adrian gave him a warm smile.

"You want to color with us?" he asked, reaching into his bag and pulling out a thick coloring book lined with cartoons and wild shapes, then unzipping a pouch overflowing with markers and colored pencils.

Jay's gaze fell on the pencils, and for a long moment, he just looked, eyes filled with curiosity. Then he nodded.

But he started watching them longer. Holding onto the toys they brought. Sleeping with the green stuffed turtle clutched to his chest. Waking before dawn to wait by the door, just in case they came.

And slowly, the questions started to come, in the form of uncertain words.

"Are you together?"

"But you're both boys."

"Where are you going?"

"Will you come tomorrow, too?"

It was slow. Uneven. Sometimes forward, sometimes back.

But with the quiet guidance of the caseworker, and the steady, patient hands of the psychologist and psychiatrist, Logan and Adrian stayed.

Every single day, they returned. No skipped visits. No broken promises.

They brought small gifts, not the kind that overwhelmed or asked for anything in return, but tokens that made the sterile world around him a little softer. A puzzle. A book about the ocean. Adrian's favorite blanket, still scented faintly like home. A ball for the courtyard. Small things. Steady things.

They sat with him in stiff plastic chairs, kept their voices low, and either played random games or watched cartoons when he was too tired. They didn't press for words or affection. They simply watched. Waited. And when Jay inched slightly closer, when his fingers brushed the edge of Logan's sleeve or curled, tentative, around Adrian's wrist as they handed him a juice box, they noticed, but they didn't make it into something more than it was. They let him decide how much he gave. And when he said nothing, they didn't try to fill the silence. They just stayed. Day after day, visit after visit, letting time do what pressure couldn't. And slowly, almost imperceptibly at first, the edges began to soften. The walls cracked, not in collapse, but in the way that lets light seep through.

Then, just when things had begun to shift, Jay was moved again. Transferred to a children's psychiatric unit for further evaluation and treatment. It was protocol. Necessary. But to Jay, it was just another abandonment.

Logan still remembered the moment he was told. How Jay had clung to the stuffed turtle, silent and stiff, his small face gone blank, not angry, not defiant, just... *guarded*. As if he already understood that this was what had happened. That once he let his guard down, he got left behind again.

They accompanied him through the transition, walking beside the caseworker into a new ward, with new walls and new rules. Adrian gripped Logan's hand so tightly that the blood had stopped moving through his knuckles. And when it was time to leave—they didn't.

They stayed.

All day. Until the sky darkened and the hallway lights buzzed low. Until Jay's eyelids began to flicker with exhaustion and his little body started leaning against the bed like he couldn't keep himself upright anymore. And even then, before leaving, they promised that they'd be back first thing in the morning.

And they were.

Again. And again.

The caseworker watched. The psychologist took notes. Jay began to respond. With small signs. He no longer flinched when Logan walked through the door. He stopped shoving Adrian's hand away when he tried to help him with a zipper. More questions came.

"Will you be here tomorrow?"

"Can I keep this?"

"Do you have to leave yet?"

"Can we go play outside?"

And with the caseworker watching, assessing how Jay responded to them, and trusting them, they slowly became his people.

They waited for official approval. It took a lot of navigating the systems and signatures, making the case that they wouldn't be another stop on the way to nowhere. And during that time, they just kept showing up.

They watched Jay begin to test them, not out of malice, but out of history. Waiting for the moment they'd pull back. Waiting for love to expire. And when it didn't, something in him began to shift.

And then—finally—the day came.

Jay stepped out of that hospital ward holding onto that turtle like it was the last stable thing in the world, with a small, worn backpack that contained his small belongings, things he had from previous foster homes. When Adrian offered his hand, Jay took it. Not with confidence, but with the kind of quiet desperation that meant *he wanted to believe*. And when his fingers closed around Adrian's, tight and trembling, Logan had to turn away for a second, because something in him couldn't quite hold the weight of that gesture.

Logan assisted him into the car seat and secured the straps of his booster seat, gently maneuvering his fingers around the tightly clenched turtle.

He wasn't the boy they had been warned about.

He wasn't angry. He wasn't wild. He wasn't defiant.

He was scared. He was quiet. He was trying.

A year earlier, Logan and Adrian had bought a house outside the city—a place that wasn't temporary, that wasn't a waiting room or a halfway point. It was a home meant for a *family*. They hadn't known what the future would look like when they bought it, only that they wanted one. And now, Jay was part of it.

They showed him his room, being careful not to overwhelm him. A small bed, a desk, a few shelves. Nothing overstated. A few toys. A couple of books. And Adrian, kneeling beside him, had said gently, "You don't have to like any of this. We'll go shopping. You can pick what you want. Whatever makes you feel like this is yours."

Jay had nodded, barely, his green eyes scanning the space. But what lit up his face wasn't the toys, or the bed, or the books. It was the room itself. The fact that it was his.

That night, after they tucked him in—blanket pulled up to his chin, hair smoothed back with the lightest touch—and read him a bedtime story, Jay whispered something into the dark. So soft Logan almost missed it.

"No one ever did that before."

And Logan, who had spent years learning how to hold steady through grief, barely made it down the hall before he collapsed into Adrian's arms and let himself fall apart.

It wasn't easy.

Those first nights were long. Jay cried, sometimes uncontrollably. He screamed in his sleep. He sat bolt upright at two a.m., his eyes wide, waiting for the other shoe to drop. Some nights, he didn't sleep at all. Just sat there, silent, staring at the door like he was memorizing it in case he had to run.

He had regular visits with the caseworker. Ongoing therapy with a child psychologist, twice a week, sometimes more. Logan and Adrian learned more about trauma than they ever thought they would. They adjusted. Recalibrated. Failed. Tried again.

One night, Logan woke to the light brush of a small hand against his arm. He sat up instantly, heart jolting, eyes adjusting to the dark.

"What happened?" he asked softly, leaning toward the little figure at the edge of the bed.

Jay stood there, clutching the stuffed turtle tight to his chest, his eyes red and swollen, his cheeks streaked with tears, a thin line of snot trailing from his nose.

"I had a bad dream," he whispered, voice cracked and wet.

"Oh, buddy... come here." Logan opened his arms, and Jay folded into them without hesitation, pressing his face into Logan's chest as his small body trembled.

Logan held him close, rubbing circles on his back, whispering quiet reassurances. "It was just a dream. You're safe now. Nothing's gonna hurt you."

After a while, when the shaking slowed and the sobs faded into hiccups, Logan reached for a tissue and gently wiped Jay's face, brushing the damp hair back from his forehead.

"Do you want to sleep with us tonight?" he asked, keeping his voice even and soft. "I'll keep watch over the bad dreams."

Jay nodded without a word, still sniffling.

"Okay," Logan said with a smile, lifting him carefully and settling him between himself and Adrian, who stirred only slightly at the shift.

Logan turned on the small night lamp on the dresser, casting a warm, golden glow across the room, then tucked the blanket around Jay's tiny frame. The turtle was still in his arms, gripped tight like a lifeline.

And after that, most mornings, before the sun even rose, Jay would crawl into their bed without a word, his small body slotting between theirs like it belonged there, seeking closeness, warmth, the kind of safety that only existed in the dark when no one was watching. Other mornings, he would shadow them through the house, never straying too far, his green eyes scanning the room to make sure they were still there, still real. That kind of trust didn't come in declarations, it came in footsteps, in glances, in the quiet decision to stay close.

There were moments Logan held onto from those first few months like touchstones. The first time Jay smiled without hesitation, wide and unguarded. The first time he laughed so hard his whole body shook, collapsing in on himself like the sound had startled him. The first time he reached up—small fingers grabbing onto Adrian's shirt, holding tight—instead of pulling away. Those memories stayed with him. Soft, steady reminders of the bond they were building, of Jay's life with them.

But there was another memory. One that didn't feel like a milestone. One that carved itself into Logan's mind with the permanence of a scar.

It happened during the second week Jay had come home.

Logan had gone into the office that morning, just briefly, only for a meeting he couldn't reschedule. He had left reluctantly, checking his phone every ten minutes, stomach tight with guilt, even though Adrian had reassured him that everything would be fine. When he got home around midday, the house was quiet, too quiet, and Jay was already asleep—curled up in his bed, arms tucked in close, the stuffed turtle held tightly to his chest.

His sleep schedule back then had been unpredictable. Some nights he didn't sleep at all—his body buzzing with something he couldn't explain, pacing from room to room like he was afraid the floor might vanish under his feet. Other nights, he would crash without warning, his limbs heavy with exhaustion, worn out from the sheer effort of making it through the day.

That afternoon, Logan had peeked into his room, smoothing a hand gently over his messy blond hair, careful not to wake him. Jay hadn't stirred. So Logan had stepped out, letting him rest.

And then, later that evening—

The screaming started.

Logan had never moved so fast in his life. Adrian was right behind him, both of them running toward the sound like instinct had taken over. They reached Jay's room in seconds, and what they found stopped them cold.

Jay was thrashing in his bed, tangled in the sheets, his tiny body slick with sweat. He was clawing at the blankets, at the mattress, at the air, like he was trapped in something they couldn't see. His eyes were wide open but wild, not registering the room around him, not seeing them. And the sounds—those screams—were guttural, raw, torn straight from somewhere deep inside him. There was no fear like that in adults. That kind of terror only lived in children.

"Jay!" Logan called out, already stepping forward.

But the second they came too close, Jay lashed out, his fists flying, his heels kicking at the mattress, his back pressed hard against the headboard like he was trying to disappear into it. He sobbed so hard his breath came in hiccups, his voice breaking apart in pieces, not words but noise. Panic made him smaller. Not quieter—*smaller*. As if he were folding in on himself, trying to vanish.

Adrian raised his hands slowly, carefully, his voice soft, low. "It's okay. You're safe. No one's going to hurt you."

But Jay couldn't hear that. Not yet.

He wasn't okay.

He was terrified. Cornered. Lost inside something he didn't have language for.

"No!" he screamed. "No!" he yelled again as they started to cross the threshold into the room.

And Logan, watching him come apart, had never felt more helpless in his life. No amount of training or love or hope had prepared him for this—the harsh reality of a child who was so afraid of being loved, so traumatized in his brief life, carrying that sorrow and pain within him.

He didn't know what to say. He didn't know what Jay needed. He just knew they couldn't force their way in.

So they didn't.

They didn't leave. They gave him space, but not distance.

They sat just outside his bedroom door, backs to the hallway wall, close enough to be seen but not felt. And for what felt like hours, they waited. Not speaking. Not moving. Just there. A silent declaration in the quiet: *we're not going anywhere.*

Inside, Jay screamed until his voice cracked, until the sobs gave way to gasping silence, until the fight in his body drained out like breath leaving a balloon. He thrashed until his limbs gave up, until his shoulders slumped forward and the trembling took over. Until there was nothing left but the aftermath of fear and exhaustion, curled in the chaos of his sheets.

And then he moved.

Not much. Just a shift. A step. But it was careful. Cautious. The way someone walks through a house they don't believe they're allowed to be in. He came toward them like a child approaching something dangerous. Like he already knew how this was supposed to end. Like this was the moment they gave up. Like he'd seen it play out a dozen times before, in other rooms, with other people, and now he was just waiting for the pattern to repeat.

Logan couldn't breathe.

He didn't speak. Didn't flinch. He just opened his arms.

He stayed there, knees pulled in, arms wide, heart open, eyes stinging, chest aching—waiting, offering.

Jay stood still, silent, eyes darting between them. His fists curled at his sides. His lower lip quivered.

And then—he ran.

Straight into Logan's arms, fast and desperate, afraid the moment might vanish if he hesitated. Logan caught him, crushed him close, wrapped both arms around him and held on as Jay collapsed into him, burying his face against Logan's chest, his entire body still shaking with the aftershocks of too much grief, too much fear, too much *everything*.

And then Adrian was there too, arms encircling them both, drawing them into one tight, unbreakable hold. Logan pressed his lips into Jay's hair, Adrian's hand traced slow circles down his back, and the three of them sat there in the half-darkness, breathing together, tethered not by words but by the undeniable truth of presence.

"They take me away," Jay whispered, voice raw and almost too soft to hear. "I dream they take me away again." The words shattered something in the silence.

"No matter what you do," Logan said, voice cracked at the edges, his hand firm and gentle at once, "no matter what happens—"

"You're not going anywhere," Adrian finished.

Logan kissed his forehead, rocking him back and forth slowly. "From this day forward, you're ours. Okay? This is your home. Just as much as it's ours, it's yours too."

Jay didn't respond. He didn't nod. He didn't speak.

He just held on tighter.

And Logan knew. Without question, without hesitation, without any doubt at all.

They would never let him go.

Time moved forward.

At some point, things just... became normal.

Jay started pre-school. It had taken time—weeks of catch-up at home, learning the basics most kids his age took for granted—but when the day came, he walked in without delay, his backpack too big for his small frame, his eyes wide but steady.

He made friends. Real ones. The kind he laughed with until he was breathless. The kind whose crayon drawings—dragons, stars, lopsided houses—were proudly taped to his bedroom wall, always a little crooked. The kind who shouted his name from across playgrounds and invited him over after school just to play and be loud and be kids.

He had a bedtime now. He had a favorite snack. He had inside jokes with Adrian, silly routines with Logan, and a way of running through the house, feet pounding the floor, voice echoing down the hallway, belonging carved into every corner.

His playful side bloomed with ease: loud, full of mischief, always curious. But when it was time to sit down, to sound out words or finish math problems, he could ground himself, grumbling, maybe, but doing the work.

Their house slowly stopped feeling like a question mark and began to become just another home on the street. Not the one with the troubled foster kid. Not the one with the complicated story. Just a house where a kid lived. With two parents. With pancakes on Sundays and lost homework under the couch cushions.

Logan found himself sliding back into work with his father, preparing quietly for the day when he'd step in fully, when his dad would finally retire. There had been a time when the idea of that—of boardrooms and spreadsheets and carrying someone else's name—had felt like a cage. But it no longer felt that way.

Not with this life waiting for him at the end of the day.

Not with Jay's voice echoing down the hall, asking him to play or help with math homework or tie the knot in a surf leash.

Not with Adrian's hand in his, steady as ever.

This was it.

Not the end of the story.

But the part where it all began to settle.

Adrian had gone back to studying, piece by piece, pushing through coursework, lectures, and long nights of reading—quietly rebuilding parts of himself that had gone unused for too long. He earned his certification through the National Academy of Sports Medicine and soon began training clients, first at a local gym and then privately at their homes.

When the idea of opening a small studio was discussed, Adrian hesitated. He didn't want to live off Logan's money, not after everything Logan had already given him.

But one day, Logan pulled him aside and said gently, "I know you've got the whole proud thing going on, and I respect that. I do. But you're not applying for a loan when your husband makes more money than he knows what to do with—"

"But—" Adrian began.

"Shh." Logan kissed him. "You want to open a studio, and you should. So let me help."

"Maybe as a loan—"

"We're married, Adrian. We share a bank account." Logan said it slowly, as if he were explaining gravity to a six-year-old.

"I'll pay you back."

"You'll be paying *yourself* back," Logan replied, amused. "Any profit goes into *our* account."

"But the money in there is—"

"Shh," Logan said again, kissing him a little firmer this time. "I'm proud to be a provider. I'm proud I get to take care of you. Stop spinning this into something it's not. We're married. Get that through your thick skull."

Adrian smiled, finally letting the fight go. "Okay."

"Good," Logan said, reaching for his keys. "Now let's go pick up Jay. My mom's waiting on us for lunch."

The studio was modest but deeply personal. He focused on veteran clients, offering trauma-informed fitness and Krav Maga training rooted in his own military background. Adrian had reached out to local shelters and youth organizations, offering low-cost and free sessions for LGBTQ youth, a space where kids could move, sweat, and feel safe in their own skin, no questions asked. He wanted them to know what it felt like to be welcomed without hesitation—to belong without needing to earn it.

And through it all, Jay grew.

At first, he called them by their names.

"Logan."

"Adrian."

And that was fine. That was expected. Trust doesn't arrive with a title—it arrives slowly, after enough days pass without doors slamming or footsteps retreating. They hadn't minded. They would've waited forever. But somewhere along the way, without anyone really noticing the moment it happened, something shifted.

Jay started calling them Dads.

Not in ceremony. Not in a big reveal. Just... quietly. Tentatively. Like he was trying on the word to see how it felt in his mouth. The first time it happened, Logan had been sitting on the couch, a book half-finished in his lap, while Jay—sleepy and warm from the day—was curled up between them, his head tucked beneath Logan's arm, his fingers absently twisting the hem of his shirt while some kids' movie played in the background.

"Daddy?" Jay had murmured, eyes shut, his voice gentle with sleep.

Adrian and Logan paused, unsure who Jay was addressing, but it didn't matter.

They exchanged glances, silently savoring this moment.

"Yeah, buddy?" Adrian had whispered, being cautious not to disturb the spell surrounding them.

Jay had simply mumbled sleepily, "I'm thirsty."

But that was the beginning.

After that, the word began to find its way into sentences. Slipped out naturally. Softly. With time, it stopped sounding like something borrowed and started sounding like the truth.

And then, one evening, ordinary and unremarkable, the three of them sitting around the dinner table, Logan had looked up at Jay mid-conversation, smiled gently, and said, "You know, Adrian also speaks Hebrew. In Hebrew, kids call their dads Abba. You can use it. That's how Adrian calls his dad."

Jay's eyes had gone wide, round and bright like Logan had just given him a secret he hadn't known he was allowed to keep.

"Abba?" he repeated, testing it.

Adrian had stilled completely, his fork suspended midair, his eyes locking onto Logan's like he wasn't sure whether to laugh or cry.

"Yeah," Logan said, grinning. "It means Dad in Hebrew."

Jay beamed. Not just smiled—*beamed*. And the very next morning, when he came shuffling down the hallway in his dinosaur pajamas, hair flattened on one side, rubbing the sleep from his eyes, he yawned and said it without hesitation:

"Abba."

Adrian lost it, and Logan had barely managed to tug him into the kitchen before Adrian collapsed into him, burying his face in Logan's chest, his hands gripping his shirt like he needed something to hold onto.

"He called me Abba," Adrian choked out, breath hitching, tears spilling quietly down his cheeks.

"Yeah, baby," Logan whispered, kissing his temple, holding him steady. "He did."

From that day on, it became a rhythm, a truth as natural as sunlight.

Adrian was Abba.

Logan was Dad.

Sometimes Daddy.

And together, they were home.

A sudden splash and the sharp, familiar sound of Jay's laughter pulled Logan out of the memory and back into the present. The ocean gleamed under the late morning sun, gold spilling over the rolling waves like the sky had tipped a jar of honey into the sea. The breeze carried warmth and salt, curling through Logan's hair as he watched Jay tumble off his board with a shriek of delight.

He resurfaced a second later, grinning widely, shaking the seawater from his hair, splashing water all over. The ocean had claimed him the way it once claimed Logan, the way it claimed Adrian.

And here, on this shore—on the very beach where everything began—it felt like everything had come full circle.

Logan felt the past crash into him, uninvited, dragging him back and forth through memory. The years apart, the pain, the silence, the ache of wanting and not having, it had been another kind of drowning.

But now, standing in the ocean, salt clinging to his skin, his husband beside him and their son laughing as he jumped in and out of the water, it felt like everything they had endured had led to this. Like this moment—this small, golden sliver of joy—was what they'd been swimming toward all along.

Jay clung to Logan's shoulders, shrieking with laughter, as Adrian guided the board across the surface of the water, making over-the-top sound effects—low rumbles, crashing whooshes, dramatic wipeout noises—that sent Jay into another fit of giggles, his head thrown back in wild delight. "Hold Daddy tight!" Adrian called, grinning, and Jay's small hands gripped Logan's shoulders with all his might as the board sped forward. In perfect rhythm, Logan lifted Jay into the air, letting him ride the rise like it was a real wave, his laughter rising above the wind. Then, with a dramatic dive, Logan dipped him into the water before pulling him back up, soaked and beaming, as Adrian cheered them both on like it was the greatest performance he'd ever seen.

And then Jay turned toward them, face glowing, eyes lit up with something fierce and bright and completely his own.

"I wanna do it alone this time!" he shouted, gripping his board.

Logan and Adrian exchanged a glance, the same one they'd shared a hundred times before—quiet agreement, soft understanding—and nodded. They didn't let him go into the deeper water, of course. That wasn't the point. They walked with him to the edge, where the sea barely touched his ankles, the kind of surf that only looked big if you were five.

"Water break first," Logan announced, crouching beside him and holding out the bottle, waiting until Jay drank enough before handing the board back to him. Only then did they step back, giving him space, but not distance. Always close. Always watching.

They stood where the sea met the land, where the tide curled in around their feet and the horizon stretched open and endless before them. Jay stood ahead of them, small but fearless, ready to face the waves on his own terms.

Logan dropped down into the sand, stretching his legs out toward the water, letting the sun press into his skin. He drank from the bottle, then passed it wordlessly to Adrian.

Adrian sat next, settling between Logan's legs, his back pressing against Logan's chest like it was the most natural thing in the world, because it was. Logan wrapped his arms around Adrian's waist without hesitation. The way the tide always pulls the sand. The way love, when it's real, doesn't ask permission to stay.

Adrian leaned into him, his head tilted just enough to rest on Logan's shoulder, the weight of him grounding Logan more than any shoreline ever could.

They stayed like that, in the soft breath between waves, watching their son chase the sea.

With a gentle touch, Logan turned Adrian's face toward him, his fingers brushing along the familiar curve of his jaw, tracing the sun-warmed skin with a reverence that hadn't dulled, not after all this time. "I haven't even had a chance to give you a proper good morning kiss," he murmured, voice low, roughened by affection, though his gaze flicked toward Jay, who was still just a handful of steps away, completely absorbed in "surfing" ankle-deep waves like they were towering giants.

Adrian chuckled, the sound soft but deep, a vibration that rolled through Logan's chest where their bodies touched. "Well," he said, leaning in, his voice laced with that quiet mischief that always made Logan ache, "that's just unacceptable."

And then their lips met.

The kiss was deep, slow, *intentional*—the kind of kiss that wasn't about heat but about memory, about presence, about *everything* they had weathered to get to this morning on this beach, alive and whole and together. Logan's hands came up to cradle Adrian's face, thumbs brushing the sharp edges of his cheekbones, anchoring them both in the moment. Adrian melted into him, one hand braced on Logan's thigh, the other curling behind his neck as their mouths moved in a rhythm only they knew—an echo of years, of silence, of reunion.

Logan cut the kiss for a moment, still holding Adrian's face and just looked at him, eyes dazed, and he bit his lips as he took him in. "God," he murmured and crushed their mouths again. He kissed him like it had been months, not seconds. Like something hungry had lived in his chest too long and finally, *finally*, was being fed. His mouth crashed into Adrian's, fierce and open and claiming, as his hand slid into the back of Adrian's hair, pulling out the hair tie and letting his hair cascade around him like water. Their lips parted as one, and Logan surged forward, his tongue sliding into Adrian's mouth, tasting him, coaxing his tongue into a slow, circling dance, until every cell in his body thrummed with the electric joy of contact.

Adrian gasped into it—just a sound, but it made Logan groan, deep in his throat, as he tilted his head further back and kissed him harder. Deeper. Their tongues slid together, hot and slick, and Logan felt Adrian melt into him, the tension in his body dissolving as he leaned back fully, letting Logan take. Letting him *have*.

There was nothing tentative about it.

This wasn't careful.

Logan completely owned him.

Adrian kissed back like fire, mouth open and desperate, matching Logan's intensity beat for beat. Their bodies shifted with it, with the friction of memory and want, of *you're mine* and *don't you dare stop*.

And when they finally broke apart—panting, lips swollen, foreheads pressed together, eyes heavy with something too deep for words—Logan didn't move.

He just looked at him.

At his husband. His partner. His miracle.

"That is a good morning kiss," Logan murmured, voice hoarse.

"That was... a kiss meant for the bedroom, ahuv sheli, not for public display." He whispered in reply, his cheeks reddening as Logan ran his tongue over his lips.

"You're salty," Logan murmured, and then the words unraveled, for once again he lost himself in Adrian's gaze, in that golden whiskey catching the sun, amber burning like scripture. Once he had sought solace at the bottom of a bottle; now he was drunk all over again, not on the liquor, but on the fathomless fire of those eyes.

Logan would never forget the words that gave him his love back, the words that struck like thunder and yet whispered like grace: *in remission*.

In those syllables surged a thousand shocks of resurrection, a jolt that tore through marrow and vein, igniting every hidden chamber of his heart. That sentence was no mere diagnosis; it was a benediction, a reprieve, a promise that Adrian would remain.

It was September 2022. They had sat trembling before Dr. Tierney, lungs locked and hands trembling. Then he smiled, almost gently, and spoke: "The scans are clear, your counts are steady, the biopsies came back negative." And with that, Adrian was declared "in remission."

The world, which had been holding its breath with them, finally exhaled.

Logan remembered sitting there, staring at Dr. Tierney, his breath caught in his throat, the taste of forever, of life with Adrian on his tongue. It was surreal, like the moment before a wave crashes, the heartbeat of silence before the rush of water takes you under.

He had turned to Adrian, wide-eyed, as if waiting for permission to believe it. But Adrian just smiled, his eyes shimmering like the sea under the afternoon sun, and with a quiet certainty, there was so much hope there. "You beat cancer?" he asked Adrian.

"We beat cancer," Adrian corrected.

It was a simple correction, but it carried the weight of the universe. *We.* Not *I*. Because they had fought this together, every moment of pain, every sleepless night, every uncertain breath. Adrian had battled the disease, but Logan had been there, holding him through the storms, tethering him to the light when the darkness tried to swallow him whole.

It wasn't perfect. There were still months of hospital visits, ongoing medications, and follow-up treatments aimed at reducing relapse risk and protecting the new marrow. The path after the transplant was rarely smooth, but each test offered a moment of relief and a fragile hope that he might finally be safe.

And then, two months later, on November 12th—*Logan's birthday*—Adrian gave him the greatest gift of all. They had their wedding ceremony. There was something almost poetic about Logan's birthday, a day that had marked so many turning points in their lives. The day he had run from the greatest love he'd ever known, terrified of its depth, only to realize later that love had already drowned him in the most beautiful way. And now, it was the day he vowed to never run again. The sand was warm beneath their feet, and the ocean sang its eternal song in the background, waves kissing the shore like a lover's promise.

"So when the end draws near and life leaves you, I'll be here, waiting to save you."

"Happy birthday, ahuv sheli," Adrian added, his voice carrying over the wind, the waves, the heartbeat of the world.

The morning air was thick with the scent of salt and sun-warmed sand, the ocean stretching before them in endless ripples of blue and gold. Adrian lay against Logan, their fingers woven together, bodies tangled in the warmth of the rising sun. The waves whispered secrets to the shore, retreating only to return again, like lovers who could never truly part.

"Today, we're moving to a new hotel," Adrian murmured as he traced idle patterns on Logan's arm, the way water carves stories into the sand. "Right?"

Logan hummed in response, pressing a slow, lingering kiss to Adrian's cheek, the warmth of his lips like sunlight melting into his skin. "Yeah," he said, his voice thick with affection. "That room's not exactly made for a kid; he needs his own bed."

Adrian smiled, shifting slightly, feeling the rise and fall of Logan's breath against his back, steady as the ocean's rhythm.

"Oh," Logan added, a smirk curling at the edge of his words, "and I need a lock on the door."

Adrian tilted his head, feigning curiosity, his lips twitching. "Any particular reason why you need a locked door, Mr. Vaughn?"

Logan's chest rumbled with laughter. "Oh, yes indeed, *Mr. Vaughn*," Logan teased, his voice dropping lower as he nosed against Adrian's neck. "I want to do some very, very dirty things to my husband at night, and I need to lock the door." He punctuated his words with a playful bite to Adrian's skin, tasting the ocean's salt still clinging there. The briny tang was inseparable from Adrian in his mind, the scent of the sea lingering on his skin like a memory that refused to fade.

Adrian threw his head back and laughed, the sound rolling over the breeze like a crashing wave, wild and free. It filled Logan's chest, sent something warm and boundless spilling through him.

"You're impossible," Adrian said fondly.

"Abba! Daddy! Look at me!" Jay shouted, his small voice pitched with triumph as he stood on the surfboard wedged into the sand, arms flung wide, knees bent slightly, a picture of pure confidence as though he were balancing on a wild sea.

They cheered, laughter breaking over them, and Logan's hand twitched with regret. "I can't believe I forgot my camera in the room," he muttered.

"Want me to run and grab it?" Adrian asked.

"Nuh, we'll head back soon to get ready for lunch. I just wish I had more shots of him like this... on vacation."

Adrian's lips curved. "I know, ahuv sheli."

"I love seeing him like that..."

Adrian hummed in response.

"I love the chaos of mornings, the spilled cereal, the endless questions, the tiny socks that vanish into thin air. I love it when he crawls into our bed in the middle of the night, even if he throws a leg in my face at four a.m. I love waking with him there, hearing his laugh before the day even begins. I love how happy he is. And I love when he sleeps through in his own bed, when the nightmares don't come. That's how I know he's healing."

"You are such an amazing father," Adrian replied. "I love it too, every moment of it."

Adrian leaned deeper into Logan's embrace, sinking into him the way the tide melts into the shore. His eyes softened as they drifted over the beach, over the place where the water met the land, and a quiet sort of nostalgia flickered in his gaze.

"I actually like the idea of going back to that cabin..." he murmured, his voice quieter now, suspended somewhere between memory and longing. He lifted a hand, pointing toward a distant curve of the shoreline. "I think it was there."

Logan followed his gaze, the past unfolding in his mind like an old, sun-faded photograph. The place where it all began. Where Adrian had once pulled him from the depths of the ocean, and where, without even realizing it, he had also saved him from drowning in something far deeper: his own fear.

The tide had come and gone a million times since that night, pulling them apart, only to bring them back to each other again.

"Yeah," he murmured, his voice barely above a whisper, his gaze locked on the spot where it had all begun. Where the ocean had tried to claim him, and Adrian had refused to let it.

The sea before them was calm now, a wide sheet of sapphire glinting beneath the late sun, dotted with swimmers and boarders who trusted the water to hold them. But Logan could still see it—the ghost of that storm. How it had torn across the horizon without warning. The wind screaming. The waves towering, rising like liquid walls, furious and merciless.

He remembered the moment his board slipped out from under him. The cold snap of water. The weightless free-fall. The silence. The sudden knowing: *this is too deep, I'm too far, no one will reach me in time.*

And then—Adrian.

Logan could see it, still. Not in fragments, but whole. Adrian sprinting from the beach, carving through the waves like something pulled by instinct alone. Fighting the tide. His body a defiant, unwavering line against the chaos. And then his hands—finding Logan beneath the surface, holding him fast, dragging him from the deep with strength that didn't just come from muscle, but from something else.

Something that said: *I will not lose you.*

A life given, for a life taken.

The way he had breathed life back into him.

Logan swallowed hard, blinking against the sting of salt in his eyes. He could almost see his younger self, sprawled on the shore, coughing up seawater, wide-eyed and dazed as he looked up into the face of the man who had just saved him. A stranger then.

His whole world now.

In the present, reality blurred. The sounds around him—the chatter of beachgoers mingled with Jay's laughter, carried effortlessly on the breeze—began to fade. Even the warmth of the sun, which gently kissed his skin, felt clouded for a fleeting moment. Logan found himself suspended in time, eight years younger, gasping for breath as he stared up at Adrian for the very first time. In that split second, before he could fully grasp its meaning or name it, something profound shifted within him.

Beneath the surface of the ocean, a treasure lay concealed—a gift quietly bestowed by the depths, disguised in chaos. On that clever subterfuge of waves, something unfolded for him, something sacred and strange, hidden beneath the performance of danger. The current whispered like a lover, sweet nothings braided with warning, luring him in with a siren's promise. It danced around him, feigning death, pretending to drag him under—when in truth, it was offering him something far deeper.

It had given him Adrian.

And in a single breath—in the blink of an eye—Adrian went from stranger to something else entirely. A lighthouse in the storm. A constant in the pull of an unpredictable world. A gravity he could never escape, even when he tried. His past. His present. His future.

"But I can't with that room..." Logan's voice wavered as he exhaled, his grip tightening around Adrian's fingers. The weight of the past settled in his chest, a bittersweet ache he couldn't quite put into words. "I almost cried when I woke up. Too many memories... ones I *love* to think back on, but in that room, it's not just remembering them—it's like I'm *reliving* them. It makes me..." He trailed off, shaking his head, lost in the vastness of everything he felt. "I don't think I can explain it."

Adrian squeezed his hand. "Try."

Logan closed his eyes for a moment, letting the words rise and fall inside him, before finally speaking. "It pulls me back into those moments, and they were beautiful—so much love, so much... everything, so much confusion too. And being back in them feels overwhelming, because I can feel it all again, not just in my head, but in my *body*. It's like time folds over itself, and I'm *there*. But then, I remember what comes after, and suddenly, that beauty—" He inhaled sharply. "—that *overload* of joy and love turns unbearable. Because I know what's coming next."

Silence wrapped around them, heavy and fragile as sea glass. Logan stared at their joined hands, his grip firm, as if holding on to Adrian was the only thing keeping him from drifting too far out into the past.

Adrian turned Logan's hand over, pressing a soft kiss to his palm, his lips warm against the skin. "You explained it beautifully, ahuv sheli," he whispered, reverence in his voice, like he understood every piece of Logan's heartache without needing to ask for more.

Logan let out a breath, a small, tired smile curling his lips. And then—

"Dad! Abba! Look at me!" Jay's voice rang through the air again, bright and full of laughter, pulling them both back to the present. Arms spread wide, knees bent in perfect imitation of the surfers he saw, he leapt from the board into the sand, a child's barrel ride ending.

Logan and Adrian erupted into cheers, clapping and whooping like he had just won a championship, their love for him as boundless as the ocean.

Jay grinned, basking in the attention, and Logan let the joy of the moment wash over him.

The rings on Adrian's hand glowed softly in the light—one an engagement ring, the other a wedding band, symbols of the vows they had once spoken with salty kisses and teary laughter. On Logan's wrist, the lifesaver bracelet sat just above his tattoo, the ink permanently marking a promise, the bracelet carrying a piece of the past that had rewritten his future.

His heart swelled, bursting like a wave crashing against the shore. Love, in its rawest, most undeniable form, surged through him—love for this man, who had refused to let go, even when Logan himself had tried to. Love for the home they had built, not just in walls, but in laughter, in touches, in whispered confessions beneath moonlit skies. Love for the journey, for every crash and every calm, for the storms they had weathered together.

Because now, standing on this beach, watching Jay jump from the board to the sand, Logan understood.

The hardships, the heartache, the running, the return—it was all part of it. The ocean had to rage before it could be still. The tides had to pull back before they could kiss the shore again. Bliss could only be recognized in contrast to pain, and they had tasted both in full.

"I'm glad we took that time off," Adrian murmured, his voice soft. He knew, as Logan did, that soon life would pull them back—Logan to the demands of work, of meetings and calls and late nights; Adrian to his own world of schedules, clients. But this moment, this stolen stretch of peace, was a memory they were weaving together. One they would carry long after the sand was gone from their shoes.

Logan exhaled a low, quiet laugh, his fingers tracing idle circles along the bare skin of Adrian's stomach. "We should go on more vacations," he echoed, not really joking.

Adrian lifted their joined hands to his lips, pressing a kiss to Logan's knuckles like it was a reflex, like it was the easiest truth he knew.

Logan's gaze shifted to the water, where Jay had just fallen—again—but was already climbing back onto his board, soaked and grinning, teeth flashing beneath the sun.

"Look at him," Logan said, voice thick with something close to awe. "He fell, and he's just... getting back up. Like it didn't even faze him."

Adrian followed his gaze. Jay was already trying again, standing on the board and jumping into the shallow water, splashing with his tiny feet.

"He's so happy," Logan whispered.

Adrian smiled, the expression soft and full. He leaned further into Logan's warmth, pressing back into the shape of him, letting the steady heartbeat behind him remind him of everything they had reclaimed. The scent of salt and sun lingered on their skin. The hush of the waves curled around them like a lullaby.

Logan brushed his lips against the flushed skin behind Adrian's ear, lingering there, before resting his chin on his shoulder.

"I'm happy too," Adrian murmured, his voice barely louder than the breeze.

Logan turned his head, letting his lips ghost over Adrian's temple, slow and reverent. "Me too."

"You know, Logan... it took me a long time to realize that when I decided not to treat the cancer back then, that decision didn't come from a clear place. I think—I know now—I was depressed. I didn't want to admit it, maybe I couldn't. But I was in a really dark place, and I made that choice from inside the fog."

Adrian paused, his voice low, steady.

"And then you showed up. You fought for my life in a way I hadn't. You fought harder than I ever did. You didn't beg, you didn't push—you just refused to let me go. You reminded me that life is something worth fighting for. That *I* was worth fighting for."

He looked at Logan, eyes shining with something quiet and raw.

"You gave me my life back, and not just survival, not just more time. You gave me a life I actually want to live. And I'll be grateful for that for the rest of it."

Logan wiped at his eyes, the tears slipping faster than he could catch them, then leaned in and kissed Adrian—soft and slow, like a promise.

Silence stretched between them—not empty, but full. Full of memory. Full of love too large for language. Everything around them faded until it was just the sound of the ocean, the echo of their breath, and the boy who had made them a family laughing somewhere just ahead.

"Thank you," Adrian whispered. "For never giving up on me. I wouldn't have made it through cancer without you. You believed, even when I couldn't. You fought for me, for us, for everything we had left. You made it true. You loved me when I hated myself so much."

Adrian turned to look at him then, just slightly, enough for their eyes to meet.

"I always will," Logan smiled, a little uneven, a little breathless. "Old and gray, remember?"

And in that promise was the tide—steady, returning. The moon, unwavering in its pull. The quiet truth that no matter what storms came next, no matter how rough the waters turned, they would always find their way back.

"I have a crazy idea... one I've been thinking about for a while now," Adrian confessed, his voice quiet, uncertain.

Logan's arms tightened around him instinctively, a smirk tugging at his lips. "I *love* crazy ideas," he mused. "But they're usually mine. I think I'm becoming too responsible with this whole parenthood thing..." His voice softened, his breath warm against Adrian's skin. "What is it, love?"

Adrian shifted slightly in his arms, his breath hitching just enough for Logan to notice. It was subtle, but Logan knew *him*—knew every nervous tick, every pause that meant his heart was speaking before his mind caught up.

Adrian exhaled, the sound nearly lost in the breeze. "What do you think... about a baby?"

Logan stilled. He felt Adrian's hesitation in the way he tensed just slightly, in the way his eyes flickered toward Jay, watching their son with something deep and longing in his gaze before daring to glance at Logan. And when he did, Logan saw it—the want, the *hope*, shimmering there like sunlight on water.

"Our baby?" Logan asked, his voice quiet, and a smile was spreading before he could stop it.

Adrian nodded, swallowing, his fingers tracing slow circles over Logan's hand. "Yeah, yes, *our* baby." He took a steadying breath. "I think we could do that. And Jay, he'd love a brother or a sister."

Logan grinned, his happiness breaking free. He bit down lightly on Adrian's shoulder, laughter bubbling in his chest.

"Yeah," he said, nodding against Adrian's skin. "I *love* that idea." He turned Adrian's face slightly, pressing a kiss to his temple. "I love it *very* much, actually."

The words felt bigger than the moment itself. They held the weight of a new beginning, of another chapter they were already writing without realizing it. The idea of a baby—*their* baby—settled between them like something inevitable, something meant to be.

Laughter burst between them, genuine and overflowing, mingling with the sound of the waves and the distant shouts of beachgoers. They kissed between smiles, between whispered words that didn't need to be spoken to be understood.

And every few moments, Jay's voice would ring through the air—*"Daddy! Abba! Look!"*—and they would turn without hesitation, watching him stumble, watching him rise, watching him chase the ocean like it was his best friend.

Logan squeezed Adrian's hand, their fingers still intertwined. "Another little one running around, huh?" he murmured, glancing at Jay, imagining what their life would look like in a few years.

Adrian chuckled, leaning back into him, warmth spreading between them like the glow of the setting sun.

"Yeah," he whispered, smiling softly. "Another wave to ride."

The little boy came running up the shore, grains of sand clinging to his skin, his blond curls plastered against his forehead. His laughter rang through the air, uncontainable and bright, as he tossed the small surfboard onto the sand, right next to Adrian's, as if he were mirroring his father without even realizing it.

Without hesitation, Jay launched himself into their laps, his tiny body crashing into them like a rogue wave, all limbs and boundless energy. Adrian caught him easily, arms wrapping around him instinctively, pulling him close as Jay wiggled excitedly, his breath coming in quick bursts, eyes wide with exhilaration.

"You won't believe what happened!" he declared, his voice full of urgency, as if he had just conquered the ocean itself.

Logan bit back a smile, exchanging a glance with Adrian, both of them amused at the way Jay spoke as though they hadn't been watching his every move the entire time.

"Oh yeah?" Adrian grinned, brushing damp curls and sand from Jay's forehead. "Tell us everything."

Jay took a deep breath, dramatically preparing himself, and then launched into his story, arms waving wildly as he recounted every second—how the water tried to push him back, how he *almost* stood up for real this time, how a tiny fish swam right by his foot (*it almost touched me, Abba!*), how he fell but *totally did it on purpose* because surfers *do* that sometimes, obviously.

Logan listened, captivated—not because he didn't know the story, but because it was *Jay* telling it. Because the wonder in his son's voice, the way his eyes sparkled, made even the simplest moments feel like the greatest adventures.

The world around them seemed to soften, the rush of the ocean blending into the rhythm of their breath, into the quiet rise and fall of Jay's small chest against Adrian's own. The boy had finally begun to settle, his endless energy momentarily tamed by the comfort of his fathers' arms, his head resting over Adrian's heart, listening to its steady beat.

Logan's arms wrapped around them both, the warmth of his touch grounding Adrian in a way nothing else ever could. Their voices drifted together, exchanging soft words, answering Jay's excited whispers, but Adrian's gaze was drawn beyond them, to the vast, infinite stretch of the ocean.

The water shimmered beneath the high sun, waves rolling in a slow, steady rhythm, each one kissing the shore before retreating, only to return again.

He had always believed the ocean had a language of its own, a force that moved with purpose even when it seemed chaotic. And now, staring out at the endless horizon, where the sky bled into the sea in seamless shades of blue, he *knew*—the ocean had *brought* Logan to him. The currents, the tides, the invisible hands of fate had pulled them together, even at the cost of risking Logan's life.

Because the ocean had *known*.

It had known Adrian would come for him.

A life given for a life taken.

Adrian had lost so much before—his mother, his soldier, friends in battles, his health, years that had slipped away like water through his fingers. But in return, the ocean had given him *this*—his second chance, his love, his family.

Every wave that rose and fell before him was part of something greater, a pattern far too vast to see up close, but now, from where he stood, he could see it in its full, breathtaking design. The ocean followed its own rhythm, a song of its own making, and somehow, in the ebb and flow of it all, it had carried him right *here*.

He closed his eyes, letting the wind brush over his face, inhaling the scent of salt and sunlight.

Thank you, Mom, he whispered in his mind, knowing, *feeling* that she had a hand in all of it. That she had been watching. That she had been the tide pulling Logan toward him, ensuring that the man who had saved his life would never be lost again.

When Adrian opened his eyes, the world before him was more vivid than ever. The endless blue of the sea, the golden shimmer of the sand, the painting of sky and waves merging in the perfect balance of light and motion.

And in the center of it all—his *son*, resting against him, safe, warm, wrapped in love.

His *husband*, the man he had once thought lost to fear and time, a man that Adrian had no idea how he managed to get, now holding him like a vow, like a promise kept.

It was as clear as the tide beneath the sun, just as the ocean had created life, *they* had created *this*.

A family.

A love that had defied storms, survived distance, and now stood as unshakable as the shore.

Logan kissed his temple, whispering something small, something warm.

And Adrian smiled, knowing that the waves had done their part.

Logan caught his lips in a kiss—deep, brief, electrifying—before pulling back just enough to flash that devilish, all-consuming smile. The one that was all white teeth and mischief, the one that Adrian hated just as much as he loved because it meant Logan knew exactly what he was doing to him.

And oh, how Adrian was utterly mad for him.

He fell in love a little more every single time Logan's silver eyes found his, like moonlight slicing through the darkest night, like the glint of sun on the crest of a wave before it crashes—powerful, untamed, breathtaking.

And when Logan laughed—oh, when he laughed—Adrian was lost. Completely, irreversibly, helplessly, his prisoner. Because that sound, beautiful sound that had once been buried beneath years of loneliness, was something Adrian would go to war for, something he would fight to protect.

Logan Vaughn was truly something else.

Something extraordinary, something so wildly unique that to love him, to have him, was to fight, to break, to dive into the deepest trenches of the ocean, to surrender to the tide and trust it would carry you back to shore.

Logan Vaughn was the essence of everything good.

Fierce and loyal, relentless in his love, forged in struggle yet soft in the ways that mattered most. He had come so far, through the wreckage, through the storms, through the waves that had once tried to swallow him whole.

And Adrian? Adrian was mesmerized, captivated, entranced.

Utterly *bewildered* by the man currently holding him.

The man he had saved once.

The man who had *saved him* right back.

And eventually, the streams of water decided to take me back to you. Through every storm, through every tide that pulled me away, through the currents that tried to drag me under—somehow, the ocean always knew where I belonged.

It let me drift, let me lose myself, let me crash and break and rise again, but it never let me go too far. Because no matter how far the waves carried me, they always brought me back to you.

Like the tide returning to the shore, like the moon pulling the ocean close, like the salt in the water that never fades, you were always there. The gravity that held me steady, the lighthouse that never dimmed, the home I didn't know I was searching for until I found myself in your arms.

THE END

Author's note

If you've made it this far—thank you!

It wasn't an easy journey, but we made it.

I wanted to share a few things about the story you've just read. The first draft of this book was written back in 2018, during my second year of my BA. I spent that year studying and drafting, pouring myself into the early shape of this narrative.

Interestingly, the original idea didn't start with just me, it came from my husband. He suggested a story about two surfers, far from home, who fall in love. That seed grew into something much bigger.

The very first scene I ever imagined, the one that sparked everything, was Logan falling to his knees, begging Adrian. Back then, it wasn't set in a hotel; it was just a single, emotional moment between two nameless and faceless people. That image stayed with me, and from there, their story slowly unfolded.

Since then, this book has been rewritten 21 times. And by "rewritten," I mean every single sentence, from the first page to the last. With each version, I went deeper. I made it longer, more complex, more human. The eleventh rewrite came after I had completed my doctoral dissertation. I had taken a four-year break from fiction writing, dedicating myself entirely to academic work. But during that time, I changed, as a person and as a writer.

That growth shaped my perspective on this story. When I finally returned to it, with new eyes and a new voice, I realized these characters needed more. More depth, more vulnerability, more truth. And so I gave it to them.

Because the person who wrote the first draft is not the same person who wrote the final one.

During my BA, I wrote other books too, ones I now plan to revisit and rework. But this one... this one is special. It held on. It waited for me. And I hope it found a place with you, too.

If this story stayed with you, I would be grateful for a review or rating on any platform you use. It helps independent authors, like me more than you might think.

Some of you may remember Sasha, the tattoo artist, and Lucian. Their story is coming soon.

Curious about what's next? Come say hi on Instagram, I'd love to connect:

AUTHORDRMICHALGUTER

About the Author

Dr. Michal Guter is a criminologist, victimologist, academic, and author with a deep passion for exploring masculinity, trauma, male sexual assault victimization and rape and resilience. She is also a dedicated teacher and researcher, often found at her computer working on either a book or an academic article, it really depends on the day. Addicted to coffee and in love with words, Michal has published in peer-reviewed journals and finds joy in reading dictionaries and grammar books just for fun, and occasionally turns to graphic design as another form of storytelling. But most of all, she loves to read stories, and you'll rarely find her without a novel or audiobook close at hand.

www.ingramcontent.com/pod-product-compliance
Lightning Source LLC
Chambersburg PA
CBHW030838030726
47495CB00005B/1275